*Pour the Dark Wine*

# DINAH LAMPITT

# *Pour the Dark Wine*

MICHAEL JOSEPH
London

MICHAEL JOSEPH LTD

Published by the Penguin Group
27 Wrights Lane, London W8 5TZ, England
Viking Penguin Inc., 40 West 23rd Street, New York, New York 10010, USA
Penguin Books Australia Ltd, Ringwood, Victoria, Australia
Penguin Books Canada Ltd, 2801 John Street, Markham, Ontario, Canada L3R 1B4
Penguin Books (NZ) Ltd, 182–190 Wairau Road, Auckland 10, New Zealand

Penguin Books Ltd, Registered Offices: Harmondsworth, Middlesex, England

First published 1989

Made and printed in Great Britain by
Richard Clay Ltd, Bungay, Suffolk

Typeset in 10/12pt Sabon by
Cambrian Typesetters, Frimley, Surrey

A CIP catalogue for this book is available from the British Library.

ISBN 0 7181 2995 4

For Antony White – in friendship and
gratitude for taking that first gamble . . .

# Contents

# Acknowledgements

My thanks are due to several people: Nicholas Fogg and Michael Gray who took me to Merlin's Mound on one of the few hot days of 1987, Frances and Ken Ivens who made Marlborough such fun, Dominic Stoker with whom I first saw Stonehenge, Stephen Weekes who invited me to Penhow Castle and loaned me precious books about the Seymours, Wendy Davies and Iris Morgan who arranged my visit to and conducted me round Sudeley Castle on one of the few hot days of 1988! Bob Howell, who let me stay in his home in the converted stables of Wolfhall Manor, and Patricia Keen, upon whose well researched painting of the original Wolff Hall, Melvyn Warren-Smith based his cover illustration. Thanks, too, to those who make my life easier – Anna Foinette, Geoffrey Glassborow, Peter Jeffrey of Barclays Bank, Erika Lock and Shirley Russell.

*Prologue*

# THE WISHES

A T NOON THE RIVER burst into flames. Or that was how it seemed to the four children who stood solemnly staring down at the fast flowing Kennet, watching as it suddenly became suffused with every golden light in Christendom, dancing and shimmering with an almost blinding sparkle.

The youngest – a scrap of a thing with eyes that looked bigger than she – cried out, 'It's a sword, a jewelled sword!' while the other girl exclaimed, 'No, it's not. I think it is a ring, a golden wedding ring.'

The eldest – a boy of sixteen, already a young adult – ruffled their hair and laughed. 'What strange creatures you are. All I see is the sun on water. What about you, Tom?'

The fourth turned his head to look at his brother. Even at ten years of age his face was spectacular: lively bright eyes dancing above a strong shapely nose, and lips that would tease women when he grew older.

'I see the ruins of a castle amidst its moat. I see the town of Marlborough but most of all I see a damsel walking out of her cottage. Don't tell me you didn't notice her Edward!'

'For shame!' answered his brother with a smile. 'Try to concentrate on the scenery.'

'Is she not part of it?' Tom asked innocently.

Edward ignored him. 'I promised to bring you to the top of Merlin's Mound,' he said to the girls, 'so now you are here, tell me what you find. Jane first.'

The elder gazed down at the small round hill on which they stood, thinking that it looked like an inverted green basin. 'I had expected more,' she said. 'It merely seems part of the castle to me.'

'No, it is the wrong shape for that.'

Tom said, 'So you really believe there is a burial vault within?'

The youngest child, who had been listening carefully, gazed at him from the enormous eyes which had given rise to her nickname, for they were the purplish blue of summer clover. 'It is true,' she said earnestly, 'Merlin *is* in there!'

Tom smiled lazily. 'Who told you that, Cloverella? Your Romany grandam?'

But even while Edward and Jane said 'Shush', the little scrap answered seriously, 'Oh yes. She brought me here once. She spoke to him, asked for his help. I know. I saw her.'

Jane stared amazed. 'You saw her speak to Merlin? He was *here*?'

The child blushed. 'Not exactly. She put me to sit beneath that ruin' – she pointed a grubby finger at some crumbling stones, once the castle's massive keep – 'then went off to seek his help. And it wasn't long afterwards that she left me at Wolff Hall and Dame Margery took me in. So, you see, he *did* work magic, for that is what my grandmother asked Merlin to do.'

They all stared at her in silence, differing expressions upon their faces: Edward, amused and tolerant; Tom appraisingly, as if he could see the beauty that would one day bloom in her; Jane nervously, half believing what she had just heard.

Eventually, Tom said, 'So you are telling us that if you make a wish at this spot it comes true?'

'That is what she said to me. That Merlin, who sleeps in a crystal cave at the heart of the mound, will hear your voice in his slumbers.'

The boy laughed, the sun picking up the reddish glints in his hair as he threw a stone skimmingly towards the moat. 'Then in that case I shall do so.'

The other three stared at him, envious of his exuberance.

'What will you wish?' Jane asked.

Tom smiled at her. 'That I shall know and love many beautiful women and end by marrying the highest in the land.'

His sister pulled a face. 'What a thing to say.'

'Then what would you ask for?'

The girl hesitated. 'To defy the fact I am the ugliest girl in the world and marry a king. Then I could turn the tables on those who call me plain Jane.'

'You are *not* ugly,' answered Cloverella gallantly, flinging her small body against her cousin's and throwing her arms about her

4

neck. 'I think your eyes beautiful, for whoever saw three colours in one?'

And she was right. In Jane's lily-pale face, in which for a fact there were few redeeming features, lay a pair of light blue eyes which held a trace of green and yet were circled by a rim of deep and vivid indigo.

Jane hugged her fondly. 'Sweet Cloverella! What would you wish, my little dear heart?'

'For wisdom,' said the child solemnly. 'For wisdom to sing to the earth and the stars and let them yield up their secrets. My Romany grandam knew some of those things but I would like to learn even more. I wish for a quarter of Merlin's knowledge.'

The other three laughed not only at her words but at the child's earnest face, for she was the skeleton in the Seymour family's cupboard; the bastard they had adopted; the child of Dame Margery's sister who had sinned with a gypsy servant and died in childbed for her crime, left at their kitchen door for them to take or reject. Dame Margery, however, had known at a glance that the changeling was indeed her sister Elizabeth's very own flesh and blood.

Now Jane hugged her cousin even more tightly and said, 'Then I hope your wish is granted for if so, you will be able to guide the lives of us all.'

Tom turned to Edward. 'And what of you, brother? You are very quiet. Are you now too old and studious for such childish things as wishes?'

His brother smiled wryly. He had been at Oxford for two years, studying grammar, rhetoric and logic. He was Sir John Seymour's second son and the most serious of all the children.

'Yes, I believe I am,' he said.

'Oh do wish, please,' begged Jane.

She moved closer to him and Edward thought that despite her lack of attraction his sister had a pleasing way with her when she so wished.

'Oh, very well. What shall I ask for?'

Tom smiled his lazy smile. 'There must be something you want. Even if it is only a goodly woman.'

Edward shot him a dark look. He had no intention of discussing the secrets of his heart with anyone, not even his brother. 'I'll think,' he answered slowly.

5

From where he stood on the top of Merlin's Mound there was an incredible view: the majestic Wiltshire countryside spread out before him, dark with forests and light with sweeping hills; a countryside mysterious as death itself, with strange standing stones and a fantastic white horse carved into the very face of the earth.

'I wish I could own all this,' he said impulsively.

'But to do that you would have to be King,' Tom answered. 'And that could never be.'

'Indeed,' said Edward. His eyes swept over the distant views. 'Nonetheless, it would give me pleasure to feel that everything I could see was mine.'

Jane turned to Cloverella. 'I believe our wishes are too ambitious. Could Merlin possibly grant them?'

'Oh, he *could*,' answered the child in whom flowed both royal and Romany blood. 'But as to whether he will or not we can only wait and see.'

'Time we went home,' said Edward. 'The shadows are beginning to lengthen.' He hitched Cloverella onto his back and started to descend the steep sides of the strangely shaped green mound that had given the town of Marlborough its name.

Thomas and Jane followed more slowly, a touch of their destiny laying its finger upon them.

'Does he *really* sleep in there?' asked the girl quietly.

'You know the town's motto.'

'*Ubi nunc sapientis ossa Merlini.*'

'Where now are the bones of wise Merlin,' translated Tom. He patted the grass slope of the Mound. 'Make my women beautiful, old man,' he said.

'Don't tempt fate, Tom,' answered Jane.

But she was laughing as she walked with her brother into the fine clear light of an early springtime evening.

*Part One*

# THE PRIMROSE BRIDE

# Chapter One

AT ANY TIME A GLIMPSE of the King's Fool could be a little frightening but this night he was grotesque. On his head Will Somers wore a bronze helmet which completely obliterated his face, only the glint of a snapping brown eye behind those already painted on bore witness to the fact that there was a man inside it at all. From the side of this terrible headpiece two twisting horns reared up, while the mouth was set in a permanent grin of cruel metal teeth. The effect was monstrous, unreal, and as Will jumped across the great hall to where sat the ladies of the Queen's household there was not one who did not consider him a hobgoblin and draw back slightly, even though they laughed.

Cackling hollowly from within the mask, Will dropped on one knee before one of them and snatched her hand to the grinning mouth, his hunched shoulder even more apparent in that position.

'Will you marry me, fair maiden?' he whispered.

The girl pursed her thin lips and did not reply.

'What! Won't you be my sweetheart?'

She took her hand away and said clearly, 'And be wife to base metal? No, I think a brighter coin would be more amusing.'

There was a roar of laughter and Will Somers loped off to find another victim while Jane Seymour, pleased with herself but letting no expression cross her pale face, turned her attention once more to the food set before her. It was Christmas, it was 1529, and for this great occasion King Henry and Queen Katharine were dining formally together before the whole court, everything being merry to celebrate the twelve days.

Or so it would seem. But beneath the splendour seethed a tension to which, these days, every man, woman and child attached to the glittering court of King Henry VIII was subjected. And on this particular occasion the threat to them all – dark and mysterious and quite the most dangerous woman in the kingdom – was near at hand. For Anne Boleyn had left her beautiful mansion of York Place, even now being renovated and enlarged to suit the Lady's tastes, and taken up residence at Greenwich, to be near her sovereign at Christmas time.

Jane, surreptitiously raising her eyes from her plate again, wondered whether Anne might yet put in an appearance, swarm into the banquet and beg forgiveness for lateness, cast her dark eyes over the assembled company and smile, as if she knew something that nobody could guess, and then take her place at a discreet distance from the King, as though she had no care in the world.

In a way Jane hoped that the Lady *would* come. Mistress Seymour had been at Court three months now, having ridden through a Savernake Forest crimsoned by autumn, to London; leaving behind the peace of Wolff Hall to be a Maid of Honour to Queen Katharine – a post to which she had been introduced by her cousin Francis Bryan – and so far she had not set her eyes on that creature whose name was on everyone's lips. It was a situation designed, at the very least, to arouse curiosity in a young woman who liked to make up her own mind about events.

For there were those who whispered that the old Queen had had her day, that Katharine was a worn-out drudge, incapable of bearing a living child, while others said that Anne Boleyn was an evil whore, so fired by ambition that she was prepared to subject the King to almost any ordeal in order to gain the throne.

Jane found a small smile forming on her careful lips. How intriguing it was! She and Edward – who treated her as grown-up these days – had laid a wager on the outcome of it all. He had maintained that the Queen would hold out, that the King would never get an annulment of his marriage, and would, in the end, tire of the Kentish knight's daughter. But Jane had declared that a clever woman could win the world if she so desired, and had put her money on Anne as future Queen of England.

'And what then?' Edward had said.

'What do you mean?'

Jane's brother had turned to look out of the window of the long gallery of Wolff Hall to the great paled garden that lay below.

'Surely Anne Boleyn is like a forest deer to the King. The faster she runs the hotter he goes in pursuit. But when he catches her up the game will be over. And that will be the end of her.'

With a frankness that only country children know, Jane had said, 'So the King has not taken her into his bed?'

Still with his back turned, Edward had answered, 'I doubt he has. But not for any strong principle on her part. No, she's too clever to give him the one thing he desires most. She'll resist as long as she can. She's no silly slattern.'

His tone was bitter and Jane had crossed over to him and given him a hug. Edward – head of the Seymour children since his brother, the sickly John, had died in 1520 – had married young and lived to regret it. While he had been fighting in France with the Duke of Suffolk, for which escapade he had received a knighthood, his wife, Katherine Filliol, had taken a lover and Edward had never acknowledged her sons as his. Nor would his Catholic principles allow him divorce and now he was at stalemate; Katherine languished in a convent while he loved nobody, all his energies taken up with the countryside pursuits he enjoyed so much.

Thinking about him now made Jane stare down the length of the great table to where Edward sat, come to Court for Christmas, dark, intense and clever. For a moment she envied the vivid looks of her brothers and sisters – and then she remembered her promise to herself. That, despite all odds, plain Jane would shine at everything and so dazzle with her wit and intelligence that some great match would fall into her hands. Her mind dwelled briefly on Sir Robert Dormer's son and their whispered words of affection before his mother snatched him away, declaring Mistress Seymour too lowly and ordinary for her priceless boy.

Jane steeled herself not to think of it. Crying made her nose and eyes swell and this was not the occasion for even the most surreptitious tears. With an enviable strength of will, she turned to her cousin Francis Bryan who sat beside her. 'What will happen if the Lady comes?' she whispered.

'The Queen will be acutely distressed: the King less so; Anne herself, not at all.'

'Is she so hard?'

Francis Bryan's lips curled into a smile but his unblinking grey eyes did not move. 'Not hard, merely disciplined.'

'Disciplined,' repeated Jane wonderingly. 'I would like to be thought of as that.'

'Why?' asked her cousin, slightly amused.

Jane remained silent, pondering her answer. She had no intention of revealing her private thoughts to her enigmatical cousin. 'Because it sounds well,' she said eventually.

He was going to question her further, she knew it. And indeed Sir Francis was opening his mouth to speak when a loud blast from the King's musicians, who had been playing throughout the banquet, heralded that the King would lead the way to the masqued dancing which would continue well into the early hours of next day.

Relieved, Jane stood up. 'I must talk to Edward before the revels. Will you excuse me, cousin?'

'Gladly, cousin,' he replied, his cold grey eyes appraising her neat and well-rounded figure without emotion. 'If only she had another head on it!' he muttered unkindly as she vanished. Then his attention was distracted elsewhere and he thought no more of his unattractive kinswoman from Wiltshire. But her brother, seeing her breathless approach, thought Jane looked well that evening, her cheeks unusually pink and her eyes sparkling.

'You are radiant. I hope you have not had too much wine!' he said, half joking.

She stopped short. 'I declare you are becoming a killjoy, Edward.'

He smiled. 'Now, now. Such anger could disguise a guilty conscience.'

She paused, her unusual eyes dark, struggling between laughter and wrath. 'Have a care. I am a grown woman of twenty years. Not some chitling to be ordered about.'

'Then in that case I concede. Come, spare a dance for your poor brother fresh from the country and knowing nothing of courtly ways.'

Jane smiled. 'Then put on your disguise and come with me.'

Taking each other's hand the two Seymours made their way to the outer hall where, having donned masks — Jane's attached to an elaborate wig of fiery red curls — they joined the other dancers, pacing out the measured steps of a pavan. The King, in gold brocade with silver lining, was at his most hearty, laughing loudly and making a to-do of neatly placing his feet. Jane, looking at him through the mask's enlarged peepholes — especially cut wide that her best feature might be on show – thought him frightening; a colossus with mighty shoulders and legs, an altogether suffocating man. She wondered whether Edward was right, whether the Lady Anne had held him at arm's length all these years, or whether the delicate creature had succumbed to the King's desire and been crushed beneath that mighty weight. Jane gave a small shudder of disgust, a little angry with herself that the thought should fascinate her so much.

The music changed to a galliard – the after-dance of the pavan – and Mistress Seymour was astonished to see the King change partners and go whirling through the women, exchanging a few steps with each one. Realising that he would be in front of her in a moment, Jane braced herself, but before she could so much as drop a curtsey another dancer, heavily masked and gorgeously attired in deepest blue, seemed to appear from nowhere and stood directly in Jane's path.

Why she reacted as she did the girl could not tell but, suddenly angered at the intrusion, she pushed in front of the other woman and, as the King came dancing up, almost flung herself into his arms. She saw his look of surprise and then saw that bleak blue eye crease with amusement.

'Well, well, well,' he said.

'Forgive me, Your Grace, I stumbled,' Jane muttered, in an agony of embarrassment, glad that the red wig and mask totally disguised who she was.

As if reading her thoughts, the King said, 'Comely women should not hide their faces. Which of the Queen's ladies are you, my dear?'

'Jane Seymour, Sir,' she muttered, raising her pretty eyes to steal a glance at him.

'Seymour, Seymour?' he said. 'Would that be Sir John's daughter?'

'Aye, Your Grace.'

'Tell your father I shall see him one of these days. I love to hunt at Savernake.'

Within her mask Jane blushed, almost incapable of further speech, and it was then that she felt the King stiffen and saw his gaze go to the dancer who had almost stolen her place. Without further word he gave Jane an abrupt nod and whirled to the other woman, catching her to him as a starving man might snatch a bone.

13

Jane heard a low musical laugh and caught a whiff of musky scent as the couple danced by her. So the Lady Anne Rochford, born Boleyn, had come to the revels after all. Fascinated, Jane stared from the safety of her disguise.

The Lady was smaller than she had thought; altogether thin and flat where Jane's breasts swelled. But she had the most beautiful hair, thick and luxurious, scantly disguised by her exotic headdress. She seemed very delicate to be holding an entire kingdom to ransom, Jane thought, and then wondered whether Edward would be right; if, when Anne finally granted the King his heart's desire, he would tire of her.

'What do you think?' she asked her brother, as he came breathlessly to her side as the music ended. He followed the direction of her eyes. 'Is it the Lady?'

'Yes, I'm sure of it. She would have taken my place in the dance had I not stepped in front of her.'

Edward laughed. 'Bold little Jane. When I am next at Wolff Hall I must tell the others how you pushed her aside.'

'Wolff Hall, how I miss it!' answered his sister with a sigh. 'How are they all?'

'Tom pursues maidens, Henry pursues game, Elizabeth does her embroidery and looks thoroughly bored, while Dorothy spends her days mooning over father's new horse.'

'And what of Cloverella?'

Edward gave a tolerant smile and Jane suspected, not for the first time, that her brother had more than a soft spot for their strange little cousin.

'Wandering about barefoot, crooning to the moon – or would be if Mother gave her the chance to do so.'

'I thought she would forget all about the Romanies as she grew older.'

'The blood is in her,' said Edward with a note of sadness. 'It will never go away.'

'And that worries you?'

He turned slightly, not answering, and Jane found herself wishing that his adulterous wife would die in her wretched convent and leave her brother free to marry again with honour. She regarded him as one of the most noble people alive and deserving of a happy future.

But all further thought was prevented by the abrupt departure of

14

the Queen, who rose from her chair – signalling to her younger women that they may remain to enjoy themselves – and swept from the room accompanied by her closest attendants, some of whom had served her since she had come to England as a young princess all those years before.

'She has recognised the Lady,' Jane whispered.

'Not difficult,' answered Edward, gazing to where the King stood talking to the masked woman with a look of utter adoration on his features.

'What price our wager now?'

Edward looked dubious. 'I don't know.'

'But His Grace is utterly besotted.'

'It is not difficult for love to turn to hate,' her brother said bitterly, 'and the greater the love the greater the hate can be.'

Jane nodded but said nothing, not wishing to hurt him more, and their conversation would have ended as each turned away to dance with another partner had she not seen the Lady move away from the King, giving a light laugh and tapping him on the forearm with a tapered finger, as if in mock reproof.

'She's coming over here,' Jane whispered frantically and, sure enough, the Lady Anne Rochford was making her way through the dancers, accompanied by a taller woman, in the direction of the young Seymours.

Suddenly nervous, Jane looked for an escape route but it was too late. The Lady stood before them.

'My dear,' she said – and Jane felt that a laugh, and not altogether a kind one, lay just below the surface of her voice.

'Madam,' she answered stiffly, giving a formal curtsey.

'In your clever disguise it is impossible to recognise you. Nor do I know this gentleman . . .' She nodded to Edward. '. . . but so many people are at Greenwich for the twelve days that it is impossible to know all the masquers. Pray, will you reveal the secret of your identities?'

Jane never knew afterwards how she had the courage to answer as she did but she found herself saying, 'Gladly Madam, on the condition that you also reveal yours.'

That Anne, for all her covering headgear and mask, was certain that everyone knew her was apparent, for she visibly stiffened as she answered curtly, 'I am Anne Rochford, the Earl of Wiltshire's daughter.'

15

There was a pause which seemed to Jane to last forever. She stood, staring at the Lady, her thoughts in turmoil, knowing for certain that she had taken an instant dislike to this slight, dark creature who could attract men just by tilting her head. But overriding this powerful reaction came another. In common with most of her generation and the older as well, Jane had learned almost by instinct that in order to survive in the maelstrom of Tudor life it was often essential to hide one's feelings. And it was to this course that she now unerringly steered.

Hating herself but knowing that plain Jane could never triumph if she made powerful enemies, Mistress Seymour dropped a respectful curtsey and said, 'Forgive me, Madam. I am new to Court and know little. Allow me to introduce my brother, Sir Edward Seymour, and myself, Jane. Our father is Sir John Seymour, Warden of Savernake Forest.'

Anne Boleyn appeared to relax for she said, 'And this is Anne Stanhope, one of the Queen's ladies.'

The woman with her curtsied politely and Jane got a vivid impression of creamy skin and a fall of auburn hair. Yet beneath her mask Anne Stanhope's mouth showed itself to have a slightly drooping underlip as though its owner were not easily contented. But now she had her attention turned to Edward and, as the music began once more, she laughingly extended a hand to him and led him away. His sister noticed with amusement that his neck had gone a brilliant shade of red.

Jane lowered her eyes, afraid that her true thoughts about Anne Boleyn might be revealed in their depths. But she need not have worried. At the first notes of the dance, Anne was suddenly surrounded by gallants all begging her to accompany them. Sighing with envy, Jane left the hall and made her way to where the cold night air from the Thames would cool her flushed face and also give her a moment to consider whether she had done the right thing in ingratiating herself with the Lady. But once outside she forgot everything, for she stood in a magical night; a frosty, freezing, splendid creation of winter stars and ghostly mist-hung moon.

Behind her Greenwich Palace, bleached white in the starshine, reared like a castle of ice, its sloping roofs, turrets and spires picked out delicately against the crisp blackness of the frost-filled sky. Long, low and spreading, built round three interconnecting

16

quadrangles – known as Fountain Court, Cellar Court and Tennis Court – tonight the Palace was brilliant with candlelight and noise as the celebrants of Christmas grew drunker, wilder and even more uninhibited as the evening wore on.

Turning, Jane saw reflected in the river a mysterious and gentle palace, its lines wobbly beneath the water, its inhabitants – the jumping luminous fish – altogether more circumspect. Then a roar of laughter and a burst of song made her face the original once more, a rather prim frown turning to a smile as an enormous codpiece – bejewelled, decorated and obviously of great importance to its owner – came floating from an upstairs window and landed at her feet. With a naughty expression, Jane threw it over the wall that separated the riverside walk from the Thames, and watched it gently float away in the direction of the sea.

She felt suddenly uplifted. Despite the chill, despite everything, Jane snatched off her disguise and let the breeze blow hard into her face, relishing the taste that it left on her lips and the hard sting in her nostrils. Her pale hair, the colour of apple blossom, lifted on the current and flew out about her head so that just for a moment she looked unearthly, beautiful almost. Then the illusion was gone and, her small mouth compressed, she turned to go back into the Palace, before some instinct made her draw back into the shadows as another sound came in on the breeze. A single pair of oars was rowing a small craft up to the steps of one of the landing stages. A late visitor was coming to Greenwich.

From her hiding place, Jane watched as a man climbed up and stood for a moment looking out over the river, his head blotting out the moon. She could see little of his body, for he wore a flowing cloak that hid his shape but his face, as he turned, was remarkable. Jane saw a mass of black curling hair, a broad powerful nose, and a set of strong white teeth as he smiled to himself. She thought that she had never seen such a vagabond and yet there was something captivating about the stranger for – or so it seemed to her – he radiated an inexplicable charm and energy. Moreover, he obviously had excellent sight because he had noticed her, where she stood in the shadows.

Not knowing quite what to do, Jane stepped out and said lamely, 'I am taking the air. It is so hot in the Palace.'

He bowed very low, the top curls on his head almost sweeping the ground. 'It is always preferable to breath freely,' he answered,

17

in some manner making her think that he knew of her recent encounter and falsehood.

'Yes, quite so,' answered Jane Seymour as the stranger bowed again and made his way into the Palace without another word.

# Chapter Two

A FAR-STANDING OBSERVER, WATCHING the figure that climbed up the slope of Merlin's Mound in the clear September sunshine, would have been forgiven for thinking that he was looking at a child, for the body – though showing a delicate curve to both breast and hip – was small in stature, while its owner moved lightly, one hand inelegantly bunching up the skirts of its dress, as if she was not bothered by a woman's weight. But woman she was and if the observer had drawn closer he would have seen that, though made on a small scale, she was a rare beauty for all her size.

An elegant bone structure supported an elfin face dominated by two enormous eyes, a strange purplish colour in shade; while from the girl's head a mass of waving black hair, unconstrained by a headdress, rippled halfway down her back. Her diminutive stature – a bare five feet in height – was her only fault and yet, in another way, it was one of her greatest attractions. At twenty years old Cloverella Wentworth was a charming figurine and only her doubtful origins and the fact that her cousins the Seymours were considered parvenus had stopped her from achieving a good match.

Now, staring all around to check that she was quite alone, Cloverella took in at a glance the wide breathless sweep of landscape, giving particular attention to that area where five miles to the west stood another mound known to most as Silbury, larger than that of Merlin. That another great man – or woman – lay buried there she felt convinced. But who? Could it be Morgan le Fay who had brought about the destruction of Merlin, as it was said? Or could it be King Arthur himself, slumbering near his guide and mentor, the most powerful wizard of them all?

Thinking that no one could ever know, Cloverella sank down onto the grassy turf and patted it with her hand. Then almost as if she was listening for an answering voice, Cloverella flattened herself on the ground and put her ear to it. But there was no response and she was just about to get to her feet when she heard a distant shout. Looking up cautiously, Cloverella saw that her cousin Tom Seymour stood at the foot of the mound, staring upwards, one hand shielding his eyes from the sun.

'Cloverella, you wretch,' he called, 'I know you are up there. Come down at once. Mother urgently needs your help for the wedding party. Now come *on*, or by God I'll climb up and box your ears.'

But he was laughing as he spoke and Cloverella did not hesitate to stand up and wave her arm.

'I *knew* it,' he cried triumphantly. 'I said to Mother that this is where you would be. You really must stop your awful habit of wandering off. There are footpads and ruffians everywhere. It will serve you right if one catches you up.'

Sticking out her tongue, Cloverella started the precipitous descent, her feet almost slipping out from under her as she ran down the half mile of pathway and collapsed, laughing and breathless, into Tom's arms. He hugged her tightly, as he hugged all women, and they looked at one another.

She had not seen him for six months, as nowadays he was attached to the retinue of Sir Francis Bryan and had spent some considerable time with his cousin in France. But looking at him, Cloverella thought how well the boy's spectacular looks had blossomed with manhood, so that now he was all dash and splendour and fit to capture the heart of any woman in the kingdom. And he knew it! Every gesture, every turn of his head and tilt of his eye, was calculated to gain him admittance to hearts and bedchambers. And as for his hands, why even though he and Cloverella had been brought up together, he could not resist letting them linger for a moment about her waist before he finally released her.

'You are a shocking flirt, Tom,' she remonstrated, laughing. 'One day it will get you into trouble.'

Even as she said it, Cloverella felt that lurch of her stomach which always accompanied a premonition her words might come true. 'You are a rogue,' she burbled on, to cover the horrid clutch of fear. 'You should try to behave.'

Tom laughed, the sun gleaming gold in his hair and his eyes a sudden glory of ocean blue. 'Must I? Why? It is much more fun to be a little naughty, provided it hurts no one.'

'Aye, that's the nub of it. But be careful. It is when you play with fire that you'll get burned.'

He caught her to him, his smiling mouth an inch from hers. 'Is that a prophecy, gypsy girl? If so I've a mind to kiss you.'

'You can't,' protested Cloverella, 'we are like brother and sister!'

Tom laughed again. 'Aye but we're not, are we?'

It was useless to protest. His mouth was on hers, drawing out the passion that burned fiercely in her Romany blood and making her want to give herself to him, there and then in the sunshine.

'I thought you were wild,' he said, drawing away. 'There is more in you than meets the eye, Elizabeth Wentworth.'

Angry with herself, Cloverella frowned at him. 'I am glad you called me that because if anybody kissed you it was *she*, Elizabeth. Not Cloverella, who is far too sensible to allow such a thing to happen.'

He slipped his arm round her waist, leaning down because she was so tiny. 'Whoever you are, you must come home now. Dame Margery is in a turmoil and running about wringing her hands.'

'I am sure that is not true.' Cloverella gave a joyous laugh. 'But it will be so wonderful to have Edward and Jane at home again. I haven't seen either of them since Anne Boleyn became Queen. Is his new bride a beauty?'

Thomas grimaced. 'I met her at court once. She was an attendant to the Lady before she became Queen. She is very handsome, but . . .'

'But?'

'I will leave you to judge for yourself, cousin. You are supposed to be able to see into people's hearts. You can tell me what *you* think.'

'Yes,' she answered slowly, 'I will.'

'And as you know so much' – Thomas smiled as he lifted Cloverella on to her horse – 'tell me whether the Queen will produce a healthy son.'

His cousin looked at him seriously, her eyes suddenly darkening to purple. 'She will produce a healthy child, yes. Very soon. But it will be a girl.'

Thomas turned a shocked face to her, then slowly a grin spread

21

over it and his eyes twinkled. 'I think you're wrong, gypsy. Every astrologer in the land predicts a boy.'

'Wait and see,' she answered calmly, and drumming her heels into her horse's sides, sped off in front of him into the heart of Savernake Forest.

Even though fine weather still lay upon the land, the first hint and breath of autumn had come to the woodland. Looking up to the glimpses of clear deep sky that could be seen through the silent army of trees, Cloverella noticed that the leaves etched against it already held in their depths a hint of russet, a foretaste of what was to come when the land blazed with splendour and every vivid hue from scarlet to crimson consumed the mighty forest and turned it into a living anthem, heralding the end of the year.

Not wanting to talk to Thomas but to think instead of what the ending of this particular year might bring, when Queen Anne Boleyn produced a daughter instead of the son the King so longed for, Cloverella rode on fast to where, standing it is own parkland and surrounded by three arboured and trellised gardens, Wolff Hall glowed mellow in the late afternoon.

The house, considerably altered and added to over the years, had originally been built in the thirteenth century by the Esturmys, from whose line a daughter had married Roger Seymour just over a hundred years before. Cloverella's uncle and aunt – Sir John and Dame Margery – had inherited the property in their youth and it was they who had added a building known as the laundry, and outbuildings on the higher ground to the east. As a result of their endeavours Wolff Hall was now sprawling and spacious; an imposing half-timbered mansion with an impressive long gallery, a chapel – in which this night James, the family priest, would bless the newly-married couple – and an entrance courtyard. Nonetheless, it was to the Great Barn, set beyond the house, that Cloverella now followed the army of servants who were busily scurrying backward and forward, their arms full of goods and chattels, and their faces all agrin and agape.

Once in the barn's entrance door, however, she stopped short, her breath quite gone with the surprise of the transformation that Dame Margery had brought about. Every wall of the thatched and boarded building had been hung with a tapestry, fastened on by tenter hooks, and down the centre ran a table – large enough to seat a hundred – already laid with plate and eating irons. Fresh garden flowers filled the empty corners and the smell of these in the confined space was overpowering.

'Why, Aunt,' Cloverella called, clapping her hands at the same time, 'it is like a palace. I have never seen anything so splendid.'

Dame Margery Seymour spun round, her cheeks flushed and a wisp of hair descending from her cap. 'Cloverella, you've come at last! Where have you been?' Without waiting for an answer she went on, 'Do you really think it looks fit for a wedding feast? You don't think Anne Stanhope will think it beneath her?'

Cloverella walked slowly round the table, examining everything. 'How could she? Why the King himself could dine in here.'

'I hope you're right. If only I had met her more often and knew her likes and dislikes.'

Her niece looked thoughtful. 'It is strange that Edward brought her here so little. Why do you think that was?'

'Because that woman' – Dame Margery never mentioned the adulterous Katherine Filliol by name – 'was still alive. Poor Ned! Why, Jane told me that he met and fell in love with Mistress Stanhope at Christmastime four years ago but hid all his feelings until *she* finally had the good grace to die.'

Cloverella smiled. Her aunt's most endearing quality was her intense loyalty to her children who, in her eyes, could do no wrong whatsoever. She had given birth to ten, four now gone – one as a young man, one as a boy, and the other two of the Sweat – and adopted another. To Cloverella, Dame Margery was exactly what a mother should be, comfortable and round and rosy, a sweet loving bundle to cuddle up to on a winter's night – so unlike the wayward slip who had made love to a stable boy and borne Cloverella as a result.

How her daughter wondered what she had been like, and how she dreamed of her! Her dead mother could come to her at night, wandering in a misty landscape, a will'o-the-wisp with laughter like music and eyes deeper than an unfathomed ocean; a sprite who should never have borne a child and who had died in agony when she did.

Cloverella collected herself as her aunt spoke again. 'I do hope Edward will be happy this time. Why, my heart will break if he does not find contentment.'

'I think he will – in his way,' Cloverella answered slowly. But Dame Margery did not notice the hesitation and further conversation between them was halted by a small voice saying, 'Cuckoo,'

23

from the doorway. Aunt and niece turned together and simultaneously let out a cry, for there stood the daughter of one, the cousin and friend of the other. Jane Seymour had returned to Wolff Hall.

After the initial kissing and hugging, Cloverella finally held her childhood's companion at arm's length to see the changes in her. And, indeed, there were some. It was true that Jane was no prettier than before, yet now she had a certain style, a certain elegance, brought about partly by the beautiful clothes she wore and partly by her manner. She had softened somehow, become more of a sympathetic listener, an intelligent foil. Standing in certain lights, talking with animation, one could almost believe she was beautiful – a trick that perhaps she had learned from Anne Boleyn.

'Well?' she said, for Cloverella's approval.

'You look transformed, quite wonderful! I suppose you have many suitors?'

Jane inclined her head to indicate that she would reveal nothing before her mother, who was fluttering over the table in the background but listening hard all the while. Loudly she said, 'Mother, with your permission, may I rest for an hour? I have ridden hard today.'

Dame Margery clucked over her like a goose to its gosling. 'Why, of course, my chuck. Cloverella, you go with Jane and see she is comfortable. She is to have her old room all to herself.'

The two girls smiled as they crossed the short distance to the house and went up the imposing stairway. But it was not until Jane had removed her travelling clothes and stood in her nether garments that she finally pulled a face and answered, 'There are no suitors. Attending on the Queen's Grace leaves little time for anything else.'

'But surely you are surrounded by men?' Cloverella said in surprise.

'Yes, but the Queen is usually the centre of attention.'

Cloverella nodded. It was quite obvious already that her cousin had a hearty dislike of the woman she was sworn to serve.

'Is she such a wretch?' she asked.

'She *is*,' Jane answered fiercely. 'Oh, Cloverella, if you had been at Court and seen the banishment of the old Queen – or the Dowager Princess as she is now called. It was pathetic.' She turned to look at her cousin earnestly. 'I am young and have no memory or allegiance to old times. And yet it tore my heart in shreds to see that poor worn face – a face that once belonged to a pretty Spanish princess, remember – crying silently, all beaten and done for. I think of it still.'

Cloverella shook her head wonderingly. 'But the new Queen must have some redeeming feature.'

Jane sat down on her bed and her cousin felt she had never seen her more thoughtful. 'Sometimes, just very occasionally, she looks quite defenceless. As if events ran away with her and she could not stop them. Do you understand what I mean?'

'Very well,' answered Cloverella softly. 'I often wonder whether my own mother felt like that.'

Jane smiled. 'You should not dwell on it. It is all in the past. Now, what of the future? How is your magic gift?'

She said it with amusement, rather as if she were mentioning some comfortable family joke. 'It improves,' replied Cloverella, catching her inference, 'I will be ready soon.'

'For what?'

'To help people know the truth of things.'

Still smiling, Jane said, 'And what do you predict for the Queen? I suppose another triumph and the birth of a son?'

'On the contrary, it is a girl. It is also the beginning of her downfall.'

Jane's face changed dramatically and just for a second there was a delighted gleam behind her eyes. 'I hope so,' she whispered. 'She has dealt out enough blows and cost enough good men their lives, God knows.'

'But we are not judge and jury,' Cloverella answered. 'That is for a greater power.'

'Oh pooh,' said Jane, only just joking. 'If you go on like that I will have to box your ears. Now don't speak of that woman any more. Instead tell me everything that has happened at Wolff Hall since I have been away.'

Ever afterwards, the residents of the manor house were to remember the day that Sir Edward brought home his second wife. Not only because of the immense joy that this gave to his family but also because of news of a greater event, that indirectly was to effect the lives of every one of them, and of which they learned that night. Just as Dame Margery had planned, a grand banquet followed the blessing of the marriage in the Seymour's private chapel, the actual ceremony having taken place at the bride's home. It was a banquet that would have been too large to encompass in the hall and so had been prepared in the Great Barn, used for celebrations when the number of guests was too great to be encompassed within the house. And what a success such a venture proved. The guests had packed in with a will and even though, much as Dame Margery had dreaded, Anne Stanhope's haughty eyes had run over the place with an air of disparagement, even she had finally thawed out and allowed herself to have a good time.

She was very much as Tom had hinted; beautiful to look at, powerful as a tigress – and utterly domineering. Gazing at her beloved cousin Edward, Cloverella's heart bled for him. He was obviously wildly in love, all his affections, sublimated while his erring wife Katherine Filliol eked out her last days in a convent – at last given full rein. He who was so serious and so honourable could hardly keep his hands off his bride and his eyes, whenever Anne looked at him, went bright with emotion.

She'll be pregnant in a twelve-month, thought Cloverella, and for once needed no flash of second sight to know that she was right.

And Edward, already the nominal father of two boys, neither of whom he believed was his, looked good and ready to settle down to family life at last. His present position as a Squire of the Body – an appointment he had held for the last three years – involved him in daily personal attendance upon the King and it was obvious that Henry liked him. For Edward had not only good looks and courage but also the charm that was the gift of all the Seymour children. He was quite definitely one of those young men about the court who were destined to ride high – provided they made no important political enemies. He had also more than his share of integrity to help him; as if he had taken all of Tom's and added it to his own.

Yet this night even the bridegroom's attractive manner was nothing compared to that of his younger brother. For Tom, eyed by all the eligible females in the company, was in his element. And when the table was pushed back and the dancing, country-style, began, he seized women and girls by the waist and twirled them round until they were breathless and had no option but to seek his support. Finally he came to Cloverella and picked her up like thistledown, holding her with straight arms high over his head.

Enough wine had been drunk for no one to care and she could do nothing but laugh as he slid her down the length of his body and said, 'Well, little cousin, what do you think of my new sister-in-law?'

Cloverella hesitated. 'Edward must keep a tight rein on her, of that I am certain.'

'Why, will she be unfaithful?'

'No, not that. It isn't that.'

'What then?'

'She is so powerful, stronger than he is. She could push him into all kinds of trouble.'

Tom grinned. 'What *are* you talking about?'

'I'm not certain – yet. It is just that I love Edward and want him to be happy.'

Tom pulled her close to him. 'And do you love me?'

In a split second she was weak and trembling, longing to be his, yet knowing at the same time that Thomas could do this to all women, that there was nothing special about his feelings for her.

'Well?'

She couldn't answer, realising that both her parents must have lusted as she was doing now in order for her to be conceived.

'You are silent,' he persisted.

'Because you give me little choice. How can I be expected to answer sensibly in all this heat and noise?'

'Then step outside,' he answered, close to her ear.

She would have done so. Would have gone with him into the forest and lain down naked beneath the stars had the most extraordinary thing not happened. Just as she stepped towards the door, Cloverella saw a reflection in the great punch bowl. She glimpsed a man's face, saw the great mass of dark curls that surrounded it, the glowing amber eyes that seemed to look straight through her. Then the vision faded and with it her terrible passion. Cloverella was herself again, quite calm and composed, and looking at Tom as she had always done, like a dearly loved brother.

'I might get cold,' she said with a laugh, and then added, 'You have not danced with Jane yet. Look, she is quite alone.'

And it was true. Tom's sister sat rather sadly, isolated in all that merry dancing pack, her small hands folded in her lap and not speaking to a soul.

He shot Cloverella a penetrating look, saying, 'Then can we step outside tomorrow?'

'Who knows?' she answered carelessly. 'I doubt that I shall have the time.'

He would have retorted, said something quite sharp to her, had not there been a general call for the bedding to take place. Having been cheated of the merriment after the actual wedding, the guests were calling for a reinactment to take place now, and Edward and Anne were laughingly giving consent. There was a general hurrying and scurrying as the female guests surrounded the bride and took her, smiling and flushed, her colourful hair escaping from her headdress, out of the barn and through the cool darkness of evening into Wolff Hall. Behind her, at a respectful distance, followed Edward and his supporters, and it was not until the couple were cheered into a bed blessed by James, Sir John's priest, that some semblance of decorum returned to the guests who, certain that the bridegroom was doing his duty, returned to the barn to dance through the night.

It was as dawn came up over the Wiltshire landscape, suddenly cold and fierce, throwing pools of mist over the fields and wreathing clammy fingers around the ancient stones which stood so silent and mystic and totally puzzling, that the rider from London, the last guest to appear, came exhausted to the doorway of the barn, calling for ale.

The women had long since gone but old Sir John drank on, toasting his son's happiness, while Tom still seemed bright as a button, as if drink and companionship were all he needed to keep him merry. He looked up as the newcomer crossed over to where he sat, then jumped to his feet and embraced his cousin, Francis Bryan.

The unblinking grey eyes looked into his unsmilingly as Francis said, 'I could not get here before. As it is I've ridden all night. The Queen was in labour and I simply had to stay to see the outcome.'

The few remaining guests went silent; this was momentous news for them all. A prince at last to satisfy the wants of both King and commoners.

'Well?' It was Sir John, half rising to his feet, who spoke.

Sir Francis rubbed the back of his hand across his mouth, making a smear. He suddenly looked drained and colourless.

'A girl,' he said shortly. 'The Queen's Grace was delivered of a girl during the afternoon.'

'God's teeth,' exclaimed someone, 'how fares His Grace in all this?'

'Cold as ice,' answered Bryan, remembering only too vividly the frozen expression that had come over that great face as the physicians had broken their news. 'But he is trying to remain calm. Already he speaks of the prince that is yet to come.'

'She had better oblige,' said Sir John, from his cups. 'She had better oblige if she doesn't want to suffer the same fate as the old Queen.'

'Or worse,' put in a voice from the shadows.

They all turned to look at the speaker but it was only old mad Will who had served Sir John since both had been young men, and was nowadays regarded by most to be simple.

'Well, I'll drink to the new Princess,' said Tom, breaking the mood. 'Come on, who'll down a toast with me?'

The diminished wedding feast rose solemnly to its feet, some swaying more than others. 'The Princess,' they chorused, and drained their cups.

'May she soon have a brother,' added Francis Bryan.

'Amen to that.'

'And now to serenade Edward,' said Tom. 'He's had long enough to complete his business. A song would not come amiss. Come on, wake up,' he shouted to the minstrels who slumbered in a heap of humanity, some asleep on each other, others with their heads on the table, cradled by their forearms.

Blearily, they rose to do his bidding, staggering across the small courtyard to the house and slumping down again beneath the window behind which the newly-weds slept.

'A dance,' instructed Tom, leaping over the flagstones. 'A dance for a new-born Princess.'

Ever afterwards he was to think of that. How he had danced, alone and tipsy, on hearing the news that the flame which was entirely to consume his heart, the only creature to stir his passion beyond endurance, had drawn her first breath in the world. That the glory which was to become Elizabeth had been born.

# Chapter Three

IT WAS A DELICIOUS AWAKENING, at first abrupt and fearful, making the sleeper sit bolt upright, terrified that she was late for her duties; then, almost at once, followed a glorious sinking back on to her pillows and the realisation that she was at home, that no one was about to call her; the initial shock suddenly worth the suffering, by virtue of the pleasure which ensued. With a small sigh, Jane Seymour closed her eyes, and considered going back to sleep. But oblivion had no wish to come. Instead, through her mind raced all kinds of thoughts and memories, which seemed to Jane to take the form of a waking dream.

For no logical reason the girl found herself recalling her first meeting with Katharine of Aragon, when Jane had been barely twenty and the Queen over forty and threatened on every front by the power of the King's dark lady. Yet despite all that turmoil, Katharine had managed a considerate smile for her shy young maid-of-honour and had helped her to rise from her curtsey with her own hand. It was something that Jane had never forgotten; the kind face, once pretty, looking at her so earnestly and smiling.

Even now, lying comfortably in her bed at Wolff Hall, Jane shied away from the next memory, in fact pulled the pillow over her ears as if to drown out a sound that was in reality only in her head. Yet nothing could take away the memory of the terrible cry that had come from the Queen's lips on that stark dawning in Windsor when Katharine had awoken to find both her husband and his lady slipped away in the darkness. How the Queen had guessed that this signified the end of her marriage, that she would never see Henry again, Jane could not imagine. But that dreadful howl of anguish, enough to freeze the blood of all who heard it, would never escape her. For the fact had been that in her own quiet way, Jane had loved the Queen; a little humbly, a little undemonstratively perhaps, but nonetheless loved and respected the daughter of the Queen of Castile who had been so ill-used in the country of her adoption.

Jane sat up in bed, though still with her eyes closed, wishing for a time now beyond counting, that she had been powerful enough to defy the Lady in the days that followed the Windsor parting. Days when Katharine had been requested by the council to leave her apartments in the castle and move on to the disgraced and dead Cardinal Wolsey's former home at the More, there to hold a pathetic little court of her own, her household and retainers whittled away to nothing, all her young maids-of-honour, Mistress Seymour amongst them, removed from her service.

But to Jane, despite all the degradation that Katharine had been forced to endure, she was still Queen. For Mistress Seymour would never, could never, mentally accept the woman she detested as the true Queen of England. In spite of all directives, Jane still thought the poor creature, little better than a prisoner, now eking out her existence in Kimbolton Castle, to be England's sovereign lady.

To try and stop the wicked turn of her mind, Jane got out of bed and, crossing rajdly to her bowl, washed herself hard, as if scrubbing her skin could take away the guilt of having hidden her feelings and accepted a place in Anne Boleyn's entourage when Katharine had been exiled. But it was useless. As she trickled the water slowly through her fingers it seemed to her that they were the old Queen's tears.

'How could I have done it?' Jane said under her breath. 'I should have had the courage of my convictions.'

But how would she have dared to make a stand? She could have brought trouble not only on herself but the whole of her family. How would they have survived when good men like Thomas More and Bishop Fisher had gone to the block?

'No,' she thought, 'I did the only thing possible. Looked meek and waited for the moment when I could do her a disservice.'

Now, calling for her waiting woman to help her dress, Jane thought with a certain grim satisfaction that since the birth of Elizabeth two years earlier, the fortunes of the mighty Anne had plummeted, with no help from Mistress Seymour or any other of the Lady's detractors. It was common knowledge about the Court that the King was losing interest, had had a passionate affair with one of Anne's ladies when the baby Elizabeth had been barely a year old – a fact that had sent the Lady into hysterics before a

31

startled Admiral of France – and was presently visiting the easy-virtued Madge Shelton in her bedchamber.

Jane pulled a face. To her mind Madge was a hackney, for the King was not the only one to taste her fruits. It was rumoured that the Queen's own brother – to say nothing of several other young courtiers – all beat a track to her apartments.

'And good luck to them,' muttered Jane. 'Anything that puts that wicked woman's nose out of joint can only be for the good.'

'What did you say, my lady?' asked her servant, kneeling on the floor adjusting her mistress's kirtle.

'I was talking to myself, Meg.'

'About the King's visit I suppose?'

Just for a second Jane looked at her blankly and then drew a sharp breath. She realised now why she had been lost in thoughts of Katharine. The colossus at the heart of all the old Queen's suffering had announced his intention of hunting at Savernake as part of his progress, and it was to Wolff Hall that he was probably already making his way at this moment.

'Merciful God!' she exclaimed, 'I had forgotten.'

'Forgotten?' Meg stood up, looking thoroughly startled. 'How could you?'

Jane gave a naughty smile and her pale features took on a pixie-like life, making them suddenly fascinating.

'I see His Grace nearly every day, remember. This visit is of no great excitement to me.'

Meg gave her a shocked look. 'It is a good thing Dame Margery can't hear you. Why, she's been planning for weeks as to how she will entertain His Grace.'

Jane patted her hand. 'I know, I know. That's why I've been sent for.'

'Yes, your mother thought he would be pleased to see a familiar face.'

Jane turned away, sitting down before her mirror and leaning forward to examine her reflection.

'Familiar face, you say? Why, he hardly knows I exist.'

Meg came to stand behind her and picked up the hairbrush. 'How can that be? You said you see him daily.'

'He walks past me daily, as he does all the Queen's ladies who are plain and uninteresting. It is only those with their fair share of beauty that he will stop and speak to. Then it is all smiles and winks.'

Meg gave her a smack with the hairbrush. 'Jane, hush. Things like that should not be said aloud.'

'Why not?' Jane studied her reflection again. 'Look at me, Meg. Last April I was twenty-five – and what have I achieved? A sweet courtship when I was little more than a child – and nothing since. And the cause? That' – she stabbed at her nose – 'and that.' She drew her lips into an even thinner line than they were naturally. 'And my terrible pale face. Why in certain lights I look almost green!'

Meg stood silent, at a loss as to what to say. It was true that her charge, given to the servant to look after while still a babe-in-arms, had nothing to commend her in the way of beauty, except for her eyes.

She opened her mouth to reply but Jane cut across with, 'And if you are going to mention my eyes, please do not do so. Nobody even notices them when they are so busy hurrying past me. Plain Jane is my role in life – and plain Jane I shall die.'

Meg had had red hair in her youth and now her sudden temper exploded. 'For shame on you! If you think you are so uninteresting it is small wonder that no one bothers with you. There are other things beside looks. What of your wit and grace and intelligence? And what of your childhood pledge to outshine all and make a grand match.'

Jane smiled wryly. 'You mean my wish on Merlin's Mound? I should not have told you of it. It was obviously unlucky to do so.'

With all the familiarity that only a trusted servant would dare display, Meg answered, 'I shall speak to you no more, Mistress, until you are in a different mind. Now, would you like me to brush your hair?'

Jane stood up, pulling a light gown over her kirtle. 'No, I shall finish dressing later. I think I will go into the garden to see the day.'

Meg looked a little chastened. 'Are you angry with me, sweetheart? I spoke only for your good.'

Jane smiled. 'I know that. But it is difficult to bear such plainness when beauty seems to unlock every door, and the things said which are meant to give cheer somehow only serve to make it worse.'

Meg wrestled with some important thought but finally settled for saying, 'Then shall I return in a while?'

'Yes. Then you can dress me in my best in case His Grace decides to surprise us all and arrive this morning.'

'Is he riding from London?'

'Yes, so there is little chance of his getting here early. I will have plenty of time to take the air.'

And with that Jane Seymour descended the stairs and made her way through the lofty quiet of the great hall – called the Broad Chamber in the days of the Esturmys – and out to the gardens in the centre of which stood the manor house.

The buildings which comprised Sir John Seymour's family home were laid out in a rectangular pattern, a great court in front, and behind a small court round which were clustered the outbuildings and the stable block. A short distance from the small court stood the Great Barn and to the left of the house itself was the chapel, built by Sir William Esturmy in the Middle Ages, where the priest Sir James officiated for the salary of £2 per year and all found.

At this early hour the gardens were at their most delicate, wreathed with tendrils of mist which rose a few feet above the lawns and through which Jane glided like a ghost. Above her head a gemstone sky was also veiled by vapour but the sweet sun shot through glinting rays, proclaiming that this September day of 1535 would be fine and fair. A blackbird rose almost from beneath Jane's feet and carolled a song for her delectation from the branch of a nearby elm. So it was with a smile on her lips that she sat down on a stone seat and looked around.

The gardens were extensive. Before the great court lay the walled garden, its neatly planned flowerbeds and walks culminating in a central circle in which stood the sundial. Yet although Jane was fond of its symmetrical beauty, it did not appeal to her as much as the sweetly perfumed Young Lady's Garden, made especially for her as the first-born girl, and in which she, her sisters Bess and Dorothy, and Cloverella, had played so many innocent childhood games. Here, roses and gillyflower grew side-by-side with sweet smelling honeysuckle and great bushes of lavender, while in the spring dark mysterious shrubs burst forth vivid splashes of colour. It was a place for pastimes and pleasure unlike My Old Lady's Garden where, beside the flowers, and at some points intermingling with them, grew the herbs; golden marjoram, dill and rosemary, wormwood, pennyroyal and sweet cecily, the beds edged with sage to give an aromatic scent overall.

Behind Wolff Hall lay the Great Paled Garden, fenced with wooden staves as the name suggested and occupying an acre, beyond which lay the orchards, the arable fields and the park lands – the Horse Park, the Red Deer Park and undulating Soden Park. All told, Sir John owned an extensive holding but nonetheless not one large enough to house Henry and his entire entourage. In fact, in order to put at the King's disposal the best suite of rooms in the house, Sir John was sleeping in a minor chamber while Dame Margery and Jane had been moved out to nearby Topenham Lodge and were to take up residence there this very afternoon, while the Great Barn – freshly painted for the occasion – was once more to act as the dining hall.

The sun broke through the mist and Jane leaned against the back of the stone seat and closed her eyes. She was not really looking forward to the forthcoming visit. There was something about His Grace which frightened her; perhaps his enormous height and shoulders and the arrogant masculinity of him. Whenever Jane saw him at Court she would lower her eyes in pretended modesty and hope that he would not pick her out to speak to. And her wish had been granted; since that night six years ago when she had danced with him amongst the other masquers, they had not exchanged a word.

Let the beautiful ones bear the brunt of his lechery, Jane thought. I could not stomach to be the butt of Anne Boleyn's vile temper.

And as this idea went through her mind she remembered the tantrums and hysterics, the irritability and outbursts of violent anger, caused by the fact that Henry's eye had wandered even when Anne had still been pregnant.

'And that is exactly what she deserves after all she did to Katharine,' Jane muttered to herself as the sun came out in full and flooded My Young Lady's Garden with all the brilliance of a fine September morning.

Nearly all the county of Wiltshire was drenched with a swirling ground mist that dawning, and the last places from which it cleared were those in which the ancient and mysterious stones reared up to pose their eternal questions. Dampened by fog they stood, grey and massive, silently brooding over the surrounding countryside, looking out to where Silbury Hill, the ultimate enigma, caught the first rays of the sun on its smooth green slopes.

Observing it from a distance and writing down what appeared to be calculations in a large book, a man stood with his back leaning against one of the stones of Avebury, singing to himself as he worked. To assist his freedom of movement, his cloak had been discarded along with his doublet and he was dressed, despite the fact that the day was still chilled by fog, only in his shirt and stocks.

The cloak which lay on the ground beside him was of a sombre black hue but the doublet thrown down upon it was a harsh shade of green, almost distressing to the eye, while his upper stocks – paned with panels of vermilion – glowed a vivid shade of purple. His dress was bizarre, indeed quite terrible to look at, yet he had a certain quality that defied derision, an indefinable strength that would have made an onlooker pause before they passed him by as a motley fellow.

His face was squarish, displaying a strong jaw and nose and a contradictory mouth, tough yet sensual, the mouth of one who could both fight and love, yet if it had not been for the wild mass of black curls that sprawled round his head, his eyes would have been the most outstanding thing about him. But as it was, hair and eyes equalled one another; the one dark as pitch, suggesting tainted blood of some kind; the other amber, golden almost, largely set and clear, yet capable of giving the wink to a maiden should their owner so wish. For here was a creature who possessed the most captivating thing in the world – an abundant energy for life made endearing by a childlike wonder. It was a deadly combination when all was said and done.

Without pausing, the man continued to make his calculations until the sun was well risen when, the glare being too great to allow him to do more, he called his horse, contentedly cropping nearby, and throwing his unworn clothes over the saddle, made off through the trees in the direction of the town of Marlborough, passing the church of St Peter and St Paul, where the son of an Ipswich butcher, named Thomas Wolsey, had first been ordained priest.

As he trotted by on his way down the main thoroughfare, the man looked back over his shoulder, thinking how that same priest had risen to be Cardinal, Archbishop of York, and Chancellor of the Kingdom before His Grace had finally turned his back on him, furious over Wolsey's failure to bring about an annulment of Henry's marriage to Katharine. Just as he had done to the old Queen at Windsor, so the King had treated his prelate at Grafton. The anxiously waiting churchman had been told that His Grace

36

had gone hunting and could not receive him but, in truth, the King was never to set eyes on his mighty Cardinal again. Sixteen months later, Wolsey had been dead, some said of a broken heart. Shaking his head at the cruel course of such recent events, the man entered the alehouse known as the Bear.

Hurrying forward to serve the stranger, bobbing a curtsey even while she walked, the keeper's daughter was all excitement as she greeted him with, 'Are you from court, Sir? Has the King already arrived at Savernake?'

The man bowed politely. 'I am little there these days, madam, and must confess I was not aware of His Grace's visit to these parts.'

The girl poured out a measure, burbling eagerly as she did so. 'Oh yes. He has announced his intention of hunting in the forest and is to stay with the Warden of Savernake, Sir John Seymour, up at Wolff Hall. It is a great honour for all the family. Mistress Jane has even come home from court.'

The man nodded slowly, one black curl freeing itself from all the rest and falling forward over his forehead.

'And Her Grace is not with the King?'

'Oh no, Sir. It is said that she expects a child next spring and is taking good care of herself.'

The man smiled quizzically. 'As indeed she needs to.'

'Oh yes, Sir. The King so longs for a Prince.'

'Yes,' answered the man, downing his ale and holding out the rough drinking vessel for more, 'he does indeed.'

Without knowing quite why, the girl asked, 'Do you think he will get one?'

The man's face was in half-shadow as he answered softly, 'Oh yes, His Grace will have a son. Of that I'm certain.'

'So the Queen will be lucky?'

'No,' he answered, still partially hidden from her, 'this Queen will never be lucky. She must pay her dues.'

The girl stared at the stranger, mystified. 'Dues?'

He stood up and a sprite-like smile crossed his face, making him normal and merry once more. 'I am talking to myself, forgive me. But I thank you for what you have told me. I find it very interesting to learn that the King has once more gone hunting in earnest.'

Any hidden meaning escaped the girl, and she answered enthusiastically, 'Oh yes, Sir. There's red deer in abundance in

Savernake Forest. To say nothing of wild boar. I am sure he will have good sport.'

'Perhaps he will,' the man said quietly. 'Perhaps the time has come for the wheel to start turning.'

She gaped at him but he would say no more, merely brushing her fingers with his lips before he left the room and, taking his horse from the stables, headed away towards London.

The cavalcade mounting the hill climbed at speed, the sun catching the bright metal of spur and bridle as the twenty men who made up the party raced to see who could attain the summit first. Well to the fore, as tact and discretion decreed that he surely must be, Henry Tudor, King of England, his mighty legs astride a powerful horse, shouted with glee in the sunshine, free for once from all the gnawing thoughts of discontent that nowadays beset him almost daily.

Yet despite his high spirits and lively retinue, this was no elaborate progress to Wiltshire, but in fact a hunting party. In place of a vast following of royal guards, chattering courtiers and brilliant women, Henry had chosen on this occasion to surround himself entirely with a hand-picked group of men: men with whom he could hunt till he dropped with tiredness; who would feast and drink well into the night with him; who would listen while musicians played the King's own compositions and raise their masculine voices in song. For this was the very relaxation he felt he needed these days, away from the worries of kingship and the nagging voice of she whom once he had loved so well but who had so subtly changed on attaining the pinnacle of power into something dark and sinister.

Even now at this moment of supreme enjoyment, Henry thought to himself that his new Queen had not been equal to the great position to which he had so ruthlessly raised her – and most certainly had not fulfilled even half of what he had dreamed and hoped and believed she would be like in their marriage bed.

Or rather, he qualified, so she became after her coronation. It was as if, having achieved her heart's desiree, she had no longer needed to act a part – though at the time she had blamed her coldness on being pregnant.

Pregnant! All that he had been through and all that he had endured just to be fobbed off with another girl at the end of it all.

But now there was hope again, unless it was another false alarm, as there had been last year. He had been certain then, and still was, that Anne had made up the story of her condition just to keep him at her side, when all he had been longing for was to crawl into a soft bed with a willing warm-bodied woman and forget all the agonies he had suffered to make Anne his consort, and then see everything he had striven for go sour.

Disappointment suddenly raged within, driving away his mood of elation, as Henry reached the summit of Topenham Hill first, briefly wondering if the others had let him win the race, and saw spread below him on the sloping ground across the valley the gardens, fields and manor house that comprised Sir John Seymour's beautiful estate of Wolff Hall.

'Well, well,' he said, his small eyes narrowing beneath their silly arched brows, 'I had not expected anything quite so fine.'

At his elbow, Sir Nicholas Carew, one of the hunting party, asked, 'Have you not visited Wolff Hall before, Your Grace?'

'Strangely, no. Yet I like old Sir John and his sons, and I'm told the hunting is good, so I cannot think why not.'

'They are a loyal family and very sound. I have known Edward for years; in fact I consider him one of my closest friends,' Sir Nicholas answered somewhat irrelevantly. Then in a more casual tone added, 'You will be acquainted with Jane of course, Your Grace.'

Henry looked slightly surprised. 'Will I?'

'She is one of Her Grace's serving women.'

'Jane Seymour?' Henry said under his breath, then added, 'Is she the little fair one, rather plain of feature?'

Nicholas gave a wry smile. 'I suppose one could describe her so, though she has remarkable eyes. But you are right, Your Grace. Her main attraction lies in her quiet charm and intelligence.'

Henry frowned. 'Was she not there when I met the French King in Calais three years ago?'

'Yes. She was one of the attendants to the Marquess, as Her Grace then was.'

The King did not answer, merely nodding his head and screwing his eyes up to look at the flowing landscape, while Nicholas Carew took a calculated guess as to what his sovereign was thinking. The expensive charade at Calais at which Anne Boleyn was meant to be

39

paraded before Francis of France in all her glory – yet, in fact, took three days to put in an appearance and, when she finally did so, came fully masked – had been a triumph. The French King had risen to the deception and been completely won over by the Lady's teasing charm. And Henry had been so proud and happy, wooed and flattered by Anne's brilliance, never suspecting that within that tempting mouth a shrew's tongue might lie concealed.

Carew smiled grimly. He had had personal experience of Anne's violent swings of mood, had been present when at a state ball given the previous year for a special embassy from King Francis, Anne had broken down on seeing Henry laughing with his current mistress. If he had not disliked her so much, been utterly opposed to the Boleyn faction and their influence on his king, Nicholas might almost have felt sorry for her, but having watched her climb to power from his place within the Court he could feel nothing but bitterness.

The King suddenly spoke, startling Carew from his thoughts. 'I think they've seen us. There seems to be activity.'

From the distance that separated them, the inhabitants of Wolff Hall appeared as mere dots and Nicholas watched with amusement as one dot, obviously a look-out, scurried into the house, while several others ran about nervously, rather as if they did not know what they should do.

The King smiled, 'I think we have taken them by surprise.'

He had done it deliberately, spending the night at Woodstock Palace in Oxfordshire, and now seemed gratified that the Seymours had been thrown into some confusion by the promptness of his arrival. He even chuckled aloud as a particular dot, very small and obviously female, went scurrying in from one of the gardens where it had, but a few moments before, been taking its leisure.

'We must proceed slowly, gentlemen,' he called. 'Otherwise I fear there might be scant reception for us.'

But there Henry Tudor was wrong, because as the cavalcade descended Topenham Hill and crossed the valley, they distinctly heard the ebullient note of the Esturmy horn – the ancient symbol which signified the badge of office of the Warden of Savernake, always blown when the monarch came to the forest – and saw the upright figure of Sir John Seymour, surrounded by an escort of hounds and horses, making his way on horseback towards them. And if Henry had indeed caught him unawares there was no sign of it as the Warden drew alongside the King's party, blew the triumphant horn once more, slung as it was around his neck by an elaborately decorated strap, and drew to a halt.

'Greetings, Sire,' he called formally. 'Welcome to Savernake Forest.' And with that he leapt from his horse with a nimbleness that would not have been unbecoming in a man half his years, and made a reverential bow.

He was a reasonably tall figure, made to look older and more dignified by a long grey beard which hung well down his chest and belied the fact that he was only sixty-one years of age. Nicholas Carew suspected that somewhere behind Sir John's mournful eyes must lurk a twinkle for the man had sired eleven children, one a bastard of his adventurous youth, and the others legally by Dame Margery. He had been a fighting man, too, and knighted in the field for his part in putting down the Cornishmen's Rebellion at the Battle of Blackheath in 1497. He had also seen service in France before he retired from military life and became a respected figure around the Court, a friend to both the present king and his father, a quiet unassuming diplomat.

'Rise up, Sir John,' said Henry heartily, and Carew realised with a strange pricking of his spine that the sovereign with whom he had been on familiar terms for over twenty years was about to act a part for the benefit of his host – that of the bluff friendly king, approachable and human, abroad with no purpose other than to enjoy himself.

'If only they could see him at the other end of the scale,' thought Nicholas, remembering the vicious snarling figure, choking with rage whenever its desires were thwarted. And his mind went to Fisher, More and Wolsey, once beloved of the King and now dead as stones because they had dared put obstacles in Henry Tudor's merciless path.

John Seymour straightened himself, smiling, and so did his escort who had bowed in their saddles.

'And now, Your Grace, if you will be so kind as to accompany me to Wolff Hall, my home, I believe that you will find all in readiness.'

With a suspicion of a wink at his entourage, Henry fell into step beside Sir John and they rode side-by-side, leading the cavalcade of courtiers, huntsmen and Seymour retainers.

'An interesting name, Wolff Hall. Is its origin taken from a pack

41

of roving wolves in the forest?' The King was obviously in conversational mood.

'No, Your Grace. It comes from the Saxon name Ulf. It appears as such in the Domesday Book.'

'Really?' Henry seemed interested but Nicholas, riding directly behind the leaders, suspected that the King was already beginning to wonder how lavish the entertainment provided might be in such a remote spot, and in truth had very little concern in the manor's history.

They were drawing nearer, the house growing larger by the second, and it could be seen that several figures already anxiously hovered in the great courtyard and that another was hurrying out of the entrance doorway to join them.

The troop of horsemen clattered over the cobbles and the servants rushed forward to hold the horses' heads. Giving the smile that Henry knew full well could dazzle anyone, he dismounted and went to stand before his hosts, raising up first Dame Margery.

'Welcome to my home, Your Grace,' she said, her high round cheeks pink with a combination of strain and excitement.

'May I present my wife, Margery?' said Sir John, a fraction too late.

'Indeed you may,' answered Henry heartily, kissing her hand.

God's teeth, thought Carew, he's set to charm the birds from the trees. If only Jane could do the same to him.

He had thought, even as they left London, that the Seymour daughter, with her quiet unassuming ways, might attract the King's attention by her very contrast to Anne Boleyn. For no two women could be more unlike, one dark as night, the other pale as a flower; one taut, tense and nagging, her counterpart gentle and charming.

'My daughter Jane, Your Grace,' Sir John was intoning even as the King jumped in with, 'But we are old friends. Mistress Jane has served us at Court right well.'

He stooped to raise her from her respectful salute and for the first time since they had danced together at Greenwich, Jane felt the touch of his hand and all the great bulk of him hanging over her. For one terrible moment she thought she was going to faint at Henry's feet as a frightening sense of suffocation engulfed her. As always, it was the very size and masculinity of him that she found so distressing, accentuated as it was by vastly padded shoulders and a curving codpiece.

'I am honoured, Your Grace,' she muttered, pulling herself up straight on his hand and still not daring to raise her eyes.

'You have served us right well,' he repeated and Jane received the vivid impression that he could think of nothing else to say. She had no choice but to glance at him then, and as she slowly raised her eyes she saw that he was staring at her in an odd manner. Knowing that the last thing her face could take was close scrutiny, Jane felt the blood rush to her cheeks in desperation. She withdrew her fingers hastily, muttered, 'Your Grace's unworthy servant,' and half turned towards her mother, but there was no help at hand there.

'Jane will take you to the great hall, Your Grace,' Dame Margery was saying. 'There you will find refreshment awaiting you and after that we await Your Grace's instructions as to when you would like to dine.'

Henry paused. 'We shall hunt for two hours, Dame Margery, and then return. There is something – restful – about Wolff Hall and we are anxious not to leave it for too long.'

'At Your Grace's pleasure,' said Dame Margery and curtsied again.

Over her mother's bent back, Jane Seymour at last looked the King full in the eye, drawing her courage up so hard that her heart began to race. 'If Your Grace would be good enough to come with me.'

'At any time, Mistress Seymour,' he answered playfully.

And it was as well that all bowed as he walked through the great door into Wolff Hall, so that the slow smile which was spreading over the features of Sir Nicholas Carew was thus carefully concealed.

# Chapter Four

THE FIRST EVENING HAD GONE SO unbelievably well that Dame Margery could hardly believe her eyes. Instead of a monarch drumming his fingers and casting his gaze about at the inferior size and fitments of the great hall, Henry Tudor had evinced every sign of enjoying himself enormously. Ignoring custom and at his own insistence he had sat at the head of the crowded table – the Great Barn being reserved until the King gave gracious permission for Wiltshire neighbours to join the throng – and had eaten and laughed his way through the entire meal. So that now, Jane's mother – seated on Henry's right while Jane occupied the space on his left – triumphantly smiled at her daughter and took another sip of wine, not caring that it was bringing a flush to her apple cheeks.

And it seemed to Jane, gazing at Dame Margery's ample proportions and button face as if for inspiration, that she had the finest mother in the world. For though noble blood flowed in the lady's veins, her great grandmother being a daughter of Harry Hotspur and a direct descendent of Edward III, Margery had the simplicity of a country woman, born and bred. She was wise; could heal a cut, wipe away a tear, cope with the deaths of four children, as easily as she could listen to problems. In Jane's view, her mother was quite the most splendid creature in creation, her only fault that she had not passed on some of her early beauty to her eldest daughter.

Knowing herself watched, Dame Margery looked up again and caught the girl's eye and they exchanged another brief smile before Jane once more dropped her gaze to her plate, where it had determinedly remained throughout the meal in a frantic effort to avoid the King's twinkling glances. For Henry, for mysterious reasons of his own, was indulging in an obviously false and sickeningly roguish attempt to flirt with her. In fact, never in Jane's life had she seen such a performance and all done, she felt sure, to prove to the King's enormous ego that ugly women could fall in love with him just as easily as beautiful. Realising that he was leaning across her mother to talk to Sir John and that she was momentarily safe, Jane risked a swift glance at her sovereign lord.

At close quarters like this – closer than she had ever seen him before – every detail of his face could be observed and Jane's eyes lingered on the red hair, almost hidden beneath the jewelled hat, and the scrubbish ginger beard growing outward from beneath his nostrils like a widely-spaced moustache. She thought she had never seen a face so huge, so moon-like, with no sign of cheekbones but instead a straight line from enormous chin to balding forehead; the whole thing made to look bigger by the King's finely arched brows, which somehow seemed plucked and effeminate. The eyes above which these ridiculous brows danced were of a dark blue shade, very heavily-lidded, and had a marvellous way of going hard as pebbles, so that it was impossible to know what their owner was thinking.

From where she sat it was not easy for Jane to see more of the King's body than his gigantic shoulders, rubbing against both those of her mother and herself whenever he turned in the confined space. Yet she knew that his stomach now had a coating of fat and that it would be essential for him to exercise long and hard if he wished to keep a reasonable physique. In a way she found Henry almost obscene, enormous in every respect, and yet, though she could hardly bear to admit it to herself, there was something about him that excited her. The very suffocating size of him aroused something base that she could not identify, nor had any desire to. The truth was that she was attracted to the King, frightened yet fascinated all at the same time.

Whether he had seen her watching him out of the corner of his eye Jane could not tell, but Henry suddenly switched his glance from her father to herself and stared at her boldly. To have dropped her eyes at once would have been tantamount to rudeness and Jane found herself forced to return his gaze without flinching, yet praying all the time that he would look elsewhere. But this he obviously had no intention of doing. Henry Tudor was going to make the most of the opportunity to stare Mistress Seymour out.

That the king was arrogant, considering every woman his prize by reason of *droit de seigneur* was blatant; the reasons for his teasing Jane were not quite so clear, though she was sure her guess was right, that he considered it good practice to charm any female, plain or fair. If he had been anyone other than her sovereign, Jane would have allowed herself the luxury of glaring. But as it was she gave a faint smile before she, yet again, lowered her gaze to her lap.

'Mistress Jane, have I angered you?' The tone was light, bantering, but she knew at once what it really meant. Henry was not going to let her get away with dropping her eyes.

Both Sir John and Dame Margery looked faintly uncomfortable as she answered, 'Your Grace, how could you think such a thing? What have I done?' and returned his move neatly.

He laughed, appreciating her response. 'Madam, to make amends for my fault – though I can swear with hand on heart that I know not what it is – I shall sing you a song of my own composition. That is if it would please you?'

Sir Nicholas Carew, sitting to Jane's left, inwardly cringed. He had never seen his friend and monarch play the coquet quite so hard, which he knew from past experience meant that Henry had no genuine interest whatsoever.

He allowed a small sigh to escape as she answered dully, 'All Your Grace's compositions are tuneful. It would be a pleasure to hear any one.'

Jane felt sickened even as she spoke. For all she really wanted to do was to make an excuse and leave for Topenham Lodge and the privacy of her bed, away from this stifling man who mocked her with his pretended overtures and made her a fool with every winking glance.

'Then will you choose the song, gracious Jane?'

She thought she was going to scream as she answered, 'To do so would be presumptious, Your Grace. I leave the choice to you.'

He seemed content with that and called to one of his own musicians to bring him a lute. Whether Henry had not trusted Sir John Seymour's minstrels to make a goodly enough sound was a moot point but the fact remained, he had brought six of his own best men and had added their number to Sir John's troupe, the whole contingent having played throughout the evening from the gallery above the hall.

Now they were silent as the King's great fingers, surprisingly delicate as they plucked the sensitive strings, sent the thrilling sound of a love lyric into the sudden hush. Carew thought afterwards that obviously this was the moment when everybody realised Henry was flirting with Jane, for he saw a pink Dame Margery stare round-eyed at her husband who, in his turn, shot a look of total astonishment in the direction of the King himself. And amongst the others at the table there seemed to run a cold chill, a tension, a silent yet somehow audible in-drawing of breath.

'If only the great lecher really meant it,' Carew caught himself thinking, then mentally crossed himself at the word he had used to describe his sovereign.

It was Jane herself who made no response. She sat in her customary pose, hands in lap and gaze cast down, hardly seeming to breath as the light, easy voice rang out words of love into an atmosphere suddenly electric with unspoken thoughts. But when at the end of the song her remarkable eyes suddenly swept up, Carew noticed that the green aspect of them was predominant.

'Thank you, Your Grace,' she said simply, and stood up. 'And now, with your kind consent, I must beg leave to withdraw. A terrible headache has come upon me this last hour and I feel that I should go immediately to Topenham Lodge and not inflict myself further on this merry company.'

Whatever Henry really thought he masked it well and played the innocent. 'Topenham Lodge?' he repeated, furrowing his brow.

'A place of ours in the village of that name. My mother and I are staying there during your visit, Your Grace.'

He's going to get annoyed, thought Carew with a sinking heart. The silly chit is pushing him too far.

Henry turned to Dame Margery who was looking horror-stricken. 'Alas, my Lady, I do not think my compositions fall well on the ear of your daughter. But her leaving us does not mean that we will be deprived of your charming company also?'

'Oh no, not at all Your Grace,' she fluttered, obviously greatly distressed by her child's extraordinary behaviour. 'The servants will ride back with Jane. I shall remain as long as Your Grace wishes.'

He turned back to Mistress Seymour. 'Then all I can do is wish you a speedy return to health, my dear, and bid you goodnight.'

The girl sank into a respectful curtsey and the gentlemen present made to stand politely at her departure but not before Henry rose rapidly, still agile for all his increasing girth, and offered his hand to help her rise. For a frightening moment Carew thought she was going to ignore it but Jane obviously thought better of such a slight and placed her fingers in those of the King. He bent his head and it was only Jane who knew that as he kissed her hand his naughty tongue, swift as a serpent, darted out and drew up the skin for a moment. Nor could anyone know except the young woman herself, how a wicked thrill of response, which seemed to shoot upwards from the most intimate part of her body and consume the rest, made her weak on her feet.

With amazing self-control Jane hid her feelings, pursing her lips severely to give a thoroughly spinsterish expression.

'I thank Your Grace for your understanding,' she said primly.

In a voice so low that nobody else could possibly have overheard, Henry answered, 'Let us hope that your headache is recovered tomorrow, Jane. For I do not intend to pass this visit deprived of your company. Do you understand me?'

She wanted to answer that she would do as she pleased and could refuse to be the butt of his cruel joke if she so wished but, of course, that was impossible. Instead Jane chose to greet his remark with silence but, of their own accord, her eyes looked up and flashed a warning. At that moment she was beautiful, flushed and breathless, her irises varied shades of jade and indigo.

'Till tomorrow then,' said the King of England.

'Indeed,' replied Jane Seymour, and left her parents' hall without looking back.

Great with child as she was, it was not easy for Anne Seymour to find a comfortable position in which to sleep, nor was she helped by the fact that Edward – beside whom she was lying in their splendid marriage bed – was breathing heavily and noisily, and occasionally gasping. In fact to keep still was becoming so difficult that it was with a sense of relief that Anne slid her legs to the floor and finally stood up.

The room was full of silver, and warm, despite it being early September, and Lady Seymour padded on silent feet towards the mirror, turning her body to see her swollen shape. Her breasts, always one of her best features, still rose high and exciting, clearly visible through the thin nightrobe, but her belly was heavy and the child in it already low, questing to be born.

Anne hoped it was a boy. The passionate marriage which she and Edward enjoyed to the full, had embarrassingly produced a daughter, little Anne, almost nine months to the day from their wedding. And now, only two years from their anniversary, another was on the way. Smilingly, Anne peered at her reflection closely.

The fall of auburn hair, unbound and turned to silver tissue in the moonshine, was lustrous, and her face had improved, if anything, with motherhood. In fact it was generally considered that her looks these days were better than ever. With her red lips curving into a smile, Anne moved away from the mirror and, passing quietly out the door, descended the great staircase of Elvetham – the young Seymours' new home in Hampshire – in search of a cooling drink and some fresh night air.

Yet she was not the only one awake, for as Anne neared the bottom step she distinctly saw a shadow separate itself from the others and furtively cross the small hall, making for the great door that led to the courtyard and thence to the gardens and parkland beyond.

Anne froze, sinking back into the pools of black shadow and watching intently as the figure reached a patch of moonlight, thrown from a high window on the landing above. Rather as she had suspected, the face of Edward's cousin, now personal companion to herself, came into view. Cloverella was also stalking about Elvetham in the silence of midnight.

Anne frowned. She did not like the girl, feeling that she had been foisted on her when Cloverella's Romany blood had debarred her from obtaining a place at Court. Anne also, rather jealously, did not care for the girl's good looks or for Edward's obvious affection for her. At the time she had argued hard against his cousin joining the entourage of the newly married Seymours, but for once Edward had stood up to her, showing a ruthless streak that Anne did not know he possessed.

'She's coming and that's an end to it. I'll hear no more,' he had said, and Anne had been forced to give way, resolving that she would marry Cloverella off to someone, anyone, as quickly as possible; though so far without success, despite two years' effort.

Now Anne enjoyed seeing her victim leap in terror as she whispered, 'What are you doing? I can see everything, so be on your guard.'

Cloverella spun round, her eyes searching the shadows.

'Here,' said Anne, stepping forward like a phantom. 'It is I who speaks.'

Cloverella put her hand to her breast, which heaved with fright. 'Oh Anne, thank goodness. I wondered what it was.'

'As indeed you might,' answered Lady Seymour, hard-eyed, 'when you stalk about the place in the dark of night.'

Her tone and the very way she stood, arms folded and chin high, demanded an explanation, especially as it could now be seen that Cloverella was fully dressed and carried a small bundle of possessions.

'Running away?' asked Anne sarcastically. 'How romantic!'

Cloverella rallied somewhat and stood her ground. 'If you must know I was leaving, yes. This very night I dreamed that Jane was crying and calling out for me . . .'

'So you were making for Wolff Hall?'

'Yes. The dream was vivid, real. I knew it must be true. Jane is in trouble.'

Anne smiled. 'Cloverella, you will *not* go to Wolff Hall. I will not have you riding out into the night nor even the day for that matter.' Pausing portentously, she added, 'There is no possibility of Jane being in tears, for at this very moment the King's Grace is visiting Wolff Hall and all is fun and frivolity.'

Cloverella looked thoughtful. 'Do you really think so?'

'Of course I do,' snapped Anne. 'Your dream was caused by too many rich stuffs taken when you dined.'

Cloverella nodded. 'If you say so.' She leaned forward to embrace her cousin and as she did so her hand accidentally slipped against Anne's distended belly. 'Why another girl,' she exclaimed with apparent pleasure. 'Another fine daughter for you, Anne. My Romany blood is never wrong in divining the sex of an unborn child.'

Lady Seymour looked as if she would like to hit the girl. 'Stuff and nonsense,' she answered roundly. 'You are just saying it to annoy me. Now go to bed, Cloverella, this very minute, before I get angry.'

Her cousin seemed sad. 'I was only trying to be helpful. Goodnight, Anne.'

She walked slowly up the stairs, her head drooping forward, but once out of sight of Anne's narrowed eyes, Cloverella ran silently along the landing to the fine bedchamber in which Edward slumbered, totally unaware of the disagreement between his two favourite women, and nestled down beside him on the bed.

'Edward,' she whispered into his sleeping ear, 'I want to accompany you to Wolff Hall when you dine with the King. You will take me with you. Do you understand that?'

Edward stirred and nodded his head but did not wake up.

'Thank you, dearest Ned,' said Cloverella and dropped a kiss on to his quiet lips before she scurried off to her own room, and away from the prying eyes of Anne Seymour.

The morning was horribly fine, bright and merry and full of brilliant sunshine which strained Jane's puffy eyes and made her want to pull the bedclothes up over her head and lie all day in a curtained room, rather than rise and be part of it.

She had cried all night, sick to the heart of Henry Tudor's mockery, and frightened quite horribly by the awesome sensation which had swept her when the King's tongue had flickered over the spaces between her fingers. So intense a reaction had forced her to admit to herself finally – for she had long had a suspicion which she had furiously thrust from her mind – that, despite her prim appearance, she was passionate.

Looking at the matter without emotion, which she found hard to do, Jane presumed that she had inherited such violent fervour from her father, whose youthful indiscretions were something of a family joke amongst his children. And if she had, she was not alone in this, for Thomas made no secret of the fact that he had lost his virginity at thirteen years of age and had been pursuing women ever since. Indeed, at the time he had proudly boasted of his early conquest to his brothers, a fact which the girls had soon got hold of and giggled about – and had been quite revered in the Seymour nursery as a result, as there is nothing more attractive than naughtiness.

Jane, on the other hand, had firmly put such feelings from her and was as innocent now as she had been as a child. Yet with the passing years her longings had ceased to be vague and had now begun to rage within her, brought to a head, or so she thought, by the overpowering and somehow monstrous attraction of the King himself.

She could have wept again, would have done so, had not she heard her door opening and the heavy footsteps of Meg advancing to the bedside. Jane closed her eyes but not quite quickly enough for her servant said suspiciously, 'Jane, I know you are not asleep so don't pretend. Just you get up, slug-a-bed. The King will be hunting soon and you should be there to wave him off. Your mother has already left.'

Jane opened her swollen lids painfully. 'I can't go,' she answered hoarsely. 'I'm not well.'

51

Meg leant over her saying nothing but taking in every detail of her mistress's pale and ravaged face.

'I don't believe you are ill at all,' she said eventually. 'I think you have been weeping, and most of the night, judging by the look of you.'

Jane remained silent, not daring to utter, and after a moment Meg sat down on the edge of the bed, took one of Jane's hands in her own and said in a different tone, 'What is it, my dove? Are you unhappy? Tell old Meg your troubles, like you always used to.'

It was too much! The one thing guaranteed to send Jane into another fury of tears was kindness; she put her head in the servant's lap and wept wildly for what seemed an age. Meg said nothing, simply stroking the blossom-pale hair, until finally Jane quietened down and only the occasional sob disturbed the silence. Then she spoke.

'This has something to do with the King's visit hasn't it? Has he said something to upset you?'

Jane shook her head violently but Meg went on. 'Old Will told me that His Grace took a fancy to you. Sang a song especially for you. Is that right?'

'Old Will is mad,' Jane answered furiously. 'His Grace did nothing but mock me.'

'In what way?'

'He thought it diverting to see if a plain woman would succumb to his charms as easily as any other.'

'Hmm,' Meg said thoughtfully. 'Now I'd always believed that King Henry was a man of the world.'

'What has that to do with it?'

'Well, if he is, he would *know* that a plain woman would fall into his arms twice as fast as a beautiful one because she would be so grateful to him. So I doubt that was his ploy.'

Jane's tear-stained face peered into hers and she said slowly, 'I had not looked at it like that.'

'No, I don't suppose you had, Mistress, because you are so busy believing yourself ugly that you don't stop to think at all.'

'What do you mean?'

Meg did not reply at once, pulling Jane towards her by the shoulders and holding her none too gently. Then she said, 'I mean what I say. If the King flirted with you it was because he genuinely wanted to. Listen, I saw Nan Bullen once when I went to Court to serve your mother. I tell you she has no looks at all. She is thin, has no comely breasts, hides a hand she is ashamed for anyone to see – and yet she once had the King of England at her feet. And do you know why?'

Jane shook her head.

'Because she is clever, so full of style and artifice that she makes people believe she is beautiful. She tosses that great mane of dark hair and flashes those eyes and men fawn over her. Well, Jane, do you not have hair light as flax and eyes sea-blue? Why can't you do as she does and hide your bad points beneath the good ones?'

It was all so sensible and somehow so relevant that Jane was almost convinced. Sensing her advantage, Meg persisted.

'You serve the Lady at Court. You have seen her early in the morning. Be honest Jane. Is her beauty a true one?'

The answer was a little hesitant. 'Not really. In fact some call her the Night-Crow.'

'There you are then.' Meg was triumphant. 'And what is the opposite of a fierce dark crow? A little fair dove – my pet name for you, Jane – that cooes so sweetly for all to hear.'

She had done it! Meg could tell by the girl's expression that she believed every word she had heard.

'Now, let me wash your face and put some of Cloverella's lotions and potions on it. If you cannot wave farewell to the hunting party at least you can greet them on their return.'

Jane nodded slowly. 'Yes, Meg, you are right. I must be there to receive them. It is only polite after all.'

The days in which summer finally concedes to the first sweet fire of autumn have a sunshine, a mellowness, all their own and that September afternoon in Savernake Forest was no exception. In the air hung the smell of recent harvests, of apples ripening in the orchards of Wolff Hall, of heavy dark plums groaning on their trees; and the light itself, filtering through the branches of the formidable oaks, was gold dust, full of dancing motes and sleepy insects, a foretaste of the half-mist it would later become. Everywhere, despite the warmth, there was a sense of slowness, as if the urgent brightness of summer, with its days of river sports and outdoor food and lovers' trysts, was gone and the earth was settling to a more leisurely pace to herald the dark, still months that lay before it.

And for once, as though his mind was more on the season's mood than hunting, the King rode in an almost unhurried manner, spurring his horse to give chase but then easing it again, as if he needed time to think, and the speed of pursuit distracted him. And that this was true became abundantly clear when, as Sir John Seymour and the other hunters sped away surrounded by his pack of yelping hounds, in fast pursuit of a buck, Henry restrained Sir Nicholas Carew by the arm and said, 'Let them be. I would like to rest.'

Nicholas, only two years older than his king but with his wiry crop of hair already grizzled grey, looked anxious.

'Are you not well, Sir?'

'Never better, Nick. Never better,' Henry replied, a shade too heartily. 'It is just that I am in the mood to converse and with whom better to do so than yourself?'

Nicholas bowed in his saddle but said nothing.

'How pleasant it is here and what good hosts the Seymours,' Henry went on. 'As you said when we arrived, a sound family, every one of them. I have a great regard for young Edward, as you know, and Thomas has proved himself an excellent courier for Francis Bryan.'

'Yes,' said Carew, thinking that Henry was going all round the point to get to what he actually intended to say, and having more than a sneaking suspicion that the King really wanted to ask about Jane.

'I know that you have been friendly with them for some time,' Henry continued, 'and probably know more about them than anyone else at Court.'

'I expect that is true, Your Grace. What is it you wish to learn?'

A blue Tudor eye looked at him shrewdly for a second before it became masked by its hail-fellow-well-met expression.

'The girl, Jane. Is she spoken for in any way? I would presume her father has pre-contracted her to someone or other.'

'Not that I know of, Your Grace. I have never heard of such a thing, though I have been on intimate terms with them a long while.'

Nicholas kept his voice completely level but inside his jerkin his heart had doubled its pace. So his plan, created more in jest than anything else, had succeeded. Quiet, mousy Jane had attracted her sovereign's attention despite the disastrous events of the previous evening. Her contrast to that scheming bitch Boleyn had been both noted and approved.

'Strange,' Henry was saying. 'She is such a self-possessed little thing I would have thought she would have made an excellent wife. I must look out for someone for her when she returns to Court.'

Carew shot him a hasty look, sure that the King was bluffing. By leaving the banquet and not succumbing to his advances – a technique used so many times by Anne Boleyn in the past – Henry had felt himself challenged. Mentally Sir Nicholas Carew rubbed his hands together and made a conscious note to contact Edward Seymour as quickly as possible.

'That would be most kind of Your Grace,' he said aloud, tongue firmly planted within cheek. 'I believe she is a virtuous girl – or so her brother says – and many consider this essential in a wife.'

'Yes,' Henry answered thoughtfully. 'Provided that it is not carried to excess, of course.'

The King's thought process was crystal clear. It was said by those who knew that he had lusted after Anne Boleyn when she had first come to the English court from France at the age of fifteen. It had been ten years before that lust was finally satisfied; ten years in which Henry had put aside a Pope and a Queen in order to finally possess his *idée fixe*.

Nicholas Carew smiled grimly. He had been an intimate of both Henry and Katharine since the reign began. It had been he who had thrust his short muscular body into disguise to dance in the Queen's bedchamber during the Christmas celebrations of 1514 while Henry's partner had been Elizabeth Blount, a nubile fifteen-year-old from Shropshire. Three years later the girl was to bear Henry's only living son, the bastard Henry Fitzroy, and Katharine had had to bear the humiliation of the King showing the baby off at Court and weeping tears of joy. Nicholas had been there, and Nicholas had suffered with the Queen, muttering into his beard as Elizabeth – now married off to Gilbert Tailboys so that the child could have a nominal father – had walked about almost purring. He wondered now if this had been the moment when an intense loyalty to Katharine had been born, or whether his feelings sprang from resentment at the Boleyn's all-powerful hold on the King.

'. . . Nick?' Henry was speaking.

'I'm sorry Your Grace? My thoughts were elsewhere.'

'I asked if Mistress Mouse could sing.'

'Mistress Mouse? Oh, Jane. Yes, I believe so. Not very well I think, but she certainly makes an effort.'

'I must teach her one of my songs before I leave Wolff Hall,' said Henry smiling, and Nicholas realised that the King's extraordinary mood of joviality was returning.

With his thoughts starting to race and the fervent wish that Edward Seymour was present and not stuck away in Hampshire, Nicholas Carew, Master of Horse to Henry VIII, yet loyal supporter of Queen Katharine and her daughter Mary, bowed his head and said, 'I am sure that Mistress Seymour would be only too delighted with that and any other favour that Your Grace might wish to bestow on her.'

And both men were smiling as they turned their horses towards Wolff Hall and cantered off through the gentle afternoon.

The shadows of evening lengthened the gold-dust day and crept into the great hall until the light was soft as iris flowers. Dame Margery, seeing the beauty of it, ordered that not too many candles should be lit, and so there was a mellowness about the whole room when Jane Seymour, later than she thought she would be, joined the banquet at which the King was already seated.

Though apologising greatly, this night there was a serenity about her and she was not covered in blushing confusion as her mother had feared. Nor did Jane falter as she took her place on Henry's left hand and, looking at her closely, Dame Margery saw that her daughter had taken so much trouble with her appearance that a tremulous confidence had been born in her and was, for the moment at least, holding sway.

Jane had dressed in blue – a colour that enhanced her eyes – and wore a French hood set well back on her head so that her hair, the colour of lilac blossom in the deceptive light, draped her face. It was Anne Boleyn who had first lengthened her eyes by clever painting and now Dame Margery saw that Jane had emulated her and had both darkened and lined her lashes. She had also laboured over her face, for her cheeks had lost their normal pallor and were pink as fruit, while her lips shone as if she had just kissed a rose.

'You look charming,' Jane,' the King murmured, his voice a trifle thick.

Carew watched and saw to his relief that instead of casting her lashes down, Jane fluttered them as she said, 'Your Grace is kind to flatter your humble subject.'

This, then, was the pattern for the evening: the King noticeably complimentary and attentive; Jane smiling a great deal and using her eyes to such good effect that they seemed to pick up something of the sparkle of Sir John's finest plate and reflect the brilliance of the candlelight.

And when all the eating was done and the King once again entertained the company with a song of his own composing, it seemed natural enough that Jane should join in. It was as Nicholas Carew had said: her voice was light and of little consequence, a far cry indeed from the accomplished performances of Anne Boleyn, but the sound was true and bright and Henry seemed well pleased, applauding loudly and kissing her hand for her endeavour.

It was as he was thus stooped that he said quietly, 'I would like some air before I retire, Jane, and I have not yet seen the gardens of Wolff Hall. Would you stroll with me before you leave for Topenham Lodge?'

She looked at him closely, for a moment losing her new-found confidence and suspecting that he was mocking her again. But she could see by the expression on his broad face that he really meant what he said.

'If that is what Your Grace wishes, then I am his to command,' she answered demurely, thinking all the while that Meg had been right: that the King of England could be blinded into believing a woman beautiful if she was clever enough. Her old wish on Merlin's Mound flashed through her mind: 'To marry a King even though I am the ugliest girl in the world.' Jane could not help a smile crossing her features and, unknown to her, the transformation that turned her from a cygnet to a swan took place.

Henry Tudor stood up. 'Dame Margery, Sir John,' he said. 'I feel the need of some gentle exercise to help me sleep and your daughter has agreed to show me your gardens. Let the company remain and listen to the music but I will take my leave of you for a while.'

A sea of astonished faces stared at him and then the entire assembly lurched to its feet as he walked purposefully from the hall, Jane's hand resting lightly on his arm.

'Good gracious!' said Dame Margery so loudly that her husband let out an equally audible, 'Ssh.'

Under cover of everyone reseating themselves, Sir John continued,

'Think little of it, my dear. It was always His Grace's custom to stroll in the gardens before retiring for the night.'

'Yes, but John, with Jane alone? Do you not think he has taken some sort of fancy to her?' asked her mother frantically.

'No I don't,' answered Sir John roundly. 'She is far too plain for him.'

'How could you!' exclaimed Dame Margery but her husband was not listening. Looking round the assembled courtiers to gauge their reaction, he was horrified to see Sir Nicholas Carew look straight at him and slowly wink one of his eyes.

'God a'mercy,' said Sir John.

But knowing nothing of the sensation they had caused, Henry and Jane were already walking towards the Young Lady's Garden and appreciatively sniffing its wafting night scents, while a thrush who had sung to welcome the day's end now added a few notes into the dusk.

'Paradise,' said the King, the part of him that wrote love songs and was capable of such passion as he had once given Anne Boleyn, filling him with sentiment.

'This garden was made for me when I was born,' said Jane. 'I was the first girl, you see.'

'Where are your sisters now?'

'Both married and gone. Though Bess will be here on the last night of your visit to pay her respects, as will my brother, Edward.'

'How well I like your family,' said Henry very slowly. 'And you, Jane, are its most precious jewel.'

She turned away from him and he saw to his amazement that the girl looked near to tears.

'What is it?' he said. 'What have I done to offend you?'

'How can I speak frankly?' she answered wretchedly. 'You are my sovereign lord.'

'But I am also a man, Jane. Please tell me what is wrong.'

She looked at him, then, and had a vision of Henry Tudor that would never leave her. She saw him as an eager boy in a huge man's body; a boy who had been misled by a scheming and wicked woman, and dragged into a net which had forced him to commit ruthless deeds in an effort to extricate himself. At that moment Jane Seymour knew that it would not take a great deal to stir the passion that lay just below her apparently austere surface and make her fall in love with the colossus who towered over her in every sense.

She decided to tell the truth. 'Because of my looks – or lack of them – I have a fear that men deride me. And I have it now about you, Your Grace.'

'How could you?' he said almost angrily. 'It is not my way to trifle with women' – that this was patently untrue did not occur to Jane, who felt more afraid than anything else – 'and I most certainly would not do so with my host's daughter.'

'Forgive me, Your Grace,' Jane answered, truly in tears now. 'I spoke out of turn. I think perhaps I had better go indoors.'

'As you will,' said Henry Tudor, 'but I would prefer that you stayed with me.'

Just for a moment Jane hesitated and in that was lost. Her future was sealed and the whole course of her life altered as she brushed at her eyes and said, 'Then in that case I will stay, Your Grace,' and the King of England took her hand in his and together they walked in the gardens of Wolff Hall until the moon rose.

# Chapter Five

IT HAD LONG BEEN SAID in the Seymour household that Savernake Forest held within its acreage places so dense and dark that if a man were to injure himself and not be able to crawl to safety, he might well be dead before any search party could find him. Further, it was rumoured that in its secret heart the forest had glades in which no mortal man had ever set foot, and – though this came from Old Will and, therefore, could not be trusted – hidden right away at the place where the trees grew densest of all, was a house inhabited entirely by dwarves.

'Have you seen it?' the Seymour children would ask him when they were still young: and he would answer 'Aye, just the once. And sitting on the doorstep and rocking a babby no bigger than my thumb, was a little woman scarce three feet high.'

Though forbidden by Sir John, who well knew the dangers of the woodlands of his wardenship, Edward, Henry and Thomas had gone looking for it. But though they had found nothing, they had happened on a remote clearing, completely hidden by trees, the ceiling of which was formed by interweaving branches and the carpet, lush grass. They had called it the Cave because of its mysterious green darkness, and had never taken their sisters or cousin there, so that it had remained a place for young men alone, where they could have secret meetings far away from curious eyes and eavesdroppers.

The quiet of the Cave was difficult to comprehend and to speak in loud tones while hidden in its leafy secrecy was impossible. So small wonder that the two men concealed there presently, murmured to one another, even though there was not another soul within a mile who could have overheard them.

'You are quite sure of this?' whispered Edward, his brilliant eyes wide with astonishment as he gazed at Nicholas Carew.

'I am positive – and I tell you, Ned, I am not alone in this. There is not one person in the hunting party who has not noticed it.'

Edward paused, one hand stroking the neat, dark beard which grew beneath his full and sensuous mouth. 'Tell me again, slowly,' he said.

'I thought at first it was a charade,' Nicholas answered, plucking a blade of grass and squeezing its juice between his teeth. 'Then I realised it was more than that. That the King must have been absorbing what I said about Jane's character and consequently took a genuine fancy to her. Now it has reached the point where he walks with her alone in the garden each evening.'

'God's head!' Edward's clenched fist punched the air. 'Is he trifling with her?'

'Who can tell? That he is tired of the Boleyn woman we all know, but Anne could yet redeem her position by bearing a son.'

'So he is dallying with Jane.'

'If he is he must be stopped,' Carew said emphatically. 'If Jane lets him tumble her his interest will end. We saw it before with the Night-Crow. Bluntly, the moment the King had had her, he lost interest.'

'There's little fear of that,' Edward answered, laughing a little. 'My sister is prim as a nun.'

Nicholas looked noncommittal. 'That's as may be. But many a high-minded woman has been dazzled by power. No, Jane's path is clear. She must prize her virtue above all else.'

'But what for?' asked Edward in exasperation. 'His Grace is married and his wife is pregnant. Why should Jane bother to play politics?'

A sly expression crossed Carew's face. 'His Grace was married when he met Anne Boleyn. Who could have envisaged how that would end? I'll swear it only needs the birth of another girl for him to put her aside.'

Edward frowned. 'I cannot see it myself. I know he is hag-ridden but the King is only too aware that if he divorces the Queen he must take Katharine back.'

Nicholas nodded. 'Very true. But he is a wily fox and a determined one. He cannot be stopped when there's a pretty woman involved.'

'But Jane isn't pretty,' said Edward, perplexed.

'But Henry thinks she is and there's an end to it. Before long we must get her on one side and coach her in the role of favourite.'

Her brother still looked unconvinced. 'I cannot believe she has such a role, despite all you've said.'

Carew turned on him a face suddenly ruthless. 'Then we must make sure that she gets it. Someone in sympathy with Katharine and poor Mary must obtain the King's ear. Otherwise their future is bleak.'

'I'll not have my sister used as a catspaw,' Edward said vehemently.

'That she won't be,' answered Nicholas. 'On the contrary, I think she might play for the highest stakes of all.'

Edward stared at him wide-eyed. 'Is there a chance?'

'If the game is played correctly,' said Nicholas Carew slowly, 'there's the greatest chance in the world.'

The two men gazed at each other in silence before they threaded their horses through the labyrinth of trees and by separate paths made their way back to Wolff Hall.

From her place beside the King, Dame Margery stared round the Great Barn triumphantly. Tonight, before all her neighbours and family, she felt that she had earned the honour of the most successful hostess in Wiltshire for who, looking at the decorated barn glowing with candlelight and transformed by rich-hued tapestries, could think anything else?

If the first night of the visit had been memorable, it paled in comparison with this grand ending. For in honour of the hunting party, now swelled by the Darrels of Littlecote, the Dowager Lady Hungerford, Master Wroughton, Edward Seymour, Cloverella, Bess and her husband Sir Henry Oughtred, to say nothing of all their retainers, a banquet of Roman proportions had been served.

For the assembled company, numbering some hundred in all, Dame Margery had chosen a table of two freshly killed beefs, twelve muttons, to say nothing of incidentals like cygnets, a variety of capons – some good, some coarse and some fine Kentish – and a selection of pullets, chickens, quails, egrets, swans and storks, these last presented cooked and sewn back into their plumage. For those of lighter appetite she had also produced a shield of brawn, pheasants, partridges and a delicacy of peachicks, snipe, larks, brewes and fifteen stuffed gulls (some nestling on black cherries, some hidden beneath crisp dark crusts).

Beer and ale had been served and also Gascon wine, sweet wine, and spiced wine, and to freshen the palate at the end of the meal there were doucettys, spiced tarts, frittours, blancmangers and vast glistening puddings nestling beside uncompromising pies of mammoth proportions. A repast fit for a King, and a King who nobody present could remember ever seeing in a better humour or, for those who were casting eyes on him for the first time, could fail to like and honour.

On this most important night of all, everyone present wore their finest clothes though Henry seemed to have eyes for nobody other than Jane, dressed in a gown of deepest blue, a French hood with sparkling billiments on her head. In view of the King's attentions, Edward, whilst scarcely crediting half of what Nicholas Carew had told him, had to admit that Henry paid his sister a great deal of court, the huge face with its little eyes constantly turning in her direction, almost to the exclusion of Dame Margery.

Not that Mother cares, thought Edward with amusement. Tonight she has scored before all her women friends and neighbours. She is a credit to us all.

He looked at Dame Margery fondly, smiling at the way her plump form bulged in the square neck of her gown, making her breasts high and round as full moons.

And why not? They fed all us children, he thought, unfashionable as it had been at the time. Edward could remember her now, sitting in her garden, constantly with a suckling babe, a comforting sight somehow.

He felt a momentary sense of disappointment that his wife had chosen not to feed their children and had had her breasts bound after the recent delivery of their second daughter – a fact which had kept Anne away from this evening's celebration and allowed a smiling Cloverella to go in her place.

Edward's thoughts ran on to the child that the Queen was now carrying and whether it would be a boy – and her saviour – or whether she was to be as disappointed as his wife had been.

And where does Jane stand in all this? he thought. What part can she possibly play? She is no cheap whore like Madge Shelton – or Katherine Filliol.

He rarely thought of his first wife nowadays but still found himself shuddering at her memory. To think he had discovered her infidelity by seeing the very act of adultery performed through the medium of a crystal ball, just for a moment allowed a glimpse of something taking place hundreds of miles distant. He would not have believed it possible, having a hearty disrespect for the supernatural until that moment. But nowadays Edward admitted freely there were forces at work of which he knew nothing, and at that moment came to a decision to seek mystic advice regarding his sister.

'Dancing,' the King was calling. 'Let there be dancing.'

A dozen willing hands pushed the trestle tables back against the walls enlarging the square in their midst, and the King himself was on his feet, raising up Dame Margery and capering about with her, amidst cheers and laughs.

Without seeing him arrive, Edward heard Carew at his elbow. 'This is going to be a rowdy night and His Grace has had plenty to drink. In some way or other he is bound to declare himself to Jane.'

Edward frowned. 'I don't like the thought of it. She must promise him nothing.'

'Then warn her,' hissed Carew – and vanished into the midst of the throng.

But Edward had no chance to seek out his sister, for a tug at his sleeve revealed Cloverella, her eyes full of laughter, her lips asking him to dance with her. Smiling, he gathered her into his arms, wondering, as he often did, what would become of such a delicious scrap of humanity with its incongruous mixture of both bad and royal blood.

'You look serious,' she said. 'Are you disappointed that Anne did not have a son?'

'Of course not,' he answered, playfully tickling. 'We have plenty of time yet.' His voice changed and he added, 'Anne told me that you predicted another girl. Did you really know, or was it just a lucky guess?'

Cloverella's eyes softened to the texture of pansies as she answered, 'I have the Romany gift, Ned. Long ago I wished for it to grow stronger – and it has. I truly believe I now have second sight.'

Thinking of the experience in Calais when a rumple-headed youth had, by what Edward could only call magic, let him see Katherine Filliol in bed with a gentleman of his acquaintance, Edward nodded. 'Then you are fortunate.' He smiled and added, '*Will* Anne and I have a son?'

'More than one,' she answered.

'And the Queen?'

His cousin's face went dark. 'No more children.'

'But she is pregnant now.'

'I know. Yet I feel certain I am right. I do not believe Anne Boleyn will bear another living child.'

She felt Edward stiffen. 'Then that could put a different slant to the whole thing,' he murmured.

'What whole thing?'

He smiled down at her, then kissed the tip of her nose. 'If your gift has not told you, then I have no intention of doing so. Go and consult your cards or scrying glass or whatever it is you use for divination. And when you have found the answer come and tell me.'

Cloverella looked cross. 'I think you are teasing me, Edward.'

'Now what makes you say that?' he said, and laughed, suddenly looking as young and charming as he had as a boy.

'Oh you!' answered Cloverella in a fury, yet half smiling as she pummelled Edward's chest before whirling him off at double speed, so fast that they nearly fell over and thus created a diversion which hid the moment when Henry Tudor and Jane Seymour left the Great Barn.

'May we walk outside? It is hot within,' the King said as they slipped quietly through the door.

'As you wish, Your Grace,' answered Jane, putting a prudish expression on her face to hide the fact that her heart had started to thump hard at the very thought of being alone with him.

He nodded but said nothing, staring up to where the moon hung low above them, dark with the colour of harvest, lighting with an uneasy glow the outline of Wolff Hall and its many outbuildings.

'I would be private with you,' Henry said quietly. 'Where may we walk that we will not be disturbed?'

'Perhaps in the orchard. I doubt anyone will come there.'

Her voice was calm, clipped, almost icy, but in reality she was terrified. Tonight, she felt sure, the King would ask her to be his mistress when she returned to Court. Would tell her that his affair with Madge Shelton was over, his marriage empty, that only she could fill the space in his bed. And though many Court beauties would have thrilled to hear those words, Jane shrank from the very thought for reasons more complex than she would have dared admit.

She walked on nervously and as the couple drew away from the

65

house, the noise of festivity grew less and other sounds drifted in: an owl, a nightjar, the leaves on the orchard trees, the silence of Wiltshire by night. Smells, too, filled the cool, sharp air. Ripened fruit, the ciderish tang of rotting apples, the keen sweetness of purple plums.

'Jane,' said the King urgently, drawing her to a halt beneath a tree laden with low hanging fruit. 'Why are you still so formal. We have walked together every night this week. Could you not call me by my name?'

'But you are my sovereign', she said, turning away, her face harsh and stiff-looking. 'I could not presume such familiarity.'

'Jane, Jane, Jane,' Henry answered, taking her by the shoulders and turning her to face him. 'I give you permission. You are to call me Henry when we are private together. You need only be formal in front of others.'

'When you would be ashamed to admit we were on first name terms.'

The words were out before she had had time to think about them and she dropped her eyes, her usual ploy, not wishing to see the thundercloud on his face.

But strangely he answered mildly enough. 'It is not that. It is just that I like to keep my private business to myself.'

Jane looked up. 'What private business, Your Grace? There is nothing of that nature between us.'

'No,' he answered, tightening his grip and pulling her roughly towards him, 'there is not. But I would wish it otherwise, Jane. I would wish that we were close friends.'

'Close?' The word hung in the air like a sword.

'You know perfectly well what I mean. I want you, Jane.'

She was frighteningly near him, in such proximity that she could scarcely draw breath. Much as she had feared, the extraordinary size of him had its usual effect. Her unsteady heart beat even more quickly, her legs grew weak and the divine sensation that she associated with passion shot through her and would not go away. She fought to draw back, struggling in his embrace regardless of the fact that he was King of England.

'Don't, please let me go,' she gasped.

'Why? Do you find me distasteful? Is that it?'

Jane stood stock still, shocking him by her sudden rigidity. 'No, no, it's not that.'

'Then what, you capricious creature? What is wrong?'

He had half released his grip on her and Jane turned away, her face hidden in shadow. 'It is something that I would rather not put into words.'

Inwardly Henry groaned, wondering why it was always his fate to encounter difficult women. If it had not been for their utter disparity it could have been Anne Boleyn who spoke to him out of the gloom. He released his hold on Jane and shook his head. 'As you will. I'll question you no further.'

His indifferent manner had its effect and the girl looked up at him. 'Your Grace, I owe you some kind of explanation.'

The massive shoulders shrugged. 'Yes, but being a woman it is unlikely you will give it.'

She gave a careful smile. 'In that you are wrong. I was afraid because I am still inexperienced. I have no knowledge of men for the simple reason that it is my wish to be taught the art of love by my husband, whoever he will be and when I finally meet him. I have seen enough of those who give their favours freely to conclude that they are thrown out like old shoes when their purpose is served.'

Henry closed his eyes. Once before, in the gardens of Hever Castle, he had heard an almost identical speech.

'God protect me from virtuous women!' he said, only just under his breath.

If Jane heard she gave no sign. 'I am sure you will understand, Your Grace.'

'Yes, I understand,' he answered bitterly. 'And some of what you say is true. Though it is not my custom to ill-use the women I have loved.'

It was on the tip of Jane's tongue to ask him how he would describe his treatment of Katharine of Aragon but she trembled at the thought of such treason.

'So if Your Grace will excuse me, I am afraid I must decline what you suggest.'

'By God,' he shouted, suddenly furious. 'I've suggested nothing — yet!'

And with that he abruptly snatched her into his arms, right off her feet and suspended her in the air like a helpless child before he finally lowered her to a level with his demanding mouth and swept her lips to his. Every sense, every nerve, every beat of life, seemed to stop in Jane as she strained against him, unable to help herself. It was all as she had feared it would be; she was on fire; a grasping greedy sensualist, prepared to experience every sensation in the universe and then demand more.

He knew, of course; knew by the way she responded exactly what she was. And as he lowered her to the ground there was a smile of pure pleasure on the face of Henry Tudor, and he gave the laugh of a child on seeing a present still unwrapped, or that of a navigator glimpsing an island, as yet uncharted.

Despite this, she ran from him. The daughter of the house at which the monarch of the realm was being entertained, turned on her heel and without so much as a perfunctory salute, sped away. Tears of shame stung Jane's bitter cheeks as she hurried through the sweet-smelling darkness and a great sob escaped from her bruised and trembling mouth; and there was no peace until she entered the dim and kindly darkness of the confines of a deserted Wolff Hall and, eventually, passing beside the house, the cloistered tranquillity of the family chapel.

Yet there was no frown of anger on the face of the King who had been left thus abruptly. On the contrary he grinned, boyish and excited, his blood stirring as it had done once before, long ago, when the dark daughter of a Kentish knight, little more than a girl, had first come to his Court and cast her lovely eyes on him. With a whistle, Henry Tudor straightened his attire and strode off towards the Great Barn and the revels that had continued most merrily despite his absence.

It was Cloverella who found her cousin, asleep and lying at full stretch on one of the pews. The last of the revellers was making his way to bed, the King had long since retired, the dawn was up and spicing the sky above the Great Barn, when Cloverella crept into the aromatic darkness and not altogether to her surprise caught a glimpse of Jane's bejewelled headdress.

So the girl had not left for Topenham Lodge, a victim of yet another headache, as Henry Tudor had so stoutly maintained. A question mark formed in Cloverella's mind and after a while, standing alone in the reverential silence, the answer came to her. With a very serious expression, Cloverella went to sit beside her cousin and relentlessly woke her up.

'Good gracious,' said Jane, obviously amazed to see her

surroundings. 'I must have come here to rest and instead fallen asleep. What time is it?'

'Daybreak, and the King will leave in a few hours. Perhaps you should go to Topenham Lodge and change,' Cloverella answered quietly.

Jane sat upright, looking guilty. 'What happened when I did not return to the banquet? Was Mother angry?'

Cloverella grinned. 'No, your fellow conspirator covered up for you. We all thought you had long since ridden home.'

Jane stared at her. 'My fellow . . . ? Oh you mean His Grace. I see.' And she had the good grace to blush.

'Dearest cousin,' said Cloverella, more directly than she had ever spoken to Jane before. 'I came on this visit because I dreamed that you were weeping and needed me close at hand. And now that I am here I find I am right. Do not be afraid to answer me because it is the Romany part of me that speaks to you now. Is the situation between you and the King as dangerous as I think it is?'

Jane turned away, her pale face so ashen that she looked only one breath away from death. 'I believe it is,' she said.

'He wants you for his mistress, of course.'

It was a statement not a question and beneath Cloverella's shrewd glance, Jane had no option but to silently nod her head.

'I see. Listen, we must both go at once to Topenham Lodge. I have the magic cards there and we can learn much from them. Then we can return here to wave His Grace farewell and no one need suspect that you haven't been there all night.'

Jane looked dubious. 'Cloverella, I don't think I want to be involved with witchcraft.'

'It is not evil to consult the cards. All Romanies do it. Really, you are quite foolish sometimes.'

'Yes, I suppose so. Nearly everyone at Court confers with astrologers and soothsayers, after all.'

'Even the King did so before Elizabeth was born.'

Jane nodded. 'Yes, and they all got it wrong. With one exception.'

'Who was that?'

'Dr Zachary. A very odd young man. And he was imprisoned in the Tower for his pains.'

'Was he executed?'

'No, later the King had him released. Apparently he is a bastard

69

child of that old fox Norfolk and the Duke exerted his influence on his son's behalf. I believe these days he lives in Greenwich.'

'A bastard!' repeated Cloverella, her eyes shining. 'So he is very much like me?'

'Yes,' Jane answered thoughtfully. 'There is a similarity, now I come to think of it.'

'Then let us see if I have half his wisdom.'

'I think perhaps that might be rather hard,' Jane said with a smile.

But there Mistress Seymour was not right for, having ridden nervously through the whispering forest and begged the porter at Topenham Lodge to keep secret their late return, she was amazed at the skill with which – having first made Jane shuffle them – Cloverella laid out the magic cards in the shape of a great tree.

'Where did you learn that?' she asked, smiling a little but for all that amazed.

'From my grandmother. These are hers. I kept them hidden until a few years ago.'

'Well, well,' said Jane. 'And what do you see?'

Cloverella made no answer, an extraordinary expression crossing her face. She seemed to her cousin to have gone deathly white and her eyes had grown both large and dreamy. She bent over the cards, caressing them like children, and her voice, when it finally came, was little above a whisper.

'He is drawn to you, Jane. There is something about you that fascinates him.' Cloverella glanced up and Jane saw that the girl looked astonished. 'In some way, though it is quite extraordinary, you have something in common.' She gave a low laugh. 'And I believe it to be physical passion.'

Jane was glad that she sat in shadow and Cloverella could not see her face growing ever pinker. She made no reply and her cousin went on, 'Do you know, I think the King is about to fall in love with you.'

Jane gulped. 'Surely not!'

'I mean it. And there's something else here too.' There was a long silence then Cloverella said, 'God's blood. I don't believe this,' and sat back hard in her chair.

'What is it? What do you see?'

Cloverella shot her a look of shocked surprise. 'These cards tell me that you will one day sign yourself "Jane the Queen".'

'As a joke? Does it mean that I will do it for a joke?'

'No,' said Cloverella, shaking her head. 'If I am to believe what I see here, you are destined to be Queen of England.'

They stared at each other in horror and it was difficult to say which was the paler of the two.

'They must be wrong,' said Jane eventually.

Cloverella shook her head, the dark hair flying. 'That is not so. It is not possible for these cards to lie. They are of ancient wisdom and can tell nothing but the truth.'

'But what of the Queen?' asked Jane in a whisper.

'It does not say and I am not skilled enough to know. All I can tell you is that you will wear her crown.'

Jane stood up. 'I cannot listen to any more. It is too much for me to grasp. How could such things be?'

'His Grace will love you – and you will love him. And he will be determined to make you his consort once that has happened.'

Jane shook her head in bewilderment. 'You are quite sure?'

'I am positive,' said Cloverella. 'But perhaps you should consult one more knowledgeable than I in order to learn more.'

'But who?' said Jane, shivering with fright.

'Why, obviously, Dr Zachary.'

'Yes,' Jane's voice was the merest whisper. 'You are right. I must go to him. Soon.'

In the brightness of morning it could be seen that the great courtyard in front of Wolff Hall was packed with horsemen, while its corners rang with the shouts of departing guests, their cries mingling with a strange cacophony of neighing animals, barking hounds, excited yells and, drowning all, a series of blasts upon the Esturmy horn. The King was taking his leave after a visit that had lasted two days more than originally intended.

Cloverella had never seen such a colourful throng. Henry's fellow guests, each one a trusted member of his personal retinue, swung into their saddles one after the other, while Robert Cheseman, the King's falconer, his bony face dominated by his long hard nose so that he resembled a bird of prey himself, held Henry's best bird on his wrist, the tinkling of the creature's bells adding to the general uproar.

'A triumph, Sir John,' Henry was saying enthusiastically. 'I cannot remember so successful a hunt.'

He was brimming with unspoken thoughts which obviously were of a highly gratifying nature, for his eyes sparkled and his small, full mouth beamed. And though he bade farewell to everyone with extreme courtesy it was for Jane that he reserved his greatest charm, leaping out of the saddle with alacrity at his first glimpse of her.

But by way of response Mistress Seymour merely lowered her eyes demurely, put on her most prudish expression, and dropped an impeccable curtsey at the King's well-shod feet.

'Madam,' he said as he stooped to raise her up. 'We await your return to Court with anxiety. Will you remain long at Wolff Hall?'

'A few days only, Your Grace,' Jane replied.

'Until we meet again, then,' Henry said, and it was difficult to gauge his mood as he turned from her and heaved his bulk into the saddle.

Jane merely bowed her head in acknowledgement as the hunting party, the King in the lead, turned away from Wolff Hall and clattered out of the courtyard. But just as they were almost out of sight, the enormous figure heading them turned back for a final look and, waving his hand, saw that Jane Seymour alone stood still watching and gave him an answering salute before she slowly turned back into the house.

# Chapter Six

DURING THAT AUTUMN of 1535 the dreaded illness known as the Sweat, which could claim its victims within two or three hours, emptied the city of London of those who could afford to travel to the country, only the poor and the foolhardy being left behind to face the risk. The King, worried as always for his safety, had removed both the Court and his pregnant wife out of harm's way to Surrey, but finding that the plague had preceded him to Shalford and then Farnham, the royal party went on to Hampshire where they descended unexpectedly on Edward and Anne Seymour at Elvetham.

How wry, thought Sir Nicholas Carew, watching Henry and Anne, Edward and his wife, all sporting together, that he should bring his pregnant Queen to the brother of the woman he truly desires.

And Edward Seymour, seeing the royal couple go off together to hawk, thought that, after all, the King's pursuit of Jane had been nothing more than a diversion to while away what could have been a rather boring stay in the company of the elder Seymours.

But when he said as much to Carew, the other shook his head. 'If you believe that, Ned, you are not as shrewd as I thought. While the Queen is with child he will put on a show, but Henry's heart is really set on Jane.'

'But only as a mistress surely?'

Sir Nicholas smiled slowly. 'That is up to her, I think.'

Edward would have discussed the matter further but Carew refused to be drawn and Seymour had to content himself with writing to Jane, still at Wolff Hall because of the dangers in London, and beg her in very veiled terms – for who knew where a spy might strike next? – not to take the King's flirtation too seriously.

But while the Court and the Seymours stayed away from the city there were those who were glad to remain behind, able to move freely abroad without the fear of prying eyes and ears. So it was that, without even a glance over his shoulder, the President of the Council of England, Thomas Howard, the mighty Duke of Norfolk himself, rode with only one man as escort, to a house that stood barely two miles from Greenwich Palace, yet was as remote and secret as any dwelling in the realm, and bade his servant knock on the door. Then the Duke waited, a smile playing round his mouth, to see what would happen next.

First a serving girl came to the door to gape open-mouthed, but no sooner had she disappeared than two children, one a girl of five leading by the hand a staggering infant not yet two, hurried to meet him.

The Duke dismounted, picking up the little boy and stroking the girl's hair. 'Well, well, my jewels,' he said. 'And how is it with you?'

Though these, his first grandchildren, had the *baton sinister* running through their coat-of-arms he loved them dearly, always thinking of their grandmother when he looked at them, remembering her honeyed skin and wild-flower eyes and how much passion she had aroused in him; more than any other woman before or since.

'We are in good health,' said the girl. 'And you Grandfather, are you not afeared of the Sweat?'

'I have had that illness and now believe myself immune. It was your father cured me of it.'

'Yes, so he told me,' she answered nodding.

In some ways, Norfolk thought, his granddaughter was almost frightening. It was as if an adult lurked within her small compass and the Duke would never, and could never, forget how the child had persuaded the King to release her father from the Tower by what had appeared at the time to be the use of magic. Her grandmother had been burned by the people of Norfolk as a witch and Howard frequently wondered if some strange strain had been passed into her, as it had her father, his son.

'Who stands waiting to greet you,' said a voice, almost as if it had read the Duke's thoughts.

'Zachary,' answered Howard, and opened his arms to his beloved son, patting the rough hair and kissing him on the cheek.

'You are well, Lord Duke my father? It is not dread of the Sweat that has brought you to see me?'

74

'No, my boy, not at all. In fact I have come to bring you a present. My visit is purely social.'

Zachary smiled and the Duke was vividly reminded of the night, over twenty years ago, when the boy had first been brought to Kenninghall Castle after his mother had been burned to death.

'You are pleased?'

'I always enjoy presents, Lord Duke my father.'

They went into the house where Zachary's wife, Jane Wyatt, bustled about her tasks.

A good enough woman, thought the Duke, but dull for my son. Too commonplace by half.

Yet Jane smiled and curtsied sweetly enough and the Duke nodded his head and called her daughter, wishing all the while that his son had chosen someone else to marry. But still he took ale from her before he went with Zachary up the steep stairs to the sloping room beneath the roof where his son said he always felt closest to the stars.

Though he had seen it many times before, this place always laid a finger of fear upon the Duke's spine and now, as he looked at the strange symbols and charts, the table cluttered with measuring devices, cards, and a gleaming crystal, he shivered a little before, without saying anything, he drew from a deep pocket an object wrapped in a velvet cloth, and put it down on the table. 'Here is the gift I spoke of. Open it my son,' he said.

For a moment they looked terribly alike as they stared at the thing, the Duke relaxed and smiling now, Zachary eager and boyish, his teeth white in his dark, clever face.

'You hesitate,' continued Norfolk. 'It will not bite you. Come now.'

'I feel its wonder even before I have seen it,' answered his son, and pulling off the velvet covering, revealed a dark crystal, gleaming black as quartz in the shadowy light.

'Christ's Book, but it is awesome, Lord Duke my father. Where did you get it?'

'It comes from Venice, from the island on which glass is blown. I bought it off a trader recently. He told me that it was very powerful and should only be in the hands of a master.'

Zachary looked up from his contemplation of the glistening sphere. 'And you think that of me? Thank you, Sir.'

'It is not just I, as well you know. You have become something of a legend.'

Zachary smiled wryly. 'Not always an easy thing.' He picked up the crystal, bending close to it and then running his lips over its surface.

'Why do you do that?'

'I greet its spirit, the power that lies within its heart.'

'Chuff,' said the Duke, 'such talk!' But he was secretly more than a little gratified that his gift had been so well received.

'So you are pleased with it?' Zachary nodded and the Duke went on, 'And what does it say to you about Anne the Queen? If she is to die, as you have so often assured me she must, who will come to replace her?'

Zachary put the crystal down. 'When I first scry this, Father, I have to be alone. You must forgive me on this occasion. But I can tell you all you want to know without its mediumship.'

'Yes?' The Duke was suddenly agog.

'Recently I was in a very ancient place, full of mysteries and magic. I wandered amongst the standing stones at Avebury . . .'

His eyes twinkled as the Duke said impatiently, 'Get to the point, my boy.'

'. . . and while there, happened to take ale at the Bear in the town of Marlborough. Do you know the place?'

'You are perfectly aware that I do not,' answered Norfolk, to which Zachary grinned openly.

'A pity, you really should visit it.' The Duke looked as if he were about to grow dark, and Zachary, thinking better of it, went on, 'It was while there that I received two interesting pieces of information, one given to me as fact, the other guessed at. The first was that the King was hunting in Savernake Forest and was staying with Sir John Seymour, whose daughter Jane had returned from court especially to be present . . .'

The Duke was frowning. 'Jane Seymour?'

'I believe you might have seen her. She was serving woman to . . .' Zachary hesitated over saying 'Dowager Princess Katharine' and instead said simply 'Anne's predecessor. She then followed the pack and is currently Maid-of-Honour to the Queen.'

Norfolk frowned all the more. 'I can't place her. What is she like?'

'Small, fair, and very pale. She has no beauty except for her eyes.'

'And are you trying to tell me that His Grace . . ?'

'I am sure of it. Convinced in fact. It came to me so strongly that when I returned I checked in every way I knew possible. Lord Duke my father, Jane Seymour will be the next Queen of England.'

'God's Wounds!' exclaimed Norfolk, and in his astonishment shot to his feet. 'It is scarcely credible. A woman of no influence nor beauty. Are you absolutely certain?'

'Positive.'

The Duke sat down again, looking thoughtful. 'This Seymour girl, she doesn't by any chance have a brother called Edward who married Anne Stanhope?'

'I believe so. Why?'

'He is what is generally referred to as a coming man. Most tedious!'

Zachary laughed. 'Well, he'll be arrived if his sister marries the King.'

The Duke smiled despite himself. 'These little self-seekers, they're everywhere, like mushroom crops. No sooner do you see off one lot than there are more of them creeping up from nowhere.'

'If the Seymours take the place of the Boleyns you will surely be pleased?'

The Duke of Norfolk's dislike for his cousins, particularly Anne, was legendary.

Norfolk put his head on one side, the broad Howard nose falling into shadow like a beak. 'I am never pleased when surrounded by parvenus. They are without fail inclined to be nuisances. But, Zachary, how soon will all this take place?'

'In a way it has already started.' Zachary's expression became distant. 'Already there is something between Jane and His Grace that is difficult to describe. A bond of some kind . . . I do not yet know quite what. But when the Sweat has passed she will return to Court and then there will be changes. Mark them well, Lord Duke my Father.'

'Indeed I shall,' said Norfolk nodding his head. 'Indeed I shall.'

It was cold when the King finally left Hampshire and headed back for a London free of epidemic. Beside him in a litter rode his Queen, declaring that her pregnancy was now certain and established and she must take the greatest care of herself, for not one thing must jolt or shock the Prince who grew in her belly. Some who heard her say this were impressed and whispered amongst themselves that Her Grace was back in favour and that Henry must surely fall in love with her all over again. But others, not so kind, answered that he had tired of his consort utterly and only the birth of a son could save her from being finally discarded.

In the midst of all this gossip and conjecture, Jane – feeling small and ugly and demoralised – set off from Wolff Hall to join her royal mistress at the Palace of Whitehall, believing, yet not quite believing, that Henry Tudor had made a fool of her, and that she had made an even bigger fool of herself by allowing him to see the passion that smouldered beneath her apparently austere surface. Yet, there had been something so intensely enjoyable about those kisses in the gardens of Wolff Hall that it was hard to accept Henry had not experienced it as well. Jane supposed with a sigh that Edward had been right, that His Grace had been indulging in a flirtation and she must think no more of it.

It was with all these thoughts very much in the forefront of her mind that Mistress Seymour entered Anne's apartments on the morning after her return, only to stop motionless where she stood; even at this early hour the King was not only up and dressed, washed and trimmed, but calling upon his wife. In a flurry of confusion, Jane curtsied, only to find as she rose that Henry's eyes were fixed firmly upon her.

'Ah Mistress Jane,' he exclaimed jovially. 'You have returned to us at last.'

'I was delayed at Wolff Hall, Your Grace, by reason of the plague.'

'Quite so, quite so. For the same cause I stayed with your brother in Hampshire.'

'So I believe, Your Grace. I trust you had good sport.'

She said it in all innocence but the King at once lowered his voice, whispering, 'Not as good as at Wolff Hall, Mistress.'

Jane looked up, startled, and understood at once what he meant. Rather than forgetting what had passed between them, it would seem that Henry Tudor wanted to remind her of that last scented night in the garden; the night when he had swept her off her feet in every sense, kissing her trembling mouth and running his hands over her body.

Suddenly at a loss, Jane turned away but a movement from the Queen's bedchamber put an end to further conversation as the former Nan Saville, now Lady Berkeley and one of Anne's most intimate friends and attendants, came out, curtsied to the King and said, 'Her Grace is ready to receive you, Sir.'

'Good,' answered Henry abruptly, and without another word strode off, the doors of the room closing behind him. Nan turned on Jane with a look of pure triumph. 'You see,' she murmured, 'how he cossets her. Now that she is with child he cannot do enough for her. Her Grace has seen off the wretched Madge Shelton for once and for all.'

'Is she no longer at Court?' asked Jane, surprised.

'Oh she is here all right but on the point of becoming betrothed to Henry Norris, though she still shares her bed with Francis Weston.'

Jane's eyebrows rose. 'So His Grace has tired of her?'

'Indeed. These days he can't be bothered even to look at her.'

Jane smiled and nodded. 'Her Grace must be delighted.'

'She is triumphant.'

She would be, thought Jane. Can nothing ever go wrong for her?

Then she remembered the birth of Elizabeth and how Anne's power over Henry had diminished as a result, and almost felt a moment's pity. And later that day as the Queen consulted her ladies about her plans to celebrate the Twelve Days of Christmas, Jane found herself watching Anne with an extraordinary mixture of emotions. Her dislike of the woman, ingrained over so many years, was now tempered with a certain guilt, a furtiveness, almost as if she had allowed the King the greatest intimacy of all, rather than just a few stolen midnight kisses. Added to this was an extraordinary sense of rivalry, a bristling as if the Queen was a much despised wife and she – Jane – the reigning mistress.

From beneath lowered lids, Mistress Seymour studied Anne carefully, taking in every detail of the Queen's appearance and noticing things that she had never consciously observed before. As with all women – and men at that – there were divided opinions as to Anne's attractiveness. In the past Jane had been bitterly jealous of the vivid dark eyes and tossing mane of black hair, coupled with Anne's extraordinary ability to make any man fall in love with her. But today, perhaps because she had kissed the woman's husband, Jane looked at her appraisingly, without envy, and was quite surprised to see that Anne was, after all, just an ordinary female, approaching thirty, rather sallow, very thin and flat chested, with a large mole on her neck which she hid with a band of ribbon, and a rudimentary sixth finger on her left hand.

Jane stared amazed. It was as if a blindfold had been removed from her eyes. Though she had never thought the Queen a true beauty she had always considered her stunningly attractive but now she saw that she was nothing of the kind.

Feeling someone's eyes on her, Anne looked up and caught Jane in the very act of glancing away. The Queen smiled. 'Mistress Seymour, I see you have returned to Court. When did you get back?'

Jane curtsied. 'Yesterday, Your Grace.'

But Anne was already turning away, no longer interested in the boring little creature from Wiltshire who would find difficulty in booing a goose and whose face could crack a mirror. Without looking at Jane again Anne said loudly, 'Ladies, His Grace has announced his intention of dining with us in the Chamber tonight and I intend to give him good company. Will all of you present please attend us at six that we may dine and dance and sing to amuse the King's Majesty.'

Somebody whom Jane could not identify whispered behind her, 'She is determined to woo him back.'

'From whom?' muttered another voice.

'Who knows. He is finished with Madge Shelton . . .'

'. . . the great whore.'

'But it is murmured the King is in amorous mood and already has his sights set on someone else.'

'God's head, who can it be?'

'There's the mystery.'

The anonymous speakers drew to an abrupt halt as the Queen rose and, following suit, so did all present. As she curtsied, Jane twisted her head a little, trying to see on whom she had eavesdropped but with a room full of women it was difficult to pinpoint the culprits. Yet, whoever they were, their conversation was extraordinary and Jane felt her heart gain a little momentum. Could it possibly be . . . She shuddered from the idea that the subject of their conversation could possibly be herself, her lack of confidence making her grow cold at the thought.

But within a few minutes something was to happen that was to make her, at last, realise her own importance. For as she made her way to her own apartment to prepare herself for the evening's festivities, not being required to serve the Queen that afternoon, somebody – she never had time to see who it was – accidentally bumped against her and when they were gone, the girl found a note had been put into her hand. Glancing round and seeing that she was alone, Jane opened it.

'My dear Friend,' she read, 'be advised that I have forgotten nothing of the matter and intend to pursue it further. Your servant and sovereign, H.R.'

Jane stared at the paper blankly then, as something of its import began to dawn on her, folded it and did not open it again until she had reached the privacy of her own room where, with her thoughts running crazily, she read it once more. That the King was referring to their brief liaison was obvious; indeed he could be writing of nothing else. With a gratifyingly warm sensation, Jane read and re-read the words 'intend to pursue it further'. So both she and Edward had been wrong; Henry Tudor had not been indulging in mere dalliance; he intended to continue the affair and pursue it to its inevitable conclusion. With a sigh of ecstasy, Jane fell back on her bed and allowed herself to think wicked thoughts until she slept.

When she awoke it was growing dark and she rose at once and sending for her servant, Emma – a Wiltshire-born girl from the Wolff Hall estate – took great pains to make herself look as near to beautiful as Jane could ever get. Dressed in a soft shade like that of lilac blossom, a French hood trimmed with pearls on her head, Jane carefully painted her face with Cloverella's preparations, rubbing on to her eyelids a liquid derived from the flower periwinkle, which served to enhance their natural brilliance.

'You look pretty, my Lady,' said the girl.

'But still pale. Give me some of that rose petal powder.'

Determinedly Jane brushed it on and as her cheeks bloomed with colour was finally content.

'That might well do,' she said and, smiling to herself, made her way towards the Queen's apartments.

In the days of the King's father it had been the custom for all men and women who lodged at Court to eat together in the Hall and it had been Henry himself who had started the fashion to do otherwise by dining privately in his privy chamber with only a few personal friends and attendants. This notion had been eagerly copied by Katharine of Aragon who had also allowed chosen companions to dance in her bedchamber, and then, of course, the new idea had been fastened on avidly by Anne Boleyn. Jane remembered, as she hurried along, how Anne's apartments had buzzed with excitement when her star had been ascending, while those of Katharine had been dull and empty.

'The heartless wretch,' Jane found herself muttering, 'if I am to be her retribution then so be it. There is nothing too bad for Anne Boleyn after all the pain and suffering she inflicted on the true Queen and her daughter.'

She stopped in her tracks with that thought, wondering yet again what were Henry's intentions towards her. If he were to divorce Anne, as some whispered behind their hands, then he would be obliged to return to Katharine – there could be no doubt about that. But then if Anne were to bear a son . . . With her mind in total confusion, Jane entered the Queen's apartments to find most of the intimate circle of both Henry and Anne already arrived, dressed like peacocks and conversing noisily. Feeling dowdy in comparison, Jane looked round for an ally and at that moment heard a voice at her elbow and was relieved to see Nicholas Carew.

'My dear Mistress Seymour,' he said, giving her a secretive smile, 'how very charming you look. Come . . .' And with that he propelled her into a corner out of earshot. 'Remember everything I say,' he continued in a fierce whisper. 'His Grace is enchanted with you but on no account must you ever become his mistress.'

'But . . .' Jane answered, perplexed by the suddenness of every-thing.

'No buts. Come to my chamber tomorrow and we shall have further discussion. Now farewell.' He laid his finger to his lips and hurried away, leaving Jane shaking her head in bewilderment.

The arrival of the Queen from her bedchamber, splendidly arrayed in a flowing gown which Jane felt deliberately accentuated the fact that Anne was expecting a child, caused a much needed diversion. But as she curtsied respectfully, Jane felt herself being scrutinised and looked up to see Thomas Elyot, an old friend of Edward's, watching her thoughtfully. Embarrassment fought with a certain pride as Jane realised that for the first time ever, in the eyes of one or two people, she was the focus of attention. Composing her small mouth into an enigmatic smile, she stared back and then graciously inclined her head.

If Fate intends me to be a favourite at least let me act the part, she thought.

But the arrival of Henry and his gentlemen, and the knowledge that he must by now realise that she had read his note, threw Jane into a total fluster. She shook when she made her curtsey, blushed an unbecoming shade of red, then slid her eyes away from those of the King when she saw them momentarily rest upon her.

I am a fool, she thought miserably. Now he will think I am displeased.

Fortunately her place at the elaborately decorated table was at the opposite end from the royal couple, seated next to Sir Henry Norris on one hand and Thomas Elyot on the other. Thus situated, Jane had ample opportunity to study the inscrutable Norris, whom everyone said had only agreed to take Madge Shelton in betrothal in order to please his Queen. And, indeed, how the principal gentleman of the King's bedchamber could bring himself to marry such a trollop, whom the King had used to serve daily or so rumour had it, was beyond Jane's comprehension.

An exciting train of thought started up; of the virility of the King; of how she might one day receive his favours; of how her passion could soon be satisfied. And then Jane's speculations came to an abrupt halt as she remembered what both Edward and Sir Nicholas Carew had told her; that she must on no account give herself to the King unless she wanted to be thrown aside like Elizabeth Blount, Mary Boleyn and, now, Madge herself. Pursing her lips slightly, Jane looked up to see Henry Tudor watching her.

His very glance told her everything. He had had no need to write a note, his eyes quite clearly announced that he wanted and would pursue her however hard she ran and in the first flirtatious moment of her modest life, Jane responded. Looking him straight in the eye she gave the King a naughty smile before she demurely lowered her gaze once more to the table.

There was a slight quiver from Thomas Elyot before he cleared his throat and said, 'Madam it would seem that all is well with you.'

Jane looked at him innocently. 'Sir?'

'You know what I mean,' he answered, lowering his voice.

Despite the fact that he was her brother's long-standing friend, Jane felt somewhat irritated. 'Indeed I don't, Sir,' she answered, 'but I take it that you refer to my recent escape from the Sweat and, if so, I thank you for your concern.'

Elyot gulped. 'I am sorry, Mistress Seymour, I believe we speak at cross purposes so I will say no more. But listen to Nicholas Carew,' he added in a trenchant whisper and then looked away.

Jane smiled to herself as the last course of jelly, blancmangers, pears with caraway, scraped cheese and clotted cream with sugar, and quince pie was cleared away. Now the wafers and hippocras, a cordial of spiced wine that heralded the end of the meal, would be served. Then the musicians would play music for dancing and the evening would finish with much laughter and amusement.

As was customary when all was ready, the King offered his hand to his wife but Anne protested that she must do nothing to put the unborn baby at risk, defensively laying a hand upon her belly as she said so.

'Dance with who you will, my Lord,' she added, slanting her eyes at him. 'For I know that you love the unborn Prince as much as I.'

Henry smiled and took for partner Lady Berkeley, while Jane moved off with Thomas Elyot noticing that Mark Smeaton, Anne's lutanist and personal favourite, had gone to sit beside his Queen at her smiling request.

'Too familiar,' muttered Elyot.

'Who is?' asked Jane, startled.

'Her Grace should not be on such friendly terms with Smeaton. He is, after all, nothing but a carpenter's son.'

'Just as her enemy Cardinal Wolsey was a butcher's.'

Thomas Elyot looked at her in surprise. 'Your brother had not told me you were a wit.'

Jane smiled as the music of the pavan continued its measure. 'It is the dancing, Sir. I believe it makes me brighter.'

'Then I look forward to stepping out with you again,' said Thomas, and bowed as the music ended, to be followed by the lively tones of a galliard.

Jane knew even before he spoke that Henry Tudor was making his way towards her; could see the little ripple amongst the courtiers as they parted ranks to let him through; felt the warmth of his presence as it approached hers; sniffed the arrogant male scent of him underlying the fine oils and spices in which he had bathed himself this night.

'Mistress Jane,' he said behind her and she spun round to curtsey low before him, her cheeks pink and her heart racing so that she was breathless.

'Will you grant me the pleasure of this dance?'

'I am Your Grace's humble servant.'

'In everything?' he whispered as he raised her up.

'In everything,' she answered quietly.

And with that they whirled away in lively fashion, Jane feeling small as a doll as the massive creature lifted her clean off her feet when the music increased its speed.

'You are a dainty little thing,' he said. 'As well as beautiful.'

Jane looked at her sovereign through narrowed eyes. 'I could never be that, Your Grace.'

'You are to me,' he said, so simply that Jane at last realised he meant it.

'You got my note?' he added softly.

'Yes, Your Grace.'

'I meant what I said. I shall not rest until you are mine.'

Jane longed to say, 'That could be tonight for all I care,' but remembering what she had been taught, answered, 'That might be never, Your Grace. I value my virtue too highly.'

'We shall see,' Henry answered with a smile and, as the dance ended to the sound of laughter and applause, did not move from her side.

'We must part company, Sir; before we are observed,' whispered Jane frantically.

'Indeed,' he whispered back. 'But at midnight I shall be on the river walk by the banqueting house. Meet me there.'

'It would not be discreet, Your Grace,' she mumbled nervously.

The blue Tudor eyes became a little hard. 'Be there at midnight,' he said, and with that Henry turned on his heel and rejoined his Queen, leaving Jane attempting to control the attack of trembling which had so suddenly and violently seized her.

How she survived the rest of the evening, she never afterwards knew. She felt that every eye was upon her, that every whispered conversation muttered scandals about herself and the King. And, in truth, several people did look Jane's way and once she caught Anne's great dark eyes running over her appraisingly. Then she saw the Queen's lips twitch and her thin brows raise.

She's thinking, 'Not that plain thing', thought Jane wretchedly and looked away as Henry, suddenly announcing that he was tired, bade goodnight to the assembled company, and left the room accompanied by his gentlemen.

Sir Nicholas Carew appeared as if from nowhere. 'What did he say to you?'

Jane longed to tell him to mind his own affairs yet at the same time was grateful for any advice that might come her way.

'He wants to meet me at midnight.'

Carew's lips formed a soundless whistle. 'Does he by God? Then you must go, Jane. But no over-familiarity remember.'

'Why?' said Jane crossly. 'Why not, Sir Nicholas?'

'Because,' he answered, 'we are playing for the highest stakes of all.'

'We?'

'Yes. All supporters of . . .' His voice dropped so that it was scarcely audible, '. . . the Princess Mary and her mother are behind you in this. Their future lies in your hands, Mistress Seymour.'

'What can you possibly mean?'

'Marriage, Jane. You must hold out for marriage.'

The room went black and spun and she clung to Carew to steady herself. 'It isn't credible,' she said, and then remembered Cloverella's words: 'One day you will sign yourself, Jane the Queen.'

'Why not? Another has done it before you.'

'Please, no more,' she answered, suddenly too frightened to think. 'Please leave me, Sir Nicholas.'

He bowed, raised her hand to his lips, then bowed again more formally as the Queen rose from her place at the table, Mark Smeaton helping her to get to her feet.

'I bid you all goodnight,' said Anne, allowing a moment's pause before she dropped her eyes to her rounding belly. 'For the sake of the Prince I must now take some rest.'

There was some laughter, polite from the Queen's enemies, sympathetic from her friends.

'I'll swear she has a cushion stuffed in there,' said a whisperer hidden from Jane's view, as Anne left the room with Smeaton.

'Perhaps,' came the murmured reply. 'But who knows if there might not go the child's father.'

Realising that for the second time that day she was an eavesdropper, Jane strained her ears.

'You mean . . .?' said the first speaker.

'But of course,' came the reply, together with a light laugh. 'They say there is no one better at siring a healthy son than a peasant lad.'

'Christ's Holy Blood!' came the reply, followed by, 'Someone is listening. Quickly!'

Jane realised that she must have made a small movement of some kind for the speakers sped away before she could get a glimpse of them. In a certain amount of growing excitement she considered what she had just overheard, admitting to herself that it was true enough. Cloverella, fathered by a gypsy stable boy had always been the healthiest of all the Seymour children, despite her diminutive stature. Could it be possible that Anne Boleyn in her desperation to produce a son had allowed Mark Smeaton into her bed? After all, Jane thought wryly, the King had been so busy serving Madge Shelton he would hardly have had time to notice if his place had been usurped. Feeling that she had a great deal to consider, Jane asked Lady Berkeley's permission to withdraw, and left for her own chamber.

As a serving woman of long standing Jane was lucky enough to have private quarters, unlike the younger women, and she had never been more grateful for the privacy than now when, realising that there were only a few minutes left before midnight, she changed into a warmer cloak and hurried out again, slipping quietly through one of the side doors that led to the river walk.

A cold wind blew from the Thames, a wind full of smells of tide and salt and wooden hulks; a wind that spoke of snow to come, of hanging icicles and logs pulled into halls. There were sounds in the wind too: of gulls wheeling in the darkness, swooping to pull out fish and causing showers of luminous drops as they disturbed the flatness of the river's snake-like skin; of a solitary heron stretching its neck and opening its wings before it slept; of the distant song of a boat-load of homeward bound revellers.

Jane was vividly reminded of the night six years before when she had stood almost in the same spot outside Greenwich Palace and first set eyes on the strange young man who had later been pointed out to her as Dr Zachary. The urgent need to consult him had never been more apparent than now and Jane determined that somehow in the next few days she must beg leave of absence and go upriver to his home.

'Yes,' she said out loud and jumped as a huge shadow detached itself from all the others. 'Is that word for me?' it asked and, without waiting for a reply, bent to kiss her.

It was Henry Tudor, sensual and magnificent, caressing her with lips, hands and body.

'I knew,' he breathed against her, 'I knew that night at Wolff Hall that at last I had found a woman to match me. That the little fair mouse was merely a disguise for a full-blooded nymph.'

'You think of me as that?' she said, struggling. 'It is not so. I have never given myself to anyone.'

In the darkness the King smiled. 'But soon you will to me,' he said.

'No, no . . .' answered Jane, and then gave up the uneven contest as all the want coursed between them like a stream and they became lost in one another's kisses, two very different beings drawn together by an attraction that knew no boundaries.

'I have got too possess you,' he gasped as they finally separated. 'Jane, will you have me?'

A certain dignity restored itself to her and she answered gravely, 'If I do, Sir, it must be with honour.'

'So be it,' he answered and drew her into his arms again, feeling himself utterly bewitched by this funny little girl whose primness concealed such a wealth of ardour, and whose plain face glowed with so much endearing charm.

'Oh Jane, Jane, it would be so easy to love you,' whispered Henry Tudor into the winter night, unaware that a shadow had slipped away from a concealing wall even as he spoke, and was making its way in haste towards the apartments in which Eustace Chapuys, the Spanish Ambassador and enemy of Queen Anne Boleyn, resided at Greenwich that night.

# Chapter Seven

IT SEEMED TO THE TWO people leaning over the dark crystal that for a moment it glowed red. But then, as they stared at one another in surprise, their heads – one pale as flowers, the other dark as a rook's – close together, they thought they must have been mistaken, for it had at once resumed its usual glittering form, with no sign of a crimson pulse.

Nonetheless, Jane Seymour looked at Zachary Howard hard and said, 'I thought the sphere changed colour. Is that possible?'

He shook his head. 'Perhaps. It is still new to me and its mysteries have yet to be revealed. But I too believed it glowed.'

'What does that mean?'

Zachary frowned. 'It could be one of several things, Mistress, but as to which I am not sure. Now, in what way can my scrying be of service to you?'

Jane hesitated, her delicate skin colouring a little. 'I am still a maid, Dr Zachary, but the years romp on regardless. I have come to you to know if I will ever be a wife.'

It was true enough and there was no reason for her to blush further but as Zachary shot her a sideways glance, Jane felt her cheeks deepen. Was it possible, she wondered, that this rough-haired rascal had read her thoughts and knew perfectly well why she had come through the bitter January weather, rowed up the Thames by a solitary wherryman despite the ominous threat of snow.

'I would so like to marry . . .' she went on with a nervous smile, but her voice trailed away as she realised that the astrologer was no longer listening to her, his head sinking forward over the scrying glass as he stared into its twinkling heart.

'I will do my best, Mistress Seymour,' he answered softly and Jane felt herself grow faint. She had used her mother's name,

Wentworth, in order to try and hide from him her true identity.

'How did you know?' she asked unevenly.

Dr Zachary's shoulders shook and he spun round to look at her, his curls flying about his head as he burst out laughing. 'Because I used to observe you around the Court, Madam.'

Jane drew in a breath, struggling between irritation and amusement, but the astrologer merely grinned at her disarmingly before he once more bent his attention to the gleaming orb on the table before him, his eyes half closing as he stared into it.

Jane sighed somewhat petulantly, wishing that she had not come, thinking that the astrologer was probably a charlatan yet terrified lest he might tell her something she had no wish to hear.

Again as if he had read her thoughts, Zachary said soothingly, 'Do not be afraid, Mistress Seymour, for what you desire most in all the world will be yours.'

The girl gave a muffled gasp. 'What do you mean?'

'What I say, Madam. The man you love will become your husband, there is nothing that can prevent it.'

He looked up at her, his large amber eyes suddenly gentle. 'Mistress Jane,' he said quietly, 'many great people have sat where you are now and I have told them their destiny, be it for good or ill. There is only one thing I ask of them in return.'

'And what is that?'

'That they trust me with their secrets. For if you and I are to continue to play shill and shall together there is little point in this meeting.'

'Dr Zachary,' said Jane forthrightly, 'you are of the house of Howard, or so it is said. That means you are kin to the Queen.'

'Mistress Seymour,' came the answer, 'you knew that before you came. So why did you choose to consult me?'

She looked young suddenly, the plain face crumpling like a child's and the great eyes swimming with tears. 'Because I need help,' she whispered. 'A destiny too great is being thrust upon me.'

Zachary rose and silently poured a golden liquid from a stone bottle, giving Jane the phial to drink.

'What is it?'

'A herbal remedy that will restore you to calm.'

The girl smiled faintly, then drank. 'It was wrong of me not to trust you. I'm sorry.'

'Forget that and listen to me. Mistress Seymour, you have come to see me on the very day when all events must change. By tomorrow morning the King will at last know which path he is free to take.'

'What are you saying? How can this be?'

'Some hours ago the Princess Dowager Katharine of Aragon died in Kimbolton Castle. The news will reach London at daybreak.'

Jane stared at the astrologer, her lips trembling. 'She is dead? That good woman whom I once served?'

'Yes, I fear so, may God have mercy on her unhappy soul. And now a chain of reaction will start which will culminate in your ascending the throne of England as consort to His Grace.'

'But Anne,' said the girl frantically, 'what of her?'

At that moment the crystal suffused the colour of blood, they both saw it together and there could be no doubt.

'Mistress Seymour,' answered Zachary, gravely, 'it is not meant that this part of the consultation should continue. A dark crystal is a powerful thing and today it is best that we leave it alone.' He covered it with its velvet cloth but Jane saw the orb glowing through the material for a second or two before it once more turned black.

'Now let me read the ancient cards.' The astrologer laid them out, then hunched over them, seeing as he did so all the great destiny of Jane and all the great tragedy of her as well. With enormous care and a kind of love, for he had warmed to this mouse with its sad little face and sweet, generous heart, he told her some of what lay before her. Yet never once did he mention the brutality of Anne Boleyn's end nor the suffering of Jane's own. Instead Zachary Howard told the girl a story of love triumphant; of the great gift of a Prince which she would give not only the King but the entire nation; of all the sweet things that were there just for her to reach out and grasp.

Yet when she rose at the end, flushed and beautiful, transformed by her happiness, still she asked, 'But what of Her Grace? How will she go?'

Zachary looked grave. 'With any parting there is pain, Mistress. Anne will go savagely.'

She took it to mean that the Queen would fight like a cat when Henry demanded divorce, and nodded her head. 'I can imagine that well.'

Zachary stood up also. 'The session is at an end, Mistress Seymour. I can tell you no more.'

She pressed a bag of money into his hand. 'I thank you. And I apologise that I did not deal straightly with you at first.'

But he was not looking at her, instead staring out of the window, his dark head cocked slightly as if he were listening to something.

'Is anything the matter?' Jane wondered at once if she had been followed.

'There's an oarsman coming this way and yet it has started to snow. Who could be calling here on such a bleak evening?'

Jane went to stand by the astrologer, peering out on a charcoal landscape in which river and sky blended into one beneath a thick fall of flakes. In the gloom it seemed as if Zachary's house were the last dwelling place on earth but sure enough a small craft containing two figures, a forlorn boatman and his cloaked passenger, was making its way towards the landing stage.

Though the huddled shape of the traveller was hardly visible, concealed by a huge fur hat and mass of rugs, nonetheless something about it struck Jane as familiar.

'Who is it?' she asked anxiously.

'I believe an intimate of yours,' answered Zachary, smiling.

Jane stared at him astonished. 'Who?'

'Why, Sir Edward Seymour I imagine.'

She shook her head, totally bewildered. 'But what could my brother be doing here? It is impossible.'

'On the contrary,' answered Zachary. 'We met in France a great many years ago when I was little more than a boy and he a young soldier.'

Jane's eyes grew wider. 'The rumple-haired youth who showed him by magic means Katherine Filliol in bed with another man. It was you!'

Zachary bowed. 'The same, Madam.'

Jane stared at him astounded in the lengthening shadows, until Edward Seymour's feet were heard mounting the stairs.

The news of the death of Katharine of Aragon swept England like wildfire. Many said that she had been helped out of the world by the administration of some slow and cleverly composed drug; others were more circumspect in their thoughts, believing Henry's insults, neglect and cruelty to be the cause. But whatever their view many genuinely grieved, mourning the loss of a good and harmless woman who in the opinion of most had been much sinned against.

The King, wild with joy because of the freedom Katharine's death had given him, wore yellow for the mourning, and stuck a white feather in his hat, while Queen Anne adopted the same colour and dressed her small daughter likewise so that the family could appear to be at one.

Those few days when Henry fussed over little Elizabeth, and Anne, proudly displaying her four-month pregnancy, never left his side, were the most difficult that Jane had had to endure since those first agonising times at Wolff Hall when she had believed the King to be making a fool of her. Despite everything that Zachary had said to her – and despite her brother's assurances that the astrologer was the most gifted man in England – she believed that the Princess Dowager's death had in some extraordinary way brought the Lady and Henry close once more, that Anne's exultant cry of, 'So I am indeed Queen' on hearing of Katharine's death, had been justified. Because of this Jane avoided her sovereign at the celebrations, not only sick at heart for her own sake but also that Henry Tudor could bring himself to order a Mass, a banquet, dancing and jousting, all to celebrate poor Katharine's end. In fact, to a very small degree, Mistress Seymour's passion for her master cooled.

In the extraordinary way that lovers have between them, he knew: knew that his little mouse, as he now so tenderly thought of her, was keeping out of his way; knew that in some manner she had grown cold towards him. At first he was mystified, then, being a man of Henry's temperament, felt a violent sweep of anger. But inevitably, just as it had so many years ago with Anne Boleyn, her indifference intrigued him and the King's mind, once the celebrations were done, constantly turned over the way in which he could catch Jane alone and tax her with behaving coldly.

Yet there never seemed an opportunity. Almost as if she was doing it on purpose, which Henry strongly suspected, Jane was constantly in the company of her fellow courtiers and other than a polite letter thanking him for the costly presents he had sent her for Christmas, made no communication. With the elusiveness of his quarry thoroughly engrossing him, the King took to entering rooms alone and unexpectedly, hoping that he would chance on Jane, preferably by herself. And as fate would have it, with only ten days left until the end of January, 1536, he succeeded.

She stood by the window, turning the leaves of a book, and Henry thought he had never seen his love look sweeter, the winter sun lightening her hair to snow and her skin delicate as mistletoe.

He had planned all along that when he finally confronted her he would be stern, rebuke Jane for her cruel treatment of him, but now the King found himself hurrying across the room, his arms outstretched, a rather foolish expression on his full-moon face.

Mistress Seymour spun round, her cheeks flushing, and Henry saw that she was frowning and pursing her lips, ready to reply formally. Then she did something which he never afterwards forgot and which was to endear her to him for ever more. The bottom lip of the tight little mouth trembled and just like a child, Jane Seymour's face crumpled as she burst into tears.

'Darling,' he said, reaching her side. 'What is it? What has upset you?'

She did not answer, burying her head in the waist of his doublet, which was as high on him as she could reach.

'Come, come,' he said, sitting on a chair and pulling her on to his lap. 'What is the matter? Please tell me.'

Jane wept quietly while Henry, rather inexpertly, made dabs at her face with a linen handkerchief. 'Won't you confide in me?' he said.

'I thought you had lost interest,' she answered between sobs.

'I lose interest in you?' he replied. 'Never.'

The answering kiss was inevitable, fierce and intense, speaking as it did of all the sensual pleasure that awaited these two, and it was with a thrill of carnal excitement that Jane felt the King's great hand slip within the bodice of her gown and close round one full high breast. She knew at that moment that she should fight him off, behave primly as befitted her virgin status, but instead Jane fell to kissing Henry Tudor as if they had been lovers for an age, all her longing for him at last flowing freely.

They were too lost in one another to hear the door open and it wasn't until a scream like the crack of ice filled the room with its fury that Jane and Henry finally and almost reluctantly drew apart.

The Queen stood in the doorway, wild-eyed, her face contorting in a combination of expressions, for on it despair, anguish and violent anger fought for supremacy. Just for a fleeting second, Jane felt guilt and pity chase one another through her heart, but then fear overcame both as Anne Boleyn flew at her in a frenzy. Henry with amazing speed for someone of his size, rose to his feet and thrust Jane behind him for protection. Nothing daunted, Anne rushed at him, raining a flurry of blows onto his impervious chest.

'You monstrous bladder,' she shrieked. 'You cheating, lying son of a whore.'

Jane could not believe her ears. That *anyone*, even the Queen of England, should dare to use such words to the King's Majesty was beyond credulity. It flashed through Jane's mind that Anne was putting herself in mortal danger by this exhibition and would have felt guilt again had it not been for the thought that the Lady had openly celebrated the death of one who had died friendless and alone, not even allowed the comfort of her daughter's presence at the end.

'Quiet,' Henry was saying calmly. 'Anne, be quiet.'

'I will not,' she screamed, striking him afresh. 'And as for you, you whey-faced trollop, you may hide behind your lover's skirts but you'll never escape my revenge. Never, do you hear me?'

'Jane,' ordered the King evenly, 'Leave the room now. We do not wish you to hear more. Now go.'

Avoiding Anne's flying fists, Jane fled past him and out, her face the palest it had been for years. Henry, watching her scuttling away, almost smiled. Even her hasty exit held an engaging mouselike quality that delighted him.

With a sigh he turned to his wife.

'Will you be calm, sweetheart? I merely kissed the girl for amusement. It meant nothing,' he said soothingly.

'What! With your hand stuffed in her bodice and she lapping it up, the great suet pudding. God's blood, how I hate her,' came Anne's stinging retort.

'My dear, don't excite yourself so. Remember the child. I tell you Jane Seymour is a woman upon whom I merely smiled. That is all. Just as you smile on Mark Smeaton. It means nothing.'

Anne's eyes flickered and looked away from him, a meaningless enough movement but one on which, in times yet to come, Henry was frequently to dwell. But now he thought nothing of it and went on. 'That's better. Be at peace, sweetheart, and all shall go well for thee.'

Anne gave him a look that years ago would have left him gasping with desire. 'Aye, all will go well when that Seymour wench is sent packing.'

The massive Tudor face seemed to set like stone. 'What is that you say?'

Foolishly, poor Anne blundered on. 'When that girl is sent from court then indeed shall I be well again.'

Henry's preposterous eyebrows rose. 'In that case, my dear, I shall consider your wishes of course. The welfare of the child must override all else.'

She ran to him, flinging her arms around him and hiding her dark head in his chest. It was as well for her, then, that she could not see the expression on Henry Tudor's face nor read his cruel thoughts.

'Then she will go?' Anne asked in a muffled voice.

He put her from him gently. 'I said I would consider it.'

The clever face that he had once thought so captivating grew mutinous. 'There'll be no peace for my child until Jane Seymour is shown the door.'

'And there'll be no peace for you if you continue to give me orders. Know your place, woman, as others have done before you,' the King answered coldly.

'Aye, I know my place,' hissed Anne furiously. 'I am Queen of all England.'

'And I am he who put you there. So have a care lest I put you out,' Henry threw back, and strode from the room without another word, leaving Anne, her hands clutching her swollen belly, to stare disconsolately after him.

Many thought that Katharine of Aragon had, even in death, been finally revenged upon the black-haired lady of Hever who had stolen away her husband and thereby ruined her life. For it was by the strangest coincidence that on 29th January just as Katharine, 'relict of our natural brother Prince Arthur of famous memory', was laid to rest in Peterborough Cathedral, the Queen who had usurped her place went into premature labour and delivered a dead son of about fifteen weeks gestation who lay upon a towel like a changeling and in his death also condemned his mother.

The King, who had fallen in the lists some days earlier and hurt his leg, limped into the Queen's apartments and upbraided her for losing his child, snarling that she would have no more boys by him.

Anne had bravely fought back, saying that it was Norfolk's fault, that he had told her the King had fallen and died; that this, coupled with the shock of seeing him kiss Jane Seymour, had made her miscarry. The growled reply had been that Anne should have emulated her predecessor, Katharine, and not looked for trouble. And, at that, the Queen had turned her long dark eyes to the wall and said no more.

After this scene a terrible silence had fallen over the Palace and while from the King's apartments had come the distant sound of a whole host of his gentlemen trying desperately to restore him to calm, from the Queen's there had been none.

Sir Nicholas Carew, his grizzled head close to the King's own, had whispered, his voice drowned by the musicians, 'Forgive me, your Grace, if I speak out of turn, but I did wonder if a little feminine company might ease your suffering. I hope I am not too bold.'

A bleak Tudor eye had regarded him with suspicion. 'You mean Mistress Seymour?'

Nicholas had bowed. 'Indeed, Sir.'

Henry had shaken his head slowly. 'It would not be fitting tonight – and yet . . .'

'Shall I ask her to come to my apartments, your Grace, that you might speak with her privately?'

The blue eyes had grown warmer. 'Do what you can, Nicholas. If her finer feelings will not allow . . .'

'She will thrust those aside in order to comfort you, Sire,' Carew had answered firmly, and bowed his way out.

He had found Jane in the chapel, weeping quietly where she knelt, and one look had Carew instantly guessing, incorrectly, what was wrong.

'His Grace will recover his humour soon,' he whispered urgently, dropping on his knees beside her.

She opened surprised eyes. 'Oh, Sir Nicholas, it is you!'

'Yes, and come on the King's business, so dry your tears.'

Jane stared at him perplexed. 'But does he not hate me for causing Anne's miscarriage?'

Now it was Carew's turn to look astonished. '*You* caused it! How?'

Jane dropped her eyes. 'The Queen found us – together – and flew into a violent rage.'

Nicholas scowled. 'Together? You weren't . . . ?'

'No, no,' Jane answered hastily. 'We kissed, that is all. But she was angry – and now this has happened.'

'Norfolk blames himself, you blame yourself,' said Nicholas impatiently. 'The fact is the woman isn't built for breeding and that's all there is to it. There is nobody to blame but her. Thin hips never produce good sons.'

In spite of the wretched circumstances, Jane smiled. 'Then if that is the case I suppose one should pity her.'

Carew snorted. 'Don't waste a morsel. The vicious hack deserves everything she gets – and more.'

'And His Grace does not hate me?'

'On the contrary. He has laid the blame where it belongs, at the feet of the Lady. It is *you*, my dear, whom he wishes to see to give him comfort. In fact he has asked you to accompany me to my apartments that he may speak with you privately.'

'Oh!' Jane's hands fluttered in the air and Nicholas grinned secretly.

'I think you are in love, Mistress.'

'Perhaps, Sir Nicholas.'

'Then, if so, this would be a good time to express your feelings.'

'What do you mean?'

'Box clever, little Jane, and the throne will be yours. The King is sick with grief that the Night Crow has lost his son and has told her she will have no more boys by him. Yet he longs for a Prince more than all the world. He is intent on a new wife, mark my words.'

Jane's eyes shone. 'Do you really think so?'

'I do, Mistress, I do. Now come with me and comfort him sweetly, but remember my words. Do not give him your body until you lie safe in the marriage bed.'

Sir Nicholas wondered why such an unemotional little thing as Jane should look away, and then decided it was embarrassment when she mumbled, 'I will heed what you say.'

But how could she, she asked herself half an hour later when the King, smelling of wine and blurred in his speech, swept her into his arms and allowed her to see a tear roll down the vast expanse of his enormous face and fall away into his beard.

'My Jane, my own sweet Jane,' he said thickly. 'You are all I have left. That evil woman has killed my son. She has taken everything from me.'

Just as she had once before in the gardens of Wolff Hall, Jane again saw the King as a misled boy and, standing on tip-toe, kissed him tenderly.

'I will make recompense.'

He looked at her eagerly. 'But how? How will you do so?'

'It has been foretold that *I* will have a son,' she answered, scarcely above a whisper, wondering if she had gone too far.

'Then pray God that I am his sire,' said Henry, so passionately that Jane thought she might cry aloud with triumph. He bent close to her ear. 'Sweetheart, I believe that I was seduced by witchcraft into my marriage and that it is null and void. It is obvious that God intends to punish me for it by denying me a boy. So clearly I must rid myself of the evil before I can ever find favour again in His eyes.'

Jane stared at him, wondering if what she had just heard was an extraordinary proposal of marriage.

'You believe that Anne is a mistress of Satan?' she said, wide-eyed.

'It is obvious. How else could the sidling bitch have so blinded me?'

'God a'mercy,' breathed Jane. 'I think you must be right, Your Grace. Think of all the good men who lost their heads because of her.'

Henry's face went to granite and the blue eyes lost their gentleness. 'Quite so,' he said abruptly and a finger of fear laid itself along Jane's spine as she realised that she had said the wrong thing, that the King did not like to be reminded of all the men he had sacrificed in order that he might achieve his wishes.

Timidly she said, 'What do you intend to do, Sir?'

'I shall see Secretary Cromwell and ask him to find grounds for a divorce. I cannot go on like this. Why, Jane' – his voice changed again and sitting down, Henry lifted her onto his lap and held her against him – 'she kept me waiting years before she finally allowed me to her bed. I would not have suffered such treatment long if I had not been bewitched. You would not do such a thing, I know.'

Wretchedly, Jane said, 'But I am a virtuous woman, Your Grace. I must protect myself until I marry.'

'Would it not be easier by far,' replied Henry Tudor soothingly, 'to let *me* protect you?'

'I suppose,' answered Jane slowly, all the advice she had been given still ringing in her ears, 'it probably would, Your Grace.'

'Then that shall be my task for this new year,' said the King. 'To cherish little Jane Seymour until finally she can be mine.'

# Chapter Eight

THE CLUSTERING HEDGEROWS THAT garlanded the rambling fields of the Wolff Hall estate were, in summer, suffused with scarlet where the wild fuschias grew in sweet abundance, attracting lazy bees and filling the air with a delicate scent of petals. But though now, in icy February, nothing flowered beneath their close shade but the heroic snowdrop, it seemed as if the sky remembered the glories of June and took on fuschia shades at both morning and night. Brave as a battle, the dawn had come up in vivid shades of pink, red and purple, and Cloverella, watching from her window, had dressed hurriedly and gone out into the freezing air to be at one with it all.

The girl was in a curious mood, convinced that far-reaching changes were about to come to the Seymours, and already viewing her own move to Court with a strange mixture of fear and elation. Naturally, Edward's wife had not wanted her as part of the entourage, bound for London to take up residence, following Edward's new appointment as a gentleman of the King's Privy Chamber.

'Her father was a gypsy,' Anne had said acidly, when the subject had first arisen. 'Cloverella is not suitable for court life. Edward, where is your common sense?'

'Here,' he had shouted, striking his heart with his fist, 'here is where I keep my sense; my sense of what is right and just. My cousin is a Wentworth, Anne, and as fit to go to Court as you or I. I'd advise you to watch your tongue.'

Anne had glared at him furiously, the fact that she was feeling slightly sick and wondering whether she was pregnant again not helping her disposition.

'I believe you are in love with her, Ned. I think there is something between yourself and the little wretch. You always take her side against mine and that is indicative in itself.'

101

Edward's saturnine features had grown dark. 'Take such evil thoughts from your head, wife. It is true I love Cloverella but not as you infer. She was brought to my mother as a defenceless child and all of us have cherished her since. I'll not have her left behind in the country to rot. Let her find a good husband at Court and be settled for life. If that happens she will be out of your way for ever,' he had added pointedly.

Anne had taken the remark at its face value. 'That is very true. I'll make no further objection.'

Edward had rolled his eyes to heaven. 'There are times, my dear, when you try my patience to the limit. Good evening to you.' And he had strode out of the room.

He thought now, as he walked the gardens of Wolff Hall where he had brought his family to stay on their way to Court, that his wife was a beautiful shrew, a haughty cat who deserved spanking. Then he suddenly grinned, the dark eyes lighting with secret memories. He had been known, from time to time, to lay his hand to those superbly rounded buttocks, and what shrieking and lovemaking had ensued. With a wicked grin, Edward stopped in his tracks and whistling a merry air made his way back into the house.

But even while he and Anne engaged in horseplay, Cloverella was staring at a flight of magpies and remembering a rhyme taught by her Romany grandam. 'One for anger, two for mirth, three for a wedding, four for a birth, five for silver, six for gold, seven for a secret never to be told.'

She shaded her eyes, the colour of brook iris in the morning light, and counted the magnificent swoop of jet and snow as the birds wheeled above her head before settling in a tree to argue. Three of them! So there was to be a wedding. But whose?

Cloverella smiled to herself, quite sure that the old fable of a serving maid who married a prince was about to be reinacted in her cousin's case. But even as she thought it, her face grew dark. It seemed to the girl that she had a cruel vision of Anne Boleyn, her face white but proud, seated in a high chair facing a multitude of unsmiling men, the peers of the realm come to try her for her life.

Cloverella's hand flew to her mouth. She suddenly knew for sure that there was to be brutality and death before Jane could achieve her heart's desire. Looking up, she saw that the magpies had added four more to their company and Cloverella shivered. The day had grown cold and the sky the sharp clear blue of a winter's day.

Pulling her shawl round her, Cloverella turned back in the direction of Wolff Hall and the warmth and comfort of Dame Margery's kitchen.

Beyond the mighty walls of Greenwich Palace lay green meadows, and at this time of year, with February running into March, wild crocuses and snowdrops had thrust their way upwards and carpeted the place with splashes of vivid colour. But though these delighted the eye of most who walked there, today a solitary figure, leaning against a tree almost as if for support, seemed not to see them, instead blindly staring out over the Thames and ignoring the flowers that grew so prettily around her feet.

'If only,' sighed Jane Seymour into the wind, 'I knew what I ought to do.'

And yet in her heart, though she went through the pantomime of indecision because her conscience demanded it of her, she was perfectly aware of what course of action she would take next. The faction that surrounded Princess Mary could advise her till their beards turned blue, Jane had defiantly determined to yield up her virginity to Henry and face the consequences. For now she felt reasonably certain that she would not be discarded as had all those others who had surrendered to him in the past. Jane may well be an innocent girl but yet she had shrewdness, and to her it seemed clear; the last thing to happen must be that she was in any way compared with Anne Boleyn.

Mistress Seymour closed her eyes and just for a moment did something that not many people dared – she looked at herself without deception and examined her motives. The fact was that she wanted Henry desperately, would have got into his bed long since had it not been for all the unsolicited advice that now poured into her ear almost daily. She was wildly passionate, that was the truth of it; a female version of her brother Thomas who seduced all and sundry without caring a fig.

And I don't either, she thought defiantly. Why should it be men who pleasure themselves all the time? Why should what is right for them be wrong for women?

The little mouth curved into a smile. 'I'll tell him today, this very day. I'll keep Henry' – she still had difficulty in actually daring to say the King's name – 'waiting no longer. Why, I am certain it will only make him love me more.'

But really she was still afraid, thinking that men like Carew and Elyot – men of the world who had each known a great many women – must be right. Yet how could one deny that wonderful feeling, that sense of yearning that was almost a physical pain, when the King held her in his arms, holding her tightly against his powerful body.

'Fiddle, faddle,' said Jane aloud, suddenly showing the steel that was the inheritance of all the Seymour children. 'I can endure this indecision no longer. My maiden state has become a burden to be discarded.' A naughty sparkle came into the deep blue eyes. 'But I must make haste about it. My brother will be here within the week and have me under lock and key, I shouldn't wonder.'

She straightened and turned, her mind made up – or almost! – and headed back towards the Palace with a certain determination in her tread.

'You do not think, do you,' said Anne Seymour, riding uncomfortably in a litter beside Edward's horse, 'that Jane has . . .' Despite the fact she was so free with her husband when their bedroom door was closed, she had the extraordinary inhibition of one who had been trained at Court, finding difficulty in discussing intimate matters.

'What?' answered Ned, his mind running over the beauty of the countryside and vaguely dredging up a memory of his wish on Merlin's Mound that he might one day own it all.

'You don't think that Jane is *intimate*' – Anne whispered the word – 'with His Grace?'

Her husband turned on her an amused glance. 'I presume you are not referring to friendship, my dear. And the answer is no. How could a meek little rabbit like my sister even consider such sinfulness?'

'Rabbits consider it frequently,' Anne answered scathingly.

Edward smiled. 'You know perfectly well what I mean. Jane is quite the primmest girl I have ever encountered. Why, one look at her mouth reveals her attitude to such things.'

Anne moved her lips into a frosty smile, a chill running through her at the swiftness of her friend the Queen's downfall. 'Have you not heard the old adage of the depth of still waters?'

Edward shrugged. 'Even if that were true, Nicholas Carew watches her virtually non-stop and if he is not there, Elyot is on hand.'

Anne lowered her voice again. 'One could almost pity such a prisoner.'

'Well, she'll have you and Cloverella for company soon.'

With a bitter irony, Anne said, 'I am still not convinced that *we* are the company Jane truly desires.'

'What Jane desires and what is good for Jane at this particular time may be different matters.'

'Don't talk so loudly,' said Anne angrily, 'the servants might hear.'

'No doubt they'll hear that and worse before this affair is over,' answered Edward, and kicking his heels into his horse's sides, rode off to be with Cloverella.

Despite March's bitter weather, the King announced his intention of hunting and almost at once set off for Windsor with certain members of his Court, leaving Anne Boleyn to pass her hollow days with her ladies, her lap dogs and pet birds, her apartments as empty as once had been Katharine of Aragon's. Only the sound of the Queen's joyless laughter and Mark Smeaton's lute broke the stillness.

When Henry and Anne had stayed at Windsor while the King had still been married to Katharine, all three of them had lodged in their own separate apartments, Henry sending dainty dishes down to where Anne supped alone. And it had been from Windsor that the King and his love had finally stolen away before daybreak without so much as a farewell, leaving the Queen solitary, neither of them destined ever to set eyes on her again. But now, in the way of a sublime revenge meted out by fate itself, Anne's old rooms were cleaned and dusted for a new favourite; for Mistress Jane Seymour was one of the few ladies who had been asked to accompany the gentlemen courtiers on this particular sortie.

For the occasion Henry had bought his companion an expensive pair of hunting gloves, and as Jane first drew them on she exclaimed in surprise at the pretty ring that lay concealed in one of the fingers.

'But, Your Grace, I cannot accept anything so valuable,' she had said modestly.

'If you do not I will be displeased,' had come the answer, and one look at Henry's face had warned Jane to let argument cease and to keep the gem with good grace. But afterwards in the luxurious bedroom set in one of the castle's towers she could not resist laughing to herself with pleasure. Her hand had never looked so elegant or shapely as it did now, bearing the King's sparkling ruby.

'Why, my Lady,' said Emma, coming in quietly and catching her mistress in the very act of waving the ring in the air to see it sparkle, 'What a lovely thing. Was it a gift from His Grace?'

Jane compressed her lips. 'That is none of your business.'

Emma refused to be chastened. 'I've been talking to the Castle servants, Ma'am, and do you know what?'

'No.'

'You know that these rooms once belonged to Anne Boleyn, as she was then, and are directly below the King's.'

'Yes, what of it?'

'There's a secret staircase in the turret, Ma'am, so that he could send her down dainties. Dainties!' Emma clasped her hands over her mouth and rolled her eyes wildly, hysterical about the double meaning.

Despite the fact that she was interested, Jane looked reproving. 'You should not gossip, Emma. You work in a position of trust and if you continue in this manner you will leave me no alternative but to send you back to Dame Margery at Wolff Hall.'

Somewhat chastened, Emma bobbed a curtsey, muttering, 'Sorry, my Lady.'

'So I should think. Now where is this staircase?'

Emma was at once restored to her usual spirits. 'The servants said it was built behind the main spiral and that you get to it through a wooden door that's almost concealed.'

'Well I forbid you to go searching,' said Jane sternly. 'Wherever it is, it is privy to His Grace's apartments and it is not for us to go meddling in things that do not concern us. Now run along to your duties.'

As the girl left the room, Mistress Seymour turned to the window and looked almost blindly at the breathtaking view, wondering if Anne Boleyn had stood in the same spot and gazed on such warm and natural splendour, and how she had felt when the King had come at nights down the secret stairs and into her apartments, his eyes full of love and his arms open, begging her to relent and give him his heart's desire.

How could, thought Jane, how *could* she have spurned him? I would not have been able to do so in such circumstances.

She realised then, with a sudden jolt, that at any time the

circumstances could be repeated and even as she thought it, with one of those incredible coincidences that are supposed never actually to take place, the door leading from the main spiral staircase slowly opened and there stood the King.

Jane gaped aghast, saying idiotically, 'But it's daytime.'

He frowned, somewhat perturbed. 'So I have noticed, sweetheart. Is it not permissible for me to visit you whilst it is light?'

Colouring violently, Jane curtsied. 'Your Grace, I . . . I am sorry, I was just thinking . . .'

'What?' He walked over and stood looking down at her. 'That I would creep below like a thief in the dark and rob you of your precious virtue?'

'No, Sir. I . . .'

Henry turned abruptly away, gazing out of the window as she had done a moment earlier. 'All that,' he said savagely, 'all that is mine. Look!' He grabbed her by the shoulders and turned her round. 'All of it. Tell me Jane, what do you see? What do you see of that great and mighty kingdom that has no prince to inherit it and no Queen worthy of the name?'

'I see a bustling waterway, the River Thames,' she answered slowly.

'Yes, go on. What more? Tell me about this river.'

His tone was harsh and Jane felt that she was being put to some kind of test. Rather nervously she slipped her hand into his vast paw and, still not looking at him, started to speak.

'I see that the Thames is calm and strong as its King, rolling through lush pasturelands green as parsley, though at dawn the water turns pink, the colour of a May Day garland or old man's hawthorn. But as the sun rises in glory it changes and the river is golden.' She stole a sideways look at him and saw that the King was smiling, his eyes fixed on the far distance.

'But at noon, or so it is said, the river is full of rainbows and it is then that kingfishers sit beneath the willow trees and sing love songs to the breeze.'

Jane heard Henry laugh gently at such foolishness.

'While in the evening as the day dies, the water is the colour of a gentian, reflecting a sky full of strange white, wheeling birds. But at night, when it is time for lovers to greet one another, the river is black as ink, full of mystery and secrets, dark as a Moor and just as exciting.'

'Bravo.' The King clapped his hands, his humour restored. 'You are a poet, Jane. A weaver of dreams.'

She turned to face him. 'And what is it, Sir, that you dream of?' she asked defiantly.

He stared at her, his eyes hardening. 'Of fathering a healthy boy, of loving a wholesome woman, not one diseased by evil and greed.'

Jane took a calculated risk. 'And do you dream of me?'

Henry's expression changed dramatically as he gathered her roughly into his arms. 'I dream of nothing else and you know it, you capricious child. Why, I would lay myself at your feet if you would have me.'

'I will have you,' she answered quietly.

'What did you say?'

'I will have you, Sir.'

'Do you mean . . .'

'Yes, now, here, in the joyful afternoon. If you want me, I am yours, Your Grace.'

He could hardly comprehend what she was saying and it was Jane who actually took him by the hand and led the King towards the great draped bed in which once Anne Boleyn had slept.

'Teach me everything, Sir,' she said, both humbly and endearingly. 'I know nothing of love though you will find me a willing pupil.'

But it was as if she had, in fact, always known; as if the appetites that had been there all along, masked by her prim appearance, quite naturally took over every other sense so that she moved in harmony with Henry's great body, throbbing with pleasure as pain, the frightening feeling of being torn asunder within by something large and unyielding, finally gave way to an exquisite pulse, a paradise into whose realms she had never entered before. She was complete with him, overjoyed to hear him triumphantly exclaim as his moment finally came and the King's leaping seed flowed within her.

Afterwards, of course, while Henry slept and she lay in the crook of his arm, Jane panicked. She had given him her much-prized virginity, she had shown him in the way she moved and shouted and pleaded, that she was wanton, as free and fierce as any courtesan. Every word of warning that had ever been said came back to Jane now with horrid clarity. She could almost see Nicholas Carew throwing his hands in the air and declaring her an utter numbskull.

And yet, she thought, looking at the huge figure slumbering

beside her, its face relaxed and younger-looking in sleep, how could I say no to him when his every touch arouses me?

It occurred to Jane, for the first time, that she might actually be in love with Henry, that the vast physical attraction he held for her was in reality something even stronger. And the thought that she could well have ruined her future chances of ever becoming his wife now brought her to the edge of tears.

Nor was the situation made any better when Henry woke abruptly, exclaimed that he was late, dressed himself in haste and hurried back to his apartments by way of the secret staircase. At this harsh leaving, Jane could have indulged in the luxury of sobbing but she, too, had little time. Tonight, Henry was to give a special banquet in honour of the Spanish Ambassador, Eustace Chapuys, until recently not popular at Court because of his loathing for Anne Boleyn – whom the Ambassador sneeringly referred to as the Concubine – but now markedly reinstated in the King's favour.

With a shout, Jane called for Emma, sloe-eyed with suspicion for having been locked out of her mistress's apartments all the afternoon.

'Are you not well, my Lady?'

'I am a little tired, that it all. Now help me dress. Ambassador Chapuys has probably arrived by now.'

'Such a fuss,' said Emma, peering into her mistress's face closely. 'Why, you're quite flushed, my Lady. Nobody would think of you as pale any more.'

'No, nor as maid any more,' muttered Mistress Seymour under her breath.

'What was that, my Lady?'

'Nothing,' answered Jane firmly, and refused to be drawn further.


'An excellent repast, Your Grace, and such excellent company,' said Chapuys, dabbing his small pointed beard with white napery. 'Why, if I may make so bold, I have not seen you in such high spirits for an age, Sire.'

His pale blue eyes, rimmed with a faded ring of grey, twinkled innocently but behind them one of the shrewdest brains in Spain was working at twice its normal speed. It had been he, Eustace Chapuys, who had been sent by the Emperor Charles to handle the increasingly difficult situation in England, when the King seemed determined to divorce his Spanish Queen, apparently on the point of breaking with the Holy Roman Empire, the great-eyed daughter of a Kentish knight waiting ominously in the wings.

To report back faithfully all that had occurred had been Chapuys' brief and this he had obeyed to the last word. Through thick and thin, when Katharine had been rejected and exiled from Court, when the Concubine had been raised up in triumph, the Spanish ambassador had written to his master and told him everything, be the news for good or for ill. And now, at last, the wheel of fortune was moving and it was the Concubine's turn to go down. Chapuys' nest of spies had told him everything. There was a brand new favourite and this one seemed destined for success. Mistress Seymour's star was firmly in the ascendant.

Glancing at her down the table where she sat, rather pink in the cheeks and breathless, Chapuys could not think why. To him, Jane Seymour seemed rather a nonedescript little person, quite mousy and frail. But then, of course, it never did to judge by appearances.

It was at precisely this moment, feeling somebody staring at her, that Jane raised her eyes and looked straight at Chapuys, who gazed back with some astonishment. The girl certainly had beautiful irises, a dark purplish blue, almost the colour of wild violets. And the expression in them. Catching her off guard like this it seemed as if, for a moment, Chapuys could read her.

She would make a wonderful mistress. Watch your future, Concubine. Retribution approaches.

And he chuckled silently before he saw something else which left him more astonished. The King, who had been concentrating on his other guests until that moment, suddenly exchanged a glance with Jane, the meaning of which left the Spaniard in no doubt.

'Well, well, well,' thought Chapuys, 'so she has not held him off after all.'

Chapuys' spirits lowered a little as he remembered how Henry's earlier indiscretions had been discarded and only the frigid Concubine had actually achieved marriage. Would Mistress Seymour end on the dung heap with all the others?

Trusting his fine judgement above all else, Chapuys leant forward. 'Your Grace,' he said smoothly, 'I do hope that tonight we are going to be treated to one of your own compositions, and hopefully sung by yourself. I cannot remember when last I heard one of your love songs.'

Henry smiled graciously. 'Of course, my dear Ambassador. Will you make a personal choice, or will you leave that to me?'

Chapuys waved an airy hand, leaning back in his seat. 'To you, of course, Your Grace. Sing whatever song enhances your mood.'

He would have staked his future that lovers and lasses and all that takes place in the springtime would have been the theme, and Chapuys was perfectly right. With his blue eyes soft with emotion, Henry – accompanying himself on the lute – sang of wooing and winning and love that lasted forever.

To watch Jane was an education in itself. She reacted to every word, at one moment shy, at another tremulous, at yet another bright with recent memories. Chapuys narrowed his eyes. I think that this one has Henry Tudor exactly where she wants him, he thought. But does she know it? That is the important question.

He decided there and then to try and give her some cryptic message during the course of the evening's festivities. And the opportunity came as the assembled company made their way to dance and Jane, just for a moment, stood beside him.

'Madam,' said Chapuys, raising her hand to his lips, 'I cannot remember when I last saw His Grace in such good humour. You are to be congratulated.'

The girl shot him a glance in which the Ambassador was convinced he saw fear. 'What do you mean, Sir?'

'Why, nothing untoward,' he answered easily. 'It is just that your friendship with the King is regarded by many as a Godsend.'

Jane seemed relieved. 'I thank you, Sir.'

'And, of course, it is obvious to me that you have great influence on His Grace.'

She looked thoroughly startled. 'Then if that is so, let God be thanked.'

Chapuys stood silently a moment, wondering what it was that was troubling her and how he could possibly set her mind at rest, but before he could say anything further Sir Nicholas Carew came up and bowed to them both.

'Ambassador Chapuys, Mistress Seymour, what pleasurable company we keep.'

'Indeed, Sir Nicholas, indeed. I relish the rest of my stay at Windsor.'

Carew smiled. 'You are joining the hunting party, Excellency?'

'Yes, Sir Nicholas. I look forward immensely to the sport.'

The clever Spanish face was expressionless and the unusual blue eyes innocently bland.

'I'm quite sure you do!' said Carew grinning, and gave the Ambassador another small, almost imperceptible bow. 'And now, if I may, I wonder if you would forgive me while I have a private word with Mistress Seymour.'

Both men were rather surprised by what happened next. Jane, her plain face transformed by a look of grim determination, said over-loudly, 'I'm afraid I cannot speak with you tonight, Sir Nicholas. I have a headache and am about to ask His Grace's permission to retire,' and with that turned on her heel and left the two of them staring after her.

Chapuys raised his brows. 'A formidable little creature, that one.'

Carew nodded slowly. 'I'm beginning to think so, Excellency. I only hope she does nothing foolish.'

Chapuys' expression became even blanker, if that were possible. 'Who knows, Sir Nicholas, who knows? That is something one can never be sure of with women.'

The move to London was complete. Edward's personal retinue – excluding of course his children who were at Wolff Hall in the charge of Dame Margery – had finally unpacked all their goods and chattels and settled into truly magnificent apartments within the Palace of Whitehall, with talk of grander yet awaiting them at Greenwich and Hampton Court. Even Anne, now fairly certain that she was expecting another child and consequently contributing very little to the effort of shifting homes, was content, and that evening allowed an intimate family supper to take place with both her personal servants and Cloverella in attendance. All was harmonious as they kept candles to the minimum and allowed the fire's soft light to sooth away the weary day.

'I really think,' she said with a sigh, 'that I shall enjoy London again. Why, what sport we had all those years ago.'

'Not so long,' answered Edward gently, watching the firelight echoed in his wife's autumnal hair which, this night, she wore loose about her shoulders in preparation for retiring.

'It seems an age,' she answered, sighing once more.

'Are you not happy with your lot, my dear?'

'Of course I am,' Anne smiled up at him and stretched out her hand. 'It is just that I wish I had my youth back.'

'You are not yet thirty,' said Edward briskly. 'It is I who am getting old.'

It was the pointless kind of discussion in which families engage when they are all weary and can think of nothing else to say and it was left to Cloverella to stand up, bob a small curtsey to her cousins and say, 'Anne, Edward, with your permission I would like to retire. I'm afraid that my eyes are growing heavy.'

Anne's servant, Agnes, also rose and begged to take her leave and so the Seymours were left alone, Cloverella gladly going to the small room, within the main apartments, which had been allotted to her as her bedroom.

Whitehall Palace had once been York Place, a mansion house owned by Cardinal Wolsey, but when the disgraced churchman had hurriedly left London, Henry had given the property to Anne Boleyn and extensive alterations and enlargements had subsequently been carried out, so that now the massive building and its lands extended over some twenty-three acres. Many of the courtiers' lodgings were situated round the various courtyards with which the Palace was amply supplied, and it was over one of these that Cloverella's bedroom window looked. Now she stood peering through the leaded glass, down into the winter darkness, wondering what turn of events would beset the Seymours next.

It was a brilliant night, the moon full and frosty, throwing a vivid beam of light everywhere, so that only the corners in deepest shadow remained unilluminated. It was from one of these that the watching girl saw a man step out, before making his way across the quadrangle, heading for a massively studded door that led to the grandiose apartments of the Duke of Norfolk. As the moonshine fell full on him, Cloverella saw a broad nose and alert face, full of interesting quirks and hollows, all set beneath a tangled mass of black curling hair. The eyes, shadowed by his dark curving brows, were hidden from her but suddenly, just as he drew in direct line with where she stood and observed, the man stopped and glanced up, as if he knew that somebody unseen was watching him. Cloverella drew back but not before she saw the brilliance of the gaze that swept over the silvered stone. Hardly daring to breath she watched the man stare round, unsure that he was indeed alone, before he went to the door and gave it a gentle rap. She heard murmured voices.

'Zachary, is that you?'

'Yes, Lord Duke my Father.'

The door opened and the man went inside, and though she strained her ears, further conversation was lost to her. Cloverella left the window and drew the curtain, undressing rapidly and jumping into bed in a state of joyous excitement. So she had actually seen the great Dr Zachary, the man who, like herself, was half Romany, and whose knowledge of the stars was greater than that of anyone living, or so it was said.

She closed her eyes but could not sleep, instead wondering how Jane – who disappointingly had not been there to meet them – was faring on the hunting trip. Then, as her mind began to concentrate hard on her cousin, a certain conviction came to Cloverella, a conviction that could not but make her smile naughtily as she finally drifted off into unconsciousness.

'But it is only natural to love like this,' murmured Henry in the darkness as Jane, quivering with a mixture of dread and desire, felt yet again the glorious sensation of his hardness pounding within her.

An hour after the castle had finally grown quiet, he had come down the secret staircase, waking her up and putting round her neck a jewelled locket, hidden in which was a miniature portrait of himself. And she, despite all her fear and resolution, had let him into her bed and kissed him until they had made love.

Even in the act, Jane knew that she would regret everything at some later stage, knew that she was putting her whole future in jeopardy. Yet, she could not stop herself.

Had I been born to a lower station, she thought, I might well have walked the streets.

So what hope for one whose uncontrollable passion for the King was leading her into deep and frightening waters?'

'But Sir,' she whispered fearfully, 'do you not think the less of me for this?'

His answer was not reassuring. 'You are one of the best lovers I have ever had, Jane'

'But . . .'

'No buts, sweetheart. Just let us enjoy each other while we can.'

The words hung in the air, frightening Jane witless, until Henry pulled her close to him, so that she could think of nothing else and further conversation turned to the pleasures of love and she did not dwell at all upon the future.

In the silent castle one candle, at least, was still lit. At a small table beside his bed, Edward Chapuys the faithful correspondent, was writing to his royal master.

'March 6, 1536,' he began. 'I can report that the King's amours with the young lady, of which I have already informed you, are proceeding well and that her brother will shortly be arriving at Court; this appointment, I believe, made to please her. It would seem that the Concubine's days are numbered and that in some way she will be brought down.' Chapuys paused, not wanting to say yet whether Henry was Jane's lover, not wanting to say anything that was not strictly true. Nonetheless, the Ambassador could not resist a final touch. 'Though the young lady is, as I have reported, of no great beauty it would seem that this is no deterrent to His Grace, who I feel certain would be glad to serve her in every way.'

With this *double entendre* Chapuys was finally satisfied. Let the Emperor work it out for himself. After all, it would only be a matter of days before the Ambassador wrote again to give him the latest instalment.

With a small cynical smile upon his face, Chapuys blew out his candle and contentedly fell asleep.

115

# Chapter Nine

THE HUNTING PARTY WAS OVER and the various partici-
pants had gone their diverse ways; Chapuys to his official
London residence; Sir Nicholas Carew to his home seven miles
downriver from the capital, where family business called for his
attention; Jane and Henry, journeying separately, to the Palace of
Whitehall, at which place she was caught up in a somewhat
emotional family reunion. For though she kissed her sister-in-law
sedately enough, and did the same to her brother, taking great care
to avoid looking him directly in the eyes, Jane flew into Cloverella's
arms in a positive flurry, and when they finally stopped hugging
one another it could be seen that the older girl wept. After this,
however, formal behaviour became enforced as Edward was, yet
again, summoned to the Privy Chamber by the Marquis of Exeter
to be schooled in the most particular duties and standards of
behaviour required by gentlemen who had been so fortunate as to
be elevated to the chosen few who served His Grace in private.

Thus left alone, Anne Seymour spent the entire day on her toilette
in preparation for making her curtsey to the King that evening and,
having dispensed with Cloverella's services, the two younger
women were left to explore the Palace, Jane acting as guide to her
wide-eyed cousin.

'And was it exciting?' asked Cloverella, 'to hunt the beasts in
Windsor Forest? Or did Herne the Hunter come for you and throw
you over his saddle.'

Jane smiled thinly. 'You have been listening to too many fairy
stories, Cloverella. Herne the Hunter is a creature of legend.'

'How do you know?' came the immediate reply.

'Because I do. He doesn't exist.'

'In a minute you will say the same of Merlin.'

Jane smiled, enchanted all over again with her tiny cousin who

116

stood her ground like a defiant doll when it came to matters of the unseen.

'I could never say that of Merlin. Nobody could who comes from Wiltshire.'

'I am glad to hear it,' answered Cloverella, adding firmly, 'and I hope the ways of Court will never make you forget your heritage.'

'Never, I promise.'

The March day had brought sunshine, bathing the earth with an intensity of light in which bulbs and buds seemed almost to grow visibly as its warmth engulfed them. The sky was the fine pale blue of early spring, filled with jolly, puff-cheeked clouds sailing nonchalantly across the heavens like coracles on a fresh tidal river. Everywhere, England was a pattern of varying shades of green and brown, like a higgledy patchwork, with occasional splashes of yellow from burgeoning fields and blobs of white where sheep, late to bear their lambs, grazed fatly.

The smell of earth and water and fleece was everywhere, as exciting in its way as a musky Arabian scent, while from the trees came great bursts of song as nests were built and feathered. It was no small wonder that those who walked beneath felt a fever, a wonderful sense of renewal, as the earth with an immense sigh of awakening, came back most pleasurably to life.

The two girls, walking together, both more than aware of the excited mood of nature, had by afternoon traversed almost the entire length of the enormous palace, passing by the great courtyard and the cockpit, then down the side of the bowling alley and through the yard behind the kitchens, skirting the edges of the small tennis court where Sir Francis Weston, supposedly the most handsome man in England, was thrashing another young courtier who poured sweat despite the fact that there was still an edge of chill in the air.

'They are friends of the Queen,' whispered Jane, and Cloverella stared.

Having left the players still lithely running, the cousins went through the ornate Cockpit Gate and at last found themselves in the Great Privy Garden, still being worked on by the master gardener and his men who had laid it out most formally, with neatly shaped beds divided into diamonds and squares, all surrounding central beds, perfectly rounded. In the middle of all dominated a fountain brought from Italy, consisting of a central pillar patterned with a twisting stone rope, down which were suspended four gushing dolphins, spewing forth sparkling water into a pretty bowl which bounced it out again, broadcasting droplets for some distance into the air.

Cloverella looked on in frank amazement at it all as the two passed through the perfect rows of flowerbeds to reach the comparative wildness of the orchard which lay to the south of the Privy Gallery. At this time of year the trees were tightly budded but soon the place would be a mass of heady-scented blossom and zooming bees, and shade would be sought on the stone benches, scattered as if at random, but in actuality placed strategically so that beautiful blossom-filled avenues could be glimpsed from all directions. Some of the seats, however, were more discreetly positioned so that lovers might take advantage of the leafy arbours and hide themselves, and it was to one of these that Cloverella now firmly made her way and sat down.

Her look was very direct as she said, 'Jane, you are transformed. Love has turned you into a rare beauty.'

Jane shot her a startled stare before she dropped her gaze to her lap. 'How am I changed?'

'You no longer believe you are plain and that in itself has made you beautiful. By loving you, a man has proved you are desirable. And not just any man, but the most important in the land.'

Jane said nothing, only her lips trembling slightly.

'But it frightens you that you have given yourself to him completely,' Cloverella went on without pausing, fixing her lilac eyes firmly on her cousin.

Still Jane made no answer but the trembling had now spread from her mouth to her entire frame and she pressed the back of one of her hands to the thin line which until a few minutes ago had been a smile.

'Please,' said Cloverella earnestly, 'tell me why you are so unhappy.'

'If I do,' answered Jane in a tortured whisper, 'do you swear upon your life that you will never tell the secret?'

'Seven for a secret never to be told.' Cloverella saw again the milk and pitch of the magpies as they swirled about her head. 'I'll never tell it,' she said. 'I swear upon Dame Margery's life and upon your own, as well as mine.'

'It is him; the King. I allowed him into my bed. All the time while

118

we were at Windsor. Oh God, God's blood. It is the very thing that they all warned me about . . .'

'They?'

'Edward and Nicholas Carew. They said if I gave into him without marriage he would see me as a hackney, like Mary Carey or Madge Shelton or Bessie Blount or any of those hideous creatures. Oh Cloverella, Cloverella, what shall I do?'

She flung herself, all pink nose and ashen face, into Cloverella's lap where she sobbed without control.

'Hold him off until he is promised to you,' said her cousin into the tumult.

A watery eye turned in her direction. 'What did you say?'

'Now that he has tasted you, hold him at arm's length until he has offered marriage.'

Jane straightened up. 'How vulgar you can be sometimes.'

Cloverella grinned. 'Half a gypsy always a gypsy, I suppose.' Her voice changed and the little face was suddenly serious. 'Jane, he *will* be yours. I told you once before at Topenham Lodge, you will sign yourself, "Jane the Queen".'

Jane let out a gusty sigh. 'You are not alone in your belief. I have been to consult Dr Zachary.'

Cloverella's eyes glistened. 'I thought I saw him the other night making his way to the Duke of Norfolk. All dark curls and dancing brows. A right rogue of a fellow. Would that have been he?'

'Indeed it would,' said Jane, nodding. 'A pretty rascal if ever there was one. But clever, or so Edward thinks; and Zachary, too, said I would wed His Grace.'

'Then why,' asked Cloverella impatiently, 'are you making such a spectacular fuss?'

'Because of what the others say.'

'The others, pooh!' retorted Cloverella, standing up. 'What do they know about it? The King has tasted the fruit and obviously found it delicious. Now keep him dangling until he must climb to pluck the lower branches.'

Jane's eyebrows almost reached her hair. 'Cloverella, I believed you to be a maid! How do you know all these things?'

'I am a virgin still, Jane, in answer to that question. And as to the other, well, even a child listens to adults.'

'And this is how the Romanies go on?'

'Of course they do,' said Cloverella, laughing. 'Before my

grandam handed me back to Dame Margery she told me the secret way of capturing any man I choose.'

And with that she was off, skipping lightly amongst the leafless trees, her dark hair escaping from its formal headdress, and the sound of her song drifting back to where Jane Seymour stood, slightly nonplussed.

Within one of Whitehall Palace's many beautifully appointed rooms, staring momentarily out of the window with more than just a tinge of envy, a man sat behind a desk on that fine March afternoon when Cloverella and, later, Jane skipped in the orchard; a man who by his very dress and bearing could be recognised as one of the most important people in the land, and whose white broad hands, the index finger of the left bearing a blue ring large as an eye, worked constantly over the sea of papers which swarmed the desk before him, even while he looked beyond.

For him there was to be none of the joy of sunshine and fine air but instead documents to sign and learned books to consult and a day that might end some time around midnight before he could finally lock away in drawers his more secret and confidential work and make his way wearily to his house in Stepney or, if it was too late for that, his private apartments in the palace.

But then, even then, for Thomas Cromwell, principal Secretary of State to Henry VIII, who had started his career as Cardinal Wolsey's steward and climbed a ladder of people ever since, it could not be entirely guaranteed that his leisure time would pass without interruption. On many occasions he had just kicked off his shoes and changed his clothes for a loose-fitting robe, when a messenger had come to summon him urgently back to whichever palace the King's Grace was residing in at that time. And there had even been one occasion when he had been about most private business with his wife, only to hear a thundering on his bedroom door and a shouted voice telling him that the King awaited him below. Henry's eyes and his had met man-to-man as he had descended the stairs, and there had been a great deal of bluff laughter from the King in which he had been forced to join, but Thomas Cromwell in truth had resented the intrusion, while his wife had hardly spoken to him for a month following.

Yet, despite that, despite all the inconvenience which being one of the principal men in the kingdom involved, Cromwell enjoyed the sense of power; enjoyed the moment when the annointed King turned to him for advice and he, Thomas, would lean forward, his fingertips together, his eyes partially closed, and carefully weigh his reply.

When the King had decided to rid England of the Pope it had been Thomas Cromwell's visionary tactics which had brought about the final break and there could be little doubt that he, and he alone, had altered the face of kingship, bringing England's government out of medieval darkness and into the brightness of modern administration.

Smiling a little at this memory of achievement, Cromwell ceased to look out at the sunshine and bent over his work once more, his eye running over pages and pages of royal accounts, his brain sifting and sorting them, even while his ears took in all the extraneous sounds of palace life; a shout from the tennis court, a roar of laughter from the bowling alley, somebody sneezing repeatedly and heavy footsteps in the corridor. Even while adding up figures, Cromwell's agile mind took in the fact that the sound was heading straight towards his room and his left hand, the blue ring catching the light as it moved, rapidly hid some confidential papers beneath a book.

The footsteps stopped outside the room. 'Come in,' called Cromwell, but the door was already being flung open without ceremony and the Secretary, raising his head to shout his annoyance, saw that the King himself stood there, straddling the entrance like a colossus, looking in some way that Cromwell could not possibly have defined, both more arrogant and overtly masculine than usual.

'Your Grace,' said Thomas, jumping up and bowing silently, refusing to mutter pleasantries when the King was in such an obviously distraught mood.

'I've come to a decision,' answered Henry without preamble and lowered himself, groaning a little, into a chair. Looking at him narrowly, Thomas observed that Henry was putting on weight and knowing that his fall in the lists in January had seriously curtailed the royal exercise, said, in all innocence, 'Did you have good hunting at Windsor, Your Grace?'

The answer was something of a surprise. 'I expect you know that already, you dog.' And a blue eye winked.

Cromwell stared at his sovereign blankly, wondering what that remark could possibly mean. Then daylight dawned. The Seymour girl had been at Windsor too and no doubt had leapt into bed with him, as easy-virtued as most of the sluts at Court.

'Well, that will be the end of her,' thought Thomas. 'Henry never bothers about women who give in too easily.'

With this in the back of his mind, the King's next remark rocked Cromwell to the soles of his feet. 'Mr Secretary, I want a divorce from the Queen. I told you in January that I was almost certain she had used witchcraft to ensnare me. Now I am positive of it. I want an annulment.'

Cromwell sat down heavily, putting his fingertips together. 'Your Grace, I . . .'

Henry's expression hardened. 'I will not take no for an answer, Thomas.'

The lawyer in Cromwell rose to defend himself. 'Your Grace, it is not going to be easy. I do not believe that the charge of witchcraft will be taken seriously and to claim that your second marriage was as illegal as your first will hardly appear valid. At the time your marriage to the Queen was regarded as perfectly legal.'

'Then find another way,' said the King harshly.

Cromwell sat in silence, his narrow brown eyes reflective. 'I take it that Your Grace would wish to marry again, should your present marriage be annulled, for the sake of the succession.'

'Yes. And don't beat about the bush. With your vast network of spies I expect you know everything about my relations with Mistress Seymour.'

Cromwell smiled knowingly and nodded his head, making a mental note to speak at once to his principal informer at Windsor Castle.

The King leant forward, lowering his voice to conspirator's level. 'She is remarkable, Mr Secretary, in *every* way.' To his alarm, Cromwell saw the man-to-man look reappearing in the small glinting eye opposite his and attempted to adopt a similar twinkle. 'I want to marry her, Tom. Though you moot that abroad at this stage on pain of death.'

Cromwell nodded briskly, everything now being abundantly clear to him. 'Your Grace, give me a few weeks, eight at the most.'

'No sooner?'

'No, Your Grace,' he answered firmly. 'The reason for ending your marriage to the Queen must be seen in the eyes of the whole world as valid. There must be no shadow of doubt, even in the minds of your adversaries, that you had no choice but to put her to one side. I cannot find such a case in a matter of days.'

Henry stood up. 'Well said, Mr Secretary, well said,' he answered gruffly. 'You lawyers know best, as always. But free me of that evil woman, Thomas, I beg you. I was blinded and seduced but now at last my vision is clear and I know I must marry sweet Jane.'

Hmm, thought Cromwell with asperity, but aloud said, 'I will do everything in my power to bring about such a splendid outcome, Your Grace.'

'Make sure you do,' answered Henry with that edge in his voice which always made Cromwell shiver. 'Make sure you do.'

And with that he stumped from the room leaving the principal Secretary to wrestle with a problem to which, at that particular moment, there seemed absolutely no solution whatsoever.

It was evening, that eventful March day finally drawing to a close, and Chapuys, as often present at Court as he could manage in these highly charged times, thought to himself that all the chief players in the drama were present. For on one side of the table – the King for once dining in his Hall with as many courtiers as could attend him – sat the Queen, sallow and shrunken, with eyes that burned with hatred and pain, flanked by her brother Rochford and all her intimate set of friends. While opposite them, like an opposing army drawn up for battle, was the Seymour contingent, gawdy with triumph; even the shy daughter of the house tonight wearing a tantalising smile which reminded the Ambassador of that of Anne Boleyn in the distant days.

Adopting the blank expression which always meant he was thinking furiously, Chapuys studied Jane Seymour. To him she seemed suddenly assured, full of new confidence.

Like someone with a plan, thought Chapuys.

Phrases from the letter he would write to the Emperor when he returned home that night, began to drift through his head. 'The King has put into his chamber the young lady's brother, to the intense rage of the Concubine.'

He glanced at Anne Boleyn now, the loathing he felt for her concealed by his empty face.

How true, he thought, the adage that pride comes before a fall.

123

You were the proudest in the kingdom and look at you now. God's justice is at work.

Mentally, Chapuys crossed himself before turning his attention elsewhere. But all present, and some a great deal less observant than the Ambassador, sensed the atmosphere in the Hall, alive with unspoken threats and curses and on a knife's edge, most felt, of actual violence. So in a way it was no surprise when the Queen rose, even in the middle of a love song, passionately sung by the King's favourite musician, James Hill. As etiquette demanded, everyone else stood too and watched, almost in a frozen manner, as Anne slowly made her way down the length of the table until she came to stand beside Jane Seymour.

Chapuys noticed in a half amused, half shocked way, that a delicate girl with dark hair and eyes the colour of flowers, made a tiny movement towards Jane, almost as if to protect her. While James Hill, though aware of the frisson, continued to sing on gamely as Anne raised her voice to a shout. 'Well, Mistress Seymour, what is this pretty bauble you have about your neck? Will you not show it to me?'

And a thin hand shot out and grabbed the diamond encrusted locket that nestled intriguingly between Mistress Seymour's round and beautiful breasts. Jane started back as if she had been slapped and momentarily the Queen hesitated. Then she leant forward and tugged the locket sharply, so sharply that the clasp loosened and it flew from Jane's neck, the chain wrapping round Anne's hand like a whip and causing one of her fingers to bleed. There was total silence except for poor James Hill who gallantly continued to sing, though not a soul listened. Into the hush came a click as Anne found the catch on the side of the locket and opened it.

'So,' she said in a terrible hiss that was far more frightening than a scream, 'the King's paramour wears his likeness round her neck. I pray to God it chokes her.'

And with that she flung the locket down the length of the table in the direction of Henry, the blood from her damaged finger spilling ominously on to the whiteness of the cloth. There was an intake of breath like a collective sigh as the King, the only person still remaining seated, rose in his chair. Chapuys, watching, thought the man would never stop uncoiling for suddenly he seemed doubled in size, both in height and girth. In fact he loomed so hugely that all around him were dwarfed, cowering almost. The Ambassador who had known the King for some considerable years felt a moment's fear.

Henry's eyes became menacing slits, searching the table's length for Nan Saville and finding her.

'Lady Berkeley,' he said in a commendably even tone, despite his furious glare, 'The Queen's hand is bleeding. I pray you take Her Grace to her own apartments and send for Dr Butts.' Then without looking at Anne again, Henry turned to James Hill, who had finally given up in despair, 'Sing your last air once more lad,' he called, then sat down and calmly continued to eat.

Again, everyone drew breath as the Queen burst into hysterical weeping, burying her head in Lady Berkeley's shoulder.

'You should be ashamed,' Nan hissed at Jane. 'Look what you have done, you heartless creature.'

'I have done nothing,' answered Jane spiritedly, 'that has not already been performed by others long since.'

And she glowered at Anne's retreating back as Nan led her away. With a general thumping of chairs the assembled company sat down again, though it was noticeable that George Rochford, the Queen's brother, and her various sprinkling of friends looked on the point of going, had not courtesy decreed otherwise.

'Dancing,' shouted Henry jovially, 'let us dance away our sorrows. But first I must return something to its rightful owner.'

And with that he stretched his massive arm along the table and rescued the locket from where it lay beside an enamelled bowl. Then, suddenly, as nimble as if he had been in his youth, Henry rose lithely to his feet and almost skipped to where Jane sat, still pale from her recent encounter.

'Wilt thou dance, Mistress?' he asked playfully, and thereby set the pattern for the rest of that disastrous evening.

Jane stood up, smiling bravely, and dropped a pretty curtsey. 'Gladly, Sir,' she answered and was rewarded with a grateful smile.

Chapuys, watching all, concluded that Henry was more shaken by the Queen's outburst than he was prepared for anyone to know. And the proof lay in the slight trembling of the King's fingers as he defiantly and publicly refastened the locket around Jane's neck.

'So . . .,' said a voice at the Ambassador's elbow and turning he realised that Cromwell had come silently to sit beside him.

'Mr Secretary,' Chapuys bowed his head.

'I would speak with you, Excellency,' Cromwell answered, 'but not here, in fact not even in this Palace. Would it trouble your Excellency too greatly to dine with me in my house in Stepney tomorrow?'

Chapuys bowed again. 'I should be delighted, Mr Secretary. I take it' – His pleasant voice, considerably accented, dwelt over the next few words with relish – 'that the matter is of some urgency?'

'Indeed, it is, Excellency,' answered Cromwell, and raised a thin dark brow. 'Indeed it is.'

The dancing went on into the early hours of the following day; Henry in a kind of frenzy, enjoining all the assembled company to be on their feet, making merry, though gradually the older courtiers, one by one, begged permission to retire, leaving only the youthful to applaud the flagging musicians and beg for more.

The Queen's brother and his associates had all left, with the exception of the beautiful Francis Weston who seemed quite happy to dance the night away. But Anne Seymour, claiming fatigue, requested leave to go to her chamber, at which Cloverella, who was feeling the strain of her first week at Court, also made her excuses and slipped out of the overheated room, sharp with the smell of sweating bodies, and made her way with Anne to the quiet of the Seymour apartments.

Yet, having helped her cousin undress, after preparing a soothing lotion for Anne's forehead, Cloverella found that she was too full of nervous energy to sleep and decided that only a walk in the open air would restore her calm. So, now knowing her way round the palace, she crept down the stairs and crossing the great courtyard, hurried past the kitchen to the small walled garden beyond.

It was a bitter night, though clear and fine, every star in the universe shining against a backdrop of curving ebony. Already there was a sprinkling of sugary frost and Cloverella trod carefully as, tiring of the walled garden's confines, she made her way towards the Thames.

The river air was full of sounds, the rushings of creatures and the splashing leaps of fish imposed upon the muted noise of revelry, still audible. Cloverella bent her head back to see the heavens and in that move saw that another stood on the landing stage, having just moored a small boat at the Duke of Norfolk's steps. Dr Zachary had come to Whitehall Palace and was alone with her in the moonshine.

126

Acting almost on compulsion, Cloverella stepped directly into his path so that as he turned towards the palace he must see her. 'Greetings, Master,' she said in the Romany tongue and made a reverence.

He jumped with fright, quite unaware that he was not alone. 'Who goes there?' he answered in the same parlance.

'A friend,' she replied, 'one who seeks the truth.'

'A friend indeed,' he said, advancing, 'who speaks the language of my mother.'

'Aye, and of my father too,' answered Cloverella and curtsied again as he stood before her.

They surveyed one another frankly yet with caution, like two animals of the same breed, come nose to nose.

'Who are you?' asked Zachary, still addressing her in the language of their forebears.

'Elizabeth Wentworth, cousin to Jane Seymour, come to court with Edward.'

Zachary nodded, the amber eyes taking in every detail of her appearance. 'They call you something else though.'

'Cloverella. That is my Romany name.'

'I am Zachary, kin to the Duke of Norfolk.'

Cloverella smiled. 'I wished once on Merlin's Mound that I would one day know much of the law of the universe. Maybe, through meeting you, that wish might yet be granted.' She put her hand on his arm impetuously. 'Take me as your pupil.'

'I have no time,' he said sadly. 'My life is already filled with all I must do, often to the detriment of my family.'

The great eyes swept his face. 'I did not know you were married.'

'Aye, long since. Have you never felt the need to combat the forces of the unseen with a little normality?'

'Not yet,' answered Cloverella seriously. 'I am not far enough advanced to have such needs.'

He touched her hand which still lay gently on his arm, aware of her disappointment.

'I will compromise. Whenever I have some hours free I will send you word and then you must come to me at Greenwich. In that way I know I can bring you safely to the world of magic, for there is great power about you already.'

Gravely, Cloverella said, 'Thank you, Master,' and kissed his hand.

Zachary was struck to the heart, full of sudden emotion that he, still young, should be addressed thus.

'God keep you safe,' he answered and went to go on towards the palace, then turned back. 'Give me your blessing,' he said.

'I bless you with all my power.'

'Thank you,' he said, his face very serious. 'Then I shall leave you until we meet again.'

'Until we meet again,' answered Cloverella and watched his retreating figure as it disappeared into the darkness.

# Chapter Ten

THE OBVIOUS WAY OF making the journey between the King's two waterside palaces of Whitehall and Greenwich was by river and normally Nicholas Carew would have enjoyed nothing more than sitting back in the late March sunshine, listening to the rhythmic sound of oars, and watching the evergreen banks of pastoral land slide gently past his delighted eyes. But today, for an uneasy reason that was based on what his Scots grandmother would have termed a beggar's hunch, Carew decided that speed was more important than pleasure and led his horse on to the ferry beneath Whitehall's landing stage and went across to Lambeth, not far from Thomas Cromwell's home. Here he made haste, cutting across country through the wild open lands to Deptford, then on past one or two pretty hamlets until finally, built where the Thames looped into a vast U, the turrets and towers of Greenwich Palace became visible in the distance.

Carew halted for the first time, allowing himself a few minutes in which to take some ale at a tumbledown inn, and wondering what it was about the contents of his saddlebag, to be delivered by him personally into the hands of Jane Seymour, that was giving such cause for concern. He reviewed recent events, knowing that the clue to his unease lay there.

That Henry would remove Jane Seymour from the Queen's company after the incident of the locket had been obvious, and it had not been many days before the Court had departed for Greenwich, leaving Anne Boleyn alone at Whitehall. Then, matters of some urgency had recalled the King to London, his favourite left behind with her brother to while away her time.

But this morning, Sir Nicholas, who as Master of the Horse had followed his sovereign to Whitehall some days later, had been summoned to the Privy Chamber where Henry, looking decidedly ill-tempered – or so Carew had thought – had shooed his gentlemen out so that he and Nicholas could be alone.

'How is Jane?' the King had asked abruptly and Carew, with a sinking heart, had thought he detected an edge in his voice.

'Well, Your Grace. In fine spirits. Though I am sure,' he had added hastily, 'that she misses your presence, Sire.'

'Hmm,' Henry had answered and Nicholas's panic had mounted. 'Well, I have a letter and a gift for her. Would you be so good as to take them, Nick, and be sure that they are put directly into her hand and given to no other.'

Mightily relieved, Carew had bowed. 'Your errand shall be done, Your Grace.'

'You can leave at once if you wish,' Henry had added, far too casually. 'There is no need for you to stay at Whitehall, as I shall be going to Greenwich just as soon as affairs permit. You can wait for me there.'

Nicholas had smiled. 'As you wish, Your Grace. Now if I may have the package.'

Henry had unlocked a drawer in his desk and withdrawn a sealed letter and a small leather bag, pulled shut by the strings at its neck. Even as he took it from the King and weighed it in his hand, Nicholas knew that it contained money and his heart had plummeted once more. Money was given to a discarded mistress for her paying off, a trollop's wage, a harlot's hiring fee.

Oh, God's Holy Blood, he thought, has the silly wench lain with him, after all I said?

And he must have sighed aloud for the King had asked, 'Is anything wrong?' and Nicholas had been forced to collect himself and grin cheerfully, despite the fact that he was seething with doubt.

Now, sitting briefly within the smoky alehouse, he recalled Jane's odd behaviour at Windsor, her constant refusal to be alone with him, as if she had something on her conscience. Nicholas plunged his head into his hands, utterly sure that he was right, torn between a mixture of anger cold as steel and hell-hot despair. As a secret supporter of Princess Mary, born of his old alliance to Katharine of Aragon, Nicholas Carew knew perfectly well that only by the disposal of Anne Boleyn, who hated Henry's elder daughter to the point of obsession, could the wretched princess ever have any hope of being reinstated in her father's affection. And it seemed to him that only through Jane Seymour, who also bore love and loyalty to the dead Queen and would certainly help her living daughter, could this ever come about.

'What a crazy thing it is,' he mused wretchedly, 'that the human race will sacrifice everything that is of true importance and merit to that irresistible urge which consistently rises between their loins.'

And in a mood of black despair he ordered more ale and arrived at the Palace far later than he intended.

Jane received him with a great show of decorum, insisting that both Edward and Anne Seymour were present to entertain him, until Nicholas was finally forced to put on a charming smile, shrug his shoulders apologetically, and say, 'My dear friends, I am sorry but what I have to say is for Jane's ears alone.'

The beautiful Anne Seymour, grown haughty since her return to Court, raised her languid brows, but Edward, now with a beard, darkly interesting against his serious face, said 'Instructions from His Grace, Nick?' and gave the merest suggestion of a wink.

Nicholas inclined his short-cropped head which he felt had acquired more grizzled hairs than ever on this particular journey.

'Indeed.'

'Then we must obey. Come Anne.'

So, they were left alone: two people who now had rather come to regard each other as something of an enemy. For a moment there was silence and then Jane opened play with, 'You left His Grace in good health, Sir Nicholas?'

'Aye, Madam,' came the terse reply, 'though somewhat short on temper.'

'And why is that?'

'Who knows? Who knows? But temper or none, he has asked me to give you these.'

And with that, Sir Nicholas delved into a pocket in his jerkin and produced the bag of money and the letter, and as good as thrust them under Jane Seymour's nose.

'A purse of sovereigns and a note,' he said unnecessarily.

He had never seen anyone lose colour so fast. A normally pale person became the colour of one who had been dead twelve hours.

'Sovereigns?' she repeated, a note of hysteria in her voice.

'Yes, Madam, sovereigns. A gift to you from the King's Grace and a note to accompany them.'

'What is in it?'

'I have not read it, Madam,' Nicholas replied between gritted teeth.

Instead of answering, Jane cried, 'Oh help me!' and, sitting down on a nearby chair, covered her eyes with her hands.

Nicholas advanced on her mercilessly. 'You have disobeyed my every instruction, haven't you Mistress Seymour? You have given yourself to the King and now you are reaping the reward of your folly. You know as well as I do that he is paying you off!'

'But I thought he loved me,' she moaned.

Carew's fury reached boiling point and exploded. 'Love! Love! You know as well as I do that His Grace's feelings can change like the wind. Look at all his discarded women! Even an idiot would not join their number if she had the choice. But you, Mistress, have destroyed everything in one swoop. I despair for your future.'

Jane rallied slightly. 'You are jumping to conclusions, Sir Nicholas. Surely there is some honourable way for me to retrieve the position.'

He did not answer, standing with his back to her and staring out of the window, his small powerful body quivering with rage. After a few moments of indecision, Jane went to him and gently tugged his sleeve.

'Please, Sir Nicholas, forgive a foolish girl who gave too much too quickly. Have you never led such a dance as I have yourself? Can you not pity what must be a common fault?'

He calmed down; loyal creature that he was, he forced himself to smile at her, though he could have wept at the entire situation.

'I daresay I have in the past.'

'Then advise me, Sir, and this time I will heed every word you say. I swear it upon my oath.'

'I think, perhaps, if you do exactly what I tell you, there might yet be a faint chance.'

'I will do anything. Just tell me.'

'Then return the money and the letter unopened and I will inform His Grace that you thanked him but said you were a gentlewoman of honourable family with no greater prize than your virtue. And that you could only accept money when you had made a match.'

'But he knows my virtue is gone.'

'Ah, but he may well read into such a message that he can have you no more until he marries you. And unless he is totally bored the whole idea might yet intrigue him.'

Jane's eyes brightened. 'But that was what I planned to do anyway. Withhold myself from now on. Here, give me the letter.'

She pulled it from Carew's grasp and rather dramatically sunk to her knees, 'Tell His Grace that I can accept nothing from him. I am a woman of high virtue and can receive no present of money until God enables me to make an honourable match.'

Carew clapped his hands silently. 'Excellent. I'll take a change of horse and return within the hour to Whitehall.'

Jane stood up, then kissed the letter before handing it back. 'I pray God this tactic will work, Sir Nicholas.'

'Unless he has truly tired of you and is turning his attention back to the Queen . . .'

'May that day never come!'

'Amen . . . he cannot help but be intrigued by such a show. But Jane' – Sir Nicholas's face took on almost a cruel look – 'if you go back on your word and consort with His Grace once more, then look for no help from anyone, for I swear by God that even your own family will turn against you.'

'I give you my word I will not do so.' Jane suddenly looked frantic. 'You are not going to tell Edward, are you Sir Nicholas?'

'On this occasion, no. But if you dare . . .'

'I swear, I swear,' she answered hastily. 'You have my oath.'

'Then I'll make haste. I shall send a servant back to you this very night with an account of what transpires.'

'Then God speed you, Sir, for I shall be in an agony until I know.'

And so you should, thought Carew bitterly, so you should, who has brought all our plans to the brink of ruin.

Jane was never able to tell when she looked back on that extraordinary time in her life which emotion had been more intense; relief at the fact that Henry had no intention of disposing of her, or joy that the King had been truly in love with her all along. At the time the two things had fused into one enormous sense of respite from danger, of an unspoken threat hanging over her meek fair head, and she had fallen on to her bed and wept and laughed until she finally fell asleep from utter exhaustion.

Nicholas Carew had had his revenge, of course. He had not sent a messenger to Greenwich that night or even the next day, but two days later had appeared himself and been shown, unsmiling, into Jane's apartments.

'Well?' She had stared at him white-faced.

Carew had shaken his head slowly. 'His Grace was most astonished that you saw fit to return his gift. He simply could not understand your attitude.'

'Did you give him the message exactly as we planned?'

'Yes.'

'And what did he say?'

'He sighed and remarked that the world had come to a pretty pass when a lover could not send his lady money to buy pretties for her wardrobe without high-flown talk of virtue and marriage.

Jane had sat down weakly. 'So it was foolish to return it. I might have known. But Sir Nicholas, have you not the feeling that whatever decision we had reached would have been the wrong one?'

'On the contrary,' he had answered, his brilliant smile like sunshine after a downpour. 'His Grace was so mortified that you could even consider his gift in such a light that he has forthwith decided to mend his ways. He has already seen Master Cromwell, who is to vacate his apartments in Whitehall at once, allowing your brother and his entourage to move in. You, Jane, are to keep your own rooms but are to be taken to Edward whenever His Grace wishes to call on you. In this way you will be constantly chaperoned.'

He did not add, 'So now you simply won't be able to fall into bed with him, you silly little wretch.'

But Jane had read his mind. 'Then I am safe; safe from myself too.'

'Yes.'

'And all because he wanted to buy me clothes.'

'Keep your head, young lady, and the King will be giving you a great deal more than paltry gowns. Now there is only one thing you must aim for, always remembering that the fate of an unhappy girl lies in your hands.'

Jane tilted her head back, almost as if the weight of a crown were already on it, her eyes glittering like opals and her sudden radiance almost tangible.

'Sir Nicholas, am I going to be Queen?'

'Yes, I now believe that you will, Mistress.'

'But how?'

Carew ran his hand over his grizzled head. 'I think we had better leave that to Master Cromwell, don't you?'

Jane nodded slowly. 'Yes, I suppose that he who saw off the Pope can just as easily cast aside a Queen.'

'I should imagine,' answered Nicholas carefully, 'that to do so would be even simpler.'

'April 1st, 1536' wrote Chapuys, his quill pen scratching over the parchment, 'and my most respectful greetings . . .' He hurried over the first part of the letter, anxious to get to the point which would please the Emperor more than anything his Ambassador had ever written to him before. And a few paragraphs later Chapuys arrived there, his face breaking into a smile as he put the words, '. . . he sent her a purse full of sovereigns, and with it a letter, and the young lady, after kissing the letter, returned it unopened to the messenger, and throwing herself on her knees before him, begged the said messenger that he would pray the King . . .'

He continued the tale, omitting to say that the envoy had been, in fact, Sir Nicholas Carew, arch-plotter extraordinary.

'. . . that by this the King's love and desire towards the said young lady was wonderfully increased, that he had said she had behaved most virtuously, and to show that he only loved her honourably, he did not intend henceforth to speak with her except in the presence of some of her kin; for which reason the King has caused Cromwell to remove from a chamber to which the King can go by certain galleries without being perceived, and has lodged there the eldest brother of the said lady with his wife . . .'

Chapuys stopped for a moment and allowed himself a chuckle. Somehow he did not quite believe the story that was circulating like wildfire in both Whitehall and Greenwich: that the King was so struck by Jane's virtuous behaviour that he had moved Edward and Anne Seymour into Cromwell's old apartments, that he might only meet Jane in the presence of chaperons.

More likely, thought the Ambassador, because the rooms are connected to the Privy Chamber by a secret passage and the King can come and go as he pleases.

He stroked his chin thoughtfully, convinced that there was more behind it than he was as yet aware. Yet be that as it may, it was now certain that Jane was playing for the highest stakes of all. He picked up his pen again.

'. . . that she must by no means comply with the King's wishes except by way of marriage; in which she is quite firm.'

'I'm well sure of that!' said Chapuys to himself.

Yet all this talk of virtue and honour did not quite fit the picture that had formed in the Ambassador's mind; that of a passionate little woman who had been actually caught by the Concubine in the very act of embracing the King, and who had happily accepted all his other gifts bar this one. To Chapuys, Jane Seymour's latest move, masterminded he had no doubt by Nicholas Carew, sounded more like a change of tactics.

'But then I am an old cynic,' the Ambassador said in Spanish. 'I so rarely give anyone the benefit of the doubt!'

And he smiled again, wickedly, as he once more picked up his pen.

On the night of St George's Day, the Duke of Norfolk, riding a black horse and wearing a cloak and hood that concealed his identity, made his way with only one bodyguard to a house in Stepney. At the same time, Lord Chancellor Audley, who had succeeded to his office when Sir Thomas More had been put to death, was making for the same destination, being rowed across the river by an anonymous wherryman, his own private barge still riding at its moorings; finally, the Duke of Suffolk, a hat of fur pulled well down about his features, and blowing into his beard, saying it was the coldest April he could remember, borrowed his steward's horse and rode alone through the darkness, relying only on his dagger to protect him from any footpads that might assail him on his journey to Thomas Cromwell's private residence.

The meeting of the four men began when most honest folk were taking to their beds and Norfolk, looking round the room grimly, was reminded of Zachary's description of witches' coven meetings, as the shadows distorted the features of his fellows, turning noses into hooks and eyes to burning pits of coal.

There was a sense of portent in the air, a feeling of high drama in which the opening players were already assembled, and for a moment not one of these great men dared speak, but sat, uncertainly, waiting for their cue. Finally it was Norfolk, the principal peer of the realm, who cleared his throat prior to saying, 'Mr Secretary, you have called us here in the greatest secrecy. May we be told the nature of this meeting?'

Cromwell drew breath. 'Gentlemen, we are here to discuss the future of the monarchy. It is the avowed intent of His Grace to end his marriage to the Queen.'

'We all know that,' boomed Suffolk. 'I hope to God you've not kept me from my bed just to tell me old news.'

Cromwell put his fingers together, his blue ring reflecting the firelight. Ignoring the Duke he continued, 'Tomorrow I shall present the King a document for signature. It is a patent appointing a commission to inquire into any treasonable action taken against His Grace.'

'Treason!' exclaimed Audley, 'you speak of treason, Mr Secretary. How does this affect the matter of the Queen?'

'Quite simply, my Lord. If she has taken a lover it would be an act of treason against His Grace's person.'

There was an incredible silence. Then Norfolk said down his breath, 'A lover! So that's it!'

While Audley came in with, 'God's life! Who would dare?'

'There may be more than one,' answered Cromwell smoothly, 'but so far my information brings forth at least a name.'

He was playing with them, relishing the moment of suspense, but Suffolk ruined everything by crowing, 'Smeaton, I'll warrant. I never could abide that jackanapes musician. But *she* seems to dote on him, silly puff that he is.'

Norfolk and Audley stared at one another, the logic of the thing suddenly, frighteningly, clear. Anne's over-familiarity with her special friends had often been remarked but now everything appeared in a new light; she had actually committed adultery with her lutanist, possibly with them all.

Suffolk rubbed his hands together. 'She's done for! Good for you, Tom. But *are* there others? Was she loose with the lot of 'em?'

'That will be investigated by the commission,' answered Cromwell.

'And who is to be on this panel?' asked Norfolk.

'It will be headed by you and me, Sir, and will consist of peers and judges, in the main.' He hesitated. 'I am afraid that of those peers, Wiltshire is one.'

'Oh dear,' said Audley, and there was a short silence.

The Earl of Wiltshire was not only Anne Boleyn's father but also the Duke of Norfolk's brother-in-law. Or rather *ex*-brother-in-law, as the Duke preferred to think of it, disliking all the Boleyns as he did and having disapproved heartily when his sister, Lady Elizabeth Howard, had married a nobody from Norfolk of that name. But, even though Elizabeth was now dead, there was still a blood tie with her three children and, though it stuck in Norfolk's craw to do so, he grudgingly had to admit that the youngest of them had done very well for herself to rise from nowhere to the status of Queen of England.

But how he hated her! Thomas Howard's loathing for his niece was something spoken of in hushed tones in the corridors of the Court.

'A pity about Wiltshire,' he said now. 'But he'd do anything to save his face; even condemn his own daughter if he thought it politic. The yellow-stomached dog.'

Despite the solemnity of the occasion, Audley allowed a wintery smile to cross his features, while Suffolk guffawed delightedly and slapped his thigh.

'He's all mouth and hands,' he said. 'Can't stand the fellow.'

'Nonetheless,' Cromwell put in, 'his presence on the commission is not one that I welcome.'

'I imagine,' answered the Lord Chancellor drily, 'that he will say very little when it is pointed out to him that both his daughters have the moral standards of alley cats.'

They all sniggered at that, for Mary Boleyn, who had married the wretched William Carey, had been a plaything of the King's until he had discarded her for her sister.

'And where,' Norfolk asked when calm was restored, 'does Ambassador Chapuys stand in all this?'

'The Ambassador has dined with me here,' answered Cromwell, 'and I put the entire situation to him and asked that he might assist my endeavour to have the Queen brought down. He agreed to do so, provided the Princess Mary concurred, which she did, saying that she had ceased to care whether her father had lawful heirs or not, and the Ambassador should do everything in his power to set aside the Concubine.'

'So the Princess knows what is afoot?'

'Indeed she does.'

'Then it would seem,' said Audley, 'that we have little left to discuss until the commission is formally appointed.'

'Except of course' – this from Norfolk – 'to ask you, Mr Secretary, who else you suspect?'

138

Cromwell looked thoughtful. 'It isn't easy, that. There are quite a few in her coterie and she certainly can't be sharing her favours with them all.'

'Why not?' said Suffolk but Norfolk was already drowning him with, 'Wyatt, Weston, Brereton? I wonder. Even Norris perhaps?'

'No, no,' said Audley. 'He is His Grace's Principal Gentleman. He would never betray the King's trust.'

'Don't be too sure,' answered Norfolk. 'That wretched creature could sidle her way round anyone.'

'Whatever, all will become clear within the next few days,' said Cromwell. 'My informers are well primed, there'll scarcely be a conversation that isn't noted down lest it contain something of interest.'

'I can see,' answered Norfolk, with only the merest hint of an undertone, 'that you intend your case to contain no weaknesses, Mr Secretary.'

'You are right,' Cromwell replied calmly. 'His Grace asked me to terminate his marriage and terminate it I will.'

'I feel in my bones that when the lid comes off this particular pan there will be a mighty mess of pottage within,' said Audley with a sigh.'

'So you believe that the Queen is to die for adultery?'

'Yes, and in my view it will be a fitting end,' said Suffolk. 'She climbed high and now she's fallen. Serve her right.'

And at that remark, thinking of all that lay ahead of them, Norfolk found that he did not know whether to laugh or to cry.

## Chapter Eleven

JANE HAD NEVER SEEN Savernake Forest so shrouded in mist nor realised that the undergrowth had grown so dense, curling and thorning around the trunks of trees and catching at her skirt like human fingers, as she walked past. Vapour was everywhere, sometimes in a sheer wall through which it was impossible to see, sometimes in strips which seemed to hang in the air like ribbons. Everywhere was the total and dense silence of fog, the only sound in that unnerving quiet the beating of Jane's leaping, breathless heart.

The song when she first heard it was almost expected. She had half thought she could not be the only one abroad in that magic forest in which time appeared to have stood still. It was a sexless voice which rose into the air, not singing so much as chanting some air of mystic origin.

The sound sent a thrill of fear through Jane and she began to hurry, but whether towards or away from the singer she could not be certain. As she stumbled through the trees, branches tore at her and it seemed that she traversed a carpet of thorns which pricked her feet through her shoes. And then, quite suddenly, the trees were no more and Jane found herself in a misty clearing, peering through the veil-like vapour at a figure reclining on a tree stump. She had found the singer, for the chant continued, rising and falling in unearthly cadences, both beautiful and terrifying to hear.

Jane took a step forward and at that moment the haze seemed to dissolve magically and she found herself staring straight into the face of Anne Boleyn. But it was an Anne transformed, for though she was human to the waist, from there down she had become an enormous and terrible snake whose vast, obscene coils wrapped round the glade, writhing and undulating continuously.

'No!' screamed Jane and turned to run, but a sinuous loop caught and held her fast.

'Help me,' she called frantically, her puny voice drowned by Anne's terrible song.

This time, Jane caught some of the words. 'For I am Eve and I'm the serpent, come lie with me, give me your life.'

The choking coil tightened its grip and Jane knew then that she would have been dead if the King had not appeared suddenly, rushing through the trees with his sword drawn from its scabbard. Without even looking at Jane he ran straight up to Anne and cut her head off neatly, with a single stroke. The head rolled towards Jane, then came to rest at her feet, and Anne's midnight eyes looked up at her reproachfully before one of them slowly winked.

'Christ have mercy upon me,' screamed Mistress Seymour in dark fear and woke to find that a sheet had wound itself round her and that her head was hanging uncomfortably over the side of the bed.

Jane lay where she was for a moment, trying to compose herself and taking deep, gasping breaths, then a flash of lightning lit her bedchamber, followed by a huge clap of thunder directly overhead, and she realised that while she had dreamed a storm had come up over London which was now at its full ferocity. Very slowly, Jane got up, freeing herself from the encircling sheet and rubbing the back of her neck which felt wrenched and uncomfortable. Crossing to the window she managed to release the catch and cautiously peered out.

The sky was the colour of grapes, shot with trees of fork lightning which slashed through its fabric and cut into the dark earth below. Everywhere wailed a great wind, coming in up river, bearing drops of water on its breath, while from time to time, brilliant flashes of light suddenly illuminated the palace and houses, showing them unearthly, bleached of all colour by the screeching tempest.

'God save us,' said Jane, and, shutting the window tightly, crawled back into bed, listening from the safety of her coverlet to the discords in the sky and the gale's wild, unnerving shrieks.

Eventually the rain came, torrents and gallons of it, hurtling, swelling the river to flood proportions, splintering boats and craft against their landing stages, setting some of the smaller vessels free to whirl out to sea. All the while, forks of light bombarded and thunder growled round heaven as if the Hound itself had broken free.

It was just as she was attempting to drop off to sleep again, that Jane heard a faint tapping on her door, and calling out, 'Who is it?', heard her sister-in-law's voice.

'Come in, the door's not barred,' she answered and, somewhat wearily, sat up in bed.

Anne Seymour bustled through, a loose gown over her night-clothes, and a look of importance on her face.

'Jane, Jane, you must get up and come at once. His Grace has arrived by way of the private corridor and has asked to see you. He thought you might be afraid of the storm.'

Jane yawned affectedly. 'Must I? I would far rather go to sleep.'

It was worth the small deception to see Anne's face, over which a look of unmitigated horror now spread.

'How could you say such a thing, you ungrateful wretch? I can't believe I am hearing correctly.'

Jane smiled. 'I am only teasing. I will come.'

Anne gave her a beady-eyed look. 'You are in a caustic mood, my girl. I cannot say that I care for it.'

'I'm sorry,' said Jane, getting out of bed once more and putting a covering robe over her nightdress. 'In fact I apologise. It must be the effect of the storm.'

Slightly mollified, Anne closed the door behind them and the two women made their way through a palace that had lost a night's sleep, for candles burnt everywhere and the courtier's apartments were alive with conversation.

In the sumptuous rooms which until only recently had been occupied by Secretary Cromwell, everyone was astir, servants hurrying to fetch food and wine for His Grace, despite the fact that the day was only three hours old. Jane, somewhat surprised by all the activity, followed Anne into the beautifully appointed principal chamber to discover Henry sitting in a chair, resting his chin on his fist, his face somewhat pale. Without saying a word he took Jane's hand and led her to the far corner of the room, well away from any listening ears.

This had been the pattern of their meetings since the incident of the returned money. On every occasion Anne and Edward would sit discreetly at one end, studiously averting their eyes, while Henry and Jane would speak in hushed tones at the other. It was wretched for all concerned, yet the King seemed masochistically determined to prove to the world that he was courting Mistress Seymour as a gentleman should, with both decorum and dignity, allowing no breath of scandal to besmirch either of their names.

Now, having reassured himself they were not overheard, Henry said in a whisper, 'Sweetheart, something of tremendous import has happened. Something that will change our situation, I believe.'

'What?' she asked, equally quietly.

'I cannot tell you here. All I can say is that everything is working to our advantage and I think the next few weeks may see a tremendous turn round of events.'

'But how?' she persisted.

Henry ignored the question. 'Tomorrow, darling heart, I require you to leave the Palace of Whitehall.'

'You wish me to go to Greenwich?'

'No. I want you to leave Court.'

Jane stared at him mystified. 'You are sending me back to Wolff Hall?'

'No, I don't intend that either. Sir Nicholas Carew, loyal friend to us both, has a house just seven miles from here. I have already spoken to him and all is arranged for you to go there. I do not want you about when the storm breaks.'

'I don't understand.'

'Trust me, sweetheart, and do as I say.'

'Very well,' answered Jane and gave a small curtsey.

Henry picked up a lock of her hair, turning it this way and that in the candlelight. 'Spun gold,' he said, 'straight from the gates of the sun.'

She smiled, her face, until that moment rather strained, suddenly relaxing into an impish look.

'I shall sup with you tomorrow evening,' said Henry softly, then, slightly louder, 'I must tell your brother of my plans.'

'Is he to come with me?'

'No, my dear, I cannot spare any of my Gentlemen at a time like this. Sir Nicholas and Lady Carew will have to be our guardians.'

They stood staring at one another, smiling rather foolishly, remembering all the tenderness that had passed between them in the past.

'I think,' said Henry abruptly, 'that soon we may no longer need chaperons.'

'Why is that?' asked Jane, startled.

The King laid an enormous finger across his lips. 'No more, my dove. All I ask is that you continue to love me.'

'That I will always do,' she whispered. And she really meant it, entranced with everything about him, flattered and dazzled by his attentions.

He took both her hands in his. 'One day soon . . . ,' he said, then abruptly turned away and strode to where Edward and Anne sat patiently, their backs ostentatiously averted.

'Sir Edward, Lady Seymour, tomorrow I have arranged for your dear sister to leave Court and stay indefinitely at the home of Sir Nicholas Carew.'

Anne looked frankly astonished but Edward, more than aware that the sore, which had been festering since the Queen miscarried her son was just about to erupt, nodded and bowed.

'As Your Grace commands,' he said.

A few days later in the fields of Greenwich, now rich with daffodils and primroses, two people walked together in the morning sunshine, talking most earnestly.

'I learned of magic from my Romany kin,' said Cloverella, 'but I was returned to the Seymours while still very young so, after that, was forced to teach myself.'

Zachary nodded. 'That is not altogether a bad thing. I too studied on my own.'

'And now I learn from you,' Cloverella shook her head wonderingly. 'I can hardly believe my great good fortune.'

How she had persuaded Anne Seymour to let her leave Whitehall and go with Jane to Sir Nicholas Carew's home beyond Greenwich, Cloverella would never know, though possibly Edward's hand could be seen in the coil somewhere. For Anne had released her without argument and now, here she was, walking with Zachary Howard, who had finally sent for her to come to him as he had promised.

Cloverella went on. 'What task have you for me? What shall I do, Master?'

'Go and collect herbs while I rest beneath this tree. Then tell me both the medicinal and magical properties of each one.'

Cloverella looked slightly disappointed. 'You are not coming with me?'

'No. I want to see how much you can do for yourself. So go to, and wake me on your return.'

Zachary rolled up his doublet, which Cloverella could not help but notice was of a very lurid purple, quite painful to the eye, and putting it as a cushion behind his head, firmly closed his eyes. Rather disconsolately, Cloverella wandered off to do her errand, glancing back at him once or twice and wishing that the astrologer was with her, as much to guide her as to be her companion. But he seemed to be in a deep sleep already and eventually she gave up and concentrated on the task in hand.

Zachary, however, was watching her intently through lids that only appeared to be closed, appreciating her delicate figure and mane of dark hair, and tolerantly accepting his weakness for pretty women, so at odds with the rest of his life. But then, of course, he was born beneath the sign of the great archer, with hooves so very earthily on the ground yet arrows that shot beyond the stars, the centaur's vision and mysteries eternally combining with his delight in pursuing the unobtainable. Zachary knew only too well why he behaved as he did, and was unrepentant.

Though he had been married to Jane Wyatt for six years and had kept a mistress, Rosamund Banastre, in Calais for three – both of which young women had borne him children – Zachary felt much as he had done ten years before when he was twenty: his two great sources of pleasure gazing at the heavens or wooing women.

So it was with a very small sigh that the astrologer presently took himself to task for entertaining wicked thoughts about his pupil, an honourable sprig of the house of Seymour who had put herself into his hands in all good faith to learn the lore of magicianship.

I shall be honourable, as befits my dignity, he decided to himself, then wondered if he was becoming pompous.

Whether it was such a dreadful notion or just a restless mood suddenly come upon him he did not know but Zachary found himself unable to lie still any longer and rather crossly pulling on his doublet, made his way to the riverbank where his attention was drawn by a cluster of marsh orchids, already blooming in the early sunshine, their purplish flowers in vivid contrast to the small yellow-leafed meadow buttercup.

He stooped to examine the plants more closely and staring at the orchids, magically spotted with vivid red to prove that in nature all colours are compatible (a theory Zachary constantly strove to emulate in dress) reminded him at once of his vivid kinswoman, Anne Boleyn. Years ago, when she had first attracted attention at Court, Zachary had foreseen her ferocious end and wept for her.

And now he knew with certainty that her last days had come and there was nothing he could do to help her, that her very brilliance had fated her to die young, as if so much force and power must be extinguished before it destroyed all those who drew near.

He thought of little plain Jane, whose cousin Zachary could now see wandering back into view, and shook his head sadly. If the King had searched high and low he could not have found a greater contrast to his splendid wife. Yet Jane had a charm undeniably all her own.

Though not nearly as much, thought Zachary, as this pretty thing making its way towards me.

He picked an orchid and stood up, holding the flower out to her. 'For you,' he said, and bowed.

She smiled gravely. 'Thank you, Master. I shall press and treasure it.'

'I am honoured. But I protest against the formality of the title you give me.'

'Formality has nothing to do with it,' Cloverella responded quickly. 'It is what you have achieved that gives you the right to be spoken of thus.'

Zachary pulled a face. 'I would rather you regarded me as a friend than a tutor.'

Cloverella dropped her eyes. 'I already do, Sir.' When she looked up again she had a certain thoughtful expression. 'I think I must soon return to Jane. So, if you are ready, may I show you the herbs I have gathered?'

If Zachary was chastened he did not show it, merely inclining his ebony curls. 'Certainly, please proceed.'

Cloverella reached into her basket. 'This is St John's wort.'

'Aye, so it is. Do you know its use?'

'To bathe varicose ulcers.'

'From which the King's Grace will shortly suffer, so for Jane's sake be sure to make a preparation of it, adding burdock roots and camomile flowers and pounding in both chopped mallow and walnut leaves.'

Cloverella's eyebrows rose slightly but she said nothing.

'And the herb's mystical uses?' Zachary continued.

'To see off the Devil and, if picked on Midsummer Eve and thriving next day, to ensure a chance of marrying well.'

'Did Mistress Jane gather it last year?' asked Zachary softly.

146

Cloverella gave him a penetrating glance. 'My cousin was not familiar with His Grace last summer. Their friendship began in the autumn.'

Zachary frowned. 'To the detriment of *my* cousin.'

Cloverella went pale. 'I don't understand, Sir. *Your* cousin?'

The astrologer nodded grimly. 'Yes, Mistress. The Queen is my kin. I am the natural son of the Duke of Norfolk.'

The girl took a step back. 'Then we are of opposing houses, Master.'

'In a way, yes.' Zachary smiled again, his fascination tangible. 'But do not brood on it. My father hates poor Anne and on this occasion is very much for the Seymour cause.'

'But you do not feel as he does?'

'No. When I was young I imagined myself in love with her; then, years later, the Queen sent me to the Tower for predicting that Elizabeth would be a girl and our friendship ended. But despite everything I still have a fondness for her.'

'So you are opposed to Jane?' asked Cloverella stiffly.

'I am opposed to no one, Mistress.'

'Then I trust you will do nothing to alter events,' Cloverella said quietly – and the first coldness between the two of them was born.

Zachary bowed. 'I took you as my pupil, Mistress, to teach you all that I know. But if you have no trust in my integrity it is better that we part company now.'

Cloverella hung her head. 'I am sorry, Master. I am young yet and still speak out of turn.'

'That is something you must control if you are to become a great woman.'

'I will try.'

She looked up at him, her eyes dark as sea caves and saw a fantastic smile turn his face from scold to scamp.

'Be merry. You are too good a pupil for me to lose now. Show me the rest of your herbs and forget what has just passed between us.'

Cloverella rootled through her collection. 'Why, here's early flowering vervain,' she said with studied innocence, drawing out a small lilac-petalled flower.

Zachary regarded her solemnly. 'And its uses?'

'As an ingredient to aid digestion.'

'Anything else?'

Cloverella surveyed the plant, holding it up almost level with her face. 'Not that I know of.'

'It is the same colour as your eyes as I am sure you have often been told. But that is incidental. It is, in fact, a very powerful love potion and charm against enchantment. Bathe in water containing vervain and you will not only be able to divine the future but every wish you have will be granted.'

'Really?' said Cloverella, widening her gaze. 'Have you ever done so, Master?'

He solemnly winked an eye. 'What do you think, my dear?'

The cream of Cloverella's cheek suddenly bloomed into rose, as, without answering, she busied herself once more with the herbs in her basket.

In between St George's Day and the next great festival of May, it seemed as though a lull lay over the Court, and so no one was surprised when, on the evening of April 27th, the King left Whitehall by water for an unknown destination accompanied only by Sir Nicholas Carew, who had most recently been honoured as a Knight of the Garter whilst the Queen's brother, Lord Rochford, had, strangely, been passed by.

The inner circle of courtiers knew, of course, that Mistress Seymour was lodged at the home of the Carews and so no wagers were laid as to where His Grace was going. Rather, and more sinisterly, money was changing hands as to when the newly appointed commission to investigate treasonable acts against the King's Majesty would strike at the Queen, who resided almost permanently at Greenwich these days, and was rarely seen at Court.

In the whispering gallery of Tudor life, rumours were flying and, though Thomas Cromwell himself retained a flint-like composure, it was said by those closest to him that he had obtained certain evidences, though exactly of what nature was not as yet clear.

But to Sir Nicholas Carew, sitting opposite Henry in the barge's small cabin, the King was about to unburden himself.

'Nicholas, I am a cuckold,' he said with a deep sigh, and when Carew jumped up in shock, went on, 'Cromwell took a statement from Mark Smeaton this morning. He has signed a confession. He has enjoyed carnal knowledge of the Queen.'

'God a'mercy,' gasped the astounded Sir Nicholas, mopping his

148

brow with his sleeve and hardly believing his senses. 'How can that be? Has the Lady gone mad?'

Henry shook his head, his face pale as a pudding. 'God knows what is in the evil shrew's mind. Perhaps a notion to kill me. At least that is what Mr Secretary believes. There may be other men involved too. Smeaton mentioned more names.'

Carew narrowed his eyes, thinking of the great soft fool of a musician and guessing without too much difficulty how the confession had been extracted.

'Your Grace,' he said, sitting down again slowly. 'Had you any idea this affair was going on?'

The big face went blank. 'None, Nick, none. I am as amazed as you are. I was cuckolded beneath my very nose and knew nothing of it.'

Carew shook his head and just for a moment, a moment that would never come again but which he never afterwards forgot, the King's eye held a gleam of something intangible which, when he thought about it, convinced Sir Nicholas that Henry was prepared to accept absolutely anything as truth in order to get rid of his wife.

'These others?' asked Nicholas suspiciously. 'Have you any idea who they might be?'

'The members of her set,' answered Henry portentously.

Norris, Page, Weston, Wyatt, Brereton, considered Carew rapidly. *None of them very likely. There's something suspect about all this. But who cares so long as the bitch is disgraced?*

Aloud he said, 'I sympathise wholeheartedly with Your Grace's situation, of course. But . . .' He let his voice float away as if he had thought better of what he was saying.

'But . . ?' repeated Henry.

'Pardon me, Your Grace, but privy as I am to your tenderness for Mistress Seymour, I cannot help but feel that the Queen's scandalous behaviour might now open a door which has previously been closed to you.'

A sentimental look, which Carew found extremely offensive, came over the King's features. 'Indeed, indeed.' He lowered his tone to a confiding whisper. 'Knowing what I do, Nick, I now feel free to declare myself. Tonight I intend to make Jane a formal proposal of marriage.'

Distaste, delicacy, doubt, all went for nothing as Carew realised

149

with a great swelling of his heart that Katharine of Aragon had finally been avenged; that when Jane Seymour was Queen of England she would do everything in her power to rescue the dead Queen's daughter from her wretched conditions.

Nicholas jumped to his feet yet again, all smiles and winks, every inch the carefree courtier. 'May I be the very first to offer my congratulations, Sir?' he said heartily. 'There could not be a more splendid match,' and with that he made a florid bow and falling on one knee before the king, kissed his hand.

Genuine tears sprang into Henry's eyes. 'Oh Nicholas, Nicholas,' he gulped. 'What a storm that wicked hack has led me into. Thank God that at last I can sail into peaceful harbour.'

'Amen, amen,' intoned Carew, bowing his head to hide his triumphant smile.

'Now stand, my friend. You who have been so good to both Jane and myself has no need to kneel.'

Carew took his time before rising. 'Your Grace, would it be permissible to inform my wife of your betrothal? I thought perhaps a small celebration later . . .'

'My betrothal,' beamed Henry. 'How good that sounds. Why I truly believe that this will be my first marriage, for the union with my brother's widow was illegal and this one will be proved null and void. I am a lover, bound for his mistress to win her hand. In a sense I am reborn.'

The sovereign's earlier pensive mood had vanished altogether for now he tapped his foot with impatience.

'Tell those men to row faster, Nick. I long to be with my sweetheart.'

Slightly sickened, the hypocrisy smarting in his mouth, Carew said, 'Will you marry soon, Your Grace? Because of the succession,' he added hastily as Henry frowned.

'The Queen has yet to be tried by her peers, Sir Nicholas,' the King answered pompously, with one of those strange changes of tack that was so typical of him. 'As you know it is high treason for the monarch's spouse to have unlawful intercourse. And it is for treason that she will eventually be arraigned. But, it is the law that she is innocent until proved guilty. I am not yet free.'

'Of course,' murmured Carew and said no more, realising that he had made a false move. Henry, however, rumbled on.

'If the Queen is found guilty then it is a capital offence and justice

150

must take its course. In that eventuality I will wait for Parliament's request that I marry again, then I shall, of course, obey the wish of the country.'

Nicholas again murmured, 'Of course,' and wished the words did not stick quite so hard in his throat. With a mighty effort he cleared his mind and thought only of Princess Mary.

'Then may I tell my wife, Sir?'

'I would not have it otherwise. Cut off from Court as she is, Jane must have another woman with whom to share her joy.'

'But her cousin attends her here, Your Grace'. Henry wrinkled his brow and Nicholas went on, 'A funny little thing with an impossible name. She has apparently lived with the Seymours for years, and came to Court with Anne and Edward.'

'A tiny gypsy creature, quite dark?'

'Yes, Your Grace.'

Henry smiled tolerantly. 'A touch of something odd there. Born with a *baton sinister* in her coat of arms, I shouldn't wonder.'

'Indeed, I believe that is true.'

'Ah well,' said Henry, 'if her presence makes Jane happy then I am delighted.'

'Indeed,' answered Nicholas, and relapsed into silence, watching the oarsmen.

The evening was mellow, not fiercely bright as in the height of summer but full of a warm peach-coloured glimmer. As the King's barge rounded the river's serpentine bends it could be seen that the water was sprinkled with gold-dust, while over to the west the sun resembled an orange as it gracefully sank amidst bands of rainbowed clouds. In the gardens of Carew's house, now clearly visible as the craft approached his territory, dusk was already gathering, the host of spring flowers standing out pale as ghosts in the dimness, while the sundial – ever present to remind man of his mortality – pointed a thin white finger at the sky.

In the gloaming people could be seen making their way towards the landing stage and Carew, peering, made out the figure of his wife, tall and stately of movement, her dark face, as always, secretive and shuttered, and that of Jane, gloriously informal, her hair which streamed flaxen and long, about her shoulders. Behind them at a respectful distance walked the wisp of a girl, Cloverella.

As the King's oarsmen slid the barge easily alongside the mooring

151

ring, Henry stood up, his face lit by a smile, his small mouth at full stretch. Looking at him, Lady Carew, who had sported in Katharine of Aragon's chamber and mopped the Queen's brow when she had been brought to bed of a boy who died as he saw first light, felt once again the familiar swell of hatred. She had loved Katharine deeply, been her friend and associate. They had laughed together as young women when, playing the part of a lady from Savoy, Lady Carew had danced for Katharine in her bedchamber, dressed in blue velvet, a bonnet of burnished gold upon her head. The Queen had been pregnant and had not dared risk cavorting, so the King had been partnered by Elizabeth Blount, fifteen and holding her slut's mouth provocatively close to that of Henry. Even now the memory of that night and of the Queen's distress when Elizabeth had later presented the King with a bastard boy, made the loyal woman shiver. Sir Nicholas had nicknamed her Eve, for he said her looks reminded him of dusk, and now, indeed, she grew dark.

'Lady Carew,' said the King gustily, stepping ashore and giving her a cursory greeting, whilst his eyes immediately sought Jane's and then misted with sentiment when she smiled.

'Your Grace,' answered Eve and felt herself grow astonished. Mistress Seymour, far better known to her husband than Lady Carew, and whom Eve had rather suspected of being nothing more than a little opportunist, was alight with love, her eyes fervently starring into those of the King, her cheeks paling and blooming with every breath.

'Your Grace,' tried Eve again, 'welcome to our home. Would you care for refreshment immediately?'

He turned on her a strange look and Lady Carew remembered how she had been ostracised, frozen out, when she had refused to come to Court after Henry's love for Anne had been made public. Now he loved another and by Fate's sweet jest it was one who had also loved Katharine. Eve hooded her eyes to hide the thoughts within them as she waited for his reply.

'First, Lady Carew, I would take a turn about the gardens with Mistress Seymour. I have something of great import to impart to her.' The play on words obviously echoed his mood, for he laughed feverishly.

Eve curtsied her acquiescence and at that moment her husband came to stand beside her, having nimbly jumped ashore from the barge. Without his even touching her, Eve felt a current of excitement pass between them and knew, as couples of many years standing often do, that he was telling her something important. She swept him a brief glance and in it read that they were about to triumph, that this night would see an irrevocable change in events, that there was now no doubt left that Henry would marry Jane.

'Then all will await Your Grace's pleasure,' Eve said pleasantly. 'Come, husband, let us go within.'

She turned and laid her hand on Nicholas's arm, noticing that the oarsmen had already alighted and were making their way towards her kitchens. With a silent sigh of relief, Eve realised that the King and his lady would be private together for this great occasion, then remembered Cloverella and looked round for her. But the girl had gone, slipping into the dusk as silently as one of the deepening shadows.

'So,' said Henry, watching the departing figures, 'now we are truly alone. Oh my sweet mistress, you will never know how I have longed for you.'

'And I for you,' answered Jane. 'Will this separation ever come to an end?'

Knowing from Carew how things were turning against Anne Boleyn this was said as a test of her lover's affection, a bait to draw him out.

'Very soon now,' he answered huskily and snatched her into his arm, crushing her against him. Where another woman might have struggled, Jane only pressed closer and her sensuality drove Henry to frenzy. Barely able to control his passion, he now knew quite certainly that he had found his soulmate at last, that Jane was the wife he had always sought.

'I vowed I would not touch you again until I could honestly make you my betrothed,' he breathed.

He felt the girl tremble. 'Are you saying that the moment has come at last?'

'It has, sweetheart, it has. For reasons that I cannot yet tell you my marriage has finally ended.'

She broke free of him and ran towards the river, now gleaming crimson with the sun's last defiant rays. Already the moon was up, soaring in triumph as the sun died, and it was in her beams that Jane now bent her head and sobbed.

Catching her up, Henry wiped her eyes. 'Why do you weep, sweetheart, on such an occasion?'

153

'Because,' she said, half crying, half laughing, 'If you truly want me as your lady it finally proves to me ugliness is unimportant and my ordeal has ended.'

He looked at her through the eyes of love, and saw that in the moonlight her hair was spun silver, her eyes diamonds sparkling in ice, while her skin was as fresh and clear as a snow-covered rose.

'May I have the honour,' said Henry Tudor very slowly but very true, 'of asking the most beautiful woman in the world to become my wife?'

There was no sound other than that of a swan opening its wings on the riverbank. Jane Seymour quietly answered, 'Yes.'

# Chapter Twelve

WHEN THE INDICTMENTS against the Queen were made public there were those, even amongst her enemies, who found some of the charges difficult to believe. That any woman, short of a Roman empress, could have had so many lovers simultaneously for over three and a half years and kept the fact from her husband was barely credible, but that the Queen could do so, surrounded by her ladies, in the very heart of a Court where rumour and whisper were matters of every day, seemed almost impossible.

The gathering storm had broken swiftly after the arrest of Mark Smeaton. On May 1st, with every courtier present at Greenwich for the May Day tournament, Henry and Anne had appeared together in public for what was to be the last time. Apparently angered by the Queen's dropping of her handkerchief for Sir Henry Norris to carry on his lance, the King had left early and on the journey back to the Palace of Whitehall Norris had been arrested. On the next day the Queen's uncle, the Duke of Norfolk, had come by water to escort Anne Boleyn to the Tower, and her brother Lord Rochford had been arrested a few hours later from Whitehall. As if this were not enough, within twenty-four hours the prisoners were joined by Sir Francis Weston, Sir Thomas Wyatt, William Brereton and Sir Richard Page.

It had all been so quick and, to the ordinary people, very unexpected. And when the charges of adultery and incest were given out, many a solid citizen shook his head; for the Queen to have lovers was one thing, but for her to have had intimate relations with her own brother, was a different matter entirely.

And it was not just the common folk of England who were incredulous. Doubt, like a slow poison, struck everywhere and would not go away, consuming the one person in the kingdom who should have been at her happiest. Yet, like a canker, the thought that Anne Boleyn might be innocent of the charges laid against her and merely being put to death to make way for her, Jane Seymour, began to torture the girl to the point where she could no longer carry the burden alone and asked her brother Edward, also removed from Court to stay with the Carews until the tempest was over, if she might speak with him both privately and urgently.

'What about?' he had asked. But Jane would not answer him, merely laying a finger to her lips, and putting a note into his hand which read, 'I cannot speak here. Take me rowing this afternoon, as once you used to do on the Kennet.' And so, avoiding Anne Seymour and Cloverella, and politely excusing themselves to their hosts, Edward and Jane had clambered into a small craft moored at Sir Nicholas's landing stage, and he, removing his doublet, had sculled out into the middle of the river.

'Well, now,' Edward said, smiling, his dark eyes twinkling very slightly at the sight of Jane's anguished face, 'what can be the matter, child? There you sit, the future Queen of England, looking as if you're on your way to a funeral.'

He wasn't prepared for the answer at all. He personally had given little thought to the question of Anne's guilt or innocence. He was a King's man, through and through, and would serve the crown and his own advancement at one and the same time. But here sat his younger sister, her funny face crumpled and slightly streaked, daring to put into words thoughts that could only be described as treasonable.

Edward heard her in silence but as soon as she had finished speaking burst out with, 'For God's sake watch your tongue, girl. What if His Grace should learn of your fears? Why, you could ruin your entire future.'

She looked at him miserably. 'But what if what I think is true? What if the entire charges are a concoction? A tissue of lies invented by Secretary Cromwell.'

Edward was silent for a second or two, pulling slowly at the oars and staring beyond Jane to where the river bent gracefully.

'A fine time to start thinking such thoughts. What can be possessing you?' he said, then knew a brief pity, wondering how he would feel in Jane's shoes if so great and weighty a matter hung over him.

'Smeaton confessed,' Edward added after a moment's silence, 'don't forget that.'

'But they say he was tortured.'

'Who says? You've not been anywhere to listen to rumours.'

Jane picked at her nails. 'I heard Sir Nicholas whisper it to Eve. They did not know I was eavesdropping.'

Edward stroked his small black beard. 'What else have you overheard?'

'Nothing.' His sister suddenly looked defiant. 'But I have a brain, Edward. I can actually think. I have been at Court for longer than you, remember, and I know all the people involved.'

'So?'

'So I have opinions and it is mine that none of those men are likely.'

A furious expression crossed Edward's face. 'By God's Holy Blood am I brother to an idiot? You'll finish us all if you go on like this.'

Jane looked undecided as to whether to hit him or cry. 'Why do you think I asked you to bring me here? I have expressed these views to no one, not even Cloverella, and I have no intention of doing so. I begged you to give me help yet you do nothing but upbraid me. I see that I must carry this burden alone.'

The diplomat in Edward Seymour rose to the surface instantly. 'Sweetheart,' he said soothingly, 'tell me your fears and let me allay them.'

'Sir Henry Norris, Ned, is the King's Principal Gentleman, the only person in the kingdom allowed into his bedchamber. Would he betray His Grace? Sir Francis Weston has a beautiful and lively wife; why should he be unfaithful? But the worst, Ned, oh the worst . . .' Jane stopped short, pressing her fists hard against her mouth. '. . . is George Rochford. It would be like you and I . . .' Her voice faltered and died away while her face went the colour of blood.

Edward nodded slowly. 'I know, dear heart, I know.' He leaned forward and took her hands from her mouth, patting them gently. 'Why don't you take a very private decision, never to be repeated to His Grace, that you don't believe that charge. That it is too unspeakable for you even to credit.'

Jane looked at him attentively for the first time and he went on, 'As for the rest, why I think that can be easily explained.'

157

'You do?'

'Yes. She was not up to the position, Jane. She flirted and played with men and that is not fitting behaviour for a Queen.'

'Yes but playing and flirting are one thing, adultery is another.'

'But how easy to step over the limits. I have no doubt that she had liaisons with them all just to flatter her ridiculous vanity.'

'But not George?'

It was a question not a statement and Edward paused, mulling over what he actually thought and putting aside his feelings of indifference as to whether the Queen was guilty or not. Eventually, having come to no firm conclusion about the wretched woman, he said what Jane wanted to hear.

'Certainly not. But never repeat that, Jane.'

'Then do you think Lord Rochford will be found not guilty?'

'Quite likely he will.'

For the first time a semblance of cheerfulness came over Jane's face.

'Then you do not believe that all this has been done in order that His Grace might marry me?'

'Would Smeaton confess to please you? Now stop it. You have said enough. A wicked woman is to be brought to justice and the law must take its course. I'll hear no more.'

'Thank you,' said Jane, 'thank you, dearest Edward. I could not have lived with those thoughts much longer.'

'Well now they are gone, dead and buried. You have shared them with me and I have taken them away.'

And with that, Edward closed his mouth determinedly and began to row for the shore.


In the hearts of everyone concerned, the outcome of the state trials was already known. On 12th May, the four commoners – Norris, Weston, Brereton and Smeaton – were marched from the Tower to Westminster Hall to be tried, and the specially chosen grand juries of Middlesex and Kent did what was expected of them and found the prisoners guilty. Wyatt and Page, released for want of evidence against them, heaved sighs of relief, and the Queen and her brother – to be tried three days later by the peers of the realm – on hearing the verdict from their gaolers, knew that all was up with them. Secretary Cromwell's timing of the trials was masterly; with Anne Boleyn's putative lovers found guilty what hope could there be for her? It was generally agreed that only George Rochford had a chance of escape.

Sir Nicholas Carew, who had taken his place in Westminster Hall to hear the trial, rather wished he had not gone. To the last, Sir Henry Norris, Sir Francis Weston and William Brereton protested their innocence, though offered mercy if they would but confess. Only Smeaton, who many believed had been racked, confessed to adultery. A strange thought had gone through Carew's mind at this: had Anne allowed the musician the honour of her bed in order to try and breed a healthy son?

Yet even more disturbing had been the presence of Francis Weston's wife and mother in court, listening to all the filth being poured out about their dear one. Carew had shuddered seeing their ravaged faces, wishing he was not involved, and believing if it were not for his secret pledge to Katharine of Aragon that he would always protect her daughter, he would have got up and walked out, not waiting to hear the verdicts. But he, like all his fellow courtiers, was always caught up in intrigue of some kind or other and there was no escape from it. Unhappily, he had sat there throughout and drawn the only comfort from the verdicts of guilty; that this day would finally doom Anne Boleyn and clear Jane's path to the throne for once and for all.

'Victims,' he had said to Eve on his return home that evening. 'Today I believe I witnessed four lambs go to the slaughter.'

'Four?'

'I am sure that Smeaton was tortured.' Sir Nicholas had suddenly buried his head in his hands. 'Oh, God's blood and wounds, I hate the Concubine and all her wicked deeds, yet who am I to judge these men? There was a look of innocence to them all, only Smeaton confessed and it was he who named the others.'

Eve had stood up and come to him, putting her arm about his shoulders. 'These are hard times, husband. Men will be sacrificed and Queens brought down before order can be restored.'

'And she,' asked Carew, jerking his head in the direction of the chamber in which Jane Seymour slept, 'will she bring peace in her train?'

'Who knows? But at least she is malleable. She will do all she can for Mary.'

'Has the King been to visit her today?'

'No, and he has given Jane instructions to move within a day or two to a house only a mile from Whitehall. He wants her to be close at hand if the Queen is condemned.'

'If?' said Carew, and in his laugh there was the sound of bitterness as well as that of jubilation.

Up to this day Norfolk had believed himself beyond tears, sincerely thought that life in the service of his monarch had hardened him to a point where public displays of emotion were no longer possible. But now, standing beneath the canopy of state, facing the dark girl from Hever whom he would have sworn, even to himself, was his avowed adversary, he felt his eyes grow suddenly wet. The moment had come, the peers of the realm had found the Queen guilty by unanimous vote, and now it was the duty of the Duke of Norfolk, Lord President of the Council and High Steward of England, to pronounce sentence upon her.

They stared at each other, uncle and niece, and he thought how pale and thin she was, her eyes so enormous and dark that they seemed to fill her face with shadows. Horribly unbidden, a memory came: Anne as a small girl, all elfin and fine, a magical little creature, feeling in his pocket for where the Duke had hidden sweetmeats.

Norfolk swallowed hard and the tears fell faster, and then he saw that Anne, who up till now had seemed almost unnaturally still and frozen, was watching him cry and was about to lose her nerve. In a moment of enormous compassion, Thomas Howard dropped his eyes and stared at the papers in his hand.

'Madam,' he said, his voice ringing unnaturally loud in a hall completely hushed and still, 'you are sentenced to be burned . . .'

He paused and cleared his throat, glancing up as he did so, and seeing that she was gazing at him like a stricken deer, her eyes afraid and haunted. At that moment he would have changed places with any man in the room rather than go on. There was a tremendous silence before the Duke finally found his voice and continued, '. . . or beheaded at the pleasure of the King's Highness.'

She looked away from him, down into the body of the hall, and Norfolk found himself wondering if she had seen the King's messenger, Sir Francis Bryan, standing in the doorway ready to go the moment he heard those words. But whether she had or not he never afterwards knew for his attention was caught by the fact that somebody was leaving the room, ill and retching. The Duke vaguely perceived the shambling figure of Harry Percy, the Earl of Northumberland, rushing blindly through the door.

'Once Harry loved me,' Anne whispered to herself, so low that only Norfolk heard. Then he saw the Queen brace up and turn back to him, her face completely white. 'Goodbye, my uncle,' she said quietly then, utterly calm and composed once more, began her final speech, never realising that her kinsman Bryan had already left the hall and was, at that precise moment, mounting the fastest horse from the King's stable, to ride at full pelt to where Henry Tudor awaited the verdict in the Palace of Whitehall.

That day, the day that Anne Boleyn so courageously faced her judges, had not started well for Jane Seymour. At once, even on waking, disruptive thoughts had returned to her, thoughts that a woman could be facing trial only because of herself and that she, plain little Jane, might after all be an angel of death. It had taken a great deal of effort to put herself into another frame of mind. Only by repeating over and over again that Henry believed it all and that she must too if they were to find lasting happiness together, did she finally bring herself round to any sort of humour. And then, even though it sickened her, a frenzied kind of excitement entered the proceedings.

Almost as soon as Jane was dressed, a messenger had come the short mile from Whitehall Palace with a note from Henry.

'My own dear Mistress, You know that you, and you alone, are uppermost in my heart and affection this day and I greet you. I will send you word of all that transpires in the Tower by three o'clock and, if it is God's will that you and I be united, not only in thought and love but also in marriage, then I will sup with you this evening that we may set down what is to be done.

Hoping shortly to receive you in these arms, I end for the present, your own loving servant and sovereign, H. R.'

After reading this, the awful waiting had been tempered with frantic preparations for a banquet. Since Jane had moved from the Carews' home to the house near Whitehall, Henry had sent her not only beautiful gowns and jewels but also his own cook and kitchen lads, servants and grooms, to ensure that she should live as comfortably and well as befitted the future bride of a King.

In a bizarre fashion the day of Anne Boleyn's trial had about it the extraordinary atmosphere of a grotesque festival, the feeling in the air so electric that Jane was glad she had left Cloverella behind with Edward. Her cousin, so full of magic and mystery, would have undoubtedly considered these events as preparatory to a blood sacrifice and been unbearable company.

As three o'clock came near, Jane found herself drawn to the window to watch for a horseman, and as a distant cloud of dust told her that one did indeed approach, her heart lurched and began to beat in an unsteady rhythm. Her thoughts flew, death and marriage, brides and corpses, all jumbled hopelessly together and, overriding all, her hopeless passion for the King which had not been fulfilled as both of them so urgently desired for quite some considerable time.

Pretending a composure she did not feel, Jane – as soon as she realised that the messenger was her cousin Sir Francis Bryan – went to sit quietly in the receiving chamber, her hands folded in her lap, allowing one of the servants to greet him and show him into her presence. He stood bowing in the doorway.

'Madam.'

Jane stared at him amazed. 'Francis, you are very formal.'

He came towards her, his pale grey eyes not moving from her face. 'Madam, I have news of great importance.' He went down on one knee before Jane and raised her hand to his lips. 'An hour ago the Queen was sentenced to die. It will only be a matter of days now before you and His Grace are free to marry. He begs me to tell you that he will sup with you tonight as arranged.'

She stared at him, utterly breathless, the tears stinging her eyes like bees. 'Did he say anything else?'

'He asked me to give you this.' Bryan pulled from his pocket a sapphire-encrusted pendant, dangling on a golden chain. 'And begged that you wear it tonight to please him.'

Jane took it from him silently. 'Were you there . . . at the Tower?'

Francis looked guarded. 'Yes, why do you ask?'

'Because as you are the only person at Court who is kin to both the Queen and myself I wondered how you could bear to be present.'

The unmoving eyes stared expressionlessly into her own. 'I found that I could,' Bryan answered shortly, and stood up.

Jane did likewise. 'Will you take some refreshment?'

A fleeting smile crossed her cousin's face. 'No, Jane. His Grace commanded that I return at once with your message. What is it?'

Jane turned away from him for a moment, looking out of the window to where the swirling Thames came up to the house's foundations.

'Tell him that I await this evening with great pleasure and that I shall count the hours until he is with me.'

She turned back to look at him, laughing a little breathlessly at her flowery words, still not quite able to comprehend that soon she would be both bride and queen.

Bryan did not smile. 'I shall relay your message faithfully, Madam.'

And with that he was gone, bowing his way out, already behaving as if she had higher station than she actually did. Jane, looking at the space where only a moment before he had stood, shivered. It was true she owed Francis Bryan much, for he had first introduced her to Court, but the details of his deliberate quarrel with George Boleyn, Lord Rochford, when he had seen the fortunes of that family begin to ebb, were frightening.

I pity anyone against whom he turns, Jane thought, and went a little cold.


Chapuys, a contented smile lighting his wise blue eyes, sat by an open window in the Palace of Whitehall, and thought that at last God's justice had been finally rendered. His beloved Queen and friend, Katharine of Aragon, had been revenged, the Concubine was to die and a good Imperialist – as he liked to think of Jane Seymour – was to take her place.

He hummed a snatch of song as he picked up his pen, about his usual task of keeping his royal master informed of events. 'You never saw prince nor man make greater show of his horns, nor show them more pleasantly,' he wrote, and then grinned broadly, even his beard seeming to shorten, for how true that description was. Since the arrests of the accused, the Queen's cuckolded husband had hardly spent a night in, speeding off by boat or horse to sup with his new mistress – and the shrewd old Spaniard was more convinced than ever that Jane was this in every sense – or to feast with other friends. That the whole affair was a happy release for the King was being made patently obvious.

The Ambassador stood up, stretching his arms and yawning,

feeling that he had been writing letters for years, and in a moment of petty rebellion crossed to the window and leaning on the sill, looked out. To celebrate Anne's condemnation her husband had organised a water pageant and from where he stood Chapuys could see the royal barge which was to lead the procession, already packed with musicians and singers of the Chamber. Cultured aesthete that he was, Chapuys felt his stomach turn. He had been at Court throughout most of Henry's hot-eyed pursuit of Anne Boleyn, had witnessed the many indignities heaped on Katharine. And now, only three years after the King had married his heart's desire, there was a pageant to celebrate the woman's denunciation.

Fat oaf, thought Chapuys with enormous satisfaction and wondered to himself that passion could transcend all, that Jane Seymour could actually have a fancy for a man not only twenty years older than she was but who was also rapidly gaining weight. He nodded cunningly, musing on the fact that even funny little women like the future queen were equally as capable of scheming their way to power as their more alluring counterparts. But, at this point, a noise from the embankment below caught his attention and Chapuys, opening the window fully, leaned out to see the sights.

The sun was not so much going down as being killed by dagger-dark clouds, for there was blood everywhere, echoing the death sentence so recently meted out to six hapless people. The river trickled uneasily, a sludgy dark crimson, on its back riding not only the King's barge, garishly garlanded with flowers and favours, but every type of craft, tastelessly glimmering and gleaming, ready to accompany the bridegroom, as their owners no doubt already thought of him, the short mile downriver to where his sweetheart lay waiting. That a lot of celebratory drink had been partaken of that day was obvious, for though the musicians sang and played sweetly enough, they had a counterpoint of other songs, both discordant and lewd.

'Christ's blood,' said Chapuys beneath his breath.

Despite the fact that he found the whole gawdy exhibition rather vulgar, he continued to watch and was rewarded a moment or two later with a sight of the King, dressed in white satin and gems, his vast codpiece embroidered with golden threads as if to boast to the world of his virility, his hat plumed with a waving purple feather. There was a huge cheer from all the attendant courtiers as with a jaunty step, like that of a man half his age, Henry stepped aboard the waiting barge.

At exactly that moment, or so it seemed to the watching Ambassador, the sun went out. A huge cloud, black as a moor, crossed its surface and hung there while in the distance thunder rolled. The atmosphere suddenly became stifling as little winds rushed everywhere, preparing for a storm. The King, refusing to be alarmed, looked up to the rapidly darkening heavens, strode into the cabin of his barge, and gave orders to cast off. The last glimpse Chapuys had of him was sitting resplendent, surrounded by his musicians, while the craft and its attendant flotilla headed out for midstream.

At long last they were alone and clasped in each other's arms, Jane almost lifted off her feet as the King smothered her aching mouth with kisses. Since the incident of the purse of sovereigns they had hardly met without chaperons, behaving so virtuously that Henry might almost have known of what profligacy his wife would be accused and, by way of reply, kept his own actions accordingly chaste. But now, with the musicians and servants dismissed and nobody present to witness what he did, he wooed Jane with intensity, determined to take her to bed before the night was out.

It had been reported to him verbatim what Anne's brother, the elegant and likeable Viscount Rochford, had said at his trial: that the King was unable to have relations with his wife for there was no virtue or potency left in him. Up till that moment men had been betting ten to one on George's acquittal, the charge of incest sticking in the craws of most and Rochford himself making a brilliant defence. But those fateful words doomed him and stung Henry to the quick, raising in his mind doubts and fears to which a man of forty-five, albeit somewhat heavy through lack of exercise, should not be prey.

Now, holding Jane away from him and looking down at her, both aware and proud of his magnificent height, he said, 'Tell me, sweetheart, have the words of Lord Rochford at his trial been recounted to you?'

Jane, with her inherent dislike of the very thought of incest, answered, 'No, and I have no wish to hear them.'

'But he said things of me,' persisted Henry gloomily. 'Things to which only you could give the lie.'

A pair of puzzled eyes looked into his. 'What things do you speak of?'

For the first time in their acquaintance, Jane saw a redness deepen Henry's cheeks. 'That I am impotent,' he answered gruffly. 'Past pleasing a woman.'

She said the best thing possible to restore the King's hurt pride. 'No doubt the man was jealous.'

'Jealous?' he exclaimed. 'How could George Rochford possibly be jealous of me.'

'Henry,' said Jane, still finding it an effort to call her sovereign by his name, 'your reputation with women was one that I am sure any gallant would envy. Nobody could resist you. Nor still can,' she added softly.

Sentiment poured from his eyes as the King wept. 'My little Jane,' he said huskily, 'you who are to be my first true wife, I shall love and protect you until my dying day.'

It did not seem quite the moment to Jane, whose handling of Henry grew ever more subtle, to ask exactly what he meant by the word 'first'. Instead she cuddled her arms more closely round his great waist.

'And I shall care for you, too, until I die.'

At that instant a freakish draft sprang from nowhere and every candle in the room flickered, some even going out.

'Oh dear,' said Jane, 'I hope that is not an omen.'

'If it is,' Henry answered solemnly, 'it denotes the passing of evil from my life, for outside it is bright.'

With his arm round her waist he led her to the window and threw back the heavy curtains. The night was still, the moon shining on the river, its counterpart glowing back from the depths, all sign of the storm now gone.

'There,' said Henry, 'the Thames, who always befriends us. Do you remember telling me its story at Windsor when first we became lovers?'

Even at the memory affection suffused her. 'I do remember,' Jane answered softly, 'I remember everything. And let those who insult you on that score come to me for the truth.'

'My sweetheart,' he said gruffly, and once more they kissed.

By the fire in the Hall the two of Henry's gentlemen who had accompanied him that night, slumbered in chairs; while the musicians and singers slept where they could. On the river the

166

master of the King's barge snored in the cabin, his oarsmen in the kitchens asleep with the scullions. Only Henry and Jane were left awake so that there was nobody to see them when, with their hands clasped together like children, the King and his beloved softly blew out the remaining candles and quietly made their way together to her own most private bedchamber.

It was at the breaking of the next day's violent dawn, all poppy-red with a suffused and angry sun lumbering up over a black horizon, that the solitary figure of a horseman streaking over the dark fields surrounding the village of Greenwich could be seen making its frantic way homeward. And it was just as the first sinister rays lit the house near the water's edge that Dr Zachary clattered into his stables and, for a brief moment, seemed to lose all his power, his boney face white beneath his tumbling curls and his body shrunken. Over his saddle, in a confusion of arms and legs and trailing hair the colour of daffodils, lay another shattered human being as weak as he, and the sight was so terrible to behold that the stable boy screamed and ran to the steward for help.

They lifted down their master and his daughter and carried them into the house, but instead of taking them to their beds, laid them down carefully on bedding near the fire. Strangely, no wife and mother came bustling in to tend her charges and no small boy rushed to greet his father. Instead only a nervous silence pervaded; a silence so still and heavy that after several hours it seemed to clang like a bell, and it was then that Zachary awoke.

'Coker,' he called weakly, 'Coker,' and when the steward came running murmured, 'Sapphira, how is she? Does my daughter live?'

'She does, Master, aye,' the man answered, 'she breathes calmly though she has not as yet awoke. What ails the child?'

Zachary shook his head. 'She has been rendered speechless and left as good as finished. And all through my fault.'

'But how, Sir? How?' asked the steward fearfully.

'Because I, may God forgive me, took her to a ritual for which she was not ready. She tried to lift a curse which was too strong for her. It took away Sapphira's speech – and only I am to blame.'

Coker had never seen Zachary weep but he had supposed, as in all things with his capricious master, whose very company exhilarated all who came in contact with it, that when he did there would be a storm, and indeed he was right. Zachary sobbed broken-heartedly, begging Sapphira both in words that Coker could understand and others said in heathenish tongue, to open her eyes.

The steward, with a great effort, braced himself for what must come next. 'Doctor,' he said firmly, 'save your tears.'

Zachary turned on him a wild and stricken face. 'What are you saying?'

'There is worse than Sapphira's plight in this house.'

The astrologer stared blankly and then Coker saw him realise the truth, though whether by magic means or guesswork he could not say.

'Jane,' said Zachary, 'my wife!' And with that he seemed to regain his strength and fled upstairs, leaving those below to try and bring his daughter back to consciousness.

In the dimness of their bedchamber, Zachary saw at once that the curse which he had tried so desperately to exorcise had not only struck his daughter but also his wife, for Jane Wyatt, the poet Thomas's sister and cousin of Anne Boleyn, lay dying.

In the single leap that it took him to get to her side, the astrologer berated himself for everything: for leaving her to concentrate his energies on other matters, for being so greatly attacked by nervous exhaustion that he had not clairvoyantly known she was ill; for being unfaithful to her with Rosamund Banastre; for the million and one things that he should or should not have done during their time together.

Once in the past Zachary Howard had saved his father the Duke from the Sweat, and now he recognised its symptoms and knew that he was too late to help his wife.

'May God forgive me,' he said again and took her cold hand in his.

An hour later Jane left her earthly shell, never speaking to or looking at her husband again. Yet he, believing that she could hear him, spoke to her; spoke of the woods of Hever where he had married her by gypsy rite, spoke of her cousin Anne whom they had both loved in those far off distant days, spoke of his joy in their partnership that she had been so patient with all his eccentricities.

As Jane breathed her last, he made the sign of the cross on her brow and then – and not in the least irreverently to Zachary's uncomplicated mind – spoke the Romany words of blessing for the dead. Then he wept. In a day and night his wife had been taken from him, his daughter as good as, and his father had sentenced his cousin to die. As Dr Zachary rose to pull the curtains against the grey and humourless day, he had never felt more alone.

Blades fell swiftly and the Grim Reaper smiled. On the 17th May the five men sentenced went to their deaths, amongst their number George Rochford. Two days later the Queen, dressed in grey damask, elegantly cut and trimmed with fur, a small hat with ornamented coifs binding up her lively hair, knelt at the block while the executioner from Calais struck off her head with one blow of his sword, even while the Queen was still praying for mercy on her soul. It was finished and done, the enchantress from Hever would never again weave her fascinating spell, the husband who had once loved her was a widower.

At four o'clock the next morning, Jane Seymour rose in the darkness and was dressed most splendidly by a bevy of waiting women. Her freshly washed hair was bound up on her head and a circlet of gold, glittering with gems, was placed upon it. Then, when she was finally robed like a Queen, Jane was escorted by musicians and servants to the royal barge, which tugged on its moorings at the very foot of the house in which she stayed.

As they cast off and made their way down river to Hampton Court, she thought that she had never seen such a morning. In the fine and glistening dawn, so different from the ominous weather that had brooded all the days Anne Boleyn remained alive, Jane saw the merry sails of craft, the waving fishermen standing knee-deep, the plunge and fall of the bending shore line. Above her head gulls plummeted and wheeled, spearheads of white, flashing against the pink and jade of sun-up; while on the banks, first villages, then churches, were lit with sparkling gold as the great orb climbed. Everywhere there was blossom, tossing and laughing as the river breeze played amongst it, curling it with its fingers and sometimes throwing down a shower of petals fit to greet a bride.

Jane laughed. Her life was complete. The ugly cygnet had become a swan. Now she could stand fearless in the daylight and lift her face to the sun. She knew that she was beautiful, that May was her very month, as delicate and fair as she. As she ascended the water steps at Hampton Court to discover that the whole world seemed to be bowing before her, her little mouth curved into the happiest smile of her life. Whatever followed from this moment, whatever sadness lay ahead of her, she would cling fiercely to this split second of time and cherish the memory even as she died. In all the beauty and splendour of her arrival, Jane Seymour stepped forth into the Palace of Hampton Court to receive a ring of betrothal from the King of England and with him to pledge her promise of marriage.

# Chapter Thirteen

AROUND THE NECK OF Sir John Seymour the Esturmy horn, symbol of office of the wardens of Savernake Forest, hung like a Welsh harp, its silver sheen nestling against the darkness of his black jerkin. The medieval craftsman who had fashioned it had crumbled to powder long before Sir John had been born but it, in the manner of all inanimate objects protected against the march of time, still glistened argent, its enamelled bands as clear and proud as the day they were fashioned by those skilled hands.

To blow upon the horn was the ancient greeting given to the monarch upon entering the forest and today Sir John, his long beard lifting in the wind like that of an old testament prophet, waited upon Topenham Hill for his first sight of the royal party, with a heart that beat at double its usual pace. Behind him all dressed in their finery were his two sons, Edward and Henry, and his son-in-law Sir Clement Smith, his other being too sickly to attend. And what smiles there were upon their faces and how grandly the old man swelled his chest, sitting his horse like a lord, for today no ordinary visitors came to Wolff Hall but His Grace himself with his affianced lady, the daughter of the house, Mistress Jane.

Sir John's faded eyes were blue as fresh sheets of linen wind-blown on a line, and they had never watched the distant view so acutely. Nor, when the royal party finally did come into sight, would he ever have raised the Esturmy horn to his lips more eagerly, waiting for that first thrilling moment when they would come into earshot and he could welcome them with all his heart. At home, he knew, Dame Margery had prepared Wolff Hall as never before and the Great Barn, in which the pre-wedding feast would be held, had been swept until it glowed, while on the tenter hooks, all replaced and shining, hung not only the Seymour tapestries but some borrowed from the mighty Wentworths themselves.

Watching his father, Edward could have laughed and also wept. Pride had rejuvenated the dear veteran to such an extent that Sir John even joked with his sons of dancing the night away at Jane's betrothal feast.

'If only Thomas were here,' he said and winked a merry eye so broadly that Edward immediately had a hint his brother must have returned from France and be about to make a surprise appearance. But he played along, 'If only,' he replied – and then winked back.

The visitors were a sudden line of colour in the distance and the moment had arrived. With a grand gesture Sir John raised the ancient horn to his lips and blew a blast that should have had the dead jumping clean from their graves. Back from the royal party came an echoing greeting and with that Sir John kicked his heels into the side of his mount and, raising his hand for his sons to follow him, charged down the slope at full speed, his beard flying out over his shoulders like wings.

They met in the valley below Topenham Hill and Sir John could hardly believe the change that he saw in his daughter. An elegant young woman, beautifully dressed and jewelled, her face superbly painted, rode in a litter beside the King, who besat an enormous horse, brightly caparisoned. Having not seen him for some eight months, Sir John was struck by the way in which his sovereign had increased so greatly in size. Jane's father knew, of course, about the King's accident in the lists which had prevented him from exercising as once he used, but nevertheless he was not prepared for the fact that even Henry's face had broadened whilst his eyes seemed to have receded slightly into his head.

Fat eyes, thought the mischievous old man. By God's teeth and toenails, His Grace has got fat eyes!

Just for a second he wondered what his daughter saw in such a gross fellow and then the generations of feudal blood that ran in his veins gained dominance and he guessed, incorrectly, that Jane was in love with the very ambience of the King rather than the man himself. Jumping from his horse lithely for a man of his advanced years, Sir John approached his daughter's litter, bowed first to the King then to Jane, and kissed her hand. There was a flash of bright eyes and then she laughed.

172

'Father, no kiss for my cheek? All this formality!'

'You are a King's future bride,' said Sir John quietly. 'Soon I must greet you as Queen.'

'But not yet,' answered Jane, 'not for a few days. May I not be ordinary Jane on this visit?'

'No,' replied her father solemnly, 'it is not possible. You can never be ordinary Jane again.' And with that he turned to the King before whom Edward, Henry and Clement were making reverence and made a secondary bow which put the others to shame. 'Your Grace, my heart is almost too full to allow me speech but know that the honour you have brought my family by asking for my daughter's hand will be spoken of with awe until there is no longer a Seymour left alive,' he said grandly.

Henry, who had not dismounted, extended a hand. 'We thank you, Sir John, and give you greeting. Now, as we have ridden hard, let us to Wolff Hall for refreshment.'

Once again the old man found an irreverent thought in his mind – 'he can't wait to get at his vittals!' – then he gave himself a mental kick. Such naughtiness was unbecoming in a man of his years and could be potentially dangerous. He must control his private fancies lest one day in his cups he might actually speak them aloud.

Yet the look on Dame Margery's face as the huge retinue clattered into the great courtyard was revealing to Sir John. Just for a second she gazed aghast at the colossus who was soon to be her son-in-law, before she remembered herself and hid her thoughts behind the excited fuss she was making of Jane. But later that evening, as she and Sir John dressed for the banquet, the comfortable Dame did allow, just briefly, her thoughts to be put into words.

'His Grace looks *older*, do you not think, husband?'

'Older?' answered Sir John in a pithy whisper. 'He looks gross, if that is what you mean.'

'Poor Jane,' sighed her mother on her breath.

'Poor Jane, nothing,' said Sir John, very quietly indeed. 'She is going to be Queen.'

'Yes, but . . .'

'There are no buts in it, Margery. She will be the first lady in the land.'

His wife looked at him, her country-fresh face quite sad. 'But she is so delicate . . .'

'No more,' answered Sir John firmly. 'We will be late for the feast. Put such ideas from your mind.'

If Dame Margery had triumphed on the King's first visit to Wolff Hall, now she excelled even that occasion. It seemed as if the entire county of Wiltshire – or those of importance who dwelled there – must be present, for the Great Barn was packed to the doors with people, servants, musicians, not forgetting the Seymour's personal priest, Sir James, now grown old and tipsy, and Will Somers, the King's favourite jester. Though the banquet was officially to celebrate Jane's betrothal, it had the atmosphere of a wedding feast and, what with Will's jokes about bride beds and maidenheads, and the many love songs that were sung, sentimental tears ran down many a flushed cheek and propositions were made amongst the guests that would have shocked Dame Margery had she overheard.

That the King and Jane were besotted with one another was glaringly obvious and Dame Margery would have spent the rest of the evening mulling over the incredible fact, had not there been a sudden thunderous knock at the door, closed against drafts as the guests tackled their fish supper – eight pikes, five salmon, seven tench and nine lobsters, to say nothing of an assortment of pike, eels, trout, bream and carp – it being a Saturday and no meat allowed. Everyone looked up, startled, except for Sir John who made a furtive signal to his minstrels. At this they broke into a noisy fanfare and the door was thrown open to reveal a cloaked figure, standing motionless, the hood of the garment pulled well down over its face.

A woman guest screamed and several men rose to their feet as if to put the intruder out but, as the welcoming music blasted forth, the newcomer threw back his hood and, half walking, half dancing, entered the barn. There was a flash of bright hair and the sound of an infectious laugh.

'It's Thomas,' exclaimed Jane, rising to her feet and, turning to her betrothed in a way that her mother considered bold, tugged the King's arm, 'Your Grace, it is my brother returned from France.'

Thomas sauntered up to the centre of the huge table and made a fanciful bow. 'Your Grace, forgive my somewhat precipitate entrance. I have ridden, even now, from Bristol, where I have been about my business. But what brother worth the name could miss the wedding of his sister?'

George Rochford walked over the King's grave and for a moment

Henry stirred uneasily as his spine crawled with fear, then he said, 'I greet you Thomas. All the relatives of our affianced lady are as dear to us as they are to her.'

They looked at each other and just for a second each had a premonition of the love that Thomas would one day have for two of Henry's women, both wife and daughter, and their gaze grew icy. Then the moment passed as each man shook off the presentiment and the feeling was lost amongst the mirth and merriment all around them.

On the 20th May, 1536, the day of Jane Seymour's betrothal, Jane Wyatt, wife of the Duke's son Zachary, was laid to rest in the Wyatt family tomb at Allington in Kent; the *baton sinister*, the sign of bastardy running through her husband's coat of arms being enough to make the idea of internment in the Howard vault untenable to the rest of the family. Thus, Jane was buried alongside her ancestors, with her brothers and sisters – still in mourning for their friend and cousin Anne Boleyn – standing uneasily at the service with the wild-headed husband whom none of them particularly liked.

As soon as the funeral was done the astrologer left them, sweeping away on his dark horse with no more than a farewell. And the next morning Thomas Wyatt was astonished to hear that Zachary had sailed with the tide to France that very night, his two children with him, the house in Greenwich closed down all but for one servant, the only clue to his destination a short letter to his father stating that his son would be placing the children 'in the care of a good woman of Calais' for the meantime.

The Duke had chuckled to himself, 'He's taking them to that slut, Rosamund Banastre, of course.' And he had been perfectly right.

The mistress that Zachary kept in Calais was now nineteen years of age, having been seduced by him four years earlier and having borne him a son, Sylvanus, who was three years old. She, in her very embodiment, was part of Zachary's guilt and yet he needed her naughtiness. Where Jane Wyatt had been all that a wife should be, Rosamund was the perfect mistress with her lovely slut's mouth and desirable breasts. But now the wife was gone for ever and Zachary was in Calais to come to terms with his future.

He had sworn to himself that he would resist Rosamund's charms on this visit but, of course, he could not and they had gone to bed together as lovers of old, and there he had wept bitterly for Jane in the security of Rosamund's warmth. Then they had talked late into the night, the candles burning low and the wine in the flagon slowly disappearing.

'I feel craven,' Zachary said slowly, 'for I deceived her over you and yet I never could resist you, you little witch.'

Rosamund looked at him long and hard. 'I think we couple well and I think that it is difficult to forgo a good partner. But soon, my well-beloved, you will have to do so.'

He stared at her, astonished. 'What do you mean?'

Rosamund pursed her beautiful mouth. 'My hand is sought in marriage and my mother has given her consent.'

'What!' Zachary was furious. 'Who is he? What is all this?'

'He has a title and money and he is French. Need I say more?'

Zachary grinned wryly. 'So you have a suitor. I should have guessed. But what of Sylvanus? Does your lover want him too?'

'No, our child shall remain here in Calais with my mother. But there is nothing wrong with that. Surely it is the custom in England for the grandmother to care for the children while the parents are at Court?'

Zachary frowned. 'That is so. But I am not sure, as yet, that I approve of your arrangements for my son.'

Rosamund threw her arms round him. 'You are getting very pompous and old, my dear. Why, I can see some grey in your hair.'

Zachary nodded. 'You are right. He is your son too and I have no right to interfere. Lady Banastre will bring him up well, I have no doubt.'

'You could not take him, astrologer.' Rosamund often called him this when she was at her most teasing. 'I would have thought you to have enough trouble caring for your own two. Why, what are you going to do now that they have no mother?'

Zachary smiled just a little forlornly. 'I had thought, though selfishly, it is true, that perhaps you . . .'

Rosamund put a finger over his lips. 'I believed till now you knew me well Zachary, but obviously not! I am far from maternal. Why, I only had Sylvanus because I knew of no way to abort him. No, I shall do my duty by Monsieur le Duc and give him clever sons and pretty daughters, and then hand them straight to the servants.'

'You are a heartless baggage, though a very sweet one.'

'Then make love to me.'

'In a moment. First, I must ask you one favour.'

'Which is . . .'

'That you shelter my children while I go on pilgrimage?'

Rosamund looked astonished. 'I did not think you pursued that kind of thing.'

'While I am in France I wish to visit the Black Madonna of Rocamadour. I feel in need of spiritual cleansing and she has enormous power, or so it is said.'

'His Grace of England would be displeased, turning as he is against all Catholic superstition.'

'His Grace of England will never know,' answered Zachary, smiling. 'Now will you take my two poor waifs into your household for a week or so?'

'Of course I will. So kiss me.'

They spoke no more, making love in a bitter-sweet mood, knowing that this would be one of the last times before Rosamund became a bride. And because of this the feel of Zachary inside her, familiar though it was, took on an exhilarating excitement, so that Rosamund felt herself lift to a height of sensation that she had never before experienced. In that moment she thought she would end her betrothal to the French Duke and stay with the astrologer always, just for the pleasure of his bedtime company but then, as they shuddered and gasped their way back to normality, she realised that this was an illusion and that truly he was not the man to give her the things she really wanted out of life.

And Zachary, too, as he fell back on the pillow, filled with pleasure, knew guilt again that he should be coupling hard while his wife lay newly dead. He sighed in the candlelight and Rosamund said, 'She wouldn't mind. They want us to know joy. My mother told me that when my father died.'

'You are right, of course. She, least of all, would begrudge me anything.'

'Then so be it. Go on your pilgrimage and come back refreshed. As best I can I shall mother the three of them. But not if Monsieur le Duc comes calling of course.'

'Of course,' answered Zachary gravely, and with that they fell asleep, curled round each other like sleepy cats, totally at ease, wishing, in a way, that it was not necessary to part for ever, but knowing that very soon they must.

\*       \*       \*

177

It took the wedding party several days to make the journey from Wolff Hall to London, for though the old people did not come, Jane's brothers and sisters, as well as Cloverella and certain servants, set out to take part in the celebrations, forming quite a large group in all. Jane and Henry, anxious for a little privacy during these last few days before they were finally wed, made a leisurely detour through the ancient town of Winchester and finally arrived in London with only two days until the wedding itself.

On the day of Anne's execution Archbishop Cranmer had issued a dispensation for the marriage of Henry and Jane without publication of banns and it had been Cranmer, too, who had held a special court in Lambeth Palace to pronounce that Anne Boleyn's marriage to Henry had been null and void because the King had previously had her sister Mary for mistress. And though nobody in the world could have been less cynical than Jane, even she felt her eyebrows rise when, on the wedding eve, returned late from their first official appearance together, Henry suddenly repeated his strange remark that she was to be his first bride.

'The other misfortunes were no true marriages at all. In both cases the women concerned' – Jane realised with a start that he could not bring himself to say the names of Katharine or Anne any more – 'were within the prohibited degrees of affinity, the Princess Dowager being my sister-in-law and the other one's sister having been my mistress.'

I do hope, thought Jane in a moment of great unease, that if I should die before he does he will not have similar difficulty in referring to me.

But the idea was drowned by Henry's next words. 'As part of your wedding gift, sweetheart, I am giving you one hundred and four manors situated throughout the realm, five castles, several chases and forests, and land in London too. Will that please you?' She could hardly answer, utterly overwhelmed, but Henry rushed on, 'And for your family, the title of Viscount Beauchamp for Edward, and for Thomas an appointment as a Gentleman of my Privy Chamber.'

Jane pressed her forehead with the back of her hand. 'I don't know what to say, Your Grace. You have lifted me and my brothers into such high esteem.'

He was beside her in a second, huge and overpowering. 'It is the least I can do for she who is to be the mother of my sons, my first true and legal wife.'

A moment of terror struck Jane to the quick, thinking of what her fate might be if she should fail to produce the longed-for heir, and what reason could possibly be found for *her* disposal. Then she remembered Dr Zachary's prophecy and screwed her courage up.

'I will be a mother as soon as God wills it.'

'And what pleasure there will be in the begetting.'

Henry was winking a heavy eye and Jane felt herself growing hotly uncomfortable, seeing herself as a brood mare and he a sweating stallion. A feeling of unease was enveloping her, triggered by the thought that Henry was far from tolerant of wives who failed him in the serious business of producing princes. Suddenly Jane felt suffocated by the very thought of being his bride and wished that it was not too late to turn back. But it was, by far. She was caught and now there was no escape.

Faintly she said, 'Your Grace . . . Henry . . . tomorrow is my wedding day and it grows late. I pray you excuse me for I would take to my bed in order to have a fresh face in the morning.'

He was all contrition and smiles, ringing a bell for her ladies and insisting that she be given a cool towel for her eyes and forehead.

'Till tomorrow,' he said, waving his fingers, then adding roguishly, 'as this is the first time I truly take leave of my bachelorhood, I would sit an hour or two with my Gentlemen. If you have no objections, sweetheart.'

He was playing a heavy-handed game of already being hen-pecked for the benefit of Jane's ladies, who all giggled obligingly, only Cloverella having the wit to say, 'I thought that stags at rut needed no permission to consort.'

The King shot her a withering glance but Cloverella was smiling so sweetly at him that he decided it must be a joke and roared with laughter, as did the rest of the assembled company. Jane had never been so glad to leave anywhere and proceed to her luxurious apartments, very different from the ones she had first occupied in the Palace of Whitehall. As she snuggled into bed, longing for sleep, she dismissed even her sisters, only Cloverella staying behind to tuck her in, as if they were girls again, laughing together in their bedroom at Wolff Hall.

'Will you read the ancient cards for me?' asked Jane, tired though she was.

179

Cloverella shook her head. 'Dr Zachary told me not to do so.'

'Why was that?' Jane said swiftly, very slightly alarmed.

'He said it is not wise to read for members of one's own family. That it gives insights that one is not meant to have.'

The same sense of unease that had afflicted Jane earlier, returned. '*He* is not going to do away with me, is he?' she asked in alarm.

'That I know will not happen.'

'How if you have not looked?'

Cloverella laughed. 'Because Dr Zachary told me so. He said that you would bear a prince for England.'

Jane smiled. 'He told me that too.'

'Then what are you worrying about?'

'Because he might not be right.'

'Dr Zachary,' answered Cloverella firmly, 'is very nearly always right.'

Jane slanted her eyes. 'I believe you have a soft spot for him.'

Cloverella's cheeks took on the shade of a springtime camellia. 'What nonsense! I admire him for his greatness as an astrologer, that is all.'

'Oh, I see,' said Jane with a smile, and almost immediately fell asleep.

In the hour just after midnight the wedding day began for the Palace servants, who were up and preparing the feast even before the King and his Gentlemen had stopped singing songs, some a little bawdy if their ears served them correctly. Even as Henry Tudor blew out his candle, the master cook was ordering more light by which to see the concoctions and confections forming beneath his skilled but overworked hands. It was not until the first fine threads of day pierced the gloom of the kitchen that he finally took some rest and wandered outside to see the dawning.

The day of the wedding was glittering, for there had been a heavy dewfall some hours before dawn and the grass and flowers shone like glass. The sun, emerging from the indigo east, was a circle of flame, piercing the vapour which floated veil-like, just above the river's surface, while the waterside Palace glowed rose red as the early rays struck its walls.

The bride, who had risen with the dawn, looked out and thought that such a joyful morning could be nothing but a good omen, and her natural good spirits returned as she thought of the glorious life that spread in front of her. Almost before it was light she had been bathed in musky oils, her hair washed and brushed until it shone like gilt, perfumed with such a heady mix of jasmine and herbs that when the King came to kiss it he would surely be driven mad with passion.

Beneath her garments Jane wore hose of silver and on her feet little silvered shoes, but nothing could be so fine as the satin wedding gown, made in a shade of light clear blue, like ice, the overskirt and sleeves elaborately embroidered in silver threads, the underskirt and undersleeves clustered with real pearls and trimmed with frothing lace. Round her neck Jane wore a choker worked with gems, the links in the shape of the letter J, and a longer necklace, encrusted with sapphires. Her hair, hanging loose about her shoulders, was crowned with a simple circlet, in which glowed one great sapphire at the front; while on her hands sparkled six rings, the one for her betrothal bearing a diamond as big as a quail's egg.

'Madam, you are the fairest bride upon whom it has been my pleasure to look,' said Norfolk, come to lead her to her wedding and now bowing fulsomely in the doorway.

Jane bobbed him a small curtsey – she was not Queen quite yet – and answered, 'I thank you, Sir.'

'So now if you are ready . . .'

'I am indeed.'

Laying her hand upon the Duke's arm and without further ado Jane Seymour set forth, her family walking in procession behind her to the Queen's private room in Whitehall Palace, where Henry and Archbishop Cranmer awaited her.

She thought afterwards that she had gone into the place plain Mistress Seymour and had come out again Queen of England, but that she herself felt no different, not even fully taking in the fact that the enormous man who sat beside her at the wedding feast was now her husband. Not even at that embarrassing moment when ribald jokes were told and she was led off by her woman relations and the female guests to be prepared for bedding, did anything seem quite real.

Jane stood meekly, clothed in a white nightgown, hoping that she looked virginal, while Cranmer blessed the marriage bed and prayed for a prince from the union of the King's Highness and the Queen's Grace.

Everyone, thought Jane dully, has to endure this awful public display, from the meanest ploughboy to the King.

But it made it no easier to bear.

And now, amidst a welter of bawdy noise from his Gentlemen, the King was taking off his robe to signify that all must leave. With Henry Norris dead, there was no one in that room, other than Jane, who had even glimpsed him in his nightshirt, or was allowed to, so it was Henry himself who drew the curtains round the great bed and waited until all grew quiet.

'My bride,' he whispered sentimentally. 'Oh Jane, do you realise, that you are at last my wife?'

'Not until consummation,' she answered provocatively, and sighed with delight as he immediately fell to kissing and touching her. In his lovemaking she could forget her fears and give herself up entirely to sensual pleasure, and this night was to be one of that indeed, as Henry almost lazily entered the deep and secret part of her body and slowly began to thrust both himself and her towards fulfilment. It seemed to Jane that this wonderful coupling would never stop, that her new husband was full of renewed strength as he explored and caressed every part of her body.

'In the morning they will look for virgin's blood,' she breathed.

'Let them,' answered Henry languidly. 'I know who spilt it and that is all that matters.'

A moment later it was over as together they reached the wild and breathtaking climax of love and slid down from it into a wondrous calm, Jane moulded against Henry's body like a child in a cradle. Afterwards she slept, her hair clouded round her face, her breasts bedewed with drops of sweat, her mouth still soft and smiling from the memory of lovemaking.

Let her be the mother of my boy, prayed Henry, staring into the moonlight. 'Let Jane be the one to bring forth a son.'

Then, quietly, he fell asleep too, as the last of the guests from the wedding feast made their way home and saw a star blaze forth in the firmament before shooting across the sky and fall away in a burst of sparkling drops.

## Chapter Fourteen

WITH A CHEERFUL WHISTLE escaping from his pursed lips, Signor Eustace Chapuys, letter-writer extraordinary, picked up his pen and with a flourish wrote, '1st January, 1537, Greetings to your Imperial Majesty at the start of another year.' Then he smiled to himself, thinking how well things had gone in the last twelve months for the party in whom he was interested and deciding, even though he had kept his royal master Charles, King of Spain and Emperor of the Holy Roman Empire, up to date with events as they had happened, to give him nonetheless a brief resumé of the past six.

'As Your Majesty will remember,' Chapuys wrote, 'a great deal of hope was raised when the King married Mistress Seymour that the Princess Mary would be reinstated at Court, and you will recall that after a great deal of trouble on the part of the new Queen, this came about. Yet not before the Princess, following the advice of myself and Secretary Cromwell, who explained to her bluntly the danger in which she lay, copied out a letter dictated by the Lord Privy Seal word for word in which she acknowledged her father to be the Supreme Head of the Church, I assuring her that the Pope would absolve her of guilt if she made secret confession to him.'

Chapuys smiled slyly. The effort to get Mary back to Court had been enormous. The Queen had begged for the Princess's company but Henry had refused even to see her. Finally, the poor wretched girl, the only thing left to her her beliefs, persuaded by her advisers that all she said and did would be pardoned by Rome, gave way and begged her father's forgiveness. On June the fourteenth, Henry's elder daughter had been summoned to Court where, lying prostrate at her father's feet, she had put her submission into words.

'How fond the King is of his child it is difficult to say,' the

183

Ambassador continued, 'but while she says and does all that he commands, he seems affectionate enough! But much is owed to the Queen who, in July, as Your Majesty will remember, presented the Princess with a valuable diamond, thus chivvying her father into giving the girl, so sorely neglected for so many years, a thousand crowns to buy her little pleasures.'

Chapuys smiled quizzically, his opinion of Henry daily becoming more and more contemptuous.

'No doubt,' he continued, 'you still smart from the letter which the Princess wrote you, informing Your Majesty that she had submitted to her father, but please remember the danger in which she lay and which she finally did realise, for she fainted at the King's feet on hearing him say to his councillors "Some of you were desirous that I should put this jewel to death", meaning herself.

'Of the other news, there still is no sign of the Queen being with child which, since the death of the King's bastard the Duke of Richmond, at the age of seventeen, puts Princess Mary closer to the throne. The other little bastard, the Concubine's daughter Elizabeth, is also back in the fold but dines at a separate table to that of the King, Queen and Mary.'

He stopped and poured himself a pitcher of wine, wondering if the King had no power left in him, as George Rochford had averred, and feeling just a little sorry for Jane, even though it suited the Imperialist cause for her not to bear a son. He picked up his pen again, and went on. 'The Queen herself, despite the fact she has not yet conceived, has had a merry summer, out and about with His Grace, but her Christmas keeping was tinged with sadness for her father, the venerable sage Sir John Seymour, died on 21st December and she was unable to attend his funeral, instead having to take part in a grand occasion, riding with the King in great state through the City.' Chapuys frowned and added, 'She has not yet had a coronation, the plans being postponed for fear of the plague, and now some say she will not have one at all as she is unable to conceive. As I have already told you, Majesty, I believe that no children can be expected because of the complexion and disposition of the King himself.'

He put down his pen, feeling that he had said enough, ending the letter with hopes that the Emperor fared well during the rest of the festivities and that the new year would bring him continued wealth and prosperity, coupled with good health.

His task done Chapuys crossed to the window of his apartments in Greenwich Palace and looked out on a landscape so bleak that the very sight of it set him longing for his native Spain. In all his years in England the Ambassador had never known a colder winter and to move around the palace was agony for him, scuttling down the draughty corridors through which the wind whipped raw from the Thames, to the nearest fire, then warming himself before he braved the next part of his journey.

It had started to snow on Christmas Eve, which even the Ambassador had had to admit lent a certain softness and sparkle to the start of the twelve day celebration. But since then it had barely stopped and Greenwich had turned into a winter palace, dripping with crystal cascades, its rooves and turrets sparkling beneath the moon, its windows traced with delicate diamond patterns of frost even by day.

Outside the land had been cleansed, purified, by the virgin white which covered it, familiar landmarks hidden and smoothed out so that Chapuys felt he dwelt in a strange anonymous country, far from anywhere known or charted. Only the trees, clad in their magnificent vestments, heavy with diamonds, stood to mark the places they had always held, proud and imperious; pleased it seemed with their glistening transformation. On the Thames, usually so fast flowing and swift, patches of ice had begun to appear, at first like spun glass, delicate and fine, a whirl of rainbows. Then the ice had started to thicken, white and dense as bridecake, yet hard as an axe.

It won't be long, thought Chapuys, looking from the window after rubbing his sleeve on a pane to remove Jack Frost's fine lacework, before people are on that skating. Who would believe it possible?

He turned back to his desk and added a postscript to the letter. 'It is small wonder, Majesty, that this is a land of strange occurrences and the King needs new wives to keep him warm, for the River Thames that runs through the heart of the capital looks upon the point of freezing over! With what fond memories do I remember the winters at home. E. C.'

And with that the Ambassador threw another log upon his already roaring fire and shivered at the very thought of making his way to the Princess Mary's apartments to dine with her that evening.

*　　*　　*

Even before she had fully awoken, Jane knew that during the night it had started to snow again, for there was an unearthly stillness everywhere and a lavender light at the window which meant that a dawn full of white flakes, swirling and dancing against the panes, lay beyond the walls of the palace. She thought then that there was no more pleasant thing in the world than to lie beneath a fur coverlet in a comfortable bed, watching the flames of the fire dance in shadow on the ceiling, and to think of the outside world, so bitter that every beast in creation had gone to its lair to survive.

And I am in mine, she thought, the cosiest lair in the kingdom.

She drifted into a doze and pretended, just for a wicked moment, that she had conceived a son and Henry had died before his birth so that she, Jane the Queen, became Regent of England, assisted by her brothers. Then a snore from her right-hand side reminded her that her husband was very much alive and that so far there was no sign of the longed-for prince.

Oh God help me this year, Jane prayed. I dread the next twelve months if I do not get with child.

The picture she had had of herself as a mare and Henry a stallion had in a twisted way come true, for he heaved at her at almost every opportunity and she, who had loved that side of their life together so much, now began to dread it. Every month as her flux came and she had to tell him again that they had not succeeded, a hard Tudor eye would glint at her, reminding Jane of a vicious old boar deprived of his feed. The conviction that one day he would dispose of her and take to wife some nubile creature still in her teens and bursting with fecundity started to haunt her nightmares, and every time the moon's cycle came and went and still she was infertile, Jane wept.

Once, but only once thank God, she had suffered the terror of the King's wicked fury. In the autumn of last year the northern part of the country had rebelled against Cromwell's dissolution of the monasteries; Lincolnshire and Yorkshire suffering much at Mr Secretary's vandalising hands. The insurrection, known as the Pilgrimage of Grace, rose to implore that the monasteries be restored, and the Prioress of Clementhorpe in Yorkshire had written direct to Jane to beg her intercession to save the nunnery. In a torment, for in her heart the Queen believed in the old faith and hated the rape of the abbeys, Jane had actually gone on her knees to

Henry and begged him to spare the northern monasteries, believing the rebellion to be a punishment from God.

Now, lying in bed beside him and remembering, Jane's teeth chattered. The King had turned on her such a look that she had known at once the fear which must have clutched the hearts of her two queenly predecessors. His face white as suet and as moist, his eyes two splits of spleen, Henry had raised his hand as if to strike.

'How dare you,' he had whispered, 'how dare *you*? Know your place, woman. I raised you up to give birth to my son not to interfere in matters that do not concern you. So hold your tongue, for you have no boy to save your head as neither did she whose crown you now wear.'

It was the first time, ever, that Henry had been angry with her, let alone threatened her life. She had felt so faint that she had been glad she knelt. Jane had lowered her lids, knowing that her pale face was bleached to the colour of snowdrops, and muttered pleas for pardon. But inside, even while she mumbled, a kind of hatred had been born out of the death of her trust.

Jane propped herself up on one elbow and looked down into the King's sleeping face. Her love for him had received a wicked blow that day and had never recovered since.

For after all, she thought as her sense of injustice rankled, I have been a good mother to his children, even getting Anne's bastard accepted back at Court, to say nothing of my endeavours on behalf of poor Mary.

The bulk beside her gasped in its sleep and turned over, pulling the fur coverlet and other bedclothes with it. Devoid even of covering on this bleak morning, Jane shivered afresh. Remembering how easily her husband could switch from lover to tyrant had frozen her to the bone and now she had nothing at all to warm her. With a muffled sound of annoyance she got out of bed and went to the fire, throwing on more logs to set the embers roaring up once more.

Though both the King and Queen had separate apartments in all of their palaces Henry, no doubt through his feverish desire to sire a son, had taken to spending most of his nights with her, only keeping apart at the time of her flux or when fatigue rendered him incapable. The matter of *her* fatigue, she noted bitterly, did not matter and even if she was half asleep, Henry would thrust away for dear life if he so desired. How George Rochford could ever have thought him impotent, Jane could not understand.

187

Unless, she wondered as she crossed to the window and gazed out, he meant it in the other sense; that the King can no longer beget children.

She shook her head, tired of worrying about it, and concentrated instead on the prospect outside. Before her stretched fairyland, a glittering winter landscape of frost and snow. The early morning fall was already dying away, leaving the ground utterly pure and unmarked except for the fresh prints of an animal and, sure enough, even while she looked she saw him. Jane watched as a beautiful red fox sported and rolled in the crispness, his coat picking up the flakes and dappling him white. Then he ran off, sinking thigh deep, as his hunger forestalled play and the quest for food became paramount.

She turned back to look at the bed where her husband stretched, just prior to waking up. Ever since he had vented his fury on her, Jane had adopted a certain way of dealing with him and now she stared slightly beyond him as she spoke.

'It is a fine crisp morning but cold, Your Grace.'

Henry yawned. 'Is it, my dear? Then you will have to wrap up warmly.'

He, too, had changed in manner since his outburst. Now he would often sound paternal, almost as if he was underlining the twenty years that lay between them. Jane sometimes wondered if it was his way of saying he was sorry.

'We can't have our sweetheart catching cold.'

The King was coy and his Queen felt a terrifying combination of revulsion and delight in being cherished. To hide her feelings she turned away, once more to look outside.

'I shall not be cold, Your Grace, for surely tonight the largest crowd of all is to be at the Palace to celebrate Twelfth Night. The very press of people should keep me warm.'

It was an answer that meant something else and Henry knew it.

'I was hoping my presence alone might protect you from the chill.'

Jane swung round to look at him but did not meet his eye. 'Of course it will, Sir, for in the company of yourself who could feel anything but heated?'

Henry got out of bed, pulling a robe about him. 'You are very formal today.'

Jane bobbed a curtsey to emphasise the point. 'Am I, Your Grace?'

He came to stand beside her. 'Yes, you are. I have obviously offended. What can I do to make amends?'

Jane thought rapidly, knowing that if she told him the real truth he would probably have her killed. 'Your offence is in your thinking, Sir, but if Your Majesty would enjoy a morning's sport, might we ride across the Thames?'

He stared at her, puffy eyes goggling. 'What do you mean?'

'I believe it to be frozen solid – or at least that is how it looks from here. When we were children, all of us at Wolff Hall, we would skate on the Kennet and run and ride on the ice. It was a wonderful sensation to walk on something that is another element entirely.'

The King stroked his chin. 'But supposing you are with child, might it not be dangerous?'

Jane looked at him boldly. 'I do not believe I am, Your Grace. Why, the last time you favoured me I was so tired I could scarce keep awake. My fault, of course, for walking far that day,' she added hastily. 'Still, I believe the mother must be participating for a child to be conceived.'

Henry turned on her a face of thunder. 'Then you must not allow yourself to get so fatigued. We have been married almost eight months. I sometimes despair of having a son.'

Jane crossed over to him, a small bit of her sorry for the heirless King. 'I am sure we will soon. It has been foretold me.'

'Then pray God the prediction is right.'

'Amen.' Jane paused then said, 'It is a wives' tale that if the woman is happy and relaxed her chances will be better. So may we ride upon the river?'

He nodded. 'Why not, if it pleases you. And let everyone come. I shall give it out that it will be today's pastime.'

'A rare treat for Twelfth Night.'

'Indeed.'

Two hours later the entire Court, in all its splendour, set forth. It seemed that everyone capable of mounting a horse was there, and in their winter trappings of furs and velvets, Jane thought she had never seen a finer sight than when the brightly dressed cavalcade crossed over the ice to the far bank to where an enterprising pedlar had set up a brazier and was roasting crabs. Several of the men, and some of the women too, had brought skates with them and, having reached the other bank, put them on and began to whirl about, cutting patterns in the ice. The King's Gentlemen, however, had with them sticks and a ball which they hit from horseback as they rode. With the colours of their clothes reflecting in the river's glassy surface and the fiery red sun above, Jane thought it looked as if they were all inhabitants of the Ice King's realm, quite unreal in their frozen splendour.

With a laugh of excitement she dismounted from her horse and took a pair of skates from a waiting groom. Then she was off, skimming like a butterfly down the centre of the Thames, with never a backward glance at her royal husband. In all that speed and elation she suddenly felt free, powerful, as if she could skate on for ever and never again have to worry about becoming pregnant or upsetting the tyrant; as if, if she went on far enough, she would find an undiscovered country upriver where she could dwell in peace amongst beautiful flowers, her companions sylvan characters who were merry all day long.

It seemed as if her fantasy was coming true, for she suddenly heard laughter behind her and turning, Jane saw that Edward, Thomas and Cloverella had left the throng and were skating fast to join her. She stopped and let them catch her up, then all four linked arms and skimmed gracefully along.

'What does this remind you of?' said Cloverella.

The other three looked at her, thinking she seemed radiant, her black hair escaping from her hood and her skin glowing with the cold.

'Skating at Wolff Hall?'

'Yes, that too, but more the day we saw the Kennet turn to gold and made our wishes on Merlin's Mound.'

'Mine has come true,' answered Jane slowly. 'Do you remember that I wished to be Queen?'

'How odd,' said Thomas. 'I had forgotten. But you are quite right, you did.'

'Well I wanted to own land and I certainly do now. So perhaps mine has as well,' put in Edward.

Thomas turned to him. 'But you said "all this", as if you meant the whole of Wiltshire.'

Edward smiled. 'Perhaps it has come half true.'

'I suppose mine has too. For I asked to know many beautiful

women before I married the highest in the land.' He laughed joyfully. 'And I have known several already!'

Jane tried to purse her small mouth but could not help but laugh instead. Out here in the middle of the winter wilderness, safe from Master Cromwell's spies, and with only her closest family near her, she could say and do exactly as she pleased.

'Well, the highest eligible woman in the land is the Lady Mary.'

Thomas crinkled his sea-blue eyes. 'Hmm, not very pretty – too short and gruff and bustling, and her gaze does stare so.'

Jane laughed gently. 'That is because she is short-sighted, poor thing.'

'And she is not completely restored in her father's favour despite your efforts, which must make her nervous.'

'I think she may yet be *fully* restored if I do not conceive soon.'

The other three stared at Jane in pity and eventually Thomas spoke high treason. 'Is it him? There are rumours . . .'

Jane blushed deeply but kept her head up; they were, after all, four country people. 'He is not impotent, if that is what you mean.'

'Aye, but can he breed children? None since Elizabeth, I reckon.'

'But what of Anne's miscarriage?'

'Smeaton's,' said Tom shortly. 'I've always thought so.'

None of them wanted to pursue that line of conversation, so Cloverella changed it. 'I will mix you a potion the Romanies use. I had heard my grandam speak of it, but Dr Zachary reminded me of its properties.'

'Zachary,' said Edward musingly. 'What has happened to him? He's not been seen since the death of his wife.'

'I believe he went to Calais with his children. No one has heard from him since.'

'A shame. A good fellow.'

'Yes,' said Cloverella very wistfully, and Jane shot her a searching look.

There was the sound of distant hailing and looking back, the four saw that some of the King's Gentlemen were drawing near.

'I think they want us to go back,' said Tom.

'His Grace has probably missed me.' And Jane sighed.

'Courage,' answered Edward. 'Take Cloverella's potion and we will probably end up with twin heirs.'

'Now that,' said Jane, 'would solve every problem I have.'

She felt a moment's intense happiness then, thinking how

191

glorious was freedom, before she linked arms again with her beloved family and they slowly and deliberately, without too much show of concern, skated back to where the King and his courtiers awaited them.

That night, being the last of the twelve days of festivity, there was to be a special banquet, a masque, and an entertainment of mummers and players, together with tumblers and a fire-eater. The Queen's brothers had organised the masking between them; a new venture for which they had begged permission of His Grace. More conscious than any other of the present strain on their royal brother-in-law and his wife, the Seymours had chosen a romantic theme for the entertainment, one of love in peril, happily rescued by a loyal heart. It was an old idea but knowing how well the King had once enjoyed a like display, Viscount Beauchamp, as Edward had now become, had commissioned from the carpenters a castle borne on wheels, complete with towers, cannon, a gate and a dungeon. In it, imprisoned, sitting amongst her ladies would be Jane, dressed in clothes of an earlier century, weeping into a handkerchief.

As soon as the banquet was underway, Edward ordered that the amazing contraption be pulled in and there was a moment's stunned silence whilst Henry, who had half guessed there was to be a surprise when Jane excused herself from the table, was seen to stare aghast before he, too, joined in the thunderous applause. Not since the days of two wives now dead had there been such a display and when Edward and Thomas, disguised as knights, came to the King's high chair with knightly clothes for him, he willingly joined the fun and donned his costume and mask.

It was some time since he had danced nimbly when similar masques had been arranged but now, despite the pain in his leg and his increased size, Henry entered into the spirit of the occasion, and with the other men made a mock assault on the castle. As the first signs of attack were heard, Jane's gaoler – none other than Sir Nicholas Carew disguised as a Turk – led her to the 'dungeon' where she wept all the more.

The Seymour brothers had already thought of the one possible flaw in the proceedings – Henry's entry into the castle to rescue his lady – and had organised that the boarding plank be specially reinforced. So that now with much goodwill and chuckling, having danced a few steps with every lady in the room, regardless of the pain it cost him, Henry hastened to the gangplank and into the wheeled contraption and clambered with difficulty down the ladder into the dungeon where Jane sat smiling at him.

It was hot and airless in the wooden castle and the King saw that his wife, in fifteenth-century clothes, had loosened the lacing on her bodice, thus exposing the tops of her breasts.

'My dear,' he said, laughing and keeping to his character, 'you are very forward. Should I leave you in prison? Perhaps you might overwhelm me.'

Continuing the pantomime Jane said, 'Oh, my lord, please rescue me, lest the cruel Turk ravish me. I would far rather die – unless you did take me,' she added in a lower tone.

Henry felt such a wave of excitement that it occurred to him that his drink might have been spiced with an aphrodisiac. 'I can hardly wait,' he said, realising as he did so that he was starting to tremble.

'You must,' replied Jane in a whisper. 'You must wait until this night is ended.'

As Sir Loyal Heart brought his lady out of the castle there was a tremendous cheer which was the sign for all the assembled company to dance. Everyone, old and young, stood up and jigged away at great pace. Henry, realising that his leg was no longer hurting him, bounded off with enthusiasm, vaguely aware that he was being watched by the little dark scrap attached to the retinue of Edward Seymour.

'She's a funny creature that,' he said to Eve Carew, who had picked him as partner in the general throng. 'Do you know, Her Grace told me the girl was stolen by her father, a stable boy, within hours of her birth, and was brought up by Romanies.'

'Yes, but her mother had died,' said Eve, and as she did so, for no apparent reason, went so cold that she shivered and Henry, thinking that perhaps there had been a tragedy in her family, danced her off at double speed, forcing her to concentrate on her flying feet.

The culmination of the masque had been carefully planned by Thomas and Edward: the rescued ladies would lead their knights off into the castle for refreshment and, amidst renewed cheering, it would be wheeled away. Whether the couples inside wished to return to the entertainment or discreetly vanish was left entirely to them.

'The potion you gave me to put into his wine, is it strong?' hissed Thomas into Cloverella's ear.

His cousin, her eyes sparkling, answered, 'The Romany girls use it to bring a lover to them and also to give him power.'

'What's in it?' asked Thomas, fascinated.

'Periwinkle, leeks and earthworms.'

'Ugh! Tell me no more for God's sake.'

The time had come. The six ladies, dancing all the while, were taking their partners towards the castle, while everyone else clapped. The King, his face transformed with passion, was being led by Jane like a lamb, unprotesting and very meek.

'It must have been that additional worm,' whispered Cloverella, at which Thomas turned his brilliant blue eyes on her, winked, then pretended to vomit.

Slowly the castle began to trundle off and the laughing crowd were left to see how many couples returned. Of the original six only two pairs came back and it was with a sigh of relief that the Seymours saw that Jane and Henry were not amongst them.

'May Dr Zachary's potion work,' said Thomas softly.

Cloverella looked at him innocently. 'Oh, that was not one of his. His is to aid conception and is made from raspberry leaf. It must be stored for use during the winter. But I had none. This is a special one my grandam used to sell.'

'It makes men of boys, I presume?'

'Dearest Thomas,' answered Cloverella, kissing him on the nose, 'it makes rams of goats!'

'Then for sure I don't need any,' he answered, and laughed, his eyes wandering round the room and settling on the Princess Mary who, even in the midst of making merry, still bore a gruff, unhappy air.

'If you will excuse me,' he said to Cloverella and bowed.

'Be careful, Thomas. Don't reach for the stars.'

'If I do, at least I'll touch the moon,' he answered lightly, and was off, the glow of the candles burnishing his hair to the colour of autumn gold.

By the light of the moon, Henry and Jane were making love as once they used; every movement, every touch, bringing them a million pleasurable sensations, every kiss a million joys. He, having drunk his fill of Cloverella's potion, felt young again, and took Jane as if

194

she were his bride, while she once more knew the passion she had originally felt for him. Tonight the terrible need for a son was forgotten by them both and they made love for pleasure, for desire and fulfilment, forgetting the pressures of the world about them.

'My sweet young wife,' whispered Henry, and Jane, forgetting his ferocity, answered, 'Dear husband.'

But as together they sought and found ecstasy Jane felt sure that there was something different, that tonight, as the twelve days of Christmas came to their brilliant end, she had achieved her heart's wish, that a new life, the life of a Tudor prince, had at long last been sown within her.

# Chapter Fifteen

EVERY BELL IN ENGLAND was ringing; in every church throughout the realm, from mighty St Pauls to the smallest Saxon cot, a solemn mass followed by a Te Deum was being celebrated for the quickening of the Queen's child. In every town and village bonfires blazed and hogsheads of wine were being put down, that all might drink without charge to the babe that was on its way. The Lord Deputy of Calais ordered celebratory guns to be fired off, and Sir William Sandys in Guisnes did likewise. Festivities abounded and there was no one in the kingdom who did not pray for the safe deliverance of a prince, particularly the delicate mother herself, who knew that her entire future depended on the outcome of this pregnancy.

As always in the summer months, an epidemic of the Sweat had broken out and Jane had been removed to the safety of Hampton Court with her entire entourage of ladies. And it was from there, with the Palace windows open and the Queen gone into the gardens to hear the sound of celebration, that the first bell rang out, only to have its message picked up and taken the length of the land, even the Regents of Scotland draining a quizzical dram as the Pursuivant of Berwick brought them the news.

All this, she thought, standing by the river and feeling the warm air blow through her loosened hair, 'all this and I am not yet open-laced. Oh God, let me not abort my baby now.'

But to the King standing beside her, bluff and big and definitely moist of eye, she said nothing. Jane had, by this pregnancy, moved into the position that every woman must envy; the pampered sweetheart of the King's majesty, the capricious wife whose every whim must be catered for. Quails had been her desire and quails had been sent for from Lord Lisle, the Deputy of Calais, from London to Dover, from Dover to Calais, with the order that if there be no fat birds available then the Deputy's servants were to speed to Flanders for them. Boxes of fat live fowl had been shipped across in a matter of days, that the Queen might have her wish and feast on dainties.

And now she stood by the river on Trinity Sunday, almost exactly a year from her wedding day, and felt the sturdy baby kick her hard. Laughingly she put her hand to her body.

'He is moving now,' she said, and saw Henry weep with pure joy.

'God grant us deliverance of a healthy son,' he said.

'Amen,' answered Jane fervently, 'amen, amen.'

And with that they joined hands and walked together to the chapel that they could pray, not only in company with the assembled Court but with the entire nation, for the prince that all hoped was to be safely born that autumn.

In the warm sunshine of that same spring François, King of France, walked with his pretty butterfly courtiers through the pleasure gardens of the Château of Chambord, that extraordinary turreted palace of four hundred and forty rooms, which boasted a chimney for every day of the year. The exquisite who was King liked to refer to Chambord as his hunting lodge, though this nonchalant description was pure affectation, for the Château was without doubt the finest in the valley of the Loire, while the gardens were splendid, a triumph and tribute to the men who had created them. Great golden beds in the style of the fleur-de-lys rose up out of vivid blue backgrounds, while amongst flowers like tongues of flame grew others in the shape of the royal crown or François's personal emblem of the salamander. Fountains leapt and cascaded everywhere and mirrors of water reflected the sky and all the sweet gaudy creatures who passed by them.

The King, who had once said that a court without women was like a spring without roses, walked surrounded by them, his vivacious favourite Anne, the Duchesse d'Etampes, on his arm. Behind him at some distance came the chillingly beautiful Diane de Poitiers, once the King's mistress but now the object of the Dauphin's obsessive adoration, despite the fact the widow was nineteen years his senior.

All of them, as they trooped past, were splashed with drops from the fountain and Anne d'Etampes stopped to count the rainbows in the sparkling plumes of water as she walked beneath a showery arch. It was a day of sheer enchantment and François, happy and relaxed, a handsome laughing peacock, was not well pleased when a liveried footman from the Palace came hurrying to find him, a look of some perplexity on his face.

'Well, what is it?' asked the King, thinking it would have to be a good reason for interrupting this blissful interlude.

'Sire, forgive me. I did check first with Monsieur le Comte, your aide, and he said you might wish to know.'

'Know what?' said François, intrigued.

'That there is someone at the Palace asking for Your Grace.'

'Who?'

'He looked a vagabond Romany to me, Majesty. Yet he claims that he knows Your Grace. He says he is Dr Zachary from England.'

'Zachary!' said the King, a grin spreading over his thin features. 'That old fox Norfolk's bastard! Show him into the gardens. I should like to see him very much.'

'But Sire,' answered the footman, somewhat distraught, 'he has children with him and they do not look well washed.'

François roared with laughter. 'And neither is he, I'll warrant.'

The servant smiled tentatively. 'Not very, Majesty.'

'You see!' said the King and laughed again until pretty Anne asked impatiently what could be the joke.

'An astrologer has arrived from England, my dear. And a good one at that. I think you will like him.' He turned to the footman. 'Tell him to clean himself up and then ask him to dine with us.'

A quickly masked look of surprise crossed the servant's face. 'And the children, Sir?'

'Let them be washed, too. Then they may go to the nurseries.'

Anne d'Etampes stared at François, astonished. 'You are asking a gypsy man to dine?'

'Zachary is not quite that, my dear. His father is the Duke of Norfolk and as to the man himself, why, I met him at Calais when our brother of England paraded the whore Boleyn for all of us to see. I spent a whole day with him. He is one of the most interesting creatures I have ever encountered.'

'I can't wait to meet him,' said Anne, wrinkling her superb little nose as a wicked smile came and went.

And an hour later when a freshly laundered Dr Zachary made his bow, she thought him attractive and gave him a searching look from beneath lashes that swept up long and thickly, partly due to the aid of a small round stick with which the Duchesse curled them both morn and night.

Anne d'Etampes guessed the astrologer to be in the early part of his thirties and liked his strong, squarish build, his broad nose and features and the tumble of blue-black curls that crowned his head. His eyes she thought a little frightening, for it seemed to her that they ran the gamut of every shade between green and gold, and could alter expression at will, capable of being both hard as steel or exciting as a new flirtation. At the moment, however, the look in them showed obvious appreciation of her charms, which pleased her. Anne gave a gracious inclination of her lovely head and the Doctor bowed so low that his hair brushed against the floor.

'Well, my boy,' said François, when Zachary had made his reverence. 'What are you doing at Chambord? Or even in France for that matter, I had thought to see you safely settled in England, tamed and domesticated.'

Zachary smiled and Anne appreciated the glint of strong white teeth. 'It would be difficult for me to be either, Majesty, but indeed I did try while my poor wife lived. But, alas, the plague claimed her last summer and, having nothing left to tie me, I brought my children to Calais to see whence fate might take us.'

François looked to where, sheltering behind their father but peeping round his legs, stood three children: a girl, fair as daffodils, with eyes the same fine blue as could be seen inside a church in summer, when the high sun casts down the reflection of stained glass. The two small boys the King took at first to be twins, though there were certain puzzling features in that conclusion. One was raven-dark with Zachary's Howard features and old Norfolk's light brown eyes, a clever child; the other round-faced, comely and cheerful, with golden hair streaked by red, and round eyes like forget-me-knots.

'*Are* they twins?' asked François, puzzled, and Zachary had the good grace to blush.

'They are half-brothers, Sir, for that one –' he pointed to the jolly boy – 'is the son of my mistress, Rosamund. While the other is by my wife. Only a few months separate them, but strangely the younger –' again he pointed to the golden-haired child, who grinned merrily – 'is the larger.'

'Well, well, well,' said François, raising a thin dark brow towards his hair, 'you *do* spread your talents about, astrologer!' Then he burst out laughing while the Duchesse giggled uproariously into her hand.

Zachary smiled too. 'It was profligate of me I know, Sire, but I have always found it hard to resist a pretty woman.'

He looked directly at the Duchesse who lowered her lids and smiled.

'Well, there are plenty of those at my Court, Zachary. I think it might be good sport if you and your brood stayed for a while this summer. There are many ladies here who would enjoy having their horoscopes cast, and your time could be profitably passed – in one way or another!'

The thin brow was rising again and Zachary felt his heart lift with it. He went down on one knee.

'Majesty, I will gladly take your offer. My children and I have travelled like Romanies across France, for that is the way in which I felt they could best learn. I myself lived roughly, as a gypsy, until my mother – died . . .' He hesitated over the word and the King wondered why. 'After that the Lord Duke my father sent me to a tutor and I became civilised. My children were born to better things but I wanted them to see the wonder of life before they grew too old. But now, like myself, they need to rest.'

'Then so be it. Welcome to my Court, Dr Zachary. Let us hope that we will learn much from each other.'

'Much!' echoed Anne d'Etampes and laughed naughtily once more while the children, at a nod from their father, came forward to be presented to the King of France.

The summer continued hot and long, ridden with Sweating Sickness, with London too dangerous a place to visit until the cold weather killed the infection.

Jane, who in early June had finally unlaced her bodices, filling in the ever-increasing gap with decorative stomachers of substantial size, roamed the gardens of Hampton Court with her ladies, thoroughly bored. Only the presence of her sisters, the young, but recently widowed Elizabeth, now in the full flower of a love affair with Gregory Cromwell, Master Secretary's son, and the boisterous Dorothy, Lady Smith, helped to pass the time with any modicum of pleasure. There was not even Cloverella to amuse them, for Anne Seymour, having borne a child in February, had temporarily retired from Court life, taking Jane's cousin with her. However, all were to assemble again in September in time for the Queen's confinement. Meanwhile, Jane passed the interminable months of waiting by supervising a change of wardrobe for her ladies, insisting that every one should have exactly one hundred and twenty pearls in her girdle and wear decorative hats, well trimmed.

Indirectly, a piece of interesting information came into Jane's possession through this preoccupation with clothes, for when Lady Lisle of Calais sent over two of her daughters with a view to their joining the Queen's entourage, the name of Dr Zachary, last heard of in that town, arose during the conversation, and the sisters saw a gleam come into the Queen's eye.

'So you know the astrologer's whereabouts? I would like to consult him at once. Where did you say he is now?'

'I believe he has been with the French King all summer, Your Grace,' answered Anne Bassett, the elder of the two. 'He came to Calais to see Lady Banastre's daughter' – the girl's cheeks deepened slightly – 'he has a child by her, you see. But then he went off, taking all three of his children with him, not even asking Lady Banastre's permission to remove the boy.'

Jane smiled. 'That sounds rather typical. But where is the Court at the moment?'

'I am not sure, Madam. Perhaps in Paris. But when the King goes to hunt in September they are bound for Chambord.'

'I shall write to him there and bid him return,' answered Jane determinedly. 'And you may take the letter with you and ask your father to despatch it with a fast rider. I want Dr Zachary here before the birth of my child.'

'Yes, Your Grace.'

Jane smiled again. 'But if, my ladies, you want to join my retinue this autumn then you will need to get yourselves different clothes. Have new bonnets made, edged with pearls, and two black gowns, one of satin, the other of velvet. And buy more material, less coarse than at present, for your smocks.'

Inwardly the Bassett sisters groaned. Their mother had kitted them up with an entirely new wardrobe for this visit and now everything in it seemed to be wrong.

'Of course, Your Grace,' said Anne, while her sister Catherine merely curtsied her downcast acceptance.

'Is the Queen not too fussy for words?' she asked later when they were alone.

Anne looked at her wisely. 'I believe that all of this is caused by worry over the forthcoming confinement. She has nothing else to think of at all, so she spends her time on frivolities.'

'Then we must get the letter to Dr Zachary. His arrival should take her mind off fashion for a while.'

'It is strange, is it not, that he has not returned to wish her well?'

'Yes,' answered Catherine Bassett, nodding. 'It is almost as if he is deliberately keeping away.'

The French hunting party was in Chenonçeau, the King's château built on foundations which rose up out of the very water of the River Cher itself, its only connection with land being a stone bridge. Tonight they were celebrating *en fête*, for the Queen had organised a masked ball by torchlight and the glittering reflection of the chateau, brilliantly lit, shone in the calm waters of the river as dusk fell over the valley of the Loire.

Lord Lisle's messenger, making his way from Chambord, whence he had been first directed, stopped his horse for a moment and stared. It was like fairyland, the little castle – so beautifully made with battlements and towers that were purely ornamental – rising up out of the water like an island. He thought to himself that he never had seen so lovely a sight, and decided when he had delivered the vital letter, bearing the seal of Queen Jane herself, that he would beg a night's sleep with the servants and see the miniature château at first hand.

On the bank, guarding the King's exquisite residence, loomed a round and formidable tower and it was to this that the messenger first reported, there being given permission to leave his horse and proceed on foot across the bridge and into the castle. Here he was once again challenged by sentries.

'I am about the Queen of England's business,' he called, 'and have ridden from Lord Lisle at Calais with a letter for Dr Zachary.'

'Then pass friend, all's well.'

But this was not quite true, for into a room leading from the left of the vaulted stone vestibule, a room with a balcony built out over the river on which the astrologer and the King stood in companionable silence, there passed through both men a sudden frisson at the distant sound of the messenger's voice.

Zachary sighed. 'What I have been expecting has happened. A letter had come for me from England.'

Frankly astonished at his companion's acuity, François stared at him blankly and Zachary continued, 'But I must not take delivery of it. I ask you to shield me, Majesty.'

Quite unable to follow, the King simply asked, 'Why?'

'Because the letter comes direct from the Queen of England.'

François shook his head, more puzzled than ever. 'Then why not read it?'

Zachary turned to face the French monarch, the reflected lights from the river shining in his face and hair, giving him a strange unearthly look.

'Sire, there is more to my reluctance than is apparent.'

'What do you mean?'

'When I told you the Queen would bear a son, I did not tell you everything.'

'Well do so now.'

'Her Grace is doomed to die, Majesty. She will not survive the birth of her boy two weeks.'

François looked aghast. 'My God, what a terrible fate. You are sure?'

'Positive. And that is why I cannot go back, as she has commanded. I cannot bear to face her when the end of her life is so near.'

The King stroked his long nose. 'No, you are right. It would be intolerable for both of you. I will have the messenger turned away, tell him you have already left us. He can sleep at the inn this night.'

Zachary squared his shoulders. 'But soon, Sire, when you leave to hunt, I must say farewell. I have accepted your hospitality long enough. This autumn when everything is ... finished ... I must return to England.'

'And your children?'

'They will go with me, of course. I want Sapphira well schooled, for one day I feel that by some miracle her speech might return.'

'You should pray to the Black Madonna of Rocamadour.'

'I already have, Majesty,' said Zachary, and smiled a little sadly.

'And what?' asked François, turning back to stare moodily over the darkening river, 'what future for our greedy brother of England?'

'Greedy in every sense,' answered Zachary sternly. 'For there will be other wives and yet another death.'

'Christ's mercy on us,' said the French King softly, 'tell me no more of it.'

And with that he strode from the balcony and into his study, holding his hands out to the fire that blazed in the hearth of an evening, shaking as if the night had grown suddenly cold.

Autumn came softly. The leaves on the trees ripened to richness and the sky at sunset was tinted the colour of wine. The air smelled golden, of harvesting, and gathering plums, and in the lofts apples were laid out in trays to keep for the winter, adding their crisp aroma to all the others. The long grass was cut for the last time that season and put aside to dry for fodder; everywhere preparations were in hand for an end of year that might well prove severe.

In the city the pestilence raged, even though the days shortened and the air grew cooler; while at Hampton Court a tremendous quiet fell over the palace as daily life seemed almost to come to a halt. It hung over Jane like a pall, all the heavy silence as she walked past interspersed with whisperings, then discreet stares, as though everyone constantly conjectured upon which day she would actually go into labour.

Dr Butts, who had once saved Anne Boleyn from the Sweat, now hovered the corridors of the Palace like a black moth, ready or so it seemed, to leap forward and attend the Queen, should she so much as hiccough. These were the most difficult times the girl had ever had to endure, living as she did in a state that swung violently between the extremes of hysterical anticipation and the crushing boredom of a guarded prisoner, no diversion capable of raising her spirits.

September was the happiest month, with the hottest days gone and both the Queen's husband and brothers returned from their various hunting parties. But still there was no sign of the summoned astrologer, who had now been in France some fifteen months. Longing for help, Jane suddenly found that she could be quite as imperious as her predecessor, and wrote to her sister-in-law, commanding Cloverella's immediate release from Edward's household so that she may permanently serve Her Grace.

'As I should have done months ago,' sighed Jane to herself as she signed the letter 'Jane the Queen', and put it into the hand of a messenger already dressed to ride.

'This is all, Your Grace?' he asked bowing.

'Yes,' she said, then changed it to, 'No'. 'Take another to my cousin who is also residing at Wolff Hall. I have certain instructions for her and I bid you ask her to fulfil them for me before she comes to Hampton Court.'

The man bowed again as Jane scratched the words, 'Go to Zachary's house and see if you can take possession of the black crystal from Venice. If he has it with him in France I know not what steps to take, for my letter cannot have reached him, yet I must know for once and for all if this is a boy that leaps so heartily within.'

'Go to, fast, and you shall be well rewarded,' she said as she pressed her seal into the wax. 'If you can be at Wolff Hall this night, all the better. But you are not to leave without Mistress Wentworth. You are to escort her to Greenwich to the house of the astrologer, thence to me. Make sure that this is done.'

The man bowed. 'Mistress Wentworth will be at your side within two days, Your Grace.'

Jane looked jubilant. 'Then I shall know all,' she said as the rider hastened to do her bidding.


The old woman who was acting as caretaker in Zachary's absence looked at the girl with the cloud of midnight hair who had come knocking at his door, with some suspicion.

'What do you want of him? He is in France and has been this year past. State your business.'

'My business is on behalf of the Queen's Grace,' came the quick reply, and the crone thought grudgingly that her lack of size in no way diminished from the girl's air of authority.

'So what is it, Mistress?'

'I have come to borrow his scrying glass that I may gaze for the Queen.'

The servant stared at Cloverella with her mouth dropping open. 'What?'

'You heard me well enough. I was once the Doctor's pupil and now I have come to consult his crystal. So let me pass if you will.'

'Aye,' said a burly man, appearing from nowhere. 'Let the Queen's lady pass.'

'He'll have my hide,' said the old woman furiously, 'if I so much as let you through this door.'

Cloverella turned on her a glorious smile. 'Tell him that his pupil has bathed in vervain and now nothing can be denied her!'

'But what of me?'

The dark-haired imp, already rushing up the stairs to Zachary's sloping room beneath the roof, paused. 'Don't be afraid. Whatever I borrow shall be returned within a night and a day. He will never know.'

'But he has taken the dark crystal with him, Mistress.'

'I thought as much. But something of his must remain, and I shall find it. It is my duty to know the Queen's future and whether she will bear His Grace a son.'

'Please disturb nothing. Dr Zachary does not like his study entered. Even I only go there to dust.'

And not very often at that, thought Cloverella as she panted up the final spindly staircase and swiftly entered Zachary's room, closing the door behind her while she looked round.

It was as if the astrologer had only just left it, just gone downstairs and would be back at any second, for his ambience within the place was tangible. Cloverella could almost smell his bodily scents, the herbs that he rubbed into his skin for cleanliness, the exotic perfume that he wore when attending Court. She felt that at any moment he would step out of a dark corner and touch her.

Boldly walking to the small window, Cloverella wrenched it open and the fresh air from the river entered the room, banishing some of the mustiness but doing nothing to dispel Zachary's presence, though the shadows lightened as the dusty panes were thrust back.

'Don't begrudge me this, Master,' said Cloverella aloud, and behind her something stirred.

She had never been more frightened, and in horrid response every nerve in her body leapt, while her heart lurched downwards. With the hairs rising on her neck Cloverella turned to face whatever had crept in behind her, making the sign of the cross as she did so. A fearsome cat with a knowing look on its face sat in the doorway.

Cloverella laughed in sheer relief. 'Oh, so you have sent your familiar out to do your bidding, have you?'

The cat slowly winked an amber eye, reminiscent of the colour of Zachary's own.

Cloverella advanced on it. '*Are* you his familiar?' It rubbed round her legs, arching its back and purring. 'Why, I believe you must be.

Then help me find his scrying glass or else his ancient cards. Though *I* know – and your master also – that my cousin Jane will bear a son, she needs reassurance.'

The cat backed away, its ears flat to its head.

Cloverella stared at it. 'What is wrong? What did I say amiss?'

She bent to comfort it but it retreated from her, jumping up on Zachary's desk and knocking something to the floor. Cloverella saw with a coldness of spine that it was a skull that rocked from side to side, disturbing the spores of dust. Yet again she stooped and then saw that the death's head concealed a small crystal. Picking up both, she took Zachary's seat and closed her eyes for a moment before she began to gaze.

For the rest of her life, Cloverella wished that this point had never been reached and yet could clearly see that it had been inevitable, to allow her to progress along her chosen path. She had asked Merlin for wisdom, had begged Zachary to take her as pupil, and now the consequences had come and she must face them with courage. But it was so hard and so painful, for even as she held the glittering sphere in a nerveless grasp she knew what she would see even before she stared into it.

Jane lay on her great bed, asleep and yet not. The paleness she had exhibited in life nothing compared with the wonderful waxiness which now consumed her. But it was not Jane any more, only a doll that she had turned in to.

'Oh God,' said Cloverella bleakly. 'I did not know. I did not know until this moment.' She must have spoken aloud, for the cat gave a mournful wail to echo her words.

The vision was changing. A voice was calling out, 'Edward, by the grace of God, right excellent and noble Prince.' And now a funeral bell tolled, sonorous yet bleak.

So that was how it was to be! The living child would kill its mother. Plain Jane, who had achieved so much, was to be snatched away in her moment of triumph. Endgame had been reached.

Cloverella never afterwards knew how long she sat motionless at Dr Zachary's desk. Hours probably, for the sun had sunk beyond the river and the room was almost in darkness, when the serving woman finally came up the stairs, the expression on her face both fearful and curious.

'Your manservant bids me to seek you, Mistress. He was afeared for you.'

Cloverella turned stiffly. 'Tell him to be at peace. I shall come down now.'

The woman shuffled in the doorway. 'What will you be taking with you?'

Cloverella shook her head. 'Nothing. There is no need. I know all that I must.' She stood up. 'Be careful not to imprison the cat.'

The servant looked puzzled. 'The cat?'

'There was one here.'

But of course it had gone, as silently and darkly as it had arrived. Perhaps Zachary had indeed guided her towards the truth, albeit almost too terrible to contemplate. With a puzzled sigh, Cloverella left the astrologer's home at Greenwich a wiser woman, and with a heavy heart rode through the darkness towards Hampton Court and Jane.

## Chapter Sixteen

IT SEEMED TO DR BUTTS that the screams coming from the Queen's apartments had somehow become frozen in the air so that, even with his hands over his ears, the echo of the terrible sounds was still audible to torture him.

Never, he thought, as near in his life as he had ever been to publicly weeping, has man or physician been placed in so intolerable a position. For the treatment of my patient is no longer my decision. Only the King can choose her fate.

He stood in the anteroom leading off Jane Seymour's bedchamber, listening to her calling to him through the open door. Calling and screaming; begging him to put an end to her suffering and make the child that was tearing her apart be born. And all he could do, for all his longing to rush in and crush the baby's head so that it could pass through the too-small space, was tell the exhausted woman to be calm, to let nature take its course. Had it been any other child he would have killed it immediately and let the mother live. But how could he lay hands upon the future Prince of Wales or, if matters came to the worst, the King's own legitimate daughter? Dr Butts shivered. If he lived to the ripest age the sufferings of Jane Seymour and his consequent predicament were something he would never forget.

Right from the start it had struck him, after a delicate examination of the Queen's abdomen during which her ladies had clustered round her, hiding her privy parts with cloths, that the child might be too big for its mother. He saw immediately that the stretching involved for one to leave the other would be an enormous effort for one so delicately built as Jane. And now, three days later, he was positive he was right, that the baby simply could not get out and that unless he cut the mother surgically and took the child away, it might well die.

Butts shuddered where he stood. The risk to the mother of such an operation was enormous and though he might, in less important cases, have saved one or other of them, now it was beholden on him to ensure that both survived. To make the situation a thousand times worse the King, nervous of the plague, had fled to Esher and could only be contacted by messenger. Jane had not only had to bear her agony alone but wait unendurable hours while riders thundered from one place to the other.

'Because I will not,' Butts muttered to himself, 'cut the mother open until I have His Grace's written consent to do so. I will not be forced to make such a momentous decision alone.'

He had performed the Caesarean operation twice before, the name – or so legend had it – coming from the great Roman leader Julius who had been taken live from his mother's womb. Yet on both occasions when Dr Butts had practised this particular surgical skill the mother had been dead and it had been only a matter of saving the child. There had been none of the tricky business of stitching the woman up that she might live on and healthily bear more children. The doctor felt faint at the very thought of what might lie before him. Not only was this mother alive, she was also the Queen of England.

His train of thought was interrupted by a bustling midwife plucking at his elbow. 'You must come at once, Dr Butts. Her Grace looks fit to leave the world.'

'Is she losing blood?'

'Not yet. But her breathing is laboured and shallow. I reckon we'll lose both mother and child if this labour goes on much longer.'

'She is too narrow to deliver the infant, that is the problem.'

'I know that, Sir. And I know the remedy for it, though it may be against the teachings of the Church.'

The physician rounded on the woman. 'Mind your tongue. I cannot listen to such treasonable words.'

'That's as may be. But the point is, how are we going to save them? Will you cut her open, Doctor?'

'Not without the King's permission.'

'But while you wait for that the Queen might breathe her last – and then what?'

The doctor's heart shrank. If the Queen was to die while he hung on for instructions from Esher, he could be in even more serious trouble.

'It seems to me, Dr Butts, that it is as dangerous to wait as it is to proceed,' said the midwife, speaking his thoughts.

Butts crossed himself. 'Then I must try to save them both. I have no choice. Prepare a strong caudle laced with enough poppy essence to render Her Grace insensible.'

'You're going to operate then, Doctor?'

'What other decision can I make?'

'None, Sir. They are both at last gasp.'

Even while he rolled back the sleeves of his long physician's gown and passed his knife through a naked flame, bidding his assistant Dr Chambers be ready with needle and gut, Dr Butts prayed, Let His Grace's message come soon. Let me be delivered from this final terrible verdict, God.

But the situation was not to be made easy and it was with great trepidation that Butts and Chambers, flanked by four midwives, stood on either side of the inert figure of the Queen, and contemplated the task that lay before them.

Rising like a small pale globe, Her Grace's abdomen, stretched tightly over the distended womb, looked inviolable. But seeing how still lay the child within, Butts knew he must act, though it was not lost on him that the early hours of the morning were the very time when the soul was most likely to fly the body.

'I pray for the safe deliverance of both mother and child,' he said aloud and as the midwives crossed themselves, plunged in his knife. In her sleep the Queen stirred and groaned but did not regain consciousness.

'Quick,' said Butts to Chambers, 'staunch the flow.'

And as his assistant gallantly leant across with towels, the abdominal wall opened to reveal the womb beneath. Now there was nothing for it. Dr Butts cut rapidly, instantly revealing the baby's shoulders.

'Quickly, let me get the head,' called the midwife and almost thrusting the doctor aside, eased the child gently upward and out through the incision.

'Oh Christ's Holy Mother,' said Butts, bursting into tears. 'It's a boy. We have a Prince.'

'Aye, and let's hear him shout,' and with that two of the other women took the new-born infant and while one cleaned his eyes, nose and mouth, the second tapped him on the buttocks to bring him to life. The child let out a lusty cry and every adult in the room wept with him, for a moment forgetting the Queen who lay unattended and bleeding on her bed. It was Dr Chambers who suddenly remembered his other patient, and swinging round, began the primitive business of stitching her back together again with catgut taken from the intestines of a sheep. As he did so her eyelids fluttered and the doctor could but hope she would remain unconscious long enough for him to finish his task.

Outside the bedchamber the Palace was beginning to erupt with noise as the news spread like wildfire that the Queen was delivered of a healthy son. Courtiers hastened from their beds to foregather in the great hall, while the Seymour family, who had not retired at all, surged towards the royal apartments, demanding to see their sister, only to be pulled up short with the news that she was resting.

'There's nothing wrong is there?' demanded Anne suspiciously, to be assured by Dr Chambers that the Queen was in fine spirits but still recovering from her ordeal. Yet the truth behind the closed door was very different as Jane swimmingly regained her senses to know by the soreness of her body that the child had been finally ripped from her and now there was nothing further to do but lie exhausted on her pillows, almost forgotten in the tumult.

As soon as he had satisfied himself that the Prince would live Dr Butts dictated a letter to the King, which went off at post haste to Esher.

'Tell him,' said the physician happily, 'that he may ignore my other communications. That I acted as I thought best and my decision has been justified. For the operation has been completely successful, both Her Grace and the Prince being in marked good health.'

It was a gross exaggeration of course but Butts dare not risk putting doubt into the King's mind about his physician's ability. If anything untoward should happen it could be blamed on so many things – eating incorrectly or getting cold, to name but two.

Yet, thought the doctor, I must do my best for the poor soul. And he hurried off determinedly to supervise the brewing of a strengthening caudle which, with luck, might bring some colour back into the Queen's ghastly cheeks before His Grace arrived and demanded to see her.

The news of the birth of a healthy Prince swept the length and breadth of the kingdom and there were few who did not fall into

212

bed consumed with liquor on the night of the announcement. Bonfires flared everywhere, church bells rang crazily, Te Deums were chanted to attempt a show of solemnity, and guns boomed forth in all the King's territories. There was not one unhappy person in the land. Only the infant's mother wept as she tossed uncomfortably in her great bed, every stitch throbbing as if it were on fire.

Her family had seen and congratulated her and in their hour of triumph none had noticed that her usual pallor was now the colour of wax, with two high bright circles of red on each cheek. Only Cloverella, lingering longer than most, had managed to whisper a request that she might treat her cousin's wounds with herbal remedies, to be overruled by the doctors and midwives who considered the Queen their property and wanted no interference from a Romany, however well connected. There had been an actual confrontation between the insolent sprite and the eminent Dr Butts when it had come to the subject of Jane's involvement in the infant Prince's christening.

'You cannot subject her to such an ordeal only three days after you have cut her open. It might kill her,' Cloverella had said angrily.

Dr Butts had smiled down urbanely at the great-eyed girl regarding him so fiercely. 'Madam, the Queen is my patient, not yours. Furthermore, as you well know, it is the custom of our realm that a Prince's mother take part in the ceremonial of his baptism. So I would urge you to put aside your objections.'

'My objections,' Cloverella had answered earnestly, 'are based on a precognition that my cousin Jane might well die.'

Dr Butts had looked at her horrified. 'You speak unspeakable words, Lady. I would suggest that this conversation is terminated.' And with that he turned on his heel, refusing to converse with Mistress Wentworth further.

So, ignoring better judgement, they had lifted the exhausted Jane up out of her sick-bed and dressed her in a mantle of crimson velvet furred with ermine, the great weight of which pressed into her wounded body like knives. Somebody had painted her face unnaturally bright, a doll's vacant look blotting out the lines of suffering beneath a layer of enamel. Then she had been placed on a state couch, decorated with the crown and arms of England and draped with a counterpane of scarlet and a coverlet of white lawn, which had been hoisted high into the air and carried to an ante-chamber. There her husband had awaited her, boisterous, merry and somewhat inebriated, and thus Jane had remained, while the long line of guests filed past to be presented before forming up into a great procession making its way to the chapel.

The plague which had kept the baby's father away from his wife's side while she was in travail, had also curtailed the number of guests. Nonetheless, a vast multitude packed the Palace to see the parade set forth from the Queen's chamber and note how well she looked, her cheeks so vivid and her eyes so sparkling, bright from the potion she had drunk to strengthen her for the ordeal.

Amidst a blare of trumpets, every note of which seemed to burst in her head, Jane watched the cavalcade set forth. First went the King's Gentlemen, accompanied by the squires and knights, carrying candles which would remain unlit until the ceremony was over. Behind them walked the clerics, the members of the Council, the great lords, the officers of state and the foreign ambassadors, Chapuys twinkling amongst them. Next strode Thomas Cromwell, now Lord Privy Seal, with Lord Chancellor Audley and Cranmer, the Archbishop of Canterbury. Behind them progressed a figure much despised in certain circles – Anne Boleyn's father, the Earl of Wiltshire, walked solitary, a towel for use at the ceremony hung about his neck.

Less painful than an axe, thought Norfolk, whose place, as principal peer of the realm, was directly behind that of the Lady Elizabeth, now four years old, and clutching in her arms her half brother's chrysom, his golden christening robe. Because the King's daughter was so small she was carried shoulder-high by Edward Seymour, the Prince's uncle, to be created Earl of Hertford later in the week. Directly behind walked Thomas Seymour, winking his eye at the little redhead and making her smile, he, too, to be honoured at the special investiture with a knighthood. Almost at the very end of the procession, behind the Queen's ladies and midwives, snuggled into the arms of the Marchioness of Exeter, whose husband was first cousin to the King, came the infant Prince himself, carried beneath a canopy of gold, the four corners of which were supported by the Marquis, the Duke of Suffolk, the Earl of Arundel and Lord William Howard. Finally walked the Princess Mary who was to be her half-brother's godmother.

With another loud trumpet bray the procession vanished out of Jane's sight, proceeding along drafty corridors, through the Council Chamber, the King's Great Watching Chamber and the Great Hall, whence it threaded its careful way down the stairs into Clock Court and through the cloisters to the chapel door, where it halted and entered in reverential silence.

The baby was released by the Marchioness to the Archbishop, who himself performed the ceremony, assisted at the solid silver font by Sir Nicholas Carew, Sir Francis Bryan, Sir John Russell and Sir Anthony Browne. But it was Mary who held the baby tightly, almost as if he were her own, during the rest of the ceremony, his parents not being present by decree of ancient custom.

Around midnight Garter in ringing tones announced, 'God of his Almighty and infinite grace, give and grant good life and long to the right high, right excellent and noble Prince, Prince Edward, Duke of Cornwall and Earl of Chester, most dear and entirely beloved son to our most dread and gracious lord, King Henry the Eighth,' and the long ceremonial was finally over. Torches were lit and the trumpets burst forth once more, to announce the return of the newly christened child.

In the Queen's ante-chamber poor Jane, who seemed in a frightening state of elation, forced herself to even further effort, for it was her voice, and hers alone, that must be the first to welcome the Prince by name, giving him the maternal benediction. Turning to Cloverella, who had refused to go with the others to the chapel, preferring to stand for the whole two hours behind her cousin's couch, she murmured, 'Prop me up a little, sweetheart, for I feel I have slipped down low to greet my son.'

But though it was said in a whisper, the King had overheard and was on his feet, placing his great hands on either side of his wife's shoulders and heaving her into a sitting position. Cloverella saw Jane wince with pain as she was pulled so abruptly by a man too powerful ever to be really gentle.

Cloverella leaned over her cousin. 'Your Grace, you don't look well. Is there anything I can get you?'

Jane smiled. 'I am *very* well, my dear. Why, this is the most exciting moment of my life; to greet my little son fresh from his baptism.'

'But after you have blessed him you must go to bed. Please, Madam.'

Jane gave Cloverella an unreadable look. 'Oh yes, I shall. I think afterwards I will sleep for a very long time.'

Her cousin went cold, remembering the doll-like creature in the crystal and thinking how like it Jane looked now, her garish face beginning to run slightly. But Cloverella was unable to reply, for the King, huge with pride, was suddenly jumping to his feet, shouting, 'I believe they are returning. Why, yes, I can hear the trumpets.'

He thundered a kiss on to Jane's scarlet lips and then hugged her impulsively. Cloverella watched, powerless, as sweat broke out on the Queen's brow and would have intervened, even telling the King himself to watch what he did, had not the tinny trumpets blown at the very doors, which swung open to reveal the whole motley crowd.

With enormous pomp Edward was carried to where the Queen awaited him and while the Ladies Mary and Elizabeth, hand in hand, curtsied before their father and stepmother, Jane blessed the child and wished him a long and happy life, then kissed him on the brow. It was over! The baby was handed back to the Marchioness and amidst cheers of elation and a royal fanfare, Jane's couch was lifted shoulder-high, that she might return once more to her bedchamber.

As the crowd formed into two lines, all making reverence as the Queen and her ladies passed through, Cloverella was swamped with the knowledge that soon these very same people would be assembling again to make a final act of homage to the dead.

Five days after the Prince's birth, which had been on St Edward's day, 12th October 1537, the Queen of England became ill and received the last sacrament, much to the astonishment of those who had thought how brilliant she had seemed at the child's christening.

Her brothers, both to be honoured that very week, flew into a panic which was typical of neither of them, and met together in secret to discuss the awful probability of the death of their sister.

'I simply can't understand it,' said Edward, 'she seemed to recover from the birth so well.'

'But she was cut open, Ned. That is far and away more dangerous than the normal delivery of a child.'

Edward, several times a father himself, answered, 'I know that,'

216

while Thomas was silent for a moment, shaking his head and stroking his guinea-gold beard. 'I love Jane,' he said eventually, 'and now I fear her end is near.'

'Have you spoken of this to Cloverella?'

Thomas looked bleak. 'No, it is my own intuition. Jane and I were close, Ned. We played together. It was you who always seemed elderly and grand to us.'

One of Edward's rare and beautiful smiles crossed his normally serious face. 'That is because I was . . . and still am.'

Just for a moment the two brothers shared an enormous affection, Ned ruffling Thomas's hair, while he mimed punching Edward in the chest.

'I pray she lives,' said Ned, pulling his brother close to him.

'Amen to that.'

They stood quietly, arms round each other's shoulders, relishing the bitter-sweet sharing of sorrow. And then, slowly impinging on their consciousness, came the distant noise of heavy running feet to break their mood. The noise stopped at Edward's door and turned into a moderate but persistant knocking.

'Who is it?'

'Me. Dorothy. Your sister.'

'Then come in.'

Lady Smith needed no further bidding but flew through the entrance in a state of great excitement.

'Jane has rallied,' she said, 'Her Grace the Queen has sat up in bed and demanded quails, her favourite food.'

Thomas and Edward gazed at each other in a rare astonishment that slowly turned to laughter.

'Then may God be praised and thanked,' said Tom, visibly wiping his eyes. 'She had me frightened, the little wretch.'

'Remember of whom you speak,' answered Edward smiling. 'We'll brook no familiar talk of the Queen's Highness.'

'Queen's Highness be damned,' whispered Thomas, pulling the other two conspiratorially close. 'She'll always be our funny little sister, won't she?'

'Always?' echoed Dorothy, and was surprised to hear that she had spoken the word as a question.

Dark hours beyond midnight, and a small dark person escaped into the Palace gardens to sit beneath a tree and stargaze, to look upon the icy firmament and wonder. Beneath its inexorable, eternal stare she became diminished, unimportant, seeing the work of the immortal hand and wondering at its vast, incredible, impartial meaning. Simultaneously Cloverella was at one and at odds with all she saw and felt.

Within the Palace of Hampton Court, her own dear cousin, her childhood friend and confidante, lay dying, there was no doubt about that. Jane had rallied briefly, attended the state christening which had been too much for her and had, in fact, killed her, then had grown stronger and ordered her favourite foods. But now, one short week later, it was obvious that the little owner of such cut and painful flesh could struggle no more and was about to slip quietly away.

'Jane, Jane,' sobbed Cloverella as she suddenly found that, unbidden, the Romany blessing for the dying was on her lips.

'Only prayer can save the Queen's Grace, Sire,' said Dr Butts solemnly. 'If she can fight through these dark crisis hours and see the dawn, then she will live.'

'God's Holy mercy,' answered the King, hiding his face behind his hands, 'it is too much to bear. Why must my great joy be so diminished by grief?'

'Take heart, Your Grace,' answered Butts soothingly. 'There is still hope, though it be but a slight one.'

From where he stood it was impossible to see the King's expression behind his shielding fingers, so the physician, though wary, was not quite prepared for what happened next. Henry suddenly lowered his hands and Butts realised aghast that his expression had changed from that of grief-stricken husband to one of furious accuser. His eyes were glinting slits, like those of a charging boar, and a fleck of saliva dappled his lip.

'Butts,' he hissed dangerously, 'is this your fault? Have you killed the Queen's Grace by ripping her asunder?'

Inwardly the Doctor shuddered, though his face remained impassive. 'Your Grace, if I had not removed the Prince's Highness by surgery then I fear he would not have survived. An infant grows dangerously tired if his mother labours long,' he answered expressionlessly.

'Oh,' replied Henry gruffly. 'I see.'

Hit him on the raw, thought Butts. He would rather sacrifice a dozen Queens than lose his precious heir.

Aloud he said smoothly, 'Her Grace no doubt has somehow taken a chill and perhaps been fed incorrectly. Allowing her to eat quails was madness, and against my wishes.'

'Then why did you let her?' Henry asked coldly.

'Because I was not consulted, Majesty. The damage had been done long before the matter came to my attenion. These foolish waiting women . . .'

He allowed his voice to fade away, having no wish to name names and make accusations when he knew full well that the Queen was dying of something he had observed often before, a type of fever that set in after childbirth, usually with fatal consequences. As to what caused it, Butts had no idea, but he was certainly not going to tell the King the truth, thus giving his sovereign an excuse to accuse him of negligence.

'But where there is life there is hope, Sire. I shall not leave the Queen's side until she is out of danger.'

'In one way or another!' Henry answered heavily. 'But what of her family? Should they be called?'

Butts hesitated. It was his own certain conviction that the Queen would not last the night, yet the last thing he wanted was to alarm Henry unduly.

'If they could bid her goodnight perhaps. I would not want the Queen's Grace disturbed by their remaining long.'

'But *I* shall keep vigil,' answered the King fiercely. 'You'll not turn me out, Butts.'

'Your comforting presence is a different thing entirely,' the doctor said uneasily.

They were summoned from their quarters: Edward and Anne, Thomas, Dorothy and Clement Smith, Elizabeth and Gregory Cromwell. Only Cloverella was nowhere to be seen as the family gathered round the bed to stare down at the small shrunken figure, its eyes closed, its face like tallow, that breathed so stertorously, obviously fast hastening out of life.

The two brothers stared at their sister bleakly. She had done so much, raising them up to high degree and making them two of the most important men in the realm, the uncles of the future King of England. At that moment they grieved not only for the dying Queen but also for what her loss would mean to their future ambitions, while Anne Seymour, to her eternal shame, only thought that in

219

future she would not be able to claim a Queen for her sister-in-law.

It was Elizabeth and Dorothy, hugging each other as they sobbed, who suffered most, crying for all the splendid time of youth, before Jane grew up and left them to go to Court.

And as though this set a train of thought in motion Elizabeth asked, 'Where is Cloverella?'

It was Thomas who answered, 'Gone out to grieve like a gypsy,' to which Edward whispered, 'Would Jane like to see her?' knowing as he said the words that they were meaningless, that his sister was beyond seeing or talking to anyone ever again. For whatever fever had held her in its grip had now driven her beyond delusion to dreams. Jane lay without moving, her eyes firmly closed.

'Let it be,' said Thomas. 'Let it be.' Then he wept.

Edward turned away for a second, before bracing himself. 'We must bid Jane farewell,' he said. 'His Grace waits in the ante-room for us. I fear that we shall not see our sister again in this world and we must pray for her immortal soul.'

The Bishop of Carlisle, Jane's almoner, stepped from the shadows by the great bed and sank to his knees with the others as they begged God to look with love upon all that was left of their sister Jane Seymour, the plain little girl who had, in the manner of fable, become a Queen. And while they prayed, in the cold October moonlight Cloverella picked autumnal flowers fit to lay at the feet of one whose life was finished and done.

'Oh my cousin,' she said, stroking the petals as if they were fingers, 'remember all the golden days of childhood. Think of them now, my darling, as you start upon your lonely journey.'

In the Queen's bedroom, from whence all the Seymours were now gone and only Henry Tudor waited by his wife's side, a faint smile seemed momentarily to play over her waxen features.

'Look, she moves,' called the King to Dr Butts.

'Alas, Sire, I fear it to be the last great sigh of death.'

'Oh no,' said Henry into his clenched fist. 'Don't let her go, who has given me so much. Don't let Jane die.'

The Bishop of Carlisle, hovering and anxious, at this raised a questioning brow to the doctor and at his nod began a solemn chant for the Queen's passing spirit; while beyond the Palace Cloverella, feeling Jane's departure, sang to the moon of death and birth before she fell to her knees and prayed like a Christian.

Only the Queen, who lay in her hair spread like a halo, and in whose marble face two vivid eyes had slowly opened to stare sightlessly at the intricate carving of the ceiling, seemed supremely tranquil and undisturbed as in the darkness a grieving King wept for her loss alone.

# Part Two

# The Ardent Swain

## Chapter Seventeen

DURING THE NIGHT a wind with frost on its breath blustered over the Channel, whipping up wild horses and showering their manes with drops of ice. It boomed in the sheltered harbour, driving the ships at anchor into a frenzy, leaping and dancing an enormous hornpipe, pulling at their moorings as though they would break free and sail home, while behind the fortified walls the town shivered at the onslaught as slates, lashed by the tempest, crashed down from roofs on to the cobbled, winding streets below. The flags which presently hung festively from all public buildings and many private, whirled round their poles like dancers, while the timbers of the ancient houses creaked and the sails of a great mill standing on the cliffs beyond the city walls spun like a wheel.

Beneath the attack the town of Calais seemed to close in to protect itself, the wooden houses and taverns – The Sign of the Ship, The Three Heads, the Crosskeys – leaning anxiously towards one another. In the Exchequer, the stout building in which illustrious visitors to Calais were traditionally lodged, the Lady Anna of Cleves turned her solemn face, scrupulously scrubbed and shiny, into her pillow to block out the sound of the wind.

Sir Thomas Seymour, playing chess late with his pale-eyed cousin, Francis Bryan, in lodgings a mere stone's throw from where lay the royal bride, looked up from the board and crossed to the window.

'I doubt there'll be a sailing tomorrow if this goes on,' he said over his shoulder.

'It's less than two weeks to Christmas. I hope we're not holed up here for long,' came the immediate reply.

Thomas turned and smiled, his splendid eyes shining. 'Would you miss your friend?'

'You may leave her out of the matter. I was thinking only how difficult it would be to entertain the Lady Anna for several days when she speaks not one word of English.'

'And, if rumour is true, has no ear for music either.'

Francis raised his brows and shook his head, saying no more, and it was left to Thomas, after checking that there was no one lurking outside, to whisper, 'Moreover, it is not as if she is endowed with beauty to compensate for these lacks. By God, I would have thought her to be the last bride on earth for His Grace.'

Once again Bryan shook his head in silence and Thomas chuckled. 'Afraid to comment, Francis? Have you grown lilyish?'

Bryan's grey eyes looked at him without blinking. 'One day, Tom Seymour, I swear you will lose your head. You play risky games. Until His Grace has denounced the Lady Anna as the ugliest whore in the Kingdom I shall sing her praises night and day.'

Thomas laughed wryly. His sardonic cousin had always used that trick, speaking slanders in the form of rebuke.

'Aye, aye. Sing away until the tune changes.'

'Which I vow it will,' answered Bryan softly before returning his full attention to the chessboard, while Tom left his contemplation of the bitter night and threw another log on the fire before mulling his spiced wine with a hot poker.

'At least he mourned her decently,' he said to himself as much as anyone. 'At least poor Jane was given time to grow cold before His Grace took another bride.'

Francis Bryan nodded but did not reply. He knew as well as did Tom Seymour, delude himself as he might, that enquiries had been afoot for another wife for the King before Jane had even been laid in her grave, but that despite Henry's longing to refill swifly the royal marriage bed it had nonetheless taken two years to find a suitable bride.

The beautiful Christina Sforza, sixteen-year-old widow of the Duke of Milan, had been Henry Tudor's first choice, but that spirited girl had answered that only if she had *two* heads would she put one at the disposal of the King of England! Greatly rebuffed, Henry had cast round the whole of Europe to find a wife.

Bryan smiled to himself. Henry Tudor had sufficiently poor judgement to suggest to François, King of France, that he should bring the three sisters of Guise – Marie, Louise and Renée – to say nothing of Anne of Lorraine and another nubile princess, to Calais, under the chaperonage of François's Queen, there to parade before him.

In a bizarre beauty contest, thought Bryan wryly.

The French King's reply had been satisfyingly stinging. No noble woman of France would trot out like a hackney at a fair to be inspected by Henry. His brother of England must seek a bride more decorously.

The negotiations with young Duke William of Cleves, Juliers and Berg for one of his sisters had been opened by Thomas Cromwell, the man who had so caustically nicknamed Bryan 'The Vicar of Hell' for his part in the downfall of the Boleyns. Both Amelia and Anna of Cleves were at present available on the marriage market, and flattered by a King's interest. Master Hans Holbein, Henry's court painter, had accordingly been sent out to strike their portraits in oil, and Cromwell had virtually made the King's choice for him. Anna in particular had a beautiful face and figure and outshone Christina of Milan as the sun did the moon, or so Thomas said. The King had been convinced. Without setting eyes on his future wife he had signed the marriage treaty on 6th October 1539.

And yesterday the welcoming party, led by the Lord Admiral the Earl of Southampton, arrayed in their finest clothes, had received the Lady Anna into the pale of Calais. The Admiral himself had been resplendent in a coat of purple velvet, cut on cloth of gold, tied with great aiglettes and trefoils of gold. Thomas Seymour and Francis Bryan had, however, almost eclipsed him, each wearing such a glinting mass of chains about their necks and shoulders, Thomas's in particular being of most unusual design and great value.

The Lord Admiral had made low obeisance before the Lady Anna, who had blushed scarlet, aware that the eyes of everyone in the welcoming party were upon her. Then, while the guns of the town boomed and an answering salute fired from the King's ships lying at anchor in the harbour, his bride had been escorted into English territory through the Lantern Gate.

'God's blood but she's plain,' said Thomas, remembering. 'But then so was my poor sister. The Lady Anna may yet please.'

Carew took Thomas's rook before he looked up. 'I think not, Tom. Remember His Grace is not far off fifty now and swelled up huge.'

'So?'

'So it will need a beautiful woman to arouse passion in him these days. That, or a wanton.'

227

Thomas guffawed, repeating the word 'wanton' before he said, 'Keep your voice down for the love of Christ. *You'll* end a traitor yet.'

Bryan smiled slowly, his cold eyes unblinking. 'That could happen, I suppose.'

'Perhaps the Lady Anna is skilled in the arts of love,' whispered Thomas as he resumed his place. 'You know what they say about ugly women.'

'We shall see,' said Bryan, as he thoughtfully refilled his wine cup.


On Christmas Eve, just as the Milk Gate into the town of Calais was being closed against the night, the watch bell having sounded for half an hour to give due warning, and one of the porters having raised his staff to knock upon the gate to mark its closing, a party of four travellers hurried through, the great gale which kept the royal bride still marooned in the city puffing at their heels.

The Controller's Clerk – always present at the opening and closing of the entrance into Calais – pulled his hat closer about his head, raised his lantern to see the late arrivals, and called out to them for their names, it being his sworn duty to mark the coming and going of all visitors to the King's citadel. Then, having noted down that they were the family of Howard, father and three children, passing through Calais prior to sailing for England, the Clerk signed them in for the night telling them where they could find Strangers' Lodging.

'Though the town is full mark you,' warned the Clerk, 'the Lady Anna's retinue and welcoming party taking up a great deal of room, plus those who have come into the city to pass Christmas.'

'But there is space somewhere surely?' asked the man, the light from the Clerk's lantern shining on his broad nose and coarse tangle of black curls.

'Try the Widow Lucas's or, failing her, Adrian Dogan's house. According to my records they have beds.'

The stranger nodded his thanks, marshalled his tired little flock about him, and strode out of the lantern's range into the bleakness of the night.

'Howard,' said the Clerk thoughtfully, staring after him. 'Zachary Howard. That name seems well familiar.'

And he was still puzzing over it as he packed up his things, the watch having now been set beyond the walls by the Marshall's

Deputy and the wickets of both the inner and outer gates securely locked and barred for the night. The order of the Keys was already forming up – the Master Porter, the Gentleman Porter and ten others – ready to carry them into the town to the King's Deputy, Lord Lisle. And it was behind this small procession that the Clerk and his assistant now marched to rejoin their families, and the fish supper that every burger of Calais was enjoying that night, it being a religious feast and therefore a fast.

This eve of Christmas the Lady Anna and the Lord Admiral were dining with the Deputy in his residence, while the rest of both bridal and welcoming parties fed in their lodgings. Tomorrow, to start the twelve days, there would be a costly banquet and a joust and, no doubt, games of cards which the Lady Anna enjoyed. But tonight was kept quite quietly and there were not many on the streets when Zachary, having seen his three children safely to bed, went out to The Sign of the Ship to arrange for a sailing to England.

The violent wind almost lifted the astrologer off his feet as he walked down Lantern Gate Street, usually bustling with noise from the leather, swordsmiths' and goldsmiths' shops, but tonight silent and dead, except for chinks of light coming from those shops behind which their owners lived. In the harbour, frothing and roaring, bounced the King's vessels, the *Lyon* and the *Sweepstakes*, each bedecked with over a hundred banners of silk and gold on the day of the Lady Anna's entrance, but now wisely stripped of decoration.

And, indeed, so fierce was the night that on entering the tavern Zachary thought at first he had ventured in vain; the owners of the fishing craft who also ferried travellers across the Channel must have all kept to their hearths. But on looking more closely he saw that one sea-dog, quite a youngish fellow with wild ocean-coloured eyes and a broken nose and teeth, had braved the gale to drink to the Christmas festivities that lay ahead.

'Friend,' said Zachary approaching, 'I'll buy your ale and reward you well if you'll get me and my family safe back to England.'

The blue eyes looked him up and down. 'You'll not be meaning before this wind blows out?'

Zachary stared through the grimy window and shook his head. 'No. Weather that can imprison the King's bride must be respected. I'll ask that we may sail on the same tide as the Lady Anna when she does go.'

The fisherman grinned. 'That I'll do, and certain. But by my reckoning that'll be some while yet.'

'Who knows?' Zachary stretched his arms above his head, shaking all over, dog-like. 'Yet suddenly I'm impatient to see my homeland. I sailed from England three and a half years ago, meaning to be away six months at most. Now it seems like a lifetime.'

'You say you have family. How many should I leave room for?'

'Three children, all under twelve years.'

'And no lady?'

Zachary shook his head with a small, sad smile. 'No lady, alas.'

The fisherman grew brisk. 'Then meet me here, Master, on the day that the Lord Admiral pronounces the Channel fit to bear the Lady of Cleves to her wedding, and I'll ferry you across behind her.'

Zachary nodded. 'I'll give you half payment now and the rest when we have crossed, if that is acceptable?'

'It is.'

'Then I'll see you a few days short of the end of the year.'

The fisherman's brows met his grizzled hair. 'Why do you say that? Are you a sea-faring man?'

Zachary grinned. 'No, it's merely a feeling I have. Would you care for a wager on it?'

The man shook his head. 'I reckon you're right. She'll blow out and change with the moon.'

'Yes,' said Zachary, 'I think she will.'

And with that the two men forgot the weather and fell to downing ale and speaking of all that had taken place in both Calais and the world in the years that had passed since Zachary last set foot in the citadel.

On the first day of the new moon, being the 27th December, the royal bride having kept her Christmas at Calais amid much merriment, the gusty wind finally dropped and was replaced by a keen, hard breeze that spoke of England. The Earl of Southampton, the Lord Admiral, rose early to inspect conditions, then ordered that the *Lyon* and the *Sweepstakes* be dressed overall with the hundred silken banners, golden in colour, that they had displayed on arrival. It was fair wind to sail. With enormous relief the welcoming party, their horses and servants, complete with the Lady Anna's entourage, boarded the flotilla of fifty ships that lay waiting in the harbour. And around noon, amidst the roar of Calais's cannon, the Lady herself embarked, and the Admiral ordered full sail.

Behind the royal fleet followed its parody, as every fisherman in Calais, deprived for days of his livelihood, took to the water in a ragamuffin flotilla which accompanied the Lady Anna as far as the fishing grounds, though some, bearing passengers, crossed with her, ready to fish on the return journey. And with the wind as fine and keen as it was, it was only four hours before England was sighted and the royal bride, only too aware of her own shortcomings, retired to her state cabin to adjust the wig of flaxen curls which she believed made her more comely in the eyes of men.

Zachary, his three children pressed close to him, peering out from beneath his cloak which was draped over all four, stood at the rail of the herring boat which carried them and stared at the milky coastline with tears in his eyes.

'We have been away too long,' he said to Sapphira, who tapped her own sign language into the palm of his hand, meaning, 'But happily returned'.

The boys, meanwhile – Sylvanus, sturdy and rosy and staring with round, forget-me-not eyes at the strange shore and Jasper, dark and youthfully saturnine – together answered, 'Never mind!' They were growing close as twins, these two Howard sons with different mothers, though physically more and more unlike.

'It's the Kent coast ahead,' said the fisherman. 'The Lady Anna is putting down at Deal. Will that suit you too?'

Zachary nodded. 'One harbour is as good as another. I'm headed for London. Unless . . .'

'Unless?'

'Unless His Grace the Duke of Norfolk be on hand somewhere about to greet the bride.' He stroked his chin and said no more, staring thoughtfully at the white cliffs which grew nearer with every rolling wave.

To come ashore within the wake of the Lady of Cleves was excitement itself for the children, who ran about scooping up the paper flower petals which had been thrown in lack of the real thing. Sir Thomas Cheyney, Lord Warden of the port, had greeted Anna on her arrival with a company of horsemen, so there were other things lying on the ground of a less prepossessing nature, as Zachary was swift to point out to his sons. But they only grinned and looked as if they would have indulged in dreadful games had he not clipped an ear of each and kept a watchful eye on them as he negotiated the purchase of two horses for the next stage of their journey.

Though only country creatures were paraded out before him, both took Zachary's fancy; one being a broad beast, an extraordinary pewter colour, with a beady eye which it fastened on the astrologer, for better or worse. The other appeared docile, a small neat mare of the type known as strawberry roan, though this was complimentary.

'They'll do,' said the astrologer and, without argument, gave the stabler the money he asked for.

'They'll get you far as London tonight, Master. And they'll ride well all their lives.'

'Umm!' Zachary raised a quizzical brow. 'Enough of that. Is the Lord of Norfolk expected here to greet the Lady Anna?'

'She's only resting in Deal for an hour or so, Master. Then the Duke and Duchess of Suffolk will conduct her to Dover. I know nothing of any plans for the Lord of Norfolk.'

'Then he probably keeps his Christmas at Greenwich, attending His Grace,' said Zachary, but to himself. The stableman had turned away and Sylvanus, far stronger and more capable than his age would admit, had already helped his sister mount the mare and had scrambled up the blocks behind her.

'I think,' said Zachary, calling them to attention, 'that we should make for Canterbury and spend the night at a tavern, the monastery guest hall no doubt now being closed down. Tomorrow we can ride to Greenwich and home.'

'I can't remember it,' said Jasper, but Sapphira gave a smile and nodded and her father knew that she could recollect all the things that had taken place before they sailed for France.

'It will be a home again,' said Zachary, just to her. 'We shall have a warm comfortable house just as we had when your mother was alive.'

Again she smiled, a little wistfully, and his heart wrenched for her that such a beautiful doll of a creature, all fine and fair, should have lost her speech attempting to ward off dark forces.

'Then lead the way, Sir,' said Sylvanus, 'and I'll follow sharp behind you.'

His father lost his grin in the hood of his cloak which he pulled up over his hat to ward off the cold crisp evening.

232

'Sylvanus, all of you, pull your caps well down. I think the new moon will bring us frost.'

And having obeyed him, the gallant little party set off, wondering as did everyone who had arrived in Deal that day, just what change in fortune the year of 1540 – ahead of them by only four days – would bring. But none wondered more so than the jolly, kindly lady upon whom every eye was turned, and who wept a little as she changed her clothes in the tower apartments of Walmer Castle, wondering how, with her lack of both looks and talent, she would ever win the heart of her monstrous bridegroom, the King of England.

## Chapter Eighteen

THE SUN, WHICH BY tradition always shone on a May Day tournament, at last came out from behind a cloud and instantly the tilt yard at Westminster was transformed. The flowers, hanging in garlands round the canopied stand in which the audience perched on rows of tiered seats, took on their full colour, as did the rich materials of the courtiers' clothes, while the armour and weapons of the contestants instantly glistened in the brightness. Nearly everyone present felt their spirits lift. It was going to be a sunlit jousting after all.

Already mounted but waiting patiently by the combatants' tents, Thomas Seymour, one of the forty-six challengers due to enter the lists that day, felt a smile broaden his face. It had not escaped his attention that the stands were packed with a great many ladies and he felt a surge of confidence in his ability to shine in their eyes. After all, these days was he not considered to be the most handsome man in England, the only other contender for the title having gone to the block accused of adultery with Anne Boleyn? Thomas felt at that moment, with the reluctant sun finally shining on him, that there was very little he would not dare, and very few women he could not win.

Despite the fact that he was now thirty-two and his elder brother Edward constantly urged him to marry, Thomas Seymour preferred to remain a bachelor, to love and then leave his ladies. For his childhood wish to marry the highest in the land had never gone away, having magnified, rather than diminished, with the passing of time. Two years ago he had cast his eyes on the Duke of Norfolk's daughter, Mary, the neat and pretty Duchess of Richmond, widow of the King's bastard Henry Fitzroy. They had had a short idyllic affair, kept most secret from Thomas Howard but guessed at by Norfolk's son, Mary's brother the Earl of Surrey.

After discovery their white-hot passion had cooled to lukewarm, partly because Thomas had lost interest and partly, he suspected, because Surrey had poured poison into his sister's ear.

'Bastard!' murmured Thomas now, and looked over to where Henry Howard, in full armour, was being helped onto his horse. 'I'll see you flat on your back, and hard, before the end of the day,' he added.

The sound of his muttering echoed most satisfyingly in his helmet so Thomas whispered, 'Bastard' again, listening and laughing, before turning his attention to a further minute inspection of the stands.

Right in the centre, directly in his line of vision, sat the King and the new Queen, now known as Anne of Cleves, Anna being considered too foreign sounding.

And what a farce that marriage! thought Thomas, grimly remembering the course of events since the poor woman had landed on English soil from Calais.

Last New Year's Day, before their first official meeting, the King, eager to set eyes on his new wife, had ridden incognito with eight gentlemen of his Privy Chamber, Thomas being one of his merry crew, to where Anne stayed in Rochester in Kent. All had been disguised in identical cloaks and hoods and it had been Henry's romantic idea that he would woo her as if he were a mere nobody. Now, recalling the scene, Thomas shuddered. One look at that sallow little face with its crown of patently false yellow curls and the King had lost his good manners. Anne's New Year present of furs had remained in his hands and Henry had barely been able to give the blushing woman the time of day. As soon as he had withdrawn from her presence he declared her ugly and old and not what he had expected at all. The reign of Anne of Cleves as Queen had even then looked precarious. Indeed, Henry Tudor had made strenuous efforts to disentangle himself and had it not been for the political situation in Europe would have done so.

The wedding and bedding had been the most strained occasion Thomas had ever lived through. The long and tedious marriage ceremony done, Henry had stood by the nuptial bed in his nightclothes and robe, surrounded by his gentlemen, awaiting the moment when the royal bride should come through the door. Thomas had been in an agony, longing to bellow with laughter, controlling a great guffaw until his eyes watered, watching Henry's face as the Lady Anne, devoid of blonde wig and showing herself in all her dark and swarthy glory, had appeared surrounded by her simpering maidservants.

'By Christ,' Henry had muttered audibly, 'I've no stomach for this,' and he had held out his hand to Thomas as if he were a condemned man parting from his greatest friend. Seymour, who in his most secret heart had no feelings for his ex brother-in-law than those of a wary respect, almost felt sorry for him.

And that night had seen the beginning of a wedded partnership that could only be described as an unmitigated disaster. From that time on Henry had constantly regaled his gentlemen with full details as to why the marriage remained unconsummated.

'I can never be provoked and steered to know her carnally,' he had whimpered into his wine cup. 'For by her breasts and belly she should be no maid; which when I felt them, struck me so to the heart that I had neither will nor courage to the rest.'

In their private sanctum, well away from spying ears and prying eyes, Thomas and Francis Bryan had laughed until they became hysterical.

'He's all worm and no snake,' screamed Seymour, and in his very derision had felt twice the man himself.

'Then God send a new Queen soon,' Bryan had answered, suddenly straight-faced, his eyes expressionless.

'You know something?' Thomas had asked, but Francis had refused to reply.

But now it was common knowledge. The King, fearing impotency above all, had cast his eyes about and at Easter time they had landed on a quivering little cat of a creature, a girl whose teasing little bosom and neat, high buttocks spoke blatantly of sexual ecstasy. Whether she had submitted to Henry Tudor yet nobody was certain but of one thing they *were* sure. Norfolk's niece, Catherine Howard, had an ageing and fearful king wound securely round her finger and he, with a wife he did not love and a marriage that had never been consummated, was already thinking of divorce.

Thomas narrowed his eyes. Two rows behind the King and Queen sat the little girl in question amongst the other maids of honour, her pretty features composed demurely, only the fact that her curving lids lowered then raised again to show her saucy eyes a clue to all the mischief that bubbled in her.

'Umm!' said Thomas reflectively.

His gaze returned to the first row. Beside the royal couple sat the two princesses, Mary, older than the King's new light-of-love by some years, as unhappy and bitter looking as ever. Thomas, yet again, found his mind wandering over the idea that a good session in a bedchamber with a man of substance like himself might be the very thing to bring a much-needed sparkle into her eye.

Next to Anne of Cleves, her foxy hair flaming in the sun, sat Elizabeth, thin as a wire, turning this way and that, trying to see everything at once. Even at this age she was an attractive little nymph, a flame of a girl very much as her mother had been. Thomas found himself smiling as he watched her.

He was about to turn away, to concentrate on the tourney shortly to begin, when once more his attention was attracted. Four rows behind Elizabeth sat a couple that were new to him, people he had never seen at court before. The man was unappetising, bloated, with bullfrog eyes, an elderly wretch, but the woman, surely not his wife, was superb. Thomas Seymour found himself gazing in frank admiration at a very pretty female, years younger than the frog, whose mass of burnished hair glinted and gleamed as she moved her head. And though her complexion might be pale, roses on snow, her eyes were vividly green, the colour of wild gooseberries, or so they seemed over the distance.

'Well, well,' said Thomas appreciatively and then felt a sensation which he thought had passed with boyhood. Suddenly and pleasurably his heart began to quicken its beat.

But there was no more time to look at the stranger or anyone else. The call to arms had come and with it the signal for the joust royal with Sir Thomas Seymour and Henry Howard, Earl of Surrey, the Duke of Norfolk's only surviving legitimate son, to commence.

To score a victory over Surrey, the sneering young noble who wrote poetry yet who declared the Seymour family to be upstarts, parvenu, was glorious indeed. And it was even more glorious to ride before the stands and see the King get to his feet to applaud the victors, of which Thomas was most certainly one, and at this watch the others rise too. They were all standing; Edward, now Earl of Hertford and a member of the Privy Council; Anne, his wife, every inch a peeress; the impudent Catherine Howard, widening her eyes; the bullfrog and his beautiful lady. As he passed beneath the place where they sat, Thomas looked straight up at her and gave an almost imperceptible bow of his head, and was rewarded by the wild roses that suddenly bloomed in her cheeks and the flash of her green eyes as they swept over him before hastily looking away.

After that she haunted him, filled his mind, until Thomas could have either sworn or laughed, both at himself for being such a fool. Yet nobody could have been more relieved than he when, at the grand and elaborate banquet, given in the great hall of Durham Place by the victorious challengers for the King and Queen, the unknown lady and her husband appeared at the exact moment Francis Bryan hovered at Thomas's elbow.

'Who is the beautiful stranger?' he asked his cousin, seizing Bryan's arm hard to secure his full attention, and nodding in the woman's direction.

The cold face flickered into a smile. 'I have no idea. Do you want me to find out?'

Thomas looked at him gratefully. 'It would be a great service.'

Francis raised a hard dark brow. 'Not smitten, surely?'

Thomas managed a lazy smile. 'And if I were?'

'She's another man's property.'

Thomas laughed aloud. 'That's never stopped me before. Besides he looks fit to drop any second.'

'They are the sort who always last,' answered Bryan with great acuity. 'The young woman with an eye to a fortune who takes on one of those, invariably ends up as nurse and arse wiper.'

'Please,' said Thomas firmly, 'spare us the details.'

'It's true and you know it.' He dropped his voice to a mere rumble, his light eyes fastening on Catherine Howard. 'And there's another pert child who might yet bite off more than she can chew.'

'Quiet for God's sake,' answered Thomas. 'Your neck is not inviolate.'

'Nor yours,' said Bryan acidly as they parted company.

The evening was memorable, in some respects probably for the fact that it was the last time Henry and Anne of Cleves were seen publicly together as King and Queen. But yet there were other things that lingered long in Thomas Seymour's mind when he thought back. How Elizabeth had laughed as her mother once did, putting back her head so that the long white neck gleamed like a swan's; how Catherine Howard smiled at the King sometimes as she took a mouthful, eating as if she were consuming a man's soul; how Francis Bryan had come to him and revealed the identity of the stranger.

'She is Katherine, Lady Latymer, born Parr. It would appear that her mother makes a speciality of marrying her off to elderly noblemen. Her first husband was Lord Borough of Gainsborough, old enough to have been her grandfather. He left her a widow when she was fifteen and she married her present old beast while she was still under twenty.'

Thomas groaned. 'What's her age now?'

'Twenty-seven. She's his third wife and he's in excellent health. They live in Snape Hall in Yorkshire, by the way.'

'Then my suit seems hopeless.'

Francis looked at him curiously. 'You are genuinely interested? *You?*'

'What do you mean? Why shouldn't I be? I'm no pretty boy, Bryan.'

His cousin laughed, a cold sound. 'I know that. It is just that I am privy to your life-long ambition. To marry a princess – or a prince's widow. Surely you are not interested in the wife of a petty northern nobleman?'

'Only to bed her. But I suppose she is as virtuous as she is beautiful.' Thomas sighed. 'The attractive ones always are.'

Bryan smiled. 'My dear friend, she is an animal born in captivity, or a child that has never tasted marchpane. Katherine Latymer would not know what to do with a man of her own age if one lay beside her.'

'What a challenge,' said Thomas, grinning once more.

'Tom,' answered Bryan, putting his arm round his cousin's shoulders, 'how is it that though you contrive to look and dress like a gentleman, you have the morals of a peasant?'

'Because everything about me,' replied Thomas rudely, 'is as strong as a ploughman's.'

'Boast, boast, boast! I think you are all talk and no action.'

'Wait and see, Bryan. I'll wager that I take Katherine Latymer to bed before this year is out.'

'Done,' said Francis, and they shook hands.

'Then for a start I must meet her.'

And with that Thomas, whistling confidently, strode away from his gaping cousin and passing before the King and Queen, who sat at the high table and to whom Sir Thomas gave a very fanciful salute, he went straight to where the Latymers sat side by side, a little country mouseish in their attitude, and bowed deeply.

Bryan watched in amazement, admiring his cousin's blatant gall, as a conversation was struck up and the man sitting on Katherine Latymer's right actually rose and gave Thomas his place. Lord Latymer, the bullfrog, seemed pleased with this attention from one of the famous Seymour brothers, uncles to the heir apparent and, indeed, obviously invited him to sit with them during the banquet. Francis saw Thomas graciously decline and take his pre-ordained place on the King's table but afterwards, when most rose to dance, he returned to the couple and sought Lord Latymer's permission to lead his wife out. Bryan observed the lady colour as Thomas gave her his hand.

For sure, he is pressing her fingers, he thought, but then his attention was turned elsewhere as he himself was summoned to the King's table in Thomas's place.

It was a warm evening and through the windows of the great hall the sun could be seen dipping over the Thames in bands of pink and gilt which augured well for next day's weather. Following the tradition of the time-honoured opening gambit of many Englishmen, the great and glorious Thomas Seymour, aware of his own magnetism, his irresistible attraction for women, could think of nothing better to say than, 'It has been very fine, Lady Latymer, has it not?'

Once more the roses bloomed in the ice of her skin and Thomas considered Bryan's belief that she would not be able to cope with a lusty man. Naughtily, and because he was what he was, Thomas accordingly drew her a little closer to him as the dance began.

If she was affected by this Katherine Latymer did not show it, merely answering in a steady voice that Thomas thought most pleasant to listen to, 'Indeed it has, Sir.'

'And you are staying at Court long?'

'For another week. Then we return to my husband's estate in Yorkshire.'

'A pity,' said Thomas, looking down at her from his considerable height and gently drooping an eyelid, 'the Court is scarce of beauty these days.'

The green eyes shot him a reproving glance but Lady Latymer said nothing.

'And you are indeed beautiful, Madam, as I am sure you are aware,' Thomas persisted, watching the struggle within her with some amusement as the primness, brought on by a surfeit of elderly

240

husbands and priests no doubt, went hard to war with all the natural youth and vivacity which had been stifled so early in life.

A widow at fifteen, thought Tom, and was seized by an overwhelming urge to embrace her.

'It is kind of you to flatter,' she was answering, her lips somewhat pursed. 'But please remember that I am a country woman and not well versed in the ways of the Court. Gallantry is a little beyond me.'

'More's the pity,' Thomas answered softly. 'It is the right of every woman to be admired.'

'I *am* admired,' she answered spiritedly, 'I am a good wife and kind mother to my step-children. My family have great love for me.'

Thomas bowed. 'Then I stand corrected, Madam. Yet it was not what I meant.'

He watched her hesitate, dying to lead him on but yet afraid of all that might ensue if a devout woman like herself should dare to open a door to the unknown. Then Thomas saw her lips quiver and thought to himself that rogues such as he were attractive to all women but particularly those who led dull and respectable lives.

'What *did* you mean?' asked Katherine Latymer slowly.

'I meant, Madam, that it is the birthright of every beautiful woman to have admirers. Not children but grown men who can appreciate all that her charm entails. Admirers from afar, mark you, who will do no more than write a poem in praise of her ankle.'

'Her *ankle*?' said Katherine and pealed with laughter, a gay silvery sound.

Now Thomas could see the youth and splendour of her as her attractive face lit up with smile after smile.

'I think you're mad, Sir,' she added, but still with the same joyful note.

'I am,' he said, pulling her as close as he dared. 'I've been mad for years, that's why I have such a fierce reputation. I'm known as Mad Sir Tom at Wolff Hall.'

'And where might Wolff Hall be?'

'In Wiltshire. It was where I was born. There they know all my follies.'

Katherine looked at him shrewdly. 'I don't believe a word of this.'

Thomas laughed, at his best, a beautiful woman in his arms who

241

obviously both enjoyed and admired him. He paused for a moment to analyse his own feelings, realising the powerful effect of her physical closeness and her general attractive way. Almost without thinking he said, 'I like you, Lady Latymer.'

'And I like you, Sir.'

'Then shall we be friends?'

'That depends.'

'On what?'

'On how you behave yourself,' she said, and curtsied as the dance came to an end.

Thomas bent to kiss her hand. 'I could not guarantee my behaviour with such an exciting woman.'

'Then we must part,' Katherine said simply. 'My husband and step-children always come first.'

'Aye, we'll part – but not for ever,' he whispered as she drew her hand away rapidly and with a very small curtsey left his side.

Not everyone was at the great banquet at Durham Place that night. The Duke of Norfolk had used the excuse of a cough and cold not to be present, while Elizabeth Wentworth, known as Cloverella, had developed a diplomatic headache, though in reality all she wanted to do was sit quietly and sort through her thoughts, her problem being whether she should stay at Court ruled by her autocratic cousin Anne Seymour, or put into plan a particularly daring and secret scheme of her own.

Yet these two diverse people, the Duke and the half-gypsy, had one thing in common as to why they stayed behind. Both knew that Dr Zachary was coming to Whitehall Palace that night to see his natural father, and though he had an appointment with one the other was determined to waylay him.

Thus a hovering Cloverella, from a secret hiding place from which she could observe the entrance to the Duke's apartments, saw a dark figure knock softly on Norfolk's oak door and gain admittance equally silently, and then, before the door closed, watched the Duke embrace his visitor.

'He's here!' she breathed in relief, and prepared herself for a long wait.

'Welcome, my boy,' Thomas Howard was saying within, bolting the door and leading Zachary to stand by the fire that burned brightly despite the warm evening. 'How good it is to see you.'

242

The astrologer smiled, holding his hands out to the blaze before he took the wine cup offered.

'It is good to be here, Lord Duke. I have been too long away.'

'Indeed you have. I thought we had lost you to the French King.'

'No fear of that,' said Zachary and put his hand out to touch his father's cheek. 'My roots are in Norfolk, Sir, as are your own.'

Norfolk nodded but said nothing and they sat opposite one another, lit by the firelight, silently appraising the change that had come about in each in the years they had been apart.

In many ways the Duke, with his broad Howard nose and strong features, had fared the better, for he had never looked truly young, and now only a deepening of lines round his mouth showed the passage of time. Zachary, on the other hand, had a great sparkle of silver in his pitch-dark curls, not one single strand, but an all over spread as if winter had thrown frost upon him. He was thirty-six now, lean and tough, a dark shadow stalking in the background of his father's life: a permanent reminder of a honey-skinned girl that once the Duke had loved.

'Will you go away again?' asked Norfolk now, this being the first real chance he had had to converse with his son since Zachary's return to England.

'No, never. Father . . .' the astrologer leaned forward earnestly, his arms on his knees.

'Yes?'

'It was guilt that drove me abroad. When Jane Wyatt died I felt that I had betrayed her.'

'And had you?' asked Norfolk mildly.

'You know so. Rosamund Banastre of Calais was my mistress and bore my child.'

'Yes, yes, I was aware,' the Duke answered quietly. 'But those times are long gone now. I believe she has married and that you have her son here.'

Zachary nodded. 'I regret that you have not had time to meet him or see the others.'

'They are well?'

'Indeed, though poor Sapphira still has not spoken. But Jasper grows daily more like you. He is a Howard through and through.'

The Duke of Norfolk smiled. 'Perhaps you should take another wife, my boy. Jane has been dead a very long time. Is there no one . . .'

The astrologer shook his head. 'No one. And being what I am, full both of your blood and of Romany, I will only marry for passion, for love. I would never do it merely to provide my children with a mother.'

The Duke smiled. 'You still bear all the fire of youth. Wait till you are middle-aged and comfortable.'

Zachary gave a glinting grin. 'God forbid that time ever comes. Let me continue to learn and quest all the days that are left to me.'

'You wild boy.' The Duke impetuously leaned forward and ran his hand through the tangled mass of curls. 'Will you never grow up?'

'I hope not.' Zachary held out his wine cup to be refilled. 'Now, Lord Duke my father, how is it with the house of Howard? I hear strange rumours.'

'I think they are more than that,' answered Norfolk in a low voice. 'Will you read the future for me?'

His son grinned. 'How fortunate that I brought both the dark crystal and the cards.'

The Duke eyed him. 'You knew full well I would ask.'

Zachary's glance was sly. 'I could not believe you wanted to see me for my good looks alone.'

'Then go to. What's to happen?'

Though the Duke had seen the sight many times before it never failed to send a thrill of fear shooting icily along his spine as he watched Zachary's features change into those of a mystic, a dreamer. The rough hair drooped over the crystal's black heart as Zachary laid his father's hands upon it and closed his own over them. Then there was silence, the only noises in the room the crackling of the fire, the scratching of the Duke's hound, and Zachary's sonorous breathing, almost as if he were asleep. Finally, after what seemed an age, he spoke.

'She is here, Lord Duke my father.'

'Who?' Norfolk found himself whispering. 'Who is there?'

'My little cousin, the little girl.'

'You mean my niece, Catherine Howard?'

'Yes, yes, yes.' Zachary seemed in a trance. 'She is here in blood.'

'What do you mean?' Norfolk found that he was shivering violently.

'She will be Queen of England unless you stop it. And she will die as such. She is an enchantress, Sir, who gives her body freely when she gives her heart.'

244

The Duke sat thinking furiously, his brows drawn down. 'But Zachary, what can I do? If His Grace is attracted to her I cannot intervene. It would be disaster.'

Zachary said nothing, laying out the ancient cards with three above representing the King, Queen Anne of Cleves and Catherine Howard.

'It is here again, Lord Duke. The Queen will be put aside, not cruelly but indeed to her own advantage. And the little Cat will creep into His Grace's bed and drive him mad before he realises the truth about her. Then comes the Tower of Ruin and the Moon of Treachery.'

'But what can I do?' Norfolk repeated with an edge in his voice.

'Tell him now that the Cat has already had two lovers. That she first gave herself to a man when she was . . .'

'Enough!' Norfolk had risen to his feet and slammed his hand down hard on the table which bore the cards and crystal. 'I know nothing of this. Catherine was brought up by her grandmother in Lambeth. She has been strictly raised. Stop it, Zachary, at once.'

The astrologer sat silently, the distant look draining from his features and giving way to what appeared to be some inner struggle. Eventually he said, 'Lord Duke, if it indeed is true that you know nothing then I beg you to make enquiries that you may yet save the house of Howard from a death blow.'

Norfolk looked furious. 'What do you mean "*if* it is true". I tell you I know nothing of any scandal linked with my niece's name. I warn you, you are going too far.'

Zachary stood up, his face rather white. 'Lord Duke my father, I beg you to see reason. You asked me to read for you. I told you truthfully what I saw. Now you are angry with what has been revealed.'

'Yes,' said Norfolk from between clenched teeth. 'Indeed I am. I warn you Zachary, that if one word of this gets out . . . one word! . . . I shall disown you.' His son said nothing and he went on, 'Don't you see that if my niece becomes Queen the power of the Seymours, to say nothing of that common upstart Cromwell, will be forcibly diminished?'

'Temporarily, yes.'

'God give me strength, I have sired an idiot. Zachary, you had better go before I lose what is left of my temper.'

The astrologer rose from the table and put on his cloak without a word. As he stood he seemed smaller, as if his father had physically beaten him and now he crouched with the pain.

'Goodbye, Lord Duke,' he said, bowing very formally.

'Goodbye,' answered Norfolk tersely, his back turned as he faced the fire and furiously kicked a log.

Without another word his natural son left the room, slipping silently away and opening the great door without a creak. But once outside and down the spiral stairs that led to the courtyard below, a great sob racked Dr Zachary and he leaned his forehead against the cool brickwork as if to ease an aching head. The shadow that came up behind him was, consequently, invisible, and it was not until a small voice, speaking in the Romany tongue, said, 'Greetings, Master' that he realised anyone was standing beside him at all.

Starting with fright and brushing his hand across his eyes, Zachary turned to face the speaker and then almost laughed as the diminutive figure of Cloverella Wentworth revealed itself before him.

'Oh, it's you,' he said carelessly, 'I thought you had returned to Wiltshire years ago.'

'And more's the pity that I didn't,' came the answer, 'if that is how you are going to greet one who was once your pupil.' She paused, peering up into his face. 'Master, are you ill? There are tears in your eyes.'

'Yes, by God's ill humour there are. Oh Cloverella, he has more power to upset me than any creature on earth.'

'Who, Master?'

'The Duke, my father. I love the old dog so much.'

Now he wept in earnest and it was the easiest thing in the world, then, to fold Cloverella into his arms and shed bitter tears that no one other than a Romany would have been allowed to see. And all the while, small though she was, she held Zachary firm and soothed him, just as a mother would have done her child. Eventually the storm passed and he could talk normally again, his eyes rather reddened but dry.

'Thank you,' he said solemnly. 'Believe me I would not shame myself before anyone else.'

'Then I am honoured.'

Zachary frowned. 'But what are you doing here? I thought that all the world was at the banquet tonight.'

Cloverella shook her head. 'I was waiting to see you, Master. I

246

knew that you were coming here and there is something of great importance that I have to say to you.'

Zachary looked genuinely surprised. 'What can it be?'

'Simply that I want to become your pupil again. Three and a half years ago you left me with never a farewell and from that day to this I have learned little of the secret lore. I ask you now to teach me more and, in return, I will bring up your children as if I were their natural mother.'

Zachary stared. 'But what of your position at Court? Your cousin is raised high and will go higher.'

'I know and I love him still, sincere, dear fool that he is. But Anne cannot cope with power. Her head is dizzy with it. Every day she becomes more intolerable. Dr Zachary, if I do not become your pupil I shall go home to Wolff Hall and live the life of an unmarried daughter.'

'But how can you be unmarried, you who are so very beautiful?' Yet Zachary knew the answer even before she said it. 'Though I can guess. Bad blood, as they believe. A Romany sired you and that has been your downfall.'

Cloverella nodded, her dark hair clouding her face. 'It is true, Master.'

'Then come with me and share a home with another Romany and his children.'

'That, Master,' answered Cloverella, smiling, 'is what I want more than anything else in the world.'

# Chapter Nineteen

WITH ONLY THE THINNEST tissue councealing her nakedness, Cat Howard, flushed with wine, stood before a long mirror, and gave herself a smiling head to foot appraisal.

Starting at the top, her face, sweetly rounded and youthful, looked innocent enough but her pretty eyes belied the fact that she was still only seventeen, having a worldly-wise expression which, combined with her drooping underlip and long rich brown hair, gave rise to a stunning attractiveness. Nor could fault be found with her figure. Though very short in stature, not an inch above five feet, she was lissom where she should be, though her breasts were excitingly full, and her legs the longest part of her.

I am, thought Cat naughtily, born for love.

And so, she remembered now with a guilty flush, she really had been. For with what joy had she given herself to Henry Mannox, her lute teacher, when she had been merely twelve, giggling and naked, romping in the great dormitory she shared with the other girls of the Dowager Duchess of Norfolk's household in Horsham. They had let the men in after lights out and they had stayed till dawn, feasting and flirting and making love. Cat had thought it heavenly.

Then two years later when the Howard entourage had moved to Lambeth, she had met Francis Dereham and learned what passion was really about. He had been the Duchess's kinsman and he and Cat together had explored the limits of what it was permissible for lovers to do. In return he had showered her with gifts and finery, enough to set her greedy little eyes alight with joy. How lovely it had been then to dress in fine clothes and wear flashing brilliants, though of course none of it half as expensive or rich as those wonderful gowns and trinkets with which His Grace was showering her now. With a smile of pure avarice, Cat threw off her robe and stood only in her jewels.

About her neck was a diamond-studded collar and on each arm a mass of costly bracelets. As she moved her hands, rings glistened on every finger and the toss of her mane of hair revealed ruby earrings as large as eggs. And there would be more to follow, or so it had been whispered in her ear. More and more when she became Queen of England.

But, of course, before that happy state could come about there was something that Cat must do, and do often, to convince the King that she was his own sweet girl, his loving baby wife, his adorable little virgin. She must get into his bed and prove to him that he was still vital, that she was just the kind of wife he needed if he was to father another son.

Even at the thought, Catherine Howard shivered where she stood, the effects of the wine suddenly draining away and leaving her terrifyingly sober. This very afternoon she had been brought in great secrecy to the Palace to be put through her paces, as it were. The King was too old now, too afraid of failure, to risk not fancying another bride. This time he was going to sample the goods and see if they came up to standard. Cat's blood ran cold. How hard she must act to be both virgin and slut, to feign shyness yet make sure the old man was capable. God's sweet blood, but were all the clothes and jewels in the world worth such a prospect?

A sound in the doorway had her spinning round, forgetting that she was naked, and there stood Henry Tudor, a moon-faced colossus, his eyes so puffed out with fat that they had difficulty in opening and closing, permanently remaining at half mast, while over them arched ridiculous eyebrows, thin as a girl's.

He was staring at her with an expression on his face that was frightening. Cat saw lechery and desire, and with fascination watched his tongue flick out to moisten lips suddenly dry.

'Beauty,' croaked Henry, 'I have never seen such beauty.'

For a moment Mistress Howard stood frozen with horror and then the actress in her took over and she found herself entering into a scene she had often thought about and practised at home.

'Oh Your Grace,' she said humbly, eyes downcast. 'I would never have dared reveal myself thus. I was on the point of changing my gown.'

He did not answer, waddling towards her with arms outstretched. Cat closed her eyes as he swept her into the suffocating bulk of him and lips, wet as sponges, covered her own.

Oh Sweet Mary, she prayed silently, don't let me scream.

Now his monstrous hands were everywhere, feeling and pulling and plucking till she could stand no more and pushed him fiercely away.

'Remember, Sir,' she said rapidly, covering the error, 'I am yet young and a virgin. You must not overwhelm me.'

He laughed boomingly. 'My dear heart, of course. Shall we kiss a while?'

The thought of that was so terrible that for a moment or two Cat felt trapped and would have run. Then sense prevailed once more.

'No, no. I am eager. Take me, Your Grace, and let your poor servant learn at last what it is to be loved by a man.'

It was enough. In a trice they were on the canopied bed and something soft and silly was pushing at her privy parts. Then the next second it was over. The great mountain lay gasping and sweating with its eyes closed. Cat looked at the King in pure astonishment. Was that all she had to endure? For, if so, everything was worth it.

'Oh,' she said loudly, watching his reaction, 'oh, oh, such searing pain. Why, I am no longer maiden!' Then very prettily Catherine started to cry.

With a great effort Henry Tudor opened his eyes. 'My dove,' he gasped. 'Have I been too rough?'

'Yes, yes,' said Cat, rolling round the bed. 'You are so mighty, Sir. I never thought the loss of my maidenhead would be so fierce. You are all man indeed, Your Grace.'

She shot him a sly glance and saw the merry grin that spread like a knife in lard. 'My own sweetheart,' he said ecstatically, 'I shall not rest till I am shot of that great Flanders Mare and you are my own dear little bride.'

'Oh my sweet lover,' answered Cat softly and dropped a swift kiss on his brow, ' 'Tis honour enough to be your mistress, Sir. Your humble servant expects nothing more.'

'Heaven like this, passion like this, is all too rare,' stated Henry heavily. 'Now that I have found it, my dear good girl, do you think I will let it go? Besides,' he added waggishly, 'what would your uncle of Norfolk say that I have robbed his niece of her virginity and she but an infant still?'

Catherine looked at him huge-eyed, trembling her lower lip and contriving to lisp slightly. 'We must never tell him, Your Grace, or he might beat me out of doors. All I had in the world was my honour and now it has gone.'

She wept again, beating her wet lashes against his cheek.

'Innocent child,' said Henry thickly, 'you shall be honourable wife, mother and Queen. The next thing that your uncle will hear is that I am divorced from that Cleves woman and asking for your hand in marriage. If, dearest Catherine, you will have an old man like me?'

'Old?' said Cat, very round of eye and mouth. 'If thou art old, Sire, then I rejoice. I think of you as strong and noble, all the callow boy in you cast out.'

The ever-open eyes looked at her approvingly and then as the moist mouth closed on hers once more, she felt the huge hands sweep her from breast to buttock. It was her saving grace, perhaps, that Catherine Howard had from the age of twelve been filled with insatiable lust. For now the very awfulness of her love excited her, as though ecstacy lay in degradation. As he touched her, Cat squealed with delight and Henry Tudor felt as much a man as he had done long ago with poor, lost Jane Seymour.

As is the way with all well kept secrets it was whispered round the Court in no time that the King was totally in love with Norfolk's niece, still not eighteen, and had consequently determined on a divorce from Anne of Cleves. But for once Cromwell, who had cleared the way for Henry to break with Rome and had later hatched the plot to bring down Anne Boleyn, seemed unequal to the task. It had been he who had engineered the Cleves marriage and now he suspected rightly that the King had never forgiven him for the Lady Anne's lack of good looks. So when Wriothesely, a joint Secretary of State, determined to climb higher, asked Cromwell to organise a royal divorce, he asked desperately how. A week later, faithful servant that he had been, he was arrested and taken to the Tower.

A few days after Cromwell's arrest, the King's plain wife, terrified for her future, was sent to Richmond. Puzzled, still speaking English hardly at all, tears had run down her housewifely cheeks when it had been explained to her that the change of air would benefit her health.

'But I am not ill,' she had said carefully.

'Your Grace must go,' had been the implacable reply.

Now, with her Flemish maids departed and only her English retinue about her, Anne felt trapped and it was only by struggling through a conversation with Mr Locke, who made the plain black dresses she liked so much as a background for her jewellery, that Anne of Cleves glimpsed the smallest ray of hope.

As he knelt pinning up a hem, his bony wrists and hands sticking out from his shirt sleeves in a way that would have amused her had she been feeling normal, Anne muttered, 'Ach, Mister Locke, I worry.'

He glanced up furtively, not wanting to get drawn into anything.

'The future,' Anne persisted bravely. 'I need a seeker.'

'A what, Your Grace?' Mr Locke asked in a startled voice.

'One who seeks. You know, cards.'

The dressmaker scratched his head.

'You want to play cards, Your Grace?'

'Ach no,' answered Anne impatiently, stamping her foot. 'I want one who can see stars.'

Mr Locke said nothing, turning his attention back to the hem and muttering to himself. Then light must have dawned for he whispered, 'Do you mean an astrologer, Madam? One who can tell the future?'

'Yes,' hissed Anne, 'that is it. Have you such a one?'

'Possibly, yes,' answered Mr Locke carefully. 'There is a man at Greenwich said to be very good. But I would not wish to get into trouble, Your Grace. I do hope you can understand that?'

His voice which had a tendency to squeak when he was perfectly calm now went out of control and ran up an entire octave. Despite the awfulness of everything Anne of Cleves let out the hoot that was her laugh.

'Mister Lock, I will be silent. Just say his name.'

'It is Zachary, Your Grace. Dr Zachary. He lives beyond Greenwich in a house on the riverbank.'

'Good,' answered Anne, satisfied.

And with that she finished speaking English for the day and

252

relapsed into High Dutch, of which Mr Locke, thankfully, understood not a single word.

When they met, they recognised each other. Zachary, for sure, had stood amongst the crowds lining the quayside as the Lady of Cleves had embarked for England, and had sailed in the flotilla that followed the royal fleet. She, on the other hand, had had her eye momentarily caught by the rumpleheaded figure standing on the quay amongst a band of pretty children, waving their hands as she set sail.

'But I know you,' she said now, and then had been utterly charmed by him, her stolid warm heart fluttering with pleasure.

'Madam,' said Zachary, bowing till his hair brushed her feet, his old and favourite trick, 'I was stormbound at Calais with your gracious self. I saw you the day you sailed for England and it was difficult to assess the beauty of that occasion. Yourself so fine and all the ships grandly decked.'

Anne's cheeky face grimaced. 'Sir, are you saying that I was like a ship in full sail?'

'How could I?' said Zachary, meaning it.

'Because His Grace thinks so of me.'

'His Grace only understands English-born beauty,' answered the astrologer treasonably. 'Foreign princesses are not his meat.'

There was a certain truth in this and Anne, who had never met anyone like him since she had landed on English shores, began to smile.

'Then I am not plain?'

'On the contrary, Your Grace, now that you show your dark hair *au naturel* I think you are splendid.'

He flattered and she loved it, and over the private supper served for the two of them, Zachary found himself warming to this Flemish girl who had had the misfortune not to appeal to Henry Tudor and whose days as Queen were now so very obviously numbered.

Eventually, when the wine had flowed freely enough and Anne had assured herself that no spies lingered behind the door, she lowered her voice and said urgently, 'I am so frightened, Doctor. Will he kill me as he did his other wives?'

Out of apparent thin air, Dr Zachary's dark crystal appeared in his fingers, another old and favourite trick.

'Come, Your Grace,' he said, 'put your hands on this.'

But even before she could do so the sphere pulsed blood red as it had done once before when Jane Seymour had been alone with the astrologer. Anne of Cleves let out a shrill scream and Zachary snatched the crystal away. But there was no need for him to look deeply. Half a glance showed him the face of his sleek little cousin Catherine Howard. Covering the orb with his hand, he spoke rapidly but carefully.

'Calm yourself, Madam. There is no need for alarm. You spoke of His Grace's other wives and it was to those unfortunate ladies that the crystal reacted just now. You, yourself, Majesty, are in no danger, in fact you are born fortunate indeed.'

Anne's uncompromising face stared at him in stolid disbelief.

'I see you do not believe me. Your Grace, I must take my leave.'

Zachary rose with dignity and headed for the door, a wary eye still on the Queen's reaction. He was almost half way out before she said, 'Dr Zachary, come back. I was frightened. But I still need help.'

'I know,' he said, relenting. 'I know you do. But, Madam, please listen to me . . .'

She nodded breathlessly, motioning him to sit down again.

'If you are clever, if you admit to the world that you and the King never consummated your marriage; if you call him brother dear and dote on the little girl he has chosen for his next wife . . .'

'So, there is already somebody else!' said Anne, her eyes growing huge.

'Indeed there is. Then you will be given estates and pensions and riches more than you dream of now. If you return to Cleves you will merely be a divorced woman, here you will have love and affection showered on you as the King's own sister.'

'You see this in the crystal?'

'I see it everywhere, Madam.'

'So I am not to resist divorce?'

'You are to thoroughly agree.'

Anne of Cleves became predictably feminine. 'Who is this other? Do I know her?' she asked, vinegar mouthed.

'She is one of your maids of honour, Madam. The Duke of Norfolk's niece, Catherine Howard.'

Anne looked shocked. 'But she is so young. And the King is so . . .' She clapped her hand over her mouth as she realised what she was saying.

'That is for them to sort out,' answered Zachary primly.

'Yes, yes.' The Flemish princess looked at him earnestly. 'But will this really come to pass? Will I really have a happy life?'

Zachary forgot all about her being Queen of England and all about dignity and protocol. He leaned forward and patted her plump hands warmly.

'I assure you, Madam, on my solemn word, that you will have a far happier life than ever will poor Catherine Howard.'

'Fancy that!' said Anne, throwing dignity aside, and hugging Dr Zachary hard to her over-voluptuous bosom.

The royal marriage was, in the circumstances, very quiet and private. On the 28th July, almost at the same moment that Thomas Cromwell, who had done so much for his royal master, lost his head, Catherine Howard and Henry Tudor were married at Oatlands, a manor house near Weybridge in Surrey. There were only four witnesses, the Duke of Norfolk and Edward Seymour, Earl of Hertford, being two of them. And that particular couple of men were an ill-matched pair; the Duke triumphant that once again a Howard occupied a place on the throne of England, determined that this niece should make a better showing than his last; Edward, a little sick at heart that the days of Seymour ascendancy would now appear to be at an end.

But for all their thoughts and fears, the two men might not as well have been there. The King, like some old and doting fool, had eyes for no one but the tiny creature who accepted his wedding ring. Nor could he keep his hands off her, kissing and cuddling every second. No sooner had Cranmer pronounced them lawfully wed than great sighs and moans broke out as Henry embraced his 'rose without a thorn', while she caressed her 'pig-wig'. Edward found it nauseating and excused himself from the wedding feast early. Thomas, on the other hand, who had ridden from London in the bride's escort, stayed on and for some reason, perhaps a wry personal comment that it had only been seven months since he escorted another royal bride, got very drunk.

'Do not be indiscreet,' Edward had whispered to him as he had withdrawn.

'Me?' said Thomas, rolling up his magificent eyes. 'Brother, would I?'

'Would pigs fly?' Edward answered tersely. 'Ever since Cloverella left my protection to live with that rogue Zachary, nothing amazes me.'

'But she writes me that she merely studies with him. He has not dishonoured the name of Wentworth, Ned.'

Edward snorted. 'I would like to believe that.'

'Then do so,' said Thomas, the wine in him flowing. 'Leave the dishonouring to me. Let Zachary talk potions and notions.'

'What do you mean?' asked Edward, shocked.

'I don't speak of dishonouring Cloverella. Though I did try once. I meant that I can be the libertine of the family.'

'You'll go too far,' said Edward seriously. 'Watch your step Tom.'

'Poof!' answered his brother, and waved his hand dismissively.

It was a small feast, just as it was a quiet wedding, and with fewer people to share the drink amongst, it did not take long for every man in the room to become slurred of speech and blurred of feature. Drunk though he was, Thomas observed Henry's face appear to melt beneath the silly gold hat, with its enormous bobbing feather. First the high eyebrows drooped, then the eyes in the surrounding circles of fat closed to mere slits. The bulbous nose and the tiny obscene mouth became one and ran down the monarch's face into all his bearded chins.

'God's body,' said Tom to himself, 'but I don't envy the chance of that child.'

But the little Cat continued to laugh and giggle and strop round the King, all eyes and pinching fingers and long succulent kisses. It was almost a relief when the end of the evening came and Thomas once again found himself standing by a royal marriage bed. But this time no ugly giggling Flemish girl came in, for this latest was a demure thing, with straight brushed hair and lashes decorously lowered, her lips compressing a smile.

For no reason Tom shivered then, and he, the least intuitive person in the world, had the sudden feeling that such a combination of nubile youth and aged obesity could never come to anything but ill.

God's mercy on the Queen, he found himself praying as he left the room, and this was so very unlike him that he fell to drinking more, until at last he slumped asleep amongst the wine cups. Upstairs meanwhile, Catherine Howard, lying wide-eyed in the royal bedchamber, listened to the sonorous snores of her enormous husband and also founds words of prayer forming on her own frightened lips.

# Chapter Twenty

IT WAS AN ODD SUNSET, angry looking. Over the horizon lay a band of pale green, then above that strips of burnished gold rising to a furious crimson, over which scudded a battalion of dark clouds. The evening air was cool, a sharp wind tearing at the trees, a spray of threatening rain in every gust. It was not like summer at all in fact, even though it was August a certain autumnal look had already come to the trees.

The valley, in which the castle of Snape stood in acres of parkland, seemed to trap the light thrown by the dying sun. So much so that Katherine Parr, walking for once on her own, found that the blissful interlude when she had time for herself was coming to rather an unnerving end, as the place turned the colour of hell. Without meaning to she quickened her steps, heading for home before it grew suddenly dark or started to rain. Then, just as abruptly stood still, listening.

In the eerie glow nothing stirred and the birds that usually sang at sundown were silent. It seemed as if all living creatures were waiting for something, herself included. Katherine felt an unreasonable panic stir within and fought it down with great strength of mind.

'There is nothing to be afraid of,' she said aloud. 'Now walk back calmly and don't be foolish.'

But with every step she took she found herself glancing about nervously until finally she started to run. And it was dishevelled and panting that she hurriedly crossed the bridge over the moat and entered her husband's mansion.

Snape Hall had been built some two hundred years before but improved on by every generation that lived there so that now it was a cross between a castle and a house. As if for reassurance, Katherine let her eyes wander over the great hall's panels of carved black oak and the many tapestries that hung there. A spread eagle, worked in gold, it's head surmounted by a purple crown, caught her attention.

That is myself, she thought. Two women in one, facing both directions simultaneously. God strengthen me to overcome my weaknesses.

But no rush of divine comfort answered and almost impatiently Katherine went to the fireplace and poured herself a cup of wine from a decanter that stood on a nearby table.

'I drink to sacrifice,' she said bitterly, 'as taught me by one who knew.' Katherine raised her glass. 'To you, my good mother, who renounced your life for your children.'

She sat down, staring into the flames, thinking of Dame Maud Parr who, though only just twenty-two at the time of her widowhood, had refused to remarry, devoting herself entirely to her young family and their education − a fact of which all three of them, William, Katherine and Anne, had been reminded almost daily.

'And what fun we had!' said her daughter now. 'Latin, Greek, devotional writings. Plenty of needlework, and then the greatest joy of all − the marriage bargains.'

Even before Katherine's twelfth birthday, Dame Maud had started negotiations with Lord Dacre for an alliance with his young grandson. But she had driven too hard a bargain, been too greedy, and Lord Scrope, the boy's father, had withdrawn from the deal. And then had followed the most terrible event: an event that hurt even to think about. Katherine had been thirteen, just entering upon womanhood, when her mother had fastened on someone else. Edward, Lord Borough of Gainsborough, a widower approaching sixty, with several children, the eldest of which was the same age as Dame Maud, had offered for the thin, anxious girl who had stood in the shadowy corner, her huge green eyes fastened on him with loathing. And though Dame Maud had demanded a small fortune for her, Lord Borough had agreed. He had bought Katherine just to get his hands on a child.

Now, sitting by the fire in Snape Hall, Katherine still wept aloud at the memory and its aftermath. A butterfly had been broken on the night Lord Borough claimed her immature body as his, a beautiful soaring creature had had its wings snapped off, a wonderful loving girl had sealed up her emotions and gone into a trance. In that state she had done her duty, cared for her

259

step-children, run the house. But the true Katherine Parr had ceased to live.

She had never forgiven Dame Maud. But knowing the danger of hatred, how it can turn inwards and consume its own source, Katherine had looked for God instead, though her idea of Him was far from conventional. Certain beliefs had sprung up, beliefs that if she tried hard enough in even her unrewarding circumstances, the tide must turn in her favour. And in a way it had.

Within a few months of each other, first Lord Borough and then Dame Maud had died. Of course it would have been vastly improper to see the divine hand in this miracle but Katherine, having muttered prayers for the salvation of their souls, did add a quick request that she might enjoy her new freedom wisely. That was as far as she dared go.

But how she had run when she had at last been left alone. With her hair streaming out behind her and her feet bare, Katherine Parr, a widow at fifteen, had felt the poor battered butterfly return to life as she had sped through the parkland of Sizergh Castle, laughing and crying with sheer relief.

That should have been her moment, of course, to marry someone of her own age and have wonderful and merry butterfly children. But somehow there seemed little opportunity to meet anyone, living with her stepson and daughter-in-law and owning no home of her own. Dame Maud, naturally, had left Katherine nothing, instead concentrating every penny on buying her son William a well-connected wife. In the end, almost out of boredom, Katherine had accepted Lord Latymer when she was eighteen and he fifty-four. It was true that he was ugly and old even then, but at least he was kind. Katherine felt that the butterfly had not died so much as gone into a cocoon.

And so, she thought now, we are always the products of our parents. My mother sold me to an old man and I got so used to it I could do no better for myself. How strange life is.

Katherine refilled her wine cup and drank deeply, her cheeks glowing, remembering the saucy fellow who had danced with her at the May Day tournament. It was hard to believe that such a reprobate was the brother of good Queen Jane, who had seemed so very pale and innocent.

'But who knows,' said Katherine aloud. 'Are any of us what we appear?'

'Hah!' answered her husband from the doorway, 'talking to yourself, eh?'

'I am a good conversationalist,' answered Katherine swiftly, and he laughed at her wit, coming to join her by the fire.

'That's as well, my dear, in view of this,' he said when he was settled, tapping a parchment and its broken seal, which Katherine's startled eyes took in as being the new Queen's crest and device, *Non autre volonté que la sienne*, testifying that Henry Tudor was the only man in Cat Howard's life.

'What is it?' she asked in surprise.

The bullfrog's gaze grew bulbous. 'You have been called to Court, Kate, to act as a Gentlewoman of the Chamber to the new Queen.'

'*I* have?' said Katherine, frankly astonished.

'Yes. It seems Her Grace wants a vastly increased retinue and the King indulges her in everything. Every month, it's said, she has an entirely new wardrobe of both gowns and jewels. And every day there is some new caprice. His Grace is apparently rejuvenated by it all. He rises at six, hears mass until seven, then rides till dinnertime at ten.'

'They are still on progress?'

'Yes. But it is Her Grace's wish that you await her return in London.'

'How strange, when I hardly know her.'

'I believe that might be the very point,' Lord Latymer answered knowingly. 'Though she has some about her who served the Lady Anne of Cleves, she wants others who are entirely fresh.'

'I suppose it will mean more gowns,' said Katherine, and inside her the butterfly stirred in its sleep.

'A few,' replied her husband prudently. He had never been profligate with his money.

Katherine's lips twitched. 'Perhaps from my jointure?'

Lord Latymer did not reply, the money that Katherine had brought into the marriage now being his property.

'I'll not go dowdy,' said his wife firmly.

'No, not dowdy,' he answered, 'but most certainly not in gawdy display.'

His wife merely smiled and stared into the flames as the butterfly stretched its wings.

\*    \*    \*

Though in Yorkshire it was both cold and damp, the summer of 1540 burned fiercely in London. Between June and October not a drop of rain fell and the pestilence, the usual companion of warm weather, raged fiercely. The King and his child bride remained on progress, while at Richmond Anne of Cleves, the highest lady in the land after the Queen and the King's daughters, relished her new-found status as the King's sister. She had £500 a year to herself, had been assigned the manors of Richmond and Bletchingley to live in, and had bought fine new jewels and clothes. She had turned her life round triumphantly and to show how carefree she was, had thrown away all her black gowns and dressed excitingly in vivid colours.

For the Seymour brothers, with the King still away on extended honeymoon, there seemed little to do, so on an evening in late September, being at a loss to amuse themselves, they decided to call upon Dr Zachary and upbraid him for ruining the reputation of their cousin, thus making a little entertainment.

Yet as they set out from their lodgings in the Palace of Whitehall and took to the water in Edward's private barge, they could not have presented two greater contrasts; the elder dark, saturnine, bearded, a somberly dressed man of intelligent appearance; Thomas, tall and golden, sporting a red beard, his blue eyes alight with mischief, his clothes elegant and daring, copied by all the other gentlemen of fashion. And in attitude, too, they were dissimilar, Edward sitting upright, scanning the river with thoughtful eyes; Thomas lounging back against the cushions, one leg resting on the knee of the other, only looking up if he spotted a comely woman on the bank.

They had brought refreshment and as Thomas imbibed more and more, he began to see the funny side of their expedition.

'I'm no man to tell another how to behave, Ned.'

His brother sighed. 'She is our cousin, Thomas, not just any woman. She is a Wentworth, remember.'

'And the astrologer is a Howard. To my way of thinking they are well matched. Do you think we should buy him as a husband for her?'

Edward's eyebrows rose violently. 'What a terrible suggestion.' 'Why?'

And put as simply as that Edward could think of no reason other than his wife's reaction and his own pride in being Earl of Hertford. It was Cloverella's mixed blood that had stood in the way of her

262

making a good match and from what he had heard, Dr Zachary's mother had also been a Romany. Edward took a thin sip of wine and sat in silence while Tom watched him, smiling.

The sun began to dip over the river and the sky became the clear light-blue of glass, while the water deepened to emerald. In places there were patches of purple where the weeds grew and the colour of the fields that ran down to the bank was dark as mint. Very small white clouds drifted overhead and were reflected in the water, their images blending with those of the swans, gracefully dipping their way downstream.

'It's a peaceful night, Ned,' said Thomas slowly, the tender side of his character welling up. 'Let us not disturb the idyll of those two gypsies, for such they are and don't deny me. Let us see, rather, if we can regulate the household that they keep.'

Edward turned down his long mouth. 'Perhaps.'

But he was won over, the beauty of the evening combining with the wine to make him feel at peace with all his surroundings. And when they rounded the bend in the river that brought them to Zachary's landing stage, he beheld such a sweet sight that every angry word he had in him was finally stilled.

Two little imps, quite naked, both about ten years old, swam gallantly in the shallows, while in a boat rowed by the untidy figure of the astrologer himself, Cloverella, one arm round the shoulders of a small fair girl who cuddled closely against her, trailed a hand in the cool water.

They all looked up at the sound of approaching oars and Thomas watched as Cloverella's face became apprehensive. All his youthful love for the little thing consumed him and he called out, 'How now, dear cousin? We are come on a visit to greet you.'

He felt Zachary's amber eyes sweep over him and Thomas waved again.

'Greetings, Dr Zachary. May we rest here a while?'

'Indeed, indeed.' The astrologer waved back. 'Greetings, my Lord. Greetings Sir Thomas.'

So far everything was very cordial but Thomas did not quite trust Edward to keep the peace as they came alongside and the larger of the two little boys, hastily pulling on his hose, tied the Earl of Hertford's barge to a mooring ring.

'If your oarsmen would like to step ashore they will find refreshment,' said Zachary courteously, and the eight men who had rowed Thomas and Edward along the stretch of the Thames gladly disembarked. The astrologer, meanwhile, had moored his own vessel and helped Cloverella and the girl on to the jetty. Then, waiting for them to walk ahead, he bowed deeply and said, 'Gentlemen, I suspect that you have come to take me to task over my seduction of your cousin, but, alas, there has been no such occurrence and Mistress Wentworth stays in my house as both pupil and honoured guest.'

Edward looked amazed but Zachary, ignoring him, bowed again to Thomas.

'I feel that I may speak to you as a man of the world. I am somewhat older than Cloverella, some nine years in fact, so you may believe that my attitude towards her is that of a senior, a brother.' His smile lit his face. 'Now, my Lord, Sir Thomas, I do hope that you will pay me the great honour of having a late supper at my home.'

They could say nothing, the wind taken from their sails completely.

'Is this true?' hissed Edward, moving rapidly forward so that he could accompany his eavesdropping cousin along the path that led through the orchard to the gardens and house.

She nodded. 'Perfectly. So you must not hate me, Ned. Court life became too much for me. I am much happier here.'

Just for a minute his face took on its old vulnerable look. 'You were finding it hard to remain friends with Anne, weren't you?'

'She has grown a little proud,' answered Cloverella slowly.

'I know, I know. And yet I love her. She has borne me children and given me much loyalty. I will never desert her.'

'And neither should you. I think you are a good couple.' Cloverella's voice grew lighter. 'And what of Thomas? No marriage plans as yet?'

'He contemplated Norfolk's daughter – the astrologer's half sister!' he said with some amazement, 'but nothing came of that. Surrey intervened, little beast that he is.'

'And he,' answered Cloverella with a laugh, 'is the astrologer's half brother.'

'Anyway, Seymour and Howard could never make a match and it ended there.'

'So Tom plays the field?'

'Fiercely. The women at Court throw themselves before him. He's never short of a bed partner.'

Thinking that perhaps he had been vulgar in front of a lady, albeit his cousin, Edward's cheeks deepened slightly, though Cloverella only laughed.

'One day he'll meet his match.'

'I sincerely hope so,' Edward answered fervently.

The supper was merry, going on late into the night. Long after the children and Cloverella had retired, the three men continued to talk and drink till the candles burned low and at last Edward Seymour mellowed.

'Well, Dr Zachary,' he said, 'I have known you many a year, you rogue, and am a great believer in your abilities. Will you read your magic cards for us now?'

Zachary shook his head violently. 'No, Sir. Drink clouds my vision and I might advise you false. Let me do so another time when I am sober.'

'Very well, but I shall hold you to it. Now, while we are alone, tell me your intentions towards my cousin?'

'*Our* cousin,' interposed Thomas.

Zachary looked thoughtful. 'At present I have none. I expect I shall teach her all I can and then she will leave me.'

'I think you should marry her,' said Thomas boldly. 'You are too alike to let such a kinship pass.'

'But we are Seymour and Howard,' answered Zachary. 'Did you not say that that could never work?'

Edward smiled wryly. 'I did not realise you could overhear.'

Thomas ploughed in. 'It is true that Surrey and I have no liking for each other. I had a brief affair with his sister, the Duchess of Richmond, but he meddled and ruined it.'

Zachary laughed. 'Surrey detests me. A bastard sired out of wedlock, whom his father acknowledges and loves. He is riddled with jealousy.'

'Then there is no problem,' Thomas answered. 'You and Cloverella are well suited, regardless of family background.'

Zachary shook his head and sighed. 'But she doesn't love me.'

'Then put a spell on her, man,' retorted Thomas outrageously, and laughed till he wept.

The rest of the night was like that, all jokes and jollity and back-slapping, so that when the Seymours left in the hour just before dawn, their sleepy oarsmen yawning themselves awake, they were convinced that Zachary Howard was one of the best fellows alive.

'He must marry our cousin and that's all there is to it,' said Thomas as he settled himself to sleep on the cushions in the barge's cabin.

'But they must live quietly,' answered Edward, sobering slightly. 'It would not do to have them at Court claiming to be related to the Prince.'

'You really do act the cock at times,' Thomas's sleepy voice was oddly sharp. 'I think your wife's self-importance is spreading to you, like a creeping disease.'

'Speak no ill of Anne,' said Edward, warningly.

'God's teeth and toenails,' came the muffled reply. 'I'm going to sleep!'

Leaning out from her bedroom window, Cloverella could hear the distant voices as Zachary and his servant saw the visitors off, their lanterns lighting the darkness.

So, she thought, my cousins approve. Now I must act.

Going to a small wooden wall cupboard, Cloverella unlocked it with determination and drew out a phial of liquid which she hid in the pocket of the night-rail thrown over her shift. Then she sat down for a moment on the corner of her bed, thinking carefully about what she planned to do.

Her love for Zachary, which had consumed her almost from the moment of their first meeting on the landing stage at Whitehall Palace, was now like a forest fire running out of control. To be beneath the same roof as he, to be in his presence daily, was more than she could bear. She longed to kiss him and touch him, to lie in his arms, to be his gypsy wife and consummate her love beneath the stars.

Yet Cloverella had no true wish to stoop to devious means, though the boast she had once made to her cousin Jane had been true. Before her Romany grandam had left her at the door of Wolff Hall, she had whispered to her little grandchild the secret of winning any man she chose. And now a concoction far more powerful than the one she had given Henry Tudor that he might take Jane to bed and sire a boy, lay ready. For weeks she had prepared it, just as her grandmother had told her, and now, knowing by Thomas's wink that at least one of her cousins approved her choice, Cloverella felt ready to act. Yet still she

266

hesitated, so desperately did she want Zachary to love her without the aid of magic.

She sat agonising, wishing her decision could be made easy, but in the usual way of life, it was left to her. Then the sound of Zachary's voice as he walked through the gardens, talking to the servant, spurred her on. With a sense of great purpose, she opened the door and went downstairs.

'My dear,' he said in some surprise as they almost collided. 'Can't you sleep?'

'The sound of the departure awoke me, and I felt thirsty. Is there any wine?'

'I don't know that I should encourage you to drink in the middle of the night.'

'By the light I would imagine it is an hour off dawn. And such strictures make you sound elderly, Dr Zachary.'

'That is because I am.'

'You are thirty-five,' said Cloverella, realising even as she spoke that her voice sounded shrewish. 'Stop making yourself seem old, Sir.'

Instead of being angry, Zachary gave her an engaging grin. 'Now, now, little pupil, don't make yourself choleric on my behalf. We shall drink a toast together if that is what you want.'

He ushered her into the dining room, where the remains of his supper with the Seymour brothers still lay upon the table.

'There,' he said, pouring wine for them both. 'Now be merry.' And with that he left the room, calling over his shoulder, 'I won't be long.'

It was the chance she needed. With one quick move Cloverella took a deep sip from Zachary's cup, then poured in the contents of the phial. It was all done in a second so that by the time he came back she was sitting calmly in her own chair, smiling up at him.

'The fire is almost out,' said Zachary, then yawned rather pointedly. 'Save a tired man's bones and put a log on for me.'

Cloverella bent to the hearth, not seeing as she did so that Zachary, in his turn, swiftly poured a potion into her cup.

'There, all done,' she said, as she sat down again.

Zachary smiled. 'Then I propose a toast.'

'And what is that?'

'To the friendship of the Howards and the Seymours.'

'To friendship.'

267

They both drank deeply, then sat looking at each other as the fire blazed up. For the first time ever Zachary noticed how finely boned was the beautiful little face he was regarding.

'You are perfect, Cloverella,' he said, wondering at himself and his feelings as he impulsively added, 'Let's take the boat out. Let's see the dawn come up over the island. Will you go with me?'

Cloverella went straight to the door. 'I'll race you to the river,' she answered and laughed, a sudden carefree sound.

Like children they ran through the darkness to where the boat pulled at its rope, longing to be off with the morning river, which now swelled and rushed with the freshness of the tide.

'Get in,' said the astrologer, and Cloverella jumped down ahead of him, terrified to touch him lest the spell be broken. She had never known her emotions so heightened, her awareness so all-encompassing. It occurred to her then that she must have drunk from the wrong glass, that she had taken the love potion, not he. But yet the expression on Zachary's face belied that. He was looking at her as if he had never seen her properly until this moment, as if he could not live very much longer without kissing her. Temptingly, Cloverella lay back against the cushions of the boat.

A glimmer of red was coming into the sky, a glimmer that reflected a long crimson finger in the river. Then the heavens were suddenly suffused with gold and rose and, as if this were a signal, every sweet smell of field and flower was released together upon the air. The scents that blew freshly down the river were simultaneously both sharp and heady. Even while they stared and breathed the couple were overawed by the beauty of it all.

The island near Zachary's jetty was not much more than a large mound on which grew a few trees. The astrologer had built a little wooden shed there for the water birds but that was the only man-made thing. And now, as they moored and climbed ashore, the place seemed like Eden. As Zachary jumped out and tied the boat up, he gave Cloverella his hand to help her and from that moment on they were lost.

They remained holding each other's fingers for a long time before he finally drew her into his arms and let all the love and longing pass from his mouth to hers. And then their Romany blood took over and they enjoyed with intensity those wonderful moments of slowly revealing their bodies, one to the other. At last they stood naked in the dawn and, almost shyly, Zachary's hands caressed in turn Cloverella's beautiful breasts.

They made love with restraint at first, touching each other and then letting go, enjoying the agony of extending the moments before they truly became lovers. But then Zachary's patience finally grew exhausted and Cloverella saw his features turn dark with wanting. Now came the moment that could no longer be put off. She was on the ground, feeling the hardness of the earth in her back and the hardness of a man's penis within. But he was a gypsy and knew how to make love, be his woman virgin or whore. He took Cloverella as if she were both, so that her little cries of pain and fear, drowned by the gurgling river, turned again and again to those of ecstasy and sheer raw pleasure. As their bodies moved together, thrusting as one, Zachary, too, reached the climax of lovemaking more powerfully than he ever had before, with wife or mistress. Now he knew that he had found his perfect woman, as wild and unashamed of it as he.

'Cloverella, my love,' he said as together they swam naked in the river before returning to the island where, beneath the brightening light of the sun, Zachary, without caution or caring, entered her once more and they made love until the sun was finally risen.

# Chapter Twenty-One

ON NEW YEAR'S DAY, 1541, the Queen-bride, whose every whim was now a command, invited her husband's ex-wife, Anne of Cleves, to sup at Hampton Court, that gifts might be exchanged with the greatest cordiality. To mark the occasion Catherine Howard wore one of her finest gowns and surrounded herself with elegant courtiers, new and old. But the Lady Anne, who these days mostly arrayed herself gorgeously, entered humbly, simply dressed and alone, and at once dropped on her knees before the King, and the Queen who had usurped her place.

'Rise, my dear Lady Anne,' said Henry jovially, but the Princess of Cleves insisted on remaining where she was, addressing Cat from a lowly, reverential stance. And she remained kneeling thus until the Queen herself left her high seat and with much display of affection raised Anne up.

The Princess, appearing much gratified and overcome, gazed round her at all the unfamiliar faces now at Court, mildly remarking by way of conversation, 'There are many people here today I do not know.'

'Oh yes,' answered the Queen casually, 'they are mostly friends of mine from the old days.' She pointed to four pretty young women who stood together. 'Now they are Catherine Tylney, Alice Restwold, Joan Bulmer and Margaret Morton, all new Ladies of my Chamber. I knew them when I lived with my step-grandmother, the Dowager Duchess of Norfolk.'

'How nice,' said Anne. 'And that handsome young man, is he also an old friend?'

Cat looked vague. 'Oh him! He's Francis Dereham, a cousin of mine. I'm thinking of appointing him my Private Secretary.'

Anne nodded wisely. 'It is good to have friends and relatives close by. But where is the Princess Mary? Not at Court?'

The Queen lowered her voice. 'Dearest Anne, I do not believe she likes me.'

The Lady of Cleves looked astonished. 'Why do you think that?'

'As you know, she is three years older than I am and, frankly, I believe she is jealous of her father's love for me. She refuses to come to Court and pay her respects so, to settle the score, I've taken away two of her maids.'

Anne looked vague, a newly-acquired trick. But within she was thinking that this was the anniversary of her first terrible meeting with Henry, when he had ridden to Rochester incognito. However, she was far too clever to mention it, and she was also far too clever to interfere if Cat wanted to alienate Henry's daughter. Instead she changed the subject.

'For His Grace I have brought two new horses all tricked out in violet velvet. And for you, Your Grace, a violet necklace and earrings to match. All these to wish you a Happy New Year.'

Cat kissed the plain face so close to hers. 'Sweet sister, how very kind. Now come and receive your presents.'

'And what a happy family we all are!' said Tom Seymour softly from the doorway and was quite gratified when the coterie of newcomers, overhearing, moved away from him as if he had the plague.

He had ridden hard that day, the distance from Wiltshire to Surrey in just twenty-four hours. For this year he had kept part of his Christmas at Wolff Hall, where Edward and Anne and their brood of children had gone to be with old Dame Margery. It had seemed strange and a little boring to be in the bosom of the family, inviting local dignitaries round to feast and look at Anne's smart clothes. But Thomas had obliged out of duty, knowing that this tranquil time was to be the last for Edward for some while. Next year, with the King already announcing his intention of making an extremely long progress north, accompanied of course by the baby bride, Edward, together with Archbishop Cranmer and Lord Chancellor Audley, was to have complete management of affairs in the south, almost a small council of regency.

Everyone knew, of course, that the King hoped for his young Queen soon to be with child, to provide a brother for Prince Edward, and all the Court had had hopes that the prolonged honeymoon would do the trick. Yet there were some unkind whispers and Thomas, looking now at the pretty Cat pressing two

271

new dogs into the sensible arms of Anne of Cleves, questioned secretly the state of affairs. Once, in the past, when his family had skated on the frozen Thames, he had asked Jane whether the King was impotent. And the birth of her son had proved him wrong. But three years had passed since then and Henry Tudor's colossal weight gain and ulcerated leg could be doing him no good.

I wonder if she'll take a lover? thought Tom, and then his mind shied away from such a terrible prospect. After the horrific example of Anne Boleyn, Cat's own cousin, nobody could ever again be so foolish.

Suddenly reluctant to get caught up in public celebrations, Thomas left the hall, turning towards the quarters allotted to him in Hampton Court. In each of the palaces the courtiers had their own apartments, the size and grandeur of which depended on their importance in the scheme of things. And as uncle of Prince Edward, yet still only a humble knight, Thomas's dwellings hovered between the stately and the plain.

I'll have to marry this high-born woman of mine, he thought, if I want to live well.

And it was with this semi-serious thought uppermost in his mind that he turned a corner and walked straight into Katherine, Lady Latymer. Thomas had never been more startled. No rumour had reached his ears that she was to be present at Court for the Twelve Days; in fact he had heard nothing about her at all since last year's May Day tournament. As far as he was aware, she was still living safely in Yorkshire with her old and horrid husband.

'God's breath,' he said, and then stood staring at her while he collected himself.

Katherine curtsied deeply, bowing her head to hide the wild colour of her cheeks. 'I wish you a happy New Year, Sir Thomas,' she said.

'And I you, Madam. And I you,' stuttered Tom, for once in his life completely at a loss.

Suddenly sensing that she was mistress of the situation, Katherine took advantage. 'Her Grace informed me that you kept Christmas in Wiltshire. How nice for you to be with your family. Unfortunately, though my husband was here at Court until two days ago, he has had to return to Yorkshire to care for the children.'

Though she thought she was being clever, Katherine had actually set herself a trap, for Tom, recovering quickly, said, 'Then, no

272

doubt you will be lonely. Allow me to be your new-found friend.'

She was furious. In fact Katherine Latymer went white and with only the curtest of nods would have gone her own way if Thomas had not lain a hand on her arm.

'Lady Latymer, forgive me. The truth is that I find you one of the most attractive women on earth.' He drew himself up to his full height and put on his sincere expression. 'But as God is my judge and witness I would not harm a hair of your head. The truth is, Madam, that I regard you too highly to do one wrong thing.' And with that he strode off.

He had got halfway down the corridor when Katherine called out, 'Sir Thomas, please. I did not mean to give offence.'

'Nor I,' he said over his shoulder. 'By God, nor I.'

She hurried up to him. 'Please Sir, you must know the truth. Her Grace has called me to serve as a member of her Chamber, and this I will loyally do. But whenever I can, I must return to Yorkshire, for there my duty lies.'

'Duty,' said Thomas softly, with a glance guaranteed to melt a heart. 'I believe you know that word well, Lady Latymer. And who am I to come between a woman and her set purpose?'

'Sir Thomas?' Her voice was a question.

'Madam,' guessed Tom with unerring accuracy, 'I believe you to be two people in one. Inside the good wife and dutiful stepmother there lurks, I fancy, a bright, free creature. Something wild and unfettered.'

'A butterfly,' she murmured.

He did not hear her. 'What?'

'Nothing, Sir Thomas. I must be on my way. Her Grace wishes to prepare for the evening.'

'Is there to be a ball?'

'No, merely a quiet supper *à trois* for the King and Queen and the Princess of Cleves.'

Thomas smiled knowingly. 'A clever one that.'

Katherine raised her brows.

'The Lady Anne. Now she is a favoured sister and invited to dine. I truly believe she must be the most intelligent woman in the world.'

Lady Latymer sighed, thinking to herself that *she* had not shown intelligence. That if she had had a grain of sense she would have remained a widow until someone like Sir Thomas Seymour had come courting, instead of going, out of sheer boredom and loneliness, into another unfulfilling partnership.

Her thoughts must have been written on her face, for Sir Thomas said, 'But there, we are not all so gifted as the Lady. It is very easy to make mistakes.'

'Have you made any?' asked Katherine lightly, hiding her feelings.

'Dozens, Madam, dozens. But there is one folly that I have never committed.'

'And that is?'

'Marriage, Lady Latymer. When I was a boy I swore that I would never marry unless my heart was completely stolen away. And so far it has remained unattacked.' Thomas gave a glorious smile. 'No, that is not quite true. It has been attacked but not defeated. I await love's dart.'

Katherine Latymer opened her mouth, then shut it again, obviously at a loss as to what to say in reply. Eventually, she murmured, 'When that day comes I hope you find great joy, Sir Thomas.'

Apparent truthfulness blazed from his blue eyes. 'It will never come, Madam, unless I find the right woman – and she is free to marry me when I do so.'

For a moment Katherine stood mute, then with another deep curtsey, she hastily turned and hurried along the corridor until she was out of sight. Tom, watching her go, gave a low whistle.

'If ever I saw one itching for love, that is she,' he muttered to himself, and putting his hat at a more jaunty angle, decided that after bathing in scented water and changing his clothes, he would, after all, join his fellow courtiers that evening.

Both Catherine Howard and Anne of Cleves had also decided on a change of garments before supper, so the ladies of the Chamber were hard put to it. Catherine, like a spoiled child, insisted on wearing all her Christmas presents; a square neck piece containing twenty-seven diamonds and twenty-six clusters of pearls; a brooch which contained thirty-three diamonds and sixty rubies; a muff of black velvet, trimmed with sable and thirty-eight rubies and five hundred and seventy-two pearls.

Katherine Latymer, watching the giggling and display, could not help but wonder how long it would be before such a lively creature as Cat grew bored with an obese old man whose legs constantly oozed pus and whose bedchamber performances now must be most seriously curtailed by his enormous girth. Would all the jewels and clothes be sufficient to keep her occupied and consoled? Thinking of her own life, which had been a series of inept kisses, elderly flesh, and lovemaking that had lasted all of two minutes, Katherine hardly thought so.

Standing back discreetly and observing, she noticed that the Queen seemed to surround herself with the attendants she had known as a child. Like little partridges they swooped in and out, overtly respectful to the Queen, and yet somehow not. Lady Latymer had the strong impression that sometimes they were almost winking together.

Yet there was one old retainer with whom Cat Howard seemed on friendly terms; Jane Rochford, Anne Boleyn's sister-in-law, widowed by the axe when her husband George had been accused of incest. Lady Rochford, who had made her peace with the King during the reign of Jane Seymour and returned as a Lady of the Chamber to serve Jane, Anne of Cleves, and now Cat, hovered like a dark shadow wherever the new Queen went.

'Interesting!' thought Katherine Latymer. 'Obviously making herself indispensable. But why?'

At last the changing was done and, surrounded by a bevy of servants, Cat and Anne made their way to that room in the Queen's apartments set aside for her private suppers. Here, a table was already laid with rich plate and gleaming cups, and the Queen's musicians, grouped in the corner, were making a cheerful sound by way of greeting.

'Oh, how lovely,' said Cat, and danced a few steps on her own. Then she looked round. 'We shall need only two ladies to attend us, as this supper is most informal. Lady Latymer and Lady Rochford, if you would stay to serve us please.'

The room emptied other than for the handful of servants who would wait at table.

'Tonight there is to be a special treat, dearest Anne,' said Cat, rubbing her hands together in anticipation. 'The King of France, to show his love for his brother of England, has sent us three great pies made from the largest wild boar ever killed in his country.'

'Delicious,' said the Lady of Cleves.

They smiled together but then were distracted as noise at the door heralded the entrance of Henry Tudor, accompanied by two of his Gentlemen. Katherine Latymer could hardly believe her eyes as Sir Thomas Seymour and Sir Nicholas Carew bowed to the royal ladies, and then to herself and Jane Rochford.

But if Tom had had any idea of standing ogling, these were to be dashed. Henry, advancing on Anne and giving her a sprightly kiss on the cheek, announced, 'Tonight we will be private. Ladies and gentlemen, we give you permission to leave us.'

And with that he kissed his wife fondly on the lips before she could argue and took his seat at the table. Rather disconsolately the others took their leave, though Thomas was the least put out.

'In this case,' he said smiling, 'will you all do me the honour of supping in my apartments?'

Katherine was on the point of refusing when both Sir Nicholas and Lady Rochford accepted in one voice, considering the diversion welcome. To refuse in view of the others' enthusiasm was out of the question. Katherine inclined her head gracefully and said 'Thank you,' in a tone that she hoped was not over-enthusiastic.

Afterwards she suspected that Thomas had known all along that the King was going to dismiss them, for when they entered his dining room it was to hear four musicians and a singer already at work, and to see a host of servants swarming about with table-ware.

'What a delightful scene,' said Carew, the man whom Lady Latymer remembered as the former champion of Jane Seymour.

'I aim to please,' said Thomas, his smile sincere, and Katherine felt her opinion of him mellow as he personally seated the ladies near the fire and made sure that the servants attended to their every whim.

Not since the death of Lord Borough, when she had lived with her stepson and his wife, both older than she, had Katherine spent such a happy evening with people who were more or less her contemporaries. And never in her entire life could she remember having such a carefree time. As the wine flowed, so did the conversation, easy, witty and amusing, and more than once she caught Thomas's eye and laughed at something that just the two of them thought funny.

It did not occur to her, innocent that she was, that the tremendous surge of happiness she was feeling was due to any other cause than enjoyment. But slowly, as the musicians played love songs and the singer sang of heart's desire, it came to her that this warmth, this unbelievable glow of pleasure, was the dawning of some unknown emotion.

She looked up and found Thomas's eyes, as deep a blue as the sea and just as unfathomable, fixed upon her. But as Katherine tried to look away those eyes smiled, and she saw in their depths a wonderful expression, so warm and kind and caring, that her heart seemed to catch light. Now she could not drop her gaze, however hard she tried. Katherine Latymer sat staring at Thomas Seymour as if she had never seen a man before in her life.

Which I don't suppose, he thought inside his clever head, she ever has.

With a clap of Thomas's hands the music changed and the musicians beat out the galliard, the dance that meant contact, the man lifting his partner up on his knee. Rather drunkenly, Nicholas Carew and Jane Rochford hopped and laughed; but Thomas was serious, raising Katherine high into his arms as if she weighed nothing. And all the time he never took his eyes away from hers; one would have thought that they were the only two people in the room.

In the end it was time to go and Katherine was subject, and never more strongly, to the great divergence that formed her character. The butterfly beating its way tremulously back to life, would have spent the night with Thomas Seymour, soaring to an ecstasy she had never known. But her twin soul, the good Katherine who suffered old husbands and cherished children that were not hers, was only too grateful to make an exit with Jane Rochford, curtseying in the doorway, murmuring thanks, and then hastening away.

As they went out of earshot, Lady Rochford looked at her knowingly. 'Now *there's* a man! Was it my imagination or did he seem to be regarding you fondly?'

Katherine turned astonished eyes on her. 'I think you must have thought it, for I noticed nothing.'

Jane Rochford smiled. 'I see.'

Katherine thought it best to change the subject. 'I wonder if His Grace's supper party continues.'

Jane laughed. 'If it does it will only be the two ladies left to dance together. His Grace retires early these days.'

The words, 'He is not as young as he was,' were out of Katherine's mouth before she could stop them.

Lady Rochford turned to look at her, an odd smile playing about her mouth. 'Indeed. And now he takes the youngest bride of all.'

Katherine stared back at her, saying nothing, as Jane's voice lowered to a whisper. 'Poor little thing, how will she spend the rest of her life in need of a proper man.'

'Don't say it,' answered Lady Latymer uneasily. 'Such words are best left unspoken.'

'But still . . .' said Lady Rochford, as she turned to go into her own apartments, '. . . it must be hard.'

Katherine did not reply, instead dropping a swift curtsey and hurrying back to the meagre room which was the best that she, as the wife of a rather unimportant northern peer, could muster.

But down in the Queen's apartments, where both Catherine and Anne had drunk far more wine than was good for them, the supper party went on. As predicted, Henry had long since retired to bed, leaving the Queen and the Princess to dance together. This they did, with much laughing, as the musicians played on. And it was then that the young girl, having become indiscreet, whispered to Anne, 'You are lucky.'

'What?' the Lady of Cleves replied, puzzled.

Cat dropped her voice to nothing, leading Anne to stand by the fire where the players could not hear. 'I said you are lucky.'

'Me? Lucky? Why, dear Cat?'

'Because he never touched you.'

Anne frowned, her English still not good enough to give her command of every nuance.

'*Who* never touched me?'

'His Grace,' said Cat, then clapped her hands over her mouth and rolled her eyes just as if she were a naughty child.

'What are you saying?' asked Anne, hoping that she was misunderstanding.

'I'm saying that . . .' Cat's voice was barely audible under the music, and Anne found herself straining her ears, '. . . he can't do it.'

'Do what?'

'*It.*'

'What is *it*?' asked Anne, totally mystified.

'Tumbling a woman. Oh, dearest, don't look like that. I mean His Grace doesn't satisfy me.'

Whether the Lady of Cleves's grasp of the language actually

278

deserted her at this stage or whether that clever woman feigned complete lack of understanding, Cat never knew. But nonetheless it was fun to burble away, telling all her heart's secrets to someone who seemed to have no idea what she was talking about.

'I *know* what it's like to do it with someone young, you see. It was very naughty but when I was twelve I hid behind the altar in the Duchess of Norfolk's chapel and did it there with my lute teacher.'

Again Catherine clapped her hand over her mouth but Anne's face remained totally blank.

'And he wasn't the only one either. My cousin Francis Dereham – he's the handsome one you asked about, who has come to court to be my private secretary – did it with me hundreds of times. He used to come to the dormitory where I slept with those four girls you saw. They all know about it.'

Anne's face remained impassive. 'What are you saying, Cat?'

'I'm saying that it was wonderful and now I miss it. That's the only bit I don't like, having to go to bed with the King.'

Anne stood up, her plain face calm and undisturbed. 'Dearest Cat, I am so tired. Your Grace, do I have your permission to withdraw?'

Catherine became suddenly regal. 'Of course you may, Lady Anne.' She held out her hand and the Princess kissed it.

'Goodnight, Your Grace.'

'Goodnight, dear Anne. And not a word, you understand.'

The no-nonsense face looked at her blankly. 'What word?'

'Oh, it doesn't matter. Goodnight.'

After she had gone Catherine Howard stood for a moment as if undecided. Then she waved her hand at the musicians.

'Gentlemen, play country tunes. When I was a young girl in Sussex we used to dance to those in the Dowager Duchess's house.'

Their leader, a handsome young man in his twenties, answered, 'But surely Your Grace is not going to dance all on her own?'

Cat frowned. 'No, of course not.' She ran a seasoned eye over him. 'You'll do, whatever your name is. Let's dance the night away.'

'But Your Grace . . .'

'No buts. Come on, fellow. Don't keep me waiting.'

And with that the Queen walked over and dragged him from where he sat. The other three sat nonplussed but at the order, 'Play on' said in a somewhat strangulated voice by their leader, they blew and fiddled with a will.

And that was how the new Queen of England spent the first night of 1541, dancing and drinking with her own musicians, while in his apartments not far away, her royal husband gasped and snored in his sleep, his enormous stomach rising and falling with each breath.

# Chapter Twenty-Two

IT WAS A GLORIOUS SPRING, very swift and sudden. One day the earth had been covered with cold-smelling snow, its diamond points glittering in the sun, the next it had vanished in a sudden thaw. Green was everywhere, buds thick and plentiful, the woods carpeted with wild flowers. In the mornings there was mist and at noon the rushing rivers gleamed crystal, while at eventide the unusual warmth of the February days brought a haze to the fields.

The early spring decided Zachary Howard to take from his stables the raw-boned pewter-coloured beast purchased at Deal and journey on it to Norfolk. And though Cloverella thought it foolish, the creature having such a wild and unpredictable air about it, the astrologer insisted. He had bought the horse on the day Anne of Cleves landed in England, and though it still would, if it could, nip his flesh if he turned away his eyes, Zachary had an understanding with it. He called it Fairy, mostly to annoy it, for nothing resembled less such an ethereal and delicate creature.

But though he departed with laughs and kisses from his gypsy wife – they had indulged in a blood wedding but not yet had benefit of priest – Zachary was secretly worried about the purpose of his journey. Since the time of their great argument over the Duke's niece Catherine, not a word had been exchanged between Zachary and Norfolk. Even at the recently passed Christmas, his natural father had not communicated, and the gifts prepared for him by Zachary and his children had remained uncalled for. Now they were packed carefully into saddle bags for the astrologer to take with him.

'But if he does not see me I shall leave them behind,' he whispered to Cloverella. 'It would make the children so wretched if I return with them.'

'Oh, surely he must come round,' she said in reply. 'He has always loved you.'

'He thought that I doubted his word and it angered him far more than I would have imagined.'

'Then, in some way, he is guilty,' answered Cloverella certainly.

'You may be right about that.'

But as he rode away from Greenwich, taking the ferry across the river to the Essex side, Zachary was aware that he had not told Cloverella all the truth. The fact was that he had held off from marrying her in church, despite the terrible pressure from the Earl of Hertford, because Zachary wanted his father's blessing before he did so. And yet the rivalry between Howard and Seymour grew and the astrologer felt certain his father would not approve his choice of second wife. Nonetheless, Zachary was determined to have Cloverella, finding her his ideal woman, as clever and witty out of bed as she was in it.

The journey through East Anglia at this time of year had a strange, almost unreal quality, the lowlands swathed in mist and moisture, so that sometimes as he rode, the broad beast clattering at speed beneath him, Zachary felt cut off from the world and time. He almost could believe that the vapour might part to show him Hereward, the Fenland leader of the revolt against William the Conqueror, wading through the shallow waterways, hiding in the reeds, ready to strike at the enemy, still alive in his own century.

The astrologer was glad to leave the deserted places behind and enter the medieval market town of Bury St Edmunds, still an important centre of the wool trade; though to see the once great monastery where the martyr king was buried, now standing sacked and empty, he found distressing and pitiful. And that mood of sorrow, of wondering the future of the kingdom, still lay heavy on Dr Zachary when he arrived in Kenninghall as the shadows of evening darkened.

As with all communities built round a great dwelling place, the village snuggled at the castle's foot, and the inn where wayfarers might find accommodation seemed almost to nestle within its walls. Thus it was with an overwhelming sense of his father's presence that Zachary scratched a note, sealed it, and paid a boy to see that it was delivered into the hands of the Duke's steward, though this, of course, did not totally guarantee that Norfolk would ever get to read it himself.

Yet Zachary had other plans. It would not be the first time he would have made his way within the castle precinct. Once as a boy he had been taken there and, when he was grown, he had forced his way in to nurse his father through an attack of the Sweating Sickness. Now, if it was necessary, he would chance his luck again. But this course of action was not destined to take place.

As night came over the village and the quietness descended which meant that the only two places where life would continue after dark would be the alehouse and the castle, Zachary decided to take a stroll. Making his way through the one main thoroughfare he stood aside as the beat of hooves told him that a party of horsemen was coming, yet as they drew level with him his attention was riveted. In the midst of his escort the Duke of Norfolk was riding out in the gloaming.

With stunning alacrity, Zachary stepped forward and swept his hat from his head, giving one of his more florid bows. As he straightened up he was rewarded by the sight of the Duke looking back over his shoulder. Zachary bowed again, his teeth white in his dark face, positive that he had been recognised.

'Your move, my Father,' he said, and singing cheerfully and loudly made his way back to the tavern.

Within two hours he was amused to see a cloaked figure, obviously one of Norfolk's servants, enter and look round.

'Have you any strangers staying here?' Zachary heard the man murmur to the alehouse keeper.

'I believe you are looking for me,' said the astrologer and stepped forward before another word could be spoken.

Slightly astonished, the man asked, 'Dr Zachary of London?'

'I am he,' said Zachary, and contorted his face oddly, giving the impression he was not altogether of sound mind.

'Umm,' said the servant, very slightly alarmed. 'His Grace the Duke of Norfolk has asked that you accompany me to the castle.'

'Then I must,' answered Zachary, 'for who am I, who is anyone, to disobey an order from a Duke?'

The expression on the servant's face was abundantly clear, his master obviously wanted this idiot for entertainment and as long as the creature behaved itself, why not?

'Then come along. But no tricks, mind.'

'Tricks?' answered Zachary, a dark crystal appearing in his hand as if by magic. 'What tricks?'

'Oh never mind! Just hurry!'

They walked in silence, Zachary peering into the crystal and saying, 'Yes. Yes,' from time to time, until eventually the servant ran out of patience.

'What is it you see?'

'I see you as a married man, lad. With a goodly wife, well made. *Very* well made.' The servant stared but said nothing. 'And I see you with a lady friend, Sir, quite small, like a fairy.'

The man, who was single, looked ghastly and Zachary, who was not reading the crystal but making the whole thing up, felt suddenly guilty. 'The two shall never find out about each other, though, and you will father many children by each. You will be the envy of all your peers. You are a lucky man.'

He looked into the crystal in earnest and saw that he was not far from the truth. 'Well, well!' he said wonderingly, and with that hid the globe away as mysteriously as it had been produced.

It seemed to Zachary as he entered the castle stronghold that the women of his father's household were present in abundance this night for, from a room leading out of the great hall, a medley of female voices could distinctly be heard. Listening carefully, Zachary caught the sound of Elizabeth, his father's second wife and mother of his two children, her boring, monotonous tone quite drowning the soft voice of her daughter Mary, the widowed Duchess of Richmond. It had been Mary at whom Thomas Seymour had set his cap, only to have Henry Howard ruin everything. And Henry's wife Frances, Countess of Surrey, was present as well. She and Surrey had both been sixteen when they married eight years ago and now they were thoroughly bored with one another. In fact it was common knowledge that these days Henry Howard was obsessed with a girl of fourteen, Lady Elizabeth Fitzgerald, recently come to Court to serve Catherine Howard, much to his delight.

Wondering what the ladies' reaction would be if they knew he was present, Zachary quietly followed the servant up the stairs to the Duke's private room. As he was ushered in he was vividly reminded of that time, all those years ago, when he had been taken as a child to Kenninghall to see the father he had never then met.

Now it all seemed to be happening again as the Duke turned to

284

stare, running his gaze over him and absorbing every detail of Zachary's appearance. 'So,' said Thomas Howard after a small silence, 'you have come to see me at last.'

Zachary bowed. 'Yes, Lord Duke my father, I could not travel before because the ways were treacherous. I hoped you would still be here.'

'I was on the point of returning,' answered Norfolk coldly. 'The King will soon be leaving for the north and I am chosen to accompany him.'

'I know,' replied Zachary, and waited.

Eventually, the Duke motioned him to a chair and poured a cup of wine, saying, 'It has been a long time since we last spoke.'

'I was in the wrong then, Lord Duke my father. I implied something and I apologise for it,' Zachary answered at once.

Howard looked at him over his broad nose. 'You implied that I knew . . . something . . . of the Queen's Grace. But I assure you I know nothing of her.'

'Then so be it,' answered Zachary hastily. 'That is the best way.'

'Then you are truly suggesting . . . ?' Norfolk stopped, leaning back and putting the tips of his fingers together.

Zachary gulped his wine convulsively. 'I would rather not discuss it, Sir. It led me to fall out with you last time, and nothing is worth that.'

'Then,' said Norfolk thoughtfully, 'we'll say no more. But before I do close the subject, give me one word of advice.'

'Gladly.'

'If this young girl is not all she pretends, what then for the Howards?'

'Danger, Sir. But leave her to her own salvation. A fool is a fool and can never be helped.'

'And she is that?'

'All of it and more, Lord Duke. She is a creature that lives for excitement and her excitement only comes from one thing.'

'Which is?'

'Illicit sex, Sir. Oh, do not look so grey! Catherine is the sort who makes love dangerously, the thought of imminent discovery her stimulant.'

'God's Holy Mercy!' The Duke dabbed his upper lip. 'I pray you are wrong.'

'So do I,' answered Zachary solemnly. 'So do I.'

'I shall try to warn her,' Norfolk said thoughtfully, his face very set.

Zachary shook his rumpled head, the sheen of silver in it picking up the light. 'I would keep quiet, Sir.'

'I must do what I must. But now enough of all that. How are you, and the children? I have missed them.'

'They are well and happy. And as for me, I have entered a time of great contentment.'

The Duke's eyes met his and Zachary saw in his father's expression a certain amusement. 'A new woman?'

'A new wife, Sir.'

The Duke's glass stopped half way to his lips. 'You have *married*? Without obtaining my blessing?'

'Lord Duke my father, be calm. We have wed like Romanies, by the letting of blood. The solemnisation by priest I have delayed until you give me your permission.'

Howard looked instantly suspicious. 'Who is this woman?'

'Elizabeth Wentworth,' answered Zachary calmly. 'First cousin to the Seymour clan but half a Romany, as I am.'

The Duke said nothing and Zachary sat watching the fluttering glimmer of firelight as it played about his father's features, showing them at one moment craggy and hard, at the next warm, understanding. The room seemed full of little noises, a comforting mixture of familiar sounds, of scratchings and rustlings and cracklings, as dogs moved and mice ran and the logs shifted in the hearth, a lovely brightness flashing and dying with them.

'I wish,' said Zachary dreamily, before the mood was broken, 'that I could be forever with you like this.'

A flame burst forth picking out the Duke's face clearly for a moment, and Zachary realised that the thin Howard mouth beneath the long hawk nose was more at ease than he could ever remember seeing it.

'My son,' said Norfolk quietly, 'I wish you well with your new wife. You have done your best with life and deserve happiness. The fact that she is a Seymour I will overlook. In any event it is Surrey who fears them more than I do.'

'My half-brother fears and dislikes many people, Sir. He is not cut out for Court life.'

'No, he should have been a poet. At heart I believe him to be an unhappy man.'

286

'And though he hates Thomas Seymour more than anyone, have you noticed how alike they are?'

'No,' said the Duke slowly, 'in fact I haven't. But you are right, of course. There is almost an affinity between them, now that I come to think of it.'

'An affinity that does not auger well.'

'Does it not?' asked the Duke softly, and after that there was silence.

The lovely spring continued. The meadows near Hampton Court were full of early colour, pussy willow trees displayed clumps of soft silver fur and light green catkins danced and swayed in the woods and hedgerows. The river gleamed blue, winding clearly through pastures and hills, catching the gleam of sunshine as it went, and ignoring the boats on its back or the hearty people who dived into it, as it flowed past Hampton's great palace. It seemed to Catherine Howard, staring disconsolately through one of the upper-storey windows to where some naked urchins played in the shallows, the most beautiful waterway in the world, the spring outside the finest she had ever seen.

The pensive Queen, all seventeen years of her, had married her monstrous husband eight months ago and, until recently, had done nothing since that day but dance and rejoice, never allowing herself time to think, never for one second contemplating the endless future that stretched relentlessly before her. But then, last February, all frivolity and pleasure had abruptly ceased. Henry had gone down with a fever and the ulcer on his leg had closed. To avoid the danger of a clot the surgeons had had to drain fluid from him daily.

After that how terrible everything had become! All of a sudden Cat's pig-wig had turned into an ill-tempered, evil, invalided old man who wanted no noise and no fun and everyone, including his child bride, had had to creep round like mice to avoid his fury. Amusing guests had ceased to call while the King lay sick, and consequently Catherine had found life wretched, a chasm of boredom, the truth suddenly home as she became terribly afraid of all those long and miserable years that might lie ahead. Instead of laughing the Queen now wept daily, and if it had not been for the company of Lady Rochford, or Lady Roe as she liked to call her, Catherine simply did not know what she would have done.

Now, gazing at the river, she felt at her lowest ebb. Today was

Shrove Tuesday, the last day that anyone could eat nice things or make merry, as tomorrow saw the beginning of Lent and all the obligatory fasting that must be endured until Easter. Usually such an occasion never passed without a play or at least music, and pancakes and other traditional delicacies were always served. But now there was nothing. Just a terrible, boring silence.

At the very idea of such unrelenting gloom, the Queen screwed up her face like a spoiled child and ran to her apartments in search of Lady Roe, a willing ear to all her poured-out problems.

'Your Grace, my dearest,' said Jane Rochford as Cat came rushing through the door and hurled herself into the elder woman's arms. 'What is it? What can be wrong? Madam, please tell me.'

She had a clever way with her, this dark-haired widow, so enigmatic that nobody ever knew what she was thinking, yet capable of charming the childlike Queen by a curious combination of servility and mothering.

'It is just that everything is so quiet and depressing,' sobbed Catherine into Lady Rochford's lean bosom. 'We always made much of Shrove Tuesday when I lived in the Duchess of Norfolk's household. It was the last chance we young people had for fun. But look at it here! Is it not like a graveyard?'

'There, there, Your Grace,' said Jane, dabbing at the pretty little face that had now slid down to her lap. 'We must think of something amusing for you to do.'

'Me?' said Cat wretchedly. 'What can I do that's amusing when I'm all alone?'

Lady Roe looked thoughtful, her dark brows drawing together. Then, like summer, she smiled. 'Why not give a small supper party, Your Grace? Just you and a few of your younger ladies, with myself to attend you. You could ask Master Dereham, your cousin, to bring an equal number of gentlemen. There could be a little quiet music, a few cards, some discreet dancing and, provided nobody makes a lot of noise, His Grace need never be disturbed.'

Cat turned to look at her, her face that a moment ago had been the picture of despair, now sparkling and animated.

'Lady Roe, I swear I could not live without you. Will you go to Master Dereham with a note while I see the cook? Oh, it could be such fun.'

Jane Rochford played a trump card. 'Your Grace, my dear. As you have been upset and anxious for His Grace, naturally . . .'

Cat muttered an echoing, 'Naturally.'

'Why don't you let me tuck you up for a rest and leave everything to me? By the time you wake up, your party will be arranged.'

Cat smiled, then stretched her arms over her head and yawned. 'Dearest, dearest, Lady Roe, if the evening is a success you shall have a wonderful present.' She clasped her arms round her knees. 'Oh, Lady Roe, please make it happen. The mood in the Palace has been so awful recently that we deserve a little gaiety, don't we?'

'Yes,' answered Jane Rochford, smiling her dark, interesting smile. 'I think it is time for some fun. Now rest, Your Grace, and soon I will come with good news.'

On Shrove Tuesday, just as a welcome shower drenched the flowers so that their scent came up from the earth with the raw heady smell of spring, Zachary Howard and Elizabeth Wentworth were married in the private chapel of Wolff Hall by Sir James the priest, now old and stumbling and very nearly blind.

The dear old man, frail though he had become, performed the ceremony with much sweetness, aware as he did so that two people stood before him who could not have found their way in the world always easy, marked with the stigma of tainted blood as they were. He also loved the bride, remembering her from early childhood, for he had been there on the very day her Romany grandam had left Cloverella at Wolff Hall, Dame Margery calling on him to swiftly bless the girl and lift from her any curse the Romanies may have laid. But he had known then from its little flower face that the babe was free of evil and that the laying on of hands, though done to please the good Dame, was not truly necessary.

And now he thought, as he gazed fondly at Cloverella in her silver tissue wedding gown and pearl-decked headdress, she was hardly changed. Maybe because his sight was clouded and he was not at all the spry fellow he once had been, but to him the little creature looked the same, still possessing the great violet eyes and clouds of nightshade hair that had picked her beauty out from all the others.

The bridegroom too, or so reckoned Sir James, was a personable being; his face full of lively expressions and pleasant idiosyncracies, hair black as pitch, though shot with silver, and a mass of dancing curls like a halo. His eyes were spellbinding, golden as a bird of prey's, yet with a warmth and wisdom all their own. And their owner looked at his delicate bride as if he would cherish her all his life.

'God bless you, Sir,' said Sir James, where he shouldn't have spoken, yet not caring about the *faux pas*.

And it was then that he saw Jane. Quite distinctly, though his old eyes had to peer, the priest glimpsed Jane Seymour sitting in the pew behind her mother, dead but unflawed, smiling.

'God bless you, Lady,' he called again, and the bride and groom though saying nothing followed the direction of his eyes.

Sir James never knew afterwards whether they had seen her or not, for no one spoke. Though Dame Margery, also turning, let out a little cry, while her hand flew to her mouth. But then came the moment for the wedding ring to be placed upon Elizabeth Wentworth's finger and by the time the bridal couple had kissed and Dame Margery and Henry Seymour – Thomas and Edward's shy brother, who hated town life – had come to kiss them too, there was no sign of the pale spectre who had smiled so wanly.

Yet afterwards at the wedding feast which was small but goodly and held in the Great Barn to remind Cloverella of past days, the old priest could not resist but lean across to the bridegroom.

'Dr Zachary, my son, you may think me a blind fool but I would swear that today in chapel I saw Jane the Queen at your wedding.'

'She *was* there,' Zachary answered quietly.

That evening, just after their wedding, Cloverella took her new husband to walk in the Young Lady's Garden, made especially for Jane when she had been born. At this time of year only the early flowers were out but the roses and gillyflower were already in bud and the dark, mysterious shrubs had points of colour everywhere.

'She would sit here,' Cloverella whispered, 'over there on that stone seat.'

She pointed, and just for a split second both of them saw Jane again, dressed in white, tendrils of mist weaving about her feet. Then she was gone as quickly as she had come.

'I hope my friend is happy,' said Cloverella quietly.

'She is. She has seen you as a bride.' Zachary turned her to look at him. 'My bride, whom I love.'

'As I you,' answered Cloverella.

'If you ever stop,' said Zachary, 'I shall remind you of tonight when we glimpsed Jane the Queen.'

'Jane the Queen,' repeated Cloverella slowly. 'Now just a poor, sad little ghost.'

And near to tears she slipped her hand into Zachary's and walked back to Wolff Hall and the wedding guests.


'Poor sad little ghost,' said Catherine Howard round-eyed, 'does she really haunt the great stairs of Hampton Court?'

Francis Dereham laughed. 'Only on the anniversary of the Prince's birth, Your Grace. There is no need to be afraid.'

He looked at her with a lazy insolence, as if he still had carnal knowledge of her, smiling to think this creature of whose body he knew every inch was now the Queen of England. He would never, could never, take it seriously. His angel slut married to that living, oozing mountain of blubber when she liked lean, hard young bodies pressed close to hers.

She smiled at him. 'I think we all grow melancholy. Master Tandridge, play for us to dance, but softly mind. We dare not risk waking His Grace.'

Cat's supper party had been a great success. In the end there had only been six present; Catherine Tylney and Margaret Morton making up the female numbers; while on the gentlemen's side, Francis had invited two young members of the Privy Chamber, Thomas Culpepper, another Howard cousin, and Thomas Paston. Though the guests had of necessity been quiet, they had eaten well, with pancakes and other delights of Shrove Tuesday coming up from the Palace kitchens, and beautiful sweet things following, to say nothing of an abundance of wine which had reduced the young things to much laughter and whispers of 'shush' as the evening wore on.

During the course of the meal the Queen had left her guests and gone to the King's apartments where she had bidden Henry, in pain and consequently gloomy, a sweet goodnight.

The piggy eyes had looked at her suspiciously. 'You seem very bright, Cat. Are you feasting in your rooms?'

'No, Sir,' she had answered, curtseying and kissing his hand. ' 'Tis but myself and two of my ladies eating sweetmeats before Lent.'

He had patted her head. 'Dear child. Enjoy yourself. It must be misery for you, shut up here with an invalid like me.'

Cat had forced a naughty smile. ' 'Tis but a respite from your loving, Sir. For I vow you are such a man as would tire a young girl.'

The obese creature looking at her had managed a twisted grin. 'Wait till we get on progress, dear one. Then we'll see a brother for Edward.'

Catherine had curtsied again, her head so low that her face was completely hidden. 'I pray so, Your Grace. Now I bid you goodnight and restful sleep.'

'Come and see me when you wake.'

'I will, Sir. Nothing shall prevent me.'

She had once more kissed his hand, then fled away, glad to be out of the stench of the sickroom and back with her young and carefree companions.

The Queen had only allowed one of her musicians, John Tandridge the lutanist, to be present, and he to play softly at that. But now, with the supper done and Lady Roe and the servants who had waited at table gone, Cat longed to dance. Very gently John struck up and the six youthful people took their partners. Before the Queen's Grace bowed her childhood friend, Thomas Culpepper, as beautiful a young man as Cat had set eyes on in months. In the flickering firelight she let her eyes drink in his appearance, lingering on the lissom body with not an ounce of fat upon it, and the curling brown hair and tanned skin in which two clear blue eyes, a shade most similar to forget-me-not, looked at her from lashes that were almost black. To crown Master Culpepper's beauty was a mouth like a rose, though not silly and girlish, just well shaped and curling.

'May I have the honour of dancing with Your Grace?' he said as he straightened from his bow.

'You may,' answered Cat and held out her hand with dignity. But when he put his lips to it she felt sensation run straight from her fingers to her breasts. It was difficult for a girl still in her teens to be aloof with a handsome man not much older, and after a moment Cat relaxed.

'Your Grace still dances beautifully,' said Culpepper, his face close to hers and both his eyes and mouth smiling, reminding her of when they used to play as children.

Cat smiled back. 'And so do you, Tom.'

The dance continued until that moment when her partner had to lift Cat high on his knee. With a feeling that was so indescribably sensual, Master Culpepper put his arms to the Queen's waist and

292

raised her up. As she dandled above him Cat knew that he held her deliberately high and when he slowly lowered her, though whether by accident or design she could not say, he slid her the length of his body so that she could feel every muscle.

Dismissing Master Tandridge, the six young people, suddenly tired, sat by the fire on low cushions, Francis Dereham making sure that the wine cups remained filled.

'Are there really such things as ghosts?' said the Queen, returning almost fearfully to the subject.

Thomas Culpepper who sprawled beside her, said lazily, 'You are nervous of them I think, Your Grace.'

'No, no. It is only that my cousin, Queen Anne Boleyn, is supposed to ride a horse sometimes in Norfolk – and neither she nor it have heads. It is said that a servant once cast eyes on the ghastly apparition and died of fright.'

She had gone pale, even her merry friends could see that, and now they made moves to comfort her. The two ladies patting her hands and calling her, 'Sweet' and 'Dearest', Dereham from the privileged position he had once enjoyed saying, 'Come now, Madam, I would have thought you to have had more sense than to believe scullions' gossip.'

The others looked a little aghast but the Queen ignored his familiarity, simply replying, 'No, I am not afraid and I shall prove it to you all. Let us go on a ghost hunt now.'

'But where at this hour?'

'To the great stairs. We'll see if Queen Jane Seymour walks tonight.'

There was a general gasp at her audacity, then moving like mice yet giggling wildly, the six set out, Francis in the lead. Behind him came Catherine Tylney, her hand in his; then Margaret Morton with Thomas Paston. Last of all walked the Queen and Thomas Culpepper and as she stumbled in the darkness and felt his hand go out to save her, it seemed the most natural thing to hold it.

The touch of their fingers, one upon the other, sealed the death warrant of that couple. For never before had either of them experienced anything like it. Sensation after sensation ran through their bodies until they were weak from touching and only wanted to fall into each other's arms and never move again. But neither knew the other's feelings and poor Tom Culpepper, realising that he had the Queen of England by the hand and was a dead man if he were to do her insult, tried hard to keep himself from brushing against her body in the blackness. While Catherine Howard, a born sensualist, only wished that she were an ordinary girl that she might pull him to her in a kiss and find out, in that way, if he wanted her.

In the end the problem was solved for them as they neared the staircase and Mistress Tylney let out a little scream.

'Did you see anything?'

'I'm not sure. I thought there was a woman in white.'

'Help,' said Cat, and turning headlong plunged back to her apartments, Tom Culpepper right behind her.

Just for a moment or two as they reached the Queen's rooms, they were alone.

'Are you there, Tom?' she whispered softly.

'Beside you,' he answered and took her hand again, raising it to his lips.

It was enough. They were in each other's arms and all the wanting, all the need, locked their bodies close together.

'Oh Tom, Tom,' murmured the Queen.

'Oh Madam, you are so beautiful,' answered the poor doomed fellow and kissed Cat as he never had a woman before, parting her lips beneath his and letting his tongue find hers.

She froze in his embrace. 'The others are coming, be careful.'

'May I see you again?'

'Tomorrow if you wish. We are, after all, both beneath the same roof.'

'But, Madam, it is so dangerous.'

Very softly in the darkness, Catherine Howard laughed. 'I know.' Then she pulled his mouth down to hers and kissed him as the others drew near.

## Chapter Twenty-Three

IT HAD BEEN HOT all day, unnervingly so for September, the sky cloudless, the clear strong blue of foreign seas. Framed against it, the trees had looked almost sinful, brazen as harlots in gawdy shades of crimson and gold. There was not a breath of wind, so that falling leaves went sighing down like dying dancers, quite straight and effortlessly, touching the ground below, then no longer moving.

In the heat people and animals, in coats too heavy for them, grew irritable. Dogs barked and scratched on every corner, while hissing cats found the shade. Men and women, dressed for the day before, not realising that the weather would change, sweated and stank, their clothes sticking to hot, infested bodies. There was quite a lot of drunkenness as the citizens of London sought to slake their sudden thirsts, and this led to more trouble as drunks swore and urinated, constables were called out in several parishes, and two dozen youths in Cripplegate threw eggs at passers-by.

Supremely oblivious of humanity and its frailities the sun soared above, brilliantly gilded, striking the river with a long finger to make it glint blindingly, then casting shadows dark as death. Mulberry hues lit dusky corners, nothing escaped the glaring eye. There was no mercy, even those dying in shade were warmed before the final chill.

Then, suddenly, it ended. The sky filled with flower shades; fuschia, rose and pansy; the river turned to wine. Red pennants fluttered in the west and clouds gave signs of battle as a ball of blood hung over the horizon, shimmered, and was gone. It was evening.

Edward Seymour, my Lord of Hertford, had not wanted to wash that day, there being a certain nuisance attached to having his servants heat and bring water, but even without his brilliant wife, ever ready to tell him he was noisesome, he realised with reluctance that he must. For once, Edward had been at leisure, relaxing in his quarters in the Palace of Westminster, untypically drinking at midday, and going down to the riverbank where he had fallen asleep in the sunshine. The result was now all too obvious as Edward delicately sniffed round himself. He must strip and bath before the evening's Council meeting.

With Henry Tudor's progress north now in its third month, the meetings of the only three Councillors left in London – Edward, Audley the Lord Chancellor, and Archbishop Cranmer – had settled into a smooth routine. As the King had commanded, almost the entire Court were with him, so it was the task of the trio to continue day-to-day administration, referring all important matters to the full Council, who travelled with their sovereign.

For this was no ordinary progress, no casual hunting trip. The King, with his Queen, his daughter Mary, his Council, his Gentlemen, his henchmen, heralds, bowmen and several foreign diplomats, was really putting on a show of strength.

While Jane Seymour had been alive, the northerners had dared to mount the Pilgrimage of Grace, their voluble and armed protest against the sacking of the northern monasteries, which had been ruthlessly put down by the Duke of Norfolk, acting on the King's command. For speaking on the rebels' behalf Henry had screamed at Jane, telling her to remember her place, reminding her of the fate of her predecessor. But now he travelled to that rugged part of England to show his quelled subjects his new Queen, his pretty Catherine, the nubile eighteen-year-old who had made him the envy of all men.

Edward had heard from the messengers who constantly passed between Westminster and the progress that the ordinary working people couldn't take their eyes off her, staring at her beautiful clothes and jewels as well as her vivacious face. Apparently the whole colourful train was causing a sensation wherever it went. Nobody alive could remember such a glorious yet dignified spectacle as, amidst a brilliant shout of trumpets, Henry and his entourage entered city after city, richly robed, leaving behind an encampment of some two hundred pavilions, in the style of a Roman emperor.

Pageantry, thought Edward as, leaving his clothes in a heap on the floor, he stepped naked into a wooden tub and began to lather the dark hairs on his chest. Pageantry and show, that's all they're cheering. By the time the King leaves some of the simple ones will think he's God come down to earth.

He splashed in the water, closing his eyes, wondering why Archbishop Cranmer had called a Council meeting for this evening, specifying in a cryptic note which had arrived that morning that it would be better if they gathered after dark.

The man loves drama, thought Edward, and smiled. Nonetheless it was intriguing that the Archbishop had thought something serious enough to convene a semi-secret meeting. Very vaguely, Edward began to wonder what it was.

By the time he was dressed, pulling one of his favourite soft hats on to his head and studying for kemptness the reflection of his strong dark features, he was curious. So much so that he sent a messenger to Audley's apartments in the Palace to ask if the Lord Chancellor might see him early.

But this did not prove as useful an exercise as Edward had hoped, for the Chancellor greeted him with, 'Have you any idea why we are meeting tonight?' To which Edward could only reply, 'I was going to ask the same thing of you.'

'Well, we won't have to wait long,' Audley answered, frowning. 'His Grace the Archbishop has asked if we might be private here at seven.'

Edward took a seat where the Chancellor indicated. 'Why the mystery do you think?'

'I don't know. Yet I have the feeling it must be weighty.'

They sat in silence, lost for words and suddenly tense, and it was a relief when a hum of voices told them that the Archbishop had arrived. A second later he stood in the doorway, very solemn, his dark eyes resting on his fellow Councillors mournfully and his usual swarthy chin tonight very shadowed.

Hertford and Audley rose to pay their respects but Cranmer cut them short. 'Gentlemen, information of great importance has come most unexpectedly into my hands. I beg you be seated that we may discuss it without delay.'

The Earl and the Chancellor shot each other a brief, puzzled glance but sat at once. The Archbishop cleared his throat, then said, 'I dread this moment.'

'My Lord,' answered Audley sharply, 'your fellow Councillors are in suspense. Of what matter is this?'

Cranmer shook his head as if delaying a second longer, then said quietly, 'This information is of the most serious sort and concerns Her Grace the Queen.'

'The Queen!' exclaimed Edward, though Audley remained silent, thinking of another night meeting long ago when Anne Boleyn had been the subject under discussion.

'Two days ago a man named John Lassels came to me and said he had information for my ears alone. It appears that his sister Mary, now married, was a confidante of the Queen when she was a girl, having been a chamberer to the Dowager Duchess of Norfolk. Sirs . . .'

The Archbishop broke off, his voice quite husky and Edward realised that he was leaning forward, his hands gripping his knees.

'Go on, my Lord.'

'Gentlemen, at the age of twelve the Queen lost her virginity to her music teacher, Henry Mannox, even boasting how they made love hidden behind the altar in the Duchess's chapel.'

Cranmer sounded as if he was going to vomit and both the other men made noises of disgust.

'Not only that. She later abandoned Mannox for her cousin Francis Dereham who spent night after night with her in the maidens' dormitory. There are eye witnesses to her guilt!'

'Holy Jesus, son of God,' said Audley and plunged his head into his hands. 'I cannot bear it. His Grace will lose his reason. He dotes on the girl.' He narrowed his eyes, looking directly at the Archbishop. 'My Lord, you are certain this is true?'

'Certain,' answered Cranmer heavily. 'Both Lassels and his sister are prepared to swear it on oath.'

There was a terrible silence as the three men sat gloomily staring round the room, avoiding each other's eyes.

Eventually Edward said, 'How can we possibly tell him?'

'I don't know,' sighed Cranmer, 'I simply don't know.'

'I suppose we *must*?'

As soon as he had said it Edward knew that he had been foolish and both men rounded on him.

'Yes, Sir, we *must*,' answered Cranmer. 'To hide a truth would be morally wrong.' The righteous angel came down to earth as the Archbishop added, 'Besides, if His Grace found out from another source, our concealment of the story would be considered a crime.'

'Then who?' said Audley. 'Who dares brave His Grace?'

'I think the one to do so,' Edward answered thoughtfully, 'should be he whose veracity could never be doubted. I think you should speak to him, my Lord Archbishop.'

'But surely,' said Cranmer, 'not before he returns from progress?'

The three men looked at one another questioningly. 'No,' Audley said, after a while, 'that would be too much for the King to bear. Let it wait until he returns.'

Cranmer dabbed his brow. 'At least that gives me time to prepare myself by thought and prayer.' He seemed to have accepted without argument the fact that he should be the bearer of such ill tidings and Edward's heart went out to him.

'It is a great responsibility, my Lord, but I truly believe that you are the right choice.'

'Yes, yes,' Cranmer's thin hand once more wiped away beads of sweat. 'But *how*? What words can I use? That is the grim question I must resolve. What does one say when one breaks a sovereign's heart?'

Edward suddenly wanted to cry, 'Nemesis!', but controlled himself admirably, thinking only in the sudden stillness that nobody, from the highest to the most humble, could ever escape the inexorable mills of God.


The moon had a touch of frost about it even though the day had been warm. It was small, a dainty silvered crescent, hanging in the midnight sky above the ancient and moated manor of Holme at Spalding Moor, fifteen miles from the city of York.

The scene was so perfect, the pretty little castle sitting in the midst of its moat, the waters made mercurial by the silvery night, that it could almost have been painted. And the fuzzy outlines of moonlit sheep in the fields beyond the keep did nothing to help the air of illusion.

Sitting up in bed and watching the moon play fairies with the water, the Queen of England seemed transformed. Gone the silly giggling little girl who had married a King for what she could gain, for here was a woman. Hair, silvered by the night, hung about glorious shoulders, slimmed down and beautiful, as was her face. Now the fine bones of Cat could be seen, high cheeks and the lovely curve between them and her chin, like a valley of softness. Her breasts were bare. Two small hills of silver with dark nipples, wonderfully placed, full and firm.

But her serene expression outshone everything else. For this was a woman not only in love, tremendously and generously so, but fulfilled – one of the privileged few who had found her other self, a man so much part of her that together they had become an individual. In this way, Catherine Howard had been changed from a pretty, plump adolescent to a woman of immense loveliness, and everyone who saw her must remark it.

Now, as on the rest of that long progress, she awaited her love. Poor Tom had kept away from her after that first stolen kiss at Hampton Court, as of course he must do, mortally afraid of the terrible wrath that could fall upon him. But the pull between them had been too great. Even before they had left the Palace to go north, Thomas Culpepper had come to the Queen to possess her body and by so doing, claim her heart.

Cat had been reluctantly forced to confide in Lady Roe, for someone had to help two people who loved each other so desperately that they could hardly bear to be apart. And with her guidance they had managed. Wherever they had gone on progress she and Cat between them had discovered where lay the back stairs, the secret entrances to the Queen's apartments and what locks, when Tom was desperate, could be picked.

Catherine and her lover had lain together at Greenwich, Hatfield and Lincoln and by then, of course, her Ladies had guessed everything. But they were her faithful four from the past and held their peace, though at Pontefract their hearts had been in their mouths when Catherine Tylney thought she had observed different guards and believed that the King had set them to watch the Queen's nocturnal visitor. But it had been a false alarm and the next day there had been much relieved exchanging of looks between Cat and her four old friends.

In York, where the architecture had been somewhat difficult, Tom had been forced to hide on the back stairs and, at another time, make a forced entry into Cat's apartments. But in a way that had been part of the thrill; knowing the risks they took and how much sweeter their love was for it.

And now, here in the old castle of Holme, she awaited him again; climbing the spiral in one of the turrets, coming to her through the night, drawn as a moth to a candle, in love in the face of the most monumental risk of all.

Cat hugged her knees, a gesture left over from the time when she had been childish, gauche. But now the chin that rested on top of them was shapely and sweet. As she heard his scratch upon the door, it was a woman's voice that whispered, 'It's safe.'

That night, that cherished night in the little castle, Cat felt that she had never known such lovemaking. As they lay awake till dawn, she and Tom merely dozing now and then, Cat was completely at one with him as the hard part of his body entered her, again and again. What joy it was to lie with the man she loved above all others, what bliss to share kiss after kiss. In what paradise had been discovered the touch of his hands as they caressed every part of her? Together that night, with every fulfilment, Catherine Howard and Thomas Culpepper were transported beyond themselves and through some mystical gate into regions very rarely reached by ordinary men and women.

But then, as they slept in that one cold hour before dawn, neither of them lay truly easy and at Lady Rochford's soft call Tom was instantly awake and hastily pulling on his hose. Cat woke too and wept a little.

'Must you go?'

'I must, darling. Lady Roe has called.'

'Then hurry. It's nearly light.'

They kissed, feeling the thrill of danger as the distant footsteps of changing guards could be heard.

'Until tonight?'

'As soon as it's safe.'

Tom gave her one last long kiss, then was gone. With a deep sigh the Queen snuggled down to sleep for an hour or two before the day began and it would be time, once more, for her to smile prettily upon her royal husband.


The Council of three, almost in daily touch with the progress, all knew a moment of raw terror as the King's return to London became imminent. According to messengers, His Grace had dallied at the pretty manor of Holme for a few days, before setting out for Hull where he remained for nearly a week, showing off his lovely wife to the astonished citizens.

'Do you think the old man still does it?' one of the town's more dubious ladies had asked another, watching the radiant girl enter within the city walls.

'Well, if he doesn't somebody else certainly does. I've never seen a more contented woman.'

'Then a toast to the Queen!'

'And to whoever she takes to bed,' echoed her friend, eyeing up the mass of soldiers and retainers flooding into the city in His Grace's wake and thinking that royal progresses, whatever their true objective, were certainly good for trade.

But now that was past and the King was almost home. It was the end of October, 1541; the harvest was gathered but it seemed, or so thought Cranmer, that the grimmest reaper of all could yet be wielding his scythe.

After hours of deliberation and prayer he still had not found the answer to his appalling dilemma. Yet the facts remained and would not go away. Henry had arrived at Windsor and from there would make his way to Hampton Court. It was only a matter of days now before the truth must come out. To make the situation worse, Cranmer had received royal instructions that on All Saints Day, the 1st November, the Bishop of Lincoln was to offer special prayers for the King's safe return and for the good life he led, and trusted to lead, with his jewel of a wife. The Archbishop had cringed both mentally and physically, dreading all that lay before him.

Yet nothing Cranmer had imagined was anything like the horror of reality. In the chapel of Hampton Court he had hardly been able to concentrate on the mass as out of the corner of his eye the Archbishop watched the Queen. Burdened with knowledge, he had been obliged to echo prayers for the King's future happiness, even while he did so his gaze turning again and again to that small demure creature, kneeling in the shadow of Henry's bulk, crossing herself like the good Catholic she was, her lids cast down with much show of modesty.

It had been that, the sight of the little hypocrite, that had finally given the Archbishop the strength to do what he must. Excusing himself from one of Henry's inevitable feasts, Cranmer had left Hampton Court and gone straight to Lambeth by water, there locking himself into his study, the way quite clear. With his mind fixed firmly on Catherine Howard's smirking expression, the Archbishop picked up quill and parchment and wrote down everything that Lassels had told him. Then he sealed the statement with Canterbury's great seal and went to pray.

The next morning, waking early after only a few hours sleep, Cranmer, in full pontificals, took to his barge once more and was rowed to Hampton Court in time for the Mass for All Souls Day, the day following All Saints. This occasion was more than solemn, it being the festival when the dead were especially prayed for.

Images of long-gone queens floated before Cranmer's inner eye as he began to chant the ritual; Katharine of Aragon, assuredly killed by Henry's withdrawal of love from her, dying wretched and alone, the prisoner of Kimbolton Castle; Anne Boleyn, the wonderful nymph whom nobody could ever catch, could she really have been turned into a nagging shrew by Henry no longer wanting her?; Jane Seymour, pale and demure, hacked open to release her son and indubitably dying as a result. It occurred to Cranmer then, very heavily, that the monarch had much to answer for, but he fearfully turned the idea aside. For the good of his realm Henry Tudor had done what he did. Or was that just a cover? Was the King a vile tyrant who killed women when he no longer had any use for them?'

'Oh God, God,' said Cranmer, and fell on his knees in a torment, hardly daring to look at the congregation of great men. Then the necessary strength came to him and he rose up valorous, thanking the Lord.

'Your Grace,' he murmured as Henry lumbered up to him to take the sacrament. 'I have something for you.'

'Yes?' The King's silly eyebrows arched.

'It is a letter, Your Grace, and I beg you now, if you have ever considered me friend, to read it well and in private.'

And with that the Archbishop slipped the paper into Henry's hand.

'Surely, Cranmer, this is not the place . . .'

But the Archbishop had resolutely turned away so that Henry had only two options, to throw the thing aside or to slip it into his pocket. To the Primate's overwhelming relief he did the second.

The die is cast, may the outcome be in your hands, oh Lord, prayed Cranmer beneath his breath. But then, horrid and unwanted, to go with those images of dead queens, came another. Cranmer saw a beautiful head, its owner still a girl, cleaved from its neck, the shapely body fallen in bloodstained straw.

'God's mercy for the Queen,' was on his lips before he knew it.

With summer over and the threat of plague gone, the courtiers' wives and older children who lived in London returned from the country, including Anne Seymour from Hertford Castle. Despite

303

her pride and posturing, which Edward had to admit were sometimes irritating, he was still fascinated by Anne. So much so that to please her he had disinherited his two eldest sons, who had been born to his first wife, the faithless Katherine Filliol, and were therefore slightly suspect as to legitimacy. In their place he had nominated his son by Anne, another Edward. This was her second boy, the first having died when he was two, and from their robust marriage she had also given Edward two daughters and a new baby, Henry. Yet Anne Seymour maintained her good looks, still slender despite the recent birth, her fall of red hair as bright as it had been when they met.

Now it was the Seymours first evening together after the summer break, during which months Anne had given birth. Consequently Edward had only seen his new son twice, afraid to leave London while the King was on progress. But, very cleverly, Anne had left every single child behind, including the baby, so that she could concentrate on her husband.

While the Queen's early indiscretions had been unreported, Edward had kept the secret, but now everything was out in the open he felt free to discuss the matter. Yet a most extraordinary turn of events had taken place, an eventuality that Edward would never have believed possible. As he recounted it to his wife her eyes widened incredulously.

'You say he laughed?'

'It is hardly credible, yet it's true. The King's Highness read Cranmer's letter then laughed in his face.'

'A great turnabout since the days of Madam Boleyn,' said Anne with asperity.

'The Archbishop has been in a state of shock ever since.'

'But how did it happen? Did His Grace not believe it?'

'Precisely. He said that John and Mary Lassels were lying, that Francis Dereham was lying. He almost accused Cranmer of lying. He believes, or wants to believe, that the whole thing is a vicious calumny invented to blacken the Queen's character.'

'And who would do that, pray?'

Edward raised dark brows. 'The Seymours, or someone else opposed to the Howards.'

'God's blood,' exclaimed Anne, jumping to her feet. 'Does His Grace think that?'

'I don't know. But he believes it strange that in the Council of three left behind there was not one supporter of the Howard clan.'

'Christ's mercy,' said Anne, still fuming. 'Things have come to a pretty pass when the monarch is so infatuated with a chit that he will not listen to the advice of his own Councillors. When he accuses them of lying for simply telling the truth.'

Edward laid a hand on her arm. 'You are so loyal, sweetheart. I love you for it.'

His wife sat down again, somewhat more calmly. 'So what will happen now?'

'I shall take you to bed,' said Edward, deliberately mis-understanding.

'You know perfectly well what I mean. What does the Archbishop intend to do?'

'He is already doing it. He is interviewing witnesses and will then present to the Council that there is a case to be answered. The King will have to listen. Even he cannot overrule his advisers forever.'

'But Norfolk and his henchman Stephen Gardiner are on the Council.'

'Two men, my dear, two men. Already the Duke of Suffolk and the Secretary of State, Wriothesley . . .'

Anne muttered, 'That social climber!'

'. . . have been won over. They will see the Queen finished if they can.'

'Norfolk must be sweating blood,' said Anne with a sly grin.

'Probably, though I have nothing against the man. It is Surrey who makes trouble.'

'How did he and Thomas get on together during the mission to Guisnes?'

'I believe it was all perfectly civilised. They did not come to blows, at least.'

'Well, that's a mercy,' answered Anne, and laughed. 'And where is your brother now?'

'Just back from progress like everyone else. It is a bitter thought, is it not, that all the time the King presented his rose without a thorn to the crushed rebels of the north, there lay a worm within?'

Edward's wife shivered slightly. 'Bitter indeed. And there may yet be bitter consequences.'

The Earl stood up. 'Enough of the Queen and her follies. It will spoil our first evening together. Let us walk by the river for half an hour while it is still light.' He slipped his arm round her. 'You have told me little of how the baby progresses. Are his eyes still blue?'

'No, he is getting like you,' answered Anne, relaxing into his shoulder.

'Poor thing,' said Edward, as fathers have done since time began. Then he and his wife laughed and kissed and went on their way, fondly.

## Chapter Twenty-Four

THE PROCESSION SETTING OUT from the King's house, built near the village of Chelsea, was not one of particular importance. At the head rode Sir Thomas Seymour, a little girl sitting proudly in front of him, held in place by his arms which were wound tightly round her. Behind came several of the King's servants and two litters, one of which was empty. That was all, no particular pomp or splendour attached to this modest train bringing the Lady Elizabeth – no longer styled Princess since she and her half-sister Mary had been removed from the line of succession – to see her father.

It was strange, thought Thomas, putting his nose near the child's hair and idly sniffing the warm clean smell of it, the way the fortunes of Henry's two daughters swung from one extreme to the other. Jane had worked hard to get them reinistated at Court, particularly Mary, for both girls had been stripped of their titles long before his sister had become Queen. Mary had ceased to be Princess of Wales when Elizabeth had been born; Elizabeth had lost her status when her mother had lost her head. Now, with a girl in her teens as Queen, greatly though Catherine liked Elizabeth, both she and Mary were isolated again – just like their young brother who Henry kept away from Court, for fear of the boy contracting a fatal illness. The days of having a loving homemaker like Jane Seymour for a stepmother were well and truly over.

Yet, despite their shared sorrows, how different the two sisters were: Elizabeth so vital, Mary so sad and bitter. And with good reason. Thomas grinned, wondering whether in view of the constant failure of plans to marry Mary off even he might have a chance of the royal hand. Yet it was no laughing matter. The poor girl had been betrothed at the age of two to the Dauphin of France, only to see the promise founder. After that she had been passed like

307

a package between Charles V and various other sons of François of France, the whole sordid business adversely affecting her health.

She needs me, thought Thomas cheerfully, I would liven her up.

Almost as if she sensed that he was no longer concentrating on her, Elizabeth gave a squirm. 'Sir Thomas?'

'Yes, my Lady?'

'May I dismount? I would speak with my governess, Lady Bryan.'

'Certainly, Madam.'

Thomas swung out of the saddle, his body nimble and graceful, a fact that was lost on Elizabeth but not on Lady Bryan, mother of the notorious Sir Francis, who had descended from her litter as soon as the procession stopped. She hurried forward, looking anxious.

'What is it, my Lady? Are you ill?'

'No,' said Elizabeth roundly, then whispered in her ear.

Thomas smiled. Even to king's daughters, nature must call. With great tact he gave the servants five minutes' rest, then took advantage of the enforced stop himself. When he returned from the trees, Elizabeth was back, running after the falling leaves, her hair the same vivid hue, in some lights flame, in others the colour of oranges. In contrast with this her eyes, which should have been blue or green to compliment her colouring, were dark like her mother's.

Elizabeth, even in childhood, was the embodiment of autumn: her lithe body lean as a twig; her paleness the white of evening frost; her hazelnut eyes part of the season's richness. Her hands, too, were eloquent, speaking of late and delicate flowers, the long and perfect fingers like petals of some rare specimen that would die as soon as winter first breathed upon it.

She was alluring even at this age. Though not a beautiful child she had enormous charm, together with a certain aloofness which Tom Seymour believed Elizabeth had inherited from her mother.

'Shall we continue, my Lady?' he asked now, bowing and sweeping his hat off so that his hair, darker than hers but with more gold in it, caught the October sun and gleamed.

'Yes,' she said, quite shortly, but in no way rude.

'Then may I lift you up?'

'Don't you think Madam should ride in her litter?' asked Lady Bryan anxiously.

'I'd rather not,' Elizabeth answered without hesitation. 'I can see far more on horseback.'

And with that she held up her arms to Thomas so that he might lift her. As he stooped and took her childish waist a sudden and almost overpowering sense of pleasure filled him, which continued as he raised the girl into his arms, then on to the horse's back. Even as he leapt up behind her, the lovely feeling was still there. Then disgust with himself drove it away. Horrible words like 'lecher' and 'molester' ran through Thomas's mind as he urged the horse into a trot. And yet it was exquisite, a sensation beyond any other he had known. The woman-child in his arms seemed to exude a fascination he had never experienced before. Almost dreamily, Thomas closed his eyes for a moment and pretended she was older, fourteen, ready to receive a man's love and courtship.

He opened them to find that Elizabeth was looking at him, and her beautiful mouth – how strange he had never noticed its sensual curve – was smiling at him.

'Were you asleep, Sir Thomas?' she asked, knowingly he thought.

'If I was, I was dreaming of you, my Lady, Did you know I danced on the day of your birth, and I have rejoiced in you ever since,' he answered.

The child in her giggled, the girl blushed, and Elizabeth turned her face away and stared straight in front of her.

'How is His Grace?' she said, changing the subject abruptly. 'I look forward to seeing him. And dear Cat – Her Grace – too.'

Looking at the small averted profile, Thomas said, 'You are fond of your new stepmother, are you not?'

'Oh yes,' Elizabeth answered enthusiastically. 'She is kind to me. She is my cousin, as you know, and I am given the place of honour next to her when we are together. Her Grace is pretty, or at least I think so. Do you agree, Sir Thomas?'

'Is it proper for me to tell you? After all, she is Queen.'

Elizabeth shot him a brief calculating glance, not certain if he was teasing. 'Perhaps you are right,' she answered. 'Perhaps we should not discuss Her Majesty.'

'But I am sure she would not care.'

'You have just asked,' Elizabeth said sharply, 'whether it would be proper. Make up your mind, Sir Thomas.'

He laughed out loud, loving her quick wits and acerbity.

'I concede, my Lady. You have made me look a fool.'

Once again Elizabeth shot him a rapid glance. 'I am sorry for that, Sir. It was not my intention.'

'I think,' answered Tom slowly, 'that we should stop talking and enjoy the ride. Now, my Lady, let us see how fast I can get you to Hampton Court.'

'By all means, Sir Thomas. As long as we don't fall off.'

'No fear of that,' he answered, and gathered the child tightly into his arms, appreciating the feel of the sparrow-thin body against his chest even while he berated himself for unnatural desires.

On the day of Lady Elizabeth's visit to her father, a visit during which she spent long hours with Queen Catherine, eating sweet-meats and playing games and cards, Henry Tudor hardly spoke at all. In the way of most children, the girl immediately thought it was her fault, stealing fearful glances at her father, where he sat in his great chair, moody and irritable. But he did not glance back and nothing about him reassured her. In the end Elizabeth, who had not seen the King for months, began to review her recent behaviour, convinced that she had sinned in some way and the matter had been reported back to him. Finally she plucked up enough courage to ask, choosing a moment when Cat had left the room and they were finally alone.

Approaching the vast chair and dropping a highly respectful curtsey, Elizabeth said, 'Your Grace, Father, have I done wrong?'

He turned on her a glance that almost froze her blood. 'Not yet. But no doubt on reaching woman's estate you will.'

'What do you mean?' asked Elizabeth, taking a step backwards.

'That women are whores. That Queens are whores. And you, young as you are, will probably grow into one.'

Elizabeth's face flamed. 'I shan't, Sir, I shan't. I shall remain pure, like the Lady Anne of Cleves.'

A smile flickered round Henry's little mouth, hidden amongst the fuzz of his beard. 'You count her as a friend, do you not?'

'I love her,' answered his daughter defiantly. 'I love the Lady Anne more than anyone.'

'More than me?' he asked dangerously.

Elizabeth went even redder. 'Not more than you, Sir. You are my King and my liege lord as well as my father.'

'A great many words for a little creature! And what about Her Grace? Do you love her more than the Lady Anne, or less?'

Something in his tone warned Elizabeth to be very careful of her answer and she stood considering.

'I like them the same, Sir, though differently.'

'And what do you mean by that?'

'Well, Your Grace, the Lady Anne is rather shy and I love her like a dear little dog. But Her Grace is smooth and sleek and pretty, like a darling cat. They are both my pets.'

'Well said,' answered Henry. 'You've got her silvered tongue, haven't you?'

'Whose?'

'Nobody,' he said abruptly and, heaving himself out of his chair, left the room without another word.

For the rest of that day, when His Grace did not return, Elizabeth puzzled over the remark. But as her father did not come to say goodnight to her – she was to leave the next morning – she was unable to question him further.

'Where is His Grace?' she asked Cat, who had come to tuck her in and plant a smacking kiss on her lips.

'Oh, I think he is closeted with Sir Thomas Wriothesley somewhere.'

'I don't like that man,' whispered Elizabeth. 'He's a dark devil.'

Catherine giggled. 'You must not say things like that.'

'Why not?' answered Elizabeth. 'He is. Wait and see.'

They kissed goodnight and Cat went to her apartments, wishing that Thomas Culpepper could come to her but fearing that within the confines of Hampton Court, though they had risked it before, a meeting would be too dangerous.

Yet long after she blew out her candle and fell into a lonely and rather restless sleep, the lights in the King's apartments burned, for Henry was in discussion with Thomas Wriothesley, the principal Secretary of State. The King's great frame wedged, as was customary, into an overpowering chair, threw a shadow on the wall like a vast spider sitting amidst its web. But on this occasion, Henry Tudor was the fly and the lean stalking Wriothesley the hunter as he paced the King's chamber, words pouring from his lips in a torrent.

'Your Grace, I beg you to believe what I tell you. I have conducted a further examination of witnesses regarding the Queen's early life and it does not make a pretty tale. When she was twelve years old, Sir, she gave herself to her music teacher, Henry Mannox. Apparently the old Duchess caught them *in flagrante delicto* and beat them both, charging them never to be alone together again. But then, Your Grace, Francis Dereham, now Her

Grace's Private Secretary, took Mannox's place in her affections. He regularly used to visit the maidens' dormitory in both Horsham and Lambeth. The Duchess's keys would be stolen by one of the girls, then they would let their lovers in. After they had all feasted on strawberries or, if they be not seasonable, apples and wine, they would make love. Dereham admits, Sir, from his own mouth that he has known the Queen carnally many times, both in his doublet and hose between the sheets, and in naked bed. He says they were betrothed, Your Grace, that the Queen entered into marriage with you when she was pre-contracted.'

The bulk in the chair shifted but said nothing.

'So, Your Grace, the Council wish to meet in emergency session. They feel that this case cannot be overlooked any longer.'

Henry spoke at last. 'Wriothesley, there is no chance at all that this is an anti-Howard plot?'

'No, Your Grace. That family has enemies, it is well known. But nobody could bribe this number of witnesses. Would Dereham himself admit and risk so much just for money?'

'No,' said the King slowly, shaking his head. 'No.'

'Then, Sir, action must be taken.'

Henry nodded. 'What do you suggest?'

This was so unlike him that for a moment Wriothesley was thrown off balance. But he recovered quickly.

'I would advise, Sir, that the Queen's movements be curtailed lest she try to leave Court.'

'Yes, you're right,' said Henry almost as if he were in a dream. 'See to it, Wriothesley. But first, make sure the Lady Elizabeth leaves the palace. Have her woken at dawn and taken to Chelsea. Then put guards on the Queen's door. You may inform Her Grace yourself.'

Wriothesley bowed. 'It shall be done, Your Grace. And may I inform the Council that a meeting will be convened tomorrow?'

'Yes,' answered Henry with a complete change of manner, 'but make it the evening. I intend to hunt all day.'

The Secretary of State stared astonished. 'Hunt, Sir?'

'Yes,' said the King shortly, 'hunt. Good night, Sir Thomas.'

'Good night, Sir,' answered a bemused Wriothesley, and backed from the room, wondering if he would ever know the workings of Henry Tudor's amazingly complex mind.

\*　　\*　　\*

By seven o'clock the next day a rather sleepy Lady Elizabeth had been put in her litter, protesting that she had not said goodbye to either father or stepmother, and taken firmly away from Hampton Court. Having checked that nothing had been left behind to cause the child to return, the Secretary of State called upon the captain of the King's guards with whom he conferred in private for ten minutes. After that he made his way to the Queen's apartments.

It was Lady Rochford who received him in the ante-chamber, informing Wriothesley coldly that Her Grace was still in bed and would not see him. Smirking a little, he made a very formal bow.

'Lady Rochford, I bear grave tidings. Certain matters have come to light and the Council is now investigating allegations regarding the Queen. Madam, you must inform Her Grace that on His Grace's instruction she is to be confined to her apartments pending further enquiries.'

The look on the dark face opposite his frightened Wriothesley. Lady Rochford lost colour so rapidly that he thought she was about to faint and went to catch her. But she recovered quickly, pulling herself out of his grasp as if he had the plague. From very tight lips she said, 'May I tell Her Grace with what she has been charged?'

'Nothing as yet,' answered Wriothesley curtly. 'The Council have not completed their investigations.'

The eyes staring into his looked haunted. 'But what is it that is being investigated?'

The Secretary of State brought his face to within an inch of hers.

'The Queen's morals, Madam. It is said by many that she is a loose woman. Now what would you know about that, eh?'

Again Lady Rochford drained white but this time she was ready for the shock. 'I know nothing, Sir. Now I'll ask you to be gone. I must prepare the Queen for all that lies ahead,' she answered in clipped tones.

'Yes, do so,' Wriothesley said over his shoulder as he made for the door. 'Remind her that she stays here only at His Grace's pleasure. He could quite easily have sent her to the Tower.'

He was rewarded by a cry of anguish as he opened the door to the sound of a contingent of guards marching purposefully along the corridor towards the Queen's apartments.

An hour later the King, dressed for hunting, left his apartments and made for the Chapel to hear Mass and pray for the full recovery of his four-year-old son, suffering with a quartern ague, as the multitude of physicians attending the boy assured Henry it was. Wriothesley had already left for London to convene an emergency meeting but the fact that he had been there overnight and that there were now guards standing outside the Queen's apartments had not gone unnoticed. The whispering gallery buzzed with rumour and there was a huge attendance at the service to see if anything untoward should occur.

The King took his place alone in the royal pew and the ritual was just about to begin when a sudden uproar broke out. There was the sound of running feet and Catherine Howard's voice could distinctly be heard.

'Mercy, Your Grace, I beg you for mercy. Protect me I implore you,' she was screaming again and again. There were two doors to the private pew, one leading from the King's apartments, the other from the Queen's. Now the handle of her door turned and every eye looked aghast. But before it could open there was the sound of a fall, followed by a cry of pain. The King was seen to shudder as the noise of a violent struggle broke out, accompanied by the most terrible shrieks ever heard. That the Queen was in a state of hysteria and being forcibly dragged, struggling violently and begging for her life, could easily be interpreted. There was a noise in the chapel like a distant moan of thunder as everyone murmured to everyone else. Only the King remained silent, though beads of perspiration could be seen to run down his face. There followed a terrible few minutes in which the sounds of the Queen's agony finally grew less, then died completely away. Then Henry spoke.

'Begin the Mass, Sir Priest,' he said tersely, and if he was shaken he hid it well.

But as soon as the service was over the King, very pale and talking to no one, left the Palace for an afternoon hunt. And later that day, as dusk fell over the River Thames, he was rowed to London in the royal barge to attend the meeting of the Council. He was never to set eyes on Catherine Howard again, his last memory of her fondling Elizabeth, just as it had been of another Queen who in the recent past he had sent most savagely to her death.

The extraordinary meeting had been called in the home of Stephen Gardiner, Bishop of Winchester; a wry move indeed. For it was in this house that Henry had first set eyes on pretty Catherine, and it was here that the lovers had held their clandestine meetings, far away from Court spies. Henry tasted bitter gall as he alighted at the water steps, so full of sweet and recent memories of a pretty little girl waving excitedly when he arrived.

'By God,' he said to himself as he limped his way indoors. 'They had better have a case to answer. If my sweetheart suffered as she did today and it is all for naught . . .'

But in his heart he knew the cruel truth and as he entered the great room and looked at the Council members, already gathered and grim-faced, the King suffered the most terrible moment of bleak despair. Nonetheless, he regarded them with mean and vicious eyes, determined to prove them wrong if he could. Catherine had brought great comfort for a man in his advancing years; a pretty face and body, and constant assurances that he was virile. If it were possible at all to prove the wretched informants mere gossipmongers, with gutter mentalities only fit to spew out calumnies and lies, the King of England was prepared to do so. With a smack of defiance in his lumbering walk, Henry Tudor took the high chair and declared the Council meeting open. Swallowing hard, the Archbishop of Canterbury rose.

'Your Grace, it is my painful duty to tell you that further investigations into the allegations laid against the Queen's Highness lead this Council to the firm conclusion that they are true. Your Grace, we believe there is a case to answer.'

Henry shifted in his chair and closed one eye, the other blinking lizard-like. He said nothing.

Sir Thomas Wriothesley got to his feet for his turn. 'Your Grace, as I informed you yesterday the statement of Francis Dereham that he was betrothed to the Queen and therefore had every right to intimacy with her is sworn to by others.'

'Lies,' said Henry viciously. 'Lies manufactured by enemies of the Howards.'

The Duke of Norfolk, sitting opposite Edward Seymour, gave a slight nod of his head at this but unfortunately it was seen by the King.

'You agree, my Lord. You know your niece to be pure, am I right?'

Norfolk was cornered and knew it. Rumour after rumour had reached his ears of late and he was now convinced that his stepmother, the Dowager Duchess, had done little more than run a high-class bawdy house while the young people of the Howard kinship had been under her protection.

'Your Grace,' he said, then stopped, unable to go on.

'Well?'

'Your Grace, in truth, I no longer know. Like yourself I am plagued by rumour.'

Edward Seymour, Earl of Hertford, stood up purposefully. 'Your Grace, I believe that the matter has far outstripped rumour. Francis Dereham says the Queen only took him into her service as Private Secretary that she might assure herself he spread no word of their past. He was blackmailing her, Your Grace. Sir, the Queen must answer this case.'

There was an agonised silence during which Edward sat down again and everyone shifted their feet. Finally Wriothesley said, 'Your Grace, do we have your permission to proceed?'

The great bulk in the chair made no move.

'Sir?' said Wriothesley again.

A muffled snort was his only answer and everyone stared aghast as the King's vast shoulders heaved convulsively.

Oh Christ! thought Edward Seymour, more distressed than he had been for years, the King is crying. This is more than can be borne.

Though he longed to look away, he watched with a terrible fascination as Henry plunged his head into his hands, his whole vast body wracked with sobs. But this was more than crying, it was an orgy of weeping, of misery and wretchedness, as Henry Tudor publicly realised that he was old, that women no longer cared if he lived or died, that he was nothing but a vast blob of humanity with suppurating legs.

'God, how hateful,' said Edward to himself.

It was both embarrassing and shaming to witness such a blustering bully as the King reduced to a shambling cripple and yet, finally, there was justice in it. The Earl of Hertford found himself unable to summon up one ounce of pity as Henry blubbered and gulped, his nose emitting slime, his eyes puffing up. Then suddenly the King lurched to his feet, grabbing for his sword which, in the manner of dangerous comedy, stuck in its scabbard.

'Bring me a weapon,' the betrayed husband was calling wildly, 'I shall kill her myself, torture her to death.' Henry wept afresh. 'I regret my fate in meeting such ill-conditioned wives.' He rounded on his Council. 'It is your fault,' he screamed, waving a finger big as a bladder. 'It is you who constantly urge me to marry. How dare you enslave me with such a great whore!'

He went purple and Edward found himself wishing that the man would die, that the King's son Edward, his own nephew, could ascend the throne and there would be an end to this terrible reign of death and terror. But he controlled every thought and emotion as Henry sank back into his chair, choking.

It was Norfolk, wily as a fox, hoping to reinstate himself in His Grace's favour after the awful revelations about his niece, who stepped forward.

'Your Grace, are you ill?'

The King fixed him with a terrible look. 'If I am it would be you and your accursed clan who are to blame. Get out of my sight.'

Norfolk bowed, but said nothing, leaving the room with as much dignity as he could muster.

'Yes, Sir Thomas,' gasped Henry, turning to Wriothesley at last. 'You may proceed. Make a full examination into the life of the Queen and report everything you find directly to me.'

Wriothesley nodded. 'Of course, Your Grace. You may be assured that the enquiry will be exhaustive.'

Right at the back of his brain, taken from an early questioning of witnesses, a name was coming up with, so far, nothing to pin to it. Yet it nagged. Turning away so that no one could see what he wrote, Wriothesley scratched 'Thomas Culpepper' on a piece of paper, then added the words, 'Get further information' before he slipped it into his pocket.

On the day following the Council meeting the Queen's Grace was interrogated. Dereham, having been re-examined in the meanwhile, had sworn that he had not made love to the Queen since her marriage, for his place had been taken by another. The name Thomas Culpepper at last meant what it should. Armed with all the information he needed, Sir Thomas Wriothesley had gone to work.

She had broken down of course, the woman she had become swamped by the frightened girl Catherine had recently been. By the end of the day the Council knew everything, even down to Culpepper's only other offence, violating the wife of a park keeper in a thicket.

'Less serious than violating the wife of a King in a palace,' the

Earl of Hertford had remarked drily, and there had been a smattering of laughter.

The pathetic love letter which Catherine had written in her own hand, very laboriously because she had always had difficulty with reading and letters, was spoken aloud.

'I never longed so much for a thing as I do to see you and speak with you . . . it makes my heart die to think what fortune I have that I cannot be always in your company . . . I would you were with me now that you might see what pain I take in writing to you. Yours as life endures, Katheryne.'

The words rang hollowly off Wriothesley's tongue and even more hollowly in Henry Tudor's heart. Yet he could not bring himself to order such a pretty child into the Tower. After a week of indecision, the King decreed that her courtiers should be dismissed and that Catherine herself should be sent to Syon House on the banks of the Thames. The girl had made herself far too ill for prison, screaming hysterically one minute, then weeping the next. In spite of the cuckold she allegedly had made of him, Henry could not exact full punishment until she was charged.

The atmosphere in Hampton Court grew heavier and heavier, the imprisoned Queen still languishing in her apartments. So it was almost with a sense of relief that on November 13th, Catherine's ladies and gentlemen were called to a meeting in the great hall to be told their fate by the Lord Chancellor himself. Audley, standing on the raised dais that he might be seen, cleared his throat importantly and looked around him. They were all there with the exception of Lady Rochford and the Queen's four childhood friends, who had been taken to London for questioning. Brooding and sullen but with a terrible air of triumph about her, he saw Princess Mary standing with Norfolk's daughter, the Duchess of Richmond, and Lady Margaret Douglas, the King's niece. Anne Bassett of Calais was present, her stepfather Lord Lisle now disgraced and in the Tower. Thomas Seymour, dashing as ever, was loitering near the back, as were many of the Queen's Ladies, including Lady Latymer.

Audley cleared his throat again, then held up his hand. There was immediate silence.

'Lady Mary, my Lords and Ladies, ladies and gentlemen. As you all by now know, the Queen's Grace stands accused of various offences, and tomorrow is to be removed from this palace of Hampton Court to Syon House. It is therefore the King's wish that

318

her establishment should be disposed of in the following manner. Please listen carefully. Sir Edward Baynton is to go to Syon with the Queen and be in charge of her household there, my Lady Baynton also to go to serve her. There shall also be at Syon three other ladies of the Queen's own choice and two chamberers. These names will be announced later today.'

He paused and looked sternly at the upturned faces, listening to his every word.

'It is His Grace the King's wish that you are made aware that the charges against the Queen are very grave. Therefore if any one of you know anything that should be brought to light in the way of evidence it should be reported to me forthwith. Failure to do so will be a punishable offence. Now, to the rest. Anne Bassett, to stay with friends as arranged; the Duchess of Richmond and Lady Margaret Douglas to leave for Kenninghall immediately. The Lady Mary to choose several to serve in the household of her brother, Prince Edward; Sir Thomas Seymour to remain at Hampton Court to guard the jewels and other valuables of the Queen, now forfeit to the Crown. Then, when she be gone, to bring them to the King's Highness at Westminster.'

Chancellor Audley stopped dramatically, then said, 'The Queen's Court is hereby formally dissolved. Those of you not required to go to Syon House are dismissed as of now. You may take your leave and return to your families.'

There was a stunned silence and then a babble of voices as everyone turned disbelievingly to their neighbour. The end had come so suddenly that no one could credit it. The grandeur of the recent progress, the fun of having a young and lively Queen was all over. A joyful year had turned to dust.

'So,' said a voice at Katherine Latymer's elbow, 'your wish has been granted. You may return to your duty.'

She had no need to look up, the very tone of voice told her that Sir Thomas Seymour had come to mock her. Very coolly, Katherine made a small curtsey.

'Yes, Sir Thomas. I shall be glad to see my step-children again.'

'I'm sure. In fact I now realise that you prefer their company to that of anyone else.'

'Why do you say so?'

'Because you spent the entire progress avoiding me. Wherever we went, wherever I looked for you, you were most pointedly standing with turned back or averted gaze. I thought you wanted to be my friend, Katherine. I had no idea that you found my company objectionable.'

A pair of icy emerald eyes stared Thomas Seymour out. 'I would rather you did not raise your voice here, Sir. We are in a crowd.'

'Then prick 'em,' said Tom exploding and, grabbing her elbow, he led Katherine, volubly protesting, out of the great hall and into an empty ante-chamber put aside for refreshment.

'I'm tired of your excuses and rudeness,' he said angrily. 'I wanted to do nothing but help a stranger. I am not used to women such as you.'

'I'm sure of that,' she retorted stingingly. 'I expect that most of them fall at your feet or into your bed.'

'Yes, some do, not all. But that does not mean I cannot admire a woman sincerely. As I do you, Katherine.'

Lady Latymer stood silently, obviously choosing her words. Eventually she said, 'Sir Thomas, I am a married woman. I also believe in God. I cannot enter into a friendship with you.'

He caught her arm, bending it up roughly. 'Is that what your religion breeds? The confusion of friendship with lust? Then if that is so I am well shot of you. Good day, Lady Latymer, I shall not bother you again.'

He smouldered with rage, his eyes blue volcanoes, his lips drawn and white. Katherine Latymer almost felt afraid.

'Please, Sir Thomas . . .'

'There is no please about it. You are a cruel bitch, Madam. And I wish I had never met you.'

'But why? I am nothing to you.'

'On the contrary, you mean a great deal. I have been drawn to you since the moment I first saw you. Believe me, if it had not been for your elderly husband, upon whom you so obviously dote, I would have won the wager I made long ago with my cousin Bryan.'

'Which was?'

'To take you to bed before last year was out.'

Katherine's snow-like skin turned to frost. 'How dare you, Sir? How dare you equate me with your cheap common harlots? You go too far.'

She raised her hand furiously, perhaps to strike him, neither of

320

them ever afterwards knew. Thomas, catching it savagely, was beyond discretion or reasonable behaviour. Instead he acted out of instinct and pulled the furious woman towards him. Then he kissed her, hard and without love, while she struggled in his embrace, longing to be released.

But then everything changed as the butterfly within, the other Katherine who longed so much for passion, for beauty, for love, fought Lady Latymer off, and for Thomas, too, there was a metamorphosis. Brash, boastful, arrogant Tom Seymour was pulled up short by the fact that the woman in his arms was so soft, so pliant, so ready for love of every kind.

Releasing her mouth for a moment, he bent to kiss it once more but this time with genuine affection. Now his lips were gentle, kind, leading her to passion slowly, lingering on her mouth with such joyful deliberation, as if he had all the time in the world to make her his own dear mistress. They kissed again and again until at last Katherine and Thomas drew apart, knowing that either they must stop or else go on to consummation.

'I can't,' she said, leaning against him with her eyes closed. 'I could not live with myself. It would be against everything I stand for.'

Thomas found himself understanding and was amazed at his own goodness.

'I know, sweetheart, I know. Don't distress yourself. Time is on our side.'

She looked at him a little sharply. 'What do you mean?'

'That Lord Latymer is old, and you and I are young.'

'Do you speak of dead men's shoes?'

'No,' said Tom soothingly, 'not that. I merely speak logically. If all things are equal, then your husband will die before either of us. If that happens and neither your heart nor mine are engaged elsewhere, will you come to me?'

'You know I will,' she breathed.

They kissed their promise to each other, a promise that one day they would be lovers, that nothing could separate them when the tide finally turned in their favour.

'Now we must part,' said Thomas, for in this matter of love he was by far the wiser of the two. 'Go to your apartments, pack your things. Tomorrow, when the Queen is gone, I shall leave for London and you for Yorkshire.'

'And after that?'

'We are in the hands of God.'

'I believe that,' said Katherine fervently.

'So do I,' echoed Thomas to please her.

They walked from the room, from their sweet idyll, to find people hurrying about, the truth finally having dawned that the Court was dismissed, that everyone must collect their belongings and start their journey home.

'What a fluster,' said Chancellor Audley, coming up to them. 'I am sorry you have to go like this, Lady Latymer.'

She shot Thomas a loving glance, the first of her life. 'Perhaps it is for the best,' she said.

Then she curtsied and was gone, leaving Tom staring after her, suddenly bereft.

'A fine looking woman that,' said Audley absently. 'Now you have the jewels ready and catalogued, Seymour?'

'Yes, my Lord. Except for those that are still about the Queen's person.'

'They will be removed tonight. She will have nothing left of the past.'

Thomas shook his head. 'What a fool, to risk all that, in view of what happened to her cousin Boleyn.'

Audley looked severe. 'The case is *sub judice* and the Queen is innocent until she is proved guilty.'

'Indeed,' said Thomas, 'indeed. Nonetheless, if the lady is found wanting she is the most monstrous idiot in the world.'

'Perhaps,' answered Audley, 'she thought it all worth it.'

'What?'

'To risk everything for passion. There are people like that, Sir Thomas. Romantic people who believe that love is more important than life.'

Thomas turned to look at him and gave a slow smile. 'You surprise me.'

'You are not one of them?'

'I believe not, my Lord.'

Audley laughed and clapped him on the shoulder. 'I think you too sensible, Seymour. I cannot imagine Sir Tom getting his fingers burnt.'

Thomas smiled crookedly. 'I hope you are right, my Lord, but one can never tell. Even the most unlikely people do extraordinary things.'

And with that he and the Chancellor went together to check, yet again, that the Queen's jewels were safely stowed, while upstairs the girl who had so recently worn them cried, for her lover and all she had lost, in the gathering autumn dusk.

# Chapter Twenty-Five

A BLEAK CHRISTMAS, AND AN old king in his castle, weeping as the nights grew dark and he was alone. In the Tower the aged Duchess of Norfolk, complaining of the cold; her daughter Lady Bridgewater, her mother's child, tight-lipped and straight-faced; her son, Lord William Howard, also there, stiff as a board and speaking to no one. There were more of them too, together with servants. The Howard clan filled the Tower and overflowed into the royal apartments. Only the Duke, leaving London at speed, had managed to escape imprisonment.

In Syon House, listless and bored, eating too much and not exercising, the Queen of England awaited her fate, knowing that the heads of Dereham and Culpepper, the two men who had loved her, were already impaled on spikes on London Bridge. Archbishop Cranmer had been more than good to her, begging Catherine to say that she had been pre-contracted to marry Francis Dereham and her marriage to the King was therefore null and void. But there he had misjudged the girl. Silly and flirtatious she might have been but Catherine Howard wanted to be remembered as a Queen. She denied that she and Dereham had been betrothed and in so doing chose death: a strange twist in the tale of an apparently young and foolish girl.

As soon as Christmas was done, a grisly festival that year, the weather changed. At night the sky was one whirling mass of flakes, the wind raw and cutting, the ways too treacherous to pass for deepening drifts. By day the snow threw an eerie light so that it was never truly bright; the world transformed into an unending sea of white in which unrecognisable buildings loomed like islands, then vanished again.

The bitter weather went on through January of the year 1542 and a fierce February followed. Shivering, the Queen – against whom a bill of attainder had been brought which she had never answered – went down the water steps of Syon House and entered a closed barge. She was taken straight to the Tower and did not look up to see her lovers' rotting heads as she passed beneath them.

Now Catherine knew that the end had finally come for her and on the night before her execution asked that the block be brought to her room that she might practice how best to place her head. Then she spent the rest of the hours left with her confessor, the Bishop of Lincoln, who departed shortly before dawn, leaving her no task but to put up her hair and dress soberly.

At seven o'clock in the morning the King's Council assembled at the place of execution, with the exception of the Duke of Suffolk who had coughed and sneezed his way out of attending. Standing grimly amongst the others, black as a rook, his dark features matching his clothes, was Edward Seymour. Sworn to the Privy Council four years ago, he was obliged, of necessity, to attend certain beheadings but today Edward felt wretched, squeamish, ill-at-ease. For tough men who plotted plots and knew the risks, the axe was all that could be expected. But for this girl, highly sexed and enormously foolish that she might be, it seemed too brutal. She was eighteen and beautiful; surely divorce could have been forced upon her.

With his mind working in this manner, Edward did not know how he could tolerate what he must. And yet he was obliged to remain there, awaiting the moment he dreaded, the moment when the blood of a girl was spilled because she had fallen in love.

Uncannily, as if he could read Seymour's thoughts, Chancellor Audley murmured, 'A raw morning and a raw act. And yet she could have avoided it.'

'By admitting pre-contract?'

'Of course. Dereham swore they were betrothed; it was she who refuted it, and in so doing left herself no defence. She denied sleeping with Culpepper, admitted Dereham and Mannox. God's passion, she was a silly girl.'

'You speak as if she is dead.'

'She will be in a moment. Here she comes.' Audley must have seen Edward flinch for he added in an undertone, 'Remember she wanted it. She could have escaped.'

But nothing, thought Edward, nothing at all can ever justify this.

Though he had heard reports that Catherine had got fat in prison she had obviously not eaten since her arrival at the Tower, for now she was hollow-cheeked and so feeble that one of the four ladies who walked with her had to help her up the scaffold.

Oh God, give her strength, Edward found himself praying.

It was customary for eloquent speeches to be made at the end but this poor thing was obviously too weak to speak and nobody could tell whether her violent shivering was from fear or cold. Like a lamb in the slaughterhouse she stood, meek and terrified, while her eyes were bandaged.

Oh Christ, thought Edward, I'm going to disgrace myself.

He stared fixedly at the toes of his boots, past caring if others noticed, and if he could have blocked his ears he would have done so. But that was not possible, thus he heard her pathetic and exhausted whispers.

'God have mercy on my soul. Spare my poor family. I die a Queen but would rather die the wife of Culpepper.'

There was a vile swish, the cause of which Edward knew only too well, and two bright spots of blood appeared on his shoes. Knowing that he was facially white, Edward turned away and thus saw what was happening amongst his fellow Councillors. Cranmer was deep in prayer; Bishop Stephen Gardiner, who had deserted his protegée Catherine when she had fallen out of favour, was not. In fact he seemed almost to gloat as did Wriothesley, who had found out so many sordid and unsavoury facts about the Queen and made a great vicarious meal of them.

'Pricks!' said Edward, very quietly, and rubbed his boots clean on the frozen grass.

At last he looked at the scaffold. A cloth had been thrown over the body but already a dark red patch was forming at its neck. The head, very humble somehow with its plain white cap and bandaged eyes, was just being thrust into a wooden box.

Where is she now? thought Edward. Where is *she*? Gone, finished? Or has her soul flown like a bird's?

A sudden fear gripped him, a terrible sense of disaster, and as he gazed at the looming scaffold he found himself drenched in sweat despite the morning's chill.

Oh Christ's sweet blood, he prayed. Never let me end like this. Let me depart in my bed like a Christian soul.

'My Lord Hertford, are you ill?' said a voice at his elbow and

Edward turned to see the unattractive face of Sir Richard Rich staring shrewdly into his.

'I have a fever,' Edward answered quickly. 'If I had been sensible I would have stayed away.'

Rich grimaced. 'But would not miss doing your duty, eh, Lord Hertford?'

He was one of those terrible men who seemed to be constructed about his teeth, which were large and slimy, pinioning his lower lip and leaving permanent marks on it. His face was detestable, big and florid, with loose cheeks that swung when he talked. Edward's overwhelming urge to scream obscenities into his ear was overcome only by the sound of another small procession approaching the scaffold. The moment had come for Jane Rochford's life to end.

On this occasion, queasy though he was, Edward had to agree that the *agent provocateur* who had aided the Queen in her torrid and fatal affair deserved her fate. Nonetheless he looked away at the moment when the axe fell.

'Not up to it,' he heard Rich mutter to Wriothesley.

Edward flicked them a cool glance as the wretched corpse of Catherine's Lady Roe was swept up to go with that of her royal mistress, feeling, foolishly, that he did not care if he made enemies. But even while he stared at them, Edward felt Audley clap him on the shoulder.

'So there's an end of it,' said the Lord Chancellor briskly. 'Not much hope for the Howards now, I think.'

'You never know,' said Edward, turning to him. 'His Grace is fond of Henry Howard and the old fox Duke volubly disowned his niece and her lovers before he fled home.'

Audley's lined face creased as he grinned. 'You may well be right. We shall just have to wait and see.' He looked closely at Edward. 'You're white, man. Come within and drink something. God's mercy but it's a cold day.'

The members of the Council were breaking into groups, heading towards the Tower's private apartments where refreshments awaited. As he left with the Chancellor, Edward took one last look round. Someone was sweeping the straw off the scaffold, releasing as he did so a little pool of blood which fell like a waterfall on to the frozen grass below.

Catherine's rubies, he thought, as the sickly sun picked up their

327

colour for a moment before disappearing behind the blankness of a snow-filled sky.

The bleak winter was particularly severe in the Fens and the Duke of Norfolk's home, Kenninghall, was cut off by huge drifts and frozen brooks. Every evening a few crisp flakes would be seen floating gently in the air, only to become blizzards as darkness fell and the bitter wind rose. By morning the landscape would have changed and the red sun, peering out of leaden greyness, did nothing to melt the ice. At night there was nothing for it but to survive in a world that had become a wasteland of snow, and every creature, from the humblest hare to the noble Duke himself, huddled in its lair for warmth.

As if in sympathy with the blood sacrifice of the little Queen, the worst days of all were in the middle of February but, at last, there came a morning when the sun came out in majesty and breathed upon the earth. Rivers which had frozen into hard pathways for horses split into spiders' webs as the ice cracked; the drifts became pools, then lakes, and finally floods. Buds burst through the snow encasing them, and hidden flowers came out defiantly. Knowing that the winter was finally behind him, Thomas Howard went to his stables and ordered that his horse and two others beside should be ready for a journey on the following day. Then he had his first bath of the year, removing every stitch he wore for the first time in weeks.

It might have been guessed, or so his steward thought, that the Duke would not make for Court, from whence he had fled so fast when the King turned against the Howards. Nor was it likely that he was bound for his son Henry, Earl of Surrey, who was uneasily keeping in the King's favour because of his old association with Henry Tudor's bastard son, the much lamented Duke of Richmond who had died when he was seventeen. Very much as the man suspected, Norfolk headed in the direction of Greenwich, and the one child he could rely on to counsel him well. Dr Zachary was obviously to have a surprise visitor.

As he made his way through the ripening countryside, it occurred to Thomas Howard that it had been many years since he had seen his grandchildren, and in the case of the boy Sylvanus, never. Now he looked forward to the reunion, but there was to be disappointed. For the house was deserted, empty of servants even, the only living thing Zachary's vast and malevolent cat, glaring at him from its one remaining eye. Constant banging finally summoned a small kitchen wench who bobbed uncomfortably and said her master had gone to read for a fine lady.

'Read?' repeated Norfolk, irritably.

'The stars, Sir.'

'Oh!' He nodded, enlightened. 'And where are the young people, pray? And your Mistress?'

'They have accompanied him, Sir. But all will be back before nightfall.'

'Then I shall enter and wait for them,' said the Duke determinedly and took his place before the fire without further ado, sending his two servants into the kitchen to keep the girl company which, if the sound of distant giggling and song were anything to go by, they did well.

Left alone, Norfolk looked round for something with which to amuse himself and found, at random, a leather-bound book lying on its side, half hidden amongst some others. He flicked the pages idly and then was suddenly riveted. In small neat but unfamiliar handwriting were inscribed the words, 'To cure the Pestilence. Take a handful of sage, yarrow, tansy and feverfew, and bruise them well together. Then let the sick party make water in the herbs . . .'

Thomas Howard's eyebrows rose. 'For Emrods or Piles' he read on, 'Stew the powder of fine-beaten amber upon hot coals and let the sufferer sit down over it, so that the smoke may ascend up into the place aggrieved.'

Thomas mopped his brow. As this could not be identified as Zachary's handwriting it would seem likely that this might be the work of that other Romany who was now a member of his family.

'So,' said Norfolk to himself, 'my new daughter-in-law is as skilled as her husband.'

He flipped over several pages. 'To take away a man's memory or even to kill him, let him drink a surfeit of Black Poppy juice, also called Opium.' So she really was a powerful creature, this girl of his son's. Well, thought Thomas Howard wryly, they burned his mother; let it be hoped his bride will survive her knowledge.

The Duke closed his eyes, putting the book to one side. When he opened them again it was to see a dark-haired, pretty creature observing him from the doorway. Instantly he recognised her from the days of Jane Seymour's brief reign.

'So *you* are Zachary's wife?' he said, rising to his feet and looking at the diminutive creature along the length of his nose. 'I remember you very well. I simply had not associated the name.'

Cloverella gave a deep curtsey. 'Lord Duke, it is nice to meet you again and to be able to offer you hospitality as your dutiful daughter. Stay and eat with us, I beg you.'

'I may remain longer than that. I am not officially in London you understand.'

Cloverella smiled. 'Then stay as long as you wish, Sir.'

The Duke inclined his head gratefully, glad of shelter, for the fortunes of the Howards were now at their lowest ebb. Those in the Tower had been found guilty of treason, in that they had concealed Catherine's unchastity, and had been sentenced to perpetual imprisonment and the forfeiting of all their worldly goods. Only the Duke and his son Surrey still teetered on the knife's edge of disaster, hanging on by the merest thread.

'Thank you, my dear,' answered Norfolk formally and would have kissed the hand of his new daughter-in-law if the door had not opened to reveal Zachary's sons, Jasper and Sylvanus, staring at him wide-eyed, their contrasting looks, raven and rose, never more marked than at this moment of surprise. Behind them followed their father, holding the hand of a spectacular girl. Norfolk gaped at the transformation in Sapphira. When he had last seen her she had been a pretty child but now, on the threshold of her teens, she was beautiful.

'Well, well, well,' said the Duke, shaking his head. 'Can this lovely young woman really be my Sapphira?'

But as she rushed to him and put her arms round his neck, kissing his cheeks again and again, she was all little girl. With that cue, Jasper followed suit. Only Sylvanus, sturdily correct, made formal bows, though his face was the colour of poppies with the excitement of everything.

All that evening the three of them played with their Howard grandfather, and when the darkness came the children sat with him by the fire, roasting chestnuts and telling him of their adventures in France. In a strange way, even though she could not speak, it was as if Sapphira communicated without words. Sylvanus, once over his shyness, said enough for two, while Jasper would listen carefully and then put in a shrewd or witty observation that had the Duke wiping his eyes with both laughter and joy.

After they had gone and Cloverella with them, supervising the bedtime as she always did, the Duke turned to his much loved son.

'You have done splendidly. Those children are a credit to you. The years of learning in France obviously did them no harm at all, in fact great good.'

Zachary smiled. 'I hope so, for I love them dearly. And is not Cloverella a wonderful stepmother for them?'

'She is perfect in every way. You come from the same people and deep has called to deep. She is the wife that you both deserve and need.'

He meant it sincerely and Zachary felt it hardly necessary to say, 'And the fact that she is Seymour?'

'She is Wentworth,' answered the Duke stoutly. 'And that's that.' He took a draught of wine, then said, 'My son, would you consider letting your children come to Kenninghall for a while? In our present troubles we have a whole army of young people within our walls. They are learning so much from Surrey's old tutor and enjoying themselves at the same time.'

'And hopefully better supervised than in the Dowager Duchess's day?'

It was a wicked remark and the Duke winced, not knowing whether to laugh or cry. In the end he did neither. 'My wife is a boring woman, it's true,' he said honestly. 'But she is very honourable. She cares for her kinsmen's children as if they were her own. Under her auspices they are learning to conduct themselves well.'

'Lord Duke, my father,' answered Zachary seriously, 'I have not been a conventional parent as you know, so I will ask the children their wishes. If they would like to go, they shall. I will not stand in their way. It might be a great opportunity for them to learn courtly manners.'

'And what of Cloverella?'

'She shall be consulted too.'

The Duke leant forward confidentially, muttering, 'She is not in earshot, is she?'

Zachary looked about him. 'No, why?'

'Because I need help, my son, and would not have her know. I have written to His Grace but with no reply. Something must be done to strengthen my position if I am to return to Court.'

The astrologer stared at him blankly. 'But what can I do? I have no influence. How can I possibly help you?'

The Duke lowered his voice to a whisper. 'Magic,' he said.

'What?'

'Magic. It was done once before when you were in the Tower. Sapphira got you out.'

'Sapphira is kept away from all that now. It cost her too dear when she was struck speechless.'

'But you could do it, surely?'

Zachary stood up, pacing the floor. 'But Lord Duke, I rarely practice my arts. I am old and respectable.'

'How boring for you,' answered his father, and they both laughed, very alike at that moment.

'What do you want me to do?' asked Zachary, thrusting a poker into a tankard to mull the wine in it.

'Persuade His Grace that he still trusts and needs me.'

'Umm.' His son looked thoughtful.

'Can it be done?'

'Of course it can be done. The question is how. If the spell is to work I must have something personal of the King's.'

'Such as?'

'Hair clippings, nail clippings. Some recently worn clothing.'

'A bribe to the laundresses perhaps?'

'Perhaps.' Zachary grew brisk. 'Anyway that you can leave to me.'

'So you *will* do it?'

Zachary both nodded his head and shook it. 'Lord Duke my father, you have persuaded me. Yet what a naughty thing it is that a reformed character like myself should be led astray by his own sire.'

'But who else?' exclaimed the Duke, before once again the two of them burst into uproarious laughter.

# Chapter Twenty-Six

THE TERRIBLE WINTER DURING which Catherine Howard had gone to her death was one that none of her courtiers would ever forget. Those who had not been caught up in the scandal, those so innocent that they had not even heard a whisper of an adulterous affair until the matter was made public, found it hard to recover from the haste with which they had been summoned by the Lord Chancellor and given instant dismissal.

It had almost been a relief to Katherine Latymer. Old men had been her lot since puberty and she had never realised until the moment Thomas Seymour kissed her that within her mild and rather devout nature lurked a prurient streak. Katherine, the devoted young wife and eternal stepmother, had only known then that she was wild.

She had come home to her old bullfrog, thankful to avoid temptation, only to realise with shock that he was ill, like a dimming candle, the light of his life beginning to fade. A welter of love seized Katherine, for after all had she not accepted John Latymer because she had been bored and lonely, though he had later become her dear friend, her companion, her sweet old partner. So what did it matter if the vigour in him had long since departed?

Yet still when he had retired early to bed and she had sat alone before the fire, dropping her detested needlework on to the floor and staring instead at the flames, she had thought of Thomas Seymour. In each spark from the logs she had seen his face, in each burning ember Katherine had relived their kiss. Then, when she had finally gone upstairs and silently crept into bed beside her stertorously breathing husband, she had dreamed of Thomas till morning.

In a way, the winter in which the Queen had died had claimed John

Latymer, and probably thousands if the truth were known. Just before Katherine came home, her husband had developed a severe chest condition and never quite recovered from it. And she had known when she had first seen him that her friend of many years, the man with whom she had grown up, was now preparing himself for death.

Lord Latymer was a staunch Catholic, quite unshaken by the new wave of religious thinking, to which Katherine in the greatest secrecy leaned, and now his faith comforted him enormously throughout his long illness.

'I go to God, child,' he had said during the recent January, 'but you, who are still in your twenties, must go to man. It is my wish that you marry again and this time to someone of your age. You should have a child, Kate. Remember that.'

And she did now, staring out of the window of their fine mansion, standing only a few miles from London. For it was in the capital that her husband had finally and rather suddenly died. In some respects Katherine was glad, for his body rested in St Pauls where many more people could pay their respects to him than if he had been buried in Well Churchyard in Yorkshire, as he had originally requested.

The funeral had not been as bleak as his widow had feared, for, on the one occasion they had talked about it, her wise old bullfrog had bidden her give the mourners good refreshment so that they might remember John, Lord Latymer, with stout hearts. And this she had done, so much so that some had left the wake quite merry, while even Katherine had taken too much wine, though on her it had had the reverse effect. Instead of her spirits rising they had sunk. Now she felt lonely and depressed, wondering what move to make next.

A tap on the door revealed Katherine's stepdaughter Mary, a great deal older than she and today a most comforting presence to have around the house.

'My dear Kate,' said Mary cheerfully, advancing into the room, 'how are you feeling?'

'Tired suddenly. Would it be thought amiss if I go to bed?'

'Not at all. I shall take you there myself.'

Katherine put her arms round the comfortable waist of her matronly relative. 'Oh, Mary, I shall miss him so much.'

'Of course. But do not miss him longer than you need.'

'What do you mean?'

'My father told me often that he wanted you to have your own child, having been such an excellent stepmother. Do as he wishes, make your life rich. In that way you will give him the greatest respect of all.'

'Do you really believe that?'

'Yes,' said Mary firmly, kissing Katherine on the brow. 'Now come along. You are looking pale. I've a mind to take you back with me and make you bloom again.'

Her stepmother wept with sheer relief. 'Would you do that? Would you Mary dearest?'

'Yes, on one condition.'

'And that is?'

'That you come back to this house when you are recovered. I do not want to think of you wasting away in Yorkshire.'

'Then I promise I will.'

'In that case, put yourself in my hands.'

'Gladly,' said Katherine with a sigh. 'Very gladly indeed.'

It had been agreed by all concerned that the best time for Zachary's children to leave home for their stay in Kenninghall Castle was when the Duke of Norfolk was restored to favour. And this had eventually come about. The spell, as Zachary later admitted, though somewhat reluctantly, had been more difficult than he thought. Nonetheless, by a combination of Thomas Howard's constant apologies for his family, the Earl of Surrey's swaggering bravado and pretence that nothing was wrong, and Zachary's locking himself away for a whole two days, chanting over one of the King's cast-off gloves, a reconciliation was made. Henry Tudor received the Duke courteously but Norfolk was not deceived. From now on the Howard family must prove themselves with every step they took, though as a gesture of his magnanimity, the King released all the prisoners from the Tower, even the old and grumpy Dowager Duchess.

With their respective parents returned to their greatly depleted homes, it was felt that most of the children who had been delivered hurriedly into the Duke's care would have a better life if they remained in his custody, it being the normal custom of the time to send young people to board with a family of higher social standing than one's own. So Norfolk's youthful establishment remained intact and in the spring of 1543 Zachary Howard's offspring set off to join it.

The boys were now ten and nine respectively, though only six months separated them, while Sapphira had entered her teens. Yet though they were still young, Zachary and Cloverella took them only as far as the border with Suffolk. The Duchess of Norfolk was not overfond of her husband's bastard and the children's origins were being kept deliberately vague. So at the county boundary the young people were handed over to the Duke's steward and his escort, the astrologer riding alongside as far as he dared, then turning back to where his wife waited for him.

'It will be good for them,' she said.

'I know, I know. And yet I am uneasy.'

He looked so worried that Cloverella felt quite concerned. 'Why?'

Zachary shook his head, the rough curls flying out. 'Just a strange feeling. But I am probably being over-protective, particularly of Sapphira.'

But as he turned for home, not the happiest man in the kingdom, his offspring were trotting quite cheerfully into the courtyard of Kenninghall Castle, where their grandfather, the Duke, stood waiting to greet them.

'Jasper, Sylvanus,' he shouted and hurried forward as the boys jumped from their horses. 'Come at once to meet the Duchess of Norfolk, my wife, who will be your mother for the next two years.'

They had been taught how to bow respectfully and now they did their very best, so much so that Elizabeth Howard, a faded grey woman whose looks hid a steely nature and strong principles, was delighted with them, particularly Jasper who resembled the Duke and who took her hand and kissed it, French style.

But it was to Sapphira, being lifted down from horseback by a servant, that her gaze was drawn in fascination. The Duchess had never seen such a perfect little thing, such a living embodiment of spring, with hair like fine gold crocuses and eyes a deep mysterious iris-blue. Moreover the girl had a touching dignity, for though she was still a child she held her head well, like a woman, yet was shy.

'How enchanting!' said the Duchess involuntarily.

'That is the dumb child I told you of,' whispered her husband.

'What a tragedy, especially for one so flawless. But can she hear?'

'Oh yes, perfectly. The complaint was caused by an – accident.'

'Then perhaps she can be cured.'

'It would be a wondrous thing if so.'

But his wife was no longer listening, running forward to take both Sapphira's hands in hers.

'My dear,' she said, 'tell me your name.'

At once the poor woman realised what she had done but none of the children seemed concerned. The rosy boy stepped forward promptly and answered, 'This is my half-sister Sapphira, Madam. She cannot speak but she can read and write and will put down any answers you wish. She also uses sign language which I can teach you if you so require.'

Elizabeth Howard chuckled, something she had not done for a long time.

'I would like to learn it, Master Sylvanus. But now let me show you your quarters. The young gentlemen share two large rooms between them, as do the young ladies. All the children here are either connected to the Howards or are close family friends. We do not take outsiders.'

'But are we not that, Sir,' whispered Jasper to the Duke, 'sired as we are by your natural son?'

'The Duchess believes you have a slightly different connection. So I would rather you didn't disillusion her.'

'Who does she think we are?'

'Distant cousins,' answered the Duke vaguely, and refused to say more.

To children who had lived, albeit temporarily, in the Château de Chambord, the castle seemed a perfectly normal place in which to dwell and they made their way within quite calmly.

'It does not seem big to you?' the Duchess asked Jasper, and was astonished when he answered, 'No, Madam. When we lodged with the French King it was in a somewhat larger palace.'

'I had no idea you were so well travelled,' said Elizabeth in amazement.

'We were with our father on – er – a diplomatic mission,' answered Jasper hurriedly, then made an excuse to join his brother and sister to avoid being drawn further.

'I suppose we are now members of a huge family,' said Sylvanus, sighing a little for the informality of his father's house.

'We always were members of it, despite the *baton sinister*,' answered Jasper in a whisper, while Sapphira wrote on a parchment left for her convenience, 'This is where we learn courtly manners.'

'Well I intend to have a good time as well,' said Jasper. 'Anyway there are two of us, Sylvanus. If the other boys are rude we can punch their heads.'

'Can we?' said his brother, brightening up. 'Oh good.'

'Not good, naughty,' wrote Sapphira, but smiling.

But it was about their sister that the two younger children felt worried, afraid that those who did not understand her disability would mock and make her unhappy. As they were left alone momentarily, Jasper whispered to Sylvanus, 'We must protect Sapphira. There may be people here who would delight in tormenting her.'

'Then they shall answer to us first.'

But it was difficult to judge, thought Jasper, as they were ushered into the great hall where stood a body of other young people, who might be what, for the faces turned towards him all wore smiles. The children had been ranged in ages so that the first he met, following behind his sister, were all quite small. These, it turned out, were the offspring of the wicked Earl of Surrey, so were the Duke of Norfolk's other grandchildren. Jasper looked over the boy, another Thomas, but decided that he was too young to be of any importance, while the girls seemed hardly weaned to him.

But for Sapphira, walking beside the Duchess who was formally introducing one child to another, there was only one person in the room. At the far end of the line and therefore obviously the oldest of them all, stood a boy unlike anyone she had ever seen. Of medium height and lissom build, his fine young shoulders and chest were obviously not quite fully grown, and yet he wore his emerald green doublet with a dash and style that marked him out as someone very special. But though his body was shapely it was to his face that Sapphira's eyes were fatally drawn.

As finely boned as that of a girl, it was, though he was no more than fifteen, already strong and determined, the hair growing attractively round it, adding extra shape and dimension. Though curly like Zachary's these locks were well kempt and more blue than black. But his lashes were jet, curling round clear green eyes, the colour of sea-washed glass. And now this fine set young lordling had also seen her and was staring most intently.

My goodness, thought the Duchess, who never dwelled on that kind of thing, how those two are gazing!

And as she and Sapphira drew level with him the ridiculous notion went through her head that such a beautiful pair should marry.

She cleared her mind of all sentiment however, and said firmly, 'Sapphira, may I present Lord Joscelin Howard? Joscelin, this is your cousin Sapphira.'

He bowed politely, his eyes leaving her face only for a second. Sapphira touched her forehead, then her heart, then put her hand briefly in his before she curtsied. Somewhere somebody tittered and the Duchess whirled round like a fury while Sylvanus bristled like a lion cub, noticeably clenching his fists.

'I greet you with pleasure,' said Joscelin and smiled warmly. 'I hope we shall be friends.'

All the old wisdom of generations of wise women, the magic that Zachary had so shunned on her behalf, reawakened in Sapphira.

No, she thought, we will be lovers.

And with that a girl who had been standing half-hidden behind him stepped forward and treated Sapphira to an icy look. Then, turning on her heel, shaking her mass of carrot-coloured hair out behind her, walked away.

A month in the company of her stepdaughter, loving as she was, proved to be enough and in early April, Katherine Latymer set off in a shower of rain to journey back to London. All the way she was dogged by a host of rainbows, as the sun broke through the prism even while drops of glistening rain still fell. The sky alternated between the clear light-blue of springtime and woolly shaped clouds, black and white. Primroses and daffodils were everywhere, carpeting the woods with gold, while trees that would blossom next month were already weighted with tight buds.

There was a wonderfully trenchant feel to the day, cool and incisive, the day for people with a purpose. And Katherine, travelling in widow's black, was glad she was returning to her mansion at Charterhouse, beyond the press of the city, in the clean sweet air of the country. Here, she felt, she could re-plan her life and examine the teachings of the new wave of religion in which, it seemed to her, God was more accessible to ordinary mortals like herself. But would that future, she wondered as she neared her gracious home, contain Sir Thomas Seymour? Or was he the type of rogue who kissed a woman and then forgot her? Was the promise to seek Katherine out when she was respectably widowed perhaps not worth the breath with which it was spoken?

Yet as she entered the house she suddenly knew the answers. He had been there, she could tell by the very atmosphere. Thomas Seymour had stirred the air of the place. Why, she could almost sniff his spicy perfume, beneath which lay the true smell of him. Not unwashed and rank as were so many, but clean and masculine, slightly leathery, as if so many hours in the saddle had actually become part of him.

Katherine had travelled to Mary's home in Surrey with only a few servants so that the estate had been well attended. And now, to bid her welcome, her steward stepped from his quarters and greeted her.

'Has everything gone smoothly, Napper?'

'Yes indeed, Lady Latymer.'

'Have there been visitors?' She knew the answer before he spoke.

'Yes, Madam. Sir Thomas Seymour has called three times to offer his condolences and enquire for your welfare.'

The world grew brighter by a million suns, fairy people flew about her head, and Katherine's heart danced a galliard.

'How kind,' she said cooly, trying to keep calm. 'Did he say he would return?'

'I took the liberty of telling him you would be back today, Madam. He has requested me to ask if he may sup here this evening.'

'Of course he may,' said Katherine carefully. 'Thank you, Napper. You have done everything very well.'

So, at last, at the age of twenty-nine, her birthday being three weeks away, life was to begin. She was to be wooed by a man only a few years older than herself. Now came the challenge, for up to this moment her physical attributes had hardly counted, her elderly husbands only wanting a sweet-natured nurse, her beauty of no consequence. In a panic, Katherine hurried upstairs, only pausing to order a bath, and stripped naked before a mirror as Catherine Howard had once done.

She looked hardly touched, she thought with relief. For her body, which had endured not even a minor pregnancy, had stayed slim. In fact her waist was minute and very supple. Facially, though, she was rather pale but her unpinned hair hung almost to her waist, honey-gold in colour, and thick enough for Thomas Seymour to bury his hands in. Yet of all her features her eyes were the finest; hazel green, sometimes the colour of emeralds, sometimes of good cider, and just as sparkling now that she thought of him. She did not, Katherine thought, scrutinising herself harshly, look her age. Perhaps she had something to be thankful for that she had married elderly men. She not only felt eighteen, she looked it too.

Though she must wear black, Katherine took enormous trouble with her appearance that night, reddening her lips and colouring her eyes, and brushing her hair till it shone beneath her beautiful French hood. Then, with every appearance of calmness, she picked up her despised embroidery and stitched with fingers she pricked so frequently, little drops of blood fell everywhere.

The April evening was sublime, tranquil and mellow, yet wild with birdsong. Every feathered creature in Christendom sung its anthem as through the gentle green dusk the Adonis of Henry Tudor's court, the lion of his day, the most flattered and copied courtier alive, made his way to woo the pretty young widow upon whom he had set his heart.

Everywhere around him was a crystal loveliness. The Thames ran at spate, fresh with rain, rippling and billowing tiny waves, while the fields, as he turned inland from Temple Bar, were lush with watering, every blade of grass bearing a glassy drop. The great hall of the Blackfriars, now deserted and silent as Thomas rode past, was the colour of evening roses in the fading light.

He went on through deepening countryside, full of sweet smells and comforting rural sounds, till at last came into view the great monastery of Charterhouse. Before Henry VIII's brutal rape of this ancient Carthusian order the sound of vespers would at this hour be ringing over the fields, but the sacked buildings, once dedicated to St Bruno and named after his first monastery, La Grande Chartreuse in France, stood like an empty shell. Thomas, far from a religious man, nonetheless crossed himself as he went past the deserted and shadowy place.

But coming into view, built almost within the monastery's confines, was a sight to cheer him. The late Lord Latymer's stately house, all mullioned windows and fine towers, an excellent place to be part of a Lady's inheritance, lay ahead, its creamy brickwork turned to amber as the sun went down behind it.

Thomas reined in and swung from his horse, removing his plumed hat and combing his hair before he slowly walked his mount to the gatehouse, where he was courteously welcomed. As an ostler hurried from the stables to assist, Thomas wondered just what sort of reception Katherine would give him, with her husband but recently buried. Yet it was no dismal snatching of a man still in the flower of youth. Lord Latymer had had his full share of years, and good ones at that.

Yet I shall be solemn, Thomas thought, for she must be sad, even if only for the sake of appearances.

But there he misjudged her, for as he was shown into her private room, where she sat by the window sewing in the fading light, she immediately got up and welcomed him with a smile.

'I bring you my condolences, Madam,' said Thomas formally, bowing stiffly and wearing his funeral face.

'I miss him,' she answered with obvious sincerity. 'We were good friends.'

'Indeed, indeed!' He sighed. 'May I ask if he went peacefully?'

'In my arms, in the morning sunshine.'

'There could not be a better end,' said Thomas and kissed her hand with true respect. She was, in his considered opinion, more attractive than ever.

'I desired to know from your steward whether I might stay to sup. Will that be in order, Lady Latymer?'

'Of course it is.' Katherine laughed radiantly. 'Why are you being so formal with me?'

At last Thomas felt himself on safe ground. 'I am obliged to, pretty Kate. I would not upset your mourning for a cage of gilded apes.'

'Gilded apes?' she repeated thoughtfully. 'That would be a rarity indeed.'

'But not as rare as your sweet nature,' he said, and really meant it.

They dined alone, by candlelight, and afterwards walked in the grounds, their footsteps quite naturally leading towards the deserted monastery. The late sky was in stripes of extraordinary colour, violet, jade and indigo, while a springtime moon, very silver and seemingly distant, threw the empty cloisters into patches of deepest shadow. In the stillness of that lovely evening Thomas Seymour took Katherine by the hand.

'May I court you,' he said, 'woo you, make love to you, everything?'

She looked at him very seriously. 'But I am so recently widowed.'

'But would your husband mind that? Did he not say to you to live on and be happy?'

It was a shrewd guess but he knew he had spoken the truth by her indrawn breath.

'Yes he did say that, privately. How did you . . . ?'

'Because, though I did not know him well, Lord Latymer never struck me as a selfish man.'

Katherine burst into tears, very suddenly, just like the April showers that both of them had dodged all that day.

'He's gone,' she said brokenly. 'And now I can never ask his advice again.'

'What advice do you need?' Thomas's voice was very quiet.

'Whether to love you, Tom Seymour. Or whether to send you packing as the great rake and seducer which I know you to be, for your reputation preceeds you, believe me.'

'You do me an injustice, Kate.'

'That's not true. I was at Court, remember. I saw for myself how all the women, married and otherwise, ran after you.'

Thomas put his hands on her shoulders, forcing her to look at him and smiling at the way the moon turned her tears into little trickles of mercury.

'But if I have the choice of so many women as you say, why am I here now? Why have I picked you to love? For I do, Kate.'

'Oh Tom,' she said and cuddled into his arms, like a kitten longing to be stroked.

'My dear love,' he said, and kissed the top of her head.

Katherine looked up at him. 'Of course I want you to woo me, to make love to me, to seduce me. It is just that I am afraid you might trifle with my poor affections. You see, despite the fact I have been married twice, I am still an innocent. Oh, I don't mean virginal, they had enough potency for *that*. It is just that I am so inexperienced and you so worldly.'

'Then the sooner you let me be your lover the better.'

'Oh yes, yes, sweetheart,' said Katherine, and closing her eyes, raised her face to be kissed in the moonlight.

The very last light was going from the Thames on that splendid

April evening. Everywhere there were rushing sounds as water swirled and eddied and the creatures who lived in the river or on its banks prepared for the night. Reluctantly, because the ambience was almost too precious to leave, Zachary and Norfolk walked slowly together through the riverbank orchard in the direction of Zachary's house, sniffing the scents and listening to the sounds of peaceful approaching darkness.

'So,' said the Duke quietly, putting his arm round his son's shoulders. 'You did well. I am reinstated at Court, and my foolish relatives free. I have a lot to thank you for.'

The astrologer turned to look at him. 'But still be careful, Lord Duke my father. His Grace the King forgets nothing, nor forgives.'

The Duke nodded wearily. 'Politics, politics. How many good men will die before this reign is over I wonder?'

'How many before the Tudors are seen out might be a better question,' answered Zachary, very solemn.'

'Thoughts like that could have you in the Tower.'

'No one other than you will ever hear them.'

'Not even your wife?'

'Not even she,' answered Zachary with a sigh. 'She loves her Seymour cousins and even to her I must be careful what I say.'

'And where is she now?'

'In her garden, picking certain herbs by moonlight.'

The Duke raised his brows but said nothing.

'And how are the children?' asked Zachary, changing the subject uneasily, or so his father thought.

'Very well. The boys are in their element, riding and swimming and fighting. And learning too. Jasper is very bright. He will make a courtier yet.'

'I hope not!'

The Duke pulled Zachary close to him. 'You are in a strange mood, my son. Introspective and sad.'

'These are sad and introspective times, Sir. But tell me of Sapphira. How fares my little girl?'

'She has become friends with the son of one of my long-dead cousins, Joscelin, and with Ursula, to whom he has been betrothed since a child.'

'That does not auger well,' said Zachary.

The Duke stared at him. 'Why do you say that?'

'Because three is an awkward number in friendship.'

'Rubbish,' answered Norfolk roundly. 'The children under my wife's care are all the best of friends. Sometimes you let your imagination run riot.'

'Perhaps,' replied his son. 'But if there is any trouble, send for me at once.'

'Trouble? What kind of trouble could there possibly be?' asked the Duke, amazed.

'You seem to forget something.'

'And what is that, pray?'

'That it was Sapphira who bewitched the King into signing my release from the Tower.'

'I had not forgotten. But what of it?'

'Simply, Lord Duke my father, Sapphira is more powerful than Cloverella and myself put together. I only hope that nobody ever really crosses her path.'

'That is not possible,' answered Norfolk confidently. 'At Kenninghall our charges are one family of happy children, and so they will remain.'

'Amen to that,' said Zachary as they went into the house.

# Chapter Twenty-Seven

IT HAD ALWAYS BEEN an unwritten rule in the household of the Duke of Norfolk that its younger members received as good and as stimulating an education as any royal child. Accordingly, every day of the year barring feasts, two tutors sallied forth from their apartments to the room put aside for scholarship, to impart to their pupils a knowledge of Classics, Greek, Latin, French and Mathematics. One of them was elderly and imposing and had taught the renegade Surrey, thus achieving the honour of creating an excellent poet out of a reprehensible boy. The other was a social misfit, a blushing genius who detested children but who, unfortunately for him, had the gift in plentitude of passing on his knowledge to the unpleasant young. When in class, this unfortunate was prone to a tic in his right cheek which was watched with fascination by his pupils, and which one or two of them had attempted to copy. Thus his life was a nightmare and he would gladly have resigned it all had it not been for the fact that he quite literally had nowhere else to go.

At Christmas he had been on the point of collapse and no amount of cajoling from the good Duchess would tempt him from his quarters to join the household. Only dire necessity had brought him to the classroom in January and the miserable creature had even contemplated suicide. Then, mercifully, had come an early Easter and though he had skulked in his room it had given Master Pratt, for such was his wretched name with all its silly *double entendre*, a certain amount of time for spiritual refreshment. But during the week following had come his worst moment. Bending before a mathematical diagram he had actually broken wind and several of his pupils had sniggered aloud. He had fled from his class, almost in tears, and would never have returned had not the

Duchess actually knocked upon the door of his room and ordered him to come out and continue.

The next day news of the arrival of three more children had filled Master Pratt with dread and he had entered the study room that morning almost too afraid to speak. There had been an anonymous braying laugh as he had come in and the tutor had stood by his desk wishing that the world might instantly come to an end and the entire castle of Kenninghall, complete with occupants, be reduced to rubble. Finally, with an enormous effort of will he had managed to look up and clear his throat.

During the electric silence that followed his attention had been caught by one of the newcomers who sat near the front, smiling at him. Eyes the colour of the Virgin's mantle – or so Master Pratt romantically thought – looked into his and just for a fanciful moment he imagined himself standing beyond his body, looking at his lanky person and realising his shoulders were hunched and his gaze swift and furtive. The tutor felt a terrible sensation of fear followed by one of enormous hope.

'Good morning,' he said tentatively.

'Good morning, arse,' muttered an indistinguishable voice.

Oh God, he thought and looked at the new girl for help. She was still smiling at him, quite softly, with no malice at all. 'Tell them your first name' were the words that came into his head.

Squaring his shoulders, Master Pratt looked directly at his pupils. 'My name is Anthony, not arse. And as we have three new people with us today we shall start afresh. From now on you will address me as Master Anthony and at least one very boring joke will be over.'

'Well done,' said the voice in his head. 'Now show them your strength.'

'But before the incident is closed,' he went on, hardly knowing where the words were coming from, 'I am going to punish the person who insulted me.'

There was a small silence, then one of the little mites piped up with, 'But who was it, Sir?'

The teacher looked round desperately and then knew quite certainly, almost as if someone had told him, that it was carrot-haired Ursula Tilney's brother, Gerard.

'Stand forth, Gerard Tilney,' he said in a voice that sounded quite menacing. And when there was no response thundered, 'Stand forth I say.'

There was total stillness and Anthony saw that he was staring at a sea of small faces with amazement written all over them.

'Why should I?' said Gerard eventually.

'Because I say so, wretch. And if you will not step out I shall come to fetch you.'

And so he did, seizing the boy's already pink ear, twisting it, then leading him, using the lobe as lever, from his place.

'Now hear your punishment,' said Anthony, pulling Gerard's face close to his. 'On this April day, being so fine and warm, I was intending to take lessons out of doors. But you, Sir, you' – Anthony shook the ear and its owner enthusiastically – 'you shall remain within and transcribe Latin all day long. And get no idea of running to tell the Duchess because I shall do so myself, now. The rest of you may pick up your things and go quietly to the meadow beyond the curtain wall. Lessons will begin in a short while.' And with that he marched Gerard off to find Elizabeth Howard, leaving behind some very startled young people.

'How dare he,' said Ursula, as soon as the teacher was gone. 'I shall report him to my father.'

'Why bother?' answered Joscelin. 'It will all be too late by the time he hears of it.'

'It's a matter of principle,' she replied haughtily, flinging her red hair about.

'Really?' said Joscelin, sounding disinterested, and got up from his place, crossing to where Sapphira sat with her brothers. He bowed politely. 'May I help you to find your way to the meadow?' he asked in his best voice.

The girl nodded, putting her hand out to him, but knowing that Ursula was watching him sulkily, Joscelin hesitated. Then he took Sapphira's small childish fingers into his and sealed his future irrevocably.

'I really think,' said Ursula, sweeping up, 'that Mistress Howard would be better accompanied by her brothers than you, Joscelin. Remember that I am your betrothed. It is your place to walk with me.'

He turned on her a look that frightened her because for a few seconds Ursula could see plainly that her future husband could not remember who she was.

'What's the matter?' she cried furiously. 'Have you gone mad? Don't stare at me like that!'

He came to his senses, abruptly and with a shudder. 'Forgive me. I shall go with you to the meadow now.'

She threw Sapphira a poisonous look. 'Mistress Howard, I must advise you that it is not seemly in a maiden of your years to hold handfast with a man pre-contracted to marry another. If you wish to keep a shred of reputation it would be best to concentrate on your lessons while you are here.'

'My sister touches people because she cannot speak to them,' said Sylvanus hotly.

'And because she is genuinely kind,' added Jasper, his face menacing. 'There is no cruelty in her, unlike some others.'

Ursula would have argued then, followed the instincts of her flaming hair and had a battle of wits with the dark boy-creature but the moment was spoiled by Master Pratt popping his head round the door and saying in a most authoritative voice, 'Not gone yet? Now come *along*!' And with that they all scurried.

Beyond the shadows of Kenninghall the spring day triumphed. It was warm enough for the young people to sit on cushions and watch the sun throwing beams of light through the trees, listening lazily to Master Anthony who, in his turn, grew bored with hexameters and pentameters, and began to talk of the beauties of the seasons and the cycle of nature reflected in human life.

'You are all in the springtime,' he said, 'like this day, golden and glowing with youth.'

'But so are you, Master,' called Surrey's little girl and as Anthony shed a tear of joy, nobody laughed at him. 'You are dismissed,' he said. 'Go and pick flowers for the Duchess. There are banks of primroses in the woods.' And with that he rolled on his back and fell asleep.

'Will he lose his post?' asked Sylvanus anxiously.

Joscelin shook his head. 'No. He is a good teacher, excellent in fact. It is just that he is so nervous. But today he seems to have passed through some sort of metamorphosis. The Duchess will be delighted.' He sighed and looked round for Ursula who by now should have been approaching in a cloud of ginger hair, but she was nowhere to be seen. Only Sapphira sat, smiling and still, watching the others as they drifted off in twos and threes, delighted to have time free from their lessons.

349

'Where is Ursula?' he called to the departing pupils.

'She went back to the castle. She was suddenly tired,' came the puzzling answer.

So now, as Jasper and Sylvanus rushed off, they were alone together. Hand clasping hand, blue eyes gazing into green, they walked slowly off towards the wood, lost in their own dream world in which nobody else existed at all. Sapphira had not expected to gain love without pain and now as she and Joscelin took the irrevocable step that both frightened and exalted them, she felt momentarily hurt.

'We are lost,' said Joscelin as his very life seemed to flow into her.

Sapphira shook her head.

'I knew nothing of this,' he whispered, quite unnecessarily because Sapphira was already aware. 'I never laid a finger on Ursula. You are my first love.'

He did not have to say that she was also his last. They were one person in many ways, two halves that together formed a perfect whole. Lying in the sunlit wood, watching the sun make tunnels of light in which insects and butterflies danced for their delight, Sapphira and Joscelin clung together, already fearing the separation that lay in wait for them, putting off the dreaded hour of their return until it could no longer be avoided.

On the edge of the great Wolff Hall estate lay Topenham Lodge, a substantial hunting lodge into which guests overflowed when the main house was full. It was there that Jane Seymour had stayed when King Henry had first come to her father's house, and it was to the Lodge that Edward's mother and children had removed themselves when in 1539, a month before his marriage contract with Anna of Cleves had been signed, Henry Tudor had visited again. But when the family was not at home and there was no guest staying in order to hunt, Topenham Lodge stood empty.

Ever since Thomas's delighted realisation that the Widow Latymer was only too eager for their courtship to be renewed, it had exercised his mind constantly where his seduction of her should take place. It would have been only too easy to become a permanent visitor at her Charterhouse home, thereby giving Katherine's servants plenty to talk about. But though he cared nothing for himself, being totally devoid of any kind of shame or embarrassment or even interest in what other people thought, Thomas would not subject someone he loved to humiliation. And he did love Katherine to the limit of his raffish ability.

Topenham Lodge, with its lack of servants and isolated position, seemed to him the ideal spot for secrecy, and with Thomas's childlike adoration of plots and schemes, it was easy to arrange that he meet Lady Latymer at a pre-arranged place along the route, Katherine to travel with only one trusty male guard, and no female attendants at all.

In the months that followed, as events took an unimaginable turn, Thomas thanked a providence that he did not altogether believe in that he had observed the niceties and taken the precaution of hiding his love affair with Katherine from slanderous tongues.

To prepare the Lodge he had sent ahead his own man Jack, who would have died rather than betray his master, to fetch from Wolff Hall old Meg who had once been servant to Tom's sister Jane. She had grumblingly set about cleaning and airing the rooms and shaking out bedding, while Jack, and Thomas's cook, another trustworthy soul, had prepared the food. So on yet another pretty April evening, Katherine Latymer had arrived in Wiltshire, her secret safe, to learn about love by putting herself in the hands of an expert.

They supped romantically before a fire, the mood well set, and then Katherine went to bed with Thomas like a child, for sweetness, for reassurance, for gentleness and caring. And this he gave because of his love for her. But after tenderness followed passion, raw and rough. Beneath his touch areas of sensation which Katherine did not know she had, were made aware of their existence; the plunging within her was demanding, exciting beyond belief, and then, for the very first time, Katherine knew what it was to explode with ecstasy, to burn and freeze simultaneously, to reach for the moon and touch the stars. She was thirty and this was her first experience of completion. As the butterfly soared towards heaven it was very small wonder that Katherine's love for Thomas Seymour became obsessional.

Afterwards, they lay an inch or two apart, staring at each other. Every detail of Tom was crystal clear; the dark leonine hair, the splendid face, complete with its little lines where he laughed or frowned, the brilliant eyes, blue as oceans. While he saw her

351

comely features changed, grown experienced. With a silent chuckle Tom put out a long finger and tickled her nose.

'Well, Madam,' he said, 'how is life with you?'

'Perfect, at last. Oh Tom, I love you.'

'And I you, my dear.' He drew her close and closed his eyes and, unbidden, a vision of the child Elizabeth flashed into his mind.

Thomas must have given a small shudder of self-disgust for Katherine said, 'Is anything the matter?'

He opened his eyes and the image faded. 'I need you again.'

It was all so new to her, a powerful lover with strength and stamina.

'I will never give you up, never,' she whispered as she flew up a rainbow of delight and floated down into paradise.

'You will never have to,' Thomas answered quietly.

'Do you promise?'

'I promise,' he said, unaware that even at that very second forces over which they had no control were moving against Thomas Seymour and his new-found love.

It blazed out of them like high summer. One look at their faces, at the way they had eyes for no one but each other, was enough. It was not possible for Sapphira and Joscelin to hide from anyone, except the very young, the fact that they had become lovers.

For the rest of that afternoon they were safe enough, for they saw only each other, but as soon as they came before the older children the truth was out. Ursula, recovering from the extraordinary bout of sleepiness which had suddenly overcome her, had searched for Joscelin everywhere, and then spied him coming out of the woods with his arm round Sapphira's waist, not even attempting concealment. She had run then, hurried from the castle, so that she met them before they even entered the precinct.

'What have you done?' she asked bluntly, her face white against her violent hair. 'Why, I could kill you, you mealy-mouthed witch,' and she had flown at Sapphira with feet and fists.

In a way Joscelin felt sorry for her as he pulled her off. 'Don't Ursula, please don't. You are making it all so difficult.'

'Difficult? You are mine, remember? Our fathers signed the contract years ago.'

'But that doesn't mean we love one another. And we don't.'

352

'Speak for yourself,' answered Ursula and with that, catching him unawares, gave Sapphira a stinging blow round the face.

Zachary's daughter went pale but made no move to hit back, in fact she remained quite still, not lifting a finger in her own defence. Joscelin, sensing something of her power, said, 'Don't hurt her, Sapphira. It's not her fault.'

She nodded her head and this seemed to infuriate Ursula all the more. 'I'll tell the Duchess what you've done. Then you'll both be sent away,' she hissed, and before Joscelin could stop her, punched Sapphira in the stomach.

It was at this anguished moment that Mary Howard, the Duchess of Richmond, daughter of the house of Norfolk, came innocently upon the scene and stopped in amazement.

'What in Heaven's name is going on?' she exclaimed. 'Are you two girls fighting?'

With her attention thus distracted, Ursula Tilney never saw and never afterwards knew that Sapphira had picked a flower from the meadow beneath her feet and rubbed a petal over Ursula's hand. Nor did she see the mark where a faint smear of juice lay upon her skin.

There was a frozen pause, then Joscelin opened his mouth to answer as Ursula said, 'No, I don't think so.'

'What do you mean?' asked Mary.

'We were not fighting,' answered Ursula dreamily. 'I do not fight with friends.'

Joscelin's expression was so amazed that the Duchess of Richmond was suspicious. 'I don't trust this,' she said. 'Is the quarrel between you and your betrothed?' And she turned to the boy for an explanation.

He coloured. 'In a way, yes.'

'He is no longer betrothed to me,' said Ursula.

'What is happening here?' snapped Mary. 'There is something I don't understand. You are all three of you coming before my mother.'

And that was how disaster struck the youthful lovers. The Duchess of Richmond, widowed but still immature, might have been deceived, but Elizabeth Howard took one look at Sapphira and Lord Joscelin and felt her heart shrink within. Catherine Howard had lost her virginity when she was twelve, now here was another, not much older, and left in her charge too.

'Joscelin, go to your room,' she said. 'Sapphira, stay here. I forbid the two of you to be left alone ever again. If what I suspect is true then one of you shall be banished from this house forever.'

'God's sweet life!' Mary exclaimed, her hand flying to her throat.

'Indeed,' answered her mother grimly. 'It looks as if we have just received a nest of vipers into our bosom with these poor relations of your father's.'

'But surely Joscelin is as much to blame?'

'Joscelin is a Howard,' said Elizabeth firmly. 'I'm not quite sure what the other three are!'

'What are you going to do?'

'I shall make up my mind tonight.'

And with that the Duchess strode out, grey with rage.

Katherine Latymer, born Parr, had gone to Wiltshire as a widow but travelled back two weeks later an affianced bride. During their wonderful sojourn, Sir Thomas had both proposed marriage and convinced her that it must be soon, in the face of whatever convention decreed. Katherine returned to Charterhouse in a whirl of wedding plans, sending at once for Scutt the tailor and ordering an expensive trousseau of French, Venetian and Dutch gowns, a slope hood and tippet, to say nothing of embroidered sleeves, crisp pleats and fine linen.

Soon, oh soon, I can put aside this dreary black, she thought. Oh John, forgive me.

An invitation to attend Court came as rather a surprise in the middle of all this activity. In fact it was extremely inconvenient. But a summons to a banquet at Hampton Court could not easily be refused, so with a sigh Katherine added a new black gown to Scutt's overflowing order.

'I wonder why I have been invited,' she said to Thomas, who had called for supper but refused to stay the night until they were safely married.

'The King's bored and lonely and fat as a pig,' came the irreverent reply. 'God's passion, but you should see the stomach of our monarch. Stout as a barrel and daily getting bigger. And as for the smell from his rotting leg . . .'

'Oh don't,' said Katherine, putting her finger to her nose. 'It isn't kind. He can't help it.'

'I think he can,' answered Thomas wickedly, starting to stalk her

354

round a chair. 'I think he's brought it on himself. He's riddled with the grand pox, the French pox and every other pox you can name.'

'Oh surely not!'

'Oh surely yes.'

He made a flying leap for her and caught her, squealing, in his arms. 'Don't you let our royal brother-in-law get anywhere near you.'

'No hope of that,' answered Katherine, unaware of the portent of those words.

The invitation was for early May and she set off in the morning, riding to the river and then taking Lord Latymer's barge which was rowed leisurely upstream towards the palace from which Katherine had been so summarily dismissed fifteen months ago. Now, as she approached it, she had no emotion other than that of slight boredom. All she wanted was to get this dreary feast over and done, that she might return to Thomas Seymour and her wedding plans.

Henry Tudor, or so Katherine believed, had been bitterly hurt by the infidelity of his 'rose without a thorn', and in the months following her execution had been wretchedly depressed. But of late he had been feasting ladies once more and taking advice to be merry from his adopted sister, the Lady Anne of Cleves. Despite everything the King was doing his best to revive his old carefree way.

But with what overwhelming difficulties, thought Katherine on seeing him again. He had been obese when she had left Court and now he seemed doubled in size, a monster hobbling on a stick; so swollen in the face that his visage had almost become featureless, only the meagre eyebrows and fuzzy beard giving any line of demarcation in a sea of puffy white flesh.

God almighty! thought Katherine, and was appalled to see him limping in her direction.

'Ah, Lady Latymer,' Henry wheezed as Katherine bent low before him. 'Good to see you, Madam. We believe that these days you have turned into something of a theologian. Unless our spies play us false.'

'Spies, Your Grace?' said Katherine in some alarm, her mind not turning to religion but to her illicit weeks of love with Thomas Seymour.

'We have heard that you are a follower of the new ideas, Madam.

355

That you are very tolerant in your outlook. That you embrace the ideals of Erasmus.'

'Sir?' She literally did not know what to answer.

'We find that we tend more and more towards educated women,' said Henry, gasping his way into a chair and indicating that she should do the same. 'There is nothing more satisfying to our mind than a woman who thinks.'

'I thank Your Grace,' answered Katherine, wondering what could possibly be coming next.

'Theology fascinates us as you know,' the King went on, swaying his afflicted leg from side to side to avoid undue pressure. 'We have discussed it since youth, as we believe have you, Madam.'

'Not really, Sir,' answered Katherine, finding her voice. 'My late husband was a devout Catholic. It is only since his death that I have felt free to explore new ideas, reforms. Though my mind has dwelt on them for some years.'

To her intense dismay a vast and pudgy hand reached out and patted hers. 'Forgive us, Lady Latymer. We have not offered our condolences on the recent loss of your excellent husband. We beg your indulgence.' A deprecating smile twitched the King's little mouth. 'We have had much on our mind since you were last at Court.'

Katherine lowered her eyes, guilt running through her blood like quicksilver. 'Lord Latymer is badly missed,' she lied, wishing that she had not come, that she had made some excuse on the grounds of poor health.

'We are sure of that,' said Henry with solemnity. 'But one must not dwell in the past. That is fatal as we have discovered to our cost. Whatever one's age, however old chronologically, it is never too late for a fresh start. Or so we believe. What think you, Lady Latymer?'

The conversation was growing so strange that Katherine could hardly make head nor tail of it. 'One must always look to the future, Sir,' she answered lamely.

'Ha, ha,' Henry bellowed roguishly. 'And with that in mind I give you an order, Madam.'

'And what is that?' she asked, horror-stricken.

'We wish to see you at Court again. We would discuss at length your new ideas. We want to hear you air your views, we want to talk with clever women. Beauty is one thing, Lady Latymer –

356

though you possess that in plentitude believe me – but brains are another. We have come to the conclusion after all these years' – again that sinister chuckle – 'that to possess one without the other is useless. That no woman bears the right to the name unless she is possessed of both charm and wit.'

The King arched his nonsensical eyebrows, waiting for her reply.

'I expect you are right, Your Grace.'

'Expect,' said Henry jovially, 'expect? We know it for the truth, my dear Lady Latymer, and that is why we feel we shall *enjoy your company* so much.'

It was then that Katherine felt the teeth of the trap close about her. There could be no mistaking that leer, that vile double meaning.

Oh Christ be my salvation, she thought. He wants me for his mistress.

With an effort of will that was almost beyond her power, Katherine lowered her eyes to her lap and kept her face quite calm.

'As Your Grace pleases,' she said, and in her breast felt her courage begin to die.

# Chapter Twenty-Eight

THE DECISION OF THE Duchess of Norfolk was, once arrived at, swift and merciless. Too much trouble had already been caused for the Howards by promiscuous little girls and wayward boys. Sapphira and her brothers must leave the following morning; Joscelin, on the Duke's return from London, was to suffer a beating at the hands of the head of the Howard clan. And with that the sordid affair would be forgotten, though never forgiven, and life at Kenninghall could continue as calmly as before.

She announced her decision in a hushed voice, a strategy that Elizabeth Howard had found far more effective over the years than shouting. First the girl was ushered into her presence.

'I know you cannot speak, young lady,' the menacing whisper had begun, 'but that excuses you nothing. I thought you enchanting when you arrived. Now I consider you loathsome. You are forward beyond your years. Tomorrow you, and your brothers with you, will be despatched to whatever hell-hole you came from.'

The ancient knowledge of Sapphira could, then, have played tricks but instead she bowed her head in the silence that was her perpetual curse. After a second, during which the woman-child gained control of her misery, Sapphira curtsied deeply and left the room, aware that she must never be parted from Joscelin, were the forces of all the world to be ranged against them.

Having made sure that the girl was out of sight, Lord Joscelin Howard was led before the Duchess.

'I am aware,' said Elizabeth, in a somewhat kinder tone, 'that you are full grown and within the next two years likely to wed Ursula, but that does not forgive your seduction of a young girl residing here under our protection.'

The handsome boy went white. 'But Madam, Your Grace, it was

not like that. There was nothing vile in what we did. I love Sapphira, I . . .'

'Love?' interrupted the Duchess contemptuously. 'What in Heaven's name would you know of love? A stripling youth of fifteen. A callow boy.'

Joscelin swallowed, manfully forbearing to point out that she had called him full grown but a moment or two before.

'I could send you forth from this place, never to return, were it not for the love that the Duke and I bear your father.'

Lord John, one of the much younger sons of the house but brother to Norfolk, had died tragically early in life leaving his widow, now contentedly remarried, to cope with two sturdy infants, both of whom Thomas Howard had taken under his wing.

Joscelin gulped. 'But, Madam, my intentions are honourable. I want to marry Sapphira. I will see Ursula's father, break our contract . . .'

Once again the Duchess interrupted him but this time she went so far as to laugh in the boy's face.

'See fathers? Break contracts? My dear child, you do not know you are born. Your father signed his pledge with Ursula's while you were both still in swaddling. It is she you will marry and there's an end to it.'

'But I don't love her,' said the wretched young man, feeling the horrible embarrassment of tears sting behind his eyes.

'Love has nothing to do with it,' answered the Duchess caustically.

'Well then it should, by God it should,' said Jocelyn with spirit, then shrank at the realisation of his rudeness to Norfolk's wife.

She smiled patronisingly. 'You'll learn, my child,' she answered, still with that annoying smirk.

'If it means learning how not to love,' he answered with dignity, 'then I prefer not to do so.'

The Duchess shrugged her shoulders. 'That is your choice, Lord Joscelin. Now go to your room and stay there. I do not want you to come out again until those three wretches have gone.'

'Gone?' repeated the boy, his face draining of colour even further.

'Yes, gone. All of them will be sent packing in the morning. I cannot risk the girl staying here in view of your foolishness, and without her there is no point in the brothers remaining.'

Joscelin knew he had to leave the room, feeling tears start to run unchecked.

'I submit to your decree, Madam,' he mumbled. 'I will go as you have ordered.'

And with that he bowed swiftly and hurried out, making for the dormitory inhabited by the older boys which, at this hour of the evening, was mercifully empty.

Once there, Joscelin flung himself down on his bed, weeping bitterly, and might have remained like that for some time had not the crackle of paper sounded in his ear. A note had been pinned to the bed hangings, only visible to someone actually lying on it. With a burst of hope Joscelin snatched it from its place and ripped it open.

'Greetings to my Lord Joscelin' he read and, despite the circumstances, had to smile at the formality of the writer. 'I know you feel, as I do, that we must never be separated. Therefore, I shall be at the stables at two hours after midnight and will await you. Do not worry about the watchmen.'

Joscelin brightened. Cautiously looking round to reassure himself he was still alone, the boy began to set aside one or two things he would need for the journey. Then he lay patiently on his bed, waiting for night to come.

Around the deserted monastery of Charterhouse the orchards were in blossom and in the gardens, once so lovingly tended by the brothers, now bloomed a great mass of flowers and weeds, growing brightly side by side. Through the cloisters birds flew and nested and the vine that had been cultivated, not too successfully in the English climate, this year already showed signs of having a bumper crop. Herbs grew wild in what had once been the herbarium, where the monks had grown cure-alls for their winter ailments and delicacies to enrich the abbot's food. Normally Katherine Latymer would have gone to pick them, or at least sent one of her kitchen lads to do so, but today she walked through the sweet-smelling place with a solemn face, her hands folded in front of her. And Sir Thomas Seymour, who paced alongside appeared equally grim, his flashing smile quite lost and his eyes dull and angry looking.

'If only I could be sure,' Lady Latymer was saying. 'If only I knew what His Grace wants of me.'

'Your body, is my guess,' answered Thomas shortly. 'Though there's nothing he could do with it if it were delivered to him.'

'How coarse you are,' replied Katherine furiously. 'This is no matter for jest. I think you should withdraw that remark.'

'I do, I do,' said Thomas hastily. 'I only spoke through bitterness. For how could this happen with our wedding only a few weeks away? I cannot believe our ill-fortune.'

There was a hut in the garden, used for drying herbs, and outside it a rotting wooden seat. On this Katherine now sat, patting the place beside her.

'Whatever happens,' she said in a conciliatory tone, 'we must not quarrel. We must not let these events make us fall out, one with the other.'

Thomas sat beside her, plunging his head into his hands. 'But it is all so worrying. His Grace has recalled you to Court for some reason. Why *does* he seek out your company more and more?'

'I suppose,' said Katherine slowly, 'that that couldn't be the sum total of it? That he merely wants a woman with whom to debate?'

One of Thomas's eyes stared hollowly at her through his parted fingers. 'Not a chance, my innocent. The man may be past it but he can still dream. He wants a bed-mate, and if she can talk as well, all the better.'

'Oh my God,' Katherine said despairingly. 'If that is true, what shall I do?'

'I don't know,' answered Thomas, lowering his hands and shaking his head. 'I simply don't know. All we can do is pray that this phase will end. That he will fasten his piggy eyes on some other benighted female and that you can fade quickly into the background and marry me before he remembers you again.'

'Perhaps we should do that now,' said Katherine, breathing rather fast. 'Perhaps we should marry at once and put an end to this uncertainty.'

'I think such a move could be dangerous,' Thomas answered thoughtfully. 'If we do that it could be your head and mine on the block for some trumped-up charge.'

'Of what?'

'Interfering with the King's desires or an indictment equally flimsy, Wriothesley would think of something.'

Katherine shivered. 'That man!'

'Yes, that man.'

She looked at Thomas very earnestly. 'Are you serious, sweetheart? Do you really think we would be in trouble?'

'Until we know what is in the royal monster's mind, one way or another, yes.'

'Does that mean you want to cancel the wedding?' asked Katherine coldly.

Thomas smiled, his naughty face reappearing like the sun. 'No, of course not. Let us just tread with caution, that's all.'

Lady Latymer actually pouted. 'Have you tired of me, is that it?'

Thomas pulled her on to his knee. 'Any more of that and I shall smack you like a naughty girl. I love you, I *actually do!* And, believe me, it came as a great shock when I discovered it. So be good, sweetheart. You are the only one ever to capture my heart so you can be very sure I won't let you go now.'

'And His Grace?'

'Pox on his cod, if he hasn't already got one.'

'Really!' said Katherine. 'You *must* have more respect.'

'I don't see why,' answered Thomas seriously. 'I don't see why at all.'


Midnight came with all its ghostly quiet, and then the hours known as small, when the human spirit grows weak and people become afraid of stillness. In the dormitory shared with four other young men, Joscelin lay awake, nervously counting the minutes, listening to the breathing of his companions, praying that none of them would stir when the moment came for him to cross the long room and make his way out through the slumbering castle.

Thought after fearful thought had gone through his mind as he kept his vigil, and yet one thing overcame every doubt he had. Joscelin wanted to be with Sapphira, come what may, and if he must risk being cast out by his family and never spoken to again by any one of them, then so be it. For he loved the girl with the perfect love that seems peculiar to the very young, as if growing older and more experienced kills some precious thing that can never return.

With no way of telling the time the boy was forced to rely on counting and guesswork so, terrified of raising the alarm, only when he reckoned that it must be nearly two o'clock did he finally rise and walk on bare feet across the darkened room. Fortunately he knew his way in the blackness and there was a faint light coming through the high windows from a waxing moon. Even luckier, the floor was of stone and there were no creaking boards to betray him. Nonetheless, he bumped into a chair, making a slight thud. Hardly daring to breathe, Joscelin stood still and listened but none of the boys stirred.

As with all great dwelling places built in an earlier century the central stairs were not the only means of descent, and now Joscelin fled to a remote spiral in a little-used tower, at the bottom of which a door set in an archway led outside. Using this route meant that he could easily avoid night watchmen but the hazard lay in that he might find himself locked in. It was simply going to be a matter of chance.

Much as Joscelin expected, the door was bolted but it then occurred to him that the key could well be nearby. Reaching above his head his fingers closed on an ancient and rather rusty object hanging on a hook, and breathing a sigh of relief, he inserted it into the lock.

The noise that followed was enormous. As the antique thing groaned round it sounded as if the entire castle, let alone the echoing tower in which he stood, was blowing up. Joscelin's heart raced as somewhere in the distance he heard a voice call out.

He flung himself out into the starlight and then followed one moment of very clear good sense as he started to plunge towards the stables. Turning back, he pulled the door to and locked it from the outside. If pursuers were coming that way they were going to find themselves imprisoned.

The tug at his sleeve in the moonlight frightened him rigid. 'Sapphira, is that you?'

She stepped out of the shadows, smiling, and Joscelin saw that on the paper she usually carried with her the girl had already written, 'I've got a good horse, fresh and ready to go.'

And she had. She might look frail as a flower but as his eyes adjusted to the light, Joscelin made out the shape of a mighty creature, many times the size of Sapphira, grazing calmly, attached to a nearby tree.

'Oh, you witch!' he said and laughed, with relief as much as anything else. He lifted her up and mounted behind her, swinging in the stirrup as he ascended the enormous creature.

'Surely you didn't saddle this thing?'

She shook her head and pointed to where a shape lay on the ground outside the stables. Joscelin, peering closely, saw that it was the ostler's boy stretched out on his back, fast asleep.

'*He* did it?'

Sapphira nodded. All the tensions of the last twenty-four hours slipped away and Joscelin smiled. 'What have I let myself in for? Well, whatever it is, we must leave now. They'll be after us soon.' And with that the boy put his heels into his mount and went off at speed.

They had both been dreaming of danger, though not the same dream, yet at exactly the precise second Cloverella and Zachary woke together from a feverish sleep and clung to each other, gasping.

'What's wrong?' she said. 'Something is, I'll swear it.'

'Yes.' Zachary sniffed like a hound. 'I can smell it. There's disaster somewhere.'

'Is it for us?'

'I don't know yet.'

He got out of bed, pulling on his hose. 'I think it's the children.'

'Oh no!' said Cloverella, jumping out quickly and putting a night-rail over her bedclothes, making for the room where all the astrologer's prophetic mediums lay.

But Zachary was already ahead of her, clambering up the spindly staircase which led to his attic and reaching out his hand to the place where the dark crystal lay on its velvet cloth.

'Well?' Cloverella crouched beside him, also trying to fathom its depths.

'It isn't reacting. There's something terribly wrong.'

'Let me see.'

Zachary's wife took it from him, rubbing her hand over the sphere's glassy surface before looking into it.

'Yes,' she said, 'quick, do you see?'

She passed it to him but the astrologer shook his dark head.

'No, there's nothing there.'

'It was only for a second but I glimpsed Sapphira and a boy, a beautiful boy.'

'And . . .'

'And danger, Zachary. Great danger.' Cloverella looked him straight in the eye. 'I think it better that we start the journey to Norfolk now than sit here agonising.'

She hurried down the stairs to dress, leaving Zachary alone for a few moments. From the shadows his terrible one-orbed cat, an eye lost fighting long since, stirred and came out.

'Sapphira is in peril,' he said to it. 'If I were a true master of magic I would send you forth now.'

364

It glared at him resentfully and shot down the stairs, Zachary following more slowly. Cloverella stood waiting at the bottom with his doublet and cloak already in her hands.

'Put these on. I think we should make haste.'

Zachary looked at her. 'I am afraid, Cloverella. By God's passion, I am afraid.

'So am I,' she answered sombrely. 'But I fear inaction more.'

'Indeed,' he said, and together they left the house.

It was not easy, with the moon and stars so dim, to find one's way in unknown countryside and Joscelin found it hard going even to plot a route to Bury St Edmunds. By following the River Thet he managed to proceed to Thet Ford. But this place he avoided for fear of being seen and instead went south-east so that by first light they were near a village called Wetherenden, picking his way through a maze of little brooks and rivers. In the saddle in front of him, cradled in the hollow of his shoulder, her mouth touching his throat in what seemed like an eternal kiss, Sapphira lay asleep, her pale blonde hair spread over his doublet like a veil.

Joscelin knew as he rode that she and he must always be together, that the great sense of belonging he now experienced must last for ever. Even though he was on horseback he somehow managed to cuddle her closer, holding the reins in one hand and wrapping his free arm tightly around her.

In a way it no longer seemed to matter exactly what direction they took. They were heading south, Joscelin knew that for sure, which seemed to be enough. If anyone from the castle had been on their trail they had certainly lost them long ago, for his route had been circuitous and not altogether logical. Yet soon he knew they must stop for food and take the risk of a party of horsemen catching them by chance.

He bought bread from a woman baking in a humble dwelling by the river and he and Sapphira, now firmly awake, sat not far from her door, consuming it hungrily, while she watched them covertly from inside.

'Come a distance, Sir?' she asked eventually, looking curiously at Joscelin's fine clothes.

'From Leicester,' he said, just a little too quickly to her manner of thinking.

'Then you're well out of your way.'

'We have friends here,' Joscelin answered vaguely.

The woman eyed them. A pair of runaways, if she'd ever seen one, more than likely defying an arranged marriage. She took particular note of them, especially of the girl who, for all her beauty, was obviously dumb, conversing with her young lover by signs.

I reckon there'll be a reward offered, she thought and went back in to fetch more food to delay them. But when she came out again the couple had gone, leaving her money for a loaf they had taken.

Half an hour later a group of horsemen, all wearing the livery of the Duke of Norfolk, thundered into view and the woman watched as they slowed down, their leader dismounting and approaching her.

'Have you seen two young people, a boy and girl, pass this way?'

She put on a knowing face. 'What if I have?'

The man snapped his fingers to the rider behind and a small bag of money was handed down.

'Well?'

'About half an hour ago, Sir. A dark young man and a fair girl with him.'

'Anything odd about them?'

'The girl couldn't speak, Sir. She was dumb.'

He nodded, well satisfied, and the bag of money changed hands.

'Did they say where they were going?'

'No, Sir, but they went that way.'

She pointed out the couple's route and the leader remounted. 'That's it, men. We should pick them up soon. It will all be over by dusk.'

'God help the poor wretches,' said someone at the back.

The leader glared fiercely. 'We are not paid to moralise. We are paid to serve the Duke. Now come on.'

He held up his gauntleted hand and the troupe moved off at speed while the woman, taking her time about it, counted out the money, wishing that runaways crossed her path every day of the week.

At noon, with the spring sun high, Joscelin and Sapphira came to a pretty little brook which burst out of a small hill and went gushing away into the distance. The girl clapped her hands delightedly and both of them dismounted, giving the mighty horse a rest, and waded barefoot in the sunshine. Then they swam, naked and happy, made love sweetly, and finally dressed again and began to take the brook's course. It grew stronger and soon became a handsome river flowing between steep embankments.

'Shall we follow it further?' asked Joscelin and Sapphira nodded.

They had no idea where they were until after journeying some while they saw, on the river's right bank, a great priory and the name Kersey.

'We're still in Suffolk,' said Joscelin. 'I know that place. Shall we go and explore?'

They had almost forgotten that they were running away, for now it seemed like a marvellous game, finding rivers and hills, seeing brightly coloured fields and flowers, and watching wild animals run about their business, with no thought of hindering or hurting them.

'Yes,' nodded Sapphira, and then saw Joscelin's face change.

'What is it?' she asked, signalling with her hands.

He pointed to his ear, bidding her listen, and there could be no mistaking the sound. Not more than half a mile away, a group of horsemen rode behind them.

'Oh God help us now,' said Joscelin, a note of desperation in his voice as he once more kicked the powerful beast into action, so that it stopped its pleasant ambling and went off at a canter, its youthful passengers clinging on tightly.

'We may yet get away,' the boy said hopefully, but she shook her head. Peering over her shoulder, Sapphira had seen the front riders come into view.

In the flat Suffolk countryside the ground suddenly and unexpectedly started to rise, sloping on either side of the companionable river in the steepest embankments the young people had so far encountered. The horse reduced speed as it began to climb upwards and then hesitated when it reached the top and there was nothing before it but a drop of some twelve feet to the deep water below.

'We're trapped,' said Joscelin desperately. 'There's no way out of here. We're lost, Sapphira. Oh my darling, we're finished.'

'No,' she cried, the sound floating out, clear and triumphant, 'no. The water will carry us to where we can be together. Jump, horse, jump!'

And it wasn't until they were plunging downwards, riders and mount all together in a terrible tangle of limbs, that Joscelin realised something; that finally, in the very last moments of her life, Sapphira's voice had been restored to her.

They dived to rescue them, of course. The men stripped off their jerkins and went in, one after another. But it was too late. Though the great beast swam to the side and hauled itself out, the two young ones had gone forever.

They pulled them to the bank further downstream, where they had floated, still together, like water nymphs, their hair spread and their eyes open, hands open-fingered at their sides, as if in supplication. It was too late to get the water out of them, too late to pump their poor bodies, so they left them, their young faces staring at God, their delicate mouths curved in fragile smiles, two of His lost lambs come to pasture.

An hour later, brought back in closed litters, they lay just so, white but as yet uncorrupted, side by side in the castle's mortuary. And this was how Dr Zachary saw them, together with the boy's elder sister, Lady Margaret, who had come in haste.

'Can there ever be reason for such a terrible end?' he said eventually, having stared for an hour at the waxen doll that was once his beloved daughter. 'How could two young lives be snuffed out like this?'

Then he broke his heart, weeping so desperately that neither Cloverella nor anyone else could do anything with him.

'If only the Duke were here,' said Elizabeth Howard, wringing her hands frantically.

Cloverella looked at her coldly. 'Then the responsibility would not have been yours, would it? But it *is*, Madam. The Duke is not here and you are. What did you say to those two poor things to drive them so hard?'

'They broke the rules,' hissed the Duchess. 'They were strangers and young, yet they made love.'

'And look to what it has brought them. I do not envy your conscience, Madam. Good day to you.'

And with that she left Kenninghall, waiting beyond its walls until in the darkness Zachary and his two sons, in sombre, sad procession, brought Sapphira's body down from the castle to take it back to Greenwich.

'But where is the boy?' said Cloverella, suddenly aware of forces at work stronger than she.

'Still there. His sister is removing him.'

'But that is wrong. That must not be. They must be buried side by side as they would want. Zachary, you cannot ignore Sapphira's final wish.'

Jasper cleared his throat, speaking little above a whisper. 'It is true Father. They loved each other very much.'

'They did, Sir,' confirmed Sylvanus, his rose face withered with sadness.

'Then so be it. I must let her go.'

And that was how the youthful lovers came to be buried together, by consent of both Zachary and Lady Margaret, not in the Howard vault but in the churchyard at Kenninghall, where mild sheep and their lambs were let loose to graze in springtime, beneath the perfect blue of a peaceful Norfolk sky.

# Chapter Twenty-Nine

IT WAS, THOUGHT Thomas Seymour, one of the most sinister moments of his life. Outside, despite the fact it was May, the sky was leaden-grey, thunder rolled ominously overhead, and torrents of water fell in visible sheets from sky to earth. While within, in a Charterhouse mansion emptied of servants, white sheets over every piece of furniture except the chair on which Thomas sat, Katherine Parr was having hysterics.

'No, no, no,' she screamed, hurling books through the air. 'I cannot endure it. I would rather be dead. Kill me, Thomas, I beg you. Put me out of my agony.'

'Hush, sweetheart, hush,' he murmured soothingly, his voice drowned by her shrieks, his tenderness dampened by the missiles flying past his ear. 'Be calm, loved one.'

'Calm!' she yelled. 'Calm! You ask that of me when my life is in ruins.'

'*Our* lives are in ruins,' Thomas reminded her patiently.

She ignored him. 'You don't know what this means to me. For years I have suffered, *years* I tell you. My mother sold me when I was thirteen to a mad old man who crushed me, body and soul. Then I married John Latymer, though that was my own choice. And now this . . .' Katherine's voice dropped and she flew into Thomas's arms in a frenzy of tears. 'I never want to see old flesh again as long as I live. The thought of aged hands pawing at my body makes me feel fit to vomit. I cannot endure to get into bed ever again beside an old man with a limp thing. Oh God, help me, Thomas darling, I can't bear this terrible fate.'

'No,' he said, patting her gently and holding her close, 'it is the most revolting circumstance I can imagine. And that it should happen to you, whom I love dearly, is beyond thinking.'

'I daren't say no, dare I?' It was half a question, half a plea.

Thomas shook his head. 'It would be too dangerous. We've discussed this before. As it is we are running risks.'

The act of attainder brought against Catherine Howard had made it treason for any unchaste woman to marry the King or for a prospective bride to conceal her past. And now, with the worst of Thomas's and Katherine's fears realised, a proposal of marriage having been made by Henry Tudor to Lady Latymer, they had much to worry about. To refuse the monarch would be an insult tantamount to treason and too dangerous with life so cheap these days – even Nicholas Carew, an old and respected favourite, having gone to the block suspected of conspiring against his sovereign. Katherine had no choice but to accept Henry's offer and hide the fact that Thomas Seymour had been her lover.

'Thank God we were discreet,' he went on. 'None of those servants would tell; Meg is almost senile and Jack's faithful to death.'

'What about the cook?'

'The cook is frightened of Jack, who would kill him. I think we are very nearly safe.'

'Very nearly?' Katherine repeated nervously.

'My darling, there is always an unknown factor. The chance that somebody, somewhere, knows something.'

'I can't bear it,' she said, starting to sob again. 'This terrible proposal puts me in mortal danger. Oh Thomas, help me, help me.'

'I can't while you weep,' he said calmly. 'Be quiet, pretty Kate, and then I will tell you my plan.'

Sad green eyes, very wet, looked at him with a small ray of hope. 'You have a scheme?'

He laughed, rather bitterly. 'As good a thing as I can think of in these vile circumstances.'

'Then tell me of it.'

They sat together, arms wrapped round each other, in the house that was supposed to be closed, at this, their very last secret meeting.

'Now dry your tears,' said Thomas and gently wiped her face with his handkerchief. He was an utter rogue and ruthless with every woman except this one with whom, for some extraordinary reason, he had fallen in love.

'We must accept the truth. We have been outmanoeuvered. So

first of all, to keep our spirits up, we have to take the long view. Simply look at my royal brother-in-law, Kate . . .'

With a flash of her old spirit, she said, 'I would rather not!' and was rewarded with a hug.

'Indeed! But let facts be faced. He is vastly fat, limping, crippled by a varicose ulcer, oozing pus, and prone to blood clots. He is prematurely old, sweetheart, dying on his feet. Our separation cannot last longer than five years at most.'

'Five years' echoed Katherine dismally.

'And I will wait, sweetheart. Have no fear of that. When that old invalid dies and you are once more widowed, I will be the first man over your doorstep.'

They exchanged a deep, dangerous kiss.

'But what of now, Tom? How will we content ourselves?'

'By being practical. My appointment as English Ambassador to the Regent of the Netherlands has been confirmed. I plan to sail straight away. I want no Catherine Howard and Thomas Culpepper situation for us. I intend to stay out of the country until it is all over.'

'And what of me? How will I bear it?'

'By being a good stepmother to my nephew,' answered Thomas simply. 'Poor little boy, what has he had in the way of stability? His father hardly ever sees him, he never knew Jane, loved the Lady of Cleves, as did all the children, and then just as he gets to know pretty Cat, she is killed.'

'And what if I am killed too?' asked Katherine hollowly.

'Sweetheart, why should you be? You are not going to be unfaithful – at least I hope not! – and there is a very simple rule for survival. Simply agree with every word Henry Tudor says.'

'But I have my own views on the reformed religion.'

'Then keep them to yourself.'

She kissed him on the cheek. 'You are profoundly wise.'

Thomas grinned. 'For a foolish fellow, perhaps.'

Katherine went pale again. 'But how shall I stand him near me? How can I tolerate him after you?'

'From what I hear,' said Thomas softly, 'there's not a great deal to worry about.' Then he winked.

'Why says that?'

'Even learned physicians must talk, my dear. I think you will find that though the spirit is more than willing the decaying flesh is excessively weak.'

'I pray God it is so.'

'I too,' answered Thomas fervently. 'For to me we are still betrothed and will remain so until the day we marry.'

'Would it be dangerous for me to keep the ring?'

'The little garnet? No. Wear it on the left hand index finger and say it was from Lord Latymer.'

'I shall never leave it off.'

'Nor I the gold band you gave me.'

The moment when they must part had finally come. Thomas kissed Katherine lightly.

'I shall not say goodbye but *au revoir*,' he said. 'For I'll be back on the day you are free.'

'Do you swear it?'

'I do,' he answered solemnly and with that left her side without another word.

To the Lady Elizabeth, who had possessed her own household in Hatfield in Hertfordshire ever since she had been three months old, a new Queen meant two things. The first, and by far the most important, that she, Elizabeth, might be invited to spend more time at court, provided the lady liked her of course. And second, that it was a new woman to inspect curiously, the latest in a parade of wives since her mother had been executed when Elizabeth was only two and a half.

She could remember her, of course. Or rather not so much remember as have a vivid impression, particularly of her mother's scent. When she had been picked up in Anne Boleyn's arms and held high, Elizabeth had smelled the wonderful heady perfume which Anne had always worn at her neck. And, close to, she had seen the sheen on that heavy fall of dark hair, and the bright eyes, sparkling when they had looked at Elizabeth, so very vivacious and attractive.

Of the women who had followed her mother, and there had been three, Elizabeth liked the Lady Anne of Cleves best. She had been and still was such great fun, laughing uproariously, playing cards, fondling the little girl on her lap and giving her sweets: a wonderful stepmother for the brief time it had lasted. Cat Howard had been adorable, of course. But then she had done something awful, something which had been kept from Elizabeth because she was too young, which could be only vaguely guessed at. And now there was to be a new one. Her royal father, the hugest man in the world so people said, was to be a bridegroom once more.

'Who is she?' Elizabeth had asked her new governess, Katherine Champernowne.

'A widow I believe, my Lady. Katherine, Lady Latymer. I hear she is very well educated.'

Elizabeth brightened. She enjoyed learning because she was good at it and, much as she loved the Lady Anne, she really was rather stupid when it came to knowing things.

'And His Grace the King is betrothed to her?'

'I don't know, my Lady. But I do know that you are to go to Court with your sister to meet her.'

'When?'

'Next week,' had come the answer. 'And you are to have some new clothes.'

'Whee!' Elizabeth had shouted, jumping in the air, while her governess had smiled tolerantly. The little thing had not had much loving in her life and, if rumour were to be believed, Lady Latymer had plenty of experience with stepchildren.

Thank goodness, thought Mistress Champernowne, that the King has chosen a sober matron at last.

She was a little surprised, therefore, when in the middle of June she accompanied the two royal ladies to Hampton Court, to see not a plump middle-aged widow woman as she had imagined, but an attractive female no more than thirty.

'Well, well,' she said to herself. 'I hope she lasts!'

Her charge, of course, adored Katherine Latymer. All the more, probably, because she was young and pretty and not a fat frump as had been imagined. And poor Mary, the downtrodden daughter of Katharine of Aragon, came to life like a kicked animal suddenly given affection. She was twenty-seven, still without a husband despite years of negotiations, and tragically embittered.

'What do you think?' whispered Elizabeth to Mistress Champernowne as Lady Latymer conversed merrily with Mary Tudor.

'I think she is going to be a wonderful wife for His Grace and that she will make all of you children very happy.'

'Do you think Edward will come to Court?'

'More often I expect, though His Grace your father is naturally concerned for the Prince's health.'

'Yes,' answered Elizabeth, but she was no longer listening, remembering another occasion when she had come to Hampton Court to see her father and been removed unusually early the next morning. Sir Thomas Seymour had been her escort to the Palace on that occasion and for no particular reason he came into Elizabeth's mind quite vividly. She could almost see the long lean body, the dark golden hair, the captivating blue eyes.

'I wonder where Tom Seymour is these days,' she said aloud and was surprised to see Lady Latymer look up and glance in her direction.

'I wouldn't know that,' answered Katherine Champernowne. 'Now hush a little. I think you might be disturbing His Grace's intended bride.'

'Oh, I mustn't do that.' Elizabeth was instantly contrite. 'I want her to like me. She will, won't she?'

'Of course,' said her governess soothingly. 'As long as you behave yourself.'

'My mother didn't behave, did she?' Elizabeth felt that she was having a brain storm even before the words had left her lips.

'My Lady! You must never say things like that.' Mistress Champernowne's face and voice were furious. 'Thanks be given that His Grace is not here, for I would not be in your shoes if he *had* heard you. You would be wise not to mention your mother at Court, or anywhere else for that matter.'

Anne *sans tête*, said Elizabeth silently but to her governess she bobbed a polite curtsey and answered, 'No, Madam. I shall in future remember that my mother is dead and most certainly buried.'

On July 12th, 1543, the two people who should have been marrying one another, had they not been overruled by a higher power, started the day in exactly the same way. Thomas, in Calais, had heard from his man Jack, who had been back to England briefly to look to Thomas's house and also glean Court information, that this day Katherine, Lady Latymer, was to wed Henry Tudor.

'Oh,' he had said, continuing to comb his hair and trim his beard as his servant told him the news. 'I see. Wait there, Jack, while I finish dressing.'

Then he had gone into his bedroom, where he was lodged in the

Deputy's house, and wept bitterly. It was a terrible experience. Only once since childhood, when Jane had died, had Thomas cried, and now he felt desolated and ashamed.

A milksop not a man, he thought, and cried all the more, his ambition to marry the highest in the land forgotten in his inexplicable love for that serious little widow, Katherine.

From the dressing room Jack had called out, 'Can I get you anything, Sir Thomas.'

'Yes,' he answered in a muffled voice. 'Gascon wine, as strong as you can find.'

'Very good, Sir.'

And with that he heard Jack leave the room as Thomas, wiping his eyes, desperately tried to get himself into some sort of shape.

In her apartments at Hampton Court, Katherine wept too, also in the privacy of her bedroom, turning and turning Tom's little garnet ring on her finger, and saying under her breath, 'It should have been you, my love. It should have been you.'

As he dressed in Calais in preparation to receive his appointment as Marshall of Henry Tudor's army, so she dressed in England in order to become Henry Tudor's wife. As Tom put on a crimson doublet, all tricked out with gold, so his Kate was adorned by waiting women in bridal dress, heavy with jewels and gold brocade. As he walked the short distance to the Staple Hall for the simple ceremony, so she progressed along the corridors to the Queen's Closet where the marriage was to take place. Waiting to greet Sir Thomas was Sir John Wallop, under whom he would serve; waiting to greet Lady Latymer was the King of England, to whom she must promise her servitude. But there the similarity ended.

Thomas went into a business-like room, was given a piece of parchment which officially appointed him Marshall of the English army, then had his hand shaken by Sir John, and a brief congratulatory drink to follow with some fellow officers. Katherine entered a room full of people, glad that behind her stood three bridal attendants, the Ladies Mary and Elizabeth, and her sister Anne Herbert, as she saw the sea of faces.

Everyone of importance was there. She recognised the King's niece, Lady Margaret Douglas, Jane Lady Dudley, the Duchess of Suffolk, and on the male side many leading courtiers, only one of whom meant anything to Katherine. She stared and stared at Edward Seymour, Earl of Hertford, wondering if he had any inkling at all of the love that had passed between her and his brother. But Thomas had obviously been as discreet as he said: Edward's face did not flicker an ounce of recognition.

Overpowering all, of course, was the bridegroom himself. Dressed in a blue velvet doublet, so big that three men could have fitted into it, he loomed. Katherine thought that she had never seen anything so monstrous and wondered for a moment if she could bear to go on. But there was no escape. Feeling totally lost she stepped forward and the very next second her hand had been consumed within the King's.

Stephen Gardiner, Bishop of Winchester, who had promoted Catherine Howard and then deserted her, conducted the ceremony, asking both respondents in turn to give their vows. Henry seemed jubilant, smiling broadly and shouting 'Yea', when asked if he would take Katherine as his wedded wife. This seemed so joyful and amusing that nobody noticed how white the new Queen's cheeks turned as the wedding ring was slipped on.

Now I am at his mercy, ran her thoughts. One false move and I could end as did my predecessor.

She stared round the room blankly as all present made reverence to her. Could it be possible that she, born without title, plain Katherine Parr, was Queen of England? All she could think of in the welter of congratulation was that somewhere her greedy mother must be smiling like a cream-licking cat.

'Your Grace, I greet you,' said Henry, and almost lifted Katherine off her feet as he gave her a suffocating kiss. Only the fact that all the guests were looking stopped her from physically shuddering.

Oh Tom, she thought, if only it could have been you.

By the strangest coincidence, at that moment exactly Thomas dropped his wine cup on the floor of the Staple Hall in Calais and the contents spilled like blood.

'It's done,' he said quietly. 'I know it.'

The day wore on with much merriment. Princess Mary, happy for once, was laughing and drinking too much wine, while Elizabeth was pink and flushed.

'You must go to bed soon,' whispered her governess.

But the girl would have none of it, running to her father and whirling a curtsey before him. 'Oh please Your Grace, let me stay at the wedding feast a little longer. Mistress Champernowne says I must go to bed.'

The King turned to his new Queen, laughing indulgently. 'What say you, Kate? Shall the imp be allowed to stay on?'

'Oh yes,' said Katherine smiling faintly. 'Let the Lady Elizabeth enjoy herself.'

'Only when she has embraced you as stepmother,' answered Henry, all joviality.

For answer his daughter, having dropped a curtsey to Katherine equally as fine as that which she made to the King, climbed up level with the new Queen's chair and, putting her arms round her neck, kissed her affectionately on the cheek.

'Welcome, dear stepmother,' she said.

Katherine hugged her, almost painfully Elizabeth thought, and said, 'I will do my best, I promise you.'

Near her like that, Elizabeth could smell the new Queen's essence, so different from the musky and exciting perfume which Anne Boleyn had worn. Just for a minute the girl closed her eyes and tried to imagine it was her mother she held. But it was impossible. The two women were entirely different.

Elizabeth sighed very quietly, then said to her father, 'Well, may I stay?'

'Of course,' he answered, patting Katherine's hand. 'Never let it be said, my girl, that you did not dance at my wedding.'

So it was in this way that Elizabeth finally found herself caught up in a ritual called the bedding. By this time she had drunk far too much wine, as had everybody else, and seemed to float on a cloud. Yet the girl, not quite ten, found questions forming in her mind to which she did not, as yet, know the answers.

The principle oddity seemed, to Elizabeth's scholarly reasoning, the fact that all the ladies giggled as they decked her new stepmother, very pale-faced, in her nightclothes, when there was nothing funny about it. And why did all the gentlemen roar their approval, standing round her father, dressed in a nightrobe the size of a tent, when the new Queen was led it? And why did the Bishop bless the bed and ask for a fruitful union, which meant children?

In some way all of these things must be connected but Elizabeth, at this point, could not guess what the link might be.

'I think I will go to sleep now,' she yawned to Katherine

Champernowne as all the guests, including the Bishop, trooped from the King's bedchamber in a merry, laughing group.

'And about time too, my Lady,' said her governess, who had been waiting for her in the ante-chamber.

'But there are some things I want to ask you in the morning, Kat.'

'Yes, my Lady,' said Mistress Champernowne with a wry expression on her face. 'I had a feeling there might be.'

# Chapter Thirty

BEFORE HE WENT TO SLEEP on that particular night in the autumn of 1543, Dr Zachary Howard, silently and privately, said a last farewell to his dead daughter. Watching the swaying lantern cast ever-changing patterns of shadow as the ship's motion drew it this way and that, the astrologer had given long consideration to the real meaning of mourning the departed before he finally released Sapphira. For what right had the bereaved, he thought, to hold on to a spirit that longed to be free? And how could anyone, be they parent or partner, dwell on memory to the detriment of those left alive?

For this to him seemed the crux of the issue. Whether one believed that death ended everything, or looked on it as a new beginning, there were still the living to consider. In his own case, Zachary had two fine sons and a young wife, also bearing their burden of grief. If he became changed, morose and depressed, the quality of their lives would suffer even further than it had already. The time had now come for his daughter to take her place as a beloved member of the family who was no longer present, rather than the subject of much misery and wretchedness.

'Goodbye, my darling,' he whispered into the darkness, the lantern now put out. 'Go on your way.'

Was it his imagination that she came to him in a rushing that stirred his hair and fluttered against his cheek? Did he really hear a joyous laugh before the cabin became silent again? Did a voice full of echoes breathe, 'Farewell'? Afterwards Zachary was never certain but, whatever the case, the illusion comforted him and he fell asleep soundly, confident that when he returned to England he would lead his family back to the harmonious life they had enjoyed before Sapphira's untimely end.

He had been in Venice for some while, in consultation with the noble family of Grimani, for whom he had been casting predictions since Francesco Grimani had long ago discovered Zachary in Southampton, where the Venetian's trading ships, loaded with cloths and spices, gold and gilt, had ridden richly at anchor. But now, with his task completed and purse full, the astrologer was on his way home, his agonising for a dead child over, his heart full of hope. Yet just as he fell asleep, soothed by his sense of fulfilment and the ship's own particular lullaby, Zachary suffered a small pang of unease. A warning note sounded which he chose to ignore as he went into a deep and heavy sleep.

The first thing to wake him some hours later was the change in the voice of the wind, which had risen from the song of a siren to a booming shout. Zachary reluctantly opened an eye, felt the pitch and toss of the vessel, and immediately rose to dress. He was too experienced a sailor to stay in his cabin, knowing that the best way to avoid sickness was to become one with the motion of the ship, riding the waves with the vessel. But once on deck he realised that sea-sickness was not his primary consideration, the situation having deteriorated rapidly and the Captain fighting to keep his vessel on course.

They had left Venice yesterday morning in a fair wind and had made good progress through the Adriatic so that now they were turning round the foot of Italy towards Sicily. But in the openness of that sea a wild tempest was blowing, sending the boat away from the coastline and out into the Mediterranean. In the darkness, with no stars to chart their passage, it was still obvious that they were plunging off course.

With great care Zachary made his way to where the Captain stood at the helm, grimly wrestling as the ship climbed the waves and then smacked into the troughs beneath.

Without turning, the seaman said tersely, 'You'd best get below, Doctor. This is no night for passengers to be out of their cabins.'

'I prefer it up here,' Zachary answered firmly. 'I favour the sight of the sea to that of four walls.'

'Suit yourself. But don't go near the rail or you'll see the ocean more closely than you'd wish.'

'I'll be careful, I promise.'

And so he remained, braced on the heaving deck, until finally the ferocity of the wind abated a little and the Captain was able to leave his place at the wheel and ask his passenger to join him for a nip of the harsh, dark drink which he always kept in his cabin.

They sat facing one another, watching everything sliding about the place, and grabbing at the bottle as it careered from one side of the table to the other.

'Is the worst over?' Zachary asked eventually.

Two eyes, set in a riverbed of wrinkles, looked at him appraisingly.

'The wind will blow out if that is what you mean.'

'Yes, that is what I meant. But why do you question? Is there some other danger?'

'We're being driven towards the Mediterranean.'

Zachary looked at the Captain blankly. 'What do you mean?'

'I fear we are being blown too near the Greek coastline, Sir. Towards the ports of the Ottoman Empire.'

He need say no more; Zachary was now only too aware of what the man was telling him. The mighty Ottoman Empire, ruled from Constantinople by the Sultan Suleiman, known as the Magnificent, stretched over vast territories from Egypt and Persia in the south to Hungary in the north. With total control of the Mediterranean Sea, Suleiman's ships, under the leadership of the Sultan's most famous captain, Khaireddin Barbarossa, harried the coasts of Spain and Italy. The Mediterranean was not safe for anyone when Suleiman's ships were prowling and to be driven off course in that direction was a serious matter.

'As soon as there's a glimmer of light and a drop in the wind, I'll make for the Straits of Messina.'

The narrow strait between the toe of Italy and Sicily's rugged coast had grown increasingly popular with sea captains attempting to avoid Mediterranean waters.

'Yes,' answered Zachary distractedly, having a sudden vision of a fleet of ships with a great piratical figure at its head. 'Yes, I think you should.'

The Captain stared at him enquiringly, believing in his passenger's powers and having personally encountered many strange and inexplicable things at sea.

'Do you have a premonition of disaster, Doctor?'

'I have the feeling we should run for it.'

'If we get that chance.'

'Does Barbarossa plunder, then kill?'

382

'On the contrary,' answered the Captain, and smiled a cynical smile that deepened the lines about his eyes to valleys. 'One can't help but admire the man. He plunders, commandeers the ship for further use, then takes the men as slaves. He wastes nothing, I assure you.'

'Slaves?' questioned Zachary, with certain dreads already upon him.

'Yes. Either to be used at sea or as part of the Sultan's work force. There are Englishmen alive and working in Constantinople even as we speak.'

'Can't they escape?'

'Those who have tried have lost their heads. Suleiman hates what he terms insubordination.'

'Then pray God Barbarossa's fleet is elsewhere.'

'The prayer of every merchant who must trade with Venice or Milan or any other part of Italy.'

'But don't his ships harry Spain as well?'

'Of course. The Sultan has created the great pirate Governor of North Africa. Everything has been made easy for Barbarossa.'

Zachary's blood was already running cold with the certainty of what lay ahead. 'Captain, I fear the worst.'

'So do I. But there's only an hour till dawn.' He stood up. 'I've spent enough time on chat, Sir. I'm going back on deck.'

'I too.'

In the open it could be seen that the ship now carried no canvas and was riding the waves like a child's toy. But what greater menace lurked safely in harbour, ready to put to sea as soon as the tempest abated to pick up the spoils the wind had brought?

Zachary's mind raced quickly ahead. If capture lay in store then he must ensure that he did not end up a galley slave or worse. An impression must be made on his captors so that he could insist on being brought before the Sultan himself and there plead his case.

Rapidly returning to his cabin, the astrologer took from his chest all his magical artifacts, wrapping them in a cloth which he placed in the deep pocket within his cloak. Beneath them he thrust the purse given by the Grimanis then, last of all, hid a jewelled dagger, lethally sharp. Finally, having changed his shoes for boots, Dr Zachary went back on deck to see what the dawn would bring.

Though the violent weather had blown the ship off course it had also kept others in harbour, for as first light came there were no

383

sails visible. Yet even as the Captain ordered that canvas be hoisted and the vessel make the most of the wind, which had now dropped to moderate, the lookout called, 'Ships on the starboard bow,' and they all craned to see.

'Is it the Ottoman fleet?' asked Zachary, knowing the answer already.

The Captain screwed up his weather-beaten eyes. 'It looks mighty like it, Doctor.'

'Can we outrun them?'

'I think it very unlikely. They have powerful galleys, we rely on our sails.'

'Then capture seems certain?'

'You should know, Dr Zachary,' answered the Captain with a wry smile. And then, in spite of everything, the two men laughed spontaneously as the fleet of Suleiman the Magnificent, under the command of Khaireddin Barbarossa, started towards them like a pack to the kill.

# Chapter Thirty-One

THE RENEWAL OF THE WARS with both Scotland and France in the years that followed Thomas Seymour's departure from England, though suiting the purpose of many, brought anguish to others. Queen Katherine Parr, knowing that Tom was in the thick of the fighting, having been appointed First Master of the Ordnance and later Vice-Admiral, would daily pray for his safe return and hope that he still loved her, for their farewell meeting had been just that: Katherine had not set eyes on him since. Though he had been back to England, Thomas had remained with his ships, keeping well away from Court. Was he being discreet or had he simply lost interest?

The Queen had often longed to ask Edward Seymour how his brother fared and the temptation had been almost overwhelming. In 1544 when Henry Tudor himself had sailed for France, he had appointed Katherine as his Regent, with Edward, Lord Hertford, as one of her three counsellors. They had been thrown into almost daily contact until, mercifully, Hertford had been once more recalled to the front, and Katherine had been out of danger of indiscretion.

The Duke of Norfolk and his son, the Earl of Surrey, had definitely looked on the wars as a means of gaining face after the Catherine Howard debacle, and at first the Earl had won victories and gained splendid praise. Yet an ill-judged battle and an ignominious defeat brought a change of attitude on the King's part and his command at Boulogne was removed from him, Surrey's place being taken by the man he hated more than any other, Edward Seymour. Thus the Earl and his father, who had earlier received a similar rebuke over Boulogne, came out of the affray without honour.

The raids in Scotland and the resulting bitter reprisals came to their terrible end in the autumn of 1545 but the war with France dragged on until June 1546. Queen Katherine, at her daily prayers, begged that this would be the finish of it; that her life could resume in tranquillity; that her fears for the safety of Thomas Seymour could now be allayed for good. And though this part of her prayer was answered, her pleas for tranquillity were not heard. Something so terrible that she had not even considered its possibility was about to befall her.

Since her marriage three years earlier, Katherine had lived a blameless life. By God's great mercy Henry Tudor's enormous girth and premature ageing had put paid to any sexual relationship between them and the Queen had thankfully slipped into the role she knew so well. But her enforced celibacy had not made her foolish. She had looked at the floor when handsome courtiers were around and pointedly spent her time with reformers of the new religion, earnestly discussing theology for hours on end. Her care of the King had been exceptional and she had personally overseen his enormous consumption of medicaments and to the application of both plasters for the spleen and olive oil ointment suppositories, to say nothing of fomentation sponges for dressing his leg. In 1544, just before Henry had left for France, Katherine had moved her bed to a small chamber near his when he was seriously ill. She had been a model of kind and good behaviour, even to the point of allowing Eustace Chapuys, the venerable Spanish Ambassador, finally retiring from diplomacy overseas, to take private leave of the Princess Mary. Yet still an enemy worked against her.

In the early summer of 1546 the Privy Council had launched itself into a heresy hunt. Several people had been summoned for examination, including Anne Askewe, daughter of a Lincolnshire knight whose husband had ordered her from the house when she had been converted to the Protestant faith. Under interrogation the wretched girl had admitted to receiving money from Anne Seymour and Lady Denny, a matter that was noted by the Council though no action was taken against the two ladies. It had then occurred to Thomas Wriothesley, already planning his position when the King died and the child Edward came to the throne, that the Queen might also be involved. And what better move than to discredit the Prince's stepmother, already proving a strong influence on the boy? Lord Chancellor Wriothesley promptly ordered Anne Askewe's removal to the Tower.

But the condemned girl would say nothing further, even when racked. Bored with her lack of cooperation, Wriothesley and his friend Sir Richard Rich worked the rack themselves, until all Anne's joints were distorted and the Lieutenant of the Tower, in a panic, hurried to the King to absolve himself of responsibility for the girl's torture. Though she was later burned at Smithfield for heresy, not naming the Queen, the Lord Chancellor was still not content.

A sick old man, bored and irritable, was ideal material for Wriothesley's serpent tongue and in no time he had Henry peevishly angry at his wife's strong opinions and progressive theological views. Books in Katherine's apartments were secretly searched and the scene was finally set for Henry to sign bills of attainder against Katherine and her ladies so that they could be brought to trial.

Thinking about it now, two months later, Katherine suffered wave after wave of violent hatred. That monstrous invalid, who had taken away her one true love, had cruelly turned against her, whereas she had given nothing but devoted service to him and his children.

'You evil man,' she whispered to herself. 'You deserve what you get.'

If Fate had not been on her side Katherine might now be facing death. But there had been an extraordinary twist of events. Wriothesley had accidentally dropped the papers concerning her and the servant who found them had taken them direct to the Queen. Reading with horror that a bill for her attainder was prepared, Katherine launched into such violent hysterics and storms of weeping that the noise was audible throughout the Palace of Whitehall. Henry, much alarmed, had sent Dr Wendy to find out the cause of the commotion and by a clever move Katherine had out-manoeuvred Wriothesley in one stroke.

The following morning, clean-faced and looking penitent, she had gone to Henry and begged his forgiveness for holding any views of her own on any subject at all. The words had stuck like suet in her mouth but Katherine was desperate to stay alive, to marry Thomas when the obese mountain of flesh heaped in a high chair, its leg stuck out on a stool, finally had the good grace to die.

Then had come her touch of genius. 'Your poor leg, Sire,' she had said, fluttering over his dressing, 'why I swear it needs fomentation.'

'You have become a doctor, Kate,' Henry had answered, 'to

387

instruct us as we take it, and not to be instructed or directed by us.'

Busily unwrapping his dressings, she had answered, 'Indeed that is not true, Your Grace. But you see I only argue with you to distract you from your great pain and to learn the true doctrine from *your* lips. For it is my honest wish to obey and serve you and devote my life to nursing you back to health.'

Henry's eyes, which nowadays remained permanently only half open, had looked at her moistly. 'Is this true, sweetheart? Are those the only reasons why you argue with me? To comfort and to learn?'

'Yes, Your Grace,' Katherine had answered meekly.

'Then perfect friends we are now again as ever at any time before.'

With her face buried in bandages, Katherine had allowed herself the luxury of a secret smile.

That afternoon Wriothesley and a detachment of guards had come to arrest the Queen and her ladies from the Palace. The Lord Chancellor found her in the gardens and was just about to clap his hand on her shoulder when the King himself had reared up from behind a hedge.

'You arrant knave, you beast, you fool,' Henry had hissed, 'dare not to lay your hands upon the Queen. Begone before I have you put under arrest.'

'What a moment!' thought Katherine now. And she thanked God for sparing her with a miracle.

It was nearly the end of summer and an important few days at Court lay ahead. Admiral d'Annebault, the French King's emissary, had come to London to ratify the peace treaty and Henry was preparing to meet him with much pomp and splendour. The royal children were to be present, even Prince Edward, now nearly nine years old, whom Katherine had persuaded Henry to include more in Court affairs.

But none of this truly concerned her and not even the terrible recollection of her danger two months ago could dampen the Queen's spirits. For Thomas Seymour was to be present at the Admiral's reception. Today the lovers were to see one another again after more than three years apart.

Though she would have dressed finely in any case, Katherine now put on her new gown with pride, knowing that it suited her, that she glowed in red. Amongst all her many expensive jewels, Tom's little garnet ring twinkled humbly on her finger. But nothing sparkled as she did herself, made even more attractive by excitement and pleasure and, above all, the anticipation of seeing him.

The Queen made her stately entrance into Whitehall's great reception room only after the courtiers were assembled, and as she slowly progressed amidst a blare of trumpets, Henry hobbling beside her and the royal children including Prince Edward at her back, Katherine kept her head aloft and her eyes steadily in front. But once seated on the high chair she allowed herself to look about. She saw Tom at once, still bowing, his red hair glistening in the brilliant light. All the love came back, sweeping her from head to foot, reminding her of the magic she and he had found together. Just for a second their eyes met and all her earlier fears were banished. In one sweeping glance he told her that he still loved her, but after that did not look in her direction again.

The Admiral's entrance, flanked by his supporters, and the florid and formal speeches that followed his arrival, passed over the Queen's head. She sat in a blur of happiness, hoping that she was not grinning foolishly, and longing for the evening when a great masque, which would allow her to move about the Court freely, had been arranged to impress the Frenchman with the English Court's magnificence.

Finally nightfall came and the Queen and her stepdaughters, all three in evening gowns and fantastically masked, stepped out as the music began. They knew their role: to surround the French admiral and lead him out to dance, with much laughing and teasing. To disguise who they were, the royal trio were to be joined by nine other ladies, similarly masked, so that the Admiral would be more than confused. Elizabeth, now in her teens, thought this great sport but Mary, suffering as always from indifferent health, considered it embarrassing and wished that she had not agreed to take part.

From behind her mask Katherine watched Thomas, laughing and talking and looking everywhere but in her direction. Had she been mistaken? Had that long stare meant something else? She must find out, whatever the result. To go through further months of torture, uncertain and frantic, was more than she could endure at this stage of her life.

The twelve dancing ladies had surrounded the Admiral and he was being led out, with much Gallic bowing and hand kissing, to open the masque. When he had picked one of them to partner, the others would be free to choose a partner of their own. Katherine prayed that d'Annebault would not seek her out, thus leaving her at liberty to go to Thomas, but this was not to be. The Frenchman had obviously recognised the Queen despite her disguise and was bowing elaborately before her, so that it was Elizabeth who went sailing past, red hair glinting through her headdress, to raise Tom to his feet.

Thank God she is still a child, thought Katherine fervently, unaware that in her formal green dress, her youthful breasts flattened by her pearl-sewn bodice, her adolescent body made more shapely by her farthingale, Elizabeth's sexuality shimmered like a flame.

'You've grown up, my Lady,' said Thomas, accepting her with a slightly mocking bow.

'How do you know who I am?' asked a voice from behind the mask.

'By your little ways,' he answered, laughing.

'Do you make fun of me, Sir Thomas?'

'Would I do that, my Lady?'

'Indeed you would, Sir.'

The music was speeding up and suddenly she had fallen into his arms, reminding Thomas vividly of the time he had ridden behind her and felt the same strange thrill as he did now. So his perversion had not gone away, he was still attracted to little girls. But then Thomas realised that he was being hard on himself. It was only this one particular little girl and he had never, in all conscience, laid a finger on her. If it was indeed a perversion then it was a very mild one. But still she did attract him and he danced extra close to her, feeling the beat of her heart in the region of his ribs as the music grew to an exciting climax.

'Well done, my Lady,' he said as the breathless dancers laughed and clapped.

'I enjoyed it. May I dance with you later?'

It was said ingenuously and Thomas grinned joyfully. 'I would be honoured, Madam.' He bowed to Elizabeth as she walked slowly away.

He stood undecidedly, longing to ask his real love to dance and wondering if it would cause any comment if he did so. The Court was riddled with spies and his vow that he would do nothing to endanger either of them still held good. But yet the temptation was great and this was, after all, a masque. With sudden determination Sir Thomas strode to where the Queen chatted with the French Admiral, and made a bow.

'Admiral d'Annebault, if I steal your charming partner might it mean that the peace treaty between our two countries would go unratified?'

The Admiral made an elegant salute. 'It is up to the Lady, whoever fair creature she may be, hiding her beauty behind her mask.'

So that was to be the game. 'Her identity is not known to me either,' answered Thomas smoothly. 'But such loveliness is too tempting. Madam, will you have me?'

'Yes, Sir,' said Katherine's low voice steadily and with that she put her hand in his.

It was enough! Their locked fingers became channels for communication, for thoughts of desire, for love; their very touching triggered off a whole new set of deepest feelings.

'Don't speak,' said Thomas, so quietly that she could barely hear him. 'There are ears everywhere.'

But Katherine could not help herself. As the dance brought them close together for the last time she whispered, 'I love you,' and was rewarded with a, 'Forever,' before they finally drew apart.

But there was one thing left to say. Thomas flicked his gaze to where the King sat at the high table, a massive padded figure inert as a doll, only the movement of his boiled-egg eyes showing that he lived. Then he mouthed, 'Not long now,' and flicked his gaze once more. The nod that showed she understood was barely perceptible as Katherine curtsied and left Thomas Seymour's side for the rest of that evening.

Before Admiral d'Annebault finished the round of celebrations organised by Henry Tudor to mark the end of war between England and France, he had two private commissions. The first was very much his own; to visit a child he had fathered on a previous visit to London, long ago when Anne Boleyn had still been Queen, and take presents for her and her mother, a young widow of rank, subsequently remarried. The second was on behalf of his own King; to seek out the astrologer Zachary, who lived not far from Greenwich Palace, and obtain a year's astrological prediction, his supply of which had been badly curtailed by the war.

Because his time was very much at the disposal of the English, the Admiral found himself unable to undertake both errands and as only he could carry out the first he sent his young *aide-de-camp* Comte Lucien Harfleur to obtain the King's horoscope. Harfleur, having been informed that the astrologer's house was more easily reached by water, duly set out in one of the two state barges put at the Admiral's disposal for the duration of his stay.

The young man, on his first visit to England, enjoyed this journey downriver, watching the other craft skimming past and the fish leaping out of the water beneath the big white daisy clouds of England in late summer. Lazily he sprawled back amongst the barge's comfortable cushions, fascinated by the river-light which dappled his skin and the point of his beard, and burnished his bright, uncomfortable clothes. He was suddenly good humoured, not caring that he was to see some foolish old man in a rundown hovel, determined to make the best of everything. He was pleasantly surprised therefore, when the barge pulled up to a well-kept landing stage and a man, working in the extensive gardens, came through the orchard to take the mooring rope.

Lucien clambered ashore. 'I have come to see Dr Zachary, my good fellow,' he said in careful English. 'Would you take me to him.'

A strange expression crossed the servant's face. 'Dr Zachary is not here, Sir.'

A little of Lucien's good humour vanished. 'How long will he be gone?'

'That I could not say, Sir. If you would be so good as to step up to the house I will get someone to see you.'

Rather irritated, the Comte followed the gardener up to the spacious dwelling place, well-timbered and very expensive, or so thought Lucien, to be owned by a soothsayer.

The gardener ushered him into a reasonably sized hall and the Comte took a seat, gazing about at the tapestries and furnishings and surmising shrewdly that this particular astrologer must be very well connected. He was still looking at everything when a slight noise made him realise that somebody else had come in, and he glanced up to see what he took at first to be a child, in the doorway. But as the dark beauty approached he saw that she was older than he thought, in her late twenties, the impression of youth being created by her small stature.

392

'Sir,' she said, holding out her hand, 'I do not know who you are but I believe that you have come to see my husband.'

Lucien gasped. 'Your husband, Madam? No, I do not think so. I seek Dr Zachary.'

'I am Mistress Howard, his wife.' The little thing laughed suddenly, and Lucien got a flash of clover-coloured eyes, very big and bright. 'I hear from your voice that you are French, Sir,' she went on. 'Pray, whom do you represent?'

'I am Comte Lucien Harfleur, here on behalf of the King of France himself,' answered Lucien importantly, and was very slightly annoyed when Cloverella wrinkled her nose in a smile.

'Oh yes, of course. They were old friends. I would imagine that his French Majesty has missed his annual horoscope.'

'Yes,' said Lucien huffily, 'that is correct. But if Dr Zachary is not here . . .'

'I will cast it for you,' Cloverella put in, adding hastily as she saw the Comte's face change, 'I am quite qualified to do so. I was trained by my husband and have part Romany blood. So follow me. He always worked in his narrow room nearest the stars. Now I do so too.'

Sensing a mystery, Lucien went with her silently, climbing to the top of the house and then up the narrow stairs that led to the attic. Here he saw symbols and charts, dark corners and a glaring one-eyed cat. He caught a little of the fear and suspense of others who had come this way and very quietly drew in his breath.

Cloverella sat on the other side of the desk and poured him a generous pitcher of wine before she drew forth a pack of tattered cards.

'I have had these since I was a girl,' she said, 'and was taught their use before I was five. One of my grandmothers was a gypsy woman, the other the daughter of a peer. Blood, blood, it flows just the same as wine, does it not?'

She offered him the cards to shuffle but Lucien put both his hands over both of hers, noticing how firm to the touch her skin was.

'Madame, much as I trust you – and believe me I do' – he kissed her fingers, one by one – 'I am here on behalf of His Grace François, King of France. With the greatest respect I am duty bound to tell him why it is the soothsayer's wife who will draw his

393

horoscope and not the man himself.' Lucien looked down at the cards. 'And also why she is offering to read my future.'

Cloverella smiled. 'I thought you might be interested in that, Sir. But as to why my husband is not here, even I do not know.'

Lucien frowned. 'What do you mean?'

The small face looking into his lost colour. 'Monsieur le Comte, my husband vanished three years ago.'

'*Vanished*?' repeated Lucien in horror.

Cloverella smiled wanly. 'Oh, not through any mystical happenings. He was not whisked away by fairies.' She bit her lip. 'At least I do not think so. The fact is that he went to visit a great family in Venice and never returned. Neither he nor the ship upon which he sailed were ever seen again. I can only presume he is lying upon the floor of the ocean somewhere.'

With an acuity that surprised him, Lucien asked, 'Do you believe that? As a Romany do you sense he is dead?'

For the very first time Cloverella looked at him with real interest. 'That is just the point. I don't. Somewhere I am sure that he is still alive. The air does not carry the vibrations of his death, do you understand?'

'Yes,' said Lucien, though he didn't, not a word.

'So I have continued to keep his house running as if he will some day return to it. Monsieur, I had little money of my own, being something of a poor relation, but through using my magic arts – just as once he did – I have built a considerable reputation and patrons that were previously his now come to me. Though I have only very few servants I have kept his two sons here and have paid for them to be well educated by a tutor . . .' She said this with considerable pride Lucien noted. '. . . so that one day they will be able to go forth and get a position with one or other of my cousins. I have turned Fate round to my advantage, Monsieur, but meanwhile my quest to find my husband is no further forward.'

Lucien, who had instantly formed a passion for this young and vulnerable witch, said earnestly, 'If you will be kind enough to tell me all the details of Dr Zachary's disappearance, Madame, I will ask my royal master if any of his many spies can get information. The recent war has thrown things into turmoil but now that we are once more at peace . . .'

Cloverella leaned forward over the desk. 'Monsieur le Comte, would you really do that for me? I would be so obliged to you. Yours is the first positive offer of help that I have received.'

Lucien, both protective and passionate in one engulfing moment, said huskily, 'Be assured, Madame, that my life is at your disposal.'

Her face lit up cheekily. 'I will try not to ask for it, Monsieur. But now shuffle these cards then cut them into three with your left hand, the hand that connects with the heart.'

Unbelievably flushed, Lucien said, 'Which flutters at this moment like a trapped bird.' He kissed her fingers. 'And which, Madame, I lay unquestioningly at your feet.'

# Chapter Thirty-Two

EDWARD SEYMOUR, LORD HERTFORD, had come back from victories in both the wars as a hero; even his wife's indiscreet behaviour which had implicated her with Anne Askewe was forgotten. But by stark contrast the Duke of Norfolk and the Earl of Surrey were in sulky disgrace and on returning to England took themselves off to Kenninghall immediately, to lick their wounds and mull over the future. Henry Howard, or so it seemed to the Duke, had now gone a little mad. A brilliant boy in many ways and a considerable poet of the school of Sir Thomas Wyatt, his grip on reality had started to diminish when Sir Thomas died. A series of disastrous and unrequited love affairs had not helped; one with his Fair Geraldine, the child Elizabeth Fitzgerald, who had married the elderly Sir Anthony Browne when she was fifteen and gone off to live in Battle Abbey; the other an enormous passion for Edward Seymour's wife, Anne, a passion of which the Duke had been highly suspicious. Had the whole thing been done to annoy Edward, or had Surrey really taken leave of his senses and fallen in love with this heavily married and haughty lady?

Then there had been the incidents of bad behaviour in London when a gang of young courtiers, led by Henry Howard and Thomas Wyatt, the poet's son, had smashed the windows of churches and respectable aldermen's houses. One night they had rowed on the Thames and shot pellets at the 'queans' – their word for whores – on the towpath. The gang had frequented Mistress Arundel's cookhouse in St Lawrence Lane and eaten meat during Lent and Surrey, in his cups, had boasted that his father would stand for King should anything happen to Henry. Fortunately for Henry Howard the King was fond of him, calling him, 'the most foolish proud boy in England', and the Earl had only served a short sentence in the Fleet prison for his crimes. But these youthful indiscretions boded no good. Surrey had become outspoken and volatile to the point of idiocy, and consequently enemies lurked everywhere.

Once more the Duke of Norfolk, desperately anxious about the disappearance of his bastard son and the disintegration of his legitimate, tried to make peace with the Seymours by offering Mary Howard's hand in marriage to Thomas. But again Surrey had intervened, blaming the Seymours for all his misfortunes and savagely screaming at his sister that she should make haste to marry Thomas and then become to Henry Tudor what the Duchesse d'Etampes was to the King of France. The whole affair had been most distressing as Mary had run from the room in floods of tears. As 1546 drew towards its end the Duke of Norfolk mournfully thought that his fortunes had never been so low.

By the generosity of the King both Seymour brothers now had fine houses in London within the vicinity of Temple Bar. Thomas, granted his home in 1545 but never there for his own very personal reasons, had characteristically renamed Hampton Place Seymour Place, but Edward was more discreet, continuing to call his establishment Chester Place.

Since the Earl of Hertford's return from the wars it had become the habit of the Privy Council to meet in his house and on this particular night, with the Council still in lengthy session, the main topic under discussion was the weighty matter of the arrest of the Duke of Norfolk. Edward, despite every accusation levelled against him by Norfolk's son, still had no hatred of the clan, seeing them as a spent force. But there were others who did not agree and it was the repellent Wriothesley who put their thoughts into words.

'That old serpent will not be stayed until his fangs are finally drawn.'

'But he *is* old,' Edward argued reasonably. 'In his seventies. He can't do much harm now.'

'Father and son both should be put down,' said someone lower down the table. And as there were sounds of assent Wriothesley added, 'With Surrey under arrest in my house it is our duty to summon Norfolk for questioning about him.'

Earlier in the month Sir Richard Southwell, a Norfolk Member of Parliament, had given evidence against Surrey on matters touching the Earl's loyalty to his sovereign. Typically, Surrey had exploded with wrath, vowing to fight Southwell in his shirt. Now both men were detained for further examination in Lord Chancellor Wriothesley's home.

'I say we issue a warrant for Norfolk's arrest,' said Richard Rich.

'He is Earl Marshall of England, remember,' Edward answered mildly.

'Then he should have brought his son up better,' retorted Wriothesley, barely concealing his claws. 'Let the old man be brought to London.'

'Aye.' The voices were rumbling all round the room.

'Lord Hertford?'

Edward sat silent, his dark features unreadable, his eyes shuttered, remembering something from four years earlier: a memory of the Earl of Surrey in the throes of passion for Anne, writing poems to various parts of her anatomy which he could not possibly have seen; pursuing her wherever she went, leaving flowers and letters wherever she would sit and walk; begging her for a kiss or even a glance and planting a suspicion in Edward's mind that had never quite gone away. He was certain Anne had not gone to bed with Henry Howard, yet how had he known about that mole . . .

'Lord Hertford?' The voice was insistent now.

'Yes?'

It had been a question but the other Council members took it as a sign of assent.

'Then a warrant shall be issued forthwith for the arrest of the Duke of Norfolk,' said Wriothesley with satisfaction.

'So be it,' answered Edward, and finally raised his hand to be counted.

In its sleeping state the figure lying carelessly on a low sofa which stood, cushion covered, on a raised marble platform in a window embrasure, seemed transformed back to its youth. With one hand thrown above his head, the fingers entwined in his own dark curls, the man looked heartrendingly vulnerable, almost innocent. Sleep had smoothed out the lines of the face so that it seemed that of a very young person, on the edge of experience, not worldly. And the body was lean, taut, far from middle years.

The room in which the sleeper lay was high, vaulted, blue mosaics dominating the walls, the stones made of two different shades, one the fierce bright blue of midday sea, the other sharp as wild jacinths. The windows, set loftily and barred without, were also dominated by blue glass but this of a more complex colour. A depth was in this blue that seemed unfathomable, not midnight, not indigo nor turquoise, but something of all three. If any creature had borne an eye this shade, it could only have been an angel.

In the middle of the floor, which was made from cool marble slabs but covered with sumptuous carpets, thrown hither and thither as if they were the merest trifles, a fountain trickled softly and continuously. Made from wrought iron, a twist of leaves supporting a bowl decorated with lions' heads, it was small, being only thigh high, yet its seductive sound dominated the room. Lamps matching its simple design hung from the ceiling, which was decorated with a pattern of dark green flowers painted on a background of Reseda. Soft light was everywhere, blue as a mosque, grey as mist.

The sleeper had experienced earlier the strange sensation of leaving his body, of rising above his prostrate form and travelling through time. In his dream, hallucination, whatever it was, he relived a scene from long ago, looking up into his father's broad face, seeing it sharp with anxiety.

'Will I outlive His Grace?' came his father's distant voice.

'By a cat's whisker you will.'

The scene faded and now the dreamer stood in a churchyard looking at two graves packed closely side-by-side. On one grave had been planted a sweet briar eglantine and on the other a rambling rose. The rambler had grown into the eglantine which held it in its branches like a lover.

The dreamer turned away and walked uphill to where a lofty castle dominated the scene, passing through the external fortifications without difficulty and then entering the great hall unseen. Climbing the stairs he went directly to the room he knew so well, the room to which he had been taken as a boy, the room where his father and he had exchanged confidences.

A hunched old man sat in the room, his head plunged into his hands wretchedly. It was hateful to the sleeper to see the game old fellow weep and yet he could do nothing to stop it. Miserably he stood beside his father and saw the tears trickle down the grizzled cheeks and out through the woven fingers.

'So many years of service,' said the old man, shaking his head from side to side in a terrible bewilderment. 'So many years, to be rewarded like this.'

In great distress the dreamer leaned forward and put his hand, light as moth wings, on his father's shoulder. He did not feel it, he did not even look up.

'Father,' called the sleeper, 'Lord Duke my father. I am here.'

But there was no response and, greatly disturbed, the dreamer retreated down the stairs to where a troop of guards led by a member of the Privy Council whose name he did not know, awaited the Duke.

Arrest, thought the dreamer in a panic, they've come to arrest my father.

Then the mighty cord which attached him to his sleeping body gave a sudden tug and in dread that he might die if he did not return soon, the dreamer re-entered his mortal shell to wake panting and gasping in the indescribable light of the blue mosaic room.

Salina, his principal female slave, stood staring at Zachary anxiously. 'Master, you shouted for your father so wildly that I thought I had better wake you. You had lost all colour. Forgive me.'

She said no more, touching her forehead to his naked foot in the ultimate gesture of servitude. Zachary sat up slowly, looking about him in a dazed manner. Normally he had a smile for the girl but this day could fine none.

'I'm all right,' he whispered hoarsely, 'but get me something to drink. I feel as if I've journeyed very far.'

She nodded and withdrew, leaving him to lie back on the pillows and slowly take stock, both of his present situation and the future.

Just over three years ago Zachary Howard had been captured by the Turks and would have ended a galley slave had it not been for a very simple conjuring trick which had made the captain of the Turkish vessel laugh so much that Zachary had found himself hustled before Barbarossa in order to repeat it. His silly hobby of sleight-of-hand, done to impress the ladies of the Court, had at last borne fruit. He had apparently produced a Tarot card from out of his ear and, when asked to repeat it, done the same from his mouth. The card Zachary had chosen for this childish trick had been that of Death, portrayed as the Grim Reaper, so that when the laughter had died away a question mark had been left.

Barbarossa, who understood more English than he admitted, had consequently hissed instructions for Zachary to read his future and had not for a second taken his gaze from his captive's face, intimidating him with every glance, knowing that he, the great pirate captain with his flowing beard and black eyes, held the power of life and death between his fingers.

Zachary had never forgotten that moment, could recall it even now, the faint smell of spice which seemed to pervade both the vessel and its owner, the black hypnotic eyes fixed upon him, the sound of the ship creaking as it rode on lively anchor.

Instead of the Tarot he had produced the dark crystal which he had taken with him to Venice, the place of its origin. Even Barbarossa had given the smallest start on seeing the blackness of the orb, twinkling like quartz where Zachary laid it reverentially upon the Captain's table.

As Barbarossa had put his wiry hands upon it, so invited by Zachary, the crystal had dramatically given the blood-flush, and Zachary could have kissed it. Now it would definitely be shown to Suleiman as a marvel. Forestalling any idea that the pirate might have of purloining the orb, the astrologer had said, 'There is a curse on it. Only I must handle the crystal,' and he had uttered a low-voiced incantation.

The bluff had worked and to add to his air of mystery, Zachary's predictions for Barbarossa had struck a chord, particularly with regard to his love affairs of which, the astrologer was amazed to see, the pirate had many.

It had not been a far cry from there to Constantinople and the fabled Topkapi Palace, set like a citadel on a promontary overlooking a sea the colour of anemonies. Zachary had been marched in a prisoner through Demir Gate and thence through the Gate of the White Eunuchs to the throne room. He had come out again as a treasured guest of Suleiman the Magnificent.

In such a dazzle of jewels, of peacock fans, of sapphire glass and heavenly rubies, it had been an instinctive thing for Zachary to prostrate himself at the feet of such a being as the Sultan, to bend his rough head before the turned-up toe of the silver shoes and ask for clemency. There had been a gentle laugh at that, and a hand had come down and stroked his hair as if he had been a dog. Then the astrologer had been bidden rise and sit on a stool at Suleiman's feet and converse as one cultivated man to another. A lasting friendship, a relationship like that of father and son, had been bonded from that moment.

Now, with that day receding into memory, Zachary smiled grimly. The Sultan's friendship had extended only so far. Soon realising his prisoner's enormous potential as an astrologer and fortune teller, Suleiman, on the death of his principal wise man, had put Zachary in his place. The Englishman had been given his own suite in the Palace, his own slaves – including the beautiful Salina – and everything he could wish for, except freedom. Threats and pleading met with equal lack of success. The Sultan Suleiman always turned a deaf ear to that which he did not wish to hear.

Even now, sensing the terrible danger in which the Duke of Norfolk had been placed, Zachary knew that to go to his royal master would be a forlorn hope. Suleiman's love was selfish. As far as he was concerned, the astrologer was as close to him as if he were his own son, and the rest of the world simply did not matter.

Salina returned, bearing some golden fluid in a glass vessel. 'This will soothe you, Master. Drink a draught and be strong again,' she said, placing it on a low table beside him.

Zachary brushed it aside. 'Salina, my father in England is in danger. I know it. Yet I am unable to help him.'

She stared at Zachary in silence, her pointed brows drawn down as she puzzled. Eventually she said, 'Could you not think so hard that your wife will understand and act for you?' Though she shared his bed whenever he wanted it, and had borne him a child, Salina knew everything of Zachary's other family and cherished each one of them as if they belonged to her.

'I could try,' he answered, biting his lip.

Even as he shuddered from the idea Zachary knew what must be done. Once more he must attempt that dangerous trick of projecting his astral being out of his body, risking that it might be unable to return.

'Will you help me, Salina?'

By way of reply she put her hands to her heart, her lips and her forehead, then bowed silently; an elegant gracious creature, mistress of many feminine secrets.

Together they went outside and she settled at his feet, both of them sitting on the balcony of his bedroom, watching as the moon rose up out of the sea. From a burner set beside the astrologer blue smoke wreathed and coiled, full of a deep and drowsy incense.

402

Much as she had no wish to disobey, the slave felt the strangest sensations. She stared at the silver deepness of the night so intently that it began to dance before her and press in on her so hard that she felt she might be squeezed into eternity.

Salina reached out for Dr Zachary's hand and as his fingers closed over hers, he pulled her upright. They stood side by side on the balcony and looking behind her she saw that another astrologer and his slave sat motionless and staring, where she had been but a moment or two before. Her master turned on her the strangest look but said nothing as Salina, knowing that she was dreaming but nonetheless afraid, held on to his hand ever more tightly.

Now the dream became fantastic as she and Zachary left the Palace and entered a strange dwelling near a river. Salina saw dark timbers and white walls and looked in vain for mosaics and coloured glass. Then she dreamed that they climbed the stairs together and looked into a bedroom where two boys slept. From Zachary's description of them, the slave recognised Jasper and Sylvanus. She watched, huddling in the shadows, as her master kissed both of them and spoke softly. The boys stirred in their sleep but did not wake.

Now he crossed the landing, Salina close behind, and entered another room. In a great bed, her dark hair spreading over the pillow, lay Cloverella, fast asleep. Even in the dream Salina was glad to see his wife was alone and knew that her master would be pleased. He sat on the corner of the bed and kissed Cloverella on the lips while his slave peeped from the doorway, afraid of being seen.

'Cloverella,' Zachary was whispering urgently, 'please hear me darling. I cannot be long. I am alive and well. A prisoner but safe. One day I will come back to you. Do you understand?'

Cloverella sighed and turned over, she was still deeply asleep. Zachary put his hands on her shoulders and shook her gently.

'Please, my darling, wake for just a second.' He kissed her again on the cheek and this time she did as he bade her. Momentarily Cloverella opened her eyes. She looked at Zachary and gave a wonderful smile, then her gaze slid to Salina, who instantly stepped away so that she would not be seen. By the time she peeped again, Cloverella had gone back to sleep.

'My darling, please help my father. The Duke is under arrest and will be lodged in the Tower. Go to see him and tell him I said "A cat's whisker". Do you understand? "A cat's whisker".'

403

In her dream Cloverella nodded and it was then that Salina felt a violent shudder warn her that soon she must return to her body. She tiptoed forward and pulled gently at Zachary's hand. He looked up, startled, and Salina realised that she had been forgotten. Soundlessly her lips formed the word, 'Come.'

He did not want to leave his sweetly sleeping wife and it was only by tugging a little harder and silently imploring that Salina eventually got him to his feet.

'Master, please,' she gasped into his ear, 'my heart feels as if it might burst.'

Zachary looked from one to the other, not for the first time in his life torn between two women. But Salina's distress was too real for there to be any hesitation. Holding her to him, Zachary willed with all his might that both of them might enter their mortal bodies, and it seemed then that he and his slave both fell, down and down a never-ending tunnel at the bottom of which there was nothing but moonlight.

## Chapter Thirty-Three

O N THE EVE OF THE Duke of Norfolk's execution his closest family were allowed to take leave of him. His Duchess, who had never loved him, bid him a stony-faced farewell but wept after she had left the room, though his daughter Mary flung herself into her father's arms and cried bitterly. She had given evidence against her brother Henry, who had so incensed her with his jibes that she should become her own father-in-law's mistress – she had been married to Henry's bastard son who had died while still in his teens – that she had turned on him violently.

'Hush, hush,' Norfolk said, patting her neat head. 'I am so old anyway that the axe will make little difference.'

'But it is utterly unfair,' she whispered mutinously. 'You served *him* well.'

'He,' the Duke whispered back, 'cares for nothing and no one. He is drowning in a sea of blood.'

After she had gone, the old man prepared himself for death, groaning at the cold of his bleak cell on that raw January night of 1547 as he knelt to pray. Far away in thought, he was a little startled when the warder, coughing in the doorway for interrupting a man on his knees, said, 'Your daughter-in-law, Your Grace.'

He looked up, expecting to see Surrey's wife, now a widow as his poor colourful maddish son had gone to the block eight days earlier, but took a startled breath as the warder stepped aside to reveal the small dark beauty whom Zachary had married.

'My dear Cloverella,' he said, struggling to his feet, all thoughts of ancient enmities banished at this late hour of his life. 'How good of you to come.'

She hurried towards him, her arms outstretched, and gathered the old bear to her dimunitive frame.

'Lord Duke my father,' she whispered into his ear, so much in the way that Zachary used to speak that the hair rose on his head. 'I have come to see you on behalf of your son, my husband.'

He held her at arm's length, his weary old eyes staring into hers. 'What are you saying, my dear?'

'That I dreamt of Zachary so vividly the other night I believe him to be still alive. I know it sounds foolish, Lord Duke, but it is the truth. He told me to say to you "A cat's whisker".'

'A cat's whisker?' repeated the Duke, puzzled. 'What does that mean?'

'I don't know. I thought it to be some private code between you.'

The Duke shook his head. 'I'm afraid it conveys nothing.'

Cloverella looked crestfallen. 'You are certain? I had hoped in this way to prove he lived. Oh Lord Duke, please cudgel your memory. Do the words remind you of nothing?'

Dimly something stirred in Howard's mind and tired as he was he began to cast back, frowning with the effort of remembering. Then suddenly it came to him. He stood once more in Zachary's house in Greenwich, Sapphira a little child held tightly in his arms. He put her down and handed her to her mother, Jane, who left the room. He began to discuss the King's Great Matter with Zachary, man to man. Then out of the blue he had asked the question, 'Will I survive His Grace?'

Now he remembered vividly the look on Zachary's solemn face as he answered, 'By a cat's whisker, you will.'

'God's mercy!' he exclaimed aloud and Cloverella drew closer so that they could whisper.

'What is it, Sir? What have you remembered?'

'I asked him if I would outlive His Grace the King and he answered, "By a cat's whisker, you will".'

Cloverella stared at him in wonderment. 'But surely . . . ?'

'It is impossible I know, but I recall now how positive he was.'

'But it would have to be *tonight*,' whispered Cloverella. 'His Grace would . . .'

'Don't say it,' muttered Norfolk, drawing her as far away from the door as possible. 'Don't even breathe it. To speak it is treason.'

'But treason or no, Zachary could not be wrong about a prediction of that magnitude.'

The Duke broke out in a clammy sweat. 'My dear Cloverella, I must sit down. I suddenly feel the world spinning about me.'

She helped him on to the hard wooden chair, the only one

provided in that uncomfortable cell, then sank onto the floor at his feet.

'You really believe he came to you? That he is alive somewhere?'

'I do Lord Duke and this strange coincidence has proved it to me.'

Norfolk shook his head silently, mopping his brow.

'If what we think might happen *did* happen,' Cloverella murmured, 'what would be your position?'

'A stay of execution.'

'The cat's whisker,' she said in triumph and rose to her feet.

'Well, well,' the Duke answered softly, suddenly too weary to stand. 'We must await events.'

His daughter-in-law bent over his ear. 'If the Reaper is out stalking tonight he may find a victim even more resplendant.'

'The cruel master instead of the loyal servant?'

'Justice,' answered Cloverella softly. 'Slow, inexorable justice. The mills of God.'

Throughout January the King had grown weaker. The musicians had long since ceased to play in the Palace of Whitehall and every day the bustle of Palace life diminished. The Queen, who had been sent to Grenwich to keep her Christmas, had been called earlier in the month to take her leave of her royal husband, as had Princess Mary. The two younger children were not fated to see their father again, remembering him only as a huge terrifying figure, very much alive, for from Henry Tudor's deathbed the entire family were quite deliberately kept away. He was to die amongst his Gentlemen, in authority to the last.

It was Sir Anthony Denny, relatively new to court, who had finally had the courage to tell the King he was dying, for even to speak the word was an act of treason. But Henry would not hear of it, refusing to send for Cranmer, insisting that he would summon the Archbishop when he felt it necessary. By the time he awoke from a fitful sleep he had left it too late, the King could no longer speak.

Henry Tudor had once saved Archbishop Cranmer from a charge of heresy and now the prelate came at speed from Croydon to repay his debt and ease his royal master's passing from the world. He found a quiet room, only a handful of courtiers present beside the grim-faced physicians, several men, including Lord Hertford and

William Paget, striding the corridor outside. The atmosphere was stuffy, hot from the roaring fire, the air heavy with the smell of spices and expensive scents which disguised the odour of rot emanating from the dying hulk in the bed. Henry had taken to that bed before Christmas, now he was about to leave it for ever.

Cranmer bent over the moon face, its half-open eyes sightless.

'Your Grace,' he whispered urgently, 'Your Grace, can you hear me?'

Henry made no response and Cranmer, terrified that his royal master might leave the world unshriven, said with some urgency, 'Your Grace, give me a sign of the repentance of your sins and your faith in Christ our redeemer.'

There seemed to him, then, to be a glint in the dying man's eyes and the Archbishop, in something of a frenzy, grabbed both of Henry's hands in his. There was a definite answering movement which could merely have been a spasm but which poor Cranmer took to be a response.

'His Grace wrings my hand,' he said loudly, 'as token of his repentance.'

He made the sign of the cross on the King's forehead. 'May the soul of our most Gracious Lord, Henry by the Grace of God King, rest in peace, shriven of its sins and trusting in Christ. Amen.'

There was a murmur in the doorway as those in the corridor, realising the end was imminent, came into the room and dropped on their knees, then there was silence broken only by Henry's rasping breath.

Edward Seymour, kneeling close to the bed, found himself staring in disbelief at the mountainous form gasping its way out of the world. It was almost impossible to credit that death was coming for that most powerful of beings who had controlled the destiny of so many for so long. But if it truly was, if his royal brother-in-law was about to breathe his last, then all Edward Lord Hertford's carefully laid plans could start their fateful course.

Henry's will, made a month ago at the end of 1546, named the line of succession and the King's executors, but said nothing about the appointment of a regent or protector. Yet as uncle of the new King, and with Thomas now a member of the Council, it would seem a small step for Edward to become virtual ruler of England. The man born the son of a humble Wiltshire knight trembled with the excitement of it all and almost missed Henry Tudor's final breath.

The words, 'The soul of the King's Grace has departed this life,' jerked him back to attention and as Cranmer led solemn prayers, Edward looked swiftly round the room before taking one last glance at the corpse. The face was losing colour already, resembling a millstone in both shape and shade. Even now Lord Hertford expected one of the eyes, closed for the first time in months, to reopen and stare at him angrily. Henry Tudor had left matters so disposed that he obviously expected to rule from beyond the grave.

But alas, thought Edward, that is too much to hope for, Your Grace. The old order inevitably must change.

As the prayer ended he rose swiftly to his feet and glanced about him. 'Gentlemen, for the good of the realm I believe that all of us here present should hold a meeting immediately,' he said calmly. 'I would ask you to step into the ante-room out of respect for our late King.'

No one demurred and Edward felt the cloak of leadership slip about his shoulders as if it had always sat there. He gave one further look round. 'The King is dead, long live the King, our most noble Prince, Edward,' he intoned solemnly.

'Long live the King,' chorused the others as they left the mortal remains of Henry VIII behind them to discuss the reign which was just about to begin.

*Part Three*

# THE LORD PROTECTOR

## Chapter Thirty-Four

IT WAS WONDERFULLY COLD, exhilarating and heady, breath fluting like spun glass and cheeks rose-red. As far as the eye could see a crisp fine icing lay over the world which in daytime looked pink, edible almost. But at night the bitter flakes fell again, altering the landscape to a white wilderness, so that by morning the world had changed. Despite its beauty it was treacherous weather, threatening to travellers, big drifts blocking roads and paths. Only the foolhardy were out and of these Katherine Parr, giggling like a girl, took herself to be one.

She had run all the way from the house, plunging through the snow in the garden and kicking it up in plumes round her feet, laughing out loud and scooping snowballs to throw at a tree. Despite the fact that it had started to flutter down again, Katherine had never felt warmer or happier. For tonight, after so many years of longing, she was to be reunited with Thomas Seymour.

As soon as she had been informed by the Privy Council that she was at last a royal widow, Katherine had written to him, and he must have thought of her at exactly the same moment for his letter had crossed with hers. She knew now that the King had been dead for three days before the Council had publicly announced the fact, three days in which Lord Hertford had ridden to Hertford Castle to fetch the new King, making sure of the succession. Seymour had not broken the news of his father's death to the boy until he had brought him as far as Elsynge Hall, where Elizabeth was staying, then on bended knee Hertford had told the two children together.

Now, standing by the gate that led from the garden to the fields surrounding her lovely Dower House in Chelsea, originally built as a royal nursery, Katherine remembered it all with a certain irony.

Because of Henry's death at the early age of fifty-five years and seven months, old Norfolk had escaped the axe and she had been freed from slavery. As for material benefits, Edward Seymour had been advanced by wish of the late King to the honour of Duke of Somerset and, following a decree of the Council, 'Protector of all realms and dominions of the King's Majesty that now is and Governor of his most royal person.' Thomas had been created a Baron, made a Knight of the Garter and promoted to Lord High Admiral. And she, Katherine, had been left money and jewels, plate and household goods, as well as two Dower Houses. The servant had been well rewarded. She was now a very rich widow indeed.

Katherine had felt no emotion at the news of the King's death other than one of relief. At last the terrible man, old before his time, killed by obesity, capable of turning on anyone, however loyal they might have been, had left the world and she could breathe easily. Since the events of last summer when the Queen had come so near to arrest and death, Katherine had not known a moment's peace. But at last it was over. She had escaped with her life and was free. She had written to Thomas straight away.

They had taken the vast coffin and its contents along the river to Windsor, where it was to be interred. It had rested overnight in the chapel of Syon House where Cat Howard had been kept prisoner until she had gone to the Tower at the very end. During the night the body had burst inside the coffin which had been shaken during the journey and become unsealed. In the morning when workmen had arrived to solder the casket, they had found a dog licking up the King's blood from the chapel floor. It had been prophesied by Friar Petyo that Henry's evil ways would merit such a fate as that of the biblical Ahab and sure enough it had come about. A grinning cur had consumed his fluids.

It had taken sixteen stalwart yeomen to lower the box into the vault beside that of Jane Seymour and then the trumpets had sounded for the new King, her son. Five days later the boy had been crowned in a ceremony that had been shortened from twelve hours to seven because of King Edward's age.

Katherine had watched it all, the two royal princesses sitting beside her, for Elizabeth had been given into her care now, to live with her stepmother in Chelsea as that part of her education which required learning courtly ways. But during the coronation Katherine could only think about young Edward, with his pale face and reddish hair, struggling through the ceremony, the Duke of Somerset looming omnipresent.

I pray the Protector governs him well, Katherine had thought suddenly in the middle of all the pomp. The King is, after all, only a nine-year-old boy.

But it was difficult to tell how Edward Seymour was reacting, his dark face giving away nothing though his wife, on the contrary, already acted as if she were a crowned Queen of England.

A silly woman, thought Katherine now, and wrote 'Anne Somerset is a puffed-up peahen' in the snow before blowing it away and laughing.

It was at that moment, smiling to herself, that Katherine caught a glimpse of a lantern and braced herself. She had seen Thomas, of course, at both the funeral and the coronation but there had been no more than courtesies exchanged between them. He was being as discreet as ever outwardly but in secret it was a different matter. Tom was braving the snow, public displeasure, everything, just to be with her.

'I'm here,' she called softly, and saw the dark figure start to run as best it could.

'My darling, is that you?' he was saying, and Katherine fled to meet him. Opening the gate and hurrying into the field where she fell in a drift, laughing and blushing as he deliberately pretended to stumble and rolled on top of her.

There had never been such a kiss in the history of the world. They had been parted for so long that they had become desperate for want of love. Thomas's mouth consumed hers and Katherine savoured his in return as they embraced at long last, pressing against each other, trying to feel each other's bodies through their thick winter clothes.

'May I stay the night?' Thomas asked urgently.

'Yes, yes. You must.'

'But what of the servants?'

'We'll say you called late, anything. But we have to be together.'

'Yes I must be with you.'

He scooped her to her feet, brushing the snow from her clothes. 'Oh pretty Kate, I missed you so much.'

'Were you faithful to me?'

Thomas grinned. 'Of course!'

Did it matter if he had not? Did anything matter now that they were together again with all dangers past and behind them?

415

'It doesn't signify.'

'Nothing does,' Thomas answered, 'nothing and no one. I am going to marry you, Kate. Soon.'

'There will be a scandal.'

'Who cares?' he said.

That night in bed, locked in her chamber away from the world, Katherine and Thomas found the greatest magic of all, passing through every stage of love, every facet of relationship. At first she wept against his chest, sickened by the memory of Henry Tudor's lovemaking, an obscene pawing which had always come to nothing.

'Nothing?' asked Thomas. 'Really?'

'Vanished,' said Katherine, wondering what it was that allowed her to be so free with this man, 'disappeared. Found dead beneath a mountain.'

Now they were giggling wildly, dangerously, verging on making a noise.

'Shush,' murmured Katherine, not quite serious. 'If the servants come I am finished.'

'But this is just the beginning,' Thomas whispered back. 'I intend to be here often, to lay siege to you until you marry me.'

'In two years,' she answered, but his reply was to glide into her, reminding her with every move how many years of her life had been already wasted on feeble men, for there was nothing feeble about Thomas Seymour, every inch of his muscular body made to please women. As he slowly, easily, biding his time, led her to completion, Katherine Parr felt that it might be quite possible, in his hands, to die of sheer pleasure.

At the peak of their sensational tide of love, when in Katherine's head every bell in Christendom raised its joyful voice, they clung together, like children. But, as Thomas grew tired and slept, she became motherly, stroking his hair and fondling him until she, too, went to sleep. When they woke it was the grey dawn of a snowy February day. The widow's husband had been buried two weeks and she felt no remorse. She had been fond of Lord Latymer but unable to resist Thomas even then. Now she no longer cared.

Lord Seymour left as soon as he was dressed, hurrying away to the inn in the nearby village of Chelsea to idle the day away and come back to her that night. Very soon his duties as a Privy Councillor would give him less freedom but at the moment he had

416

time to spare and was intent on wooing and winning the woman of his choice with economic speed.

Just as he left the Dower House, Thomas looked up to give Katherine a final wave and saw a flash of red hair jump back from another window. So his young obsession was up and about and spying. Thomas doffed his hat in that direction but there was no answering response. Had he looked back again as he hurried away through the snow-filled garden he would have seen a pair of dark eyes following his every move.

So, thought Elizabeth, that's the lie of the land, is it? Well, well! Who would have dreamed it of my earnest little stepmother?

She supposed that she ought to be filled with righteous indignation, swelling up with rage that her father's memory was being thus abused, but yet had no inclination to rouse herself on the matter. This particular stepmother had been enormously kind to her, not as eccentric as the Lady Anne of Cleves nor as glamorous as pretty Cat Howard, but genuinely good-hearted to all the royal children.

And who, Elizabeth said to herself, could pretend that it has been easy for her?

She knew the facts of life by now, being thirteen and daily expecting her first flux which, as yet, had not started within. Learning everything had been fascinating and somehow compulsive, for Elizabeth could not drag her mind away from her own mother, that chic, dark being who had only to look at a man for him to fall in love with her. Would she have that power, she wondered? And yet she had considered Tom Seymour, with his teasing and laughter and over-bright eyes, had a certain tenderness for her.

But obviously not, thought Elizabeth, it is my stepmother that he visits in the night, not me.

She got back into bed, snuggling down beneath the covers, wondering what it would be like to lie with a man and whether Tom and Katherine had really done that rudest of things last night. Kat Ashley, formerly Champernowne, who had recently married John Ashley, a close friend of Roger Ascham who was already under consideration as at tutor for Elizabeth, had explained everything. In her usual intelligent way the girl had considered the facts without emotion and found a strange reaction within herself, part longing, part disgust, not helped by the lateness of her physical development.

For Elizabeth's body at thirteen seemed unusually thin and lanky, or so she thought herself. Her breasts, though forming, were still childish and her only claim to beauty so far was her hands. Elizabeth thought them very fine, long-fingered and tapering, supple at both wrist and palm. She would often spend time gesturing and posturing before a mirror to watch their swanlike movements. Now, thinking about Tom Seymour and her stepmother, Elizabeth put her fingers together to form a steeple.

'What if they were to marry,' she muttered, then laughed. Serious little Kate would never consider such a rash step.

But yet Tom *had* been there visiting, if not overnight, early for a social call. Elizabeth, now too flustered by her thoughts to sleep again, rose from her bed, anxious to get outside. She loved sporting activities, running about and being boyish. Deep in her heart she wished that she had been the male heir and not Edward. Then she could have ruled her kingdom with a childish roughness and gruffness which would have blossomed to supreme statesmanship when she had reached man's estate.

'Womanhood! Bah!' she exclaimed, gazing at her pale thin frame, before she covered it with clothes and headed out into the snow.

He was a very odd little boy, thought Edward Somerset, looking across to where his nephew, swamped by his grown-up clothes which included a prominent and quite unnecessary codpiece, read and re-read the document which the Protector had handed to him. That the child was near to being a genius, even by the advanced standards of education that he was already receiving, was obvious by the way his eyes flew across the sheet, then read again slowly to assimilate the facts.

If my nephew lives, thought Somerset cynically, he will probably be the ablest statesman ever to sit the throne of England. In truth, an extraordinary little creature.

The King was not like any Seymour that Somerset could remember. Old Sir John had been a countryman, loving the forest and hunting and loudly blowing the Esturmy horn to greet the monarch, and in a way Thomas had taken after him, being a man of action rather than an intellectual. In fact, thought the Protector very privately, Tom has moments when his rashness borders on stupidity.

The other Seymour children had been quieter, leading more settled lives, including the future Queen Jane. She had been intelligent, true enough, and witty when called for but how she had given birth to this prodigy of learning, Somerset could not imagine. Tudor blood must be carrying the seed which engendered such feats.

'My Lord Uncle,' the boy was saying, combining both Somerset's relationships to him in one title, 'do I take it from this paper dated 21st March, ratified with the Great Seal, that the power for our realm, to conduct matters of state and all business, private and public, domestic and foreign, until we have accomplished the age of eighteen, now rests with you?'

Somerset bowed his head. 'Your Grace approved such a measure.'

'Oh yes,' answered the King seriously, 'that is not the point. What I believe to be the issue is the tremendous responsibility now resting on your shoulders. Is it too much for one individual to carry such a burden?'

Somerset looked at the boy with a crazy mix of emotions, longing to pick him up and carry him shoulder high as once he had used when Edward had been Prince.

'It is indeed a great onus, Your Grace. But the Privy Council of this land are used to one person being so empowered. They found it too difficult to rule the realm by committee as it were.'

Edward screwed up his face and just for a second Somerset saw Jane peep out of his eyes.

'Yes, my Lord Uncle, but *we* rule the realm when all is finally said.'

Somerset went down on one knee. 'Your Grace, this land so gallantly brought to Reformation by the late King's Majesty must now continue on its course. I believe' – here Somerset laid his hand upon his heart, convinced of every word he uttered – 'that toleration of faith is essential, that true reform must be our goal.'

'*Our* goal?'

'The realm's, Your Grace.'

'Ah!' answered Edward, looking wise. 'I thought for a moment you meant *us*, Uncle.'

That boy is too clever for his own good, thought Somerset, rising and bowing. Aloud he said, 'The Duchess of Somerset, your aunt, wonders if you would do her the honour of dining with us tomorrow, Your Grace.'

The King's face brightened. 'Will Uncle Thomas be there?'

'He has not as yet been invited, Sir.'

'A pity,' said the boy, looking fractionally wistful. 'But then he may yet come.'

'I shall make sure that word gets to him, Your Grace,' answered Somerset, feeling unreasonably irritated that the child so obviously preferred his scampish brother.

'Then tell the Duchess we shall be delighted to attend her.'

It was all so formal, so pompous, that Somerset felt like throwing caution to the wind and saying, 'You are speaking to your uncle, boy. Just for a few moments in private you could surely unbend and let us be as once we were,' but the King was speaking again.

'We do congratulate you, Lord Uncle, on the position of pre-eminence to which you have been called and we do most heartily pray that with God's help you will act wisely as Lord Protector to our kingdom.'

'Thank you, Sir,' answered Somerset gravely, then changed his voice. 'I have recently had constructed in my garden some new butts for archery practice. I think them of reasonable standard . . .'

He said nothing further, knowing how the boy enjoyed sports, watching as the King's face grew enthusiastic and younger-looking. Briefly, Somerset experienced a moment of true compassion for the poor soul, doomed from the moment of his birth to lead a completely unnatural life, never allowed even once to be free and naughty as was the right of every other child in the land.

'I should like to try them, Lord Uncle.'

'Then perhaps tomorrow . . .'

'It will be a pleasure.'

Somerset backed his way out, genuinely depressed, wondering how he could stand another nine years of such behaviour. Henry VIII had been dead two months but his legacy lived on everywhere. If the Lord Protector was to bring the realm through the difficult years that lay ahead of it, he had to muster every ounce of strength and patience he possessed.

He thought, as he got into his barge to go to Temple Bar, that perhaps he had already made one mistake in keeping Norfolk alive. The Council had argued for three days after Henry's death as to what should be done with the old warrior, and it had been

420

Seymour's voice that had saved him. Now Thomas Howard was serving a term of indefinite imprisonment in the Tower and it was privately hoped that nature would help the Council out of their dilemma. But with spring in the land and the stir of bravery that goes with new beginnings, the last person that anyone was thinking of was Norfolk. Unless of course it was Cloverella, become important in her own right since the disappearance of Dr Zachary.

I must see her, thought Edward in a rush of conscience. I must see her and enquire after those two boys she is raising. Perhaps she could do with help regarding their future.

And then he realised that with his largely increased household and the plans he had for building a grand new house on the banks of the Thames, there could be room in his establishment for two bright lads.

'I shall seek her within the week and make an offer to place them,' Edward Seymour muttered to himself as he stepped ashore at his landing stage and just for a moment, and an irrestibly pleasing one, savoured the power of largesse and what it was like to think and act as a King.

# Chapter Thirty-Five

THERE HAVING BEEN SUCH a severe February and cold March, April by contrast was very soft and sweet, yellow with sunbeams and warm as newly-baked bread. Enjoying the sunshine and leaning out of her wide-open window, through which came the sound of all six of her daughters, the youngest still toddling, happily playing in the gardens below, the Duchess of Somerset gazed about her with certain satisfaction.

The beautiful grounds of her mansion, Chester Place, which included orchards and a paddock, ran down to the river Thames, but these already seemed paltry in comparison with the lands that were to be attached to the new home presently being built for the exalted Seymours. For Somerset House was to be not so much a family dwelling place as a palace. Not only was Chester Place to be demolished to make way for it but many other buildings as well, for the huge residence was to occupy some six acres with additional acreage in the landscaped grounds.

Unfortunately, thought Anne with a contented sigh, this house is simply not adequate for our position in the world.

With one more sweeping gaze she left her vantage point and settled herself comfortably to read a newly arrived letter, a letter which by its royal emblem endorsed, if anything needed to, how very far Anne Stanhope had progressed from being a gentlewoman of, first, Katharine of Aragon then later Anne Boleyn. Cracking apart Princess Mary Tudor's seal with a winner's smile, the Duchess of Somerset read the opening words, 'My good gossip'. Her smile deepened. To be on such highly familiar terms with the heir to the throne, let alone aunt to the King himself, was to have arrived at the peak of society.

In some respects Anne Somerset's retention of the good looks of her youth, despite many pregnancies and births, had much to do with her increasing foolishness. It had only been a few years since the Earl of Surrey had fallen in love with her and made the fact blatantly public. In her very rejection of him Anne had skilfully encouraged the man, so that though she had appeared in the eyes of others to be the hapless victim of a passion-crazed poet, she had mutely spurred Surrey on to greater excesses, that all might notice and remark her beauty and power. The affair had revitalised her marriage too, Edward being consumed with jealousy and half suspecting her of succumbing to Surrey's blandishments. The fact that her husband's first wife had been unfaithful to him had not softened Anne's heart in the least, in fact she had cleverly neither denied nor confirmed that she and Henry Howard had been to bed together.

Now the Duchess continued to read Mary's letter. 'And thus, my good Nan, I trouble you with myself and all mine; thanking you with all my heart for your earnest gentleness towards me . . .'

It was not difficult to be gentle towards a Princess of the blood royal, particularly when she was rather plain; gruff and ailing, Mary was hardly likely to compete with Anne in any way at all. But for the other two royal ladies, the two who lived in the Dower House in Chelsea, Anne had no liking. Katherine Parr, as far as the Duchess was concerned, was a parvenue who had obtained by her wiles the title of Queen Dowager, and was paid far too much attention as a result, while Elizabeth, that pale-faced skinny girl with unbecoming orange hair, stared too much. Though she had served the girl's mother, the Duchess had no liking for the daughter, whose dark eyes rested on her as if they could see through to the bone.

But Anne Somerset's true *bête noir* was her brother-in-law, Thomas. Deep down in her soul, so deep that she could no longer consciously remember it, Anne had once had a desperate fancy for him, loving his carefree looks and manner, falling under the spell of his wild blue eyes. Whether he had actually slighted her or whether she had imagined he had done so, again had been forgotten. But Anne's former feelings for him had become soured and now she hated him desperately, longing to see him discomfited and degraded. Subtly, the Duchess poured poison about Thomas Seymour into the ear of anyone who would listen, whenever she had the chance.

Mary's letter finished, Anne got to her feet again, staring out of

423

the window once more at her six daughters. Though producing sons was obviously not her strongest asset, the Duchess had two surviving and that was enough to ensure the Seymour line continued. Nevertheless, if she did not feel it would ruin her social life at this interesting stage, Anne might consider trying to produce a third, naturally asking Princess Mary to be his godmother.

The Duchess picked up her letter again. It was signed, 'Your loving friend during my life.' How well that sounded, thought Anne, contentedly contemplating her inviolate position as friend and kinswoman to the mighty.

In the late afternoon of the same day, during a very moderate but refreshing shower, Katherine Parr picked up her pen and wrote to Lord Seymour, as she very often did. The Dowager Queen was now in such a frenzy of love that she hardly knew which way to turn. Convention decreed that as a King's widow there should be a really decent interval before she married again, yet her loving but respectable heart longed to be Thomas's lawful wife. He, on the other hand, cared nothing for the niceties, urging Katherine to marry at once, determined to wear down her resistance, promising that he would woo his nephew and the Council into full agreement.

Lord Seymour had already bribed John Fowler, a member of the Privy Chamber, to ask the King casually whom Edward thought his uncle should marry. Unfortunately the boy had come up with all the wrong answers, suggesting Anne of Cleves and then Princess Mary, a fact which had sent Thomas into gales of laughter, though Katherine had not thought it funny at all.

Now, not having seen him for a few days, she was trying to be cool, writing sensibly that he must also seek approval for the marriage from the Lord Protector who, if he denied to sanction their alliance, would then look foolish if the King and Council agreed.

Frowning sternly, or trying to, Katherine wrote, 'My lord, whereas you charge me with a promise, written with my own hand, to change the two years into two months, I think you have no such plain sentence written with my hand.'

How hard it was to be cross with him even in a letter. Yet Katherine knew perfectly well that she had not agreed, in writing or any other form, to marry him in two months' time. She sighed and continued, 'When it shall be your pleasure to repair hither, you must take some pain to come early in the morning, that you may be gone again by seven o'clock; and so I suppose you may come without suspect. I pray you let me have knowledge overnight at what hour you will come that your portress may wait at the gate to the fields for you.'

Katherine added a few more sentences then ended 'By her that is, and shall be, your humble, true and loving wife during her life. Katherine the Queen.' She sealed the letter then pressed it with her device, ringing a small handbell for one of the servants, wondering just how she and Thomas would get over the enormous difficulties that faced them. Yet what could really happen? Neither the Protector nor the Council could remove their worldly goods or titles. Only the threat of ostracism hung over them and that could easily be borne by two people in love. Still, Katherine was not easy, fearing some strange revenge, some quirk of fate, that might yet harm them somehow.

There was a light tap on the door and thinking it to be a servant, Katherine half rose, the letter clutched in her hand, but it was Elizabeth who stood framed in the doorway, her dark eyes gleaming, her skin very white. In this April light she seemed iridescent, glowing from within.

'Well, dear Kate?' she said.

Katherine knew it was wrong, knew that she should have been strong and adult, but somehow Elizabeth had wheedled out of her the truth about Thomas. In a moment of weakness, Katherine had confided the secret of her love and then awaited the girl's ice-cold fury. But, strangely, it had not come. Instead there had been a toss of the head, which had instantly reminded Katherine of Anne Boleyn, and a knowing light had appeared behind the hazel eyes.

'You deserve some joy. My father was not easy, was he?'

Katherine had not answered, merely staring at Elizabeth in amazement, wondering what she was really thinking. Because one never knew with her; the pale face, the dark eyes, a strange combination at the best of times, could look positively mask-like on occasion.

But with a stunning change of subject all Elizabeth had said further was, 'Aren't you glad the wretched Wriothesley has fallen out with the Protector?'

'Er, yes, of course,' Katherine had stumbled over her words, completely taken by surprise.

'But I think Lord Somerset should have had him killed. Men like that always come back, don't they?'

'Sometimes,' Katherine had answered.

Now she looked at her stepdaughter with a half-smile and said, 'Well, what?'

'Is he coming? Is it to be all love and madness or long face and sadness?'

'How poetic,' Katherine said with a laugh. 'I think he is coming. This letter asks him to let me know at what time.'

'Then it must be sent at once,' Elizabeth whirled to the door and Katherine wondered again at the child's incredible thinness. 'Hawkin, if you please. Her Grace the Queen has an important letter. Would you see that it is taken immediately to the address inscribed.'

Elizabeth turned again to her stepmother and behind her back Katherine saw the servant roll his eyes. It was true that the Lady Elizabeth had grown more imperious since being reinstated in the line of succession, after her brother and his heirs and Mary and her heirs, and today she seemed in the mood for giving orders.

'Now, dear Kate,' she said, 'you must decide what you are going to wear for your tryst?'

With a laugh, Katherine pulled the girl into her lap, wrapping her arms round the slender waist and kissing the bony cheek.

'You are enjoying this aren't you, you little wretch? Now why, Miss Meddle Mouse? What does it matter to you if I see the Lord Admiral or not?'

'Because,' answered the girl in a burst of laughter, 'I love schemes.' She dropped her voice to a whisper. 'My mother loved them too or at least I think she did.'

Katherine grew slightly uncomfortable. 'Why do you say that?'

'Because she schemed her way on to the throne, didn't she? But then, of course, she schemed her way right off again. I wouldn't have done that. I would have made sure that having got there, I stayed.'

'Yes,' answered Katherine softly, 'I think you would.' She pulled Elizabeth close to her. 'Do you often think about her?'

'Lately I have,' the girl answered truthfully. 'And I don't really know why. Perhaps because I am beginning to grow up.' She bent over and kissed Katherine's mouth. 'But you are the sweetest mother of them all. I want *you* to be happy.'

426

'Then come with me and look at clothes. You may choose my finery. That is, should the Lord Admiral decide to come.'

'Oh, he will come,' answered Elizabeth certainly. 'He's mad for love, is that man.'

And she kept to herself the fact that he had flirted with her when she had not been a great deal younger than she was now, and that Tom's bright eyes, whenever he had looked at the girl, had held an expression in them that he could not disguise.

He is in love with Katherine, thought Elizabeth wisely, but it is I who drive him mad.

Several weeks later than he had intended, Edward Seymour set off to see Cloverella, journeying by river through a showery day. Above his head blue-black clouds dominated the sky, so that the buildings on the riverbanks seemed white and exciting, the spires of the churches glistening with raindrops, the earth black with water. Daffodils were everywhere, green and gold, and the Protector noticed at least one vivid clump of late crocuses, purple as the sky above them, yet threaded with vivid yellow, like marchpane.

Nesting birds were in full throat, a blackbird singing its song amongst the trees of Zachary's garden, clinging to a thin branch, bobbing and dancing in the wind as if it had no fear. Somewhere a storm thrush called out its high anthem, exciting and wild. It was a pagan sound, blood-stirring and raw.

The Protector shielded his eyes and looked up to find the thrush, but as he did so it started to rain, not a shower but a downpour. It was a soaking, driving rain, falling full in his face and making him wet to the skin in a matter of seconds. The oarsmen crowded into the barge's cabin as best they could, though it was far too small to house them all, but Edward plodded up to the house, enjoying himself as he had not for a long time. Something rough and rare stirred his soul at this primeval wetting, this complete return to nature, the flowing of water and tears and sweat. For he wept a little as he walked, tears of gratitude for having climbed so high, tears of sorrow that it was now too late to change his life's direction.

The two boys he had come to see, having spied him from the house, were waiting in the doorway with towels, and Somerset marvelled at their likeness and yet their dissimilarity. Jasper was beautiful, changed, fourteen years old and dark as the blackbird whose distant song could still be heard. A humorous quirky face, bright with intellect, smiled up at him. Sylvanus though, had retained his youthful rosy charm, two vivid forget-me-not eyes still shining out of a merry round face, though the golden curls of childhood had now turned quite shockingly red.

'Well,' said Edward appreciatively, 'you are two likely fellows if ever I saw any.'

They grinned simultaneously and in that their likeness showed. At that moment they could have been twins.

I wonder what the King would make of them, thought Somerset, and some perverse streak in him decided upon the introduction.

Cloverella awaited him in the hall and her cousin thought she had come a goodly way from the days of their youth. The little gypsy thing with eyes almost bigger than she, had turned into a poised and beautiful woman, very well dressed and obviously in command of her life. But there the Protector pulled himself up short. No woman as calm as this could have lost someone she loved dearly.

'Is Zachary still alive?' he burst out, even while towelling his head.

Cloverella smiled and nodded. 'He has been located by an agent of the French King based in Constantinople. My husband is a prisoner of Sultan Suleiman, unable to escape but apparently enjoying every second of his captivity.'

Edward stared at her in astonishment as she went on, 'You know Zachary, my dear cousin. He could talk his way into anything – and he has! He is now the Sultan's chief astrologer.'

They both laughed uproariously, the Protector dripping water on to the floor in an ever-increasing pool from his sodden garments.

Cloverella looked contrite. 'I forget my good manners. Come and change your wet clothes. There is plenty of Zachary's peacock garb left behind and you are most welcome to help yourself.'

It was with some difficulty that Somerset managed to find a doublet and hose of sober colour, Zachary's penchant for rainbow shades never being more apparent than when riffling through his clothes press. But eventually, dressed in a too-small outfit of dark green, Edward descended the stairs to find that a light meal had been prepared in his absence and Cloverella and her stepsons awaited his arrival.

'Seriously,' he said, as he sat down, 'can nothing be done to help Zachary? Should I open diplomatic channels?'

428

'I think,' answered Cloverella, equally grave, 'that King François had already started to do so before his untimely death. But now with the Dauphin come to the throne I do not know what will happen. Yet I feel Henri must be friendly to me for I have already received an invitation to attend Court.'

Somerset stared. 'I knew that Zachary was well established in French high society but I did not realise that you . . .'

'I have a friend there,' Cloverella replied casually. 'Comte Lucien Harfleur is my contact.'

'Harfleur? Was he not part of the Admiral's delegation last summer?'

'Yes, the same.'

'Then how . . .'

'He came to see Zachary on behalf of the King. François wanted his horoscope cast and I offered to do it in Zachary's absence.' Cloverella's dark brows drew together. 'It was not easy. You see, I foresaw the French King's death.'

'What did you do? What *do* you do in those circumstances?'

'In that particular event I said nothing. In other cases it depends entirely on the facts. But it taught me one thing, Ned.'

'And what is that?'

'Never again to read for friends or family. I can see now that it is far too dangerous.'

Somerset nodded wisely, suddenly in no need to hurry home, longing to spend hours away from his duties talking with Cloverella about the past.

'Do you remember our wishes on Merlin's Mound?' he asked.

'Yes, they all came true, more or less.'

'Did they?'

'Jane wished to be Queen, if you recall, and you, Ned, looked all around you and said you would like to own everything you saw.'

'But I don't.' Somerset chuckled. 'How could I?'

'You are Lord Protector, my dear. The nearest thing to being a King there could possibly be. In a way you own the realm, acting on His Grace's behalf.'

Edward looked reflective. 'I had not thought of it quite like that. But what of Thomas?'

'He asked to love many women . . .'

'He's done that all right!'

'. . . and end by marrying the highest in the land.'

Somerset frowned. 'Hmm! It would never surprise me if he made a play for Princess Mary, though even he could hardly think such an incompatible union would ever work.'

Cloverella's eyes twinkled. 'The wonderful thing about Thomas is that one can never tell what he's going to do next.'

Edward's face did not give a corresponding smile. 'These days, and in his elevated position, that characteristic has lost a great deal of its charm.'

'You are angry with him, Ned! Why?'

'He's too . . .' The Protector sought for the word and found, '. . . restless. He moves around as if there's something at his heels, egging him on to outdo not only himself but everyone around him. He worries me.'

Just for a moment Cloverella's mouth looked pinched. 'Be kind to him, Ned, for the sake of the family. You must always remember that Thomas is . . . just Thomas.'

Somerset changed the subject. 'And what was your wish, sweetheart? I cannot recall after all these years.'

'I wished for knowledge, for a greater understanding of supernature.'

'And has it been granted to you?'

'Oh yes, I think so. There is still a lifetime's work ahead of me but with Zachary's help and also through taking his place in his absence, I have grown.'

'In every way. You have become a considerable woman, Cloverella. I think you will be well received by France's new king. But be careful. There is only an uneasy peace between our two countries. I would not like you to get caught up in anything that might prove dangerous.'

'I have the Comte to protect me,' answered Cloverella, smiling.

'It was to the Count that I was, in part, referring,' said Edward grandly, as only a Lord Protector could, and was gratified to see Cloverella's cheeks turn a sparkling pink as she looked away from him.

Later that night – Edward still deep in conversation with Cloverella, the oarsmen asleep in the barge, Anne Somerset dreaming in Chester Place – the Lord Admiral of England took the dangerous road from Chelsea village to the Dower House. Beneath the midnight moon he galloped through the fields, fording the

430

stream at Blandels Bridge, a favourite haunt of highwaymen and footpads, and rode the path to where the wall of the house ran down into the fields. There he dismounted and walked his horse to the postern gate, at which place his porteress, as Katherine had termed herself, awaited him. As promised, Thomas had sent her word in advance and now, despite the fact that midnight had struck, she was there.

'Oh darling,' she said and flew towards him even before he had finished tethering his mount.

They stood in silence beneath a distant and dainty moon, locked in an embrace that said more than words. The very essence of Katherine seemed to enter into Thomas at that moment so that he imagined a joining of spirits. He felt that he, too, had suffered what she had done, knew well the agony of a child sold to and abused by an indecent old bridegroom, the drudgery of a woman forced to nurse elderly husbands, the terror of a queen who walked in fear. All the good in him, everything decent and fine in his character, surfaced like an anthem.

'I love you,' he said.

All her life, Katherine knew she had been two people, all the undisciplined joyful part of her contained within a butterfly, a butterfly who had been bruised and hurt, whose wings had been ripped off cruelly, but who had grown more and flown again. And now the butterfly consumed the meek earnest little mouse, the pious little woman who prayed a great deal and thought too much. It simply opened its rainbow wings and folded in the milksop, who gave a sigh and passed away without pain.

'I love you too,' she answered.

The moon was too delicate, too kind, to reveal the silvered lovers who lay beneath the canopy of a weeping willow, making love with solemnity, like priest and priestess pledging their faith. It was ritually done, without haste of any kind, the tidal wave an affirmation, the troth that followed it sacredly pledged.

'You promised me two months,' said Thomas, telling a falsehood without caring. 'But I want you to break that vow.'

'What must I do?' asked Katherine, every part of her in harmony with her lover and the night.

'You must retain the figure two but change the time scale.'

'*You* want to wait two years?' asked Katherine in horror, the idea now beyond contemplation.

'Two days,' answered Tom, and chuckled. 'I want to be married in two days' time, pretty Kate.'

'But Tom, by whom? And what of the future? To act without the Council or Protector's permission is surely dangerous.'

'Not so dangerous as leaving you a widow a moment longer in this wicked world of men. Cranmer will marry us if you ask him nicely, you and he are old friends. As for permission, I will get the King's, just you wait and see. He is my nephew after all.'

'But your brother will be furious!'

'Prick 'im,' said Tom irritably. 'I have not come this far in the world nor reached the age I have to ask my brother's permission every time I want to fart.'

'Surely you will not do that at our wedding?' answered Katherine, laughing despite herself.

'Of course not. Now, let me hear your answer. Putting aside all the obstacles, will you marry me the day after tomorrow?'

'But . . .'

'I don't want to hear but,' said Tom firmly, putting his fingers to her lips. 'Please say yes, Kate. Trust me to take care of the difficulties.'

'But I have nothing to wear.'

'Then get something. Will you marry me?'

'I think so. Yes, perhaps I will.'

'I'm very pleased to hear it,' said the Lord Admiral tartly. 'At last I can achieve my ambition.'

'And what is that pray?' asked Katherine, all light heart and amusement.

'To be respectable. An old married man.'

And with that almost impossible wish the bargain between them was finally sealed.

Because of the warm weather and consequent fear of the plague, the King and his entourage had removed themselves to Hampton Court, whose splendid grounds offered every kind of amenity to a nine-year-old boy intent on enjoying himself on a fine day in early summer. There was the river for swimming or boating, the gardens for strolling, the butts for archery practice, the parkland for riding. Any one of these pleasures would have been acceptable to Edward Tudor who stood, gloomily staring out of the window, wishing that he had not agreed to an audience with his favourite uncle or that he

432

was somebody else, the granting of either request equally welcome.

Yet it was at moments like these that the King sensed within himself an innate pomposity, for even as he thought how exciting it would be to be an urchin boy, a dirty-faced mudlark, he shrank from the very idea of not understanding Latin, not being able to discuss the Classics. In many ways the poor wretch was not happy with the child produced by the tutors and scholars with whom he had been placed since birth, yet he was impotent, unable to break free from the rigid mould they had created for him.

He wondered, even while he watched the glittering river, what Lord Seymour wanted of him and if it could have anything to do with the ridiculous questions John Fowler kept asking. Whom should his uncle marry, would this one be suitable, what about that one? The King felt he had given his answers clearly enough already; the Lady Anne or the Princess Mary, if Thomas could change his sister's religion. But not content, Fowler had persisted. What would His Grace say to a match between Lord Seymour and the Dowager Queen.

'Nothing,' Edward had answered in exasperation. 'I would say nothing.'

'Then Your Grace would have no objection?'

Edward could remember that he had been tired and bored at the same time. 'Of course I wouldn't,' he had answered scornfully. 'Why should I? It's as good an idea as any of his madcap schemes.'

That had put paid to it at the time but then, from a clear sky, the Lord Admiral had suddenly requested a private audience.

'Christ's blood,' said the King now, pressing his nose against the glass. 'God's holy passion.'

Edward rarely swore, so felt better for the oath and turned back to look into the room, only to see that the usual rigmarole surrounding a private audience had begun. Obviously the King's uncle had arrived at the Palace and presented himself at the privy chamber where a page had taken the message to a gentleman usher who, in his turn, had passed it on to one of the gentlemen-in-waiting, one of whom was now approaching the place where the boy-King stood.

Making a deep reverence, the young nobleman said shrilly, 'The Lord High Admiral, Baron Seymour of Sudeley, is here to see Your Grace at Your Grace's pleasure. May I know Your Grace's wishes in this?'

433

'Show him in,' answered Edward loftily. 'We will give him audience. And let the word be spread that we will speak with our uncle in private.'

There was a general shuffling of feet as the room cleared and then a voice from the doorway, announcing Thomas Seymour by all his titles was interrupted with, 'If you could inform His Grace that his sailor uncle is here I think that might suffice.'

Edward looked down his nose, a trick of his when alarmed. Should he laugh as he would like, or should he look askance? In the end he did neither, standing mutely and a little foolishly – or so he thought – as his uncle came towards him.

Seymour bowed deeply, his hat sweeping off and brushing his nephew's foot. 'Sire, as I am the Admiral I wondered if it might be in order that we hold this audience upon the river. It is, when all is said, hot work indoors today.'

He stood upright, very straightfaced, though Edward could have sworn he detected a wink about Thomas's eye. With a flash of inspiration the King scored a point.

'Lord Uncle, we have a better plan. First tell us quickly why you are here, without cackle as you would say, and then we give you leave to take us upon the river.'

He's learning, thought Tom, by God he's learning.

'Very well, Your Grace,' he answered briskly, 'I am here to inform Your Grace that I have concurred with your wishes.'

'Wishes?' Edward wrinkled both brow and nose. 'What wishes?'

'Your wish, expressed to me via John Fowler, that I should marry the Dowager Queen Katherine.'

The boy looked positively amazed. 'Did we wish that?'

'I believe, Sir, that you told him it was a good idea.'

The King realised with a thrill of horror that he had been misquoted but that to say so would be downright insulting.

'Well, we . . .' he muttered.

Thomas Seymour dropped on one knee. 'Then I crave the blessing of the King's Majesty. I have done as you have bidden. The Dowager Queen and I are now husband and wife.'

'You took our remarks very literally, Lord Uncle,' said Edward, with a certain acerbity.

'Your slightest wish is my command, Your Grace.' Thomas stood up again. 'Now what say you to the river, Sire? I have a new model sailing boat, a replica of my own in the fleet.'

Edward extended a small pale hand. 'We would wish to see it.'

Thomas, smiling broadly, kissed the little fingers then clasped them firmly in his own. 'Then come with me, Majesty,' he said, and with that the two of them left the stuffy confines of the Palace and ran, laughing, through the gardens and down towards the Thames.

# Chapter Thirty-Six

THROUGH THE DOOR OF THE Chelsea Dower House, being opened amidst a royal fanfare from the King's trumpeters, came the wonderful smell of spice, of cooking, of Christmas. Just for a second the boy-King paused in the entrance, sniffing, letting his thoughts wander to the mother who had died when he had been a few days old. If she had lived there would have been family Christmases every year, not the formal occasions he had spent with his father and a procession of stepmothers, or the others when he had remained in his own household, only having his sisters for company. For Jane had left him lonely, a strange little boy, very solemn and serious, happiness being something almost unknown to him.

But now at least he was smiling as his favourite stepmother curtsied to him and invited him into the house. Very formally the King bowed, accepted, and walked into the great hall to see all his family, with the exception of the Protector and his wife, bowing and curtseying to him. Without exception their eyes twinkled and the boy felt a moment of intense pleasure, secure in the thought that so many people loved him.

It was Elizabeth who rushed to kiss him on the cheek and Edward thought how elegant she looked, pale as snow yet clothed in scarlet, like holly and mistletoe, her russet hair gleaming beneath her hood. Uncle Thomas was not far behind her, tall and dashing, his bright eyes permanently smiling as if he secretly laughed at the world. The King found him fractionally disconcerting.

This Christmas being the first for Edward as sovereign, he had copied his father in everything, keeping his celebrations at Greenwich and inviting all his family to attend him on Christmas Day, which they had done in rather a strained atmosphere.

During the twelve days the King had left the Palace twice, to go

436

to a banquet given by his other uncle at Chester Place, and now to come to the Dower House. And here Edward knew already it was going to be lighthearted, gay, whereas with the Lord Protector he had felt awkward, the Duchess fawning over him to such an extent that the child had felt near to screaming. The presence of two amusing boys, distant kin to Somerset, had been the only redeeming feature. Though respectful and polite, they had obviously seen Edward very much as a contemporary and before the feast had shown him some good card tricks, while the younger of the two, Sylvanus, had taken the King on as a competitor in the butts. All of this had made the day worthwhile and Edward had extended an invitation to the lads to attend him at Greenwich, an invitation which his uncle had accepted with alacrity on their behalf.

But now his elderly half-sister Mary, who did not truly approve of her stepmother's rapid re-marriage, but was keeping part of her Christmas in Chelsea for the sake of their old friendship, was coming to kiss him too. Edward felt he was truly amongst kinfolk, much more so than at Greenwich when the Queen Dowager and the Duchess of Somerset had glared at one another in a most un-Christian manner. The only person absent from this Chelsea family gathering was his pretty cousin Jane Grey, the girl having returned to her home for Christmas. Like Elizabeth, Jane had been put into the care of the Queen Dowager to further her education.

'What is your pleasure, Your Grace, for you are voted Lord of Misrule today?' Elizabeth was calling, looking as if she would whirl him off his feet at any second, hovering over him like a flame in her gallant red dress, smiling her special smile.

'I should like to dance with you, dear sister,' the boy said politely, knowing that she was longing to jig away and as Lord of Misrule it was up to him to organise events.

'Then let it be a chain dance, Your Grace,' the Admiral put in. 'One where we change partners.'

Edward nodded agreement, the musicians struck up, and friends and family in the great hall began to cavort enthusiastically, Edward dancing with his sister then bowing stiffly before the Queen Dowager, who smiled at him kindly and went prancing away with him despite the difference in their heights.

Edward had never been sure in the end whether he had really suggested his Uncle Thomas should marry her or not. John Fowler had assured him again and again that it had been the King's idea all along. To the point that Edward had written to Katherine, 'We thank you heartily, not only for the gentle acceptation of our suite moved unto you, but also for the loving accomplishment of the same, wherein you have declared a desire to gratify us.' But he had still not been certain.

The news of the secret marriage between the Queen Dowager and the Lord High Admiral had caused a furore and the Lord Protector had reacted savagely, though not half as badly as his wife, who had been seen to seethe. Anne Somerset had always disliked Katherine, considering her common and *nouveau*. She had resented being the Queen's train bearer during the King's lifetime and now the Duchess was indignant that Katherine took precedence over her.

It had been Anne who had been the instigator of the scheme to keep the Queen's jewels, given to Katherine Parr by Henry and claimed by her as her own, though Somerset maintained they were Crown property. There had been and still was bitter wrangling over the gems, Thomas vehemently siding with his wife. For the first time open animosity between the brothers had been noticed, and the King, yet again, had been approached to intercede, John Fowler acting as go-between. Edward had felt a sudden exasperation with both his uncles but had been willing to assist Thomas, who always gave him extra pocket money when he was helpful, whereas the Protector kept him horribly short.

Now Edward bowed to Katherine and changed partners to dance with Mary, who at thirty-one was old enough to be his mother and who seemed remote and ancient to the boy. It was his other sister, whirling in the arms of Uncle Thomas and glittering with some inner excitement of her own, to whom the King felt truly close. Elizabeth and the Admiral were laughing as they danced past and Edward thought curiously that his uncle must be feeling the heat, for a sweat beaded his brow.

'Can we play Catch?' called one of the children present, and shrieked with delight as Elizabeth announced that she would be Catcher and everyone was to watch out. She fled the length of the hall, her arms outstretched while the others screamed and ran from her. But the Admiral did not run quite fast enough and ended by being caught by the elbow and held firmly, looking down into the upturned face of the laughing girl and smiling so much that eventually her eyes fluttered away and would not meet his. Edward saw colour rush into Elizabeth's pale cheeks, then wondered why she suddenly looked back at his uncle and tilted her eyes.

Uncle Thomas was not a very good Catcher for, predictably Edward thought, he seized hold of his wife and gave her a smacking kiss. After that Katherine came in pursuit of the King and he in his turn caught one of the children. Everyone was very breathless and glad to rest and have more to drink before the next game.

All the time they had danced and played, the beautiful smells from the kitchens had wafted ever more strongly until at last, with the light outside dimming but all the candles in their holders making a wonderful glow within, the great table was brought in and set and the assembled company took their places, the King at the head with his stepmother on one hand and his elder sister at the other, all watching as the banquet was carried in.

It was a culinary triumph for Katherine, or so Edward believed, feasting his eyes on two grinning boars' heads and a great assortment of poultry, all beautifully presented, many sewn back into their plumage; a particularly effective sight with the swans who appeared to be swimming on their trenchers, tricked out with blue decoration to look like water.

The wine flowed and the Queen Dowager gazed down her table with satisfaction, the first Christmas since childhood when she had been truly happy, married to a man she adored, honoured and respected by her stepchildren. All that she wanted now, both to seal her marriage and crown her joy, was to conceive and bear a child of her own, though sometimes Katherine feared she might be barren stock. She had never been pregnant, but comforted herself with the fact that her husbands had been old and past their best, though when she had married Lord Seymour she had been accused of marrying again so quickly that if there had been a child no one would have known if it had been fathered by Henry or Thomas. But the charge was ridiculous and Katherine knew it, though she had held her peace.

Now she looked the length of her board to where Thomas, a little drunk but all the more attractive and rakish for it, sat at the other end between Elizabeth and the young and widowed Duchess of Suffolk. He was showing off, capturing the attention of the two girls as he described some exploit, some act of daring.

They are entranced by him, thought Katherine, and smiled to herself, loving him all the more for his attractive ways.

439

The meal proceeded, Elizabeth eating sparsely as was her custom.

Will she ever fatten up? her stepmother wondered and also thought it was high time the girl was visited by the monthly flux. The King, however, despite his small physique, was eating well, tucking into mince pies and sweetmeats, enjoying himself thoroughly.

'If Your Grace would care to spend the night at Chelsea?' Katherine asked tentatively, turning towards him with a smile.

'We should like that very much,' he answered enthusiastically and she could have hugged him to her heart, poor vulnerable thing, weighted down with responsibilities and only allowed to be a child on rare occasions like these.

'Then let the Christmas songs be sung,' she called, 'His Grace will favour us with his presence tonight.'

'Hooray,' shouted Elizabeth wildly and Edward raised his glass to her.

They danced again when the table was cleared, and watched the Mummers and played Forfeits, but eventually all grew weary. The children nodded in the firelight and the King fell asleep with his head in Katherine's lap. His servants carried him gently to bed and he hardly woke as they tucked him in. Even the mercurial Elizabeth at last began to yawn, and it was then that Mary and the Duchess of Suffolk both stood and said they begged leave to retire. With the three girls gone and the other adults away to see to their children, only the Queen and the Admiral were left to sit by the flames, their arms around each other, comfortably seeing the day come to an end.

'A wonderful Christmas,' said Thomas softly, 'thank you, pretty Kate.' He kissed her ear. 'As soon as the flames burn lower I shall take you to bed. I long to stretch out beside you, to fall asleep gently, looking at your face.'

She smiled at him serenely. 'Thank you for all you do for me.'

'I do nothing,' answered Tom. 'It is you who makes life so sweet.'

They climbed the staircase slowly, making for their chamber, and then got into bed, cuddled one another, and slept straight away. But not far away from them, in the silence of her own room, Elizabeth stared at the ceiling by the light of a wintry moon.

From the top of her head to the soles of her feet she ached with wanting Thomas Seymour, convinced of her power over him, sure that he wanted her too. He had hardly left her alone since the marriage. Almost every morning while Elizabeth still lay in bed, he

440

would come into her bedroom, dressed in his own nightclothes, and tickle and tease her, smacking his hand familiarly across her buttocks and sometimes letting it linger a moment too long.

Poor Kate, thought Elizabeth, she thinks it all horse play but she hasn't seen the look in his eye, felt the touch of his hands. He desires me desperately, as I desire him.

He disguised it cleverly though, romping with the maidens of the household, pulling Katherine into the games whenever he could. But there could be no doubt about his motives. The Lord Admiral longed for Elizabeth, wanted to lie with her in naked bed.

Elizabeth sat up straight, her eyes wide. Her wretched body still hung on to girlhood and recently when she had run her hands over her privy parts it had seemed to her all was not as it should be. But how could she be sure? She did not undress before others, did not know exactly what she ought to be like. Elizabeth longed to confide in her stepmother but drew back from such a step. If there were anything anatomically incorrect the last person she dare mention it to would be Katherine, who just might tell her husband. The girl felt that if Thomas were to think her imperfect she would die of shame.

Unable to sleep, Elizabeth got out of bed and crossed to her window, pulling back the hangings and looking out on a frosty night. Eaten by guilt, she felt flushed and over-warm, and thought she would like to race round the gardens in the moonlight until she grew cold. But of course she could do no such wild thing, instead getting respectably back into bed and cuddling her bolster, pretending it was Thomas Seymour and that she was surrendering her virginity to him. And on that point Elizabeth wondered if she dared ask Kat Ashley about herself and what she feared, but, even as it went through her mind, decided against such a course. For the best way to keep a secret without doubt, was to tell nobody. It was a life's plan that Elizabeth intended to follow strictly.

'I really think,' said Anne Somerset furiously, 'that something serious will have to be done about those two.'

'Umm?' answered her husband, not listening.

'That conceited bitch Parr and your reprobate brother. It seems to me they win every hand. Here we are, with no adequate home, living in cramped conditions with another babe on the way, while they have sent an army of workmen to Sudeley Castle which is now, or so I am reliably informed, completely restored to its former glory

441

and newly furnished into the bargain. So Madam is content at last and moves down there next week with her whole retinue; the Princess, Jane Grey, ladies, maids-of-honour, a household over one hundred and twenty strong, to say nothing of yeomen of the guard. You would think it is she who is married to the Lord Protector, not I. And to crown it all, she's pregnant. I think that woman casts spells. She can't put a foot wrong. In future I shall refuse point blank to carry her beastly train.'

The Protector nodded sympathetically. 'It is true that Somerset House is taking an inordinate amount of time to build, but you did want a palace, sweetheart.'

'Yes, and while I wait for it, Katherine goes to live in a castle.'

'It is indeed very galling.'

'Galling!' shrieked Anne, jumping to her feet. 'It is sickening.'

The Protector and his wife looked at one another unhappily. While Katherine got on her nerves, so did Thomas get on his. It was becoming generally known that his brother, in his role as Lord Admiral, associated with pirates. Last spring, when Thomas had gone to sea with a fleet to capture Thompson, a blackguard who operated around Calais, the whole thing had ended with the Admiral and the pirate striking a bargain. Thompson's base was the Scilly Isles and Lord Seymour had not only allowed him to continue to harbour there but had bought the Scillies from the Blanchminster family, with Lundy Island to boot. Now the Isles were a haven for Thompson and for any other pirate who cared to use them, provided they shared their plunder with the Lord High Admiral!

If a charge of piracy is brought against him, Edward thought wretchedly, Thomas will have to answer for his actions himself. I will be powerless to help.

He sighed loudly and turned his attention back to Anne who had now worked herself into a full-blown rage and was weeping loudly.

'It simply isn't fair,' she was sobbing. 'We all know what he is like, an unprincipled rogue and a womaniser. It is you, Ned, who do all the hard work, who try to bring about reforms, and what do you get out of it? Trouble and grief, while Thomas sails through life as if it were all a great joke.'

'Yes,' answered the Protector grimly, and for a moment knew what it was to envy someone. On his shoulders lay the terrible burden of a troubled kingdom, torn with religious strife and economic disorder. Henry VII's legacy to his country had been a full treasury, a state of peace abroad and domestic unity. His son, Henry VIII, left behind him empty coffers, a nation with no friends and civil unrest. This had been the task that Edward Seymour had so bravely undertaken on behalf of his nephew.

But it was true, Thomas had a fine life. Handsome, carefree, married to a woman who worshipped him, who was rich as well as pretty, everything about the Protector's brother seemed to speak of charm and gaiety. And now he was taking up residence in a splendid Gloucestershire castle, refurbished and modernised, its stately grounds restocked with trees and flowers and rare birds. It was no small wonder that, just for a moment, the Protector wished they could change places.

He briskly lost his temper with his wife, the only way to overcome such negative emotions. 'Do stop whimpering,' Ned said crossly. 'When Somerset House is built it will be as fine as Sudeley, if not finer. And as for Thomas, he runs too many risks. One day, if he does not watch his step, he will get the wrong side of somebody important. So meanwhile, Anne, be quiet. You are making me annoyed.'

It was so unusual for him to criticise her that the Duchess stared at him in astonishment. 'How dare you speak to me like that when I am pregnant?'

'I doubt my words will affect you, my dear. I would think you could do far more harm by straining yourself to fever pitch.'

'You are obviously on their side,' hissed the Duchess furiously. 'It is perfectly clear that in some terrible way they have won you over. I see that I may no longer trust you with my confidences.'

'Christ's holy passion,' roared the Protector, 'you are heating my blood. I'll say good day to you, Madam, before you push me too far.'

And with that he slammed from the room, called Jasper and Sylvanus from the boys' quarters, and made for the Palace of Whitehall armed with bows and arrows, board games and cards, to give the King a cheerful and day-long surprise.

The very first glimpse of Sudeley Castle was one to take the breath away, or so thought Elizabeth, who had remained in Chelsea while Tom and Katherine had been wrangling with builders and

443

decorators, and not seen the place till this moment of arrival. Set in its own rolling parkland, just beyond the Gloucestershire village of Winchcombe, the walls looked mellow, almost amber, in the late winter sunshine, reflecting all the beauty of very old brick. There had been a house on the site long before the Norman Conquest, all trace of which original had long since vanished. But another Admiral of the Fleet, Ralph le Boteler, who had fought in the French wars under Henry V and VI, had rebuilt Sudeley with his spoils. Unfortunately, this Admiral had been on the side of the Lancastrians during the Wars of the Roses, and had been forced to sell his castle to King Edward IV when the Yorkists had triumphed, so that Sudeley had then reverted to the Crown.

It had been Boteler's castle, with its glorious banqueting hall, its towers and barbican, which the Seymours had set about restoring but, to add greater size to the original, new quarters had been built beside the castle in the shape of a square, joined on to it by the old hall, which had been badly ruined. It was here, in the east wing, that Tom and Katherine were to have their bedroom, and it was here that a nursery for the new baby had been lovingly prepared. The rest of Katherine's retinue, with the exception of her principal ladies, some three hundred people in all, were to dwell in the other wings.

As the vast cavalcade drew nearer the restored building, everyone stared in wonderment. What had once been a fortified castle had been most cleverly transformed into a gracious dwelling, gentle and mature, lulled by the song of birds, shaded by illustrious trees which had withstood the passage of centuries. Over the sweeping lawns peacocks, both white and standard, strutted and called, while on the moat, now partially blocked off, swans stretched their feathers in the pale gold sunshine.

'What a graceful place,' said Elizabeth spontaneously and Tom, who was riding beside her – Katherine being in a litter because of her condition – gave her an unreadable glance. Beneath those spectacular eyes, the girl felt herself growing warm and looked away, but too late! He had already put out his hand and tugged a long wisp of red-gold hair which had fallen out of her hat and trailed down over her shoulders.

'Fox hair,' he whispered, 'fox hair for a little vixen.'

Elizabeth felt she could weep with longing and with anxiety; anxiety that she might not be quite as other women and thus unable to satisfy the desire that burned in her so uncontrollably.

444

She slanted her eyes at him. 'Vixens have teeth, my Lord.'

'Aye, and so do dog foxes. Teeth that sink into unsuspecting little girls.'

'Unsuspecting?' repeated Elizabeth, then nudged her horse on to move to the front of the procession, tantalisingly giving him one last glance over her shoulder as she went.

She drew abreast with the gentlemen-at-arms who were clattering into the quadrangle created by building new wings on to the restored but original hall, part of a castle practically rebuilt to help make room for a household of such magnificence.

'How very grand it all is,' said Elizabeth to Katherine's steward, who was rapidly riding to the front of the cavalcade to ensure the staff already in residence were ready to receive the Queen and the Admiral.

He gave her a cool look, or so she thought, and Elizabeth found herself wondering how much he knew about the romps that she and Thomas had indulged in at the Dower House. Had Kat Ashley, who had taken the Admiral to task over his behaviour, been speaking out of turn? Did he know that Tom had tried to kiss her while she was still in bed or, if she was asleep, had put back the curtains to wake her, so that Elizabeth had been forced to retreat up the bed away from him?

Thinking of it like that it sounded sordid. And so it is, thought Elizabeth in a horrible moment of truth. But I want him. My body may be a child's but I still want him.

Feeling that the steward was looking at her even more strangely, Elizabeth dismounted and flung angrily through the great oaken door on her immediate right, finding herself in the restored hall, one of the most ancient parts of the original castle. Her stepmother stood waiting for her and Elizabeth gaped astonished, wondering by what means Katherine could have come from the middle of the cavalcade and was now within doors.

'Your Grace,' she said and curtsied.

Katherine ignored the intruder, staring straight in front of her like a sleepwalker. Elizabeth's blood felt like ice within her veins and every hackle on her body rose. She stood petrified, drenched in freezing sweat, as Katherine glided right past her, the Queen's eyes never moving, still fixed in that strange motionless stare.

'Christ have mercy!' whispered Elizabeth and plunged towards the door, only to see the Queen turn and give her one terrible, fearful glance before she, too, stepped into the courtyard. Gasping for air, the girl rushed out to find that the quadrangle was filling with lively noisy people who, quite spontaneously, took off their hats as the litter bearing Katherine Seymour came into view. And though it was not possible, *there* was the Queen, beaming with happiness, smiling at her husband as he lifted her down to stand beside him.

The steward stepped forward saying, 'On behalf of us all, Your Grace, we bid you welcome to Sudeley Castle and wish you and the Lord Admiral many happy years here,' while everybody cheered again.

Katherine raised her hand. 'Thank you,' she said. 'I know that we are all going to be happy in this lovely place.' She already had Jane Grey beside her but now she searched the crowd for Elizabeth. 'My dear,' she called gaily, 'come and be with me. I want the family together as we make our first entrance into Sudeley. Come.'

Katherine extended her hand but Elizabeth could already feel every drop of blood draining from her head as everything around her became a black void and she dropped limply onto the flagstones beneath her feet.

## Chapter Thirty-Seven

TO KATHERINE, SO CONTENTED that sometimes she sang to herself from the moment she rose until the moment she wearily, but very pleasantly, got into bed, the year 1548 was the happiest she had ever known. In February she had moved permanently, though she still visited her manors of Chelsea and Hanworth, into Sudeley Castle. And though Thomas was absent a good deal, about his affairs as Admiral, the Queen Dowager was never lonely.

Always within calling distance were her two charges; the ivory-faced Elizabeth, glittering and withdrawn, more introverted than before to Katherine, though still as fierce and boisterous with the others; the gentle Jane Grey, daughter of the Marquess of Dorset and Frances Brandon, whose mother had been Henry VIII's sister. It was an unwritten understanding that Jane only remained with Katherine, now that the Queen had married Lord Seymour, to be groomed as a bride for her cousin King Edward. Thomas, in fact, had been given the girl as ward in exchange for a fee which he was to pay Lord Dorset on the signing of a marriage contract between Jane and Edward. Katherine did not like to think about this arrangement too much, smacking as it did of the sale of the child by her father.

For these days she felt drawn to Jane, who sympathised with Katherine's pregnancy, laying her hand on the Queen's extending belly to see if the infant therein was dancing, whereas Elizabeth would have none of it, merely extending the normal courtesies and leaving the matter there. She seemed to have scant interest in the 'little knave' as Tom and Katherine had lovingly nicknamed the unborn child.

Though the weather was still cold, Katherine walked a great deal, admiring the chilling bravery of the snowdrops, exclaiming at the brilliant colours of the crocuses in the woods. Somehow they

447

reminded her of Elizabeth who was dressing resplendently at present, choosing all the vivid purples and whites of flowers to show off the colour of her extraordinary hair.

Another routine was to visit chapel where twice a day prayers were said for the Queen's safe delivery. Since taking up residence in Sudeley, Katherine had surrounded herself with those learned clerics who practised the reformed religion, her chaplain being the spiritual leader, Miles Coverdale. She punctiliously attended both services, her cheerful song changed to an anthem, and though Jane accompanied Katherine to both, Elizabeth came only to one and Thomas to none.

'I pray privately,' he had answered when Katherine had remonstrated with him. 'You've enough people to talk to God for you without me.'

There had been no arguing, for he would never take her seriously when she was angry, instead winking a blue eye and coming after her like a grizzly bear, roaring, with outstretched arms ready to hug her. Then he would put his lips to her belly and kiss the little knave. Katherine considered him the most loving and lovable man in the world, his arrant scampishness one of his most endearing qualities.

It was at times like this that she resented the sudden intrusion of Elizabeth, whose long pale face would appear at the door and put an end to the Queen's loveplay. The thought that the girl was doing it on purpose had crossed Katherine's mind more than once, and she had remembered the dark eyes of Anne Boleyn, similar to Elizabeth's in many ways, and how they would slant and stare at whoever it was she wanted to attract, just as Elizabeth's did at Thomas. A strange suspicion began to grow like a canker right at the very back of Katherine's mind.

The flowers in the woods changed to daffodils and the ancient trees were full of nesting birds. Katherine, walking more than ever now the weather was warmer, thought she had never enjoyed anything as much as the change of seasons at the castle. The month of her arrival had seen snowflakes fall and she had looked out of the magnificent oriel window in the medieval banqueting hall, heavily restored under her direction, and seen the miracle of snow lying beneath ancient castle walls. Within it had been warm, the fire blazing in the vast grate, and half closing her eyes Katherine had pretended she had gone back in time; that her huge retinue, all chattering and laughing like monkeys, were dressed in earlier clothes, had fought at Agincourt, had loved and cursed and sweated in another age.

That fancy had taken her again when the woods had borne their fine tracery of spring and she had heard the first cuckoo give his call. Had other women, budding with child, heard that same sweet, silly sound? Did all time go round and round in a never-ending circle?

These thoughts re-echoed on Passion Sunday, the fifth in Lent as Easter was late, when Mary Odell, one of Katherine's favourite and closest ladies, insisted on making Passion Dock pudding, a tradition centuries old. In a flurry of excitement all the younger girls rushed out to pick dock leaves and enjoin the gardeners to pull up nettles, while Katherine sat in the April sunshine watching them, her hand resting on her ripening body. She was just over three months pregnant and so far the little knave had not moved, a disappointment to Jane Grey who longed for that moment to happen.

As the Queen sat enjoying the warmth in her splendid knot garden, Lady Tyrwhit, one of the multitude of Katherine's stepdaughters who had now come into her service, went through the yew walk, accompanied by Elizabeth, and a snatch of their conversation drifted towards the Queen.

'. . . speak my mind whoever you might be,' Lady Tyrwhit was saying.

'. . . report you to the Queen Dowager for the common upstart you are,' came Elizabeth's angry reply.

Katherine sat upright on her stone seat, aware that they could not see her unless she stood, and suddenly, horribly, curious.

'I've watched you,' Lady Tyrwhit went on. 'I've watched you look at *him*. You're a disgrace, Madam.'

'How dare you,' the girl answered furiously. 'I am a Princess of the Blood and I will not be spoken to like that.'

'I care nothing,' Lady Tyrwhit said roundly. 'Your behaviour is a scandal, a . . .'

They were going out of earshot and Katherine was left in turmoil. Who was this man at whom Elizabeth was supposed to gaze so scandalously? And then a memory came back to the Queen, a memory of a silly incident in the garden at Hanworth, when Elizabeth for some childish reason of her own had insisted on wearing a black dress.

'You look terrible in that abomination,' Tom had said, and had

449

chased the girl with a pair of shears snatched from a gardener, until she had sought refuge in Katherine's arms, though Tom, nothing daunted, had cut the offending garment off her back. Elizabeth, squirming and squealing, had stood in her underwear and given him such a look when he had finished, a look which Katherine would never forget. Everything had been in it; hatred for ruining her clothes, adoration for being the reprehensible rake he was, and something else. At the time the Queen had been too preoccupied to pursue it further but now she recognised exactly what else had been present. That child, that girl of thirteen, had looked at Katherine's husband with lust.

The Queen went cold in the sunshine. How could she have been such a fool? She herself had been married at thirteen; beaten and raped, but married. She had made the great mistake of thinking Elizabeth a child when all the time a woman stood there, a thin boyish woman admittedly, but still a woman.

'Oh my God!' said Katherine aloud.

There was a distant shout and Mary Odell came running into the garden, an apron held up in front of her full of dock leaves.

'Oh Your Grace,' she said, panting straight up to the Queen and dropping a curtsey, 'it's been such fun. Look, we've gathered masses of leaves. Will you come to the kitchens and help us prepare?'

Katherine stood up slowly, suddenly feeling her age. She was in her thirty-fifth year, Elizabeth in her fifteenth; the gap between them yawned like a black-mouthed chasm.

'And what is this pudding supposed to do once it is baked?' she asked with a little laugh. 'Does it contain the secret of eternal youth?'

Mary Odell flashed a smile, sunny as summer. 'It makes your true love faithful if he eats some too.'

'Then save a piece for the Lord Admiral,' answered Katherine, without thinking.

Mary looked at her ingenuously. 'I should not have thought he would need it, Madam.'

'No?' said the Queen thoughtfully. 'Perhaps you are right Mary. Perhaps you are right after all.'

Rather thankfully Edward, King of England, looked at the line of feet spread out before him, considered the fact that he was ten years

450

old, and gave a wry smile. He was at St Paul's and it was Maundy Thursday, and in memory of Christ washing the feet of his disciples at the Last Supper, it was tradition that the monarch should bathe the feet of as many paupers as he had years of age.

Only ten for me, thought Edward gleefully. But I'll wager the Lord Protector takes all day to do his!

For people other than the King were also involved in this ceremony, bishops and great personages must do likewise, and the Duke of Somerset, not in his best clothes Edward noted with amusement, was next in line.

Throughout most of last year and during this as well, the boy-King's irritation with the Seymour brothers had been rankling like a prickle in his shoe. Much as he wanted to have goodwill towards them, much as he wanted to be fair, to like them both equally, Edward was finding it more and more difficult.

It now seemed reasonably clear to the King that Uncle Thomas, who was more liberal than ever with sums of pocket money, was anxious to limit the powers of Uncle Edward, who was not. Only last November the Admiral had come to the King with a draft bill suggesting that Thomas should become Governor of the King's Person, a separate entity from the Protector. But the King had been in no mood to accept. The Duke of Somerset, stingy though he may be, had fought gallantly in Scotland during the summer, when the militant Scotsmen, aided by their French allies, refused to honour a treaty which bound their baby Queen Mary in marriage to Edward Tudor. As a result it had not seemed right to the boy to treat the hero Protector in a cavalier manner. The Lord Admiral had had his first taste of the King's stubborness as Edward had firmly said, 'No.'

Since that time the King knew, quite certainly, that the Admiral had been attempting to get various bills through the Lords limiting the Protector's power. And then there was the vexed question of the Queen Dowager's jewels, the dispute over which still dragged on. Edward had sat at his desk with all its lovely secret compartments full of his own special things, in the room known as The Kynge's Secret Studie, and written his journal and quietly seethed.

'After all *I* am King,' he muttered to himself. 'I may be only ten years old but it doesn't stop me being King.'

If he had his way, Edward thought, he would have punished both the Seymour brothers for nagging him and then magnanimously forgiven them on a promise they would behave better in future.

451

Now he braced himself, looking at the feet again, and went on his knees on the carpets and cushions specially set down for him. Sighing inaudibly, Edward picked up the first foot – which had already been washed three times before by a laundress, the sub-almoner and the almoner – and shoved it into a basin of warm water and sweet flowers.

'God bless the King's Highness,' said a quavery voice.

'May the blessing of Christ be with you,' answered Edward stoically, dunking the foot in and out of several more basins, before wiping it, crossing it and kissing it. Only one foot per pauper, God be praised, he thought but all the while he kept on what he called his 'holy' face, smiling seraphically at the Lord Protector who watched with approval.

If only, thought Edward, plunging fiercely at some poor fellow's heel, those two could be combined into one person, open-handed and amusing but honourable and serious as well. Then I would have something like a really decent uncle.

The Lord Admiral returned to his stately domain on the very day that his wife, as Dowager Queen, bathed the feet of the poor of Winchcombe, kneeling heavily on her supporting cushions and repeating the action thirty-four times. Arriving too late for the ceremony Thomas nonetheless escorted her from the chapel, built in the castle grounds, and lectured her severely on doing too much, saying that she could have excused herself the ordeal on the grounds of being with child.

'But they enjoy it so, Tom. And I am not far advanced, after all.'

'Has the little knave moved yet?'

'No, but I expect him to do so daily.'

That evening all the household dined in the ancient Banqueting Hall on a feast of fish, it being a fast until Saturday when Eastertide Tansies, a delicacy of cream, eggs and juice of spinach, would be served. Tomorrow, of course, the bakers would be up before dawn in the castle kitchens, preparing hot cross buns in memory of the kindly woman who had offered Christ a loaf on his way to Calvary. Then the household, even Thomas, would go to chapel to pray for their immortal souls.

'You are very quiet, pretty Kate,' said Thomas, as the meal finally done, he got into bed beside her in their beautiful room in the east

452

wing. 'You should not have taken part in the ceremony, I do not think it was good for you.'

She stared at the ceiling in silence for a moment or two and then, quite suddenly, decided to take the bull by the horns.

'It is not that I am tired, Thomas, it is more that I am worried.'

He propped himself on one elbow, staring at her with concern. 'What about?'

'Elizabeth,' answered Katherine firmly.

Did she imagine it or was there a fraction of a second's pause before he repeated, 'Elizabeth? Why?'

'Because I think she's in love and I think it is with you.'

'Oh rubbish,' Tom answered and fell back on the pillows, grinning.

'Treat it as such if you like,' Katherine continued with acerbity, 'but I think all that teasing when we lived in the Dower House did no good. I believe she conceived some kind of passion for you.'

'Really?' Tom was looking at her with interest and the Queen was suddenly furious.

'I *knew* it would make you vainer than ever. I *knew* I should say nothing. But you asked me and, for once, I told the truth.'

'What do you mean, for once? I thought you were always truthful.'

Fatigue, anxiety, pregnancy, were suddenly all too much and Katherine burst into tears, turning her back on her husband and sobbing into the pillow.

'Listen,' said Thomas calmly, not touching her but somehow tremendously close, 'you have nothing to fear. I love you, Kate, and I always will. If some silly slut of a girl gets a fixation about me it is not my fault. The little bitch can leave here tomorrow as far as I'm concerned. But I can see that the teasing may have done harm and for that I apologise.'

He did not make a move, waiting for her to roll over into his arms which, after a second or two, Katherine did.

'Do you really love me?'

'Till death,' he answered solemnly.

Katherine shivered. 'I pray that that is many years hence.'

'Amen indeed,' said Lord Seymour and held her as tight against him as he dared without making uncomfortable the growing life within.

On Easter Sunday, with the rising sun dancing for joy at the Resurrection, that life finally moved of its own volition. Katherine, walking hand-in-hand with her husband through the yew walk, gave a cry and turned to him, her eyes shining, her face aglow.

'Oh Thomas, the little knave has moved. He has come to life. What a wonderful omen on Easter Day.'

Katherine had never seen her husband weep before, did not know the dashing Lord Admiral, that fine, fearless blackguard, was capable of such emotion. But now fierce tears sprang into his eyes and going on one knee before her he kissed the Queen's body where the baby dwelled.

'I love you, Katherine,' he said, almost harshly. 'It is you who have changed my entire life. I lay it at your feet.'

It was one of the most profound moments they had ever shared in a relationship that had been charged from its very beginning, and putting her hands to cup Tom's face, Katherine wept with him, mingling their joyful tears. It was just then, looming against the midday sun, her shadow thrown before her, that Elizabeth appeared at the far end of the yew walk, sinister and omnipresent, a stark black shape.

Tom sprang up and uttered one of the terrible oaths for which he was renowned. 'God's testicles, what does *she* want?'

His violent reaction frightened Katherine more than the sight of the girl herself. Nobody indifferent, nobody who did not care, would be so angry.

He craves her, she thought, and wondered if she was going to faint.

For a moment or two Elizabeth could be seen to hesitate and then with that determination which was already a characteristic, started to walk towards the Admiral and his wife with a normal but measured tread. She drew alongside and swept the most incredible curtsey, deep to the ground, her head bowed so as not to gaze at them.

'Good day, Your Grace. Good day, my Lord,' she said, then went on her way without looking back.

Thomas stared after her. 'How dare she,' he said. 'I'll string her up.'

'But she did nothing,' protested Katherine.

'That's just the point,' answered the Admiral furiously. 'That creature can make an ordinary greeting seem an insult.'

454

'I think,' said the Queen, very slowly, 'that you are allowing the Princess Elizabeth to affect you deeply.'

Though the days between Easter and Whitsun grew cooler in temperature it now seemed that Sudeley Castle and its principal occupants were at fever pitch. At night, though she pretended to sleep, Katherine could hear Thomas tossing and turning as if he were ill. While in her apartments, though only Kat Ashley was aware of it, Elizabeth whimpered like a wounded animal. Unhealthy forces were at work and the air was alive with longings and whisperings.

It was as if some enormous wound was festering, coming to a terrible head, and that only lancing could dispel the poison that pervaded every room, every inch of the gardens and grounds. The Queen felt there was no more serenity, no peace anywhere, except in the chapel. And she knelt there long hours, almost avoiding the house and the two people in it who were causing her such anguish.

The end was almost a relief; the boil burst; the venom was at last allowed to drain away. In that same yew walk, hidden from the castle and from onlookers, Elizabeth and Thomas, who had for days been stalking round each other like two battle-ready cats, came accidentally but intentionally, face to face.

'Right, young lady,' said Lord Seymour without preamble. 'I have words to say to you.'

'Remember to whom you speak,' she answered, all fire and ice. 'I'll have no disrespect from you, Lord Admiral.'

'By Christ,' said Thomas savagely, 'you are an evil little bitch! I'll disrespect you as much as I please.'

Her hand, strangely long and thin, shot out and delivered him a smarting blow on the cheek. 'Never, do you hear me,' she whispered fiercely, 'never speak to me like that again.'

Thomas caught her wrist, bending her arm back painfully. 'You wait,' he said, but that was all. They wanted each other too desperately to waste one more word. With a movement like flight she was in his arms, straining her body against his, eager for anything he might do to her. At long last they kissed as adults, the days of childhood and romping dead and buried. As her lips parted beneath his and their uncontrollable desire was translated into sensation both of them knew that they were found and lost, that the end of all this longing must, of necessity, be cruel.

And that was how Katherine found them, kissing hungrily, greedily, like beggars at a feast. She turned into the yew walk from the chapel and stood transfixed, her face growing pinched, her eyes dark. At that moment the devout and pious Queen was an avenging angel, and dangerous.

'You wretch,' she screamed and rushing up to Thomas hit him hard upon the nape of his neck. He fell back, half in surprise, and Elizabeth was released from his grasp.

'And as for you,' said Katherine, relishing the moment as the girl's face went ashen and her eyes widened to twice their size, 'you are an ungrateful slut, not fit to be here. And think not that you will complain of your treatment to your brother, Madam. For His Grace the King and the Lord Protector shall be the first to know how you came creeping like a whore around my husband and your reputation, not good now, will drop even lower.'

'No!' gasped Elizabeth. 'You wouldn't . . .'

'Oh yes I would,' replied Katherine. 'People speak evil of you already and will do so doubly in future. And I shall take the greatest pleasure in repeating to you everything they say. Now begone. You must be out of my house, you and your servants, by tomorrow morning.'

It was pleasurable. She who never lost her temper obviously inspired awe when she did. Elizabeth sped into the castle as if the Hound of Hell was coming after her.

Katherine turned to Thomas. 'How could you?' she said quietly. 'How could you, the father of the child I carry, do this to me?'

'Very simply,' he answered, with an attempt at noncholance. 'The girl quite literally threw herself at me. I would never have believed such profligacy possible.'

'You're lying!'

'If that is what you believe, then so be it. But I tell you Henry Tudor's daughter has an appetite as insatiable as once did he.'

And with that Thomas bowed politely and walked away, not to Sudeley but towards the open countryside, leaving the Dowager Queen of England standing forlorn and alone.

# Chapter Thirty-Eight

THE SUMMER HAD BEEN HOT, stifling, almost too much to bear for a pregnant woman not in the first flush of youth, whose peace of mind had been shattered abruptly, her physical well-being deteriorating as a result. Throughout the searing days Katherine had sat in the shade of Sudeley's mighty trees, wishing that the little knave would come into the world, yet knowing that she must wait till later in the year, certain that the babe had been conceived during that last sweet winter at Chelsea, when Elizabeth had still been a child and Thomas a faithful husband.

Katherine had forgiven him his indiscretion within days, unable to bear the mortified expression and air of wounded injustice. He had marched back from his walk later that evening, martyred and hard-done-by, refusing to speak to a soul, including his wife.

'I tell you the creature molested me,' was all he had said as he blew out the bedside candle. 'You may think what you like, Kate, but that is the truth of it.'

'You should never have encouraged her in the first place. All those ridiculous familiarities at Chelsea. You should be ashamed of yourself. A man of your age!'

The snore that answered Katherine had been most unconvincing, but Thomas was refusing to admit a thing. And so he continued, pained and suffering, until at last the Queen had exploded with rage.

'You are making me furious by this behaviour. Anyone would think it is *I* who offended, not the other way round.'

'You *have* offended by thinking ill of me, who have loved you for so many years and waited so long and patiently to marry you.'

'Which makes it harder for me to bear the fact that you betrayed me.'

A look of anguish crossed Tom's face. 'One kiss a betrayal? An amorous child accosts me and that is deceit? I see that I must leave Sudeley, Katherine. Where there is no trust there is no love and it is clear that you no longer love me.'

But she did, desperately, and that was the tragedy of it. Katherine had wept bitterly, running away from him to their bedroom, where Tom had eventually caught up with her. Lying on the bed beside her, he had taken her in his arms.

'Listen, pretty Kate, it is you I love, not that red-haired witch's daughter. I tell you, sweetheart, the girl is unbalanced. But what hope could she have with that heritage? Her father a lecher, her mother a whore. Thank God she has gone. I pray that I never set eyes on her again.'

'But you will!' said Katherine sensibly.

'I will and I won't. In future I intend to look right through her for the evil slut that she is.'

'Do you mean it?'

'Of course I do. I adore and cherish you, and I intend to show Madam Elizabeth she had better keep her distance or answer for the consequences.'

It was all bluster and bravado, big words meaning little, but Katherine was deceived, or allowed herself to be. She loved Tom too well and needed him too much, now that she was pregnant and old to bear a first child.

'Then kiss me,' she had said, 'and we will be friends again.'

His face lit up. 'Oh please, darling. I cannot bear it when you are angry. Let us go to Hanworth for a few days and forget this trouble.'

They had left Sudeley almost on the heels of Elizabeth, who had gone barely a week before, trotting off in the summer sunshine with her retinue, not even turning her head to look back. Katherine had watched her from an upstairs window, half hating, half admiring the rigidity of the girl's back. She might be leaving in disgrace but she was not showing it by the merest hint. The Queen had never seen the girl carry herself more proudly.

'Good riddance,' Katherine had said softly, but deep in her heart she had been unable to hate the foolish chit. Thomas at his most charming was a difficult man to contend with, she could hardly blame Elizabeth for loving him. And then, of course, with her usual brilliance, the Princess had made a counter move, writing a letter that twisted Katherine's words and made a brave attempt at righting the situation.

'Truly,' Elizabeth wrote, 'I was replete with sorrow to depart from Your Highness, especially leaving you undoubtful of health, and albeit I answered little, I weighed more deeper when you said you would warn me of all evils that you should hear of me. For if Your Grace had not a good opinion of me you would not have offered friendship to me that way, that all men judge the contrary. But what may I more say than thank God for providing such friends to me.'

Very clever, thought Katherine. So I am now your friend!

But the days at Hanworth, almost like a honeymoon, had revived her spirits and when Tom left for Court, attempting yet again to retrieve her jewels, he wrote to her sweetly. Katherine read the letters many times, smiling at one in particular and at the way Tom signed it.

'And so I bid my most dear and well-beloved wife most heartily to fare. From Westminster, this Saturday, the 9th of June. Your Highness's most faithful loving husband, T. Seymour.'

'Faithful and loving,' said his wife to herself and was almost reassured.

They had returned to Sudeley Castle in late June and spent a few idyllic weeks together before, very suddenly and without warning, Thomas announced that he must go to London to see the Protector.

'But why?' Katherine had asked suspiciously.

'To sort out this business with the Council.'

'What business with the Council? Thomas, what have you been up to?'

Her husband had put his booted feet on the chair opposite him and closed his eyes wearily.

'I asked the King to intercede in the matter of your jewels. The prats concerned did not take kindly to that and sent word to attend 'em. But I didn't go.'

'What!' Katherine had exclaimed in horror. 'You refused to answer a summons from the Privy Council of England?'

Thomas opened one eye and grinned. 'Yes, my dear. I said I was too busy.'

His wife had not known whether to laugh or cry. 'What did they reply?'

'That unless I explained everything to the Protector – my beloved

459

brother who likes to keep all the power to himself – I would be put under arrest.'

Katherine had sat down heavily. 'Oh Tom, why do you take such terrible risks?'

He had grinned at her, turning on his inexhaustible supply of charm. 'Because I enjoy it, pretty Kate. As do you.'

'I? Never.'

'Did the woman who gambled everything to secretly marry the Lord Admiral not relish the element of danger?' he countered swiftly. 'Did our clandestine meetings not hold a certain spine-chilling thrill? Come on, admit the truth.'

Katherine had smiled reluctantly. 'Well . . .'

'Of course they did. Life's a challenge, Kate, and by God's precious soul I am going to wrestle with it. You knew that when you married me, so don't complain now.'

'I am not complaining. It is just that sometimes you make me very afraid.'

'Nonsense,' he answered, rising and crossing to where she sat. 'The Protector will be putty in my hands, just as he always has been. I shall simply tell him I was too occupied with making love to my wife to attend the meeting.'

'That should go down very well,' answered Katherine grimly.

'Yes,' said Thomas cheerfully, 'I expect it will. Even my brother has an eye for a pretty woman.'

Katherine shook her head slowly. 'One of these days . . .'

'*I* shall be Lord Protector, just you wait and see.' And with that Tom pulled her from her chair and gave her a kiss. 'We shall be the two most powerful people in the land.'

'I don't want power,' Katherine protested.

'We'll have to face that when the time comes,' her husband answered firmly.

The river room, as Edward Seymour always thought of his study, was alive with light, all the dartings and quiverings of the Thames reflected on its walls and the brightness of the sun, glancing off the surface of the water, beaming straight in so that the Protector, who sat with his back to the window, appeared completely in silhouette. Such an effect gave him a powerful and somewhat menacing look, of which Edward, with incredible naivety, was unaware, merely moving his seat round the desk so that the sun did not shine in his eyes. Had it been his brother Thomas in such a situation, he would have done it deliberately, sat like that all the time in order to overpower his visitors.

The fantastic palace of Somerset House being still under construction and Chester Place demolished to make way for it, Syon House was the temporary home of the ever-growing Seymour family. In the middle of July, Anne had produced a third son, much to her delight, as she now considered her childbearing duties done. But this being the season for the plague she had removed the younger ones to the country, out of danger, and the riverside house was quiet, only the servants remaining. By their own request, Jasper and Sylvanus, now both aged fifteen, had stayed behind in London with their patron.

The fact that the study overlooked the river had another advantage beside that of brilliant light. Any approaching vessel was audible and the Lord Protector, by going to his window, could see in excellent time all those who approached his landing stage. Now the steady pull of oars and the time of his clock, set in a little golden globe, told him that his renegade brother was approaching and, sure enough, a swift glance down to the Thames confirmed this. Thomas, garbed in clothes of a light tawny colour, heavily decked out with amber beading, was stepping ashore.

With his hair bleached summer-bright and grown long to his collar, a gold earring piercing his ear, and a hat with a large plumed feather which shimmered in the breeze, Thomas looked lion-like, everything giving the impression of a yellow mane.

Damn him, thought the Protector, he is too attractive for his own good.

And so he was! Even the ordinary people of England would cheer Thomas Seymour in the street, idolising his marvellous appearance and easy laughter, his enormous personality and common touch.

While they think me dry and hard as seasoned leather, thought Edward wryly.

And so they did! Though it seemed hardly fair that the brother who longed for reform, and fought for it too within the confines of the Council, whose aim was to better the people in every way, was the one they did not like.

Not that that matters particularly. It is the fact of the King favouring one uncle more than the other which is really difficult to contend with, the Protector considered bitterly.

461

He returned to the desk, deliberately bending over his paperwork so that when the knock eventually came he could be discovered busy. But Thomas, as laconic as ever despite the very real threat of his arrest and imprisonment, gave the merest tap and walked in without waiting for a reply, thus catching his brother staring at the door, slightly open-mouthed.

'My dear Ned,' said the Lord Admiral, sauntering forward jauntily, 'how very nice to see you. Do I find the Lord Protector well?'

'You find him very well,' Somerset answered irritably. 'Now pray sit down. We have a lot to discuss.'

The Admiral obeyed but not immediately, first giving the most immense and florid bow which entailed sweeping off the powerfully-feathered hat and brushing it almost to the floor.

'Oh dear,' sighed Somerset, inaudibly.

'Where shall I sit?' asked Thomas, deliberately difficult.

'On the opposite side of the desk.'

'But there the sun will shine directly into my eyes and I shall scarce be able to see you. If you have no objection, that great chair by the fireplace would suit very well.'

'Then take it, please.'

'Gladly, gladly,' answered the Admiral, and arranged himself carefully within its oaken confines.

'I have asked you here today . . .' the Protector started, only to find that his brother was speaking at the same time.

'I hear that Anne has been brought to bed of a goodly son. My congratulations to you both. How amazing, Ned, to think that you have fathered twelve children and I only one – that I know of, of course!'

'It took me two wives to do it,' answered Somerset drily.

'Indeed, indeed. Whereas I married late and wisely.'

If there was a barb in that remark, the Lord Protector ignored it. 'And how fares Her Grace the Queen Dowager? She must be drawing near her time.'

'Dr Huick told her to expect the babe in August.'

'Then I wish her safe delivery.' Somerset cleared his throat and put the tips of his fingers together. 'But it was not to talk of Her Grace that I summoned you, Tom. Had I not told the Council that I would speak to you personally, you would have been placed under arrest for failing to attend them.'

Thomas crossed one elegant leg over the other and Ned found his mind wandering, wondering how his brother's hose never wrinkled when every other mortal's did.

'Yes,' said the Admiral.

'It is no good,' snapped Somerset crossly, 'pretending that this is a matter of no importance. Not only do the Admiralty accuse you of failing in your duty and increasing your yearly fee by £800, but the Council have evidence that you are trying to undermine my authority by open approaches to His Grace our nephew.'

'I merely asked him to intercede in the affair of Her Grace my wife's jewels, which are, Ned, her *personal property* and not the Crown's.'

'And that is all?'

'No,' answered Tom mildly. 'I also suggested that I should be Deputy Keeper of the King's Person rather than your brother-in-law, Michael Stanhope. There are those, Ned, who consider that too much power centred around one person is not always healthy.'

'You are jealous, aren't you?' said Somerset coldly. '*You* want to be Protector, that's the truth of it.'

For the first time Thomas looked uncomfortable. 'No, I . . .'

'Don't lie,' snarled his brother. 'You are not content with being Lord Admiral, Baron Seymour of Sudeley, and husband to the Dowager Queen. You are merely aggrieved that you haven't risen higher. I should have you arrested for treason. By God, I should.'

'No,' said Thomas, 'that would not be right. I only felt that the care of our nephew should be shared between us, rather than between you and Michael Stanhope. If that was wrong then I apologise, Ned. I could never be Protector, it would mean too much responsibility for a man of my stamp.'

'Indeed it would,' answered Somerset heavily. 'You, who consort with pirates and give yourself an increased wage when you want one, could never be trusted with our kingdom. You would bargain it away.'

He spoke with great bitterness and the remark was received similarly. Thomas visibly smouldered, his blue eyes darkening dramatically.

'If any man other than my own brother had said that to me I would have smote him,' he said furiously. 'Ned, have a care. You go too far with me.'

There was a fraught silence and Somerset found himself thinking how odd life was. Thomas was the one who deserved a reprimand, yet it was he who now admonished the Protector.

'I think,' he said, after a pause, 'that we are going too far with each other, Tom. I truly believe that for the sake of the King and the realm we must not quarrel like this. As far as I am concerned I am prepared to accept that you only approached His Grace our nephew about trivial matters and that, provided you assure me it will not happen again, I will recommend the incident be forgotten.'

'The matters were not trivial to me,' answered Thomas.

'That's as may be. But the Council await my verdict. Are you going to formally apologise or not?'

Thomas stood up, approaching his brother with a strange expression, half smile, half something more disquieting.

'I apologise,' he said, putting his hands flat on the desk's wooden surface and leaning forward to stare into the Protector's face. 'I apologise Ned, for the sake of my wife and the child she is carrying. I would not want either of them to endure the agony of my being imprisoned.'

Somerset stood also, the light from the window catching his face as he moved. He seemed careworn and haggard, looking far more than his forty-four years, a weary expression in his dark eyes.

'Then I will accept your apology and so report to the Council. But I beg you, both personally and as Lord Protector, let well alone from now on. Concentrate on family life, leave politics to others.'

There was no reading Thomas's face as he bowed his head. 'If that is your wish, my Lord.'

'It is,' answered Somerset, 'it is. Now having forgiven, we must forget.'

There was a pause then Tom said, 'If you have done with me I will return to Sudeley Castle and my wife.'

'And the Admiralty?'

'Will have to do without me until after the child is born.'

'Have a care, brother,' whispered the Protector.

'You look after your kingdom, brother. And I will look after Thomas Seymour,' whispered Tom in reply, as he swiftly left the room.

A golden, corn-bright August. Hazy mornings, lakes of mist lying at the feet of the gentle Cotswold hills, and brilliant noontimes, the wheatfields shadowed by their clear blue slopes. In the evenings hills dark as grapes, soft and purple in the fading light, the sky above them a fierce bright azure which faded in minutes to deepest indigo.

The colours in the castle echoed nature. The day nursery had been hung with twelve tapestries, each of which represented a different month of the year and was worked with dyed threads accordingly. The night nursery was vivid as sunset, the nurse's bed adorned with scarlet and crimson, the cradle trimmed with cloth of gold. Tom had hung the tapestries with his own hands while Katherine and Jane Grey, watching him, had made noises of delight.

'Oh little knave,' Katherine had said, laying both hands on her swollen body, 'please hurry. I can hardly bear to be so enormous for another minute.'

As if in answer the baby had jumped and both Tom and Jane had hurried to feel him, laughing and saying that the child inside danced the volte. But on the last day of August, just as the beaming sun let forth its first light on the Cotswolds, the little knave jumped in earnest and the Queen found herself suddenly soaked with her womb's mysterious water. This was the sign for which they had all been waiting and the midwives were called at once, while Dr Huick hovered in an ante-chamber.

Birth was not easy for Katherine Parr. In June she had celebrated her thirty-fifth birthday and though she had eaten sensibly and exercised strictly throughout her pregnancy, the natural strength of a girl ten years younger was no longer hers. Tom's Romany cousin, Cloverella, had sent a potion of raspberry leaves to drink during labour and Katherine found some relief in this. But her travail was long and wearisome and it was not until the early hours of the next day that the exhausted woman heard the small sad cry of her little knave and the words, 'You have a daughter, Your Grace.'

'A daughter?' Katherine could hardly believe it, so sure it was to have been a boy.

'Yes, Your Grace.'

And they showed her a bundle of humanity, scarcely bigger than Katherine's hand, which looked at her with surprised blue eyes, and waved its fist.

'Oh how pretty,' said the Queen, and cried with sheer fatigue.

An hour later, when both Katherine and the babe had been

washed and dressed, Tom was allowed into the chamber, looking round rather nervously, or so his wife thought.

'The little knave is a girl,' she said to him wistfully. 'No son for poor Tom, I'm afraid.'

'I know, I know,' he answered, then smiled brilliantly. 'But I have been told already that she is a stunning beauty, fit to break the hearts of every man born. May I see her?'

And without waiting for permission he crossed to the cradle, leaned over it and picked out his minute daughter.

Watching him closely, Katherine's heart swelled with love. This was no act to please her, no pretence that he did not care the child was a girl. Tom genuinely loved the tiny creature he held so gently in his arms, delighted with his little scrap of beauty.

Kissing the babe gently, he handed her to the nurse and crossed to the bed, sitting down beside Katherine and holding her close to him.

'Thank you,' he said. 'You could not have done a nicer thing for me.'

'You really like her?'

'I adore her. As soon as you are ready to sleep I am going to write to every important person in the world, telling them that my daughter is the most beautiful girl they will ever meet.'

'Then go now. I am very tired.'

Thomas bent close. 'Was it hard for you, pretty Kate?'

'Very,' she said, 'but worth it when I saw your look of delight.'

'I love you,' he answered gently, 'don't forget that, will you?'

'Of course not.'

And with that Katherine Parr snuggled down to a well-deserved sleep.

In his riverside study in Syon House, the Lord Protector sat with a letter in each hand, his brow greatly furrowed. One, written earlier that day, taking his brother to task for his naughty behaviour as regarded the Admiralty, Somerset was now regretting. The other, full of wonderful humour and joy, was from the culprit himself, announcing the birth of the most beautiful girl ever born.

'Oh, Thomas,' sighed Ned Seymour sadly, 'what are we going to do with you?'

How could he crush his errant brother with a reproof when Tom was so happy? And yet, if he did not, the Protector would have failed in his duty. He had given his word that he would write to the Lord Admiral that very day and list the Admiralty's many complaints. And Ned was uneasily aware that there were those in the Council all too ready to make capital from a rift in the family.

'I can't get out of it,' he said aloud. 'Yet it grieves me to mar your joy.'

Thus, reluctantly leaving the content of the letter exactly as it was, Somerset picked up his pen and added a postscript, frowning all the while.

'We are right glad by your letters,' he wrote, 'that the Queen, your bedfellow, hath a happy hour; and, escaping all danger, hath made you the father of so pretty a daughter . . .'

His pen scratched on.

'. . . is no small joy and comfort to us, as we are sure it is to you and Her Grace also; to whom you shall make again our hearty commendations, with no less gratulation of such good success.'

Somerset smiled at last. Perhaps there was to be a happy ending after all.

'Thus we bid you heartily farewell. From Syon, the 1st of September, 1548. Your loving brother, E. Somerset.'

He sealed the letter, then let it lie for a moment or two under his fingers.

'God willing, let Thomas behave, and be a good father to the infant,' he prayed aloud. 'And God grant good health to the Queen.'

The candle, which had been giving him extra illumination in the fading evening light, at that moment blew out and Somerset blinked a little, feeling a finger of fear as he sat for a second in total darkness, before he reached for a tinder and lit the taper once more.

The Queen made a wonderful recovery from the birth and Dr Huick, who saw her the next morning, pronounced himself delighted. The scrap of humanity, too, was thriving and the happy parents decided to name her Mary. Tom, in ecstasy, hung around the nursery suite until he was almost driven out by the Queen's ladies who wanted their charge to get rest.

Five days after the delivery, at last considering it safe to leave his wife, Tom went hunting early in the morning, wearing a scarlet coat, and cantering through the mist with his fellow riders. They

467

laughed as they rode, a merry pack of men, out to enjoy themselves as much as to stalk quarry.

'I am the happiest man in the world,' said Tom, as they stopped to drink from their flasks. 'Gentlemen, I give you a toast, the Lady Mary Seymour, the most beautiful girl ever born.'

'And Her Grace the Queen,' said one of his companions.

'The Queen,' echoed Tom.

Afterwards he wondered how no hint of disaster came to him, how he continued all that day with no idea of what lay ahead. Yet the moment he entered Sudeley Castle that evening, he knew. The very quiet of the place told him that something was wrong. With a pounding heart, Thomas shot up the stairs and into his wife's chamber.

At first he could not see her for the crowd round the bed but on hearing him they drew back, and he glimpsed Katherine, flushed and ill, twisting on her pillows.

'God's precious blood,' he said, 'what has happened?'

Lady Tyrwhit, who barely tolerated Thomas and could only be icily polite to him, stopped his headlong flight towards the bed. 'My Lord, I must warn you, Her Grace the Queen is far from well.'

'I can see that, Madam.'

'She was taken ill this morning, just after you left to hunt. When I came in she asked me where I had been so long. And then Her Grace said she felt such things inside herself that she was sure she could not live.'

'What!' said Thomas. 'What are you saying to me?'

He pushed her roughly aside and rushed to Katherine, who seized his hands fiercely as soon as she saw him.

'Oh my darling . . .' he started, but a high peevish voice, one that he could hardly identify with his pretty Kate, was whining at him.

'My Lady Tyrwhit,' the Queen was saying, 'I am not well handled; for those about me care not for me, but stand laughing at my grief. And the more good I will to them, the less good they will to me.'

Tom stared at her, horrified. 'Why, sweetheart, I would do you no hurt.'

Katherine narrowed her eyes and Tom knew, with a terrible sinking of his heart, that she was remembering Elizabeth and that fatal kiss.

'No, my Lord, I think *so*,' she answered. 'For you have given me many shrewd taunts.'

The Admiral wheeled round on Lady Tyrwhit. 'What does she mean by this?'

'She thinks you have not used her well in the past, my Lord.'

'But I love her,' answered Thomas furiously. 'She is the only thing I live for.'

And with that he went back to the bed, disregarding the cries of Katherine's attendants, and flung himself down beside her, lifting the Queen into his arms, whispering again and again, 'I love you pretty Kate. I would never hurt you sweetheart. I will make you better.'

And how desperately he tried. Demanding cool towels, Tom washed her flushed face hour after hour, pushing back the russett hair which was now as damp and limp as the coat of a sick animal.

'I love you, pretty Kate. You are going to be well. Do you understand?'

She nodded faintly. 'Yes, yes. But what of *her*?'

'May she be damned,' answered Tom savagely.

'Don't leave me, Tom, will you?'

'Never,' he answered fiercely. 'I shall hold you in my arms for ever.'

'Yes, yes,' she whispered, 'then I will be happy.'

And that was how he stayed, the Queen sleeping, until his gentlemen finally led him away exhausted. It was then that Katherine, quite clearly and calmly, asked Dr Huick and John Parkhurst, her chaplain, to witness her verbal will.

'I leave all my goods to my husband,' she said distinctly, 'wishing they were a thousand times more valuable than they are.'

After that Katherine was at peace and began to dream, a rich, strange dream of vivid colours and strong sensations. She dreamt that she was walking through a valley, dark and mysterious, filled with wonderful trees and flowers. At the end of the valley a bright light beckoned Katherine on. Beside her walked Tom for, though she could not see him, she could feel his arms round her and the welcoming cool cloth with which he sponged her face.

After a while the Queen drew nearer the light and entered it, finding that she was back in her own bedchamber and had really been nowhere at all. Looking round, she saw that on the bed lay two forms, one a waxen figure she did not recognise, the other Tom, convulsed with weeping, wild-eyed and terrible.

'She's dead,' he was saying, 'she's dead.'

'Hush, my Lord,' answered a man that Katherine recognised as Dr Huick. 'Try to get a hold of yourself. Be calm I beg you.'

'How can I?' Tom asked in a voice like a howl. 'Without her there is no one left to help Tom Seymour. Oh God's dear soul, my pretty Kate is dead but it is I who am gone.'

The brightness in the room was getting stronger and Katherine blinked her eyes, almost blinded by the power of it.

'Are you ready, my dear?' said a voice at her elbow.

She turned and saw to her great astonishment that John Latymer, the dear old bullfrog, was holding out his hand to her.

'But what of Thomas?' she answered anxiously.

'He cannot be helped now. It is you and I who must go together.'

'Will he be all right?'

'That is up to him,' answered the bullfrog, his funny old face just as sweet as Katherine remembered it. 'Now come along.'

And with that they went, hand-in-hand, out of the room and into the radiance.

## Chapter Thirty-Nine

WHERE THE SUMMER OF 1548 had been golden, now the winter raged. A week before Christmas, on the very day that the Princess Elizabeth and her retinue set out from Cheshunt in Hertfordshire for their journey to London, it started to snow. Flakes as big as fists floated out of a seal-grey sky, settling on the furs and hoods of the travellers, and a wisp of hair which blew about Elizabeth's face glistened damply, then stuck to her cheek like the tendril of a vine.

'Should we turn back?' asked Thomas Parry, the Princess's cofferer, his portly body quivering slightly with the cold.

'No,' came the indignant answer, 'there are those who await us in London. My royal brother for one, and also Lord Seymour. If he has been good enough to lend us his house then the least we can do in return is try to maintain some semblance of punctuality. Go to, Master Parry.'

And with that the Princess had pulled her hood well down both to protect her face from the snow and block the cofferer from sight, or so he suspected.

It had been a very fraught autumn, thought Thomas Parry, particularly with regard to the Lord Admiral, whose behaviour since the death of his wife had been erratic to put it at its kindest. Terrible stories had circulated. How Lord Seymour had been so drunk on the night of Katherine's death that it had taken four of his gentlemen to lift him from the floor; how he had ridden off, shrieking curses to the sky, not even to return for his wife's funeral. How Lady Jane Grey, that mousey child of eleven years, had been forced to play the role of chief mourner, draped in long black weeds and a veil, only to be rewarded for her pains by an exhibition of the Admiral's most eccentric behaviour.

In a frenzied fit of despair, Thomas Seymour had announced that he would be shutting down his houses and leaving England only, in the next breath, to change his mind and fetch Dame Margery Seymour from Wolff Hall to run his establishments for him. Jane, who had been sent home to her parents, was promptly asked back again, thrown between her father, Henry Grey, and Thomas, as if she were a ball. But this time Lord Dorset was not so willing to release his daughter, not feeling it quite seemly for her to live in the same place as the Admiral now that the Queen was dead. However, a further fee of £500 and redoubled assurances that a marriage to the boy-King would most definitely be arranged, had changed his mind and Jane had been despatched once more.

It was whispered that the girl had not been the only subject under discussion between Lord Dorset and Lord Seymour. It was said that Thomas was also sounding out the ground to see where Henry Grey's allegiance might lie should Thomas organise a rebellion in the name of the King, a rebellion to let Edward Tudor determine his own acts and do away with the Lord Protector. It was whispered further that should an uprising take place the late Queen's brother, the Marquess of Northampton, would also add his weight to such an enterprise. But they were mere rumours with probably not a grain of truth to substantiate them.

But what *is* true, thought Parry, grinning fatly and stealing a glance to where Elizabeth, a real winter Princess in white furs and scarlet cloak, rode ahead of the column, is that the Admiral is mad for love. And it is the Lady Elizabeth he wants.

Within a month of the Queen's death, Parry and Katherine Ashley had been asked to meet the Admiral in conditions of great secrecy, something which had appealed to the child in all three of them. The cofferer could remember the scene now; the Admiral, having assured himself that they were alone, throwing off his cloak and laughing, plying them with strong drink, grinning hugely.

'I'm lonely, that's the truth of it,' he had said. 'I miss my Kate and I want to fill my bed.'

Mistress Ashley had pretended to blush but it had deceived no one. 'Oh, Lord Seymour, how can you say such things?'

'Because they are true, Kat. And you of all people know how well the Princess likes me. Now, neither of you will find me ungenerous. All I want you to do is plead my cause – and do a little spying on my behalf.'

'Spying?' repeated Parry, pompous and shocked.

'Only of the sweetest sort, Sir. I desire you to find out what my Lady thinks of me. Whether or no she will have me for a husband.'

'I think she might well, Lord Admiral,' Kat had giggled, sipping her brandy.

'Why do you say that?'

'She blushes whenever we mention your name and the other night when we played the game of Drawing Hands, she chose you, my Lord, and then chased you away. We teased her greatly, did we not, Master Cofferer?'

'Yes,' said Parry, 'yes.'

He was thinking something, wondering how the Admiral could be so intent on another when the grave had scarcely closed over Katherine Parr. He slid his eyes sideways, surreptitiously staring, and noticed that Lord Seymour's face was very slightly flushed.

He's not well, Parry thought.

The Admiral had become momentarily serious. 'Tell me, Kat, why did you write me a letter of condolence and not the Princess?'

'She wouldn't, my Lord. I've never seen her so strange. She said that neither you nor she deserved sympathy but that I could write to you if I wished. I showed her the letter but she had no interest in it.'

'Umm.' Tom had stroked his reddish beard. 'She's a funny little wench.'

That had been a good evening and the sport that ensued as a result had been amusing too, the more intimate servants making it their business to see Elizabeth blush. Typical conversations had all been on similar lines.

'Of course the Lord Admiral is free to marry now.'

'Indeed he is. I've heard he'll wed the Lady Jane Grey.'

'Really? I thought it might be someone nearer home!'

But Kat Ashley had taken the bull by the horns, repeating the conversation to her fellow conspirator, Parry.

'I said to my Lady that she could have the Lord Admiral for husband if she wished to.'

'And what did she reply?'

'She asked me what made me say it. You know her way, answering a question with another.'

'Indeed I do. What did you say?'

'That it was the rumour in London that she and the Admiral were about to be married.'

'How did she take that?'

'She laughed and said it was but London news.'

A cool reply, thought Parry now, staring with mixed feelings at Elizabeth's lithe shape, sitting her horse with almost masculine ease. And a cool young woman at that. But how long would her coolness last now that they were on their way to London to keep their Christmas in Seymour Place, loaned to the Princess by the Lord Admiral for the duration of the festivities?

She had been desperate for accommodation, for over a hundred people were accompanying Elizabeth to keep the Twelve Days. And then, with Christmas only a fortnight away, Seymour had contacted Parry and offered the use of his mansion. The cofferer had never seen anyone so delighted. The Princess had smiled, showing her small, seed-pearl teeth, the ivory face turning the colour of a pink.

'He has done that for me?' she had said, looking as if she was about to whirl Parry round and round. 'The Lord Admiral has offered me his home?'

'Yes, Your Grace. He told me to tell you it was the very least he could do for a lady of such merit as yours.'

The seed-pearls had shown again, briefly. 'The Lord Admiral is a flatterer, Parry.'

'Ah, Madam, but he follows through. Those were not just empty words.'

'That is true.'

Parry had cleared his throat. 'Your Grace, I hope I do not presume . . .'

Elizabeth had smiled a scampish smile. 'I hope not indeed.'

'. . . but it has been in my thoughts to ask you whether, should the Council and the Lord Protector approve, of course . . .'

'Of course.'

'. . . you would marry with the Lord Admiral?'

The shutters behind the dark eyes had visibly closed. 'If that comes to pass, I will do as God shall put into my mind. Good day, Master Cofferer.'

It had been a rebuff and Parry supposed now that he had deserved it. Nonetheless, the cofferer had reported by letter straight away and the Admiral had declared himself delighted.

'Tell Her Grace I will come and see her at Seymour Place when she has settled in.'

'Yes, my Lord.'

Elizabeth had instantly issued an invitation of course, one which Thomas had gladly accepted. They were to have a private supper together two days after her arrival.

On a sudden impulse Cofferer Parry dropped back in the calvalcade so that he drew alongside the litter in which Katherine Ashley was travelling, the curtains drawn back so that she could see her charge, riding like an arrow with the men at the front, declaring litters 'stuffy'.

'Well?' he said.

'I think all will be,' she answered guardedly.

'Has she' – Parry's eyes flickered over the distant figure in scarlet – 'said anything?'

Mistress Ashley lowered her voice. 'We must be careful. The whole household knows what is afoot and my husband has warned me not to tease her further.'

'Why?'

'He fears that she truly bears some affection for my Lord Admiral.'

'Does he, by God!'

'Yes. So from now on we must act for Lord Seymour with great circumspection.'

The cofferer gave her a wink, his eye momentarily vanishing in the fold of his portly cheek. 'In view of what you have just said I believe there will be no need for circumspection. I think the affair will soon be public knowledge.'

Kat looked concerned. 'I hope the Lord Admiral will inform both Protector and Council before he makes a move. Think how furious they were when he secretly married the Queen. I do not think they would stand for it twice.'

Parry frowned. 'But Her Grace is cautious.'

'No woman,' answered Mistress Ashley wisely, 'is cautious when she is in love.'

It had taken hours and reduced two waiting women to tears before she had finally been pleased with her appearance. But eventually, dressed in the colours of a water nymph, the shades that suited her best, Elizabeth had been satisfied. Her kirtle, worn beneath an open gown, was of soft aquamarine taffeta, encrusted with pearls. The gown itself was green, its skirt tucked back in an A-shape to reveal the kirtle's adornment, its sleeves tight from wrist to upper arm, where they prettily puffed out. On her head was a close-fitting cap, also pearl covered, while her hair, red as fire in the candlelight, flowed loose and lustrous to her shoulders.

Mistress Ashley had stared at her charge long and hard, wondering if the Princess was really lovely or if it were an optical illusion, forgetting that this had also been the enigma of Anne Boleyn. Finally Kat had decided that Elizabeth's looks were too fierce for real beauty, the milky skin contrasting too harshly with the vivid hair and dark eyes. And yet, dressed in those soft greens, she had an unforgettable radiance, a splendour, that was quite dazzling.

Tonight my Lord Admiral will propose, thought Kat, and for a moment got carried away by a romantic vision of the mating of two spectacular beings, Adonis and Phoebe, brightness personified.

'Well, Kat?' Elizabeth was looking at her, almost anxiously.

'You look splendid, Your Grace.'

'As splendid as my mother?'

'Equally so.'

'She was fifteen when my father first fell in love with her.'

Kat smiled. 'I know that. Just the age you are now. And, of course, a great man is in love with you too.'

Elizabeth caught Mistress Ashley's eye in the mirror into which the Princess still gazed. 'How can he do it, Kat? He loved her, my stepmother, the late Queen. I know he did.'

Mistress Ashley said the most perceptive thing of her life. 'I think he loves you both, Your Grace.'

'But how?'

'One like a chair, comfortable and easy, a warm, friendly kind of love. But the other like a fire that burns in his soul. The Lord Admiral is consumed by you, Your Grace.'

'Is he?' asked Elizabeth, turning away from her reflection at last. 'Is he really?'

'I have no doubt. Now go to the reception room and await him; you will not be disturbed.'

'And later?' asked the Princess, very, very softly.

'Nor then either.'

He was now very slightly crazed, that was obvious. The second that Elizabeth set eyes on him, the first time since she had been expelled from Sudeley, she knew it. It was as if a caricaturist had over-

476

emphasised each of Thomas Seymour's features just a little cruelly. The hair, too long, separated where it touched his shoulders; the handsome face was fractionally bloated; the beautiful eyes, once so sensational, were feverish and somehow dangerous. Even the lithe body had parodied itself; where once the Admiral had walked with jaunty confidence, now he swaggered like a fop, his gait exaggerated and foolish.

The Princess saw all of it and none of it. She was desperately in love, her frenetic desire for Tom fuelled and fired by the months they had spent apart. It was all she could do to remain seated as he came into the room but with her enormous control she did so, merely glancing up and smiling. But Tom came striding towards her, his eyes blazing with open adoration.

Taking her hand to kiss it, he said, 'I have missed you, my Lady.'

Elizabeth gave him a very straight look. 'I would have thought you to be still in mourning, my Lord Admiral.'

'Mourning?' he repeated thickly, almost as if he were drunk. 'I shall never stop mourning. But that is one thing, you are quite another.'

'What do you mean?'

'That I am obsessed by you, Elizabeth. When you were a child it was just the same. Then I castigated myself for indecency, for perversion, for disgusting thoughts about a little girl. At Chelsea I couldn't keep my hands off you. But now, thank God, you are a woman and I may pay court and make love and do all the things I have been longing to do to you.'

Elizabeth smiled. 'Yes, it is true. I am a woman at last.'

But she was lying. Though her thoughts and emotions were ready for love, though she felt desire so strongly that sometimes she wept, Elizabeth's body still had not started the moon's mysterious cycle. But not even Kat Ashley knew that secret. The Princess had told her long ago that the flux had come, and pricked her finger occasionally and rubbed it on the sheets to lend authenticity.

Thomas gave her such a look at those words, as if he would have taken her to bed there and then, that Elizabeth grew nervous, for tonight there was something frightening about him.

'My Lord Admiral, a good repast is prepared for you in your own dining room,' she said quickly. 'Nor have I thanked you yet for the loan of this magnificent mansion.'

'Everything I have is yours, my Lady,' said the Admiral with a smouldering smile. 'My land, my property, my body, I lay them at your feet.'

'Then in that case, do me the service of enjoying the board prepared. My household, here in London to attend my brother, and myself mistress of your house, makes me feel that I have truly arrived at woman's estate.'

'I wish that you were mistress of more than my house,' answered Thomas softly, 'unless, of course, you were mistress of it permanently.'

Elizabeth, if she heard him, made no sign, merely rising to her feet and by a nod of her head indicating that he should give her his arm to escort her to the dining room. And there, too, he would have thought Elizabeth had planned to distance herself, for she had put herself at one end of the table, he at the other.

The fierce feelings they had for each other, the strange compulsion that triggered longing, was stultified by being apart. Tom sat in his place, savage as a bear, while in hers, Elizabeth picked at her food as was her habit.

Throughout that strained meal the Princess's musicians had played and now, with the table finally cleared, they made music in good earnest. Tom, who had drunk enough to be bold but not enough to make him foolish, deliberately moved from his isolated place and pulled a chair before the hearth, and after a while Elizabeth joined him.

Very subtly the mood between them changed again, growing comfortable, so that the girl was no longer frightened by the feverish quality that had raged in Tom ever since Katherine had died. But eventually, when wine and love songs had had their predictable effect, sentiment and sweetness slowly turned to the white-hot passion they had known at Sudeley Castle during that last fateful week. It was time for consummation.

The faithful Kat, thinking all to be for the best, had made sure that the servants kept their distance that night, so when the Princess and Thomas Seymour ascended to her chamber, really his own bedroom, they were unseen. Thus they were together at last, lying on his bed, and to Tom was to befall the task of robbing a Princess of the Blood, the second in line to the throne, of her virginity.

A long lean body revealed itself to him, as white and unexplored as arctic snow, its breasts small and beautiful, shaped like moons. While Elizabeth saw for the first time hard muscle and sinew, a

478

tanned skin, an exciting part of a man that she had never yet glimpsed. She was afraid, that strong fearless girl knew what it was to fear as Thomas, having kissed her so often that it ceased to be enough, in an almost leisurely way rolled himself on top of her.

Elizabeth had heard from Kat Ashley that love could not be bought without pain, knew that the giving up of her virgin state would hurt just once, or a few times possibly, and then never again. So now she prepared herself, gritted her teeth a little, as Thomas pushed against her.

Nothing happened. She could feel his thrusting between her thighs but that was all. There was no searing hurt as she had been led to believe, no sensation of a largeness entering within, nothing.

'My God,' said Tom, raising himself to look at her.

'What is it?' asked Elizabeth, more than half afraid already.

'I am not sure. Perhaps I have drunk too much. I cannot enter you, sweetheart.'

'Why can't you?'

'You are very much a virgin.'

Now she was terrified, the thought of her flux, or rather the lack of it, beginning to pose frightening questions.

'I know that young girls have a membrane, perhaps mine is strong.'

It was horrible. The Lord Admiral was swinging himself into a sitting position and reaching for his clothes. At that moment Elizabeth felt more degraded than the lowest member of the animal kingdom.

'It is not my fault,' she cried. 'it is you, you are not man enough to take me. I despise myself that I loved you. I do, I do.'

She burst into a flood of weeping and for a terrible, clinical, passionless moment, Thomas Seymour saw all his schemes slipping away from him.

'But my Princess, I adore you,' he said.

'Then prove it.'

Tom's mind rushed like a trapped rat. He was almost certain that there was something wrong with the girl, that where all normal females, however young, had an entrance, in Elizabeth's case there was nothing but a shallow dimple.

'I am too tired,' he answered in a lather of desperation. 'I should have drunk nothing. To avoid scandal I shall leave you, my pretty

479

sweet. But I shall return tomorrow when I am stronger, to consummate our love.'

There was silence as Tom looked warily at Elizabeth. He had never seen her so tense, bleached with shock, her hair hanging round her shoulders like a red shroud.

'I think it would be best not, my Lord Admiral,' she answered in an oddly low voice. 'My reputation is probably already gone because we are alone together late at night. I think it would be more politic if from now on we see each other only when I am accompanied.'

How can that be resolved if we are never by ourselves?'

'The future will take care of itself, Lord Admiral,' she said icily.

'What do you mean?'

'Just that. Goodnight, Sir.'

And with that the Princess Elizabeth turned her back on Thomas Seymour and feigned sleep as he slowly and in bewilderment left the room.

# Chapter Forty

HOW STRANGE IT SEEMED THAT on Twelfth Night, considered to be the most exciting of all the days of Christmas, the Adonis of Henry VIII's court, the most dashing man in England, sat sad and solitary in the banqueting hall of Sudeley Castle, drinking himself into a stupor, having long ago sent everyone else to bed; mother, gentlemen, servants, musicians, all dismissed.

Tonight Thomas felt utterly bereft, the wretched business with Elizabeth being the final blow to his hopes of replacing Katherine. For though the Princess had seen him since, as custom decreed she must, she had made quite sure that they were never alone together, keeping Kat Ashley at her side as if stuck by glue.

Thomas had left Elizabeth on that terrible night, sure that something was wrong with the girl. But now, after the passing of days, he was no longer certain. Had the fault lain with him, had he been mistaken about her? If so, he had obviously antagonised Elizabeth so greatly as a result, that Tom doubted he would ever be able to win her back. In a storm of self-pity, he wept.

'Nothing,' he said drunkenly, 'I've got nothing. My pretty Kate, my sweet Elizabeth, both gone. My brother is holding the reins of power so that I have become a laughing stock. I, the King's uncle, a pauper in every respect.'

And there had been signs recently that the little boy Tom had nurtured so carefully with bribes of pocket money was developing a mind of his own.

I've got to act quickly, the Admiral thought desperately. I've got to make a move as soon as I get back. I'll make that child a proper King if it's the last thing I do. I *must* have a say in affairs. I have just as much right, by God's precious blood, as my conniving brother and his bitch of a wife. It is time that Edward Seymour moved over

481

and made way for a younger man. And if he doesn't I would rather be dead.

It was very cold in the hall now, the temperature freezing. Tom raised his head from his wine cup and glanced about him. There was nothing to see. Yet his hound, lying at his feet, was alert too. With every hackle on its back raised, the dog whined as it appeared to watch somebody or something traverse the length of the huge room.

'Kate?' said Thomas hoarsely. 'Kate, is that you?'

There was no reply and nothing stirred, only the candle flames seeming to bend as if a breeze had just blown past them.

'Kate, are you trying to say something?' whispered Tom.

And then, by the strangest coincidence, at that moment he knocked over his wine, watching dazedly as it trickled like blood from the table to the floor below.

'Oh God's mercy,' he said and rising to his feet staggered from the room, afraid to look behind him to where the wine formed a thick red pool.

Even from the summit of Topenham Hill, where they reigned their horses in for a moment to look at the incredible view, they could hear the silence. Where once the hustle and bustle of Wolff Hall, tucked in the valley below, would have reached their ears even at that considerable distance, now there was nothing, not even the stamp of a hoof from the stables.

'We shouldn't have come,' said the Lord Protector.

'We had to,' answered Cloverella.

Yet secretly she agreed with her cousin. Too much had happened, too many sad and terrible things, for them to visit the scene of their golden childhood at this stage. Too many memories were about to be brought back by entering the very portals of the house. And yet Ned had insisted, not content to pour out his heart to her in any other place.

After such an early end to winter, with January bringing a thaw that melted every bit of ice and snow, the ways were not only treacherous but muddy. So it was two dishevelled and bespattered figures who descended the hill, crossed the valley, and made their entrance into the great courtyard, where once Henry Tudor's powerful beast had pawed the cobbles and sent up sparks from its ringing hooves. Now, a solitary ostler came from the stables to help

482

them. With Dame Margery still gallantly keeping house at Sudeley Castle only a very small staff remained behind to run Wolff Hall.

But for all that, the greeting was warm. Dame Margery's elderly steward, who had been there in Edward and Cloverella's day, came dodderingly to meet them and assure the Protector that all was well, that there would be no visitors as he had requested.

'And when you have bathed, my Lord, and Mistress Cloverella too, I thought you might like to take a turn round the gardens before you dined, knowing how fond of them you are.'

It was like a journey into the past, walking hand-in-hand, for there was a very strong bond between Ned and Cloverella that nobody else quite understood. They stood in the walled garden, sheltered from the coolness of a late February evening, its sundial telling them that there was one hour left until darkness. Then made their way slowly, stopping to sniff the herbs and admire the early shrubs and flowers, through the Ladies' Gardens; My Old Lady's somehow missed Dame Margery's comfortable presence, My Young Lady's mist-haunted and quiet as it had been ever since Jane's death. In silent accord, Ned and Cloverella made for the stone seat on which she had so often sat.

'You know how desperately troubled I am,' the Protector said without preamble. 'The realm seethes with discontent.'

'But you are trying to help, Ned. You have done nothing but good.'

'The landowners do not see it that way. By abandoning enclosures – .'

'You mean the boundaries put upon the great estates?'

'Precisely. By getting rid of those and restoring the land to tillage I have made enemies of all the powerful landowners. Both the old families and the newly rich have turned against me. And yet I must, for the good of the common folk of England, continue my reforms.'

He sighed deeply and Cloverella took his hand.

'The people are more important than the privileged few, Ned. And always will be.'

'Dear God, Cloverella, they are as near to my heart as my own family, which my enemies rejoice to see is now split asunder.'

'There is no hope for Thomas?'

'None. Not only is he lodged in the Tower but there is a bill of attainder against him of some thirty-three items, unanimously passed through the Lords as a case of treason. But what hurts me so desperately is the way he turned against me. He wanted to depose me as Protector, give Edward – that little boy! – autonomy. But when, pressurised and harried by the Council, I ordered Tom to appear before me, he simply did not bother. That was why he was arrested. He could have avoided it. He is doomed, Cousin. And I fear that in his death he might bring me down also.'

'But how, Ned, how?'

'My enemies will snatch at anything. Heaven knows where they will strike next.'

'But you are strong, you can outwit them.'

The Protector smiled at Cloverella. 'I love you for your loyalty.'

She smiled, then said hesitatingly, 'You do realise, don't you, that Tom is not the Tom we grew up with?'

'What do you mean?'

'He is unhinged, Ned. Insane. I think he loved the Queen deeply and her death sent a volatile personality over the edge of reasonable behaviour.'

'But how could he have loved her?' the Protector asked harshly. 'He was sniffing round the Princess in five minutes and terrible stories have emerged. He was pursuing her even while they all lived in Chelsea. There was bottom pinching, tickling, God alone knows what!'

'How do you know that?'

'Katherine Ashley and Cofferer Parry were arrested a few days after Tom, and the Lady Elizabeth was put under restraint. Sir Robert Tyrwhit was sent to question her and his wife is to be her new governess.'

'And they all confessed?'

'Eventually, yes. But at first Tyrwhit found a conspiracy of silence. However, Parry finally admitted that Tom was desperate to marry the Princess, and Ashley confirmed.'

'And the girl herself?'

Ned smiled grimly. 'A worthy opponent, my dear. The only time she faltered was when Tyrwhit made her read the confessions of Parry and Ashley.'

'What did she do?'

'Become breathless and blushed, I'm told. But neither of them said anything really incriminating about her. I am convinced they have all three sworn a secret pact.'

'Umm.' Cloverella looked thoughtful. 'Do you think the Princess was Tom's mistress?'

Somerset shook his head slowly. 'I don't know. He lent her Seymour Place at Christmas time and talk abounds that he visited late at night. But no one will ever learn the truth. She wrote me an extraordinary letter, you know.'

'Yes?'

'In the last paragraph she said that Tyrwhit had told her it was rumoured Elizabeth was in the Tower with Thomas, and was with child by him. She said these were shameful slanders and that she wanted to come to Court to see the King and show herself as she really was.'

'How odd!'

'I thought so. It suggested to me that Her Grace had something to hide while seeming to deny. For not once in the letter did she refer to the relationship between herself and Tom, only throwing dust in my eyes by talking about pregnancy.'

Cloverella put her arm round her cousin, holding him close to her. 'Be very careful. You are the subject of a great deal of enmity.'

'I know and I will be cautious. I promise. But what I do for Tom is more immediately on my mind.'

'You can do nothing. The Tom we knew and loved died long ago. A frenzied man will go to the block, a man who knows not which way to turn. He is cornered Ned, his reason gone. It is better he dies.'

The shadows had lengthened while they spoke and now they both shivered, though whether through chill or the weight of events was not certain. Ned stood up and held out his hand to Cloverella.

'We must go in. We shall sit by the fire in the gallery tonight and remember old times.'

'But only the good ones,' she answered, smiling.

They made their way through the dusk to the house, and as they did so it seemed to both of them that a third person, the slight misty figure of a young woman, walked a few paces ahead, as if escorting them homewards.

It was as though, on his last day, the strange partnership, the twin souls of Thomas and Elizabeth, were bonded in some way, so that she, under virtual house arrest at Cheshunt, woke with a portent of such doom that she was physically ill. Tom, waking at the same

485

moment in the dreariness of his room in the Tower, felt he could see her standing and watching him, already wearing black.

When the Princess had calmed herself a little she dressed in a kirtle and gown of ebony velvet, knowing he hated that colour, remembering how Tom had cut her dress to ribbons all those years ago when she had still been a child. Yet she must mourn him, he who would have been her lover if fate had not played its final cruel trick on Anne Boleyn, and given her a child deformed.

By pretending a chill, Elizabeth had delayed her return from London and insisted on seeing Dr Huick, swearing to Kat Ashley that she would allow no other physician near her. When they had parted company, both patient and doctor had been grim faced. Women's diseases were the province of midwives, not men, and Dr Huick could honestly say that his entire experience of pelvic examination had so far been confined to corpses. But he knew what he saw now well enough. Elizabeth Tudor was doomed to a life without men, her vaginal canal missing, a small inadequate pouch in its place.

Even before she had let him look at her, Elizabeth had made Huick swear an oath so solemn that the physician felt bound by more than his Hippocratic vow. Rumour might gather strength, but the truth would never come from his lips, her secret was safe. And the only other person alive who knew it was shortly to have that life taken away. As the Princess dressed in black to mourn Thomas Seymour, she also mourned the children she would never bear, the husband she would never have, the loving fulfilment that could never be hers.

The Lord Admiral dressed brightly for the scaffold, fearless and foolish to the end. He wore scarlet so that the blood would not show and a hat with a huge white feather to annoy the executioner. In his velvet shoes he had sewn two letters, one for Elizabeth, the other for Mary, which he had written with an aiglet plucked from his hose, and ink smuggled in by his man John.

It was windy that March day and Elizabeth, unable to bear the close confines of the house, spent most of the time in the garden, wandering amongst the winter beds and feasting her eyes on a bush of jasmine. She had no idea at what time the execution would take place, only knowing from listening to Lady Tyrwhit that it would be today. But suddenly she could picture him, standing on the scaffold, defiant and unrelenting to the last.

'No final speech, my Lord?'

'None,' said Thomas curtly, for he knew, did he not, that he died falsely accused, alone and friendless. His brother had signed his death warrant, his nephew had not lifted a finger to save him, his wife had deserted him by dying, his obsession with Elizabeth had ended in the most ironic twist of all.

But before he laid his head on the block, Thomas Seymour gave one last long look round. 'I do not accept this sentence,' he said. 'All I wanted was to see the King's power restored to him and the Protector's diminished. I die a victim of another's greed.'

He knelt and turned quickly to look for John, white-faced and trembling, but ready to serve his master to the end.

'Speed the thing you know about,' whispered Tom and then the headsman wielded his axe twice and it was over, John weeping as he climbed the scaffold to remove the shoes from the corpse's feet.

In the garden at Cheshunt, the black veil attached to Elizabeth's hood blew up over her face and for a second or two, while she fought to pull it down, she felt she could hardly breathe.

It's finished, she thought, it's done. Oh Thomas, Thomas.

She wept bitterly, then, not just for his death but also for her life sentence. The final joke had been played on them both. Never again would the dashing Lord Admiral play his love games, never in the future could Elizabeth play hers.

# Chapter Forty-One

AS WITH ALL GOOD IDEAS the basis of it came from a casual remark, a mere piece of idle chatter, said as much to pass the time as anything else. Yet Zachary Howard, the second he heard what was spoken, knew that here at last was something which might open up a chance for his escape from the Court of Suleiman the Magnificent.

This court did indeed live up to its Sultan's name, being one of the most beautiful in the world, the Topkapi Palace more superbly marbled and decorated than any other, its inhabitants more exotically and richly dressed than even the splendid courtiers of France or England. Because of its rarity and excellence, travellers came not only from all over the Ottoman Empire but also the world to bring the Sultan gifts and often to take away some prize in return.

As Suleiman's chief astrologer, Zachary was introduced to them all, often in a sense of competition, the Sultan claiming that his wise man was more of a visionary, a better divine, than any they could produce, and being proved right. In this way Suleiman came to regard his astrologer more and more highly as the years passed by, and politely but firmly refused all diplomatic attempts by both France and England to secure Zachary's release.

Then, in the autumn of 1551, came a visit from a much-travelled Indian nobleman, Lord Ravi, a minister of the ruler Sher Shah, seeking the Sultan's help to repel the Moguls. And it was by his lips that the chance remark was uttered.

'Your reputation preceeds you, my dear Astrologer,' he had said, leaning across the low table that separated them, upon which stood bowls of fruit and sweets alongside cups of a rich dark liquid known as ch'a, the origins of which lay in China, or so Zachary believed.

'Does it, my Lord?'

'But much as your Sultan admires you, I believe that we have men in India who might be equally wise.'

'Let me establish one thing,' Zachary had answered, 'Sultan Suleiman makes such claims on my behalf. I do not endorse them. I am an Englishman, brought to Turkey eight years ago. In reality, though it does not appear so as I live in the very height of luxury, I am held captive. But the Sultan does not like me to speak of it so I will say no more. But as regards boasts of greatness, I do not make them.'

'But you are an astrologer and clairvoyant of considerable repute?'

'Yes, Sir, I am. It was born in me, a gift from my mother. Fortunately, as a child I was allowed to study further and increase my knowledge.'

Ravi smiled. 'Then I would like to hear your comments on the rope trick, a thing native to India. I saw it the other day and was both amused and puzzled.'

Zachary frowned. 'The rope trick? I know nothing of it.'

'Do you not? I thought its fame might have spread. It is simply this. A magic man with an assistant boy comes into a village and collects a crowd of onlookers, who are made to stand close to one another so that they form an unbroken circle. From a basket the man produces a rope which he shows round for inspection. It is found to be perfectly normal yet at his command it becomes rigid and stands in the air like a pole. The boy climbs up and disappears into a small cloud which hovers at the top, the man climbs after him, though one can still hear his voice.'

'It is an illusion I imagine.'

'Definitely so. Because down to the ground comes, gruesomely, the boy's severed limbs and trunk. The man reappears with the boy's head and a bloody knife clenched in his teeth. He thrusts the remains into a cloth which he then stabs for good measure. While the spectators are still aghast, the magic man shakes the rope which returns to normal, while the cloth moves to reveal the boy in one piece and grinning cheerfully. So tell me, Astrologer, how is it done?'

'I don't know yet,' said Zachary slowly, as an idea was born. 'But I shall certainly experiment.'

'Do you think it is a mass hallucination? That the crowd see something which does not happen at all?'

'Probably. But the hallucination must begin with the rising of the rope, unless . . .'

'Unless what?'

Zachary grinned. 'You don't think I would tell you, Lord Ravi, surely? After all you have challenged my skills. It is up to me to prove to you that I am as clever as your magic men.'

'Very well,' Ravi said, now much amused. 'I am a man of honour. I shall lay a wager both with you and your Sultan that his astrologer cannot reproduce the Indian rope trick.'

'In how long?'

'Two weeks?'

'Make it three and I'll take you on,' said Zachary cheerfully, and held out his hand.

'Done,' answered Ravi, and shook it.

Autumn stole into summer like a thief and laid a finger here, a thumb mark there, then scurried away again. At first, even a critical observer could not be sure that they had seen a hint of yellow in the leaves of the oak tree, a splash of gold in the birch. It was settled weather, fine and warm, and yet signs were everywhere that the year had already started to wane.

In the mornings a gentle slumbrous mist rolled over the river, vanishing slowly with the sun but reappearing again at dusk. The daylight took on a special nuance of colour, the afternoons amber rather than gold. The smell of fruit was in the air, the crispness of apples, the heaviness of plums, and wasps appeared from nowhere to buzz and irritate.

Now the thief struck regularly and each day saw a subtle change in nature's tints. Reds appeared, transforming trees and shrubs, there were points of molten light throughout the landscape, scarlet berries bloomed in the hedgerows. The days were fine but cool, the mornings saw the rime of ground frost.

In tune with the mellow season, the Duke of Somerset felt a great calmness come over him, almost to the point of resignation. He took long walks by the river alone, staring into the water and seeing his own face look back at him sadly. Since Thomas's death, since that savage act of fractricide, he had become old. Though only in his fiftieth year he looked far more, his hair nearly grey, the dark saturnine features so sunken that the bones of his skull were clearly visible beneath. But the expression in Ned's eyes was the saddest thing of all; disillusionment and sorrow, misery and pain.

On his solitary walks by the Thames, the Duke found himself turning over again and again the question as to whether politicians who were sincere – or almost – for he had to admit that even the best of them suffered from *folie de grandeur*, could succeed. He, of all people, had sympathised with the labouring classes, continually fleeced by their masters, who rapaciously lined their pockets at the expense of the people. But yet his good intentions had foundered, the nobles determined to get rid of such a dangerous creature whom they accused of being both sheriff and robber, too full of social conscience whilst still the richest man in the land.

The summer following Tom's death had been a season of more uprisings and revolt, the agricultural workers taking up pitchforks to protest against their wretched conditions. In an agony, for these were the very people that he sought to protect, Ned had seen the Earl of Warwick – that dark powerful ogre of a man – set out with English troops and German mercenaries to put down the trouble in Norfolk, while Lord Russell, whom the Protector had begged to be gentle, massacred Cornishmen.

Then had come a terrible ordeal. Knowing how dangerous he was to them, the wealthy landowners, under the most capable leadership of Warwick, encouraged the merchants of the city of London to support the Earl's faction against the Protector. Ned had called on the ordinary folk to rally to his side and ten thousand of them had done so. But Warwick had massed an army of fifteen thousand men, more than the Protector could cope with. England, in the autumn of 1549, had stood on the brink of civil war.

At first, Edward and Anne Somerset had been blissfully unaware of how the situation had deteriorated, spending September together at Elvetham, their Hampshire home, in almost lighthearted mood. But in October when they joined the King at Hampton Court, Ned had realised just what peril he was in. Only a handful of the Council had remained faithful to him and with the Tower of London now fallen into Warwick's hands, it became obvious that Somerset's enemies were about to seize the King. Anne had left Hampton Court by boat while Ned made ready to ride through the night with Edward Tudor, not to the Tower, as the Protector had originally intended, but to Windsor Castle.

The King had never regarded his uncle in the same way after that escapade, furious that he had been woken up and dragged out of bed when he was suffering from a heavy cold, even angrier that the Castle was not prepared for him, having little food and a temperature like ice.

How wretched, thought Ned, staring solemnly at his reflection in the river – a drowned sad Ned, rather hopeless. I lost everything that night, even my nephew.

Warwick had captured them and sent the Protector to the Tower, of course. Had seen to it that Ned rode back to London a prisoner, watched by the silent citizens who lined the streets, Wriothesley and Lord Huntingdon on either side of him, his jailers.

How he had escaped with his life, he never knew. Warwick and the Council had drawn up twenty-nine articles of accusation against him and presented them on the day before Christmas. With his signature on the documents the Protectorate had ended and Edward Seymour had been released from the Tower, a broken man.

That had been eighteen months ago; eighteen months in which some of Ned's power had returned. He had been reinstated to the Privy Council and, later, the Privy Chamber. And when Warwick had been struck down by a serious illness, something so mysterious that Ned had suspected Cloverella of meddling, he had found himself leading opinion once more.

Warwick's health had not improved and the Earl had been too ill to attend the wedding of his eldest son, John Dudley, with Edward Seymour's eldest daughter, Anne; a marriage supposed to restore the erstwhile friends to some of their former companionship. The fact that it had not done so had been a savage blow to Ned, the King and Council's refusal to give Dame Margery a state funeral, an even bigger one. And now their message was abundantly clear, Somerset might be back amongst them but his wings had been clipped for good. Edward Seymour could remain as a puppet figure only, under the mastership of the fully recovered Earl of Warwick.

He had had wild ideas of trying to oust Warwick, of course. But somehow the futility of it, the sheer folly of attempting a coup, had pressed in on him even harder than the desire to free the country of Warwick's disastrous conservative policies. During the long plague-ridden summer, Ned had lived quietly at Syon House, almost a recluse, knowing himself to be a spent force.

Now, the reflection in the river wavered and Edward's haggard face vanished as small drops like rain broke the surface and formed ever-increasing rings. Touching his cheek, the Duke of Somerset realised that he was weeping, his spirit finally broken. Two years ago he had signed his own brother's death warrant and now the revenge of fate had been exacted in full. The social and religious reformer, the man who had wanted to leave a stable and contented realm for his young nephew to take over, had fallen foul of a huge ambition. The Earl of Warwick, sworn to care only for his own kind, had trodden him ruthlessly aside.

Talk of the forthcoming attempt at the Indian rope trick by the Sultan's chief astrologer had spread not only through the Topkapi Palace but the city of Constantinople as well. Massive wagers were being laid, books were opened, and odds for and against were the talk of the market place. In the midst of all this excitement there was nobody more delighted than Suleiman himself. As always he saw such a feat as a tribute to the greatness of his empire yet, before he laid his own particular wager, the Sultan very sensibly called his astrologer before him.

'Dr Zachary, may a thousand blessings be upon your head.'

'And a thousand thousand upon yours, mighty Sultan.'

Suleiman motioned Zachary to sit on his usual stool set at the Sultan's feet.

'My son, the honour of my Court rests in some measure upon your shoulders. Tell me, is this rope trick possible to do? Is it really a hoax or is it magic?'

'Mighty Sultan,' answered Zachary, kissing the turned-up toe of one of Suleiman's surprisingly small satin shoes, 'the answer is that it is a combination of both, or so I believe. Whether it is possible or not I am still not certain, but trust me.'

'I shall, my Zachary, but tell me exactly how I should wager, what words I should use.'

'Wager, great one, that your chief astrologer will climb the rope and vanish.'

'As simple as that?'

'I think so.'

Suleiman frowned. 'But what of the boy?'

'The boy will also vanish.'

'But the trick is that you both return?'

'Indeed it is, mighty Sultan.'

'And will you use Cem?'

'I shall, Sir.'

They both smiled, thinking of Zachary's son, born to Salina a year after she had been given to the astrologer as principal slave. The boy was Zachary again, dark and brilliant, like a jewel, suiting his name, which was pronounced 'Gem' in English.

'My Cem,' said the Sultan's chief astrologer fondly. 'If anyone can help me with this trick it will be he.'

'Your third son,' answered Suleiman, who knew Zachary's family history well. 'And the most loved?'

'No, mighty Sultan, I love all my children.' Zachary would have liked to have added that he missed his two in England but knew Suleiman would be greatly offended if he did so. Instead he said, 'They will be men now. Eighteen years old. I wonder if I would recognise them.'

'A father always recognises his children,' answered the Sultan. 'I have over a hundred, so believe me, I should know.'

'Indeed, greatest of the great,' answered Zachary, and left the Sultan's presence, bowing magnificently.

Because of the *baton sinister* in the pedigrees of both Jasper and Sylvanus Howard, the positions obtained for them by the Duke of Somerset in the household of the King of England were, perforce, somewhat lowly. Jasper, being the cleverer of the two, had become one of the King's many secretaries; Sylvanus ostensibly a falconer, though really the boy-King liked to challenge him in the butts, enjoying sporting activities whenever he was allowed time for them.

It had not been easy after the death of the Lord Admiral and the demoting of the Protector to keep their positions at Court. In fact many days had passed when both of the boys had expected to feel a hand on their shoulder and a voice telling them they were under arrest. Yet the King must have had some small influence with Warwick for Edward Tudor's two companions remained. Perhaps, thought Jasper, it was because their stepmother had been so close to Jane Seymour that her son liked to keep them in his retinue.

Yet the relationship between the Howard brothers and the odd boy that Edward had become had grown strained during the autumn of 1551, the days leading up to the King's fourteenth birthday on the 12th of October having been particularly difficult.

'Do you know, Jasper, the King has not been near the falcons or the butts for a whole week now,' Sylvanus had said when the brothers, both off duty, had met in Jasper's small apartment.

'He has not called me to work for him either. He is definitely avoiding me.'

'Something's afoot.'

'Do you think it is more trouble for the Duke of Somerset?'

'I would not be at all surprised,' answered Sylvanus, frowning.

'It is strange,' said Jasper, abruptly changing the subject, 'but I dreamt the other night that our father came back to us.'

Sylvanus's beautiful rosy face broke into a smile. 'Do you think it is an omen?'

'I don't know,' Jasper said thoughtfully. 'But my thumbs are pricking. Something is going to happen, I'm certain of it.'

He was right. On the 16th of October, having been unable to attend the masque given in honour of the birth of the King's Majesty on the 12th, the Duke of Somerset arrived to dine with his nephew alone. It was a cold, formal meal, the boy saying so little that in the end his uncle had blurted out, 'Your Grace, tell me, I beg you, if I have done anything to offend you.'

The King turned icy eyes on him and Somerset found himself hating Jane's son, the sweet boy welcomed by an entire nation who had turned, through constant treatment as a demi-god, into a hard-hearted little wretch, indifferent to blood relations and faithful servants alike.

'Nothing, my Lord,' said the brat, in a voice that meant, 'everything'.

Somerset hesitated on the brink of saying that the execution of Thomas Seymour had eventually been forced upon him by others; that the desperate night ride to Windsor, cold and miserable though it was, had been essential; that he had never tried to seize power for himself, but only for the cause of England and its long-suffering people.

'Then, Your Grace, know this and know it well,' answered Somerset bravely, 'if I have done anything inadvertently that has not been to your taste, understand that it was for the sake of the nation, for the sake of yourself. That you might take over the reins of a sound state, a peaceable kingdom.'

'Thank you,' answered the King tonelessly.

'Yes, thank you indeed,' said Ned, blood before his eyes and bitterness in his heart. 'I have brought you a fine horse for your birthday gift, nephew. See it when you have time to spare.'

He no longer cared now, ex-Protector that he was, a fallen man without hope. 'God bless Your Majesty,' he said and stood up from the table.

'Are you leaving us?' asked the King in genuine surprise.

'Yes,' said Somerset, 'I am leaving you. Farewell, Your Grace.'

He stumbled from the room, blinded half by tears, half by fury, realising that his breach of etiquette had been appalling but that the fate which lay ahead of him would be even worse. And as he reached the stables, mounted his horse and with the two servants who had accompanied him turned away from the Palace, the Duke saw that nemesis had finally come. On the road ahead, in a cloud of dusty hooves, an arresting party was galloping hard.

'By God,' shouted Ned, 'things have come to a terrible pass,' and he wheeled round to escape only to see Sylvanus and Jasper Howard, mounted, armed, and miraculously at the ready, putting their lives at risk by leaving their sworn duties.

'Go back,' Somerset shouted, 'it is treason to desert your posts. Don't side with me. I am finished.'

'Damn treason,' said Sylvanus 'and damn the pricks who have turned against you, Lord Duke. Loyalty has to start somewhere.'

And with that he unsheathed his sword as Jasper did likewise.

To look at Cem was to relive memories of childhood, for here was the young Zachary Howard, tough and courageous, sweet and steadfast, with the dark fascinating looks and rough black curls that had always made his father so attractive yet so distinctive a personality.

'Now,' said the astrologer, cuddling the boy in the crook of his arm, 'you do understand why I have to go, don't you?'

'Yes, my Lord. You must return to England to see your wife and grown-up sons who are sad and troubled.'

'Not just troubled. I believe that your brothers might be in danger.'

At the word 'brothers', Cem's face wreathed into a nest of cheerful grins. He loved the very thought of it, of having older half brothers in England, boys of importance whom one day, with luck, he might be able to visit.

'Then you must go back to them, Sir.'

Zachary leaned close to Cem's small brown ear. 'You have arranged for the boat to be moored three miles down the coast?'

'Yes, my Lord. And I have arranged also for a decoy vessel to sail at the same time with a dark-haired man wearing your clothes.'

'And the snake's skeleton?'

'Was sewn into the rope, my father, by a blind tailor who did not know what he did.'

Zachary smiled and patted his son's dark head. 'You have done well, my Cem. I shall miss your sweet presence when we part.'

'But it is their turn in England,' answered Cem philosophically, 'they have not seen you for so long. Whereas I, if I escape the Sultan's wrath and live, may one day travel to you.'

'If you do as I say, Suleiman will not be dangerous. Angry, yes, but you can charm him out of that. I think he will believe what you tell him, for several hours at least.'

'And what about my mother?'

'She will not be in danger. She is innocent of this plot and can swear so. Anyway, the Sultan would never harm the beautiful Salina.'

'It sounds like a legend,' said the boy, his eyes shining, bright as topaz.

'It will be a legend. How the glorious Salina had a child by the English astrologer, Dr Zachary, who grew up to be the famous Cem, the greatest wise man in the Ottoman Empire.'

'Will I really become that?'

'Yes,' said Zachary certainly, 'you will. Now, once again, tell me how we do the trick.'

'It will be performed by means of mass hallucination. Really you and I will climb into a tree but the audience will think they watch us enter a cloud. It will be all illusion.'

'Except for the rope. That will stand up because a snake's bones are stitched within. But after that it is up to me to persuade them, to put them into a trance.'

Cem looked at his father very earnestly. 'You will be able to, my father, I know. You are a very powerful man.'

'I only hope you are right.'

The blue Turkish afternoon was upon them, a haze softening the distant peaks, a rare loveliness coming upon the waters of the straits so that they glowed like a sapphire. The whole scene was transformed unforgettably by the light and in the Palace's largest courtyard the locked gates of the harem shone like mother-of-pearl.

Seats had been erected before the offices of the Grand Vizier, and now these began to fill with courtiers, gaudy as hummingbirds, bright as swallows. On two high chairs in the front sat the Sultan Suleiman and his Russian wife, Roxelane, her huge blue eyes fixed firmly on the area close to the Gate of Salutations where Zachary was to attempt his feat of magic.

The afternoon was very warm and somnolent, the air wreathed with a sweet-smelling vapour coming from a huge incense burner set beside the seats, and another, strategically positioned within the standing circle of people who had offered to take part. Thus it was with an effect of walking through mist that Zachary and Cem made their entrance from the Gate of Felicity. On seeing them there was an indrawn breath of excitement, followed by total silence from every member of the crowd of several hundred who had been privileged to watch.

Zachary bowed low before Suleiman. 'Mighty Sultan, glorious Sultana, today I will attempt the impossible with the aid of my son, Cem. To answer the challenge of Lord Ravi I will perform the Indian rope trick.'

There was another audible breath followed by applause then a gasp as Zachary flicked the rope and the snake's bones within locked in the strike position.

'Now,' said the astrologer, 'I want you to watch Cem. Do not take your eyes from Cem. Focus your attention. Look at him, look, look.'

Every head turned to watch the boy and now Zachary launched into rapid and incessant speech, giving elaborate and detailed explanations of everything they were doing.

'Now Cem is climbing, watch, watch.' They did so, hardly breathing. 'Now he has reached the top and . . .'

Cem had swung into the branches of a great tree but it was as Zachary suspected. The audience was in that state known as trance. They believed everything that was being said to them.

'. . . he has vanished from your sight.'

There was another audible gasp.

'Now,' said Zachary, very fast. 'I shall repeat the feat of daring. I will climb the rope and vanish. Watch me, watch me I say.' He shinned up fast and called from the top, 'I am going to vanish now . . . now . . . now . . .'

He swung into the tree, kissed Cem on the lips, cried, 'A magic carpet awaits me,' kissed his son again and jumped from the tree to the parapet of the Gate of Salutations. Below him stood a ladder,

498

held by the blind tailor who had stitched the snake into the rope.

'Help, the carpet is taking me away!' Zachary called, his voice growing faint, and descended the steep treads faster than anything he had ever done in his life before.

'Help,' echoed Cem, sliding down the rope like a monkey and sprinting to where the Sultan sat. 'Oh mighty Suleiman,' he gasped, 'may a million blessings be yours. I fear that my father's magic has worked but too well.'

'What do you mean?' said the Sultan anxiously.

'Not only has Dr Zachary climbed the rope but he has also vanished into thin air on a magic carpet. Behold, is he not the cleverest astrologer in the whole of the world to do this?'

'Yes,' answered Suleiman, shaking his head in wonderment, 'indeed he is. In fact,' said the Sultan, starting to laugh uproariously, 'I think he might be the cleverest man I have ever met. Call out the guard.'

# Chapter Forty-Two

THE PEOPLE KNEW THAT HE was for them, knew that Ned Somerset had genuinely tried to better their lives, that the charges of treason and felony were trumped up by the dictator, Warwick, who had now created himself Duke of Northumberland. They stood, hundreds of them, waiting in silence outside Westminster Hall where he was being tried for his life, and when a false rumour started that the good Duke stood free, they shouted and cheered until they had no voice left.

Others who had been loyal to Ned and who also stood trial, Paget, Arundel, the Howard brothers, Sir John Thynne, owed their lives to those stony-faced ranks of solid citizens, even Northumberland afraid of exciting angry public opinion further. But Somerset's blood had to be spilled if the dictator was to succeed, and spilled before Parliament was convened when, as Northumberland knew full well, intelligent and pertinent questions might yet be asked about the flimsiness of the charges laid against the Duke.

The only person to be feared, the one person who could still step in and pardon Somerset, was the boy-King himself. Yet there was a way of dealing even with him. The Duke of Northumberland truly believed in the adage that every man had his price, and in the case of young Edward Tudor that price was entertainment. Accordingly, the Christmas festivities of 1551 were quite extraordinary in their lavishness. Northumberland personally ordered that the best Lord of Misrule should be appointed and that he should remain in the royal household for the full twelve days, while the Privy Council of England itself planned entertainments and deliberated on fancy dress, making decisions about a jerkin for the tumbler, straight to his body. A far cry from judicial murder.

While Edward Tudor, that impossible creature, destroyed by a lethal dose of sycophancy, giggled and clapped his way through masques and tiltings, his relatives and friends kept a cold Christmas in the Tower, Ned in a bleak secure cell to which he had been moved for fear of a rescue attempt. And all the while the citizens of London and the honest people of England murmured that their good Duke was being put to death unnecessarily, that the case against him was patently false, that he was a victim of Northumberland's rapacious greed.

Cloverella, having nobody with whom to spend the festivities, closed up her house and stayed in the Bell Inn in Carter Lane, a noisy but respectable tavern where a woman might reside without annoyance. Every day she went to the Tower at the time when visitors were allowed, and so managed to see Anne Somerset, Jasper and Sylvanus, and the old warrior himself; Norfolk, still alive at the age of seventy-eight, tough as leather boots.

'My dear,' he said, rising with his customary courtesy as his daughter-in-law came in, 'how glad I am to see you, you have cheered my Christmas Day. Though I hear that the fortunes of the Seymours are now as low as those of the Howards. What times we live in. What times!'

'The Tower is packed to overflowing with Northumberland's enemies,' she answered in a low voice, ever-watchful of the omnipresent jailers. 'Including two Howards. Had you not heard?'

The Duke shook his head, his once full head of white hair reduced to spikes since his imprisonment. 'They deliberately tell us little. Who are they?'

'Your grandsons, Jasper and Sylvanus. They drew weapons against the arresting party come to take Ned.'

'My God, they're not under sentence of death?'

Cloverella shook her head. 'No, indefinite imprisonment.'

The Duke sat down heavily. 'How terrible at their age. For me it matters not a whit. When I wake in the mornings I am often surprised to find that I am still on earth.'

Despite the terrible conditions and the bone-aching cold, Cloverella laughed. 'I love you, Lord Duke, though it may be impertinent of me to say it. You have not lost an ounce of your wit.'

'Thank you, my dear, on both counts. Now, what news of that missing husband of yours?'

'None. I am beginning to think he is happy in captivity and will never return.'

The Duke stood up again. 'If you think that, you do not really know my son. He has given you his love and pledged his vow accordingly. He is imprisoned against his will, I know it.'

Cloverella twisted her lips. 'He has probably taken a Turkish wife and forgotten me.'

The old man shook his head. 'No, Cloverella. He may have bowed to nature's will now and then as men do, and women too' – Norfolk looked at her so shrewdly that Cloverella flushed from head to foot, glad that he had never at any time been her adversary – 'but he would never desert you. I am surprised your magic gift does not tell you so.'

'I do not look for myself, it is too unlucky.'

'Then you must take my word,' answered the Duke, with just the suggestion of an order.

Cloverella had bought dainties and wine to cheer the prisoners' wretched day, and herbal remedies to combat the complaints brought about by cold and damp. And one look at Jasper, lying on his narrow bed in high fever, had his stepmother hurrying for her bottles and jars.

Because of their age and lowly position, the two Howard boys had been given a mean cell, the straw on the floor filthy, a smell emanating from it that had Cloverella putting her sleeve across her mouth and nose. On the battered table, the only other piece of furniture, stood a bowl of soup and a hunk of bread, untouched, and a bottle of wine, half drunk.

'Our Christmas treat,' said Sylvanus with a laugh.

'How long has Jasper been like this?'

'A few days. It will pass though, Stepmother. It is prison fever. A lot of the inmates get it, or so the turnkey tells me. He gave him a dose of something vile which seemed at least to make him sleep better.'

Cloverella sniffed suspiciously at the bottle. 'Well, he is to have no more of it. See that he takes this three times a day, and applies this to his chest . . .' She rattled on, unaware that her stepson was struggling over something he wanted to say.

'. . . and two generous measures of this at night to help him rest.' Cloverella looked up and saw Sylvanus biting his lip. 'What is it, sweetheart? Why are you looking like that?'

'I don't know whether I should tell you,' he answered awkwardly. 'As you know, I have none of my father's gift, being too much an outdoor person. But Jasper is different and I believe has a little of it.'

'So?'

'So, just before the Duke was arrested, Jasper had a dream that father came home. And now, in his fever, he is having more. He even calls out for Zachary.' Sylvanus's face glowed with eagerness. 'Cloverella, is he coming back? You of all people should know?'

She stood on tiptoe and put her hands on his shoulders. 'My darling, I don't, truly. A clairvoyante must never divine for herself, it is too dangerous.'

The door was being unlocked and a pool of light fell on the cell's filthy floor. The turnkey stood in the opening.

'Time to go, Madam.'

Cloverella produced a coin which she thrust into his grimy hand. 'My son is not well, jailer. Please see to it that the floor is washed and clean straw put down.'

The man looked at the coin and pulled a greasy forelock. 'Very good, my Lady.'

'I shall return tomorrow to see it has been done.'

'Yes, Madam.'

In stark contrast with the boys, Anne Somerset sat before a log fire in a comfortable room with a bedroom leading off it. Her bed had fresh linen, by her washing bowl lay a good towel, and on the table, already laid for supper, were dishes and spoons, a selection of silver plate stored in a nearby cupboard.

'Such luxury!' said Cloverella, not altogether surprised.

'I sent for them from home,' answered the Duchess briskly. 'There is no point in staying here without comforts. But my selection of clothes is both meagre and poor. Cloverella, would you do me the kindness of going to Syon House and getting me some more?'

'Certainly. What items do you require?'

'Well, about a dozen gowns and kirtles. But there are two black ones I particularly want, one velvet and the other satin, both edged with jennetts. Then I would like my scarlet stomacher and velvet coat, and my partlets and ruffs and all the laces that Mistress Pursbey has in her keeping.'

Cloverella stared at her amazed. 'You will need *all this*?'

'Indeed I will. And if you could get my crimson satin box

complete with the stuff that is in it while you are there, I would be most obliged.'

There was nothing to be said. Such frivolous behaviour while her husband froze in a nearby cell, under sentence of death, was more than Cloverella could comprehend. She stared at Anne mutely and then saw something unbelievable. The firmly compressed lips were trembling, the muscles of the chin quivered.

'Oh dearest,' said Cloverella, and rushed to take Lady Somerset in her arms.

'Oh God, God, God,' sobbed Anne, completely broken. 'My Ned, my love, they are going to kill him. Oh Cloverella, I do not know how to bear it. They will not let me see him. Not even today, not even on Christmas Day. I have been granted an interview on the eve of execution and that is all. And I *love* him. I really love him.'

Cloverella wondered, then, how she could have been so foolish as not to realise that the silver plate, fine napery and beautiful clothes were simply to show the Duchess's tormentors that she would not be beaten.

'You see,' Anne went on, grasping Cloverella almost painfully, 'they fear a rescue bid by the citizens of London. No one is to visit him at all until the night before he dies.'

'Oh Ned, Ned. How pitiful!' said Cloverella, and wept also.

'Will you write to the King?'

'The letter would never get to him.'

Anne nodded dismally. 'You are right. I am clutching at straws. And the ungrateful child would do nothing in any event. I hate him.'

'But Jane was so kind. It is hard to believe that little monster is her son.'

'Ah,' said Anne, narrowing her eyes. 'But remember who his father was. Not the best-natured creature ever born.'

'So one evil begets another, in every sense,' answered Cloverella harshly. 'The Seymours have drunk from a bitter cup.'

'All their good intentions trodden under.'

'But never forgotten, I promise you. The name of Seymour will never be forgotten.'

It was just as the Duchess had said, the most rigidly guarded prisoner in the Tower was her husband. Fear of rescue had produced the most stringent conditions of imprisonment, the people of England having learned at last which of the two Seymour brothers was truly their friend. Edward spent his days alone, quietly preparing for death, looking back on his life with a clear conscience, knowing in his heart that he had tried his best for both the King and his realm.

For bribes, the jailer brought him occasional terse messages.

'Your wife says she hopes you keep in good health.'

'Will I be able to see her soon?'

'Yes.'

'When?'

'Some time in January.'

Only in this way had Ned learned that his execution was to be soon and on the evening of 19th January his long ordeal was finally over. The Warden of the Tower came to his cell to tell him that that day in Council, sixteen members being presented, a decision had been made to apply for a warrant for Somerset's execution.

'In how many days' time?'

'Three, my Lord.'

It was a relief to know; it was a relief to have the embargo on visitors lifted; it was relief beyond measure to see Anne again, to hold her in his arms and tell her for the last time that he loved her.

'But it is my fault,' she whispered.

'What do you mean?'

'I was too proud, too overbearing, Ned. My haughtiness made people dislike *you* and because of my foolishness you are going to die. I should be the one to walk out to the block tomorrow.'

'What nonsense is this?' he answered, taking her chin in his hand and forcing her to look at him. 'You have been a wonderful wife and mother. You have given me many clever and comely children. Your love and loyalty to me are beyond question.'

'Ned,' she muttered, looking away despite his forcing, 'Henry Howard's passion for me went unrequited. I did not . . .'

'I know, I know. And you never had need for jealousy of Cloverella. She was just my childhood pet.'

'Has she been today?'

'Yes. The only one of us left of the four who wished.'

'The four who wished?' repeated Anne curiously.

Ned smiled quizzically. 'When we were young, on Merlin's Mound, Jane, Thomas, Cloverella and I made wishes – Jane to be queen, Thomas to marry the highest in the land, myself, foolishly,

505

to own everything I could see. They were all granted, and yet how bitterly. It was only Cloverella, who wished for something unselfish, who escaped.'

Anne looked at her husband in disbelief. 'But it is only a foolish legend that Merlin sleeps in there. It is just a strange coincidence.'

'Is it?' answered Ned softly. 'Can you be quite certain?'

She felt utterly crushed by fate; dwarfed and impotent, a futile little figure whose magic had deserted her. As Cloverella climbed aboard her barge, moored at the Tower's watergate, in preparation for the row back to Greenwich, she experienced a moment of sheer desolation. It seemed to her that everyone she loved had been taken away in one form or another. Jane and Tom by death, Edward as good as, Zachary by captivity or desertion. And though her stepsons were alive, Jasper having recovered from his fierce fever, they were gaunt, skeletal boys, Sylvanus's rosy beauty pinched and withered, Jasper's raven darkness turned sallow.

Very briefly, as the barge pulled out across the unfriendly waters of the January river, Cloverella wondered whether to let herself slip quietly over the side and allow her sodden garments to pull her down to the mud at the bottom. But she rallied her thoughts, knowing that her oarsmen would only jump in bravely after her, getting a dangerous soaking in the raw and unrelenting wind.

Cloverella huddled in the cabin, peering out from her fur-lined hood like an elf. Even though it was only four o'clock it was already beginning to get dark and she faced the prospect of yet another evening alone, tormenting herself with visions of Ned's imminent death.

I can't endure it, she thought. I shall get the servants to sit with me. A solitary vigil is more than I can stomach tonight.

The barge rounded the bend in the river and entered the loop of water above Greenwich. There was no one to be seen, only a lone wherryman coming back from dropping a passenger. The citizens of London and the people of the surrounding villages were huddling in their homes on this unfriendly evening. Yet, as they drew within sight of her house, Cloverella saw that for some reason every candle in the place was blazing, the light shining out over the gardens, so bright that it caused a glow on the river.

Zachary's terrible one-eyed cat sat on the landing stage, rising and arching its back as the barge drew alongside.

'What do you want?' said Cloverella, cautiously bending to tickle its head, for it was a creature of fiercesome swings of mood and one could as easily get a bite as a purr.

It hurried ahead of her up the orchard path and, as it did so, from the stables the astrologer's raw-boned horse let out a sudden wild cry.

Cloverella stopped in her tracks. 'My God,' she said, 'My God,' and started to run.

They did not desert him! Despite the edict of the Council of England that every householder in London and its surrounding villages must remain in his house until after ten o'clock in the morning, long before daylight they trudged in the darkness, thousands of them, to Tower Hill. The man of the people, the good Duke of Somerset, was being put to death because greed and ugliness and ambition had come in the way, but they were going to see to it that he did not die friendless. They had come, not to gloat or gape at a side-show, but to pray as a multitude for his immortal soul.

By seven o'clock thousands of people stood in a surly silence and when, an hour later, Ned Somerset appeared, as tall and commanding as ever and wearing his very best clothes, a huge cheer went up and the crowd pressed forward, jostling the extra troops who had been drafted in especially to guard the scaffold.

'God bless the good Duke,' someone shouted, and the cry was taken up on every side. 'God bless the Duke, God bless the good Duke Ned.'

Acknowledging them with a smile, Edward Seymour climbed to the block steadily and without hesitation, and knelt at once in private prayer. Then he rose to make his last speech on earth to the people who loved him.

'I declare to you all that I have never offended against the King, either by word or deed. I have been as faithful to this realm as any man alive but I die nonetheless as an act of obedience.'

Edward paused, his attention distracted, and there was a sudden murmur in the crowd at the appearance of mounted men on the perimeter.

'A rescue,' cried a woman hysterically. 'It's a rescue.'

'Then let them through,' shouted another, and the crowd scattered frantically, some throwing themselves into the Tower Ditch to get out of the way.

But the horsemen were not what they had hoped and there was an angry roar as it was realised that these were extra guards, come to quell rabble-rousers. It was now obvious to those trying to keep order that mob violence was about to erupt and the situation could go rapidly out of control. Sir Anthony Browne turned his horse and rode towards the scaffold to try and restore calm, but the now hysterical people thought he brought a royal pardon, for it was hard for even the most callous of them to comprehend that a boy could be so ungrateful to an uncle who had served his monarch loyally and well.

'A pardon is come. God save the King,' they shouted, and caps were thrown into the air and arms waved triumphantly.

'By God's passion,' said Browne, 'there will be a riot in a moment. What shall we do?'

He never forgot Somerset's smile at that moment; it haunted him the rest of his days. 'I will calm them,' said the Duke and raising one hand he took a step forward. There was an instant hush as a thousand voices stopped simultaneously.

'Citizens,' called Ned, 'be at peace, I pray you. There will be no pardon, but I am content to die as I am, in the knowledge that I have always served the King faithfully, for I have been most diligent about his Majesty in his affairs, both at home and abroad, and no less diligent in seeking the common commodity of the whole realm.'

Somewhere a woman sobbed and there was a tense silence. Then Somerset spoke again, forgiving his enemies and begging the pardon of any he might have offended. He looked once more at the ordinary folk.

'Good people of England, the time has come for me to die and I once again require that you will keep yourselves still, lest through your tumult, you might frighten me. For albeit the spirit be willing and ready, the flesh is frail and wavering, and through your quietness, I shall be much more the quieter. God bless each and every one of you.'

He turned to the headsman. 'Get it over quickly for God's sake.'

'And your forgiveness, my Lord?'

Edward gave the man a coin, and on the executioner's instruction turned back his collar. 'I pardon you all for my death,' he said to the warden and the sheriffs, then he knelt but was forced to rise once more to remove his doublet which still covered his neck. Ned again went down on his knees, covering his face with his handkerchief. Then just as the words, 'Lord Jesus, save me,' came to his lips, the axe fell and it was over.

A solitary voice rose above the sound of weeping. 'A blight on the Tudors for all that they have done. May they be barren stock and thus their line perish.'

Nobody moved and there was no arrest, for it was not possible to identify who had shouted. Only the cry of the wheeling gulls from the Thames broke the massive silence as they screamed out at the moment of Edward's passing.

# Epilogue

THEY CAME INTO THE DAYLIGHT like moles, their eyes blinking at the brightness, shuffling uncertainly, not quite sure what was expected of them.

Anne Seymour was first, walking stiffly, her beautiful face lined and drawn, her fall of red hair quite white. Behind her came Stephen Gardiner, the Bishop of Winchester, who had always looked gaunt and so had changed little. Then, like flowers feeling the precious sun for the first time, Jasper and Sylvanus Howard, rake-thin, with parchment faces, walked out on either side of an old grizzly. He had lived and survived, he was eighty years old, he was the most venerable of them all. Thomas Howard, Duke of Norfolk, was leaving the Tower of London a free man after six and a half years of imprisonment.

Heading the party who awaited them was the Queen of England herself. Short, blunt, with bad eyesight and a gruff voice, she had triumphed over everyone and taken the crown. Mary Tudor, the ill-treated daughter of Katharine of Aragon, had come into her birthright at last.

That poor spoiled boy, her half-brother, that nonsense of a person created by fawning courtiers and zealous tutors, had died when he was fifteen, in great pain and misery. And perhaps it had been better so, for King Edward was already showing signs of the cruelty and coldness that had so characterised his monstrous father.

But Mary had not achieved her rightful place without a struggle. Northumberland, the dictator who had killed Edward Seymour, had married his son Guildford Dudley to the little mouse Jane Grey and then had claimed that under the terms of King Edward's will she was the new Queen of England. There had been fighting and bloodshed and, in a way, Ned had been avenged. For Northumberland and his son and Jane Grey, all three, had gone to the block for

510

their upstart temerity in trying to take what was not lawfully theirs.

And now it was over. Mary had triumphed. She stood by the gate of the Tower, repaying her debt to old friends. It was August 1553 and the new Queen was releasing the prisoners.

They came to where she waited, a small, sad, dowdy figure, and went on their knees to their saviour. And when Norfolk tried to rise again and felt pain in his ancient joints, it was the Queen herself who first assisted him, then passed him into the care of a dark-haired man who stood respectfully behind her.

'Zachary,' said the Duke, 'my son. Oh my very dear child.'

Slowly, moving almost as if they were in a trance, the little group began to disperse: Anne Seymour with her old friend the Queen, arm-in-arm, Mary calling Anne 'good gossip' as she had done all those years ago; Zachary with his father and sons towards the barge which was to take them to Greenwich, where he would love and care for them and bring them back to strength, together with Emily, his new daughter, born to Cloverella exactly ten months after his return.

'It is over,' said the Duke simply. 'I have been spared, to help my family prosper once more. Zachary, I want you to live in Norfolk with me, return to your roots. Will you do so?'

'If my wife agrees, yes. There is nothing left for me here. I have seen too much evil, known too much hardship. All I want now is to help my boys grow strong and see them set out on their chosen paths in life.'

He hugged them close to him, two fine young men, their faces already beginning to glow from the freshness of the river breeze.

'Then I shall pray,' said the Duke, and there was silence while he and Zachary remembered a time long ago, when a wild-headed child had been taken to Kenninghall Castle on the night his mother had been burned as a witch.

'She called you Zachary, didn't she?' he said now, smiling and recollecting.

The astrologer bent his dark head so that Norfolk could stroke it. 'Yes, Lord Duke my father,' he answered.

In the first sweet crispness of autumn Cloverella went alone to Wolff Hall, walking its empty corridors and gardens, listening to the silence, hearing the sound of herself echo and re-echo through the house that had once known so much laughter.

511

Then, having said farewell to it for ever, Zachary's wife rode to Merlin's Mound, just beyond the town of Marlborough, and there she tethered her mount and climbed to the top of the steep slope. Far below, the river Kennet sparkled and leapt with every golden light in Christendom.

'It's a sword,' said Cloverella, 'a jewelled sword.'

Was it fancy that a light voice answered, 'No, it's a ring. A golden wedding ring', that a carefree laugh rang out, that a serious voice said, 'What strange creatures you are'? That as she turned to go the river was the colour of wine in the dying sunlight and that the wind sang the word 'Remember'?

# Historical Note

About every famous person of the past there are always several schools of thought, in fact one could go so far as to say no two reference books interpret the facts in quite the same manner. Therefore, when making a study of characters from history, one is forced eventually to form one's own conclusion based on the evidence presented.

The two contradictory stories about Jane Seymour, one that she sat on the King's knee accepting his caresses with equanimity, the other that she adopted a highly moral tone when he sent her a gift of money, returning it at once, have so baffled historians that they tend to accept one or the other. Yet it seems possible that both situations could have arisen in the development of their relationship. That Jane became Henry's mistress before they married is pure speculation but does make sense of the two apparently incompatible but well-documented accounts.

That Jane gave birth to Prince Edward by Caeserean section is not believed by all historians, some claiming that it was a rumour which was circulated at the time in order to discredit Henry VIII. The dangers of such an operation were then so great that for a husband to give consent for it to be undertaken was virtually to put a sentence of death upon the mother. However, both Neville Williams and Robert Lacey state quite firmly that Jane was subjected to such an ordeal.

It is certain that Thomas Seymour was in love with Katherine Parr, stepped out of the picture when Henry VIII came on the scene, but married her secretly very soon after Henry's death. What is not so clear is his behaviour with Elizabeth at this time. One theory, believed by many, is that he proposed to Elizabeth *before* Katherine Parr and only turned his attentions back to his former love when Elizabeth refused him. The chief evidence for this lies in letters supposedly written by Elizabeth and Thomas, published by an Italian called Gregorio Leti in his *Vita di Elizabetta*. No trace of the originals exists and other letters reproduced by this author are extremely dubious. In fact Neville Williams in his biography of Elizabeth I states categorically that Elizabeth's letter 'is undoubtedly a forgery of Leti's.'

That Thomas was fascinated by Elizabeth is beyond dispute but that he actually proposed to her in the forlorn hope that the Council would permit him to marry a thirteen-year-old princess in line for the throne is hard to believe. It is far more likely that on the King's death he immediately resumed his courtship of Katherine, now a very wealthy widow of high station. Elizabeth's deposition at the time of his arrest states that Katherine Ashley said Thomas, 'would have had me [i.e. Elizabeth] before the Queen'. This merely repeats a remark of Kat's made at the time when she, bribed by the Admiral, was attempting to encourage Elizabeth to marry him. Further, if Elizabeth had *really* written a letter refusing Thomas's proposal of marriage, would she not now have produced a copy of it to clear her name?

It has become fashionable for all modern historians to regard Elizabeth's refusal to marry either as 'emotional, the result of the extraordinary strains of her childhood', or as the manifestation of a fear that any husband might diminish her power.

Yet her father's lifelong quest was to produce an heir and Elizabeth's Council certainly believed that an heir to the throne would have strengthened the Queen's position enormously. The case that Elizabeth I suffered from testicular feminisation is brilliantly presented in a paper by Professor Bakan, who states, 'Recent advances in the understanding of the process of sexual differentiation and the description of the testicular feminisation syndrome justify a reconsideration of the value of the evidence of her contemporaries that Elizabeth's refusal to marry was based on her knowledge of a physical defect.'

Another well-argued article by Robert Greenblatt entitled *The Virgin Queen*, which appeared in the *British Journal of Sexual Medicine* in 1986 asks the pertinent question, 'What did Essex mean when, railing against Elizabeth, he said, "her conditions are as crooked as her carcass"?' The article goes further, quoting Sir Walter Raleigh: 'Her minions were not so happy as vulgar judgements thought them, being frequently commanded to uncomely and sometimes unnatural employment.' A strange remark to say the least! Finally, it must be remembered the times in which Elizabeth lived. She was a Tudor Queen of England and twentieth-century views that she kept her virgin status for twentieth-century psychological reasons are not really relevant.

The opinion that Edward Seymour, though a proud and ambitious man, had the best interests of the country at heart is shared by most historians, but it is piquant to note that the Good Duke, for all his efforts, ended buried between the headless corpses of Anne Boleyn and Catherine Howard, his enemy the Duke of Northumberland being put in beside him during the following year!

Mary, the child born to Katherine Parr and Thomas Seymour, is generally considered to have died in childhood. Following the execution of her father, the baby was sent to the Protector's household at Syon House and then on to the Duchess of Suffolk's establishment. It is from there that history loses trace of her, though Agnes Strickland in *Lives of the Queens of England* presents a plausible case for Mary having survived to womanhood, marrying Sir Edward Bushel by whom she had a daughter. A painting of a solemn little girl, said to be Mary Seymour, hangs in the nursery suite of Sudeley Castle to this day.

The site of the original Wolff Hall probably lies between the present Wolfhall Manor, a dilapidated and somewhat dispiriting place, and the house known locally as the Laundry. Nobody is quite sure. Parts of the present house are indeed very old but unlike Blickling Hall and Hever Castle, childhood homes of Anne Boleyn, time and lack of care have been allowed to erase the birthplace of Jane Seymour.

Sudeley Castle, however, where Katherine and Thomas lived and had their child, stands restored and proud in its beautiful parkland, while in the chapel in the grounds the mortal remains of Katherine Parr lie in peace.

# Bibliography

*Henry VIII*, John Bowle
*The Chronicle of Calais*, The Camden Society
*The Channel*, Shirley Harrison
*Henry VIII and His Wives*, Walter Jerrold
*The Life and Times of Henry VIII*, Robert Lacey
*The Seymour Family*, A. Audrey Locke
*Annals of the Seymours*, H. St Maur
*Ordeal by Ambition*, William Seymour
*Lives of the Queens of England*, Agnes Strickland
*Elizabeth I*, Neville Williams
*Henry VIII and His Court*, Neville Williams